PRAISE FOR

As Meat Loves Salt

"Until I read *As Meat Loves Salt*, I believed Samuel Pepys' diaries offered the best portrait available of the mid-1600s in England. Now I know better. Maria McCann has captured the bloody heart of the century better even than the man who lived in it. McCann unpacks the guts of the culture like a butcher pulling entrails from a slaughtered pig. This novel is sensual in every respect: McCann makes us feel the bodily sensations of the characters—blood, sweat, tears... *As Meat Loves Salt* is a feast that will leave grease on your cheeks and disturbing images in your mind. It's the best novel I've read over the last year—a masterpiece of craft and cunning."

—*The Philadelphia Inquirer*

"A wrenching psychological thriller about a man wrestling with private demons at a time when bloody political upheaval seemed to drive an entire nation mad. Meticulously researched and boldly told, *As Meat Loves Salt* is gripping melodrama." —*The Boston Globe*

"[A] riveting, fiercely intelligent, and brutal first novel... sprawling in length, rich in period detail, and astonishing in its psychological insights, the book reads like an old-fashioned Victorian social novel with a bit of Freud thrown in." —*The Advocate*

"A brave choice, Ms. McCann's jealous, brutal hero is unattractive by traditional lights, for he personifies why wrath is one of the seven deadly sins. But Jacob, who destroys what he loves with the rapacity of his desire, is as compelling as he is appalling... the writing here is flawless. Ms. McCann captures the flavour of 17th century English, but never at the expense of comprehension; these pages flow like claret... a fat, juicy masterpiece." —*The Economist*

"McCann's brilliant debut is an eloquent narrative that is historically rich and enthralling. American readers, especially those who enjoyed Sarah Waters' *Tipping the Velvet*, will rejoice." —*Library Journal*

"Brilliant, ambitious . . . the story of a compelling anti-hero who struggles against his own violent tendencies to little avail. The scope of the narrative, the unusual conceit and the resonant writing combine to make this a powerful, unusual debut." —*Publishers Weekly*

"An inventive and vigorous debut novel set in 17th-century England at a time of revolution . . . urgent and energetic, full of voluptuous descriptions of food, paintings and lifestyles, as well as the war scenes . . . McCann creates a gripping account of 17th-century England in a climate of social change. Her language is bold and alive, and the reader is drawn into the story right from the start."
—*Independent on Sunday* (London)

"It's hard to believe that this accomplished potent historical tale is a first novel. . . . A genre-transcending, irreplaceable work: historical fiction at its very best." —*Kirkus Reviews*

"A gritty, disturbing, and erotic debut." —*Out* magazine

"A triumphant piece of historical evocation . . . McCann's unflinching descriptions of battle are matched by the power of her depiction of London in all its fetid splendour. . . . [She] shows the imaginative empathy that is the hallmark of a true novelist." —*Vogue* (UK)

"An electrifying erotic thriller . . . Part historical yarn, part picaresque tale, part poignant fable of same-sex love and taboo-breaking . . . A certain splendour in the writing makes this novel a tour de force of sensational scenes, an anatomy of violence and an elegy for lost kinship. Forbidden sensuality is searingly described by chiaroscuro candlelight. Rich in secrets and surprises, this novel has its own fierce poetry." —*The Independent* (London)

"Full of biblical allusions and echoes, *As Meat Loves Salt* is a carefully constructed allegory of temptation and betrayal. A story tense with anguish, intimacy and shame and overlooked by the menacing presence of the Devil, it imaginatively re-creates the mentality of a society racked by war and intoxicated by radical new ideas of freedom and change.... This is an intriguing and disturbing first novel which lingers in the mind; few characters simultaneously reveal and hide so much about themselves as Jacob Cullen."

—*The Times Literary Supplement* (London)

"This vaulting first novel re-creates Cromwellian England with a modern twist: an obsessive liaison between two deserters from the New Model Army at a time when homosexuality was a hanging offence. A consuming and headlong read... *As Meat Loves Salt* is highly accurate as a historical novel and electric as a story of love and war. It is an unusual and memorable achievement which the judges of the year's literary prizes made a bad mistake in ignoring."

—*The Economist* Books of the Year

"Her first book, *As Meat Loves Salt*, can only be assessed as truly remarkable. McCann also writes with a seemingly uncanny ear for the cadences and phraseology of 17th century speech and with a wonderful eye for physical detail in this outstanding debut novel."

—*Birmingham Post*

"This is an outstanding debut novel, a fresh and unusual achievement.... As the title implies, it has all the dirt, stink, rasp and flavour of the time, as much as Simon Schama at his best... But this is a brave attempt to break into a world few of us could imagine. It deserves to be a great success."

—*The Daily Telegraph* (London)

As Meat Loves Salt

MARIA McCANN

As Meat Loves Salt

A HARVEST ORIGINAL • HARCOURT, INC.
Orlando Austin New York San Diego Toronto London

www.HarcourtBooks.com

First published by Flamingo in the UK 2001

Library of Congress Cataloging-in-Publication Data
McCann, Maria, 1956–
As meat loves salt / Maria McCann.
p. cm.
"A Harvest original."
ISBN 0-15-601226-X
1. Great Britain—History—Charles I, 1625–1649—Fiction.
2. Great Britain—History—Civil War, 1642–1649—Fiction. I. Title.
PR6113.C36 A7 2003
823'.92—dc21 2002068546

Text set in ACaslon
Designed by Cathy Riggs

Printed in the United States of America
First Harvest edition 2002
DOM 10 9 8 7 6 5

Acknowledgements

I am most grateful for the help and support of Tony Curtis and Gillian Clarke of the University of Glamorgan, for the generosity of Alan Turton, who showed me the ruins of Basing House, and to Andy Pickering for passing on helpful information. Neither Alan nor Andy is responsible for any liberties I have taken with history.

Thanks are also due to my friends Frances Day, Deborah Gregory, Elorin Grey, Elizabeth Lindsay, Julie-Ann Rowell and Dana Littlepage-Smith, both for the pleasure of working with them and for their excellent taste in pubs.

for my parents

There was once a king who wished to know how much his three daughters loved him. He called the eldest and asked her. 'How much do you love your father?'

His daughter answered, 'My love cannot be measured. You are more precious to me than a palace full of rubies and gold,' and the king was pleased.

He then called the second daughter and put the question to her also.

The girl answered, "My love is beyond compare. It will endure until roses bloom in snow and fish nest in the trees,' and again the king was pleased.

He then called his youngest daughter and asked her, 'My dear child, how much do you love your father?'

The girl replied only, 'I love you as meat loves salt,' and whatever the king coaxed or threatened her with, she would not change her answer.

Insulted, the king divided the youngest daughter's fortune between her sisters, cursed her and cast her out.

Seeing how foolish their father was, the two eldest sisters began to intrigue against him, and in a short time they had seized the kingdom and cast him out in his turn. He became a beggar, and wandered across the land he had once ruled, despised by everyone he met.

One day, weary and hopeless, he came to a village where all the inhabitants were hurrying along the road together, dressed for a celebration. When he asked the reason for this he was told that not far off there was a great house, and that in this house there was a wedding, and the young couple had said that no one should be turned away. The king was very hungry, so he went with them hoping for some share of the feast.

When he arrived he was put to sit at a bench with the rest of the humbler people. For some time he thought of nothing but how much he would be able to eat, but at last, on looking up, he saw that the bride was none other than his own daughter whom he had banished. The king was too ashamed to make himself known. 'Besides,' he said to himself, 'she only loves me as meat loves salt.'

Now it happened that the generosity of the bride and groom was so well known that many, many unexpected guests had come for the feast. When the meat was served and everybody helped themselves, there was not enough salt to go round, and the king was one of the guests who was left out. He took a mouthful of roast meat and tasted it, and how he longed for salt to put on his food. Then he understood, at last, the meaning of his younger daughter's words and the love that she had felt for him, for the meat was nothing without the salt.

Contents

As Meat Loves Salt

PART I

ONE

Scum Rises

ON THE MORNING we dragged the pond for Patience White, I bent so far down trying to see beneath the surface that my own face peered up at me, twisted and frowning. The three of us had churned up the water until it was half mud and spattered with flecks of weed before I knocked my foot against something loose and heavy that lolled about as we splashed. I tried to push it away from us, but too late.

'It is she.' Izzy's lips were drawn back from his teeth.

I shook my head. 'That's a log.'

'No, Jacob – here, here—'

He seized my hand and plunged it in the water near his right leg. My heart fairly battered my ribs. I touched first his ankle, then wet cloth wound tight around something which moved.

'I think that's an arm,' Izzy said quietly.

'I think it is, Brother.' Feeling along it, I found cold slippery flesh, which I levered upwards to the air. It was certainly an arm, and at the end of it a small hand, wrinkled from the water. I heard My Lady, standing on the bank, cry out, 'Poor girl, poor girl!'

Zebedee reached towards the freckled fingers. 'That's never – Jacob, do you not see?'

'Quiet.' I had no need of his nudging, for I knew what we had hold of. Ever since we had been ordered to drag the pond I had been schooling myself for this.

'You forget the rope,' called Godfrey from the warm safety of the bank.

I looked round and saw the end of it trailing in the water on the other side of the pond, while we floundered. 'Fetch it, can't you?' I asked him.

He pursed his lips and did not move. A mere manservant like me must not speak thus peremptorily to a steward, though he were hanging by his fingernails from a cliff.

'Be so kind as to fetch it, Godfrey,' put in the Mistress.

Frowning, the steward took up the wet rope.

The pond at Beaurepair had a runway sloping down into it on one side, made in past times to let beasts down into the water. It was coated with cracked greenish mud, which stank more foully than the pond itself. We grappled, splashing and squelching, to drag the thing to the bottom of this slope, then Zeb and I crawled to the top, our shirts and breeches clinging heavily to us. Having forgotten to take off my shoes, I felt them all silted up. Izzy, who lacked our strength, stayed in the water to adjust the ties.

'Pull,' he called.

Zeb and I seized an end of rope each and leant backwards. Our weight moved the body along by perhaps two feet.

'Come, Jacob, you can do better than that,' called Sir John, as if we were practising some sport. I wondered how much wine he had got down his throat already.

'Her clothes must be sodden,' said Godfrey. He came over and joined Zeb on the line, taking care to stand well away from my brother's dripping garments. 'Or she's caught on something—'

There was a swirl in the water and a sucking noise. Izzy leapt back.

The body sat up, breaking the surface. I saw a scalp smeared with stiffened hair. Then it plunged forwards as if drunk, sprawling full length in the shallower waters at the base of the runway. I descended again and took it under the arms, wrestling it up the slope until it lay face to the sky. The mouth was full of mud.

'You see?' whispered Zeb, wiping his brow.

The corpse was not that of Patience Hannah White. Our catch

was a different fish entirely: Christopher Walshe, late of this parish, who up to now had not even been missed.

~

'He is the servant of Mr Biggin, Madam.' Godfrey tried yet again, his beard wagging up and down. 'One of the stableboys at Champains.'

The Mistress pressed her veiny hands together. 'But why? Where is Patience?'

'Not in the pond. *Not* in the pond, which is as good news as the death of this young man is sad,' fluttered Godfrey. 'Might I suggest, Madam, that it were good for you to lie down? Let me take the matter entirely in hand. I will send the youngest Cullen to Champains and Jacob shall lay out the body.'

My Lady nodded her permission and went to shut herself up in her chamber. Sir John, ever our help in time of trouble, made for the study where he had doubtless some canary wine ready broached.

My brothers walking on either side, I cradled the dead boy in my arms as far as the laundry, and there laid him on a table.

'Directly I saw the hand, I knew,' said Zeb, staring at him. He pushed back the slimy hair from Walshe's face, and shuddered. 'It must have been after the reading. Two nights, pickling in there!'

'A senseless thing,' said Izzy. 'He went out the other way, we all of us waved him farewell.'

Zeb nodded. 'And not in drink. Was he?'

'Not that I saw,' I said. 'Unless you gave him it.'

Izzy and Zeb exchanged glances.

'Well, did you?' I challenged.

'You know he did not,' said Izzy. 'Come lads, no quarrels.'

'I have yet to say a harsh word,' Zeb protested.

In silence we took off our filthy garments in the laundry and washed away the mud from our flesh. Izzy gasped in lifting the wet shirt over his head and I guessed that his back was paining him.

'Thank God Patience was not in there.' Zeb, drying himself on a linen cloth, shivered. 'But this lad! Poor Chris, poor boy. Suppose we had not looked?'

'You were wise to leave off your shoes. I fear mine are ruined,' I said.

'Dear brother, that is scarce a catastrophe here,' Izzy replied. He found a basket of clean shirts and tossed one in my direction. 'That'll keep you decent until we can get back to our own chamber.'

'Godfrey could have bidden Caro bring clothes down for us,' said Zeb. 'What are stewards for, if not to make others work?'

'I would not have Caro see this,' I said.

'What, the three of us in our shirts?' asked Zeb.

'You tempt God by jesting,' said Izzy. He limped over to the boy and stood a while looking at him. 'Suppose it had been Patience? I would not be you in that case.'

Zeb started. 'The Mistress doesn't know, does she?'

'No, but it is the first thing thought on if a lass be found drowned,' Izzy replied.

Zeb considered. 'But there were no signs – if I remarked nothing – if any man had the chance, that man was I—' He broke off, his cheeks colouring.

Izzy crossed the room and took him by the shoulders. 'They can cut them open and look inside.'

'Are we in a madhouse? Cut what? Look at what?' I cried.

The two of them turned exasperated faces upon me.

'Ever the last to know,' said Zeb. 'So Caro has told you nothing?'

'Our brother has been hard at work, Jacob,' said Izzy. 'Patience is with child.'

So that was the key to their mysterious talk: Patience with child by Zeb. The great secret, taken at its worth, was hardly astonishing – I had been watching Zeb and Patience dance the old dance for some time – yet I was riled at not having been told.

'Two days and not in the pond. She is run away for sure,' said Zeb. 'But why, why now?'

'Shame?' I ventured – though to be sure, *shame* and *Patience White* were words scarce ever heard together, except when folk shook their heads and said she had none.

'She would not have been shamed. Zeb agreed to marry her,' said Izzy.

'What!' I cried. 'Zeb, you're the biggest fool living.'

'I like her, Jacob,' protested my brother.

'Oh? And would you like her for a sister?'

Zeb was silenced. What he *liked*, I thought, was the place between her legs, for what else was there? We would be all of us better off without Patience. It was impossible any should miss her braying laugh; for myself, I had always found her an affliction. She was Caro's fellow maidservant and a mare long since broken in, most likely by Peter, who worked alongside us and was roughly of an age with Zeb. Patience and Peter, now there was a match: loud, foolish, neither of them able to read, neither caring to do so. I had a strong dislike to Peter's countenance, which was both freckled and pimply and seemed to me unclean, yet I was obliged to admit that in many ways he showed himself not a bad-hearted lad, for he worked hard and was ready to lend and to share. I much preferred him to Patience, whose constant aim was to draw men in.

She had tried it once with me, when I was not yet twenty. Coming through the wicket gate with a basket of windfalls from the orchard, I found her in my way.

'That's a heavy load you've got,' she said.

'Move then,' I told her. 'Let me lay it down,' for my shoulders were aching.

'An excellent notion,' Patience said, 'to lay a thing down on the grass.'

She had never before fastened on me, and though I knew her even then for a whore I was slow to take her meaning. My coat was off for the heat, and Patience put her fingers on my arm.

'You could give a lass a good squeeze, eh?' She pressed my shoulder so that I felt her warm palm through my shirt. 'I'm one that squeezes back. I wager you'll like it.'

'I wager I won't,' I said. 'I've no call for the pox. Now let me through or you'll feel my arm another way.'

For some time after that we did not speak, but servants must rub along somehow – they have enough to do coddling the whims of their masters – and besides, I think Izzy said something to soften her. Since then we had behaved together civilly, as our work required. Peter was come next, I was pretty sure, and had consoled her for Jacob; but she could never have engaged Zeb's interest had there been a comelier woman in the house. There was Caro, of course; but Caro was mine.

Caro. Against Patience's slovenly dress and coarse speech, my darling girl shone like virgin snow. Naturally, there were huffs and quarrels between the two.

'She's lewd as a midwife,' Caro complained to me once. 'Forever snuffling after us: does he do this, does he do that.'

But I was no Zeb. I treated Caro always with the respect which is due from a lover and never assumed the privileges of a husband. Thus I again thwarted Patience by my self-command.

Self-command was the unknown word to my brother, and could have put no brake on his doings. Foolish indulgence had ruined Zebedee. He was only four when Father died, and missed a guiding hand all the more in that his beauty tempted our mother to spoil him.

'Zeb must go on with his lute,' she announced, when it was clear we had scarce a hat between us. To be just, he played well, and looked well even when he played out of tune. We Cullen men are all like Sir Thomas Fairfax, dark-skinned to a fault, but the fault shows comely in Zeb because of his graceful make and his very brilliant eyes. I have seen women, even women of quality, look at him as if they lacked only the bread to make a meal of him there and then – and Zeb, not one whit abashed, return the look.

I lack his charm. Though I am like him in skin and hair, my face is altogether rougher and my eyes are grey. I am, however, the tallest man I know, and the strongest – stronger than Isaiah and Zeb put together. Not that Izzy has much strength to add to Zeb's, for my elder brother came into the world twisted and never grew right afterwards. 'Izzy gave me such a long, hard bringing to bed,' my mother said more than once, 'you may thank God that you were let to be born at all.'

Now Zeb was to go to Champains, as being the best rider and also the most personable of the menservants. I did not begrudge him the job, for I rode very ill and was generally sore all the next day. My own task was humbler, but not without its interest: to clean the boy's body for his master to see it, and for the surgeon. This cleaning should rather be a woman's work, but I was glad to do it for otherwise, Patience being gone, it would fall entirely upon Caro. In the chamber we dressed according to our allotted duty, Zeb taking a well-brushed cassock and some thick new breeches for riding, myself pulling on an old pair over a worn shirt.

'Just wait, we will be suspected for this,' Zeb said to me, combing out his hair. 'You especially.'

'Me?'

'You quarrelled with him that night.'

'I wouldn't call it a quarrel,' I protested. 'We disagreed over his pamphlets, what of that?'

'Jacob is right,' said Izzy. 'Hardly a drowning matter.'

Zeb ignored him. 'It will put off your betrothal, Jacob.'

Izzy turned to me. 'Take no notice. He wants only to tease, when he should be examining his accounts before God.'

'What!' Zeb was stung in his turn. 'Patience isn't dead, nor did I send her away. I heard her news kindly, sour though it was.'

'So why would she leave?' I pressed him.

He shrugged. 'Another sweetheart?'

Izzy and I exchanged sceptical looks. Like all beautiful and fickle persons, Zeb aroused a desperate loyalty in others.

'Are you not afraid for her, with a boy found drowned?' Izzy demanded.

Zeb cried, 'Yes! Yes! But what can fear do?' He buttoned up the sides of his cassock. 'Best not think on it.'

'Think on your duty to her,' said Izzy.

Zeb grinned. 'Let us turn our thoughts rather to Jacob's betrothal. Now *there* everything is proper. A little bird tells me, Jacob, that Caro has been asking the other maids about the wedding night.'

'Away, Lechery,' said Izzy, 'and mend your thoughts, lest God strike you down on the road.'

Swaggering in boots, Zeb departed for the stables.

'Talking of my wedding night and his friend dead downstairs! He's as shameless as his whore,' I fumed.

'He is always thus when he is unhappy.' Izzy spoke softly. 'His weeping will be done on the road to Champains.'

I snorted.

~

As a child I was afraid of the laundry with its hollow-sounding tubs. When later I courted Caro I did it mostly in the stillroom amid the perfume of herbs and wines, or – in fine weather – in the rosemary maze. The room where Walshe lay had a smell of mould and greasy linen, and as a rule I avoided it, not a difficult thing to do for men's work rarely brought them there.

I dragged off the boy's wet clothing and arranged him naked on the table. The silt in his mouth looked as if, stifled in mud, he had tried to gorge on it. I let his head droop from the table-end into a bucket of water and swabbed out his mouth with my fingers before squeezing more water through his hair.

When I bent down to check the ears for mud, I saw the nape of his neck strangely blackened, so rolled him onto his side. What I found gave me pause. Great bruises darkened the back of his neck, his thighs and the base of his spine, as if blood was come up to the skin. Perhaps all drowned men were thus marked. Pulling him face upwards again, I then worked down the body to his feet, which were wrinkled and colourless, hateful to the touch. As I went, I dried him on linen sheets found in one of the presses. Caro would be angry with me for that but she must bear it patiently unless she wanted to lay out the corpse herself. That I would not permit, for the thought of her tears unnerved me.

My thoughts being troubled, I was glad to work alone. The turning and lifting came easy to a man of my strength, for he might be sixteen and was as small and light as I was big and heavy. *Little warrior*. He lay utterly helpless beneath my hands.

'Where is your knife?' I asked.

The skin of his breast shone pale as cream where the flesh was unhurt. I stroked it and ran my hand down one of the thighs. So slender, so unformed. No glory in dispatching such. And no defence to say the Voice had urged me on.

Going to the stillroom for bandages, I found some ready torn. First I packed the boy's fundament, stuffing him tight. Next I bound up his jaw, and weighted down the eyelids with coins. He might as well be laid out for immediate burial, as there would be precious little for the surgeon to discover. Even a natural, I thought, could see what had done for this young man.

Christopher Walshe had been slit from above the navel to where his pale hair thickened for manhood at the base of the belly. The belly itself showed faintly green. The wound was deep, and, now I had rinsed it free of brownish water, a very clean and open one, for the blood had drained off into the pond like wine into a soup, leaving no scab or cleaving together of the flesh. Walshe had a boy's waist and hips, without any padding of fat to take off the ferocity of the blade, which had pulled right through his guts. His ribs and shoulders were dappled, in places, with blue.

There would be more bruising around his feet and ankles. I examined them, and found long bluish marks which might give the surgeon a hint, unless it were concluded that he had scuffled foot to foot with someone.

I put my finger into the wound. The edges curved a little outwards like the petals of a rose, and after an initial tension my finger slid in full length. He was cold and slippery inside. I withdrew the finger and wiped it on my breeches.

~

In the scullery every servant, even my gentle Izzy, was grown surly. That was a sign I recognised and had interpreted before I was given the news.

'Sir Bastard is come home,' said Peter, who had not been present at the pond-dragging and now stared sulkily at the table.

I groaned. Sir Bastard, or to give him his proper name, Mervyn Roche, was the son and heir and so disliked as to make Sir John popular in comparison.

'Will he stay long?' I asked. Much as I hated Mervyn, this once I was glad enough to talk of him, for I dreaded giving a report of the boy's wounds and seeing the horrified faces of my fellows.

'Who knows?' Izzy scratched with his fingernail at a crust of candlewax on Sir Bastard's coat. 'Look at this – stained all over and he throws it at me, expects it spotless tomorrow.'

'Why doesn't he buy new? He has money enough,' I said, lifting down the tray of sand.

'Drinks it away, like father like son,' said Peter. 'He is awash already.'

'Even his father doesn't go whoring.' I laid the first plate in the sand and began rubbing at it with my palm until there came a bright patch in the grey, then moved on so that the brightness spread. Usually I liked scouring pewter, but it would take more than a pleasant task to lift my mood with the weight that lay on me. And now Mervyn was in the house.

'As the pamphlet said, scum rises to the top,' I went on. It galled me to be a servant to such as he, lecherous, intemperate, devoid of wit or kindness, forever asking the impossible and, the impossible being done, finding fault with the work.

'Sshh! No word of pamphlets,' said Izzy.

At that instant Godfrey came into the room. 'I have talked with both Master and Mistress,' he announced.

'And?' asked Izzy.

'They have promised to speak to him. Peter, it were better you did not serve at table. Jacob and I will be there.'

'What's this?' I did not understand what was meant.

'O, you don't know,' said Izzy. 'Sir – ah – our young Master hit Peter in the face this morning.'

Peter turned the other side of his head to me. The eye was swollen.

'I will not ask what for, since to ask supposes some reason,' I said, and went on scouring.

'Humility is a jewel in a servant,' said Godfrey. 'It is not for us to cavil at our betters.'

'Or our beaters,' the lad muttered.

'To hear you talk,' I said to Godfrey, 'a perfect man were a carpet, soiled by others and then beaten for it.'

'And hearing you,' he returned, 'it is clear you have had some unwholesome reading lately. Take care the Master does not catch you at it.'

'How should that happen unless I left it lying in a wine jug?'

'Jacob,' said Izzy. 'Get on with your work.'

Such impudent abuses as these Roches put on us, grew out of that slavery known as *The Norman Yoke*. That is to say, the forefathers of these worthless men, being murderers, ravishers, pirates and suchlike, were rewarded by William the Bastard for helping him mount and ride the English people, and they have stayed in the saddle ever after. The life of the English was at first liberty, until these pillaging Barons brought in *My Lord This* and *My Lady That*, shackling the native people and setting them to work the fields which were their own sweet birthright. Now, not content with their castles and parks, the oppressors were lately begun to enclose the open land, snatching even that away from the rest of us. Roche, this family were called, and is that not a Frenchy name?

Though Caro thought our Mistress not bad, I had noted how little My Lady, as well as her menfolk, had trusted us since the war began. When they thought we were listening their talk was all of wickedness and its punishment. *The King has Divine Right on his side*, one would say, and another, *New Model, forsooth. New noddle, more like*, and there would be loud laughter. Then Sir Bastard might put in his groatsworth, how the rebels were *half fed* (for they thought it no shame to rejoice in such hunger), *half drilled*, *half witted*, so that the victory could go only one way.

But we heard things from time to time, for all that the Roches kept mum or even spoke in French before our faces – indeed, so stupid was Mervyn that he had been known to do so before Mounseer Daskin, the cook, who could speak better French than any Roche had spoken since 1066 – and we took heart. Servants came to visit along with their masters, and whatever their sympathies they brought news from other parts of the country. We were on our guard, however, in speaking with these, for there were those who made report of their fellows.

'It is said Tom Cornish is an intelligencer,' Izzy told me one day. This Cornish had once been a servingman, and was now risen in the world – too high for any honest means. He farmed land on the far side of Champains, and his name was a byword throughout the country for a dedication to the Royalist cause bordering on that religious madness called *enthusiasm*, and commonly supposed only to afflict those on the Parliamentary side.

'You recall the servants who were whipped?' Izzy went on.

I nodded. Not a year before, two men from Champains had been tried for being in possession of pamphlets against the King.

'Well,' Izzy went on, 'it was Cornish brought them to the pillory.'

'Impossible,' I answered. 'Say rather Mister Biggin.'

Biggin was the master of the accused men, and had made no move to defend them.

'Him also. But the one they cried out against was Cornish,' Izzy insisted. 'Gentle Christians both. More shame to Biggin, that he let them suffer.'

'You forget they had a serious fault,' said I.

'Fault?'

'Choosing their own reading. But Izzy, Cornish does not live at Champains. How would he know of it?'

''Tis said, he fees servants. Most likely, some who come here.'

It was not like Izzy to suspect a man without cause. I noted his words carefully, and I guess he spoke to the rest, for we were all of us exceedingly discreet.

Our masters were less so. Sir John, when in his cups, left his private letters lying about, and his son was alike careless. *Mercurius Aulicus*, the Royalist newsletter, appeared in the house from time to time; lately, we had noted with growing excitement, it was finding less and less cause to exult. Naseby-Fight, in June, had been followed by Langport, not a month later, and the half drilled half fed had triumphed in both. 'The Divine Right,' jeered Zeb, 'seems sadly lacking in Divine Might.'

Izzy pointed out that the soldiers on both sides were much of a muchness, for though the Cavaliers prided themselves on their fighting spirit and high mettle, they had the same peasants and masterless men to drill as their opposites.

'Besides, Sir Thomas Fairfax is a gentleman,' he added, 'and this Cromwell a coming fellow.'

Not that we were reduced solely to *Mercurius Aulicus*. Godfrey was right, I had found me some reading and was very much taken therewith, considering it not at all unwholesome.

It was begun a few months before, by chance. Peter went to visit his aunt who worked at Champains, and there met Mister Pratt, one of the servants, and had some talk with him.

'Eight o'clock behind the stables,' Peter whispered to me that night. I went there after the evening meal, along with my brothers.

Peter held out a sheaf of papers. 'Here, lads, can you read these?'

Izzy took them and bent his head to the first one. '*Of Kingly Power and Its Putting Down*. Where had you these?'

I snatched at another. '*Of True Brotherhood* – printed in London, look.'

'Will it do?' asked Peter. 'And will you read it me?'

'We shall all of us read it,' Izzy promised.

These writings became, in time, our principal diversion. After the first lot, they were brought after dark by 'Pratt's boy', that same Christopher Walshe who later lay in the laundry, naked under a sheet.

It was our pleasure on warm evenings sometimes to take our work outside, behind the stables where Godfrey never went, Zeb and Peter drinking off a pipe of tobacco as part of the treat. There we would read the pamphlets. Printed mostly in London, they spoke of the Rising of Christ and the establishment of the New Jerusalem whereby England would become a beacon to all nations.

'A prophecy, listen.' Zeb's eyes shone. 'The war is to end with the utter annihilation of Charles the Great Tyrant and the *Papist serpent* – that's Henrietta Maria.'

'I know without your telling,' I said.

'Measures are to be taken afterwards. *In the day of triumph*, er, O yes here 'tis – *The rich to be cast down and the poor exalted. Every man that has borne a sword for freedom to have a cottage and four acres, and to live free*—'

We all sighed.

'*There shall be no landless younger brothers, forced by the laws to turn to war for their fortunes, and no younger brothers in another sense neither, that is, no class of persons obliged to serve others merely to live.*'

'A noble project,' said Peter.

At that time these writings were the closest any of us came to the great doings elsewhere, for at Beaurepair things went on much as they always had, save that the Master and Mistress were by turns triumphant and cast down. We had escaped the curse of pillage and its more respectable but scarce less dreaded brother, free quarter: no soldiers were as yet come near us. Sir John was too fond of his comfort to equip and lead a force as some of the neighbours had done, so he neglected to apply for a commission and his men were kept at home, to pour his drink.

In the reading of our pamphlets we servants were, for an hour or so, a little commonwealth. Though Peter and Patience could not read, the rest of us took turns aloud so that all might hear and understand the same matter at the same moment, and then fall to discussing it. Izzy had taught Caro her letters and she did her part very prettily, her low voice breathing a tenderness into every word she spoke. I would sit with my arm round her, warming to that voice and to the serious expression of her dark eyes as she, perhaps the least convinced of us all, denounced the Worship of Mammon.

'So, Caro, the Golden Calf must be melted?' Zeb teased her one time.

'So the writer says,' my love answered.

'And the Roches levelled with the rest of us?' he pressed. 'What say you to that?'

Caro returned stubbornly, 'I say they are different one from another. The Mistress—'

'The Mistress favours you, that's certain,' put in Patience, whose coarse skin was flushed from too much beer at supper.

'And not unjustly,' I said. 'But what is favour,' I asked Caro, 'that you should take it from her hand? Why are not you rich, and doing favours to her? Surely God did not make you to pomade her hair.'

'She deals kindly with me nonetheless,' Caro retorted. 'God will weigh us one by one at judgement, and she is clean different to Sir Bastard.'

'That may be,' I allowed, 'but she trusts us no more than he does. Besides, we cannot put away one and not the other.'

'If Mammon be pulled down,' Izzy warned, 'we must take care the true God be put in his place and not our own wanton desires – the God of simpleness, of truth in our speech and in our doings, the God of a brotherly bearing—'

He paused, and I saw his difficulty. We Cullens were the only brothers present, and Zeb and myself were constantly at one another's throats.

~

The night before Patience ran off, we spoke long on a pamphlet circulated by some persons who farmed land together. Young Walshe had but just brought it, and having some time free he stopped on for the talk – 'Mister Pratt knows where I am,' said he – and sat himself down between Zeb and Peter to get a share of their pipe. I thought him overfamiliar, even unseemly, passing his arm around Zeb's waist, but Zeb liked him well and on that night he sat with his arm round Walshe's shoulders, and laughed when the lad's attempts to smoke ended in coughing, though it was he that paid for the tobacco. Patience lolled against Zeb on the other side, and a man would be hard put to it to say which fawned on my brother more, herself or the boy.

Our debate was not strictly out of the pamphlet, but grew out of something beside. The writers freely said of themselves that they shared goods and chattels, but it was rumoured of them that they had also their women in common and considered Christian marriage no better than slavery.

'Does "women in common" mean that the woman can refuse no man?' asked Patience, looking round at the men present. Except when she gazed on Zeb, her dismay was so evident that for a moment the talk was lost in laughter, not least at her sudden assumption of chastity. I laughed along with the rest, thinking meanwhile that she had nothing to fear from me. I took none of Zeb's delight in women who fell over backwards if you so much as blew on them. In

Caro I had settled on a virgin, and one whom I would not take to my bed until we had been betrothed.

'Does it mean that men are held in common too?' jested Izzy. 'It seems to me that if no woman is bound to no man there can be no duty of obedience, and so a woman may as well court a man as a man a woman. So may the man refuse?'

Peter considered. 'Obliged to lie down with all the women!'

'For the sake of the community,' said Zeb with relish.

'But whose would the children be?' asked my darling.

Zeb answered her, 'The mother's who had them.'

'Fie, fie!' I said. 'The rights of a father cast away! Whoredom, pure and simple.'

'Look here,' urged Walshe. 'It is set down, *To be bound one to the other, is savagery.*'

There was a pause. Everyone, Walshe included, knew I was soon to be espoused to Caro.

'Am I then a savage?' I asked.

'Jacob, it was not Chris that said it,' replied Patience. 'He put their case only.'

The rest looked at me.

'Am I—'

'There would be incest,' put in Izzy, laying his hand on my shoulder. 'Jacob is right. Brother and sister, all unknowing.'

'That happens now,' said Peter. 'And not always unknowing.' Zeb looked up at once, seeming to search Peter's face, but Peter did not observe him and went on, 'There's bastardy too, and many a man raising another's son.'

Zeb ceased staring. The boy, catching my eye upon him, shrank like a woman closer to my brother's side. I became aware of Izzy's fingers kneading the back of my neck.

'Bastardy there may be, but 'twould be worse where they are,' Patience insisted. 'And what of old and ugly persons? None would have 'em!' She gave her horrible honking laugh.

'Those do not marry as it is,' I said through gritted teeth.

Izzy shook his head. 'Some do, and they have rights invested in the spouse's estate and on their body. But in such a commonwealth none would live with them. They would be the worse for it.'

'They might burn, but they wouldn't starve,' Peter said. 'Which they do frequently now.'

'You cannot get round the incest,' said Izzy.

Caro said, 'I want my own children,' and blushed.

Zeb, sitting opposite her, tapped her foot. 'Don't you mean you want your own man? Want him all to yourself?'

'Stop it,' she hissed.

'I shall call you sister,' said Zeb, 'and you can call him,' he assumed a doting expression and spoke in a mincing, squeaky voice, '*husband.* O Husband, I've such an itch under my smock—'

Peter whooped. I gave Zeb a kick that would afflict him with more than an itch.

'Behold, a tiger roused!' he shouted, eyes watering. Caro's cheeks were inflamed. I kicked Zeb again and this time shut him up.

Through it all the boy watched me and said nothing. He had still not begged my pardon, and from time to time I let him see that I was also watching him.

'Our talk grows foolish,' said Izzy. 'An unprofitable choice of reading, but we will do better next time.' He got up and walked off in the direction of the house.

We were not often so rowdy, for though Zeb's spirits were usually too high, he loved Izzy and would be quiet for him if not for me. Peter was coarse-minded, but never quarrelsome. A deal of interesting matter and many ideas came first to me in those talks, for example the thought of settling in New England.

~

Now the date of my betrothal to Caro was fast approaching, and Sir Bastard back among us, the Norman Yoke incarnate. I was no more safe from his blows and pinches than was Peter, my size being no bar to a craven who relied upon my not striking back. Had he and I been servants both, he would have run a mile rather than encounter with me. I did not want to serve him at dinner, for he would be too drunk to care what he did and in this condition he was at his most hateful. That Godfrey would be there was some comfort, for the brute was aware that My Lady listened to her steward more than to any other servitor. But what was My Lady, in that house? Those who should show a manly dignity were sunk into beasts – no, not beasts, for beasts are seemly among themselves, and have even a kind of society, whereas such degenerates as these desire only a bottle.

I pressed hard with the sand, polishing out the knife scratches in the pewter, scouring as if to wipe the Roches from the face of the earth. The burnished plates I stacked in neat piles, for I hated a slovenly workman. When I did a job I did it well, and Caro was the same: I loved her deft grace as she moved about the house. Had we the wherewithal we could have run an inn or shop together, for she was skilled with all manner of things and clever with money.

Not that I was marrying her for that. She seemed to me simply the likeliest girl I ever saw, with a sweet child-like face which gave a stranger no hint of her quick wit. She was good-humoured too, able to charm me out of my melancholy and wrath. Zeb had tried over the years to win her, and failed; I looked on, defeated in advance, until Izzy spoke to me one day.

There is another brother she prefers.

What, Izzy, is she yours?

No, Jacob, nor Zeb's nor mine. Who does that leave?

At first I would not believe him. It had never fallen out that anyone, man or woman, preferred me to Zebedee. Then at Christmas we played a kissing game and I saw that she managed things so as to get in with me.

'Forfeit,' Izzy cried. 'You must give Jacob a kiss.'

Her mouth was so soft and red that I longed to put mine against it, but was afraid lest I spoil my chances with some clumsiness.

'Turn,' she whispered, and tugged at my sleeve so that my back was between us and the company. I bent down and we kissed with open eyes, Caro's utterly wide awake and innocent even as, unseen by the rest, she put the point of her tongue between my lips.

Afterwards Zeb asked, 'Did she suck your soul out?' and laughed; he told me all the company had seen me shake while kissing, and thus roused me to a blushing fit that lasted half an hour.

But I began to keep company with Caro. We had that talk which all lovers have, *Why me*, and *Since when*. She said I was a man and Zeb a boy, and during the kiss which followed her hand brushed against my body as if by chance. Like a fool, I spent days wondering did she understand what she had done to me.

Next to Caro, Patience showed cumbersome as a cow. Impossible, I thought, that she should hold Zeb, who was constantly seeking new pleasures. Whereas Caro, delectable Caro, should hold me for ever. More than once of late I had been woken at night by Izzy laughing and punching me, and when I asked him what was ado he would not tell.

'Haste and get married,' was all the answer he would give. Peter and Zeb, who shared the other bed (only Godfrey had a chamber of his own) laughed along with him. In the dark I blushed worse than before, for I suffered hot, salt dreams and had some idea of what I might have done.

I was slow with her. After *Kiss Day*, as I afterwards thought of it, after she called me a man to Zeb's boy, I was still unsure and sometimes thought that for all she said, she must like Zeb better than me, for all women did. At times I even fancied, God forgive me, that she had perhaps turned to me following an earlier adventure with him.

One day I looked out of the window and saw her talking most earnestly with Zeb some yards off. I rose and quietly opened the window a crack before ducking beneath the sill.

Caro's voice came to me: '... and sees nothing of my difficulty.'

'Jacob all over,' Zeb said. 'But to the purpose. He must be put out of hope, you know.'

'I cannot do it!' she cried. 'Two brothers ... (here I missed some words, for my ears were throbbing) ... to do something so cruel.'

'But the longer it goes on, the crueller,' said Zebedee.

There followed a silence. I rose and peeped out of the window: they had joined hands.

'Shall I undertake to tell him?' asked Zeb.

Caro cried, 'Indeed, Zeb, you are too kind!' and then, before my very eyes, they embraced, out there in the garden where any might see. I pulled the window to and sank to the floorboards, trembling.

The rest of that afternoon was passed in planning Zeb's death, various ways, and devising punishments for Caro. During the evening meal I spoke not a word to either, even when directly addressed, and saw my fellow servants exchange puzzled or offended looks. Afterwards, when all was cleared away, I sat by myself at the kitchen fire polishing the Master's boots. Zeb and Caro were most likely keeping out of my sight, and they were wise, for every time I thought of Zeb taking her in his arms, my jaw set and my own arms and shoulders became hard as iron.

The door opened and I glared upwards. It was Izzy.

'I have made a discovery today,' I said at once.

'Have you?' His voice was mild. 'Will you tell me what?'

'Acting the ambassador? Be straight. You are come to make their excuses.' I bent forward and spat into the grate.

Izzy contemplated me. 'Who are *they*? My business with you concerns no excuses.' He pulled up a chair next to mine.

'Well?' I snapped.

'Nay, I can't talk to you in that style. Would you rather I went away?'

'Zeb is courting Caro,' I burst out before I could stop myself. 'Don't you know it?'

'You amaze me. How did you make this – discovery?'

I told him what I had seen and heard. Izzy's face quickened with some inner revelation before I was halfway through.

'This is – none of it what you think,' he began slowly.

'What, not the embrace!'

He scratched his nose. 'Jacob . . . there's a thing I must break to you. Somewhat ticklish.'

I thought, *You are in the right of it there.*

'Caro has sought Zeb's counsel.'

'Why not mine?'

'It concerns you.' Izzy glanced up at the ceiling as if wishing himself anywhere else in the world. 'She has sought mine also, and her difficulty is—'

'How to break off with me!'

'She wonders why you wait so long to declare yourself.'

I was silenced.

He took a great breath and went on, 'If I may speak my mind – take note, this is none of her saying! – you make a fool of her, keeping company so long and the day not settled on. She has never wanted any but you. I thought you had a great mind to her also, and you can be sure the Mistress would be pleased. Where then lies the impediment?'

'She is mighty familiar with Zeb,' I answered slowly, and then, filling with stubborn anger, 'I will not espouse her, or any, where I think my brother might have been before me.'

That was the only time in my entire life I saw Isaiah in a passion.

'Do you ever raise your eyes and look about you?' he hissed. 'Everyone knows where Zeb's delight lies, except the hulking idiot who is his brother.'

I gaped at him.

'Besides, now is too late,' Izzy went on, his eyes gleaming, 'for such talk! You have kept company with her for months and given no hint. I repeat, you make a fool of her, and – I promise you! – if one word of your – madness – gets out, you'll make such a fool of yourself as you'll never live down.'

'He embraces her.'

'Because he sees her unhappy! And should they kiss, what is it to you? You are not espoused, and if you like it not the remedy lies in your own hands.'

I was stunned, partly at this view of the matter, but mostly at what he had said of Zeb. 'Zeb in love? Who?'

'O, a certain maid whose ear he has been nibbling, full in your view, these past months. She has two eyes and a mouth and her name begins with P.'

Things that I had taken for jests came back to me: Zeb arm-wrestling Patience, or begging a lock of her hair 'for lying on a maiden's hair brings a man sweet sleep'.

'Caro does not wish to break off, then—?' I faltered.

Izzy rolled his eyes.

I went on, 'Yet they spoke of cruelty – said it was cruel.'

'You. You're cruel to Caro.'

'To Caro . . . ?' They had talked of a *he*. I was about to explain his mistake when the truth came to me. The cruelty Zeb had spoken of was my own, and the sufferer Izzy. My elder brother had never ceased to love Caro, that was it; he had but loved her more tenderly as she turned away from the shared kindnesses of their early years towards something different with me. O Izzy, Izzy: he was the better man of us two, I own it freely, but he was not the sort of man a maid dreams of taking to her bed, and he had been forced to learn it over and over as he watched me win her. I could hardly bear to look at him as he sat there, smiling in defeat.

'Cruel to Caro, yes.' I must now conceal my pity.

'I would see her happy,' he returned simply. 'I thought her happiness must lie with you.'

He it was, I remembered now, who had first told me of her preference.

'But I begin to think *I* was mistaken.' Izzy stared ahead of him. 'Lord, what brothers I have. One eats women and the other starves them.' His voice trembled as he rose to leave the room.

'Don't go, Izzy.' I flung my arms round him from behind. 'Wait and see – I will declare myself.' Even as I said it I felt what a bittersweet promise this must be to him.

He turned to me and we pressed our faces together, the way we had always made up our quarrels as children. I had to bend down now, having so far outgrown my childhood protector. His face was damp around the eyes and for a moment I felt with horror that he was about to cry, but his gaze was bright and steady.

As he put me away from him, Izzy said quietly, 'You are near as handsome as he, and bigger.'

'Don't make me more of a fool than I am,' I answered.

'There, I knew you would not hear it.'

'You love me too well, Izzy.'

He sighed. 'Very well, think yourself ugly. But Jacob,' he went on, 'be not so harsh with Zeb.'

I said I would not.

Going to seek out Caro, I found Zeb and Patience in the scullery, his arms about her as she scraped at a dirty dish, and I wondered at my blindness for so long. My own darling I discovered moping in the great hall. When she saw me she rose, and would have quitted the room, but I stepped up to her and begged her forgiveness. Before we parted that night, our betrothal was a settled thing.

~

The Mistress furnished Caro with a good dowry. All the money I could afford for her portion had been put by out of my own sweat, and was not bad considering the little that servants such as ourselves could scratch together. Neither of us could fairly hope for more if we meant to stay where we were.

My brothers and myself had been born to better fortunes than we enjoyed, but our father, though godly, was strangely improvident. *I found my inheritance wasted and my estate encumbered*, was his constant cry throughout my childhood. *Yet all shall be paid off, and you, Isaiah, shall inherit—*

Dust and debt. There was nothing else for Izzy to come into. The day after we buried Father, I found Mother weeping in her chamber, the steward standing over her and papers scattered all around.

'Jacob,' she screamed at me as if it were my doing, 'O my boy, my boy,' and fell to tearing her lace collar. I took it for the grief, and wept along with her, until the steward came forward saying, 'Pray, young master, send your brother Isaiah to us.'

When Izzy came out from the chamber he told me that we were nine-tenths ruined. The house and lands were certain to be seized. The steward was at that instant writing a letter for Mother to sign, begging our neighbour Sir John that of his goodness he succour a distressed widow of gentle birth and her three helpless children.

Sir John Roche was not in those days the wineskin he is since become, and his wife (who inclined to a somewhat Papistical style of worship) was known for her rather short-sighted charity. Our mother was given a cottage in the village and the three helpless children were put to work in the fields on Sir John's estate. This was perhaps not what Mother had in mind.

Margett, who was at that time the cook at Beaurepair, later enlightened me. We were in the kitchen together and her forehead shone greasily as she bent over a pig she had on the spit. I thought her grey hair very ugly, but her face was kind, if wrinkled, and from her I could find out things the others kept secret.

'Your father owed Sir John a deal of money,' Margett said. 'Turn the handle there, it's about to catch. Lost a fortune by him, the Master did.'

And so he wished us to work his fields. It was every inch my mother, not to have understood this. She understood nothing but weeping, coaxing and prayer.

When we were let fall into the furrow, I was ill prepared for my new life. For one thing, I was then accustomed to the attentions of servants (though unlike Mervyn Roche, I had been taught always to address them with respect). Now I found a great abatement of rest and of comfort, whether I were in the field or cooped up in the dark cramped place that was become our home.

Most unendurable was the utter loss of all means of raising myself from the earth. My books were left behind in our old house. Weary as I was, I would gladly have had them by me. I could read well and was skilled in reckoning, knew my rhetoric and Scripture, and had begun the ancient tongues some years before.

'A forward lad for his age,' our tutor, Doctor Barton, had told my father. 'He might be trained up in the law perhaps, and become secretary to some great man.'

Now the forward lad found himself grubbing at roots, spreading dung, pulling thistles. When there was nothing else to do a boy could always be set to scare crows. Alone in the field where none could see me at it, I wept. Zeb, too young to grasp that we would be wasted in this valley of humiliation, was less wretched, though from time to time he would whine, 'When are we going home?'

The other workers were at first somewhat in awe of us, but when they understood that for all our polish we were penniless, things altered. Very soon they made no difference between us and themselves.

'Here, young Cullen, take this off-a me; don't stand there gawking,' said a man who could not read. I felt myself bitterly degraded. When I perceived that I was forgetting what I had been taught, that my only study now would be scythes and manures, terror seized me.

Izzy, finding me one day in a fit of despair, knelt by me in the field and crooked his arm about my neck. 'A man's value lies in his obedience to God's will,' he said. 'We are as precious to Him now as ever we were.'

'He does not show it.'

'Indeed He does. We eat and drink; we have good health, and one another,' he reproached me. But I lacked his greatness of heart.

Margett also told me that about this time, My Lady passing by in the carriage was struck by the sight of the three 'black-boys' labouring in her field. She made enquiries, and found that while she had thought us to be living on the charity of the Roches, her husband had reduced us to peasants.

'That was an evil day for him. The sermons!' Margett gloated. 'Table lectures, fireside lectures, pillow lectures! – until he said she might bring you to the house. A fellow was sent for you directly, before the Master could change his mind.'

I remembered that. When the man came into the field and bade us follow him, for we were now to work indoors at Beaurepair, he must have thought we would never move off. Izzy stood motionless and speechless, while I dropped to my knees thanking God, for I knew what we had escaped. Servitude inside the house was still bondage in Egypt, but we were now shaded against the noonday heat.

Caro's fortune was even humbler than my own. Margett told me that Caro's mother, Lucy Bale, had been a maid at Beaurepair in time past, a woman about the Mistress's own age and her entire favourite.

'It ended sadly, though,' the woman said. 'In the same year that the Mistress married Sir John, Lucy found herself with child. That's a fault easily wiped out, to be sure! – but her Mathias was killed. An unlucky fall.'

Later, Godfrey told me more. Lucy, it seemed, bore up under her shame with no little dignity. Sir John would have sent her away, but his wife argued that provided she showed herself repentant, she should stay, else she would surely sink to a most degraded condition.

In the event she had no chance to sink, for she died in giving birth to her daughter.

The child, which was of a rare white-and-gold beauty (both Lucy and Mathias were, said Godfrey, bright as sovereigns), was christened Caroline and put under the care of the then steward's wife, to be raised up a servant. I remembered her being shouted for, and once, when she might be six or seven, dragged by her hand through the great hall, trembling, for the steward's wife was sharp of tongue and temper. Had Mathias lived, Caro should have been called Caroline Hawks, but none of his kin wished to claim her, so she kept the name of Bale. Izzy, finding her one day weeping in the garden, took her in his arms and dried her eyes and nose on his shirt. He called her Caro for short, and Caro she became.

~

'Come along, Jacob.' Godfrey stood before me, smoothing down his collar. 'Leave that for later and wash your hands. The meat is ready to go out.'

I rinsed the sand off my fingers in a bowl of water before following him into the kitchen. The roast was set upon a wheeled table, and as fragrant as the stalled ox must have smelt to the Prodigal – a fine piece of mutton stuck with rosemary. Around it stood dishes of carrots and peas, a pigeon pie and sweet young lettuces dressed with eggs, mushrooms and oil.

'Let us hope they leave plenty over,' I said to Godfrey.

'Amen to that.' The steward poured wine from a decanter, held it up to the light and sipped it. 'Very pleasing. I will help you with the dishes and then come back for the drink.'

We trundled in with the mutton, my mouth watering. Someone, most likely Caro, had set up the table with such precision that every cup and dish was in absolute line, not a hair's breadth out. No pewter today; instead, the plate glittered. At one end of this perfection sat My Lady, her hair like string and face flaky with white lead; at the other, Sir John, bloated and purplish. To his mother's right Mervyn sprawled like a schoolboy in a sulk, tipping the chair back and forth on two of its four legs. He was far gone in drink. I silently thanked

Godfrey, grate on me as he might, for keeping Caro away. Only men and whores should serve Mervyn Roche.

When he saw us he shifted in the seat with annoyance and almost fell backwards.

'Mother!'

'Yes, my darling?'

'Mother, why don't you get a proper butler? Here's the steward serving the wine – what does he know of it? – and none but that booby to help him. If there *be* any wine.'

'It is decanted, Sir, and I am going back for it directly,' Godfrey soothed.

'I saw a man at Bridgwater carve in a new way entirely,' Mervyn announced. 'It was a wonder to see how he did it – here—'

To my amazement he leapt from his seat and held out his hands for the carving knife and fork.

Godfrey kept his hands on the trolley but dared do no more; he looked helplessly at My Lady. Sir John, seemingly oblivious, stared at the ceiling.

'Do you think you should, my sweet?' Lady Roche implored. On receiving no reply she tried for help elsewhere. 'Husband, if I may speak a word? Husband?'

'Might a man eat in peace?' the husband grunted.

Mervyn glared at his mother, then snapped his fingers to me. 'You, Jacob. Give it over here. Christ's arse, if I can't carve a joint of meat—!'

The Mistress winced at her son's foul tongue. I took the roast to him and laid the knife and fork ready. Godfrey disappeared through the door leading to the kitchen. I stood back, arms by my sides as I had been taught. He made a fearful butchery of it, hacking in chunks the sweet, crisp flesh which the cook had so lovingly tended. I saw his mother sigh. When the best part of the meat was ruined I brought forward the plates and shared out the tough lumps between the diners. *Why, O God,* I was thinking, *do You not let slip his knife?*

'A butler, I say,' he persisted, cutting into the pigeon pie with rather more finesse than he had displayed in carving the mutton.

'Where is the need?' asked his mother. 'We live in a very small way here.'

'Aye, I'll say you do!' He pushed off with his legs from the table, almost dropped backwards onto the floor, but retrieved the balance of the chair just in time. 'Where is Patty?' This was his name for Patience.

'Patty is no longer with us,' came the reply.

'What! Dead!'

'No.' My Lady began crying.

'What, then?'

'Run away. Or—' She shook her head.

Mervyn glanced at her, took a gobbet of flesh and chewed on it. 'If she's run away she's a fool. You,' he again snapped his fingers at me, so that I itched to twist them off, 'tell that Frenchified capon I've had better mutton in taverns.'

I bowed and took my chance to escape him a while. Going out of the door I met Godfrey returning with the wine and I hoped it might find better favour than the meat. Best of all would be if it were poisoned. One thing was cheering: Sir Bastard might scorn me but I had beaten him to the woman he desired. Setting aside his sulks and his drink-stained eyes, Mervyn was handsome, especially round the mouth, with its fierce scarlet lips hemming in very white teeth. In him a man might see what his father had been when young, just as in Sir John his son's fate was laid out plain – if the son were fortunate, for his whoring was proverbial and a lucky pox or clap might yet shorten his days. He had always had a thirst for Caro. If I could think at all on my wedding night, I should take a minute to exult over him.

In the kitchen the cook, used to madness in his masters, shrugged when I told him the insults heaped on the roast.

'I have a syllabub for that lad,' he told me. 'A special one. Don't you go tasting, Jacob. Barring Godfrey, everyone's helped with it.'

'Not me,' I said. I took my turn and spat in the thing too, stirring in the spittle. A voice like Father's somewhere in my head said, *Sweetly done, my boy*. I carried in the syllabubs, placed the defiled one before Mervyn and stood the picture of submission, watching him eat it.

~

The man who had joined with us servants in taking this small but choice revenge was called Mister, or Mounseer, Daskin. Between him and Mervyn was deadly hatred. We were out of the ordinary in having a foreign cook. Margett, who had told me of my father's debt to Sir John, dropped dead one day while arranging a goose on the spit, and the Mistress, who clung still to some pretence of elegance, tormented Sir John for a French cook, such as were just then starting to be known in London.

'I will have my meat done in the good old English way,' said the husband, who had no hankerings after *hautgousts*, *hachees* or dishes dressed *a-la-doode*. 'There will be no French cooks at Beaurepair while I am master.'

His next dinner taught him better: the meat was bloody, and the sauces full of grit. Sir John glared about him. 'Is the wine spoilt?' he asked.

'Not at all,' his wife replied.

'Then why have we none on the table?'

'The cellar key is lost.'

Sir John knew when he was beaten, and bade the Mistress do what she would.

His wife let him down gently. Letters of enquiry to her friends in Town brought forth a number of likely men, but she settled on Mister Daskin who was but half French, could speak our language and cook in the English way beside. He arrived in the coach one wet October afternoon, a small dapper man in London clothes, looking about him with pleasure. It was said that fashionable life had hurt his health.

'Up all night, and then working again all day,' he told me. 'Never, Jacob, never go to London!'

'You will find it very dull here,' I answered.

'Now that is exactly what I like.'

It seemed he found promise of saner living in our old stone house with its surrounding fields and trees. The first meal he cooked for the household was served to Mervyn, and I guess he was never so pleased with his bargain since.

Daskin was not bad for someone half French. He was a Protestant, and he gave good food to the servants as well as the masters. Peter sometimes assisted him in the kitchen, but more often it was either Caro or Patience, and Caro told me she had picked up a great deal of knowledge concerning preserves and puddings from Mounseer, who was not jealous of others seeing what he did. Most of what was cooked was done in the English style, for after a week or so during which her pride would not let her speak, the Mistress was forced to admit that she did not care for French feeding, and Sir John's roasts were restored to him.

~

When Mervyn had given his final belch and strewn bread about the table, the Mistress joined her hands and offered up thanks. Her son rattled off the words through force of habit, so that by happy accident I was able to hear him thank God for what he had just received.

After they had got down from the board Peter came to help me clear away.

'Look at that.' I pointed out the roast, now stiffening as it cooled. 'That's how he carves.'

'Still alive, was it? Kept running about?'

The room felt cleaner with Mervyn gone. Daskin came in and wheeled off the meat, muttering words in French that any man could translate only by studying his face. We returned the plate to the sideboard and carried the slipware to the scullery to be washed along with ours.

In the room where we had our own food there was a smell of onions and cider. Caro was laying out the dishes; Daskin bent over the mutton, trying to save what he could. I was suddenly very hungry. The syllabub could not be spoken of before Godfrey, who was there examining a fork which Mervyn had bent out of shape, but it hung in the air between us all, a secret pleasure to set against the gloom of that morning's discovery.

'There's nothing wrong with this meat,' said the cook. 'If I myself carve what's left you'll find it as tender a roast as you've had.'

'We never thought otherwise,' Izzy assured him.

'I have made onions in white sauce,' added Caro, looking sweetly on me because she knew how I relished this dish. I sat on the end of the bench next to the place she would take when she left off serving.

The meal was set before us and Godfrey led us in asking God's blessing. As soon as folk began spooning up onions and handing about the bread, the talk turned to Chris Walshe, and to Patience.

'Is Zeb back from Champains yet?' I asked.

'No,' said Peter. 'I guess they'll keep him there awhile.'

'What for? All he did was drag the pond.'

'This is fine mutton, Mounseer,' said one of the dairymaids, who seemed to have got the sheep's eyes into her own head to judge by her glances at him.

'Did Chris – was Chris hurt, Jacob?' asked Caro.

'He was,' I answered. 'Has nobody been to look?'

'I locked the laundry after you laid him out,' said Godfrey. 'It is neither seemly nor respectful for everyone to go goggling at the lad.'

'There's something in that,' said Izzy. 'But tell us, Godfrey, how was he wounded?'

The steward hesitated.

'Jacob knows already,' urged Peter.

Godfrey said, 'Well. It was no accident.' He looked at me.

'Stabbed,' I supplied.

A general gasp and then a buzz, not unlike pleasure, rose from the company.

'There are bad men about,' said Godfrey. 'Be watchful. The Mistress has instructed me to look over all the locks and bolts, and I should be obliged if you would bring me to any weak ones.'

'And still no sign of Patience,' said Caro.

'Did she quarrel with one of you? Had she any trouble?' the steward asked.

'None,' Caro said. 'No trouble.'

I turned to her and saw her face quite innocent. I pictured Zeb, how he would have answered, perhaps mopping up sauce on a bit of bread, and his eyelashes lying modest on his cheek like a girl's.

TWO

Beating

AFTER THE MUTTON and cider I felt the need of fresh air. It was Peter's turn for scouring the dishes, so I went out into the rosemary maze. I loved this maze, its pungent scent, the blue blossoms which besprinkled the dark hedges in the summer and the fragrant knot garden at its heart, where one could sit on the bench and doze. Caro went along with me, stealing a few minutes before going back to the house and Mervyn's wine-stained shirt, for he no sooner fouled a shirt than he changed it, no sooner changed than he fouled. His laundry had often robbed me of courting time.

We sat on the warm stone seat, carved with suns and hourglasses, and twined ourselves in an embrace. My hat fell off onto the chamomile behind the bench and so that we should be equal I pulled off her cap and kissed her stiff yellow coil of hair. She laughed and put her face up to mine. There was cider on her breath. I touched my mouth to hers and she looked straight at me, then closed her eyes. Very slowly, softly, she nibbled my tongue as I slid it between her lips. I closed my eyes also, the better to feel the inside of her mouth. We stayed like that some time, tasting and toying, while bees droned up and down the rosemary hedges, until Caro broke away and kissed me on the nose. 'I should go, Jacob.'

'A little longer—' I pulled her onto my lap. The skin of her breasts, as much as I could see and stroke, was like petals of the purest white roses. I wondered, not for the first time, how it must feel to embrace a woman without her stays, without even her shift. My breath came faster and I strained her to me.

Caro whispered, 'The Mistress may come out.'

'She may indeed.'

A tussle followed, with much laughter and tickling, but at last I let her go and she went back to sitting at my side. Holding hands, we contemplated the knot garden while I suffered the familiar pain which would only be eased upon our betrothal.

Once, in that garden, I had put my hand right down her bodice while we kissed, and felt the tender bud of her breast swell and push greedily between my fingers. My own flesh had straightway begun to ache, and I caught such a look in her eyes as told me plainly what would happen next if I did not stop. I did stop; I withdrew my hand, and heard her moan with disappointment. I had passed up a chance, but gained a knowledge inexpressibly sweet. Many men are wed for their purses, the man being taken, oft grudgingly, along with the money. I knew with proud certitude that this was not my case. There was no need to hurry, to take her in that furtive way in which Zeb conducted his loves. We would wait until the appointed night. It might even be that something in me took pleasure in teasing her. Sometimes, as we worked together or sat decorously side by side, I recalled that pleading moan of hers, and smiled.

'Poor Chris.' Caro interlaced her fingers with mine. 'A hideous death.'

I had forgotten Walshe. The eager shoot that was my body shrivelled as if she had thrown cold water on me.

She frowned. 'And yet—'

'Yet?'

'Now that I think on it – he was always strange. What was his business here? Wandering at night, on another's land?'

'Perhaps he was stopped by someone from the house,' I said. My stomach fluttered; I wondered would she notice the sweat which had begun squeezing from my hand.

'Folk naturally defend their own,' Caro went on. 'Or a servant who kills a trespasser by chance, shall he be blamed?'

My guts coiled within me for I thought I saw a way out of my gaol. 'So,' I put it to her, 'if it were one of us dispatched Chris, would *you* deem him guilty?'

''Twould depend why he did it.' She straightened suddenly. 'Why Jacob, do you suppose it *is* one of us?'

I hesitated.

'Yes! You have a man in mind,' she insisted.

'For myself, none. But we are servants, we must look to be suspected.'

Caro seemed satisfied with this. However, in speaking it, I had slammed the door of the gaol on myself, and now felt my courage begin to slip away.

'I saw you from the window,' Caro went on, 'dragging the pond. I had made up my mind for Patience.'

'Well, you knew what cause she had to despair,' I said. 'Her condition.'

Caro's hand stiffened in mine but she said nothing.

'I am not Godfrey, that things should be kept from me,' I said.

'Zeb asked me not to.'

There was a thunderbolt! I had thought to receive some such answer as, *I did but yesterday find out*, or *I do not like such talk*. My love, the woman I had near entrusted with my secret, with my very life, was all the while in private conference with my own brother.

I put Caro away from me and searched her face. 'Zeb told you—'

'Asked.' She looked back frankly, without shame.

'But why should I not know? He is my brother. I am the child's uncle!' I went on, growing more angry as the full sense of it came to me. Why, he had gone so far as to mock me for my ignorance.

'He said he must tell you himself,' she said quietly. 'Do you not think that was right, Jacob?'

'Aye! Would that he had told me before he told you!' I got up and retrieved my hat. Then, not wanting to sit down again, I put it on and stayed behind the bench, away from her.

'It was Patience first broke it to me, not Zeb,' protested Caro. She twisted round to speak to me; there was a flush beginning in her cheeks.

'I do not think he would ever have told me,' I brooded. 'Had we pulled her out of the pond, how happy he would be!'

'No, Jacob! How can you say such things of him?'

'Well, does he look miserable? Does he weep, is he unable to eat?'

'Not while you are there. But I have seen him weep.'

'Frightened he'd be made to marry her, most like.' I circled the bench. 'And had I known it, he would have been.'

'Well, you know now,' Caro said. Her eyes were dry and not as soft as I had seen them when we came into the maze.

'He has angered me. And so have you.'

'You are too easily angered.' She sat very straight with her fingers intertwined on her lap. 'That is why you are not told things.'

I was amazed. 'Is this how you speak to your future husband? So you have let Zeb give an account of my character!'

'No indeed. I have eyes and ears of my own.' Caro stood up and arranged the top of her gown. 'It may be he would not marry her, but to say he wishes her dead! You are too fierce with your brother.'

'Was it not you, yourself, told me of her filthy braggings? Said it sickened you? Would a man want to marry *that*?' I grimaced in disgust.

'Such women do marry. What would you have him do?' She replaced her cap. 'But you are troubled, it is natural with Chris's death. Surely that's more terrible than—'

'What has Chris to do with this?'

'Jacob! Zebedee has lost both friend and love. Have some pity.' Caro turned and walked through the first gap in the maze.

'He plays on the pity of silly maids and then he ruins them,' I shouted after her.

It is a woman of all people who should see the danger in such a fellow, and a woman who never will. I sat arguing it out with her though she could no longer hear me. She was as obstinate as Izzy, who was forever telling me that Zeb was not really bad, for all the world as if he too were a wench dazzled by Zeb's eyes.

They were both of them deluded. He would never be anything but fickle, tasting one love and flying on to another. There had been a tramping woman, older than himself and no innocent, when he was but fifteen: I had caught Peter letting him in late at night, flushed and exhilarated. Being once alerted by Izzy, I had observed Zeb's steady heating of Patience, who was only too hot already: his tickling her, putting the point of his tongue in her ear, and generally laying siege to that tottering fort, her virtue. Whenever I saw him at it, rage choked me. Had he been younger, and under my authority, I would have prescribed him a beating.

~

Back indoors, I again took up the tray and went on with my scouring, pressing the grains of sand against the pewter until each dish would have passed, at a distance, for silver. Near me sat Izzy, scraping teasels over Sir Bastard's coat to raise the nap.

'That will have to do.' He stood and held up the garment. 'What do you think?'

'You've wrought marvels with it.'

'It stinks of wine. God, how the man slobbers and sicks!' He threw it aside. It was not like my brother to let ill temper gain on him and I saw in his petulance how weary he was.

'The house is quiet without Zeb,' I ventured.

'Why do they keep him so long!' Izzy moaned. 'Is he suspected?'

'No reason he should be.' I rinsed the pewter clear of sand and began drying the pieces on a cloth. At that moment the sound of rapid footsteps came to us from the corridor. With a quick glance at me, Izzy ran to the doorway and looked out. I heard someone whispering and saw him gesture in reply. He closed the door and came back to where I was stacking the dishes.

'That was Caro. Zeb's back.'

'Has he seen the Master yet?'

Izzy shrugged. We left the scullery and made our way to the hall, where we found our brother in council with Godfrey.

'If the Mistress would be so good,' Zeb was saying.

Godfrey listened judicially, nodding from time to time. 'I will inform her. And when does he expect to have the cart, did you say?'

'Tomorrow. O, and he asks that the boy's friends here may be let go to the funeral.'

'We shall see,' the steward answered, frowning. The frown meant nothing, for Godfrey had never been known to grant anything on the first request and we would most likely get a half-holiday if we wished it. For my part I had just as lief stay home.

'That is all the message he sent,' Zeb prompted.

'Thank you, Zebedee. Now, have you and your brothers sufficient work?'

'Were we not to beat the hangings?'

'Indeed. Pray do so.' Godfrey turned and strode towards My Lady's parlour. I groaned inwardly, for if there was one task I detested, beating hangings was it. 'In God's name, why remind him of that?' I muttered as the door closed after the steward.

'I want to talk to you both, out in the orchard. Anyway, Jacob, we should have to do them some day soon, so why wait until it rains?'

'What did Biggin say?' demanded Izzy. 'Is he coming over to fetch the body? Do they know what the boy was doing here?'

'During the night? No,' Zeb returned. 'He is to be carried back there tomorrow. The most suitable cart is out at present, but they will send it over with a coffin – the carpenter is put to the job already.'

'And the surgeon?' I asked.

'They had no cause to tell me. I guess they'll call one to the house when the boy arrives. You washed him, Jacob. Did you see—?'

'Slit right up the belly. They won't need a surgeon to interpret that.'

'O, the little fool!'

Izzy stared at him. '*Fool?*'

My heart began to thump. Supposing Zeb was risen, gone to the chamber window. It was bright moonlight when I grabbed the boy's knife, and my empty bed – but no, his way of speaking to me earlier on—

'Out,' Zeb insisted. 'Let us go out. You fetch the hangings, I will set up the line, when I have once rid myself of these clothes. I am not Sir Bastard, to ruin them with dust.' He hurried off towards the stairs leading to our chamber. Izzy and myself gazed at the hangings which covered three walls of the hall, and then at one another.

~

'Hold hard – there's a corner come down – let me not trip!' Thus, standing on a chair, did I bully my brother from above. It was my task to unhook the tapestries from the wall while Izzy gathered up the edges and held them away from my feet.

'I have it,' he assured me. 'Step down.' A spider ran over my neck as I dangled one leg in the air, almost causing me to fall, but at last we laid the third hanging on the worn flags of the floor. Izzy loaded me up and we progressed along the corridor, my brother going ahead to open each door as I came to it.

'Wait,' he said as we emerged into the sun. I was glad enough to stand and do nothing as he ducked back into the house, coming out directly with the carpet-beaters. There were five of these, supposedly from Turkey, of fine withy and all different in form. Godfrey said they had been presented to My Lady by some traveller much taken with her in that far-off time, her youth. I wondered what Caro would say to such a gift. With Izzy holding up the hangings behind me like a maid holding her mistress's train, we passed by the maze where I had been scolded by Caro, by the pond where Christopher Walshe had been fished up by the armpits that very morning, and along a stony track to the orchard.

Zeb was not there. 'He is sloth itself,' I grumbled, all the while dreading the sight of him. We spread the hangings over some bushes until our brother should come up with the line. Izzy sat in the shade of a pear tree and began swishing about him with the beaters, as if killing flies. 'This for me,' he said, setting one apart from the rest. 'Do you wish to choose?'

'They're all alike.' Surely Zeb was lingering in the house expressly to torment me.

'Not in the least,' said Izzy. 'This one is the fastest, and that the prettiest.'

Sometimes, I reflected, my brother had odd notions: he had preferences in cups and candles as well as in the customary things like food and music, wherein each man has his particular taste. He had once told me that when we worked in the fields as children, every implement had for him its own character. But this was, after all, a small oddity. Apart from Caro, I loved Izzy better than anyone I knew, much more than I loved Zeb or my mother, perhaps because he never teased me.

A whistle, full and liquid, drifted over the orchard among the songs of blackbirds and thrushes.

'See, he is not so late,' said Izzy the peacemaker.

Zeb's face, solemn, even strained, was oddly out of tune with his warbling of 'There Lived a Pretty Maid'. He nodded to us, then began looping the rope he had brought over the apple boughs.

'Higher,' suggested Izzy. Zeb obeyed without question.

'We are alone,' I prompted him.

'There.' Zeb gave a final tweak to the line and turned to face us. 'If someone comes, we put up the hangings.'

'Yes, yes!' My shirt was all damp. 'But tell us, how did you break it to them at Champains?'

'Godfrey gave me a note for the master. He – Mister Biggin – called me into his study and asked me was I sure, how was the lad, dark or fair – you know how it goes. In the end I did persuade him that what we have in the laundry is the earthly shell of Christopher Walshe.'

'And did you say how he died?'

'Drowned, of course. When you find a lad in a pond—' he shrugged. 'Would I had known about the stabbing. There will be more explanations tomorrow.'

'Not from you, surely? You don't think they suspect you?' Izzy urged.

'Perhaps not of killing the boy.' Zeb picked up the hanging on the top of the pile and laid it ready. 'They kept asking me how we knew it was he, as if our knowing him were some proof of guilt.'

I felt a twist of fear. 'What did you say?'

'I told them Godfrey knew him. That was nothing but truth, Godfrey did know him from when he was sent over there last year.' Zeb took a beater (like me, not choosing for the beauty of it but merely seizing the nearest) and lashed out at the pallid face of Chastity, represented in the act of taming a unicorn.

I took the next hanging and spread it over the line next to Zeb's. 'They suspect one of us, then.'

He shot me an impatient look. 'Would they tell me if they did?'

'You said "Not of killing" him. But that's the way they're thinking. They'll fasten on somebody, if not you, then—'

'Listen, both of you.' Zeb hit his tapestry again, sending a cloud of motes into the air. 'Biggin had one of his tenants waiting in the corridor outside. When he brought him in, he called the man Tom Cornish.'

I cried, 'Not the intelligencer?'

'The same.'

Izzy and I spoke together: 'What manner of man is he?' and 'What is he like?'

'Grey-haired, with purplish cheeks. But if he were young, I'd say he was amazingly like Christopher Walshe.'

I stiffened and felt Izzy do the same.

'Cornish began crying right in front of me.' Zeb waited for this to sink in.

'The lad is – was – a nephew of his?' faltered Izzy.

'Closer.'

I gasped.

Izzy's hand flew to his mouth. He stammered, 'But – but why was he called Walshe?'

'A bastard, I guess, brought up under the mother's name until Cornish put him out to service.'

'God have mercy on us,' Izzy whispered.

Zeb went on, 'He worked for Biggin but it seems to me that Cornish had uses for him too. The servants whipped for their reading, remember? *Spiders and spies, do draw in the flies.*'

Now I saw it, the wretched little Judas bringing us the bait with which his father would scoop us into the net. There he had sat, with Zeb's arm round him, sharing the pipe of tobacco which Zeb and Peter could ill afford. I brought down the carpet-beater with such force that the tapestry leapt like a fish on the line, and I kept on cutting into it, dust settling on my face, which was already beaded with fresh sweat.

'So we are all suspected for that part,' I said. 'Nay, Cornish knows.'

'And thinks one of us put a stop to the game,' said Izzy, his cheeks pale. I felt a pang at having exposed such a gentle, upright soul to suspicion. He was innocence itself, but what was that to a spy?

'We must burn every pamphlet in the house,' I declared. 'And look behind the stables, in case we left anything there.'

'But what was he doing here at night?' mused Zeb. 'I cannot come at it.'

'I am going behind the stables this minute,' said Izzy. 'And after to Caro and Peter, to bid them burn anything in the chambers. Have you papers or pamphlets, either of you?'

'Under the bed,' I answered. '*An Answer to the Great Tyrant*. Bid Peter look near the bedhead, along the wall.'

Izzy ran off. Zeb and I continued flogging the hangings. I looked down at his lady and her unicorn. She was as tawdry a female as I have seen; only a beast disordered in its wits would yield to her its magic power. My tapestry showed the same woman strolling in a knot garden, one unlikely-looking flower held to her nose. A young man watched her from a tree. I had always thought him a lover, but now I saw he could as easily be a spy set on by her husband. I brought the beater down upon his stupid face until my arm ached.

'There is worse,' Zeb said.

This was a novelty. As a rule he avoided reposing any confidences in me, preferring to talk to Izzy. Observing him, I thought he looked sickly. Perhaps the thing could not wait, but had to come out, like the secret of King Midas's ears.

'There was a woman waiting in the corridor where Cornish was.' Zeb's voice shook. 'I saw her through the open door as he came in. She was very like Patience.'

I concealed my shock. 'Why would she go there?'

Zeb shrugged. 'I never denied the child was mine, how could I? She had a promise of marriage, and she loved me, why, she could scarce—' He recollected himself. 'That is, I thought she loved me. Suppose she was there to give evidence against us? I am afraid she was.' He rubbed at his brow with the back of his hand.

'What evidence? Peter and Caro have burnt the papers by now. But this woman's not Patience. You will see.'

'I am afraid,' he said again. 'Nothing is as I thought.'

'So it seems.' The news struck me like a chill wind. Was it possible that my beguiling brother had been beguiled? Yet it seemed more likely he was mistaken; what woman would desert Zebedee for a greybeard with purple cheeks? As for myself, I had killed not a simpleton but a practised, treacherous wolf cub. We were well rid of him. I turned to Izzy's hanging and drove the dust from it in clouds.

~

Cornish did not show himself, with or without Patience, the following day. Nor did Mister Biggin. A farmworker we had never seen before drove the cart, bearing a plain deal coffin, round to the laundry door. Caro had washed the boy's shirt and done what she could with his other garments. Izzy folded them neatly next to the deal box and I lowered the lad in my arms until he was lying snug within it.

'It's him for sure?' asked the cart driver.

For answer, I drew back the linen shielding the corpse's face. The boy's freckles showed greenish against the dull white skin.

The man took off his hat. 'That's him. God ha' mercy.'

I pulled the shroud across again, seeing in my mind the wound with its clean folds lying one against the other. The man led the horse about, mounted to the front of the cart and cracked his whip. Our false friend jogged away over the cobbles, lapped in borrowed linen and in a silence all his own.

THREE

Battles

WE NEVER WENT to the funeral, for which I was glad. But our talk was of little else, and while we tormented ourselves about Walshe, Cornish and Patience, the date of my espousal to Caro was almost upon us. Lying in bed, I gave myself up to voluptuous imaginings of my wedding night, almost too sweet to bear; but when I slept there came nightmares in which I was seized by Cornish or the officers. Sometimes Christopher Walshe walked before them, pointing me out. Starting out of sleep, I would dry my face on the bolster and consider whether I dared make away with myself, rather than be arrested. Once, when my groaning had woken both myself and Izzy, my brother whispered to me, 'Do you truly wish to be wed? Better cry off now than repent it after,' and I answered that the dreams had nought to do with my wedding, it was the boy, sunk deep into my mind. He put his hand on my brow, to cool it, and said he also dreamt of Walshe. Izzy was the only man there that ever touched me softly, as if I were capable of being hurt.

By day, these fears seemed foolishness. None had witnessed the boy's death, and none was come for me though he was laid in the ground.

~

Less than a week after the pond-dragging, I looked out of a window to see our mother crossing the courtyard. I at once ran down to her, my head filled with sudden panic, fancying that the men were in her cottage, throwing the pots about in the scullery, ripping up every bed in the house and carrying away my father's Bible.

When we embraced her cheek lay against the buttons of my coat, and I remembered how as a child I had looked upwards into her face. The tables had been turned for many years now.

'I hope there is nothing wrong at home,' I said, pushing open the stiff oak door to the hall. I would never have called the cottage *home* except to Mother. 'Or are you come to see Caro?'

Mother ignored Caro's name. When the two first met, I had seen by numerous signs, which none but sons could read, that she disapproved of my choice. Having nothing however to dispense or withhold, she was forced to bow to it.

'What should be wrong at home? I am come to thank the Mistress for a present she made me,' she said. 'So I might make a good show at your betrothal.'

I flushed. 'Do we beg money now?'

'No, son! It came without asking. O my boy – you're grown so handsome—' she pulled my head down and kissed all over my face—'she's a fortunate lass that gets you.'

Hoping that Caro would not choose this moment to come by, I held Mother off from my kiss-dampened cheeks. 'The luck is on my side, to have such a one to wife. And such a mother,' for her eyes told me that to praise Caro was, in my mother's view, to dispraise herself. 'Pray wait here a while. I'll announce you to My Lady.'

'You'll take me to Zeb and Izzy after?'

I groaned inwardly. 'Of course,' and leaving Mother near the stairs I went up to My Lady's chamber.

It was Caro who opened to my knock, and on seeing me she at once laughed. I guessed by this that I was the subject of their talk, but said only, 'Will you tell Her Ladyship that my mother is here to give her thanks in person?'

'I will come down,' called a voice inside the room. We stood aside as the Mistress swept past.

'Going down!' Caro whispered.

'Going to be fawned on for a present she made,' I returned. 'I had as lief not see it.'

'Should I not go to your mother, after?'

I hesitated. 'Let Mother see her darling boys first.'

'Very well. Come here, Signior Jacob—' Caro put her face up, and from *her* kisses I did not pull away until we heard a door open downstairs.

'You are lucky to get me. So my mother says,' I murmured as we listened for the sound of the Mistress coming back up.

She pinched my cheek. 'I'd say the luck's all the other way. My Lady has promised more—'

'But it is agreed,' I said, surprised. Lady Roche had already settled a dowry of thirty pounds on Caro, who said over and over that the Roches were none so bad after all, while I thought the money would be best spent in getting away from them.

Caro explained, 'Other things. There's a gown for the day, not so old, neither. Earrings also. And I am to have a chaplet from the gardener, with roses, or gilded wheat and rosemary.'

'Earrings? You have not had your ears pierced?' I did not want my wife's lobes punctured to suit the Mistress. Lifting the edges of her cap, I was reassured to find them still whole.

She laughed. 'The loan is only for the day. We will tie them on with silk.'

'I would gladly have got you a gown,' I said. 'But we are to have an espousal, not a church wedding.' *And I dislike the Mistress making you her poppet,* I thought.

'Yes, but since we are to be espoused *de praesenti*, where's the difference?'

'I mean only that—'

'O Jacob, you will not be thwart, I hope? There will be a bridebed and all, why not a gown? Besides, her lending it is a sign of high favour!'

'She may well favour you. No maid else could endure her white lead and belladonna.'

Nonetheless, I found myself smiling back at her. Her gown had been hard earned.

Caro went on, 'It is all of blue. For constancy. And heeled shoes, with silver thread—'

We kissed again.

'Shall I not have the ring inscribed?' Caro wheedled. 'Eh, Husband?'

'No,' I said at once. We had already been over this. I did not want a ring at all, preferring a simple and godly joining of hands before our friends, but I had bent so far to her wishes as to purchase one. I would not, however, have some doggerel such as *Our Contract, Was Heaven's Act* cut into it. I had done much that foolish custom requires: gloves had been purchased to give to all our friends, and a fine embroidered pair for Caro herself. In this last instance, Zeb had threatened that if I did not give way, he would shame me by furnishing the bridal gloves in my stead. I had also presented her with wedding knives, those scissors as necessary as the groom himself. All of it was very much against my will, not through meanness on my part, for I grudged the cost of nothing that I thought seemly, but I disliked this courting of *good luck* through gew-gaws and trifles. What have Christians to do with *luck*? Nor would I have garters pulled off by her bridesmen, or stockings thrown about in the bridal chamber. The others complained that without such brothelry (which they called *merriment*) it was hardly a wedding, but no matter for their whims.

My love linked arms with me. 'What will you wear, Jacob?'

'My best coat, the one you know with the mother-of-pearl buttons, and a lace collar to my shirt. I have had them ready a month and more.'

'And favours?' she coaxed.

'Aye, favours,' for I had gained my point over the ring and other trash, and I knew that without these trumpery bits of ribbon her woman's soul would not be satisfied.

Caro squeezed my hand. 'We will look like gentry.'

'I am gentry.' My own words surprised me. Having been a servant so long, I had near forgotten.

'But not idle like some we know.'

'Let us hope,' I said, 'that he will be away, or dead drunk in bed.'

My Lady was coming back up the stairs, grunting from a stiffness she had in the legs and hips.

'Madam, may we go down now?' I requested. 'Caro has not yet been seen by my mother.'

'What! Most certainly you must go. She is in the garden with your brothers, near the lavender bed.'

'You are all kindness.'

We bowed and curtseyed, then scampered downstairs like children.

Mother was just where the Mistress had said, standing between Zeb and Izzy.

'I always forget how pale your mother is,' said Caro as we crossed towards them. 'Where is her part in you, Black Jacob?'

'The eyes.'

'So much?'

'More than she has in the others. Zeb and Izzy have Father's complexion entirely. Yet folk say I am the most like him.'

Mother turned the grey eyes which were under discussion sharply upon her future daughter as soon as she perceived our approach. Caro curtseyed with a graceful sweep that not even Mervyn could have faulted, but to no purpose: there would never be liking between these two. My mother bristled like a dog's back. For Caro's part, as soon as she came out of her curtsey she drew herself up, Youth against Age.

'You have met Caro before, dear Mother,' I tried. 'Now you meet her as a dutiful daughter.'

Caro smiled.

Mother's glance raked her up and down as if seeking cracks in her skin, as she said, 'I will scarce know what to do with a daughter. My babes have all been boys.'

Izzy shot me a sympathetic glance.

'I had hoped we might put you to bed at home,' Mother said, turning on me. 'But you will not want that.'

'That was our first wish,' I assured her, Caro's head bobbing up and down in agreement. 'But the kindness shown, and such gifts – a servant is not a free man—'

My mother inclined her head so slightly that one might not say she nodded.

'The Mistress has given me a gown against the day,' put in Caro. 'And a pair of—'

'She has been most kind,' I hurried to conceal the last loan.

Mother pounced. 'A pair of what?'

'Earrings,' faltered Caro.

'Earrings for a serving maid.' My mother stared into the sky, her mouth sulky and closed like that of an old fish.

I was stung. 'Say rather for *my wife*.'

'Your mother thinks I intrude myself among my betters. Give you good day, Madam.' Caro turned and walked away.

'Are you now content?' I burst out. 'I mean to espouse her, and you had best—'

'Mother, will you come and see my garden?' Izzy almost shouted. 'The Mistress has given me a plot for myself, and I take cuttings of the rare plants.'

'Indeed, Isaiah, that will be very pleasant.' And off she went with Izzy, leaving me and my betrothal to come about as we would.

Zeb grinned. 'Caro is too pretty for her, and you too amorous. That sets her on edge.'

'Amorous? I did but speak!'

'It shines out of you.' He gave a sly laugh. 'For all she says, methinks she would scarce welcome the bridebed at home. And then, she once hoped we would marry better.'

'Then you must look for trouble, when the time comes.' If Mother behaved thus with Caro, she would surely take a whip to Patience.

'I have ample trouble at present.' Zeb's eyes grew miserable.

'Be easy,' I said. 'Patience cannot be at Champains. She will be found in time.'

He glanced at me in surprise. 'I have been thinking. Perhaps you are right, and I drove her away—'

I shook my head. There followed a rare moment of peace between us.

'Ah, well,' Zeb said at last, 'Mother will come round. Directly you and Caro quarrel, you'll be her own sweet boy.'

'We won't quarrel,' I replied. Zebedee clapped me on the shoulder and we began strolling back to the house.

~

'Have you seen the ceiling?' Caro pushed open the door of the unused chamber that was to be our married quarters.

I looked up. I had seen it often, without much interest. Now the other servants had cleaned both it and the walls, revealing the fantastic images that crowded there: a shameless hotch-potch of the pagan and Papistical, a whirl of naked and semi-naked forms intended to give the eye the impression of an ascent into the air above the house.

'Sir John's taste exactly,' I pronounced.

'O no,' Caro corrected me. 'Older than that. Godfrey says Sir John's father hired a foreigner for the painting.'

'And how do you like it?'

'Not at all,' she said at once.

I gazed on the bloated babes carrying lyres and blowing trumpets, the swags of painted stuff and grapes piled up here and there. In the centre, a bare breasted woman conversed like the strumpet she was with two men, one on either side of her. All three were seated on thrones shaped like shells and coloured gold.

Caro pointed. 'That's a goddess, the Mistress says.'

'You are prettier than she.'

My love wrinkled her nose. 'She is coarse. In need of stays.'

I said, 'Izzy told me these were painted so that the children conceived here might be beautiful.'

Caro burst out laughing. 'What, Mervyn—?'

Laughter seized on me also. 'Why, yes. Look there—' and I pointed out a chubby infant swilling wine from an upturned horn.

'Mervyn must have been made in the great chamber.' Caro wiped her eyes. 'The ceiling there isn't fit for a maid to look on.'

'You will get used to this one,' I said slyly, and saw her blush.

The espousal was fixed for the next day. My Lady was to send her coach for our ungracious mother, and since our fellows at Beaurepair were also our guests, servants were come in from a neighbour's house to help Mounseer with the food. Poor Mounseer, he was the only one of us not to have a holiday. But he had consolation in the form of Madeleine, a young Frenchwoman employed to dress hair. Her thankless task was to spin gold from the thin and greying locks of her own mistress, and now she had been borrowed and was to try her skill with ours. I had heard Daskin present himself to her the day before, and since then there was no good English spoken when these two were together, nothing but *parly-voo*, the two of them talking so fast you might think the words had been banking up in them and were bursting out like the autumn floods. Thus my spouse was freed of brushes, false hair and unguents for one day – a mighty sacrifice on the Mistress's part. I owned it freely, it was extraordinary how she liked Caro. She was a woman who should have had a daughter.

'We are made, you know.' Caro squeezed my arm. 'She'd let none but me have this chamber.'

'True,' I answered her. 'But when Sir John dies, and he does his best to bring it about, it will be Sir Bastard in the saddle. He's itching to debauch the maids.'

She sniffed. 'Do you not think I might refuse?'

'Would you had heard the talk in March, my love, when he brought his cronies and I waited on their late-night drunks. How the *amorous propensities* are heated by struggle, and not struggle in play neither.'

'Ah.' Her face sobered. 'He's one you have to watch, certes.'

'What, has he touched—'

'No, Jacob! He does no more than look. While his father lives, we should stick here. I am laying by money.'

'Are you sorry to change your first bridesmaid?' I asked. We had been forced in courtesy to ask Patience to carry out the first bridesmaid's duties, decking our chamber and the rest with flowers against the day, since neither of us had a sister or cousin who could decently claim precedence.

'Only if she be really lost,' Caro said. 'But there will be two bridesmaids. Peter's sister Mary will take Anne's place and Anne will stand in for Patience.' She smiled at me as if to say, *Fear not, all will be done.*

I eyed the heathens in their painted Heaven. Soon they would look down on our embracings, and I promised them good sport. Though I had never had a woman I understood perfectly what to do, and had an edge on me keen as a new blade: she would not find me shy or cold. We would sleep wrapped in one another, and wake to—

I caught Caro's eyes on me and flushed.

'The place will be sweet with all the flowers they can find,' she said. 'There were more in July, but—'

The door swung open, making me jump. It was Zeb. I expected a grin and the inevitable jest about inspecting the bed but his face was rapt as if from some vision.

'Jacob, I heard—' he corrected himself, 'and Caro – I heard something they kept from us—'

'Is Patience found?' cried Caro.

'No, Sister. Listen. Sir Bastard was in the West, was he not?'

'What's that to us?' I demanded. 'What care we where he is, so he's not here?'

'Jacob, Parliament has gained Bristol.'

I whistled.

'That's why he's been so curst of late,' Zeb went on excitedly. 'He's come home with his tail between his legs.'

'When was it?' Caro asked.

'The tenth of September. That's the fourth in a row: Naseby, Langport, Bridgwater and now Bristol.'

'They are going to win,' I said. My brother and wife-to-be stared back at me, unspeaking.

'I heard him telling the Mistress about it,' said Zeb at last. His eyes shone. 'They are all frighted now. There were stores lost from the whole of the West at Bridgwater, and Fairfax got between the King's army and Bristol.'

'And took Bristol itself! O brave Fairfax!' I could have capered with glee. 'To put down their precious Rupert.'

This prince was the King's own nephew, and had sworn to hold that city for His Majesty. There were many who considered him a kind of evil spirit, for he was monstrous tall and fearless in battle. What was more, he had been seen to converse with a familiar in the shape of a white dog, and though this dog had been killed at Marston Moor, yet the man continued cunning beyond mortal power. Once, I had overheard some guests say at table that had the King but been advised by Rupert, the upstarts and the common sort would have been crushed utterly. Now Fairfax had crushed *him.*

'We are going to see new times,' murmured Zeb. 'But fields of dead, first.' He turned to go out, pausing at the door to add, 'They slit women's faces at Naseby.'

'Lord protect us from the Cavaliers!' Caro gasped.

'It wasn't the Cavaliers did it, Sister.' Zeb cocked an eyebrow and was gone.

I pictured a face slit across. The blade would rip up lips and cheeks, catch in the gristle of a septum on its way to the eyes. Caro was saying something but I could hear nothing of it for the pounding in the back of my head. Suddenly my father spoke there and in my breast all at once, saying, *I have pursued mine enemies, and destroyed them; and turned not again until I had consumed them.*

Amen, I answered him in my heart. It was needless speaking aloud, for I had found over the years that he made himself known only to me, and though the Voice might shake the flesh on my bones, yet none but myself could hear it.

FOUR

Espousal

THE NIGHT BEFORE my wedding I was restless, jostling and kicking poor Izzy until at last he pinched me. There are few things so lonely as watching while others sleep; I lit a candle and stretched out on my back, staring round the room and thinking how odd it was that I should never again lie there. The ceiling in our chamber was unpainted, but its plainness was crazed and fissured into shapes like those seen in clouds or maps, the surface throwing up ridges and crevices as the yellow light lapped against them. A smudge in the far corner was a cobweb which had been spun in Patience's absence, and over the bed there was the familiar three-branched crack which I had seen every morning and night since we left Mother's cottage in the village.

Zeb had told me he could not remember our old house, with its pear trees and the lozenges, *gules et noir*, set in the window of the room where we slept as boys and where perhaps young brothers might be sleeping now while the Cullens, dispossessed, stewed in a fusty servants' chamber at Beaurepair.

Zeb. I had spoken gently to him, and he to me. I judged my brother and myself to be natural opposites, blended of quite different humours, yet as I lay there something I had not thought on in years came back to my mind, and ruffled it. When first we moved to the big house, Zeb and I slept together in the bed I now shared with Izzy. My elder brother turned in with Stephen, a lad who was since dead of eating tainted meat, and it seemed to me that there had been kindness between Zeb and myself. On saints' days (the Mistress still kept these, and though heathen they were not unwelcome to us servants) I had been fishing, and swimming, with him; I was sure it was Zeb, and not Izzy, who had once made me laugh so hard that beer came out of my nose and I was sent down from table. Was it when Stephen died, and Peter came, that my brothers had changed places in the chamber? It might be that Izzy had wanted the change, for Peter snored in tiny grunts like a dreaming dog; but Zeb and I were never the same again. He withdrew from me; I began to find him wilful and spoilt.

Our room was that night too hot, as it was most nights from April to October, and the grey of dawn showed that, though the casement was open, mist beaded the inner panes. The scent of hard-worked bodies hung in the air like the whiff of some disagreeable mushroom and I wondered how many pints of sweat I had breathed in over the years, along with essences of feet and farts and garlic. My Lady's grand chamber smelt of rose otto and occasionally, when Sir John had paid his wife a visit, of wine, while the room set aside for myself and Caro had as yet no perfume but emptiness and dust. I turned over and sniffed the pillow, finding my own smell mingled with Izzy's, and thought, *Clean linen for us tomorrow,* and for some reason the red glass came to mind.

When our young master, as we called him in the presence of Godfrey, might be fifteen and myself perhaps some two years older, a Venetian visitor brought him a birthday gift – a newfangled glass cup from an island where the people are expert in the crafting of such things. It was presented at the midday meal, first to Sir John that he might look at the workmanship. Standing behind the Master, I craned my neck, marvelling and longing to touch. The thing was like blood frozen and carved, all even, pure and crystalline, a scarlet flower with chains of bubbles intertwined in the stem.

'Most cunningly made,' said My Lady. 'See, Mervyn.'

The visitor took it from Sir John and put it into the boy's hand and he, being careless, straightway let it fall and it shattered on the flags. The visitor's reaction I cannot now remember, for I was so shocked that I cried out in protest as if the cup had been my own. I was told to fetch a broom. Sweeping up the fragments, I cannot swear that I did not let a tear, while Mervyn sat sullen and stupid. I guessed they had given him a tongue-lashing while I was out of the room, but I would fain have seen him hanged for the destruction of the glass before my eyes could learn it.

For weeks I kept the shards of it in a leather pouch, taking them out frequently to admire the stem, which was still in one piece, or to look through the fragments of the bowl and see the world all drenched in blood. The garden viewed thus was a scene of nightmare, its trees and plants hot curls of stone beneath the fiery skies of Hell, the black and crimson maze a trap for souls. Or, it might be, this was how Beaurepair itself would look on the Last Day.

'Your grim fancy,' said Izzy when one day I showed him the Hell Garden. 'The thing amuses, I suppose. But I would rather have the garden as it is.' Zeb would also hold or look through the glass pieces from time to time, until the day when, called to some urgent task, I left them on the floor and out of the pouch. When I returned to my treasures they were gone.

I at once suspected my brother. But Zeb persuaded me that this was none of his teasing while Izzy, looking sick, suggested I enquire of Godfrey. The steward told me that he had trodden on the glass shards and one of them had pierced his shoe and gone into the sole of his foot. 'And so,' said this wise old fool, 'I have thrown them down the jakes.'

Thus perished a lovely thing, all broken and degraded, for that it was given into the wrong hands. I drifted off remembering, and it came back to me in my dream, where I was holding it for someone to see. But it was already broken, and a sadness blew through me like smoke.

When next I opened my eyes the room was light and the other three were standing over my bed.

'It is time,' said Izzy.

We were boys again. Half asleep, I protested as the cover was dragged off. Izzy put into my hand a cup of salep, a rare treat in that house where the servants drank mostly beer. I let its thick, pearly sweetness drop over my tongue like some great honeyed oyster.

Peter had fetched us up a special perfumed water from the still-room. As bridegroom, I was first with this water, which had been infused with rosemary and lavender. There was also a washball to scrub my skin with, and cloths for drying. In the days when we still had old Doctor Barton for tutor, he showed me a print of a Turkish bath and I, being at once full of a child's desire, begged of him that we might go to Turkey. He said that it was too far off, and the people not Christians, but the picture with its men naked or draped in sheets, the spacious stone halls, the fountains and the musician in strange pantaloons and pointed shoes, plucking at a shrunken harp, stayed with me. It was still before me even when I bent to hoe Sir John's cornfield, miserably fulfilling the Word: *In the sweat of thy face shalt thou eat bread.* Now I took a dampened cloth and ran it over my body. My delight in washing and aversion to every kind of dirt was a byword in our house. Though I was called fantastical, and was much teased, yet it made me a careful servant, and I thought Caro did not like me the less for it.

While I was drying myself and lifting out my best shirt from the press, the other three all washed together, splashing the water here and there, mostly over head and hands for none but me took off his shirt. There was much fooling, much spitting of foam; the chamber floor was soaked, as was Zebedee when Peter scooped up water in his hands and threw it.

'Clodpate,' said Zeb without venom. He pulled the wet shirt over his head and came to the press where the fresh ones were kept. Almost dressed by now, I watched him fling the linen this way and that, Peter wailing that everything would be crushed. It struck me how rarely I saw Zeb naked, for all that we shared a chamber. Stripped, he showed more muscular than I remembered, but well-knit and graceful – what some called a *proper* man, one who drew women to him and had already sired a child to prove it. As for my elder brother – poor Izzy, what woman would be charmed by him? His back would never be as straight or as strong as the one that was turned to me now as Zeb dropped a shirt over his head and pulled on his breeches.

'Hold, Jacob,' said Izzy. Peter and Zeb turned to watch as he handed me a pair of hose I had never seen before, of the finest wool and such a tender white you would say they came from the mildest, purest lambs.

'These are not mine,' I told him.

'Yes they are, they're a gift from us three.'

They smiled kindly on me and the hose were straightway more precious to my heart than anything the Mistress might give or lend. I hugged my brothers and Peter, gaining a little damp on my shirt-sleeves, but that mattered nothing: the coat would go over it.

'Soft as down,' I said as I stood up, hose stretched clean and tight and my newest shoes on.

'They look well on you,' said Izzy.

'My thanks, they are the best I ever saw.' Again I suffered a pang for the sweet brother whose garments never looked well on him. Peter helped me do up the mother-of-pearl buttons on my coat, which, like Zeb, were handsome but difficult to lay hold of.

'Like a prince. She'll want to eat you,' Peter said as he slid the last one into place.

Zeb laughed. 'Be kind and let her.'

Izzy was giving a last brush to his coat. 'I hope Mounseer finds the cooks to his liking. I heard shouting from the kitchen last night.'

'Have you seen Caro's robe?' Zeb asked him. 'It is magnificent.'

I stared. 'You have, then?'

'It's only the husband that's not allowed. You'll take her for My Lady Somebody.'

'When did she show you?'

Izzy stopped brushing. 'Are we ready, lads?'

'The favours!' cried Zeb. With shaking fingers we pinned them on, so that the guests could pluck them off later – another curtsey to Dame Fortune, but one I had not dared to oppose.

'Here, here!' Peter shoved a glass of wine into my hand. 'Down in one. Go to it.'

I was glad to obey.

'Done like a man,' said Izzy.

'When did she show you the gown?' I repeated, but Zeb and Peter bounded out of the door, eager as dogs to the hare.

'This is no day for jealousy,' Izzy said, laying his hand on my arm.

'I'm not jealous.'

Peter went directly to the garden, while we brothers had first to knock at Caro's chamber. It should have been her father's house, but there was nothing to be done about that. I tapped on the door and heard whispering and a stifled laugh within. Godfrey's voice bade me enter.

She was standing in the middle of the room, her eyes glittering. A cloak had been thrown over the gown, and her hair hung down loosely as befitted a virgin bride. Mary and Anne, clutching branches of gilded rosemary, looked me over from head to toe. I took Caro by the hand as custom demanded, said the traditional 'Mistress, I hope you are willing', and allowed Godfrey, who was standing in for her father, to lead me out of the room. The bridesmaids, giggling, went on either side of me, their captive man, while Izzy and Zeb stayed behind to escort Caro.

We slowly descended the stairs. I was in a daze and my shoes, which were not well broken in, pinched. I heard Izzy and Zeb laughing along the corridor. The idea was that Caro should follow me out to the maze, where tables of food and drink would be laid out. There we would pause a while, admiring the delicacies and everybody's finery, until the time was come when Caro and I should make our vows before those assembled. Then there would be well-wishing, much eating and drinking, presents and diversions (perhaps that kissing game with which she had enticed me all those months back) to the sound of sweet music, and afterwards back into the house to gorge ourselves further until the time came for us to be put to bed. I must get through everything, showing no impatience for that blessed moment when the chamber door would shut out their urgings and jests. Then I would turn to her, trembling, aching, while outside the pastimes went on and everyone pictured, with amusement or envy, our mutual entertainment.

'God has sent you fair weather,' said Anne. We passed through the door by the stillroom and a cry went up, '*There he is!*' The company was assembled and waiting for me just outside the house. Dazzled by the sudden strong light, I with difficulty made out the Master and Mistress, and taking off my hat I bowed to them. Then I looked about me, greeting all the guests with a general bow and a smile. I remarked little Joan, who was lovesick for Mounseer, and another, older dairymaid standing further back in the group. There were also the ostler and his boys, and some of the farmworkers, both men and women, who had laboured by my side in the fields. I wondered did they remember those days, and resent my rise in fortunes.

'Your mother awaits you in the maze,' said My Lady, whose face was pink with pleasure. At *your mother* I started guiltily, for I had not missed her. We strolled in a leisurely fashion towards the maze entrance, and my vanity was tickled when I heard one woman tell another that *I* was a very proper man.

'Wait till you see her wedding clothes. Beautiful as the day,' said Godfrey, craning his head backwards to speak to me. I could not help but grin like a fool, though the fresh collar chafed my neck. I put my finger down it and pulled to loosen the stuff as we stepped between the rosemary hedges.

I am to be espoused. I am to be espoused. Bound to a woman who wondered, in her innocence, if I suspected another man of killing Walshe. The thought was enough to rob me of breath. We rounded the last corner and passed through a high dense arch. There I turned, and waited. Everyone watched me wait.

First came my brothers, pacing with branches of rosemary before them, Izzy's slight lurch a foil to Zeb's long supple stride. The sun glanced off their thick black hair, so exactly like my own, all three of us showing like gypsies among our fair-complexioned friends. Both bridesmaids turned towards Zeb as he approached, as daisies open themselves to the dawn.

Caro entered the maze in profile to us, so that I saw first her long neck and the sapphire drop depending from her right ear. Her hair hung down her back. It had been brushed and polished with silk so that it shone beneath the chaplet of wheat and roses. When she turned to face me I took the full force of her beauty, which seemed almost that of a lady, her gown cut low, her neck and shoulders of cream. This was Caro transformed indeed, wondrous tight-laced, in silk the colour of June sky – I could never have procured her such. Her brown eyes rested on me with a delight equal to my own. Drawing near, we bowed and curtseyed each to the other and a general *aah* of pleasure ran through the company. The bridal finery showed more of her breasts than I had ever seen before: I tried not to gape like a lumpkin at the delicately gleaming skin thus revealed.

'Son.' My mother's voice cut through this delectable contemplation. I went at once to where she was standing in the little gateway cut in the left-hand hedge. We embraced and she wept, saying her Elias stood before her in the flesh. That did please me. Though others had remarked on it, Mother had never yet given me so much in the way of praise as to say I was the print of my father.

'Do you not think her beautiful, Jacob?' She indicated Caro. 'The earrings show very brave against her neck, do they not?' By which I understood that the two of them had made up their quarrel.

'She is an angel,' I said, as all bridegrooms do. I scented pomade on Caro's hair and wanted to touch it, but feared to spoil the hairdresser's work. Tears stood in my eyes, I could hardly have said why.

'Pray come this way – this way, friends—' That was Peter, whose job it was to shepherd the guests to their rightful places. I turned to see him leading them to some trestle tables disposed about the knot garden. There was one table longer than the rest and he waved laughingly to me, to show that was where we should sit when the thing was done. Half stunned, I listened to the shuffling and rustling, the chatter and laughs as Godfrey helped folk arrange themselves. The field workers were put in a separate group near the hedge. I remembered the day when Caro and I had sat on the knot garden bench and quarrelled over Zeb's secret.

Holding hands, we stood in the midst of those assembled as if summoned before the officers. Before us on the cloths were light and creamy things, suitable for bride tables: chicken cullis, Devonshire whitepot, quaking pudding and (I thought of Mervyn) a row of syllabubs, each in a separate vessel with a cunning spout for drinking off the liquor. Music drifted from the far end of the knot garden, where a small group of hired players kept a respectful distance. The guests spread themselves and fluffed out their garments, the better to enjoy the warmth of the day.

'Time we married, Izzy, if this be how it is,' proclaimed Zeb from the end of the long table, and I wondered if, despite his fears, he still missed Patience.

'Do you know your words?' Caro whispered.

'Yes, but no matter if I forget.' I had insisted we should have the *sponsalia* (as the betrothal was called in Latin) *de praesenti*, for such a betrothal, even without witnesses, made us one just as if we had been joined by the priest. It needed only the swearing of vows. I had a horror of being married by My Lady's 'spiritual director', who stank of Rome, or by Doctor Phelps, the pastor of the village church, who had once preached there that the poor, being God's special care, should rather be envied than relieved, and that a poor man who complained of his lot did so at the instigation of Mammon, naked greed, 'for sure he had not the breeding to make right use of riches if he had them'. On that occasion I had sat sizing up the man of God, allowing myself – in fancy – to beat him to his knees. No one had ever fought me and won, and I did not think the good doctor would be the first. Now, with Peter's glass of wine warming me to a pleasant freedom, I felt more than ever that Phelps was best away. Wed to such a wife as Caro, I thought, 'tis a poor return to break the parson's teeth.

'Why do you laugh?' Caro pulled on my sleeve.

'I'll tell you later.' Smiling to myself, I glanced up and saw Godfrey coming over to us.

'It is now. O, I feel sick,' murmured Caro.

My Lady looked tenderly at her across the dishes of food, calling, 'Take heart, child. A few minutes and you are man and wife.'

Now I was the one suddenly sick, not for the stumbling words of a vow, or that I might speak foolishly before the company, but for the huge thing I had undertaken. There might come a time, and soon, when my wife repented of her bargain, but there was no breaking off after this, though we should prove scorpions to one another. I saw Zeb staring at me, wondering, it might be, what was become of Patience, or envious of what I had won for my own.

'Here, wife.' I put my arm under Caro's to steady her trembling. Under our feet was the flagged square at the centre of the maze, and around us the knot garden, with other stone flags supporting the trestles. The young men gawped and grinned, while their lasses dug them in the ribs and devoured Caro's gown with their eyes. Older people looked wistful, or dabbed at their cheeks. My mother sniffled. I heard speeches on my looks, and on hers, spoken out loud as if we were both of us deaf. Izzy nodded to me as if to say, it would come right. Most of all I remarked Zeb, whose features looked to be carved in stone. Though I fixed him, eye to eye, he appeared unaware; one would say he looked not at me, but through me.

'Have you the ring? Give it here.' Godfrey thrust a swollen square of lacy stuff towards us.

Caro glanced down at the lace and giggled. 'My Lady's pincushion.'

I put the scrap of gold on it. Godfrey snapped his fingers. A little boy in silks ran forward and was placed officiously to my left to hold the cushion. The steward, plainly happy in his work, stepped aside with a swirling movement and the guests grew quiet.

'Friends, we are here to witness the solemn contract of two of our company,' Godfrey announced. 'Known to us all, and respected by all as honest folk and faithful servants. We pray that their union may be long, happy and fruitful.'

'Amen,' I answered along with the rest. The moment was come. Clearing my throat, I took a firm grip on Caro's left hand. 'I, Jacob, do take thee, Caroline, to my wife, from this day forth, and do call on these here present to witness.' I then took the wedding band (the boy near bursting with importance all this while) and worked it over her finger. 'In token of which, I do give thee this ring.'

Her flesh was cold and damp: I pressed it between my warmer, drier palms to infuse her with strength. The music had ceased, and as I thus soothed her I heard jackdaws bickering somewhere on the house roof. Caro now turned to me and said in a high breathless voice, 'I, Caroline, do take thee, Jacob, to my husband, from this day forth, and do call on these here present to witness.'

I smiled at her. She immediately coughed, was seized by a spasm, and beat her hand against her lace with a frightened movement. A kindly laugh rose from the company, at which her cough cleared. She touched her finger, turning on me a joyous smile: 'In token of which I do accept this ring.'

And with those few words and that paltry circlet of metal Caro and I were made one flesh. We stood facing the company as if about to perform a dance: I was tempted to bow, and wondered if they would applaud. At last I was bidden kiss her, and a very sweet kiss it was. The Master and Mistress now stepped up to kiss her also, followed by Godfrey, my brothers and Peter's sisters, and then the folk nearest to us rose up to follow suit, so that she was mobbed on all sides as every person there present sought to give and receive good fortune. They scrambled for the favours on her gown, and on those of Mistress Mary and Mistress Anne. I felt hands pluck at my own coat and saw the ribbons snatched from my brothers also. Young men waved the favours triumphantly in the air and pinned them to their hats.

When the kissing and the snatching of favours were done, the guests made for their seats, but not until grains of wheat had been cast over my wife's head, for fruitfulness. As we walked to our seats, a young girl cried, '*Jacob!*' and something struck me on the face before falling to the path. I saw she had thrown me a candied almond. Laughing, protesting, we held up our hands as more sweetmeats, mostly raisins, pelted onto us. Some landed in Caro's hair and bosom; one or two managed to slip down my tight collar. Caro brushed off comfits as we seated ourselves at the board with our employers and attendants.

The Master and Mistress wished us a long and happy life together, at least the Mistress did, for none could be quite sure what Sir John was trying to say. The company was in high good spirits. We were brought two great silver mazers, full of sops in wine, which we drank down to the cheers of the company. They were filled to the brim again, and we were made to interlink our arms before drinking them, which was easy enough; but then they set us to hold the cups to one another's mouths. I was afraid I might spoil her dress, but then I saw the Mistress signing to me that it mattered not a jot, so I went ahead with a will and spilt only a few drops and those from my own mouth. It seemed a good game, but one best played in private.

It came to me that I had not yet eaten a morsel to mop up so much drink.

'Let's to bed directly,' I whispered to her.

Caro laughed at me, a laugh full of love, and I stored up that laugh for when we were old, when I might say to her, *Thus do I remember you on the day we were betrothed.*

In the usual way of things I would have waited on my guests, but this was neither my house nor Caro's, and simple hospitality would not fit the Mistress's notions. Little boys dressed as cupids handed the dishes round to those who could not reach them, and were much kissed and fondled by the women; I disliked this heathen play-acting, but gathering that the idea had been My Lady's and was generally considered a most happy one, I complimented her on her delicate fancy. Sir John, seated opposite us, proposed a toast to our health and happiness, in a kingdom going on *in the good old way*, every man true to his King. My mother fluttered and said I was foolish at times but not a bad lad; I smiled at Sir John and when the toast was over, silently drank off my own, to Black Tom Fairfax. They called the sweet wine *white*, but it was rather a pale gold, frilled with bubbles at the glass's edge. I had not finished the toast before another was proposed, and I was handed more wine, this time red.

Caro caught me viewing her through the glass of red wine, and again she laughed.

Sir John was in his element – the liquid one – and those around him only too willing to keep pace. This time the company was invited to wish us fine children for, said the Master, at twenty-five I was of an age when I should have issue, and he hoped he might live to see my son a loyal servant to his own, a speech that made Caro dig her nails in my hand under the table. She need not have feared. I smirked my thanks and stood to toast those who had done us so much good (the red again), after which someone toasted the House of Roche for its unfailing affability and true *noblesse* (another white). A cupid, his wings bedraggled, ran about with bottles and casks. Then by common consent we turned back to the food, and a quiet hum arose, punctuated by the occasional clink. There was cheesecake and spicecake, along with a most extraordinary dish, exactly like collops of bacon only sweet to the taste, cut from red and white marchpane, and at a separate table, a great heap of bridecakes. I wondered who would cleanse the foul dishes.

Caro looked hot. Having watched her eat a collop of marchpane, nibbling inwards from the edge and turning the thing about in her hand to make a circular scrap which she at last took on her tongue, I offered her another for the sake of such a pretty sight.

Joan came up and spoke quietly into Izzy's ear. Izzy's eyes widened, and as she moved away from our table he turned to me and whispered, 'It seems Mervyn is sick, and accuses Mounseer of poisoning him.'

I thought of the syllabub. 'And how would Joan know?'

'She took cream up to the house for cheesecakes, and while she was there—'

Godfrey was at my side again. Izzy waved his hand to say I should hear the rest when he could give it me. I glanced at the Mistress, who had not the look of a woman whose cook has poisoned her son, and concluded that she, like me, fancied the poison was rather come in a winecup.

'Jacob, the bridecakes,' Godfrey said.

Folk began banging on the tables, calling, '*Bridecakes, bridecakes!*' and Caro, no longer shy, dragged me up from my seat. Godfrey led us to the table with the bridecakes upon it, Caro on one side and myself on the other, bidding us kiss over it. The pile was just low enough for Caro to lift her lips above the highest one. I bent forward and kissed her to the sound of cheers and shouts; there was clapping of hands. Then there was a gasp, the clapping broke off, and I looked down to see that the hem of my coat had swept a cake off the table to the ground. The cheers resumed, but they were not so loud as they had been, and my wife's smile when we sat down again was shot through with worry.

'That is nothing, pure superstition,' I told her. 'Do but think, my love! Is it likely a cake, a piece of dough and spice that we make ourselves, should govern our lives?'

'No,' she answered; but her voice was uncertain.

'Jacob is right,' put in Izzy, who had overheard this. 'Besides, he is big enough to protect you, is he not! And you have now two brothers to boot.'

Caro kissed his lean cheek. 'You have always stood brother to me, Izzy.'

I wondered how he liked her saying that.

The music grew louder. Some of the young folks were for dancing, and a set was made up. They continued to dance for the sun shone bright but mild, and were ready next for snap-dragon and other nonsense. During the ceremony I had felt almost nothing, but now sat brimming with happiness. All I could see was my wife, with her trusting eyes, her cheeks made rosy by wine and the O of her lips as she watched the game. A raisin clung to the skin of her neck. Bending forward, I took it between my lips. The men near me cried, 'Hey-hey!'

'Jacob is mad passionate in love,' called Zeb. 'Pray keep him in order.'

'In order yourself,' I retorted. My collar was seized from behind and a shower of raisins fell down my back; whirling round I clapped hold of the trickster and found I had caught Izzy, crept out of his place. I jumped up and caught him in my arms. Caro rose to embrace him also.

'A very comfortable lass,' he panted. 'She doesn't squeeze like you,' whereupon Caro did squeeze him, and he her, until they collapsed in laughter.

With the day scarce begun, we had all of us drunk too deep. Sir John was singing, in a voice like boiling jam, about *a wench who had two* – his wife here put her hand over his mouth. Something dropping down my shirt, I felt inside and found a tiny heart of scarlet marchpane entangled in my chest hair.

'They get everywhere,' said Peter, giving me a lewd wink from across the table.

O could I but run away with her! I had now the right to take her openly to my bed, yet I must go instead through all the merriments of the day, which rightly seen were nothing more than tortures. That was fine sport, I guessed, baiting the eager bridegroom with dances and toasts until he was near crazy. I had never before tasted the cruelty of it. The winks, the looks, the jests all assuming me to be on fire – which I was – the constant fanning of my heat by dangling before me the delights I should come to soon, soon, soon, but *not yet*—

Caro frowned. 'Look here, my love.' She held out a finger: a pretty scarlet globe of liquid swelled from the pad, ran over and trickled down her palm. Exasperated, she put the finger to her mouth.

'What's amiss?'

'The rose chaplet,' she mumbled. 'The gardener left some thorns in.'

'Hold your hand up,' suggested My Lady.

Caro did so, but the stream of red continued. 'Fingers are nasty for bleeding,' she lamented, and put it back in her mouth before it could stain the gown.

'We will tie it up,' I said. 'Are there fresh bandages in the still-room?'

Caro stopped sucking just long enough to say, 'Aye.'

'Come on then.' I rose. There was a general catcalling and cries of, 'Hot!' and 'Caro, beware!'

'You will excuse us a few minutes, Madam,' I said.

The Mistress nodded. Caro followed me out of the maze with her hand poised above her head as if to give a signal.

The stillroom smelt sweet. I put my mouth in hers and we kissed very slow and deep, my love holding the injured hand away from our finery. Profiting by her lack of defences, I held her close to me and crushed the gown.

Caro drew back her head. 'Wait. Here's the stuff,' and she pulled away from my embrace to open a drawer full of torn linen. I recognised an old shirt of Sir Bastard's. Taking one of the finer strips, I tore it in two and bound up the finger, pausing frequently to kiss.

'The blood's almost stopped,' she remarked in a brisk voice which did not fool me, for I had felt her breathe hard against my mouth.

'Stopped? Mine is rising,' I murmured. 'Let us go upstairs and look at the chamber. Say yes, Caro,' and I bit her ear.

She closed her eyes. 'We are not to see it yet.'

'None will know. We can seek out the traps,' I coaxed, knowing she had a horror of spiders in the bed and was mightily afraid the menservants would put some in.

Caro frowned. 'Well – if we do not stay long—'

The scent of dust and emptiness was gone, the room now fragrant with roses and pot-pourri. Anne had looped ropes of flowers over the bed and walls, and doubtless managed it better than Patience could ever have done. The floor was strewn thick with rosemary. There was a nonsuch chest for our clothes – that had not been there before – and on it a great bunch of lavender. I dearly loved the perfume of this herb and went up to the chest to smell it.

'Izzy,' said Caro. 'He knows you like lavender.'

She was gazing at the tester bed. New hangings of saye had been fitted, and tied back to show the linen all clean and fair over three good mattresses. The hangings were flesh colour and yellow, signifying desire and joy.

'Did you choose the colours?' I asked.

Caro smiled and shook her head. 'I was told it would be blue.'

I stroked the bolsters with my hand and looked beneath them. On top of the cover lay an embroidered nightgown for Caro and a plainer, but still beautifully worked, one for me. Mine was very large and I knew my wife had made it specially, as a wedding gift.

'No spiders or hedgehogs,' I said, passing my hand between the sheets. I took hold of her again, and we pressed close. Her mouth was sweet as crushed strawberries.

'Enough.' Caro ducked out of my arms. I thought of grappling her to me directly, and the guests be damned. She went on, 'For every minute we stay, there will be a jest at us. It might be they are in the stillroom already.'

Reluctantly, I straightened my garments.

'Giving of gifts comes next.' Caro examined the bandaged finger. 'See, the blood is—O, what's that?'

She was staring out of the window. I went to it and saw a dust-cloud moving towards Beaurepair, along the hill road which led to the village and further on, to Champains.

'Jacob, what is it?' Her voice trembled. 'You look—'

I punched the windowsill, making her jump. 'It is Patience. And Biggin. And Tom Cornish.'

'Patience!' Caro's smile flared an instant and died. 'With Cornish? That man who – spies?'

I nodded, trying to make out the faces of their companions.

Caro tugged at my sleeve. 'What should she do with him?'

'Quiet.' I watched the distant woman's skirts rise and fall with the horse. Zeb had been right, then, and it struck me that they were hoping to catch all of us at a swoop. This was why they had lain so quiet: Patience had told them of my betrothal day and they had waited, knowing that on this day, of all others, we would not be away from home.

I turned to Caro. 'Listen, wife. There is not time to explain. These people mean us harm. We must leave.'

'What – what harm?' she stuttered. 'How can we leave – the gifts—'

'Run away.'

Caro gaped, then laughed. 'You'll not make a fool of me. You can't see them from here.'

I took her by the shoulders and spoke into her face. 'It may be that you cannot, but I can. Go get all the money and jewels there are, put them under your gown.'

'I have none but—'

'Hers, get hers,' I cried. 'These men are come for me. Then go the long way round to the stable, and wait.'

'But they are not – how are they come for you?'

'Come to hang me. Shape yourself! Stand here losing time, and you'll see me kicking my heels.'

'That can't be. A man can't just come—'

'And then it will be you. Don't you see? She has told them of our reading!'

Caro stared at me stupidly. 'To be hanged? For that? Nay, they—'

'Must I spell it out? They'll put the boy's death on us now.'

She flinched away in terror.

'Get her jewels,' I repeated, feeling myself in a nightmare wherein I was running for my life and everything conspired to hold me back.

'But she has been—'

'Obey your husband,' I shouted. Caro whirled about and ran

through the door. I heard her high-heeled shoes thud along the corridor in the direction of the Mistress's chamber.

One of the cupids was taking off his wings by the fountain. I hurried to the lad, bade him find the groomsmen, that was Mister Isaiah Cullen and Mister Zebedee, and say they should come at once, on a matter of great importance. 'And don't shout it out,' I urged, showing him a penny. 'Whisper in their ears, and fetch them back here.'

He ran off and I paced the grass, moaning with impatience. I had not told Caro the entire truth. The three persons I had named were indeed making towards us, but so were a larger group of men from Champains. It seemed my eyes were very much better than hers, for I had also seen muskets, and, hanging from one saddle, a chain.

My brothers arrived together, hot and breathless.

'Is Caro hurt?' Izzy panted as I handed the boy his penny. 'Or is this some jest?'

I waited until the lad was out of earshot before saying, 'There is an armed party coming along the Champains road: Patience, Walshe and Comish. With reinforcements.'

Never had I seen Zeb look so terrified. His warm colour drained at once. 'Coming for me?' he faltered.

'Why you?' Izzy's voice was sharp.

'Patience – the boy – but that's none of my doing! You will bear witness, I gave of my tobacco—'

'Friends do fall out,' I said. 'Can you prove you were not with him when he went under?'

Zeb grew paler still. 'I was asleep in the chamber. But we can none of us stand witness for our brothers! Who will believe us?'

'Patience? You are sure?' Izzy urged me.

'Yes! Yes! And we have no proof against her accusations.'

'Nor has she any,' he said.

'She has her belly to prove some knowledge of us,' I retorted. 'And to come thus, they must believe the rest. Let's be gone.'

Izzy said, 'We all of us went to bed that night—'

'*They* have joined together, and *we* sink or swim together,' I cried. 'Caro is gone to the stable with money and jewels. Will you seize the time?'

They stared at me, Izzy's eyes screwed up in bewilderment, Zeb's slowly clearing into decision.

'You mean run away?' Izzy asked at last. 'Now, as we are?' He looked from Zeb to me as if trying which of us would laugh first and spoil the jest.

Zeb caught hold of him. 'I see it, Izz. Come with us, for the love of God,' and he pulled Izzy along in the direction of the stable.

'Indeed I will not!' my elder brother cried, flinging about him. He knocked Zeb's hand away. 'I've done no wrong.'

''Tisn't what you've done, but what folk think,' Zeb pleaded.

'And if we cut away like a gang of thieves? What will they think then?'

'Do what you will, I am going now,' I said.

Izzy said, 'You have doubtless your reasons.' His eyes were suddenly grown cold. 'But take Caro? To what purpose?'

'She is my wife.'

'Consider the danger you put her to.'

'She is my wife,' I repeated, feeling an obscure shame in the words as I turned and strode towards the stable. Zeb ran after me, then turned back and embraced Izzy. When he at last caught me up his cheeks were wet.

'We lose time,' I snapped.

Caro waited, bejewelled and trembling, at the stable door. I coughed at the scent of piss and straw, setting myself to obey Zeb's orders for he was the only one who knew what he did.

'Courage, child,' he called to Caro as he ran about clutching spurs and whips. He was quick in saddling up.

'Get up behind me,' I called to Caro as I was about to mount.

'Behind me, fool,' Zeb hissed. 'You're too big and she needs to be with one who can ride. Give her a hand.'

'The saddle's wrong for a woman,' Caro wailed. Shaking, clawing at Zeb's coat, she put one leg across the horse, her gown bunching out fantastically on either side. The animal started forward.

'Don't squeeze him,' Zeb rapped out. 'Put your arms round me.'

'I can't do this.' She was in tears.

'O, but you will,' he replied.

'Jacob,' she quavered, 'let us stay. The Mistress loves me, she will not permit—'

'Can she turn back musket balls? There are armed men.' I urged my horse forward through the door and we were out in the stable yard. Despite having Caro behind him, Zeb soon passed me. I saw his hair whip back into her face. The cobbles shone in the sun; there was a flash, and one of the sapphire earrings dropped into the straw and muck of the yard.

FIVE

Over the Edge

I HAD NEVER LEARNT to sit a horse. Now I banged up and down, hoping only to stay in the saddle. My brother, light and easy in his seat, had his own trials for I could see how Caro dragged on him. Her face was pressed up against his coat, eyes closed, lips forced back over her teeth, and she looked to be crying. A foul smell wafted to me and I saw that she had vomited onto her gown. My own gorge rose at it, and I turned my head aside.

We were headed for the woodland which lay behind Beaurepair, and which was still unenclosed. To get there we had to go through the gate. I had not seen the keeper at the betrothal, but we might yet be in luck, for he was in love with one of the dairymaids and none too fond of his work. We pounded along the track towards this gate, leaving by the back of the house as our pursuers approached by the front.

'God be praised!' Zeb screamed. I looked: it was one of the keeper's days for courting, and the gate stood open. We were through it without his having so much as seen us, and clattering along the open road. On the horizon lay the wood, and I prayed we might reach it without being seen.

Zeb kept up the pace. My shirt was soaked, from the labour of staying in the saddle and the terror of being thrown. An ugly twist of sickness came upon me without warning, and my mouth brimmed with bitter juice; I spat, breathing hard to keep the sickness down. There was something metallic on my tongue: I had chewed my lip, and drawn blood.

I am watching out for you, came the Voice, so sudden that it frighted me.

I looked back as we plunged into the wood. There was nothing on the road. A green scent of moss and darkness closed about us and the air at once grew cool. Zeb urged his horse on between the trees until he turned into a narrow track on the right and straightway went crashing down a steep slope, then up a bank on the opposite side. I was hot and cold from feeling the ground drop under me, and I could hear Caro's sobs. They slackened as the terrain levelled out, and the track widened into a clearing. We continued more slowly. I shifted, trying to ease the pain in my thighs, and spurred my mount until it drew level with Zeb's. 'Are you going right through?'

He shook his head. Caro stared piteously at me. She was still wearing the rose chaplet and it vied for pallor with her brow and cheeks. There were blood smears behind her left ear. I reached across and lifted the cursed thing, tossing it into a bush.

'Here's as good as anywhere,' Zeb said, wheeling about. He slipped from the saddle and put up his arm for Caro. Something in me hoped he would not be strong enough to support her, but she got down leaning heavily on his shoulder. I too dismounted, hearing my legs crack as I put foot to ground. We tied our beasts to a thorn bush.

Caro sat on the ground shuddering, her face cupped in her hands. At last she lowered her fingers, sliding them along her arms for warmth, and I saw the bandage was come off. Staring at the grass she said, 'We have done a terrible thing.'

'That may well be.' Zeb looked steadily at me.

I bent to Caro and laid my hands on her shoulders. She was cold as marble. Taking off my coat, I put it round her, but she continued to shake. I remarked a vomit stain on the lace of her gown.

Zeb stood a while watching us. 'If we knew where they were,' he said. 'If I could see them, now,' and he began pushing his way through the scrub. The branches closed over him.

'My thighs are skinned,' I said.

Caro made no reply.

Feeling the lack of my coat, I walked to and fro. My wife laid her head on her knees and snuffled into her blue silk.

'I'll starve with cold,' she mumbled. 'All this is madness.' She held up the gold chains around her neck. 'We can return these, Jacob. Say we went in pursuit of thieves.'

'You know that won't wear.'

'How will we sell them?' Caro screamed. Some small creature skittered through the bushes at her back, and she collapsed again into silence.

Zeb's voice suddenly rang out, anguished. 'Jacob! Jacob!'

Caro leapt upright. I plunged through the branches where Zeb was gone before, seeing nothing but scrub and trees, my wife stumbling after me.

'There are footpads in these woods,' Caro hissed.

I shook my head. 'He's seen something.'

We stood straining our ears.

'Zeb?' I called.

And then I saw him, not far off. My hands flew to my mouth as I took it all in. Zeb had climbed a tall tree as a lookout. Now he dangled from a branch by his arms, legs kicking free. Below him, on the grass, lay a freshly broken bough. A strip of torn bark drooped like a hangnail from the trunk.

Caro's eyes had followed mine. 'Elm,' she moaned. 'Hateth and waiteth.'

I moved forwards, wondering if I could catch him. He had about fifteen feet to fall. A man dropping from that height might well break the bones of one beneath.

'He's going!' Caro screamed. I saw Zeb's hands peel from the branch. There was not time to get beneath the elm. His legs strained upwards in a wild attempt to scissor them round the trunk, but it was much too thick for him. He fell fists clenched, with a howl which exploded in terror as he struck the ground.

There was silence, broken by Caro's whining, 'O Lord, Lord, O Lord, O.' We clambered over logs and leaves. He was stretched on his back, face white and eyes closed. She wet her finger and held it to his nose and mouth. 'I can't feel anything! Jacob, there's no breath, he's not – he's – Jacob—'

'Calm yourself.' I felt under Zeb's coat and shirt, pressing my palm flat to the skin. Strangled sobs came from Caro. My brother could not be dead. He was warm. Only that morning, looking on his nakedness, I had remarked how strong he was grown.

'He lives, be at rest,' I said, feeling Zeb's heart leap under my hand.

'Let me.' She pushed my fingers aside, pressed her own to him and at once sighed. I saw her shoulders loosen and her head drop forward as if praying. Then she stiffened again.

'He's not right here.'

Here was his waist. I unfastened his coat properly, from top to bottom, and pulled up his shirt. Zeb groaned without coming back to us. I saw now that his flesh was darkened and puffed up round the lowest rib, and he was not lying straight.

'There's something broken,' Caro wailed. 'O, look there!'

I did look and saw that he had landed across a branch lying in the grass. I covered him up again, thinking that we were in the very worst plight for tending him – no surgeon, not even a blanket. He groaned again and opened his eyes.

'Zebedee!' Caro kneaded his hand. 'Do you know us?'

He muttered, 'Too well.' But even this feeble joke lost all relish when he tried to sit up and fell back crying.

'Move your foot,' Caro implored him.

His right foot flexed.

'Your back's not broken,' she whispered, but he had swooned from the pain.

'We have to go on,' I told her. 'Here we are like to be surprised.'

'He can't.'

'Do you want him hanged?' I urged.

Caro wrung her hands. 'Will you carry him?'

'We'll put him on horseback.'

We tortured him into the saddle. I walked on one side of him and Caro, trembling, rode on the other horse, at every minute afraid that her animal might bolt. Strung out like this we had great trouble in passing along the narrower paths, and our progress was slow indeed. I was close to tears, having not the slightest idea where we were headed or how we would do now that Zeb was hurt. We walked seemingly for hours, and many were the groans Caro and I heard before we at last stopped near a stream: Zeb had twice been sick, and had once fainted onto my shoulders. I stood ready to catch him as he dismounted. He gasped – '*Ah!*' – but was able to walk almost to the water, sinking down just before he reached it. Caro knelt by his side, stroking his cheek and pushing his hair out of his eyes.

'Don't put me back on the horse,' Zeb begged.

'No, no,' she murmured.

I said, 'Tomorrow we will get you a surgeon.'

'I'm thirsty.'

Caro cupped her hands in the stream and I supported him so that he could drink. Most of the water dropped onto his chest and he shivered. The wood was beginning to grow dark.

I took Caro by the sleeve and led her away. 'Sit down,' I urged in a whisper. 'What think you? Is there more than a rib broken?'

'What do I know!' Her voice came cold and dispirited. 'Why should there be?'

'He faints. I didn't faint when mine was broken,' I reminded her.

'O, *you*...!' She got up and went back to Zeb, soothing him with soft pitying noises as one might a child.

He lay staring at the branches above. I heard him say, 'Sister, I'll die.'

'Pain talking,' I said, going over to him. 'You'll not die. Now act the man.'

'I'm starting a fever.' Zeb reached for Caro's hand and pressed it to his forehead.

'He's very hot.' Caro looked at me helplessly.

'Broken bones do get hot.'

'Feel, here,' Zeb pleaded with Caro. He indicated his chest.

'Let me.' I fingered his shirt front. It was soaked with sweat.

'I can cool him,' said Caro, loosening the collar. 'Put my handkerchief in the stream.'

'No,' I said, laying my hand on hers as she began easing the shirt up over his chest. 'Best he sweat it out.'

'I'm burning,' moaned Zeb.

'He shouldn't be half naked like that. Cover him up.' I straightened Zeb's shirt and pulled his coat close over his breast. The wind, growing stronger, stirred the tops of the trees so that they hissed like a poker in ale. 'Come away and rest,' I told Caro.

We lay down together a few yards from Zeb, barely able to see one another. I took my coat from her and arranged it over both of us. It was not much of a blanket, for cold air crept in on every side. Faintly from under the stench of horse and vomit came the scent of her pomaded hair.

'How will you get him a surgeon?' whispered Caro.

I pulled her on top of me. 'We have gold.'

'But—' She checked herself. I felt her shake as she went on, 'We could go home with him. Take back the jewels, say you feared a false accusation – you were in drink. What is whipping, what is gaol, even, when Zeb may die?'

'I can never go back, and nor can you. It means hanging.'

'What, for a few pamphlets?' She twined her arms round me. 'Let me go to the Mistress. Let me beg mercy. Peter burnt all the papers – it is their word against ours—'

'Take it from me, wife, we are tarred with the same stick.'

'I can face it out!'

There was no light left in the wood. I knew what I had to do, and it was like sliding down ice in pitch darkness. I had stood on the brink of this slide for so long now I was come to desire it, was dangling the first foot over the edge. Better push off boldly, I thought, than crouch there forever.

'Caro,' I breathed into her neck. 'It isn't what you think.'

One foot on the ice.

'Patience fled for fear of me. She's out for blood, and Cornish too.'

Both feet.

Caro lifted her head. 'You? You and Patience?' Her voice was thick, stupid with baffled suspicion. 'The child! You – you—'

'No!' I shouted, so hard that I hurt my throat. 'Don't you see it? Caro!'

'Jacob, don't—'

'Caro, it was I killed Christopher Walshe.'

I had pushed off. The polished blackness of the slide dropped away to a place I could not see; I was falling out of life. Caro's breath heaved and choked. Her body lay against mine rigid as a plank.

'I heard noises and went down in the night. Cornish and Patience were in the garden by the maze, only I did not know who they were, then. I was listening. The boy jumped me.'

'Why would he!'

'I had not time to ask him,' I retorted.

Caro's breathing slowed a little. After a while she asked, 'And Patience? Doing what?'

'I told you, I did not see.'

'You did not see,' she repeated as if she had been there. 'But you saw it was Patience.'

'I saw a woman, and next day Patience was gone.'

'Not true,' Caro kept saying. 'No.'

But it was true, and not the worst of the truth neither.

~

When first the boy leapt out to bar my way he took me unawares. I thought him a man, but then the moon coming out showed me the little fool standing about a yard off, waving his dagger. Though furious at his insolence, I laughed aloud. He was so easy; I had the knife off him and his arm twisted up his back before he could make one good pass with the blade.

'Be quiet,' I said, 'and come along with me, or I'll slit your throat.' He came along like a lamb, and I marched him away from his friends, over to the large trees near the pond.

Not daring to call out, Walshe fell to whining for pardon. 'O Jacob,' says he, 'you see it is only me, pray let me go,' and all the time he was looking out for his father, but I had taken care to get the trees between us and any help that might come to him. At last he fell silent, gaping at me much as he had gaped from the protection of my brother's arm.

'What of dear Zeb?' I mocked. 'Not here, is he?'

The moonlight showed me tears on Walshe's cheeks. He was panting with fear, breast rising and falling beneath his white shirt. *Show him*, said the Voice, *what becomes of a boy who insults a man.*

'Well, little warrior.' I pushed him up against the tree and pressed my left hand hard over his mouth, and just tickled his belly with the point of the knife before driving it in. He tried to push away my arm with both of his but could not, and his struggles were so feeble that the savage fit in me was still not worked off. I pulled the knife down and out, and feeling my fingers warm and wet from the blood, I said to him, 'Let us see what Jacob will do now.'

Twisting his arm again to keep him in front of me, lest he bleed on my coat, I wrestled him over to the pond. On seeing where we were headed he turned his face to look up into my eyes, and I tightened my grip on his mouth, and smiled and nodded. By the time we got there he was very weak, and too confused to call out when he got his chance. I held him by the legs into the deep water at the side of the runway. There was not even much splashing.

~

'It was dark,' I pleaded to Caro. 'Else I should never – I took him for a robber—'

My wife clamped her hands to her ears.

'Caro, hear me.' I reached up and prised the hands away.

'You put him in the pond! O you should have brought him back – fetched a surgeon—'

'Too late, he was dead. I thought to hide the corpse. Besides, he was a Judas, they all of them meant us harm—'

Caro cried, 'O what do I care what they meant!'

'I am telling you how it was!'

'*You* killed him. And here have I been—' She began weeping again, a breathless, driven sob. 'Here have I been – wondering – if I drove Patience away. We had words that day.'

'Do you hear me? Patience—'

'Patience *saw* it.' Caro's voice was become a lash. 'And for *that* she left, and returned.'

For once her quick understanding struck fear into me.

'Who knows? Possibly she heard.' I tried to keep my voice calm.

'All this because he spoke against you!'

'Not for that, not at all,' I said. 'You don't listen.' I tried to put my arm around her but she rolled off me and lay by my side. 'Caro, I was set on in the dark, Walshe set on me—'

There was a scuffling in the leaves and Caro spoke from somewhere above my head. 'I am going back to Beaurepair.'

'Don't you understand?' I was exasperated: there she stood as if nothing had happened. 'You cannot go back.'

'I shall try whether I can or no.'

'You read the pamphlets and stole the gold with the rest of us,' I answered. 'As for Walshe, I did it for you. He would have—'

'Did it for me!' Caro screamed. There was a sharp pain in my side: she had kicked out, and not in jest. 'When you didn't know what he was! How, for me?'

My side throbbed. 'Another kick,' I promised, 'and you'll wish you hadn't.'

'Don't ever say you did it for—'

'Enough! The thing is done. You stay here,' and I sprang up.

Caro leapt back, panting. 'You let me contract myself to you.'

'You cannot go back,' I hissed. 'Do you want us to be taken?'

'You were keeping ahold of me until the betrothal. I don't know you, O God, God help me.'

'O but you do know me, Mistress.' I stepped forward to where her voice had been, but found she had moved further off. I heard her pushing through branches. Then a frenzied whisper: 'Zeb, Zeb! Zeb, wake, please, O God, Zeb—'

I closed in on her voice as it floated upwards from where she crouched over my brother's body. There was a faint slapping sound which I took for her patting his face. Zeb groaned once or twice, and Caro shrieked, 'He's here! He's—'

I was upon her before she had time for more. Pawing my brother like that, calling myself, her lawful husband, *He* . . . ! I dragged her upright by the hair and forced her along with me, ignoring her wails, until we were some yards off, tussling all the way.

'Lie down,' I said.

'Jacob, let me—'

Amorous propensities heated by struggle, whispered the Voice. Other men took their pleasure, even with sluts like Patience, whilst I, a loving fool, had waited weeks, months for a wife who at the first trial offered to leave me. I grabbed her by the waist and pulled her down. The wedding gown was heavy and in the dark I knelt on it. My fingernails tore in trying to hitch it up. A squib exploded in my head: she had hit me in the eye. I brought my fist down on her face as if chopping wood. She commenced screeching, and I gave her another, and another, until she learnt better. At last all I could hear was stifled gasps.

'Now keep still,' I said.

Her thighs under the robe were damp and cool as mushrooms. My hand gouged between them, found the soft place where I would slake myself. I undid my breeches.

'Jacob, please.' Her voice quavered; she coughed and snorted and I guessed her nose was bleeding. 'Zeb hears you.'

Again I saw her hand move under his shirt. 'Let him.'

'Please, Jacob, Jacob.' Caro's tears and spittle all but choked my name. 'How will you feel tomorrow?'

'Married.'

She whimpered, mingling prayers and sobs as I pushed into her. She had still her maidenhead; I drove in hard until the flesh gave way and I was packed tight.

'You're killing me!' Caro shrieked. 'Killing!'

I pushed harder, for mastery.

'Zeb!' she screamed.

'Keep him away if you love him,' I snarled. 'I'm able for him, too.' Let him hear that. Let him hear all – let—

The spasm was upon me and it was intense unto agony. I heard myself growl. Teeth clenched, I crushed my hips against her, the pleasure surging in me so that for a moment I was nothing but that, I was dying, and even as I let go the gasping of the flesh slowed, slackened and I knew where I was and who lay with me. Heart pounding, I collapsed onto her breast. Caro at once shifted under me so that my body slipped out of hers. She then tried to pull the gown over her thighs, but my weight prevented it.

There was silence apart from our breathing.

From the side of the stream came Zeb's voice, timid: 'Caro?'

'Don't make me come over,' I threatened.

'Caro!' There was a pause, then he commenced weeping. I made to rise and stop his noise.

Caro at once called, 'Take courage,' and the crying grew quieter.

'What should he want with courage?' I demanded. 'Have I hurt him?'

She gave no answer. I knew then that Zeb, listening to our struggle, had feared Caro was killed outright.

In time, pain in my knees obliged me to raise myself. My wife turned on her side and curled up like a child, her back to me. I lay stretched out, staring into the invisible trees. My coat was lost in the dark, and now that the animal heat was gone off the cold of the wood struck to my very bones.

It was already coming to me what I had done, the ruin I had made. Rage and lust had sharpened in me to a madness. I had even wanted Zeb to hear this butchery of a wedding night, and now my cheeks burnt with shame. Whatever it was that Zeb did with his women, it was not this.

'Caro?' When I touched her neck she shuddered. 'Wife, are you cold?'

'If you will do it again, just do it,' came her voice, crackling with hatred.

'You must be cold. Let me put my arms around.'

Caro gave a terrible laugh. 'Here, take this.' She prodded at my hand with something hard. I felt for it with my fingers and found myself holding the wedding ring.

'How can I take what's yours?' I fumbled for her own hand and pressed the ring back into it.

'Very well,' she said and I felt her body jerk. Something landed in the leaves.

'What was that?' I asked.

'The ring gone. Thrown away. Now leave me.'

I listened while she strained with sobs that went on and on like some beast mourning for its young. Tears slid out of my eyes, and my throat was contracted to an ache. It was not what I had meant. Not the boy, not fleeing the house, not this – connection – with Caro. Not what I had meant.

When I laid my hand on her shoulder she only wept the more loudly. There was nothing to do but lie and wait for sleep. Zeb did not call again. I rolled away from her in my turn and lay facing in the opposite direction, listening to the wind-battered trees, thinking of the bridal bower I might have had, and had rent in pieces at that moment when I spitted Christopher Walshe. Caro should by rights be cradled in my arms and I in hers, each drunk on the other, or sleeping innocent as surfeited babes. Instead we lay back to back, the whole of the earth between us.

At last I slipped into a dream of shifting trees and paths. Something moved, and I woke in a terror, heart clanging; but all was still. I slept again, and Father came to me, saying that my life was in God's hand, and I saw the hand with a little flame of fire in it, and was afraid. When next I woke, it was dawn, mist sieving through the trees and a pearly grey just sweetening the sky. There was a great coldness all round my belly, and feeling down there I found myself still unbuttoned. I sat up. The grass next to me was pressed flat, but Caro, Zeb and the horses were gone.

PART II

SIX

Prince Rupert

SOME DAYS LATER I emerged from the wood on the northern side, having torn every garment and twisted my shoes almost off my feet, but that weighed little against the inner torment that rent me. I would almost have been glad to be taken by Biggin and be done with it, yet the miserable cowardice of the flesh made me still listen for the sound of men and shrink down in the bushes if I heard any. On coming out of the trees and seeing the highway fair and open before me, I felt a deliverance of body if not of soul. The morning was soft and my road lay between fair green hills, so evenly balanced that I seemed walking in a picture.

Behold, said the Voice, *earthly beauty. It is nothing but seeming, for to the uninstructed eye the world appears fruitful and sweet, yet in it is nothing but a pile of skulls, showing where others were lost as they went before.*

'I am lost,' I answered, 'and can never be found again.'

Not one of us merits salvation. We are too feeble and corrupt to attain to it or form the most childish conception thereof. Yet God shows His mercy in saving some, and His justice in condemning others. Father told this to Izzy and me, and spoke to us of the Elect: he tried to explain these things to Zeb also, more than once, but the boy was too young and foolish, and began to cry. The Elect are chosen from before the beginning of time, and are known by their inner light and godly conversation. Within me all was darkness, and neither my conversation nor my conduct godly. I must look, then, to have Hell as my portion. God cuts out our path, makes a groove in the clay with His finger, and we poor blind ants slide down into it.

I was not long out from the trees when I fell prey to savage thirst. Like a fool, I had not thought to drink deep from the stream before quitting it, I was come across no other water in the wood, and now I sweated much in the sun. Men are wont to think of our England as a soft green land, nourished at the breast of many rivers; yet I can prove by bitter experience that it is possible to walk for miles along the King's highway and find no more than a puddle. On coming to the first village I dared not stop, lest word of our flight had reached there, and methought the wedding garments were like to become the mark by which all might know me and put me to death. There was a well, however, by the church, and winding up the bucket I put my head in it like a horse. Pulling out I saw a woman draw back from a high window as if she thought I would leap up to her.

Just after the last house in the village I found a sign which told me I could turn left onto the Devizes road. I had some crazed idea of walking to Bristol, now that the city was fallen. Any kind of work requiring strength was mine for the asking; in such a large place I might surely earn my bread in safety.

It came to me that if Caro and Zeb were not gone home they might also fix on Bristol as being a place where they could offload the rings and necklaces. Should I find her there, I would throw myself on my knees and beg pardon. I trudged along rehearsing a vow that all the rest of her life I should never lift a hand save in her defence. At other times I blamed her for leaving me so utterly destitute of the means to live: her loud honesty, I reflected bitterly, had not stopped her taking all the gold. Then I recalled their plight, a beautiful young woman in a low-cut gown, the only man who might protect her broken and feverish. Some kite would have the jewels away from them as easily as I had possessed myself of Walshe's knife, and perhaps do evil on them as I had upon him. But if they scaped – and here the Devil put it in my mind that they lay together at an inn. The bed was soft; she dressed his wounds and passed her hands over the rest of him. Again I saw the shirt slide up over his chest; she gazed, and gazed – she fastened the gold chains round his neck – at that I shook my head like a baited bull, to clear it, and felt her put the betrothal ring in my hand. I had searched for it on discovering their flight, but it was lost in the leaves. The memory of her flinging it away was a knife to me. I prayed that I might learn of their safety, might be delivered from my misery, might be revenged – I knew not what to pray for, and all for nothing anyway. God is not moved from His great designs by the prayers of the righteous, how much less does He care for the whinings of the damned!

~

The Devizes road was straight enough, but I made slow progress as my feet pained me sadly by now. After an hour of walking I took off my shoes and found a fat blister on the back of each toe, and my right heel split like a plum. Yet it was better than going barefoot and even limping along I could surely manage fourteen miles before dark. As I went along my conscience wrangled within me, and my sense, also turbulent, worked me to such a pitch that I passed along the road without seeing it, thus saying to myself:

She is my wife. Espoused *de praesenti*, and the – act – in the wood does consummate.

Aye, but spiritually it is clean different. Tears do not argue consent—

I AM HER HUSBAND.

Zeb will lie with her. She will be as Patience – she put her hands on him that way in the wood, they have made their game of me I perceive—

CHRIST let me think no more of this.

My thirst returned upon me most cruelly.

Once, when I was a growing boy, the three of us were allowed back to Mother's cottage for a saint's day, and while in the village I stole some walnuts from a neighbour's tree. This neighbour was a bandy, red-haired old man, whom I think now had a liking to my mother but at the time I saw it not. I took the nuts for their green shiny coats and was scratching at these the better to smell them when he called out, 'Jacob,' and the name leapt in my breast. I was already a big lad and very strong from the field work. When he came up to me he was no taller than myself, but I was sore afraid of him. He took the nuts from me and cast them on the ground along with the little knife I was carrying.

'Now get down,' said he. I had been raised to bear punishment meekly, and I knelt thinking he would beat me.

'No, lie down. On your back.' And I did indeed lie down, hoping he would not kick me. Instead of which he placed a foot on either side of my body and then hunkered down until he was sitting astride me. He took up the walnuts and the knife.

'See this boy?' He peeled one of the things before my face. 'Here, eat it.' And he pushed the unripe nut into my mouth and pressed my teeth into it. The burning made me scream and some of the nut got down my throat. In my agony I threw him off and ran home, spitting and wailing.

'Green fruit, boy!' he shouted after me.

My tongue was black weeks after.

I cannot say why this suddenly came to memory except the thirst, now growing outrageous. Still I went on up the Devizes road, having no idea how far I might be from Beaurepair. Soon I made up my mind for it that I would beg at the next door for water if Cornish himself lodged there, but it was another hour at least before I came upon a group of straggly dwellings, not even an alehouse, and the whole place strangely quiet. An elderly man stood in one of the cottage gardens and stared at me as I staggered up to him.

'Save you, Friend,' I wheezed, 'and where might I find some water?'

He looked me over and did not answer.

'I faint from the road.'

The man spoke almost without moving his lips. 'You'll be a quartermaster.'

'What?'

He gestured at my dirty wedding gear. 'With the King's forces.'

'All I seek is water, for myself. Give it me and you'll see me no more.'

He dawdled still. I observed that his body was bent over on one side by injury and the hands had twisted black nails: the hardness of long oppression.

'I wear another's clothing for all my own was stolen,' I cried. 'Don't you hear my voice crack with the thirst? Be a Christian, Friend.'

The Christian moved away from the wall and pointed silently over his shoulder. I saw, and ran to, a well. The water tasted like sucking an iron spoon but I drank enough to split my sides, far beyond the prompting of need, for I had learnt what it was to thirst on the road.

'Now get you gone,' he said. 'Those are your garments right enough; you're big like all the rich. Tell them we've nothing to eat but the scurf off our heads.'

He must be crazed with want, I thought, to fancy that a quartermaster would come with neither horse nor weapon. I started along the street and looked about me for saner company, and a house where I might beg a little bread. But my surly friend was right: wherever I looked I saw folk draw back from the windows. There were no cows, nor no grain neither, in the fields, the fruit trees in the gardens were all picked bare or even lopped and not a single hen picked a living from the clay and stones of the road. I walked on, and on, and on.

We had suffered nothing of this at home: by some stroke of luck or stupidity they had never asked us for free quarter. I had heard of it, how the soldiers ate everything they could and stole or broke up the rest, nay, debauched the women too if the commander turned a blind eye. The King's forces were the most dreaded for that their officers had precious little control over their men, but no army was welcome. Now I was seeing it for myself. At every house where I tried to beg I had the same answer in words angry or civil, and many seemed persuaded I was a spy, sent to ascertain what remained to be devoured. In the end I took to stealing by night, mostly the odd apple in a garden or griping crabs from the hedges. Breaking into the dairy at one place I found a cheese, and wept with joy. In this fashion I passed perhaps a week, and was lucky not to be put in the stocks.

But at last there were no more houses, and the torment began in earnest. The Devil lashed me onwards with ugly pictures of Caro and Zeb; he rode me hard, driving in the spurs. I had pain all along my breastbone and I thought of the words *broken heart*. My pace had slowed; I knew that beggars could walk for days without food, but I could not do as they did, being used to good feeding. What victuals I had picked up no longer sustained me. My path began to zigzag, and from time to time a knee buckled or the heel of my shoe turned aside. I was like one that has had a beating, my body tender, swerving, weakening as I went, and my throat parched. There was none on the road, and I sat for a moment to ease my blisters. When I made to get up I could not, and sprawled on the grass. It was sweet to dissolve into blackness and the earth. When daylight came back, I was talking to someone who asked me, *Is Isaiah in gaol?* I answered, *Patience and Cornish might name him. They are most hardened against Zeb and me. If they take him it will be with Caro and they must hang him in gold*. On my asking how Patience could leave Zeb for Cornish, he answered me singing, that *Zebedee was cruel to her and this makes maids devils, maids devils, maids devils.*

Aye, I said. *And devils themselves grow crueller by the continual action of pain upon them*. I opened my eyes and there was nobody with me.

The sun grew stronger on my face. Noon. My head ached as from strong drink and I wished only to remain lying and speak to none. A woman passed me with a little child, walking by on the other side. Afterwards I tried to rise, but getting upon my feet my body pitched forwards and I was again stretched in the dust. I rolled onto my back. The walnut was in my throat, burning the flesh black, but I could lose it by falling asleep. The old man stood over me, dropping something onto my face. I said to him, *They are in bed at the inn together, but he is dead of the fever*; I made to sit upright but my head was nailed to the ground. He forced another nut between my teeth, a hard one. It let something cold into my mouth.

'Keep your feet on him,' a man said. I could feel no feet on my body; was someone standing on me? There was a smell of smoke and I heard our horses run into the wood.

The sky was wet. I lay on my back and saw men move at the sides of my head before darkness closed over me again.

'His eyes opened,' said a gentle voice near me, and then, 'drink.' The hard thing was once more put between my lips and I turned my head away.

'Leave him, Ferris.'

'We cannot leave him like this.' Warm fingers wiped my mouth and chin. I looked up to see a young man gazing perplexed into the distance, his profile lean and pensive, but full-lipped and long-nosed. He knelt at my side as if watching for someone, his hand still absently stroking my lips so that I breathed its scent of sweat and gunmetal.

I coughed against his palm, and he turned on me a pair of eyes as grey as my own. Pale hair hung thick on his collar; I saw he had shaved some days before. As I met his eyes they darkened, the pupils opening out like drops of black ink fallen into the grey, then he looked away, and his fingers slid from my face.

'Let me drink,' I creaked out.

'Get on your side.' He tugged at my arm, gritting his teeth as he tried to roll me over. 'Up. Up on your elbow.' When he had pulled me into position, I reached out my hand for the water, and caught a wry look from him.

'You could have saved me a job. Here, and don't spill, this is precious.'

There was mould on the sleeve of his jacket. I took the flask, swallowed about half, and handed it back.

He waved his hand. 'Drink more,' and he stayed close as if to say, *I don't go until you do.*

I sat up and looked about me for the other man I had heard, but he was gone. On both sides of the road, pressed around small fires, were soldiers wrapped in garments that had once been bright red but now were faded to yellow or filthied to brown, except where patches had escaped the mud and smoke of battle. At one fire nearby a boy sat watching us. He smiled and waved to my new-found friend.

'We got some water down you earlier. Drink anyway. I'll fetch you some victual.' Ferris sprang up and walked off, stopping to speak with the lad I had noticed and clap him on the shoulder before passing behind a group of men and out of my sight. Pale blue smoke blew across me, smelling of home, and a thin rain, like spit between the teeth, chilled my neck. I could see now the cropped hair of the young boys round the fires. Some of them, and most of the older men, still wore theirs long. I put my hand up to my head; someone had cut my hair close to the scalp. There it lay on the grass, a knot of wet black vipers.

'Feel better?' He was back, squatting easily by my side.

'Did you do this?'

Ferris glanced at the dead man's locks on the grass. 'No.' He held something out to me, but I could not take my eyes away from what had once been myself, and was also Izzy and Zeb.

'Here,' he pulled my hand away from my shorn skull, 'best eat without looking.' It was bread and cheese, the bread hard as your heels and the cheese popping with mites, but I grabbed at it.

'Not too fast if you haven't eaten lately, you'll hurt yourself,' said Ferris. 'Easy, easy!' He snatched the cheese from me.

'Why are you feeding me?'

'Call it your ration. You're in the New Model Army.'

'You mistake. I am—'

'We lack men. What, going to lie down and die are you?' He laughed.

'But I'm weak, unwell. I've been starving.'

'Starving!' The grey eyes mocked me. 'Granted you're somewhat hungry. We see it all the time. And that suit of clothes! We thought we'd found us a deserter, a Cavalier officer. Until you spoke.'

'I said nothing to them.'

'O yes. While I was bringing you round. And struggled. We stood on your coat to keep you down.' He offered me the bread and cheese again. 'Some of the lads thought we'd caught up with Rupert of the Rhine.'

'He's a devil,' I mumbled into the tough crust.

'So they said, and they were about to take a short way with you, but I told them, Prince Rupert's not a man you'd find lying in the road. What *is* your name?'

'I – well, I have a mind now to be Rupert.'

'Aye, who wouldn't be! Roast goose for him, no bread and cheese.'

'Were you told to enlist me?'

'No. I am squeamish – would not leave a man to die of thirst on the highway – so I came to see if you were well enough to enlist. You're well enough now,' and as I made to protest, 'now.' He jerked his hand towards one of the fires. 'Yonder's your corporal – he'll teach you your drill.'

I considered. 'Is it all bread and cheese?'

'Not always that good! But there's beef sometimes, and eight pence a day – when they pay it.'

He got up and put out his hand to me, but my hipbones, dry as the ones in Ezekiel, grated as I struggled upright, so that my weight pulled him down; laughing, he was forced to leave go.

While I was lying in the road the day had passed into evening, and I was glad Ferris walked before me as it was hard to discern either form or order in the groups of soldiers lying round the fires. He stopped in front of a man whose hair was so dirty it might have been of any colour, and was soiled with more than mud: as I looked closer I saw brownish blood all down the right side of his face, cracked where the sweat had oozed up under it.

'Prince Rupert come to serve under you, Sir,' said Ferris. I bowed awkwardly. The men around laughed.

'And what might be his real name?' asked this gentleman, whose voice was pinched with pain.

'If I may, Sir,' I put in before Ferris could spoil my game, 'I will take the name Rupert, since it seems I am known by it already.'

He waved his hand as if to say, what was that to him?

I was put down in the Officer's book as Rupert Cane – the first name that came to mind – and ten shillings given into my hand.

'That's your entertainment money,' said Ferris, who was come with me.

'Entertainment?'

'Money on your first coming in. Keep tight hold, you won't see that much again.'

I was handed a red coat, two shirts, breeches, and hose; also a leather snapsack and a cap with dried blood on it, as if peeled from the head of a corpse.

'I can't get this coat on,' I said, holding it up.

The man shrugged. 'Nothing I can do there. One yard of cloth, that's the regulation.'

'Suppose you gave him two, and we got a tailor to run them together,' suggested Ferris.

The fellow was willing enough. I thanked him from my heart and Ferris took up the coats, saying he knew a man would undertake the work for a shilling.

As we walked across the camp I felt the food warming me and longed for more. To take my mind off it, I asked Ferris what would happen the next day.

'We will see to your coat... and you'll be drilled in the pike,' he added.

'*You* are surely not a pikeman!' I said, without thinking.

He stopped and gave me a hard look. 'I have outlived many pikemen.'

'I did not mean—' but my voice faltered, for I had meant it. There was a pike over the fireplace of the great hall at Beaurepair, and all the men had lifted it at one time or another. Ferris was of too slender a make to carry such a weapon. It might be, I thought, that he had some little thing to do, far from the van of the fighting. But carrying a pike was better than lying a corpse by the roadside, and for this I owed him thanks. I smiled on him and he at once returned the smile.

'If you would know,' he said, 'I was a musketeer. But a man that knew me in London thought I might be more use elsewhere.'

'Where – why?'

'I am not bad at the mathematics, and some of his best were just then dead. So now I help with artillery,' he said as we seated ourselves at a fire. 'Really it is for the cavalry to do, but what with fever and shot – well, they need men who can count without their fingers,' his mouth twisted at his own grim jest, 'fire straight, and dodge whatever comes back. When the enemy are in range, so are we.' He held my eyes and I felt myself rebuked.

'I know nothing of war,' I said.

'Would that I could say the same. It is a bestial occupation.'

'Yet it is said the men of this army are rather godly than beastly. Is it not the other side that plunders? Do they not call Rupert, *Duke of Plunderland*?'

Ferris grinned. 'Is that why you took his name? Aye, there are those who sing psalms in battle, and our commanders take pains to hold in the plunderers, but not for love of the vanquished. They see rather that armies need friends, and that soldiers once run wild are insensible of authority. Especially if they chance on Popish wine.' He threw a stick into the flames. 'A man may sing psalms, you know, yet cut the defeated in shreds with as little mercy as—' he paused for a comparison, and ended by shrugging.

Warmed by the fire, I stripped myself and tried the new shirt and breeches, Ferris watching me in silence. The shirt was coarse but almost clean; both it and the breeches were big enough. These last had pockets, a new thing for me. My old garments I put in the snapsack, but when I took off my shoes, the fine hose that Peter and my brothers had given me were worn to rags. Not without regret, I put them on the fire.

'Ferris, you said, "especially Popish wine." Is it so strong?'

He grinned. 'Any wine a soldier finds is Popish. That salves conscience.'

I gazed at him. 'Do you say there are no goodly soldiers? That all are wolves?'

'Soldiers are but men. There are many both brave and merciful—' Ferris paused to wave in greeting as a figure skirted the fire. 'As for the other side, they are more than even with us—'

He broke off and called eagerly to the new arrival. 'Welcome my lad, and did you get any?'

I looked up and saw a boy almost as tall as myself, all legs and arms. His face shone with pleasure and even in the poor light I was struck by the gem-like brilliance of his blue eyes, the kind which often go with yellow hair. This boy's hair, however, was so dark a brown as to be almost black, and I thought I recognised the lad who had waved earlier from the fireside.

'This is Nathan,' said Ferris. 'A good comrade and *not* beastly.'

'Who called me beastly?' asked the boy. 'See, Ferris,' and without awaiting a reply he pulled a cloth from under his coat and proceeded to unwrap two chunks of roast meat, the fat gleaming in the reddish light. 'There's bread too.'

'You are a marvel,' Ferris told him. Turning to me he added, 'The meat's mostly boiled.'

'I guess this was picked up at Devizes,' the boy said.

Ferris grinned at him. 'Plunder, eh? Is there enough for Prince Rupert here?'

'Prince—?' He giggled, regarding me curiously, then said, 'I think we have not met before?'

'I joined up today.'

Nathan seated himself on the other side of Ferris and began slicing the beef with a dagger, trying to make three portions out of two. To my surprise he showed no sullenness at this unexpected reduction in rations. 'Is your name really Rupert?'

I nodded.

'You're from these parts?'

'Right again.'

'I wager you'll be pikes. They always put big fellows on pikes,' and he commenced telling me the weight of a pikeman's armour. He had altogether too much to say, and his voice grated on me.

Ferris, watching my face, said to Nathan, 'He'd bear the armour well enough, if there were any.'

'Surely,' the boy agreed. He passed the meat to Ferris and began cutting bread.

'Even I could carry what they issue now,' Ferris continued with a glance at me. 'But most men don't want it. A buffcoat – that's the thing.'

'Would you wish to be a pikeman?' Nathan asked him.

'I wager Rupert thinks me unfit for any kind of soldier.'

'O, no,' I said, 'I only—'

'And he is right,' Ferris went on. 'The recruiting officers are told to find the tallest, strongest men, and what do they turn up? Seven years older than Nat, and not as tall.'

He passed me some beef and Nathan held out a piece of bread. I tasted my share and relished its very toughness as making it last longer. Ferris crammed roast flesh into his own mouth and closed his eyes, sighing as he bit into it. I watched Nathan layer his bread and meat, holding them delicately in long hands that hardly seemed fitted for soldiering.

Looking back at Ferris I found him staring at me. He said, 'For all that you think, I can put down any man my own size—'

'Nay, taller,' said Nathan.

'—and I wager that's as much as you can do.'

Nathan coughed. A morsel of bread shot out of his mouth, brilliant in the firelight, and I saw that he was laughing.

'Nat, you'll choke one of these days,' Ferris warned.

This made the boy worse. I heard great snorts as he fought to swallow his food.

'What ails him?' I asked, vexed at his silliness for I felt I was somehow being made a mock of.

'Me and my bravado. He knows I am no brawler, eh Nat?' Ferris handed me more beef. Nathan continuing to giggle, I rose, sensing myself in a false position. The two of them turned laughing faces up to me.

'Where did you get the meat?' I asked. 'I will try for some more,' and indeed I could have eaten the whole lot twice over.

'That fire over there.' Nathan pointed. 'But they won't give you any. It was a favour to me.'

'We shall see.' I made my way to the fire he had indicated and found some beef still in it, roasting on a stick. This I seized. The two whose food it was crying out in protest, I offered to fight first one then the other for it, and appealed to the others sitting around to judge if that was fair. They, being bored and ready for any diversion, said that it was. I then held myself upright and let the beef-cooks get a good look at me. 'Well,' I said, 'which of you shall be first?' and made to take off my coat. Neither budged, so I took up the meat and left them to the contemplation of their cowardice and the jeers of their companions.

Ferris and the boy were pushing one another, still laughing, when I returned with my trophy. They stopped at once upon seeing it, and Nathan gasped, 'How did you persuade them to that?'

Ferris leapt up. 'I can guess how,' he said, and he had the stick away from me before I knew it. 'I will tell them it was nothing but jest. Nat, give me this,' and picking up the cloth he strolled off towards the other fire while I stood amazed, considering whether I should bloody his mouth for him if he returned.

Return he did, cloth in hand, and after grinning at me straightway sat down at my feet.

'What do you mean,' I said, 'by – hey, you, what do you mean?' It was awkward standing thus over a man on the ground and talking to him. Nathan glanced anxiously up at me.

'Sit here and I'll tell you.' Ferris patted the grass. I squatted next to him, my anger ready to flame out at a very little thing.

'That's the second time today I've saved your life,' he said.

'Saved my life! They were near beshitten for fear of me.'

'Can you catch musket balls in your teeth? Those men are musketeers.'

I recalled Mervyn's syllabub.

'I have told them you were in drink, meant the thing as a jest and would have brought it back, only you forgot the place,' Ferris went on. 'I suppose you are not really the Duke of Plunderland? They do say he goes about in disguise.'

Had someone at home – Zeb, or Peter – said such things, he would have smarted for it. I glared at Ferris.

He looked steadily back. 'Ah, yes. You are full as big as he. Able to put me in the ground without a weapon, eh?' He began untying the cloth. 'Are you still hungry? Are you, Nat?'

A flush spread over my cheeks.

'Here.' Ferris opened up the last folds and pushed the bundle of meat towards me. 'No bread this time.'

Nathan was full of admiration. 'Brave Ferris! Where did you get it?'

'From them, of course. I begged another share as reward for bringing it back.'

'Many thanks,' I muttered.

Humbled, I finished the meat in silence and endured Nathan's prattle with as much patience as I could muster. After a while the boy said, 'Ferris, we are to see Russ before turning in for the night.'

'I forgot. Where is he?'

'Methinks on the far side of the camp.' The boy stood up. 'We should go now.'

'Agreed.' Ferris rose. 'You will be snug enough here,' he said to me. 'Warm, and plenty of comrades round you. Sleep well.'

They picked their way across the grass. The boy was indeed the taller of the two, and I observed with a pang that he put his arm across Ferris's shoulders as I used to lay mine over Izzy's. Where, I wondered, was my own dear brother? Was he suffering for my crimes? To walk with my arm round him, to seek his advice, these were things which most likely I should never do more. I looked around me. The men were sprinkled about in groups and I could see none so utterly alone as myself. *I have been loved,* I wanted to call out to them, for it felt like leprosy.

I slept that night with the others, as near the fire as I could get, and tried to ease my aching hips. The entertainment money was laid next my breast, where a thief could not lift it without waking me. Yet it was impossible to rest easy, and after a while I gave up trying. As the fire sank low, and more men drifted into sleep, I heard mutterings, sobs and rustlings all around me. Many unknowingly gave tongue to their pain: 'Mary, Mary, no such thing,' mumbled one nearby, and another screamed out in the night, 'Save him, it falls.' Later, from some distance off, I heard shrieks as if a man were having a fit. It seemed that all suffered, the good along with the bad. But then, lying dismal and quiet, I felt the surge in my head which announced the Voice, and straightway there came unlooked-for comfort:

Our affairs are all of them ordered, and shall we, with our puny efforts, direct them ourselves? You are sheltered within the Lord's own army. Rest you there.

~

Daybreak was deathly cold. Swathed and huddled bodies flinched as the drum beat out *reveille*; I watched the man nearest me open his eyes on God's sky and fall to silent cursing. He lay awhile propped on one arm, coughing up phlegm, before crawling off to the fire and laying the wood together. He then moved away, came back with a water bottle and seemed to pour it into the flames, for steam rose. After a time I understood that he was boiling a pannikin of water, something I had done countless times. The strangeness of the place had made me stupid.

A cry of 'Rise, rise' was heard nearer to us and the men commenced groaning. When we were all upright I thought I had never seen such wild-looking folks as some of the young ones. They were purple-grey with cold and their cropped hair stuck up at all angles. I passed my hand over my own head: tufts and angles too.

'Where's your lovely locks, Rupert?' one called to me.

'Sent them to his honey,' said another.

I turned away.

'Eh Rupert, want some bread?'

I limped on stiff legs to the fire. The one who had first called pointed to something like boiling slops on it. 'Bread's so old you can't eat it without.'

'Maybe *he* can,' another replied. To me he said, 'Big lad, aren't you? Are they all big in your family?'

'I'm the biggest.'

'Do they all *talk* like you?' Much laughter. Their voices came hard and unfamiliar to me but not unfriendly. They sounded something like Ferris, and something like Daskin; I could not always catch their meaning when they spoke fast together.

'We're from London,' said the last one to speak, seeing my difficulty. 'My name is Hugh, this's Philip and that's Bart.'

Bart took out a little pot and spooned some of the mess into it. I watched him blow on the brownish curds. It was the coarse bread called cheat; at home we had eaten the good white manchet, like the gentry. 'You can have this after me,' he said. 'There should be beans, but we ate them all last night.'

'And cheese?'

'Cheese, lads! No, there's been no cheese of late.'

'A man gave me some yesterday.'

'He's a friend worth having,' said Bart. He handed me the pot of boiled bread. 'Must have picked it up somewhere. Is he here?'

I looked about and saw Ferris seated some yards off, examining the inside of a shoe. Turning to the rest I was about to point him out when I noticed their intense stare, like the eyes of dogs on a rabbit.

'I don't see him,' I said.

~

That day I entered upon my training. First we learnt how to position ourselves by rank and by file, and the distances to be observed, such as touching with outstretched hands, with elbows and so on; then the various motions: *facings, doublings, countermarches and wheelings.*

The business started well enough. *To The Right Hand* was simple, for we all swung to face the right and were brought back again, or *reduced*, by the command *As You Were*. This the veriest fool could have performed without difficulty, and I began to feel hopeful; but when we passed through *To The Right Hand About* (which was still sweet and easy) into *Ranks To The Right Double*, there was some stumbling, as when young children learn a dance, and when we came to *Middle-Men, To The Right Hand Double The Front*, a sigh passed through the lines of men. The corporal was obliged to take us through this last five times at least before the move could be seen for what it was, and even then the soldiers were by no means sure of it, as was plain from their glancing about to see what their fellows did. One near to me, a thin man with yellow skin tight and shiny over his face, had been lost since we abandoned *To The Right Hand*, and could never make it up after. I saw him, baffled, whirling and stamping about. There were others equally out of tune with the rest, too slow or turning the wrong way entirely. Many seemed as raw as myself, and some few were evidently so stupid as to be hopeless of instruction.

A short rest followed, and as soon as we broke rank there came a steady rain. The men wandered about, complaining, or squatted on their heels until it should be time to begin again. I thought I had not done too badly, and that once accustomed to it I should perform my part as well as any.

Next was weapons drill, and we were now given to understand that we were already divided into groups according to the arms we would carry. Ferris and Nathan had been right, for I was handed a pike. Weighed in my hand it seemed bigger than the one at Beaurepair, some six yards long and so heavy it was hard to carry except on the shoulder. We stood in the rain trying not to jab each other as the corporal took us through our postures.

Handle Your Pike was no more than raising it from the ground, and as to *Recover*, and *Order*, those were just as a man might say, *Plant It Thus By Your Side*. Yet all around me I saw confusion, and men in the wrong without knowing it.

The corporal shouted again, 'Order your pike!'

I stood still, my right arm extended, slightly bent, to hold the pike with its base just before my right foot.

A voice not the corporal's said, 'Bring the hand as high as your eyes.'

I turned. The man behind me was a greybeard, but hale and strong, with the look of a practised soldier. He indicated his weapon. 'Thumb cocked, and your pike against it.'

'Thanks, friend.' I copied him, finding that the correct position held the pike firmly, but also (since we were made to wait a long time in this posture) made my arm ache.

At last we got on to *Advance Your Pike*, which was done in three motions. I was cack-handed here, and the movement would not come smooth. The pike, which was to be locked between my right shoulder and arm, slipped away and I had to catch it in the left hand before it brained one of my fellow scholars. We then *Ordered* the pike again, very like the first time, and went on to the next part.

'Shoulder your pike!'

As I took the thing on my shoulder the top of my shoe came away from the sole. The pike dropped backwards and the others cried out to me to mind what I did. Our corporal came up to see what was the matter.

'I can't stand level on one shoe,' said I. He told me to take off both, so I stood watching the mud squeeze up between my toes while he walked again to the front of the file.

'Shoulder your pike!'

Had I known how many postures were to be gone through that day, I would have drilled with less enthusiasm. My feet cold unto numbness, I learnt how to *Port*, *Advance*, *Charge For Horse*, and other moves, with their endless *palming, griping, raising* and *forsaking.* Nothing could ever be done with a pike, it seemed, unless it were done in three motions, and there was already some considerable doubt in my mind as to whether men could do thus in the heat of the fight.

When the full drill had been gone through, by which time the new soldiers were *reduced* not to any former posture but to perplexed misery, those who could read were given a paper with the main points set down in the form of a doggerel rhyme. This I folded up and afterwards forgot.

The corporal told me to go again to the baggage train for shoes and wrote out the order. Taking it there, I was given a pair of boots, finer than anything I would have worn at home. They were even big enough, though I felt the last man's feet moulded within them.

'Why boots?' I asked.

'The latchets we have here are too small. Give me those, soldier,' for I was still carrying my own shoes.

'The sole is torn away from this one.'

'No matter, we can make up a pair from two odds if we have to.'

So my shoes were put in the pile with the others and that was the last I saw of them. Once I was Jacob. I washed in sweet water for my bridegroom's bed. Now I was Rupert, and I took my boots for battle.

~

We broke camp in the afternoon, and I was glad of the even road for walking. While marching along I considered what I had learnt. At Beaurepair there had been an old drill manual in Sir John's study, designed to promote the use of Dutch tactics. All of us young men had studied it on the sly, sometimes snatching up a broom and posturing as musketeer or pikeman. We had pored over the engravings of classical battles wherein the troops advanced in orderly fashion, the files of pikes showing like square hedgehogs, and every kind of soldier keeping with his fellows. I had marvelled at this thing called an army. Yet our army marched in small knots and gaggles, the men seeking out their friends to pass the time. Sometimes these were comrades who carried the same arms, sometimes not, and I concluded that such books were like books of manners, written for that things were not done as they ought to be.

As we trudged on some of the men, especially the London lads, began to tell me of the fighting they had seen and of their dear hopes. I said they were most admirable at their drill, as indeed I thought.

'You would be amazed to see how they drill in London,' said Bart. 'They're trained to defend the city against attack, for the liberty of the people.'

'From what you say, there are none so good in these parts,' I admitted.

'Another thing, most trained bands won't go from home,' Bart went on, warming to his subject. 'But the London ones, well! Fifteen thousand lads, prentices mainly, regularly exercised. And they do their stuff.'

'I wager they frighten the other side,' I offered.

'The Cavaliers – to speak truth, they've some good men but they run wild. No discipline, rag tag and bobtail.'

'What are their men?'

'Great lords, poor country fools . . .' here he hesitated but I smiled, 'Papists, folks from up north where they think the King pisses perfume, Irish and Welsh rabble . . .'

'And men from the rich cathedral towns. Where you find a cathedral and a pack of fat priests, you find Royalists,' put in Hugh.

'They bring their doxies with them,' Philip said.

Another man, walking behind us, here shouted, 'He's got doxies on the brain.'

'Are there not women here also?' I asked, for I thought to have seen some near the baggage train. 'What are they?'

Hugh laughed. 'Many are wives to some man here. Others are wives to all.'

'There are women feign their sex,' put in Bart. 'To pass among the men without insult.'

Philip guffawed. 'Or to whore the more freely.'

I enquired of him what happened to these soldieresses if their men were defeated. None answered me, so I asked where we were headed.

'Now Devizes is fallen we're off to Winchester,' said Hugh.

'Fallen?'

'Aye, where have you been? And Bristol two weeks back! Your namesake was there.'

'Mine?'

'Prince Rupert. It was he defended the town.'

'I knew Bristol was gone. Is Rupert dead, then?'

'Not he. Black Tom let him go to Oxford to the King. We should have put him to the sword, but that's Fairfax for you, honourable to a fault.'

'He's honour itself,' said Bart.

'Will you show him me?' Though I felt Fairfax had done wrong, showing so gentlemanly to a necromancer, I was more eager to see him than ever.

Philip explained, 'He's gone on to Exeter. He's black like yourself; wears his hair a bit longer, mind.' Here they all laughed and I knew that one of them must have cropped me.

'You'll know him on sight,' added Bart.

'Was that why Rupert yielded? Because Fairfax was Fairfax?'

'Well. Long walls they had at Bristol, hard to man properly. And water running short. Once that happens...' Hugh waved his hands expressively. 'We got the garrison supplies, but he saved his men and the citizens.'

'Were the citizens all Royalists, then?'

'Not when Rupert left, they weren't! His men flay the people, see, and he turns a blind eye. When he came out the townspeople were shouting, "Give him no quarter!" They'd have torn him to pieces if it hadn't been for Black Tom.'

I returned to the question I had asked before. 'What happens to the women on the losing side?'

'That depends,' said Philip. 'On your commander, on the luck of the day, the class of person you're dealing with... I've seen everything. Seen them run through. There were Irish whores drowned back to back at Nantwich – that was Fairfax.'

'Not so,' Bart said. 'A false report. He let them go.'

'No?' Philip jeered. 'Naseby, then.' He turned to me. 'You've heard of Naseby?'

I nodded. I knew what was coming, the slit faces, but was curious to hear his story.

'Well, you know God gave us victory outright?'

'Indeed.'

'Cromwell said it was cutting down stubble! And after, we found their women fleeing the field, some of them English gentry and some of them Irish. Not a word of English could they speak, what did they want over here, filthy Papist whores? We ran them through.'

'What, all of them?' I could not hide my shock.

'Only the sluts and the Irish. About a hundred. They kept jabbering, calling on Satan to save them.'

I could think of nothing to say.

'They were Welsh, not Irish,' put in Hugh. 'They were speaking Welsh.'

'Irish or Welsh, they were walking bow-legged.' Philip winked at me.

I asked, 'And the English ones?'

'I told you, the sluts we paid off. For the rest, some paid *us* off, and some – well, we carved their faces for them.' He smiled at the memory. 'They were seemingly gentlewomen, but no decent woman would have followed that army. So we ploughed up their cheeks – put an end to their trade.'

'Basely done,' said Hugh, shaking his head.

'Suppose those bitches had found us wounded on the battlefield? You know what they'd have done to us?'

Roundhead. The wildest, the crop-headed prentices out for a savage holiday. They had told me that calling another man Roundhead in the presence of an officer meant a fine, it was such an insult. I remembered that Zeb could scarcely ride or walk and that Caro was tricked out in My Lady's blue gown. The jewels. Heavenly Father, let them not be overtaken by such men as this. For their sakes and mine, let me not be guilty of their deaths.

'Are you well, man?' They were staring at me. 'You were chewing your lips.'

I nodded, thinking, *This is curiosity not pity*. Izzy, how he did pity everybody. The men in front began singing psalms:

> *'O sing unto the LORD a new song;*
> *For He hath done marvellous things;*
> *His right hand, and His holy arm,*
> *Hath gotten Him the victory...'*

As long as I could fix my mind on the psalms all was well, but I could not long forbear thinking of Philip's words. I had heard before that there were plunderers and would-be ravishers in the Parliamentary ranks as well as among the King's men, but kept under a much stricter discipline. That restraint had seemed well enough, and as Ferris had said, soldiers are but men; yet I had not thought how it would be to live side by side with such. God's army! I could not go on walking next to Philip. I moved away from him and quickened my pace; it was not until I saw Ferris, walking alongside one of the great guns, that I realised I had been looking for him. He smiled at me but said nothing as we fell into step together.

'Were you at Naseby-Fight?' I asked him.

Ferris looked surprised.

I went on, 'What happened to the Royalist women who were left on the field?'

He frowned. 'They were barbarously treated,' and raised his face sharply to mine. 'Do you want to know how?'

I felt my cheeks flush.

'You already know,' he said, turning his profile to me.

'I hoped you could tell me it was not true,' I said.

'It is true. You get no more from me.'

I thought him unjust. 'Was it my sin? I was not there.'

He again lifted his face to mine. 'There are men who warm themselves at others' sins. Someone has infected you, heated you with his boastings, so you come to me for more.'

'No, indeed!'

'I can smell it on you. But you will be disappointed in me. My way has always been to show mercy where I could, to man, woman or child.'

We walked on. From time to time I glanced at my companion, but he kept staring ahead.

'Forgive me, Ferris,' I pleaded. It was the way I would sue for pardon to Izzy when I was too rough with him during our childhood games. This man had something of Izzy's way, and I should keep by him and away from the prentices – though Hugh was perhaps not a bad young fellow.

'You'll get your chance to hurt people,' he said, looking full at me.

This was mighty strange talk, coming from a soldier. I wondered if, like me, he was fallen away from some better life.

'Ferris, how did you come into the army?'

He was silent.

I tried, 'So what trade were you put to before the war?'

'A draper in Cheapside.'

'Are you married?'

His face twisted.

It seemed I could say nothing right. I battled on, 'What will you do when the peace comes?'

'I should like to leave trade and farm for myself,' came the surprising answer.

'What, like a peasant!'

'No, like a freeborn man with no master over me. London is one great Babylon, a very Sodom of cheating – O yes, the citizens' houses too! You'd be surprised what goes on there. Between prayers they find out new ways to water the servants' milk.'

'You're bitter, Ferris.'

'And you're not?'

A second time he had laid his finger on something I thought hidden. Was I then so easily sounded? No one at home had thought so, but London folk were different. We walked on a few steps, fear coiling my belly into loops.

'This bitterness of mine, can you tell—'

'I am not a soothsayer!'

'No, no. A jest,' I said. Not a good man to lie to; last year his friendship would have been a delight to me. Now, how could I tell him about the boy, or about my doings in the wood?

But even as I argued with myself, my spirit was opening to him. Again I felt how much I missed Isaiah, how I ached for a good and trustworthy friend. In the company of such a one I might mend, and live better.

'You wish to stay with me,' he said.

'Ferris! How do you know?'

'How can I *not* know! You are saying it to me, in your walk.'

'Is that a thing a man may interpret? To what end?'

'Well, it's of great help in training dogs.' He grinned and I saw that he had forgiven me. Was that because he thought of me as his dog?

'Take no offence,' he added.

SEVEN

Bad Angel

I KEPT WITH HIM from then on, except when we were forcibly separated, as for drill. By dint of frequent repetition I was now grown proficient in this, and not only joined with the rest of the men in proper form as regards rank and file, but also went through the pikeman's postures without pause or bungle. In addition I had learnt to follow the drum, and to know the beats for *Call, Troop, March, Preparative, Battle* and *Retreat*, all of which lessons I endeavoured to put into practice as best I might, for I was the same proud and careful workman I had always been.

Ferris's task, as he had said, was to help with the artillery, and there were many times when we could not be together. Besides, he had his own mates among the gunners. In fact, he had plenty of friends among all the better sort of men – after two days he had my coat ready, for one of these friends was a tailor – and he would often joke with them. But he hated certain kinds of bawdry, in particular tales of amours struck up with women obliged to give free quarter, when the men jeeringly recounted their conquests afterwards. At times, too, soldiers would chronicle some rape reported of the Cavaliers, speaking with a relish which showed them secretly envious, and this he perceived and despised.

Some of the men jestingly called him Mistress Lilly to his face, and must certainly have had a name for me too, but took care not to let me hear it. I was not so much under Ferris's sway that I was grown soft. One quick step up to a man, my eyes staring into his, settled most arguments.

'You frighten me, Rupert,' said Ferris one day after watching me see off a man who had tried to steal my snapsack.

'Have I ever picked a fight?'

'Not of late. But when I see you like that, I ask myself, will he know when to stop?'

This again put me in mind of Izzy. 'While you are there, I will always know when,' I said.

'You haven't in the past?'

He waited. I turned away.

'You should try to be friends with the men.'

I knew what he meant. Those walking near us did not care for me. More than once, coming back from the latrines or from drill I heard the tail end of some speech, perhaps my name, and then men's eyes would shutter over as I approached and the group would break up. As for their prattle, I cared nothing for it. But on occasion they would come and talk to Ferris, and he, being kind, seemed to relish it, and then I felt them squeezing me out. I had reproached him therewith, and he said that a man needs friends on the battlefield, that one of these had pulled him out from under a corpse at Bristol and that they were his companions still.

From time to time Nathan would join us, but some coolness was grown up between Ferris and him. The boy would hang about, seeming not to know what he should do, and though he spoke to me always with courtesy, I more than once found his glittering eyes fixed on mine as if I had done him some hurt. I could not recall any insult offered to him, and since his talk was wearisome, I was glad when he wandered away.

Not long after the time when Ferris said I should make me some friends, we were marching together and he asked me had I family living. That was a question I dreaded. He had once started on this tack before, but one of those fools broke in on us – the only time I was glad. Afterwards, I had chewed over my story, and now it was needed I had it at my tongue's end.

'I know not if my brothers are dead or alive,' I said. 'One of them I last saw at our Master's place in the country. He was wrongly suspected for . . . something, and I had to go without knowing what became of him.'

Ferris raised his eyebrows at me and I felt I might as well have confessed. 'And the other?'

'Wounded, the last time I saw him. Not by me. He had a fever. I lost him in a wood and when I came out of it you found me on the road.'

His eyes rested on me, grave, considering. 'You left home in a great hurry, it seems.'

'Aye.'

We walked on a few yards. I knew he was waiting for more, but when he spoke it was to ask, 'Are they like you, these brothers?'

'In their persons? Not nearly so tall. But we are all dark-skinned. Zebedee – he's the youngest – is the properest man you ever saw, gentry not excepted. Everyone that sees him, well, women . . .' I paused.

'*A black man is a jewel in a lady's eye*, eh? And the other?'

'Isaiah is the eldest, the one before me. He is weak of body and looks older than his years. But he does as much work as most.'

Ferris nodded. 'What I meant was, are they troubled in soul like you?'

'I would say, they have no cause.' It was the nearest I could get to a confession.

'If only you could find out what became of them,' he mused.

We walked on in silence. I felt his goodwill towards me. Perhaps one day I would be able to tell him everything, even that I was that detested being, a ravisher. I knew Ferris would not admit that her being my wife changed the case. He had already expressed himself more than once on this subject, and said no man might force a woman, no not his wife, for that it took away her bodily dignity. Whenever he talked of it he clenched his fists and jaw, and I at first concluded he must have witnessed many instances among the soldiery; yet when I asked him he said it was a thing, thank God, that he had never seen for himself.

'We may pass near your Master's house,' he suddenly cried. 'Who knows, they may demand free quarter there.'

I had told Ferris where Beaurepair lay, and he had frighted me most cruelly by letting me know that the army was headed back in that direction.

'I can never go back.'

'You have a new name, Prince Rupert, a new round head and a beard coming.'

'I can't disguise my height.'

'You're not the only tall man in England. I'll shave your head for you the night before.'

'Christ preserve me.' I felt my guts coiling at the idea of entering the grounds.

Ferris said soothingly, 'Most likely they'll quarter us elsewhere.' I thought of Mister Biggin's household, which was worse still. He went on, 'That means sending Fat Tommy over at night to find out.' Fat Tommy was a living skeleton who could walk as fast as some people could run. 'He can go as a beggar; you'll give him a day's bread and beer.'

'This is building castles in Spain.'

'What else should a man do on march? Come, to whom shall we send him?'

'Zeb's great friend was Peter. A manservant.'

'And your sir-name?'

'Cullen. My brothers, Isaiah and Zebedee.' It was a knell on my tongue. 'And—'

'Yes?'

'Nothing.' I could not unpack the stinking wound that was Caro, not yet. 'I need to know what the master did to Izzy, and whether they caught them—'

'Them? You said Isaiah was left at home?'

'Him, I mean. Zeb. Will Tommy remember all this?'

'Oh yes,' said Ferris. He fixed me with his eyes. 'Tommy's story will be as good as your own.'

There was a little coolness in him after this speech, but we got over it as we got over many awkward moments. He did not like my trying to deceive him, but he could also see that I was in travail with myself. As we drew near my own country I grew almost possessed: I had difficulty breathing, my head ached, and the ration, poor and plain as it was, would not lie quiet in my belly. At last, as the sun was sinking, I recognised a mound known to the folk around Beaurepair as Mulberry Hill. It was on Walshe's land. We had been approaching for some time before I knew the place, for I had only once before seen it from that side. The recognition hit as hard as seeing the gallows, with the noose knotted up for me and dangling ready.

'What ails you, Rupe?' someone called.

I was reeling as if drunk.

'Devil's in him,' came a voice from behind.

'Got the staggers,' Ferris said over his shoulder. After a few minutes he whispered to me, 'Well?'

'That hill. One lives there who hates me, who'd burn me alive.'

'Burn you alive? Burn?' He stared at me.

'Burn, hang – anything cruel.'

'Ah,' Ferris murmured. 'Courage, he won't get the chance. Who is this mighty hater?'

'A man – there's a woman too.'

'Do they have names?'

I was silent. We trudged onwards, and I managed to straighten up.

'I'll shave your head tonight,' he said after a while.

'Thank you.' I wanted badly that he should understand me, at least a little, and went on, 'Do you remember saying that some men warm themselves at others' sins?'

'No.'

'Well—' I had made an ill start, but as usual could not leave it alone. 'It was you told me about them. And I find there are others, who may be soiled and hurt by another's sins. I cannot always speak freely of myself to you. I would not infect you.'

'O, you fear my emulation? You think you're the first sinner I have met with?' He laughed. 'I do recall now our talk of men and sins. You were asking me about Naseby-Fight! Do you not think *that* might have infected me?'

'Yes of course, you have seen – things – but my own acts give me bad dreams. I would not give such dreams to you.'

'I've plenty of my own.'

'You said you were afraid of me sometimes.'

'Mostly when you talk like this. Confess, have you burnt a village in their beds?'

I rolled my eyes at him.

'Well, that's the way you get me thinking. You suffer from pride, Rupert. I wager you think God can't forgive you.'

'I did think so. But not now he has sent me such a friend.'

This pacified him somewhat. It was getting dark, and soon we struck camp. He was as good as his word, heating a bowl of water over the fire and shaving my head with surprising deftness, his hand firm on the back of my neck. I watched his face and saw there absolute concentration, the absorption of a craftsman, as he passed the razor over my skin. The blade being coarse, he could not help nicking me in places, and each time he did so he frowned.

'You would make a good barber,' I said when he was done, fingering my shorn scalp.

The firelight showed me that he was smiling, whether at my gratitude or at my strange new looks I could not tell.

'This puts me in mind of old times,' I went on. 'The servants out on a fine evening and the work mostly done. Sitting with my brothers. We were reading pamphlets,' and despite everything I warmed at the memory. 'About God's commonwealth in England. Zeb and Peter had tobacco and we took it in turns to read aloud. We would go down behind the stables and hide from the steward, and the maidservants would come too, if they could. I affected one of them, Caroline.' I hoped that in the darkness he would not see how her name made me wince.

'What were your pamphlets?' Ferris asked eagerly. 'Not stuff your master would like?'

'Not a whit! We had *All Men Brothers* and *Of Kingly Power and Its Putting Down* and some others, bits and pieces. I was rapt with them.'

'Could you all read?'

'My father fee'd a tutor for us three.'

My friend looked his surprise at me.

'We were not always servants,' I said. 'Another time I'll tell you how that was. Our Izzy taught Caro her letters when she was a child.'

It came back to me with sweetness and pain, my brother bending over her, pointing out a line in the hornbook. He had been her champion and favourite all through childhood; his reward had been self-denial and sacrifice, which I had at last trampled under my feet. He would never call his precious one '*sister*', kiss her innocently at Christmas or see her happy with his brother's babe in her arms. Somewhere, if not dead – no, that was not possible, God would not be so cruel – they must each be wondering what was become of me.

Ferris was speaking.

'I am sorry?' I said.

'In London. I wrote just such pamphlets, printed them too.'

'What, those same ones!' I wrenched my thoughts away from Izzy and Caro.

'No. But very like. I kept company with men of ideas, not useless projects but all that might bring Adam out of bondage. Our chief design was that the commons, that fought the war and bore the free quarter, might not be ridden over by little kings at home, for then where was the use of having fought at all?'

I thought of Sir Bastard and nodded.

'Now is the time,' he went on, 'when we might do just such a thing. These poor people that starve at the door of Dives, that cannot take a turf of the common ground and dig on it while all the game and suchlike is shut up in Milord's park – now is their day. The country is up in arms, and the work will be brought about!' He clapped me on the shoulder, laughing, and I remarked that thus animated, the fire shining full in his face, he was comely. I smiled back and we regarded one another an instant.

'Are you married, Rupert?' he asked.

'I am,' I answered, surprised into truth.

'I had a wife, Joanna. She helped me with the pamphlets.'

'You're a widower?'

'God rest her soul. She couldn't write, but she helped bind the pages. I was teaching her to read, from the Bible. I sometimes wish she were here, but what a place for a woman.'

'Perhaps she is with you in spirit.'

'Sometimes – as just now – I feel suddenly persuaded all will be well. That may be Joanna acting upon me. We were merry together; we liked each other well.'

'How long were you married?'

'Not long. She was but sixteen when she died. She would have been brought to bed about now.' His voice thickened. 'One day she was sick and fell to bleeding, the next the child was born dead. She never got out of bed after that, grew weaker every day. The curse upon Eve, the doctor said, agony of childbed. They see so many dead that way.'

I wondered whether Caro had fled the wood with my child within her. 'Still,' I said, 'a man must have issue.'

'The child was not mine.'

I put my fingers into my mouth for shock and wondered if I had understood aright. He was breathing fast. I looked about to be sure no one else could hear him. The rest of the men were roaring at some jest.

'It was not mine,' he repeated. 'I knew of it, she was in her fourth month when we were contracted.'

'She had been widowed?'

'Forced.'

I could scarce believe what I heard. 'Why didn't they marry her to the man that did it?'

'He was already married.'

'Why didn't her father act against him?'

Ferris laughed savagely. 'Why indeed? My manservant – he was courting their maid – dropped a few hints in my ears. The mother was long past beauty and troubled by a sickness of the womb. The father was a man of strong lusts – once word got out, 'twas no matter for her dowry. None would bite.'

'None but you?' Was it possible that he had been so pressed for money as *that*?

Ferris answered, 'I should have said, no *worthy* man would bite: there was one who offered, one who despised her. In the end I took her without the dowry.'

'Why, when the other would certainly have had it?'

'Her father disliked my butting in, and would else have concluded the thing. So I made love to his purse; it was either that, or deliver up Joanna to the other man.'

'Was there liking between her and you?'

'O yes.' His voice was grown soft. 'I had already thought of asking for her, before all this came about.'

'But you could not be expected to give a name—'

Ferris ignored me. 'They had her locked up. Every day I saw her staring at me from the window opposite. Once she looked at me with such misery that I opened the casement to talk to her, but she ran into the back of the room.'

'Afraid of you.'

He nodded. 'That cut my heart. I began to consider, whether *husband* rightly meant owner, or protector and friend. I had a thousand uses for the dowry, and refusing it meant the old man profited by his wickedness. But it was the only way.'

'You must have brought contempt on yourself as a wittol,' I whispered.

'A wittol's wife is his property, only a property he rents out,' he hissed back. 'This eternal curse of property! We own our brethren – our wives too are chattels—'

'You would practise community of wives?' I asked, shocked to think Ferris might be the author of that very pamphlet over which I had quarrelled with Walshe.

'You miss my meaning entirely! This selling the girl off was – was a second rape, and no remedy for the first. Why are good people so slow to see this? Many of my friends, calling themselves Christians, urged me to stand aside and do nothing.' He was agitated. I patted his arm and he went on, 'It would have come right. On our wedding night she put her arms round my neck and wept. I wept also, and told her that I would never reproach her with the child. I loved her, and what the godless and the heartless said was nothing to me.'

He had turned his face aside; I heard him snuffling and struggling for breath.

'And then,' he forced out, 'she died, and her father was safe. He never came to see her on her deathbed, or me afterwards. I buried her and the baby – it was a girl – sold up, left the money with my aunt, and joined the army.'

On his cheek were tears, which I wanted to dry but dared not touch. I held his hand, feeble and hopeless. I was quite unable to speak. How might a man like me comfort one like him? He had said simply that he showed mercy where he could, but excepting mere brute strength, he was beyond me in every way.

We sat together in silence as the fire burnt down and I thanked God inwardly for showing me what a Christian might be who, like the apostle Paul, considered Charity as the chiefest virtue. I vowed that if I ever had the chance I would atone to my wife and brothers, and I thought how both Izzy and Ferris, neither of them fighting men, had yet endured much to protect those they loved – but that way lay great pain for me, and I got off it. We turned in for the night and after a while I heard Ferris's breathing light and rapid. He was perhaps with his Joanna, for he laughed once or twice in his sleep and it was such a joyous laugh as I had never heard from Ferris the soldier. Sleepless, I watched the fire. When the ardour of my prayer had cooled, I found in my breast a sneaking wish that I had stopped his talk. After such an outpouring I could never, never tell him what had passed between myself and my wife, and sooner or later he would ask.

~

The next day things went on as usual for the other men. Nathan prattled of politics while I suffered an agony of terror as we drew nearer and nearer to our house.

'Courage,' said Ferris. 'None would recognise you.'

'I have others to fear for. What if the news be bad?'

At last the hills parted, as in some evil vision, to discover Beaurepair. A cold hand griped my innards as I looked down upon the buildings. They were most of them well back from the road in low sheltered land, and we were able to survey them first from the side and then from the front as we skirted the walls of the park. We crossed in front of the lodge. Behind the house I could see the gate (now closed) where I had ridden out behind Zeb and Caro, with the field and wood beyond. I wondered if the gate-keeper had lost his place. There was my old chamber window, and a man, perhaps Godfrey, slowly crossing the herb garden.

Ferris looked on the house, and on me, and on the house again. 'Did they use you well?'

'Some of them,' I answered. 'The Mistress had her good side. But Sir John was a sot, and the son . . .' I could not find words strong enough for the son.

'I was never in a house like that,' he went on, staring at it. 'So big.'

'Don't the citizens have big houses in London?'

'Here, Fat Tommy's behind us.'

We fell out and loitered. I rubbed my sore feet to colour our idleness and Ferris kept watch for the thin soldier. It was not long before he came up, bouncing a little on his skeleton's legs.

'Tommy, how would you like more rations?' said Ferris. 'Prince Rupert here wants tidings of his friends at that house.'

I showed him the different windows and doors while Ferris kept off Nathan and the rest of the men straggled past. Tommy was quick to learn. Then we got back into the lines and together went through the story, that he was a beggar. I warned him to keep mum before Godfrey. He was to try for a talk with Isaiah Cullen, or Peter Taylor, and find out what was become of the runaway servants.

'On no account say a man in the army sent you, unless you can talk with Isaiah alone,' I urged. 'Alone with him, you may give my likeness.'

'Once we strike camp,' he said, nodding. 'If I can get off.'

We agreed on a day's ration, beer included, to be paid when he brought back the intelligence. Ferris and I would try to distract attention from his departure.

'Your luck is in,' said Ferris to me as I pushed forward to my former place.

'What do you mean?' I panted.

'We won't stop here, or in the next village either. There's too much daylight left and they want to get to Winchester, then to Basing-House. Cromwell's afraid the weather will break and mire his artillery in the mud.'

'You didn't tell me this before.'

'Nathan told me while you were with Tommy.'

'Oh.' Nathan again, chattering to Ferris about the New Jerusalem.

'Why do you frown, Rupert?'

'You know, I should go back, and make restitution.'

'I said, why do you frown?'

Restitution. It had a glorious sound. I could offer myself for punishment; it was most likely only a choice of deaths, for my head might be shot off in the field. Though powerless in the matter of Caro and Zeb, I could clear Isaiah's name. But even as I warmed myself at this vision, something gnawed at me. I pictured myself back at the house and my resolution wavered: I could be brave enough now to deliver myself up, but once there, I knew my heart would fail me. At last I saw that it came to this, that Ferris would march on with Nathan, Russ and his other friends while I faced justice alone. At this thought my courage shrivelled like a withered gourd.

We put up for the night in one of those scoured villages. The men were ill content after passing more comfortable billets, and there was much grumbling as they pulled down bales of straw and spread themselves to rest. Tommy was bedded in the barn with us, which was surely the hand of God in my affairs. I asked the officer, who came round to see how we did, if this Basing-House was what they said, the lid on top of a secret hoard of treasure stolen by Papist priests.

'It's a nest of Papists entirely,' he said. 'John Paulet, that's the Marquess, is a declared recusant and he has sworn to hold Basing-House for the King. To death, if need be.'

'And the treasure? Is it really so much?'

'Who can say? They have golden idols in their churches. We'll find out, my lads.'

The men returned his grim smile.

'Why are we to besiege a house?' asked Ferris. 'When there are whole towns held by the Cavaliers?'

I saw Tommy step out through the door and close it behind him.

'It gives courage to the enemy. And, what some might consider worse, it blocks the wool trade, and there are solid citizens in London bothered thereby.' The officer's voice was steady. I looked at his creased face, the scars on his right temple, and wondered had he been at Naseby.

'Their godless riches can be put into godly hands,' he added in the same flat voice. This was a heart I could not read; I wondered if Ferris could.

We lay down in broken straw. In the night there was a storm overhead. I listened to the usual snoring, then the cough and stir of every man around me under the hammer of the rain and sudden boom of thunder. Some groaned, perhaps for the wet roads and the labour of the coming day. Waiting for Tommy, wondering if he would get back in time, I had not slept at all. When the storm went off I dozed a while, and was woken by water running down my neck. I shifted, and a hand touched mine. My messenger was wintry cold and the rain dropped from his hair onto my shaven head so that I jumped.

He whispered angrily, 'That's nothing man, it's right through to my skin.'

'I'm sorry for it, Tom. What news?'

He lay down beside me. 'Rub my hands, for the love of God. They're ice.' I did so, and blew on them. Such cold and bony flesh, it was hateful. He could hardly keep his teeth from knocking together. That was like Zeb, feverish.

'Thin folks feel the cold the most,' he said.

'Keep your mind on the ration,' I suggested, chafing warmth into his fingers. 'There, put them under your arms.' The carcass hands slithered out of mine. 'So, what news?'

'What do you most want to know?'

I was unsure where to start. 'Well. Who did you speak to?'

'I couldn't come at any Isaiah or any Peter. There's no such men there.'

My heart sickened. 'What, then?'

'A maidservant.' I almost cried out, but he went on, 'French, pretty as you'd see anywhere.'

Madeleine. If My Lady had kept her on, Caro could not be returned. Or she might be in gaol. I waited in terror to hear Caro or Patience spoken of, unsure which prospect frightened me more.

'But you asked after Isaiah?' I urged.

'To be sure. She said that she remembered him, and that he was run away; there was a great hurly-burly with the servants, just about the time you joined the army.' He laughed hoarsely, throat full of phlegm. 'There's two men run off with a maid. That was the second maid they lost, she said, and a lad found dead in the pond. Fine house, by the sound of it.'

'They've caught neither maid nor men?'

'Still looking for them. Not in the right place, eh, Jacob?'

'And the third brother? Isaiah?'

He hawked and spat.

'Isaiah? He's not dead, Tommy?'

'Not that she knew. They took him before the magistrate. He had a whipping and was turned out of the house; they said he was more fool than knave.'

Whipped. O Izzy, forgive me. 'If he was no knave, why turn him out?' I asked. 'He was a party to their going?'

'Some said this, some that. They found a great many papers and pamphlets wrapped up secret and buried behind the stables, where this young maid who gave evidence, I forget her name, said the brothers used to go and talk. But again, he had stayed, and that argued innocence. The other servants gave him an excellent character.'

And the Roches turned him out, I thought. I could remember the name of this young maid – young whore, young spy – if he could not. We had buried nothing behind the stables, all had been burnt. I knew now what they were doing that night when I killed the boy, and most likely other nights too. Poor babes as we were, burning our reading and thinking ourselves safe, when these devils had already laid a mine there could tear us in pieces. My breath came in gasps. Suppose I ever came up against Cornish again, my first thought would be to run, be he never so fat and grey.

'They *do* say one brother drowned the young lad,' Tommy added.

In the darkness it was impossible to read his face.

'They had an old mother,' I said. 'I don't suppose you have news of her?'

'You never asked for any.'

'And have they heard anything of this Isaiah since he was turned off?'

'Not that she told me.'

'No. Thanks, Tom. I'll see you all right tomorrow.'

'O, I nearly forgot. The heir is dead, poisoned.'

I thought I would faint from the shock. 'Poisoned! By whom?'

'The brothers, who else?'

Most likely Mervyn had brought the thing on himself. Or had Mounseer had the last laugh after all, and at our expense?

'God rot all poisoners, I ate some soup there,' Tommy said. 'As for you, you'll have to be cleverer.'

'How, cleverer?' I thought he wanted more of the ration from me.

'I called you Jacob a while back. You never noticed.'

No more I had. As I tried to think how to recover my mistake Tommy moved away into the darkness. I heard him snort to himself, 'Prince Rupert, forsooth!'

Anguish kept me awake afterwards. I was not sure that I had paid out my bread and beef for any good end. I could not make restitution now, be I never so willing. Izzy might be a soldier, a pressed man fighting for the other side. I shuddered. But no, I could not see either him – or Zeb – being well enough. Izzy was not strong enough to bear a whipping – he would be sick a long time after. Thanks to me, my wife and brothers were all of them destitute. I told myself that Zeb and Caro had the jewels. Did Izzy understand what Cornish had done to him? Did he try to prove that those devils buried the papers themselves?

I turned over and my thoughts flowed into a different channel. Now I marvelled at the coldness of Patience, who had lain in Zeb's arms and plotted his destruction. Carnality is of the flesh, but this was a pure deep drink of the Devil. As for Cornish, he knew who it was had killed his boy, and had doubtless laid plans for me.

There are foes against whom it is no help to be tall and strong. I was afraid of a young woman and a man past his prime, because they outwent me in imagination. Now I was possessed of a friend who might help, yet I was afraid to lose him, as I had lost Caro, in the act of unburdening myself. Tommy had said I was not clever. I had spun myself a wretched web; but I would at least try to learn from my errors. Yet it was hard to see how that might be done, and I lay sleepless long after.

~

Ferris was awake before me and shook me until I opened my eyes. 'Rupert. Tommy's back.'

'We've already talked.' I rubbed my face. 'I'm not much wiser than I was.'

'But he did get there?'

'He went all right. But all he could find was, they have whipped Isaiah and turned him off. No one else has been heard of.'

He patted my shoulder. 'You can do nothing, then. That's hard.' He was righter than he knew, for I was in no position to return the jewels.

Grey air blew in through the barn windows. My friend sat beside me in the straw; he looked weary and when I studied his profile he seemed not much fatter than Tommy. I dreaded the day's marching after my broken sleep. I could hear men outside moving carts and cooking pots, and I remembered that my rations were forfeit. Ferris opened his sack and held out a piece of bread.

I shook my head. 'No, keep it.'

'I can't eat if you have nothing. Come on.'

We descended to the farmyard outside the barn. Someone had found eggs and laid them in the ashes to cook; the farmer would be angry, not only for the eggs but for the hen, which was doubtless under some soldier's coat. Our morning food and drink was handed out, and mine went straight to Tommy. I had thought of refusing him payment, but could not in front of Ferris. My friend took some water from the cauldron in a pot he had and sopped half his bread in it, then offered the mess to me. Musty as it was, the smell of it broke my self-control and I ate, urgent as a starved dog.

'It's warm at least,' I said. I hoped Ferris would not be too hungry without it. Not far off the thief was handing hot eggs out to his friends, laughing to see the men juggle them from palm to palm. I saw Philip come up and beg for one. He waved to me and I nodded back. The thief refused him a share, and I was glad. Then the prentice pointed me out to another man. There followed a series of curious gestures, followed by laughter.

'Was that the lad cut my hair?' I asked Ferris.

'What makes you think so?'

I watched Philip pat his skull, grimacing in mock amazement. 'It was.'

Ferris shrugged. 'What does it matter? It's been shaved since.'

'You talked once of bodily dignity.'

'I've seen heads shot off.'

He seemed out of sorts. We had no drill that day, and as soon as the men had eaten and packed up their belongings we were ready to go again. Mud covered the road and we sank in up to our knees where those in front had churned it. The troops plodded on like cattle, heads bowed.

'Do you still fear action?' I asked as the soldiers just ahead moved off.

He nodded. 'So will you, when you're in it.'

'When did you last engage, then?'

'Bristol. We were there from late August to the tenth of September. We began the real assault at two in the morning, and it was eight before the Prince appealed for terms. We were two hours at push of pike. Two hours.' He whistled.

'A long time?'

'You're a pikeman. Work it out.'

'Last engaged at Bristol? I thought you were at Devizes?'

'Aye, Devizes! That was nothing. They surrendered straight off. But Bristol – first I got a blow on the head knocked me out, then a fellow who took a musket ball in the guts fell with his belly right on my face, bleeding into my nose and mouth. Russ pulled him off, else—' Ferris grimaced. 'I can still taste him.'

I shuddered as we squelched onwards.

'It was just after Devizes we found you, Prince Rupert. Some of the men reckoned you were Plunderland himself, others thought how a black man was lucky, and said you'd brought us luck already.' He grinned at the memory.

'You didn't believe it?'

'No, of course not! God decides these things, not a man's skin.'

'Amen to that.' Yet I wanted to be lucky to him. 'Why you? Why were you the one to save me?'

'O, it wasn't just me. The prentices helped.'

'You mean they cut my hair. You were the one gave me food and drink.'

'Well, you weren't very thankful just at first! They held you down while I poured it in.' He laughed, and turned to me. 'What does it matter? Rupert?'

'It matters not at all.' I felt strangely cold. Perhaps I was sickening for something.

'Are you well, friend? Nothing wrong?'

'Only hunger,' I said and vomited up the bread he had given me.

~

By the time we got to Winchester I was sweating, dizzy, barely able to walk. Ferris dragged me onwards, saying that once we arrived I could lie down.

The troops had been ordered to conduct themselves in a Christian manner, to carry nothing away nor cause any nuisance or harm to the citizens, provided we were entertained without resistance and not obliged to assault the place. We waited, armed and ready, at the city gate while Cromwell summonsed the Mayor, one Longland, and demanded access into the city 'to save it and the inhabitants from ruin'.

Word went round that Longland had half an hour in which to reply. Men picked lice from their bodies, rubbed their hands and stamped against the cold, while I fixed my mind on standing upright so as not to be trampled should we go in by force.

After a short time Longland returned to the gate, bringing the civil reply that the place was not his to yield up, but was in the gift of the Governor, Sir William Ogle, and that he himself would undertake to bring Ogle to it.

At this Cromwell would tarry no longer, and we burst in regardless of what Ogle might do or say. Their men barely resisted, so that the whole army was got in without hurt.

'Sit here,' said Ferris, leading me to a low wall. 'If challenged, you are too sick to move. I will find out where you should go.' He pushed through the mass of soldiers towards the nearest officers. I sat head in hands, wondering if I should die there without having seen action.

'Rupert.' Ferris was back and plucking at my arm. 'They are laying the sick and wounded in a church near here. We must get you in.'

I rose, dazed, and allowed him to lead me where he would. Men were swarming like ants through the streets.

'Ogle has shut himself up in the castle,' Ferris went on. 'So it's to be siege, after all. I won't be able to watch out for you.'

He was short of breath. I clung to him, afraid that once fallen, I would never rise again.

'Don't lean on me, you'll have me down,' he gasped. We staggered along; once I slipped on the cobbles and Ferris swore at me. At last I heaved myself up some steps and through the pointed archway of God's house. I heard Ferris cry, 'Help here, I beg of you,' before I sank onto the flags of the church.

During the siege I lay on a hurdle, taking nothing but sips of beer and the odd spoonful of pease which someone gave me. At times methought I was talking to Zeb. At others I was with Caro, and newly espoused. I must have said something blushworthy, for the man who was in charge of tending the wounded grinned at me whenever he saw me after. Ferris told me later that the second day of the bombardment was a Sunday, which had boggled them somewhat at first, until Hugh Peter, chaplain to the train of General Fairfax, led them in prayer and preaching even as the artillery was set off. In the midst of this I lay drifting in and out of fever, perhaps coaxing the attendant with the honeyed words of courtship.

When I came to my right reason I first saw the roof far above me, its carvings and gilt. There was a stench of blood and other foulness in my nostrils, and on turning my head I saw a line of sick and wounded laid along the nave. Their screams and prayers echoed from the walls of the church, then slackened to an exhausted muttering. Camp followers, wives and women who passed for wives, wept over the flayed and shattered bodies they were come to nurse; men crazed with pain called on long-dead mothers who could once kiss a hurt away. Near me one panted as if from a hard fight, while on my other side a man wailed something I could not interpret, the words twisting into a howl as the pain opened up in him. From time to time a young lad, burnt and slashed into fever, gabbled hoarsely to 'Jim'.

A cracked bell chimed as the ground shook under us. That was the guns going off, and I thought at once of Ferris. Raising myself a little, I saw one of the attendants bent over a man nearby. At first with my dry mouth I could not raise my voice above a whisper, so I slapped on the ground with my hand. He came over at once, and I was just able to make myself heard.

'Friend, what day is this?' I croaked.

'A great one, for you,' he replied. 'I never thought to hear you speak again.'

'But how long is it since I came in?'

'Three days, four.' He went off and came back with a cup of some herb. As I wetted my burning throat, he added, 'Your mate'll be glad to see you come through.'

I stopped gulping. 'Has Ferris been here?'

'There's a gunner came here every night. Is that his name?'

'He'll come tonight, then.'

The man smiled. 'If not, you'll be fit to seek him in a day or two.'

I drank the rest of the medicine and lay down among the cries of agony, to wait.

Hours passed. Part of the time I slept, and on waking remembered at once my friend was coming. There were tender places all over me from lying too long on the hurdle, and I fidgeted, trying to ease them. When next I woke it was night and the church roof a cave of darkness. Nearer me, candles shone here and there on the backs of pews. The wounded men were quieter, perhaps sleeping, but there was something else, something strange in the air. At last it came to me that the guns were silent.

Something echoed down the church: a hurdle banging against a door. At the other end of the nave I saw a small fair-haired fellow brought in, his face dripping blood.

'Who's that?' I cried out to the bearers. They laid down their burden, looking to see who had called. One of them shouted over to me, 'How should I know? His mother wouldn't know him now.'

I stared at the mangled features. The other bearer examined the wounded man, shaking his head.

'No friend of yours, I trust,' called out the one who had first answered me. 'He's just died.'

I turned on my side and wept in a way I had never wept before, not for Caro, nor for my own brothers. I moaned like a woman; I cared not who heard me; I rocked back and forth.

'Rupert? Do you know me?'

I opened my eyes. There was a split on his cheek where something had gouged it, the skin stiffening and all the side of his face bruised black. I looked over to the hurdle where I had seen the dead man. He was still there. I looked back at Ferris, and pulled him down to kiss him.

'Mind my wound,' he said wincing. I kissed his hands instead, and clung to them, unable to speak. He was warm and solid.

'You're a fine sight.' He smiled on one side of his mouth to spare his injured cheek. 'I did not think to find you so well.'

'You were here before,' I said.

He nodded. 'I have brought you some pottage.'

It was hard to prop myself upright, and I had lost my spoon, or had it stolen while raving. Ferris gave me his. Without hunger, I began scraping up the food.

'A man has been put to death,' Ferris said. 'In front of the entire army.'

'A soldier?' I asked between mouthfuls. 'What for?'

'Plunder. Cromwell wanted an example.' He looked about him. 'There are some sights here, Rupert—! You are lucky.'

'Lucky in my friends,' I said. 'You'll stay with me a while?'

'Not now,' he said. 'They will want to talk soon to the artillery. Since we laid siege I have been here every minute I could. I will come back.'

I dropped the spoon and seized him by the hands. To my amazement, he prised off my fingers, breaking my grip.

'See how weak you are? Eat. Keep the spoon.' He patted my shoulder and walked off, hand to his torn cheek. I slowly finished up the pottage. Whenever I thought of him prising off my hands I felt like crying. It was the weakness. I was at his mercy; but then, he was a merciful man.

~

The fever once over I came on speedily. Ferris brought me extra food – beef now, butter, whatever I could take – and I found later that he had eaten almost nothing himself. After another two days I was sent back to the ranks, where I discovered that he had also managed to beg extra rations for me, on the grounds that I was a big man and had not eaten for some days, and a few ounces of cheese might save them a rare pikeman. I devoured everything I could get, and hoped there would not be hand-to-hand fighting before I had regained my strength.

In the event my luck still held, for there was none. It might be a week after we first arrived at the city gates that Ogle sued for terms. He was let to march out with a hundred men and given safe conduct, after which the rest of the garrison were disarmed and let go. The defences were blown up with the Governor's own gunpowder, and we left for Alresford. What became of the wretches who had lain with me in the church, I never knew.

~

Things were not as they had been. I was glad that men willingly did things for Ferris, that they delighted in his friendship, and I knew full well that it was this comradely way he had that had got me the extra rations – but I liked his company best when I had him to myself, and during my sickness some of his old cronies had taken up with him again.

We were on the march from Winchester to Basing. I would have dearly loved to pass the time in private talk with Ferris, but had as usual to endure the others. There was Nathan of course, now talking constantly of Winchester. There was also Russ. I judged Nathan to be no more than nineteen, seemingly of good family, and Russ, a man in his thirties, turned out to be the very soldier who had saved Ferris from drowning in blood at the siege of Bristol. He never tired of bragging about it, as if to say, What had I ever done for Ferris that was half as good? As for Nathan, he was the merest prating youth; I could not see why he had enlisted at all, for he had little stomach for fighting. Though he interrupted everyone else, he never tired of hearing Ferris talk. These two, Nathan and Russ, gave me sideways looks but went on speaking when they remarked that I was listening, where at one time they would have fallen silent. They were squeezing me out; well, if they declared war on me, they would find me more than willing. If Nathan went on one side of Ferris, I made sure to go on the other, for I would not let them separate him and myself, even in walking. Ferris meanwhile tried to make peace, and to bind us fast friends.

'Rupert was a manservant, in one of those big houses we passed,' he said. I shook my head at him.

But Nathan was not interested in me. 'Ferris, were you at Naseby-Fight?' he asked.

Ferris said nothing.

'What was it like?' Nathan persisted. I waited to hear my friend reprove him as he had reproved me but Ferris answered simply, 'What Cromwell said. They were stubble to our swords.' He sounded weary.

I hoped Nathan would now ask about the women, thus bringing Ferris's anger down upon his head. He went on, 'Is it true that Jesus fought on our side?'

'I didn't see him,' said Ferris.

We trudged through a sticky yellow clay.

Russ put in, 'It didn't seem such a sure thing at the time. It was the first real test the New Model had, and Rupert, the Prince I mean—' he glanced at me, 'he's a cunning bastard. But in the end it was our men, not theirs, kept together.'

'How was the terrain?' asked Nathan.

'Foul, uneven, a few terrible slippery runs, hopeless for cavalry. But we got onto a hill; that helped. And we outnumbered them.'

'Two to one. And had Jesus on our side,' said Ferris.

Russ laughed, while Nathan looked abashed. Blushing, he asked Ferris, 'Did you fight bravely?'

'I didn't run.'

'Four miles of corpses, arse-naked mostly,' Russ said. 'We had need of every stitch.'

I fingered the cap I had been given.

Nathan suddenly turned to me. 'How do you find the pikes, Rupert?'

'I missed Winchester.'

'O aye, Ferris said but I forgot. Next time you'll be right in the thick of it, eh?'

I did not reply.

'Don't you feel afraid?' he insisted.

'I make others afraid of me.' I saw that Ferris, his back to us, was talking to Russ. Grabbing hold of Nathan's arm, I pulled him up until he was on tiptoe and pushed my face into his. He flinched and a tiny squeak escaped him.

'I've got more company than I want these days. Understand?' I laid my hand on my knife, let him see it, then gave him the look which had sent the snapsack thief running.

'Now make your excuses.' I jerked my head in Ferris's direction. The boy turned on me a pair of sky blue eyes, their colour sweetened by tears. He must have felt the shame of those tears, for he straightened himself. I saw that Ferris had turned, and like Russ, was watching us.

'Martin said he would mend a strap for me,' mumbled Nathan. 'I'll see if he be finished.' He whirled about, bowed hastily to Ferris and Russ and nodded to me without looking at my face. Ferris met my eyes with a cold stare.

'I'll bear him company,' said Russ and bowing to Ferris, but not to myself, he went off more slowly.

'I saw that,' said Ferris to me. His voice was jagged with anger; I flinched from his face as Nathan had from mine. We walked onwards in silence.

Behind us I heard one say, 'Nat shogged off quick enough.'

There was brutal laughter, then another voice, jeering, 'You're the man for him, eh? Step up then, say the lad's your friend, you're come to do his fighting for him.'

They laughed again, but when a third man said, 'Walk with *that* and you'll find a knife in your back,' they fell to muttering.

I began to feel afraid.

'Do you know what Russ was saying to me just before the boy left?' demanded Ferris.

I shrugged.

'He spoke to me of a bad angel. And so did other men while you were lying sick.'

I kept on walking without looking at him.

Ferris cried out, 'I stinted myself to feed you! Why are we fighting this war? Is it not for freedom, a man's right to say what he wants?'

'I only—'

'And to whom he wants?'

'Stop it. Ferris! You're like – like—'

'Yes?'

I was shaking.

'I'm not your creature, Rupert. No matter who has been.'

'You know nothing about it.'

'But I begin to know you.' Ferris tapped my clenched fist. 'Want to hit me? Well, go on. You're much bigger than me.' He jerked his face up towards mine and shouted, 'See if you can break me of having friends!'

Someone behind called out, 'Well said, mate!' I whipped round and saw all the men glaring at me. Until that moment I had not known how much Ferris stood between me and them. I crimsoned, and dropped my hands.

We went side by side in silence. Now I was the one with tears squeezing from my eyelids. When a soldier walked by I turned my head away for shame.

In time my breathing slowed. I kept looking at Ferris, but he marched on with a stride I had never seen him use before. It seemed I had gained some of his facility of reading the body, for I knew this gait was a way of shutting me out.

'You must talk to anyone you like,' I said at last.

'That goes without your saying.'

'I will go and invite them back. Courteously.'

'Keep away from them,' he snapped.

'Will you still walk with me?'

'Would you walk with a bad angel?'

'I'm a man, seeking forgiveness.'

'Say rather you are trying to keep ahold of me.'

As soon as he said this something tore within me. What had she said? *Keep ahold of me till the betrothal.*

Then we fought, and she left.

~

We camped that night at Alresford, where Cromwell's old friend and comrade, Richard Norton, kept the manor. The talk was all of sieges. They said we might be over the walls of Basing-House the next day, and spirits were high. There was even the odd bawdy song, which one of the officers stopped to reprove. He was not a stern reprover. The young man pleading that he sang for the music only, he was given leave to hum the tune without the words.

I had no heart to sing. My sole thought was how to soften and win round my friend. He kept away from me, his face averted, and looked so unhappy I would almost rather he had hit me. Going to where he sat cross-legged tearing at a bit of cheat, I seated myself opposite him and put my beef, the best part of the ration, into his lap.

'Here,' I said, 'I know you have stinted yourself.'

'I don't want your food.' He took the meat, not unkindly, and laid it on the grass.

'What can I do to prove I'm sorry?' I turned my wrists towards him. 'Here, I'll cut them.'

Ferris stared at me.

I went on, 'Anything you say.'

He shook his head and sighed. 'This is just it, Rupert. This savage way of yours, it—' He pinched his lips together as if keeping something back.

'Take the food, then.'

He took it up, only to hold it out to me. 'Here. What I would have of *you* is liberty.'

'You have it.'

He went on, 'I am sick to my soul, cannot bear more troubles. Friends, companionship – these are my only comforts. Would you take them from me?'

'*I* am a friend.'

He sighed again.

I took back the beef. 'Why are you sick?' I asked. 'Wound inflamed?'

'That, and—' He bowed his head and his hair fell forward; his body slumped like an unstringed puppet. 'The assault, for one thing. Were we nearer London, I'd desert.'

'You fear injury, death?'

Ferris raised his head and looked curiously at me. 'Have you ever known pain, Rupert – not cut fingers, but pain that makes you scream out – and no help for it?'

I tried to remember.

'No,' he went on, 'I see you never have. But you lay with the wounded at Winchester.'

'They were calling for their mothers.'

'Agony dissolves manhood like wax in a flame. This,' tapping the torn cheek, 'is but a taste.'

We were silent a while, then he went on, 'Death can be kind. There are things I dread more—'

'Infirm? I'd always help you.' I took his hand.

'More that – O, you don't understand me.' He sounded weary of my company. Offended, I loosed my grip.

'None of my friends can help me, no, not Nathan,' Ferris looked hard at me, 'but brawling and jealousy are afflictions I cannot bear.'

'Jealous – that I'm not. And I'll brawl no more.'

'No, Man of Wrath?' There was sadness in his smile. *Man of Wrath*, *Bad Angel*: I was getting myself some ugly names. Though his anger seemed suddenly burnt out, yet something had changed between us two. Ferris must know that one good blow from me would lay him flat. If he would challenge me to strike him, rather than give up Russ and Nathan, then I must bear myself meekly towards them.

'We'll have our hands full tomorrow,' I said.

'Aye. With a place like that the artillery'll be kept busy,' Ferris agreed. His face grew less melancholy, more thoughtful. 'They have it all worked out. We shall be finely placed – ours on the one side, Colonel Dalbier's on the other, or so Russ tells me. I've been moved to one of the great guns.'

'Why?'

'They've got a bigger man for the cannon. He loads faster.'

'You were never made for a soldier, Ferris.'

'I hope God made no man for a sol—' he faltered.

'But you fear I was made for one?'

'Tell me, Rupert, tell me truly. How did you come to be on that road, dressed as you were? Why can't you go back?'

I considered. 'Now is not the time.'

'Will you tell me after the siege?' He spoke softly, tilting his head, trying to win me over.

I rocked my body back and forth, longing to tell, shuddering at the memory of what befell me when I opened my heart to Caro. A hateful thought struck me: he might have heard it all from Tommy.

'There should be no secrets between friends,' urged Ferris. He took my hand; I looked away from his eyes before he could beg it all out of me.

'We'll talk of it later,' I said, feeling his moist palm against mine, and the long well-shaped fingers which had wiped my mouth. 'Pray forgive me what I did today.' I let go of his hand and stretched myself out to sleep.

'I'll tell Nathan and Russ you are sorry,' said Ferris. He rose as if to go.

'Aye, do. Beg their pardon for me. You have the gift.' I crushed down the mistrust springing in my breast.

He gazed upon me without speaking.

'Pray go to them,' I urged.

Ferris smiled. 'That's the right good way. I'll talk to them tomorrow.'

He lay down next to me.

'You're staying here?'

'It may be the last time we see one another. Goodnight, my brother in Christ.'

He closed his eyes and seemed soon gone off into a doze. I watched him as he turned his head back and forth, pursing his mouth and brow. Plainly the cut cheek troubled. His hand came up to it repeatedly, and each time fell away: I remembered his wincing from my kiss in the church. Shortly after, I fell asleep.

EIGHT

Mistress Lilly

THE NEXT DAY we came to Basing, and I found that any talk of being in there at once was madness. Only to gaze on Basing-House was to feel the terrible power in the place, for it was as much citadel as house, with lookouts on every side. These were linked by a guard wall said to be eight feet thick and stuffed with rammed earth able to swallow anything we might throw at it. If no breach were made, then up that wall we must struggle, hindered by our weapons, their men comfortably picking us off from the ramparts.

All behind the wall was of a piece – a fearsome show of strength. To one side was the Old House, of a very fine red brick. It was flanked by two great towers and encircled by a mighty earthwork. Men said the earthwork was most likely built by William the Bastard or his friends, so long had oppression reigned here. In itself the Old House looked ready to outlast any siege whatsoever; but that house was but the half of the place named Basing, for some way off was raised the New House, built in the time of Bluff King Hal. This second was a palace in itself, and though it had suffered hurt from the cannon, it was still of a size to daunt the courage of a besieger. To me it looked like a great many dwellings pushed together and topped by domes. Russ, passing by on his way to the baggage train, told me it had near four hundred rooms, which made Sir John's Beaurepair, which I had once thought so grand, a hovel to it. Some said that these Old and New Houses were joined by a long covered passageway, which made them one, and though Russ told me that was nonsense, there was no such thing, yet I could not help picturing the defenders scuttling back and forth from one house to the other, like rats in a pipe.

So much for what lay inside the wall. Outside, where the common people had lived, not a cottage remained. All had been razed lest they shelter the enemy, for Paulet, intent on the defence of his own, did not scruple to scatter the stones of humbler hearths.

We were encamped in the park, some six thousand men with little occupation until the guns were in place. A Dutchman, Colonel Dalbier, not one of the New Model but engaged with Parliament's blessing in the same enterprise, was already installed and had lost no time, for his battery had done good service. There was a great turret shot down, and part of one wall of the New House. Word went round that when the wall collapsed, goods had spilled into the court below. That sight had warmed the besiegers to their work, for every soldier had heard of the fabulous treasures within.

'Will we really sack it?' I asked a man standing near me.

'What do you think they are come for?' he answered. *They* were a crowd of folk with carts and waggons, camped well back from the field. 'Crows, all of them. The house is as good as a carcass already.'

'Surely the army will take whatever's there?'

'What they can carry. That leaves plenty.'

It was clear now why Cromwell had been on edge to fetch his artillery here before the roads grew too bad. The place was so well defended that there was nothing to do until Ferris and his mates should have smashed us a passage through the walls. I said, thinking aloud, 'But the place is a town in itself.'

The man smiled. 'Show me the town Cromwell couldn't take. Besides, the God who was with us at Naseby is with us still.'

'If God intends to make it another Naseby-Fight,' I said, plucking one foot, then the other, out of the mud, 'He does not show his love in the weather.'

'Lord bless you,' cried the other, 'that's all to the good. Soft earth for the pioneers.'

He moved off. I remained, rain soaking through every thread on my back. Those inside Basing-House, or *Loyalty House* as the Papists were said to call it, enjoyed the unspeakable comfort of a roof – two roofs – over their heads, along with wine and feather beds. I already knew that some were actors and whatnot, hardly a man among them able for honest work. There were also war-like and unnatural women who had thrown staves at our soldiers from the windows, and swarms of priests, buzzing away at their Latin spells. But we would have a good swat at them and by constant stoning of their wasps' nest we might bring it down at last. At any rate, we would not come away before one side or the other was utterly undone. Looking on the place, I only prayed it would not be ours.

As soon as Cromwell arrived he was in council with Dalbier, and the two together spent some time in reconnaissance. Ferris went with the other gunners up to our breastwork, as they called the foremost defence, built so that a man might hide behind it. Pioneers had crept forward, digging their trenches always at such an angle as to offer no clean sweep to enemy firepower, so that this breastwork was now close to their defences. From time to time came the roar of Dalbier's guns, followed by white smoke drifting across the field.

~

Nothing could be done, the first few days, but dig latrines and plant the artillery. I made trenches for the former and laid planks across them, knowing that in two days the stench would sicken me, and indeed, every time I had occasion to go there, I wished that men could seal their noses as dogs flatten their ears. Worse still was being there in company. Soldiers complained of their watery arses, their costiveness, their piles, as if any cared to hear, and I was not spared the bestial merriment which for some must accompany each turd or fart. I had never felt my fellows so gross, and would have gone almost anywhere else to relieve Nature, had it not been that, save a sea of mud, there was nowhere to go. Every so often it was bruited that such-and-such a soldier was slipped from the planks head down into the shit-pit, and in these stories I perceived a depraved relish in anything filthy and disgusting that could befall a fellow creature.

While the sky was light I saw nothing of Ferris, unless it were a far-off glimpse of a man who might be him, and whenever shot landed near his position I clenched my fists and prayed. When at last he came back into the body of the camp I found Nathan glued to him. It was the same the first night and the second. Afraid of me the boy might be, but not so much as to keep off and let me have my friend to myself. I wondered if Ferris had borne my apology as he had promised.

Men passed the time as best they could: cleaning weapons they had not fired, writing letters which might never be read, stone-throwing and wrestling. The more godly squinted at their soldier's Bibles. Those men whose wives trailed along with us were better off at this time especially, for along with cooking and mending clothes, the women had much to do nursing the sick. In addition to the usual wounds, a raw cough was spreading rapidly among the troops. All about us was wet, grey and brown. At first we had thought to forage for hedgefruit or coneys in the fields round about, but once men began crossing them they soon became nothing but one great bog of mud. Whatever could be eaten, and much that could not, was gone by the second night.

By day I avoided Nathan and Russ, but since at night they were always with Ferris I was obliged to make one of the company if I would see him at all. A fire would be found or built and our wettest clothes spread next to it. There was no soothing the misery of never being dry: the hands that we rubbed on our chapped skins were split between the fingers. Some grew so weary of damp garments that they sat naked by the fireside, holding steaming shirts and breeches against the flames. During the worst nights a man might wake and find that while he slept, his front turned to the fire, his shirt-tail had frozen stiff at the back. I wondered how many of these men were homeless and masterless, how many had a desperate and bedraggled wife trudging behind with her babes. It was now the middle of October; had there still been a call for sickles and scythes, I guess many would have run.

The long hours of darkness dragged. Russ talked of past exploits, Nathan of the new Jerusalem, and I of nothing. Ferris struck me as weary, which was natural to one in his situation, but I saw that he was fretted by more than guns and gun platforms. He seemed ill at ease, and I sensed he was waiting for me to set things right with

Nathan. It might be the third night, one blessed time when it was late and the boy still not there, that I found Ferris sitting alone by the fire. I was just about to make him a present, half a loaf of good bread, when he spoilt all by cutting into my talk.

'I have done my utmost to make peace with Nat,' he said. 'I have begged forgiveness for your knife. But what good is it, when you do nothing but glare on him?'

'I do not glare,' I cried, and indeed I had no idea of doing so.

Ferris sighed and said that Nathan was young and green, he must be gently handled, and for all he imagined himself a warrior he was but a sprig.

'Then he should not be at war,' I replied.

'I say as much to him myself. He answers that young lads are fighting everywhere—'

'Starvelings, maybe. But he can read and write, has parents, has he not? Why does he stay?'

Ferris regarded me an instant, hesitated, then said, 'To the point. He is easily faced down – as well you know – and there is something besides. He has heard some tale about you.'

'From whom?'

Vexation narrowed my friend's eyes. 'Planning vengeance already? You don't listen to me, you must go about things a softer way. In your place I would—' he stopped, for Russ and Nathan were approaching us.

'I have no need of other friends,' I complained. 'I wish to talk with you alone.'

'And if I am shot tomorrow? These are not bad men. Sit with us, and bear yourself kindly.'

Unhappy, I sat with them. Doubtless I looked ferocious, and did myself no good with the boy. Nathan no longer pestered with his talk, but pained me a new way, by asking how many men had been killed on the artillery, and how close the shot was come to Ferris. This was a thing I had as lief not know, but I held my tongue.

'One of my mates had his face blown off,' said Ferris dully. He held up his arm and I flinched to see the reddish-brown slime stiffening on it.

'What did the surgeons do?' asked Nathan.

'What could they? The men wouldn't even take him, they said it was wasting a hurdle, and I guess they were in the right of it. That was before noon and he was still alive come sundown.' Ferris spoke through gritted teeth.

'But he's dead now?' asked Russ.

'Aye. He died as soon as it got dark.'

Russ and Ferris exchanged a steady look, which I thought I understood and saw that Nathan did not.

'They give us it hot and strong,' Ferris went on. 'Barrow-loads of stones as well as shot and shell.'

'The breastworks are very close,' said Russ, adding for my benefit, 'that makes things bloody,' which was just what I most dreaded to hear.

Ferris said, 'All we can do for now is lob granadoes.' I hated to think of him doing this, for the granadoes, pottery shells full of powder, sometimes went off while still in the soldier's hand. 'But Cromwell does well with the gun platforms. We'll soon get a practicable breach.'

'What's that?' I asked.

'When the walls start to collapse,' Russ explained. 'Then you get a slope the men can run up.'

'The cannon royal,' Ferris added, turning to me, 'fires around – sixty – pounds.' His last words were smeared over by yawns.

Russ told him, 'You should sleep, lad.' There was something like tenderness in his voice. To me he said, 'It's backbreaking work. You won't see any of your milords as gunners, they'll none of them touch it.'

'You won't get your face shot off now,' said Nathan to Ferris.

'That's not the way it goes, Nat.' Ferris smiled wearily. 'Just keep praying for me. What's the password? *Sleep*.'

He lay down on his side, found he had placed his injured cheek to the ground, and rearranged himself so that the wound did not touch anything. 'It drags,' he muttered, and drew up his knees for warmth.

Grunting, the rest of us also settled ourselves in our soggy clothes about what was left of the fire. Nathan took great care to get Ferris between himself and me, as if I might creep to him in the dark and cut his throat. He made such a business of it, I was tempted to shift places and stretch out with my head in his lap.

Russ and Nathan wished me a feigning 'goodnight', which I returned; Ferris murmured, 'Sleep well, Rupert,' as if he meant it.

'Sleep well, Ferris.'

Waking some time later, I heard his breathing rattle. There was wheezing on every side; we were losing more men to flux and to inflamed, bubbling chests than to gun or sword. I dozed briefly and was straightway with Zeb, squabbling over some job left undone in the kitchen. Coming out of that dream I lay a while thinking about those I had lost, until I at last drifted off. It was a poor night's rest, full of fears and starts. Towards dawn I grew as miserable in body as in soul, and not only from cold, being unable to sleep soundly for the want of a piss and unwilling to piss because I was half asleep.

~

Jolted by some noise, I opened my eyes and saw Ferris already up, his shoulders heaving from a hard cough. After a moment he hawked and there was a hiss as he spat into the embers. None of the other men moved. His face melancholy, Ferris contemplated the sleeping Nathan. I thought he might be about to look at me, so feigned sleep. When I opened my eyes again he had put on his helmet and was pulling some bread from his snapsack. I watched as he bit it, and heard him sigh; it was evidently too hard.

'I have some,' I whispered.

Ferris started and smiled. I rose and took from my sack the half-loaf I had saved for him; he did not pretend to refuse, but pressed my hand as he took it, saying, 'Many thanks.' Then he walked off in the direction of the battery, eating the bread as he went. I watched him circle the mud pools as he moved over the grey field.

The rest of us felt the dew on our hair and clothes, swore or prayed according to inclination, and readied ourselves for another day of waiting. I relieved myself at last by pissing into the mud next to the others, and was abused for it, and wondered was I indeed that same man who had washed down his body in scented water.

~

That was the day, all our weapons being in place, that Cromwell sent to John Paulet, the Marquess of Winchester and Master of Basing-House, to know would he surrender in common sense and decency, or put his own people and ours to the danger of a storm. For, he wrote plainly, as acknowledged Papists, the Marquess and his people could expect the utmost severity if they went on to the bitter end, and their only hope of mercy, according to the law of arms, lay in surrender. But whether through stubborn pride, or fear that we were less honourable than we pretended, the Marquess could not be brought to sue for terms. The time was now come to show them some play. The order was given and our great guns commenced firing.

My fears for Ferris rarely left me, and having little else to do I had taken to standing in the field, watching each ball and shell crash into the outer walls and cringing whenever the enemy landed something near our battery. After a while I was joined by one Price, a tall man and well made, but sickly-looking and with the cough which was spreading through the camp. He it was who told me most about Basing-House and its occupants.

'Romanists, all of them,' said he. 'The Marquess pushed out his one Protestant commander. That was Colonel Rawdon, and a fool's trick it was to get rid of him. Paulet threw away five hundred men at a stroke.'

'He must have great faith in his idols,' I remarked.

'In the walls, as well as the Pope. One way and another, the place has been under siege for years.'

'And always stuck it out?' I tried to picture how much food must lie within.

'Aye. We nearly got in with the London Trained Bands,' Price broke off to cough up some phlegm, 'but it ended in disgrace.'

'How? Our men were cowards?'

'I'd not say cowards. They were over the wall – the hardest part! – and they got into the barn.' He pointed at a massy building within. 'It was full of food and drink. Would you believe the whoresons stayed there, gorging, and the roof in flames over their heads?'

'Did they burn to death?'

'The defenders turned shot and cannon on them. The rest were beaten back.'

Remembering the cheese I had stolen while tramping the road, I could well understand how the chains of duty and common prudence had snapped all at once. Such plenty, spread before men both hungry and cold, would be irresistible.

'Have the people inside never gone short?' I asked.

'We nearly had them once – they were starved down to oat porridge. A couple of them tried to get out over the wall. Paulet hanged them, else more would have followed. Desperate, they were.' He sighed. 'And then the place was relieved. No, the only way is to batter down the houses.'

'And that's what Cromwell's sworn to do?'

'He and Dalbier before him.'

I asked why, if Dalbier were set on it, he had not done the thing before we came.

'It takes time,' said Price. 'The man's no fool with his mathematics.'

'That's not to say he is a soldier,' I returned.

Price looked strangely at me. 'Do you think war is all swordwork? He's an engineer, that's what artillery needs.'

I assured him that I gave full credit to the artillery.

Cromwell's great guns shot off, then Dalbier's, then Cromwell's again, sometimes the two together, while we waited and sank deeper into the filth of the field. Those of us who were not concerned with the bombardment kept back from the breastworks and passed our time as best we could.

I walked forward once that day in search of Ferris and saw him load his weapon, body tensed with effort. He straightened up with a hand to the small of his back and seemed so far from any thought of me that I lost courage and returned again to my place. All this time the sky blackened, emptied onto us like a well-bucket, and like a well-bucket refilled itself for another drenching.

Back from spying on Ferris, I went to stand beside Price, the two of us holding our pikes and watching cannonballs sink into the walls of Basing, when suddenly he began to sway.

'How is't with you?' I stretched out my hand to him, but he suddenly bent, groaning, and spewed a vile, stinking fluid. He dropped the pike but fortunately it fell between, and not on, two men standing in front of us.

Price straightened up. 'Beg pardon, comrades.' Reaching for the pike as one of them handed it him, he straight let it fall a second time, and himself on top of it.

The man who had given back the pike crouched over him. 'Soldier?'

Price did not stir. The man looked helplessly at me. I pulled our fallen comrade up onto his knees and found him wet with blood-streaked shit.

'You'd best take him to the surgeon's tent,' said the other. I raised Price to his feet but found myself taking his whole weight, for he was as if dead.

'He's big,' I said, but none offered to help me so I heaved him over my shoulder and brought my uncleanly burden through the ranks as best I could, laying him on the rutted grass outside the tent entrance. There were no hurdles. The surgeon's mate, a little, sweaty fellow I had not seen at Winchester, came up and asked what the injury might be; I explained it was rather a case of flux than shot. He told me that practically every man in the tent had some sickness of the kind.

'Had we tents for the healthy, we'd not need them for the sick,' I complained. The man looked at me, as if to say he wished for tents as much as I did, and could do as little to procure them.

'Don't bring any more,' he said, 'unless it's wounds.'

'What if it's vomiting and flux?'

'Lay them on their sides.'

'They'll get trodden on,' I protested.

'Then don't tread on them.' He laughed. I was at first enraged, but then saw that he was half crazy having neither space nor physic for so many sick and the assault proper still to come.

Price, at least, I had got out of the action. As I left I saw another man stagger in, spewing down the front of his buff-coat, and wondered if he would be ordered back to the ranks. I returned to my place, sinking in the field up to my knees and more than once groping on all-fours to wrench my boots out of the sucking mud. As I went I looked again at the battery for Ferris, but could see none like him. From where I stood it was hard to tell one man from another, and the great guns were all in a fume. I wiped my hands on my red jacket. It was caked in filth and I recalled my wedding coat, Peter fastening the mother-of-pearl buttons and calling me a prince. Suddenly hungry to look on the coat again, I rummaged for it in my snapsack. It was gone. Most likely it had been stolen at Winchester and the buttons cut off. So it was that I lost my last remembrance of a happier time, of which there was now not a thread left.

When I got back there was another standing in line with me, holding Price's abandoned pike. At first I did not know Philip through his mask of mud and smuts.

'I thought you were muskets?' I asked, taking up my own weapon. I did not want his company.

'Blew up. Last night.'

'But you're not hurt.'

'Hugh had it at the time. He's lost a hand.'

I marvelled at the ill chance of this world, that saved Philip and maimed Hugh. To the lucky man I said, 'But you can't just come to us!'

This he ignored. There was a bursting sound as the cannon went off again, and Philip shouted, 'Like Winchester.'

'How so?'

'Made a hole wide enough for thirty to enter abreast. In a day, that was.'

'Then I'd say this is different.'

'We'll get in, never fear.' He smiled at me. 'They'll hang, draw and quarter the priests.'

I did not care to answer. Rain came down heavily; Philip turned up his cheeks to the sky and let the downpour rinse away the mud. He had a sweet young face full of kindness, God help any prisoner or defenceless woman who trusted in it. Ferris, in contrast, must look a devil by now, his wound red and smarting from the smoke. I remembered the story about his drowning in blood at Bristol.

'There's your mate,' said Philip, pointing.

My heart leapt: I strained to follow his finger, but saw only Nathan.

'Well, well!' Philip raised an eyebrow. 'He's coming your way.'

In that moment I felt I could humble myself as Ferris had asked, and waved to the boy, but he failed to notice me. Nathan was unhelmeted, his delicate features tensed as if he were distracted by some fear. His wet hair showed almost black against his neck and forehead.

'Pretty little piece, isn't he?' asked Philip. 'You know what they say about him?'

At last the lad saw me. His eyes narrowed, then he turned his head to one side and moved away from us.

'Mind this,' I ordered Philip, and put my pike into his free hand.

He gave an oily wink.

'Nathan! Nathan!' I shouldered my way through the ranks towards his red coat, which was a recent issue and still bright enough to stand out. When I finally laid hand on his shoulder he twisted away, his face pouting and pulling like that of a young child.

'Be easy, man, I want only—'

'He's on the guns, Rupert.'

'I know. He's not the one I want.'

'I haven't seen him,' he went on without listening, 'since you sat with us last night.'

'Hear me, Nathan! I am come to talk to *you*, to say I am sorry for – for the hasty words I spoke. Be so good as to forgive them.'

Cough as I might, my voice would not act the lie for me, but clanged hard and flat. I could abase myself when alone with Ferris, yet in the company of the boy himself, his twisting and whining stirred me up again. Softening my tone as much as I could, I added, 'Ferris said he would bear you my apology.'

'Aye,' he muttered. 'Many thanks, I must be gone—'

'Nathan!' I placed a hand on my heart. 'Did not Ferris tell you?'

'I swear, I've not seen him.' Nathan pulled away from me. 'Let me go now, don't hurt me.'

'I am suing for pardon, why should I hurt you?'

The words which I had meant for gentle came spiked with exasperation at his stupidity. I took him by the shoulders to compel attention.

'Please, Jacob! Let me go!'

'By Christ, Nathan—' I stopped.

A wail escaped him. Too late, he clapped both hands to his mouth.

Rage beat up from my belly. Gritting my teeth to hold it in, I put the question as if to a child: 'Who said my name was Jacob?'

The goose had not the wit to run but stood shaking, hands dropped now and limp as gloves.

'It was Fat Tommy.' I shook him. 'Wasn't it?'

A couple of men near us stepped closer; I turned to them. 'Private quarrel, friends; you see I do no more than put a question.'

'He's a murderer! He's going to kill me!' shrieked the little fool.

I loosed his shoulders, spreading my hands to show myself unarmed, and laughed to the onlookers. 'He's a boy, gentlemen, though you might not think it seeing him thus afflicted with the mother.' I appealed to them whether they had seen me do the lad any harm, whether he showed a bloody lip or a bruise anywhere. They looked at Ferris's sprig, at his trembling mouth and his tears just starting, and laughed along with me.

'Pray witness our talk, gentlemen. Now, Nathan,' I took hold of him once more, as the cat takes back the mouse, 'look at me.' I knew he would not be able to do so; he tried, but winced away.

'Look at me,' and I tightened my grip on his arms until it was sure to give pain. When he raised his face to mine I slackened the hold – not too much – and softly went on, 'It was Fat Tommy. You see I know already.'

Nathan sniffed back phlegm and tears. 'What will you do to him?'

'Nothing. What else did he tell you?'

He again looked away, down to the ground, black lashes standing out against the bluish skin beneath his eyes. I ached to strangle him.

'Has he frighted you with some tale about me?'

Nathan shook his head. When next he forced himself to meet my gaze I saw the ghost of Chris Walshe, pleading and terrified. There was no doubt in my mind that he knew, and it must follow that Ferris knew also.

I let go of his arms. 'Tommy is a wicked liar,' I said for the benefit of the men still listening. 'In proof of which, go your way in peace.'

He ran off, and I stayed a minute gaining command of myself. I could hear Tommy's gloating voice lingering on Walshe's wounds and on the last agony of Mervyn Roche, Nathan adding his squeaks the while: *He pulled a knife on me! He'll have us all poisoned!* until between them they had killed every last kindness in Ferris. I had much to repay these two. I would wait my chance during the assault, when my friend would be none the wiser.

The rain had slackened. I tramped and elbowed my way back to Philip who, being unequal to the two pikes, had stuck them upright into the mud.

He grinned at me. 'No breach as yet.'

I grinned back. 'What were you telling me about that lad? The pretty little piece.'

'It's not what I say, it's what they all say. He's more girl than boy.'

'Are you saying that I *use* him as a girl?' I kept smiling, and at the same time pushed him over backwards.

'No!' he shouted from the ground. 'Not you.' He scrambled up quickly, and I let him; I could easily knock him back again.

'Who then?' I demanded.

His face grew sly. 'Don't know as any names were mentioned.'

'Who says this?'

'Can't remember who told me. Rumour's a wicked thing.'

'Your days as a pikeman are over,' I said. 'Go and be something else, or you won't get through the siege.' A couple of good kicks and he was face down in the ooze. He rose spitting, the ground sucking at him as he staggered away from me.

'Ask your dear friend Mistress Lilly.' It was sprayed from scarlet lips in a beard of mud. I lunged at him and he dodged between two men and ran.

~

They hanged men who were caught together. When I was eight I hid behind my father as they roped up a fellow, grinning and misshapen, perhaps an idiot; the word *sodomite* came to me from the crowd but no other man was with him. He waited, raised above the people, his hands bound behind his back, while the executioners readied the other prisoner: a witch, bonnetless and with bloody patches on her scalp. One held her upright on the stool while the other fitted the noose. Her head fell forward onto her chest, giving him some difficulty, but he at last fumbled the rope into place. I saw the man in front of me scratch his arse and move forward, blocking my view. Then the people about us gasped, and laughed. My father swung round and lifted me. I saw the two of them thrash against the air. The woman's eyes were crossed and her tongue lolled from her mouth; this it was that made the people laugh. My father lowered me and led me away. I looked back before we turned the corner and saw them dangling black against the sky like the crows our gardener nailed to the trees at home.

'What's a sodomite?' I asked.

'One who mocks God and Nature.' His lips closed tight.

'What will become of them?' I meant the corpses.

'You know your Scripture,' Father answered me. 'They shall be cast into the pit.'

I did know. It meant burning, the worst pain there was. In Hell, though dead, you were as if alive, and you felt everything.

The rain came on again. The heat of my rage once abated, a leaden cold weighed on me. If I died of the flux, then farewell to Caro, Zeb, Izzy, Ferris. I ought to be more afraid of God, I knew it even then, but all my fears ran on what I had heard. That meant damnation: the soul insensible of grace and sin alike, following blindly its own rutted track to Hell. Instead of considering my eternal salvation, I picked at my filthy fear as a hungry man picks a fowl's carcass. Ferris and Nathan, it was true, was false. I would have given ten years of my life for Isaiah's advice. One thing I did at last recall: he had said that a man's character should be weighed along with his counsel. Philip had no character to speak of. Thus I resolved to consider it, but too late: the poison blade once entered, the venom was eating deep within. I stood in icy rain and up to my knees in mud, my garments chafing whenever I moved an inch, and neither felt nor saw anything of the field before me.

What I did see were pictures, each held before my eyes an instant and then replaced by another: the brightness in Nathan's face as he laid his arm about Ferris's shoulders, my friend's smile as he told Nathan to keep praying for him. Again I saw them push at one another, like boys that roll on the grass, fighting in play; again I heard that laughter which had shut me out.

And then came the last pictures, the terrible ones. I felt these coming and tried to hold out against them, against the pawing and the licking and the – the rest of it. Ferris and Nathan were all over me, they were in my mouth, they closed over my head as the pond had closed over Walshe.

For perhaps an hour I stood scarce knowing where I was or what I did. The Voice visited me once without warning, and jeered, *They play their game beneath your nose.*

There is not opportunity, I answered silently, and in saying it at once saw where the opportunities lay. The Voice was already gone, leaving me in a pitiful state, and not only for what it had revealed.

There was in this – *intelligence* – something that was not like my father. Though he had warned me when I was a boy of the weakness and corruption of the flesh, yet his talk was mainly of clean living, of the sweet perfume of chastity, pleasing to God in a man as in a maid. Never had I heard him, even in impressing upon me the force of temptation, dwell lasciviously upon the sins of any person, no, not a sinner in the Bible, much less upon the shame of one known to me. He was a man of chaste and godly conversation, too wise to sully or heat a young man by a minute recitation of vice.

I bethought me of other things the Voice had said of late, and grew still more anguished when I recalled its promptings in the wood. Had it not fired me, at a moment when my blood was already up, with a furious thirst for mastery? It was not righteousness, and as I forced myself on the woman I loved, tearing her, the Voice had uttered no word of reproach.

Show him what becomes of a boy—

At this last memory I grew cold as the lad himself, though the sweat burst out all over for sheer terror. The thing was horribly of a piece. I knew now whose Voice spoke in my head and heart; who it was that hunted me for one of His.

~

The sky grew dusk and still the bombardment went on. Ferris might be shot or half dead of the flux for all I knew. Standing fire meant exposure to flying shards which cut into men more cruelly than any sword: it was one of these jagged pieces which had laid open his cheek at Winchester. From time to time gunners were brought past on hurdles, and then I was filled with agony lest I should spy him among those, pulped or gutted, for whom death could not come fast enough.

I walked in a daze to one of the fires where two men were saying the walls would heal themselves in the night, Basing being protected by charms and the power of Satan. A third rebuked them, saying such superstitious trash was not fit to be uttered save by the priests within. 'We will have them, my lads,' said he, 'never fear.'

The ration was handed out – bread, butter and beef – and, having eaten it alone, I pulled my coat round me and lay down where someone had spread straw over the mud. Though my muscles lacked strength, being constantly stiff and chilled, I was now grown half used to wet clothes and to sleeping in boots. These last were more use than latchets, which in the boggy ground could be sucked clean off your feet.

There was a bang, then screams; looking round I saw a man hold up the bleeding stumps of his fingers in the firelight, while a second nearby had his hands clasped to his face. Another gun blown apart. Comrades gathered round the one whose face was covered, trying to prise his hands away and gritting their teeth in distress, while the man with no fingers seemed more surprised than pained. I guessed he would not feel it awhile, and then would come the torment. Philip, having passed Hugh the weapon which took off his hand, had left him. I hoped Hugh's other friends might prove more loving.

The man who had spoken of superstitious trash sat down next to me, his ration on his lap. I watched him chew doggedly on the beef and cheat, licking his fingers so as not to lose so much as a skin of grease. He was a greybeard and had the look of one that had served before. I marvelled that a man who had survived one war would wish to fight another.

The old soldier smiled to see me bedded on the straw. 'Not long now, friend, before you can lie between sheets.'

'I have forgotten what they feel like,' I answered. 'Tell me, will the artillery go on much longer?'

'They'll be leaving off soon.'

At that I pulled myself into a sitting position. 'Some say we'll be in there tomorrow.'

'Perhaps. I wager we'll see splits in the wall at least. And once the thing's well opened up – no quarter!' He punched the palm of his hand and frowned. 'Mind you, I could wish us not so weakened with the flux.'

'All this lying out in the rain.'

He nodded. 'The Scots do better. They have tents for their men.'

'Truly?' I had not thought that savage folk would take such care.

'Truly. This damnable weather is enough to turn a man Cavalier,' he went on.

'How, turn Cavalier?'

'For a leaguer-lady to bed down with. Devil take the lust, what I crave is the *warmth*!' He laughed. The last thing I wanted to recall was my lying down with a woman, but I laughed too.

The guns quietened. Lights showed in the windows of Basing-House and I wondered what the Papists saw when they looked upon us, crawling wet and muddy over the earth. A young lad came and put some logs on the fire. I was mighty grateful, for my hands were dead meat. Rising, I fanned up a blaze with my coat, and in doing so saw Ferris cross on the other side of the flames.

'Ferris, man, stay!'

He stopped and turned. I ran up to him at once but faltered when I saw his look.

'What ails you, Ferris? Is your face worse?'

'I told you to treat Nat kindly,' he said.

'I begged his pardon!'

'Indeed. His arms are all bruises.'

Cursing my own folly, I stammered, 'I meant only to keep hold of him. Don't believe all you hear – I don't credit what they say of you—' and then shuddered, having started what I could not finish; I was unable even to name the thing.

Ferris looked scorn at me. 'Did you never understand, from what I told you of me and Joanna, that I care nothing for what fools say? Knowing a man for a fool, why should I trouble myself with his maggots?'

I breathed again; he might not listen to Tommy. But there was also Nathan. If he was to Nathan what Philip had said, his hard words on fools might be meant for me.

'*You* should worry, if any should,' he went on, 'with your skill in making enemies.'

'Have I made you my enemy, Ferris?'

'You are going the right way about it, tormenting Nat.'

'But I begged his pardon,' I said again.

'Don't deny—!' he shouted, then grimaced. I guessed that the angry twisting of his countenance had dragged at the wound. He screwed up his eyelids at the pain and jerked his head away until he could bring himself under command, then turned his face up to me and said quietly, 'If you will frighten off my friends, I needs must go with them.' His hand shot out to check me as I reached toward him, and he moved away, his walk stiff in the cold. I stood torn and miserable as he stepped into a group of men and was lost to view. That night I lay down alone, and as I sought the thin comfort of sleep, I remembered that Price was still not come back.

NINE

God's Work

THERE WAS NEWS through all the camp: two of our officers were captured. The light being poor and a thick mist lying on the land, a party of enemy horse were crept out unseen and had intercepted Colonel Hammond and Major King. These two were on their way to speak with Cromwell, but found themselves instead taken inside Basing as prisoners. Some of our men grudgingly confessed the raid to be a bold move, worthy of Protestants. Cromwell lost no time, but straight made proposals to exchange them, and these being refused, warned the Marquess that should the officers be harmed, Paulet himself should not find quarter in the hour of the assault.

That hour was now come very close. The 'practicable breach' of which Ferris had spoken was made at last and I daresay filled me with as much terror as it did those within.

The first sign was a deep crack snaking down the defensive wall. Few of us saw it at once, but then a wild yell rose from the men at the guns, spreading through all the ranks, and I wondered if *he* made part of that savage cry along with his mates.

But this was as nothing: the wall itself, cunningly cut away from the base, now took blow after blow, and began to split upwards between the stones. Our cannonballs continued striking low until the thing started to collapse onto itself. Ferris, I thought, would undoubtedly get us into the house. I pictured him frowning, ramming down the powder, and I prayed that no matter what he inflicted, all their shot and shell should fall wide of him.

'This is it, soldier,' said a man standing next me in the field. 'They'll never scrape that lot together. I reckon we'll go on smashing away until we can all get in at a rush, and then it's in the hands of Jesus!'

My mouth was dry. 'Will that be today?'

Tomorrow first thing, more like. Have you seen action before?'

'This is my first.'

He laughed at me, flashing yellow donkey-teeth. 'You picked a cursed time to start, soldier. Nothing so bad as the end of a siege.'

If we came through alive then that mask, Rupert, must be lovingly talked with again, and so made flesh and blood. Ferris must be got away from Nathan. The boy was unnatural; Ferris's care of him only spurred evil tongues. Besides, Nathan had Russ, and Tommy. My need of my one friend was greater than his. And then I thought that, were I indeed one of the damned, friends were not my rightful portion, and God would surely kill or maim Ferris to spite me, and I felt a worse fear than if I myself were to be maimed: to think of him hurt was to hurt in my own flesh. Were he in need, I thought, I would do for him what he had done for the gunner with no face, though they should hang me for it, and he never know his deliverer.

There came a hammer blow upon the ear: a ball had struck the house from the artillery stationed on the other side. Our lads played their part also, and fired off a shell that hurt the Old House front. Those within gave back fiercely, and shot began to rake the gunners. There were screams, which made me feel sick; smoke blew back onto us, stinging my eyes as I strained to see who was hit. The guns fired off again and again, like a bully that rains blows on a beaten man, and methought they were faster than the day before.

'There!' exclaimed the man. 'That's it.'

'What?' I cried, for I could see nothing like a breach. 'Are we through?'

'Not yet. But when they keep it up, like that – they reckon on it not lasting long.'

Men were running back and forth, craning to see. A babble spread like a wave through the lines, from front to back: 'Going!' The great wall was sinking down into itself, and as we watched, a well-placed ball carried away part of the top. A scream of triumph went up from the ranks. Once, being very little, I heard a drunken crowd run past my father's house to seize a witch who had blighted an orchard, and they had bayed like hounds. I remembered Ferris's *worse than dead.* We saw another cannonball widen the gap; stones and earth trickled down, and again there came that terrible scream.

The next cut a gash further along the defences; our men now turned the bombardment on that, and widened it. Stones flew through the air; clouds of dust arose and mingled with the smoke. All around me soldiers were cheering on the gunners. *Brave lad*, I said in my heart to Ferris, as if this could keep him alive. To my companion I bawled, 'They do well.'

'Aye,' he called back. 'Tomorrow look to be blooded.'

We watched, deafened by crashes and shouts, my new friend hunting lice beneath his shirt as the guns beat a path for us. At last it was too dark to continue, and the mass of soldiery began pressing back towards the camp. I could not help praying, though I knew my prayers to be worthless, that somewhere unseen by me Ferris was laying down the rammer and sponge, smokestained and weary, but unhurt.

~

That last night, before retiring to his headquarters in Basingstoke, Cromwell went round pressing the men's hands, putting them in heart for the morrow. I wanted to make one of those whom he spoke to or touched, for he filled me with admiration. Not a few of the men would likewise have walked through fire for Oliver Cromwell; like Fairfax, he could win folk's belief to a degree that I scarcely ever saw in a man elsewhere, unless the man were Zebedee, and Zeb's conquests were different entirely. But Cromwell was no lady-killer; his ways were manly and direct, and the love he inspired born of merit: he was a fine tactician, and one that would undertake much for his soldiers. He was known to write frequently to London, asking that his men might have this or that. Yet he would hang any caught pillaging against orders; there was iron within the man as well as without.

I pushed to the front for the privilege of being noticed by him. When at last he caught my eye, and took my hand with the square grip of a practical soldier, saying, 'You're a fine big fellow for the pikes,' my heart beat fast as if I were a boy.

'May I do good service,' I said, blushing at the fervour in my own voice. And what was he, this hero, this Christian Mars who had so reduced me? Why, the merest sloven, if one looked but on the outside, a man with thin, straggling hair, one whose inflamed nose glowed in many a soldier's joke. Nature had made our Nolly very plain, and he did not trouble barber or tailor to hide it, but this diminished him never a jot; rather, his valour and virtue made comeliness a paltry thing. I shuffled and hemmed like one in the presence of royalty. Then he turned to speak with an officer, and passed for a moment out of my view.

We had been instructed to wait, for he had particular instructions for all the troops. I looked about for Hugh Peter, Cromwell's own chaplain and a very holy minister, come all the way from Salem to help in our enterprise. He was another man I judged to carry the seeds of greatness in him, fertile in ideas, brimful of confidence in the power of God to direct our human works aright, so that I loved to hear his talk. In Salem, he had told the soldiers, there was neither wanton ease nor beggary, but for every man both work and food. This account greatly pleased me, but cost me also some pain, for to Salem had I once thought of taking Caro.

'Where is Hugh Peter?' I asked the man in front of me.

'Gone to tell Parliament that Winchester is fallen,' came the reply.

'Silence! Silence!' the officers were shouting. There was an immediate hush. Cromwell, mounted upon a platform that all might see him, was about to speak.

'Tomorrow,' he began, 'we fall on a nest of vipers.' He looked round him at the men. 'While you sleep, I will watch and wake, and think on the meaning of Psalm One Hundred and Fifteen, on heathen and idolaters. Know you that this man, John Paulet, has scratched *Aimez Loyaute* on every window of his Papish fortress, that is, *Love Loyalty*; but his loyalty is to crazed and brittle idols. Be the house never so well defended, yet with God's help shall it be but scattered stones: think you on Jericho and Babel, and the cities of the plain, or if you still doubt it, look you to that Psalm I spoke of, One Hundred and Fifteen,' here he glanced round at the men, some of whom nodded fervently, 'before you lay you down to sleep. Every man to be up and ready before dawn. At six will be the signal for your falling on, four shots of the cannon.'

He raised his hand in farewell and dismounted from the platform. Sober, as men who were now about serious business, the soldiers began to wander away.

That *four shots of the cannon* sounded in my ears like a death knell. I could not stay alone, but went on the prowl and discovered Ferris cooking some pease. Despite our falling out, happiness sprang in me to see him alive and unhurt. Going timidly up to my friend, and bowing, I asked if I might look in his Bible. That he had one I knew, for I had seen him read it sometimes while in camp.

'So Hugh Peter directs your devotions now, along with Cromwell's,' he said. I had never seen his face so weary. He groped in his snapsack for the Holy Book and handed it me before turning back to his cookery.

'He's a godly man,' I said, glad to be talking.

'Nay, say a god and have done.' He curled his lip. Steam rose and he shielded his cut face from it.

'May I not choose my own reading? Who's the tyrant now?' I asked. 'What has Hugh Peter ever done to you?'

'To me, nothing. He exults too much over the fallen.'

'But this is God's work. You said so yourself. If God's foes fall, we should exult.'

'Ah yes,' Ferris sang out. 'God's foes!'

I was baffled. Had he not spoken of the work which was to be finished?

Ferris looked hard at me. 'Well, at any rate I don't force my doctrines with fists. I leave that to Hugh Peter and those like him.'

'Not force doctrines! You are in the army!'

'I know it,' he snapped.

'Don't you put your hand to God's work any more?'

'O yes. I can put your hand to it, too,' and he took my hand and laid it on his cheek. The skin was hot, and crusted with dry pus and blood. 'Lovely, eh? Tomorrow I'll do God's work on someone else.' As he let go of my hand I saw that the locks of hair next his cheek were singed. 'God's work,' Ferris said, 'is living in peace, manuring the land, working by persuasion.'

'But some must be persuaded by force,' I said.

'Persuaded. Do you think I love the man any better who did this to me? That's not it. And Basing-House won't be it, either.' He smiled coldly. 'Don't you know it is to be a Golgotha?'

'You don't know it yourself.'

'I can see it. There's you reading your war songs, that one over there – he's ready to break up any idol, provided it's of gold—' He pointed out a lad shouting and gesticulating, surrounded by excited listeners. 'Just as well I fed you up, got your strength back. You'll do great execution tomorrow.' He turned to the cooking pot as if it sickened him to behold me, and this I could not bear. I put my hand on his arm. He knocked it off.

'What! To me!' I shouted. I pushed him in the chest. The pottage went flying into the fire and Ferris lay on the ground.

'Leave be, whoreson!' There was a crack, and a flash. Someone had hit me over the head from behind. Pain dazzled me. My mouth had bloody needles in it: I had bitten the inside of my cheek. Someone was twisting my fingers fit to break them; as I tried to pull my hand free something was torn from it. I looked down and saw my knife on the ground, and it came to me that I had drawn it on Ferris. Despite the twisted fingers I could still feel the slap of my palm on his coat. I lowered my arms. Men rushed up to help him, but he waved them away, coughing as if winded. I covered my eyes for shame. I heard Ferris get up and come towards me, as if to embrace me in forgiveness, but he stepped to one side and spoke into my ear.

'That's been coming a long time,' he panted into the silence that was grown round us. 'But to play those games, you must get a bigger friend.'

'I can't help it!' I cried aloud.

'The worst thing you've said yet.'

I heard him spit.

Pain battered at my skull; the murmur of men's voices swelled up again. I uncovered my eyes and looked about me, the other men avoiding my gaze. Ferris was gone. At last I saw him sitting some way off, with Nathan and Fat Tommy. The pease in the fire began to smoke and stink.

'Here,' said a voice. The man behind me was holding out my knife. 'Save it for the priests, eh?'

I bowed as I took it from him.

There was nothing to colour my loneliness and shame except Ferris's Bible. I lay down, feeling thus less exposed to men's stares, and turned to Psalm One Hundred and Fifteen. The firelight danced on the holy words:

> *Wherefore should the heathen say, Where is now their God?*
>
> *But our God is in the Heavens: he hath done whatsoever he hath pleased.*
>
> *Their idols are silver and gold, the work of men's hands.*
>
> *They have mouths, but they speak not: eyes have they, but they see not:*
>
> *They have ears, but they hear not: noses have they, but they smell not:*
>
> *They have hands, but they handle not: feet have they, but they walk not: neither speak they through their throat.*
>
> *They that make them are like unto them; so is every one that trusteth in them.*

They that make them are like unto them. But Papists and other idolaters can hear and see and smell, though their idols cannot. I laid the book down to come, if I could, at the inner meaning. Then I remembered we were about to assault the house. I read on: *The dead praise not the LORD, neither any that go down into silence.*

Go down into silence. We were to leave them like unto their idols, utterly unable to see, hear, smell, touch, walk. Ferris was proven a true prophet: Basing should be made a place of desolation, a Golgotha.

I knew what it was to send down a soul into silence. There was rage, and a violent flurry of the body, and water swirling over a boy's head.

~

Though I remarked prayer and Bible-reading all around me, I saw also that men were plucking up tenderness by the root. There was a new ugliness in them; as they passed between me and the fire their faces were hard. I wondered, with some dread, what I would see on the morrow. Ferris looked sad because he already knew it; his knowledge made him thin and weary. Philip was most likely looking forward to the assault. It was rumoured there were many noblewomen in Basing-House: a feast for him, and Hugh now unable to restrain him. My own friend had seemingly cast me off.

The urge to return the Bible grew. I knew it was only so that I could speak to Ferris again, beg his pardon, and I made myself lie where I was. No one else came to keep company with the bad angel, and I could read no more after that psalm. I put the book inside my shirt and closed my eyes, seeking the way back to a time when all was full of fair promise. That day in the maze with Caro. Her tongue in my mouth, and the hissing of the bees. Caro and Patience hanging out linen the summer before; the three of us brothers side by side, teasing one another as we worked.

I turned over to ease my hips, and heard one nearby say it was ten o'clock. It would be some time before all of our company were settled for the night. I was not ready for sleep myself, wanting only to keep quiet and out of the way. Thoughts of Caro and my brothers could no longer hold me; I turned over again, and opened my eyes.

Nathan was there, his curls dropping forward almost into the flames. I watched him from under half-closed lids. He must have taken me for asleep, for he paid me no mind and swirled round the contents of his cooking pot. Pease again. I remembered Ferris's pottage knocked in the fire, and supposed Nathan come back to make a second lot.

I studied the 'pretty piece'. His hair was springing up as it dried; he had a creamy neck like a girl's, and with a girl's care he bent over his preparations, unmindful of me. His sleeves, pushed back, revealed a scholar's hands and smooth, slender arms. Not much to him in a fight: that thought warmed me. I wondered would Ferris come and help with the food, or if I would pass the night without any sight of him. He was as harsh with me as one whose love was lost for good. A draught blew on my back and all the side of me turned away from the fire. Tomorrow my body might lie out to freeze on the field, none to bury it. Well, it would be an end.

My attention caught by some flutter, I saw Nathan peering at me. His head turned away at once and his shoulders stiffened. I sat up, hope stirring.

'Nathan?'

He scuttled sidewise, getting the fire entirely between us.

'Nathan, pray hear me. I was sincere when I begged pardon. I fear you mistook.'

He nodded, and kept stirring the pot. 'And your pardon, Rupert, if *I* offended.'

'The fault was mine, I am hasty and choleric. I hope you can forgive me for it?'

'Aye, Rupert.' A flat dissembling voice: he was still afraid of me, though his lips curved upwards towards cold blue eyes. A real viper's mouth. I felt in my cheek the smart of the bitten place. *Let me once get you alone*, I swore to him in my heart, *you'll know what it is to be bitten.* It was like promising myself the best wine, and on the strength of it I smiled on him almost tenderly. 'Be so good, Nathan, as to tell our friend Ferris we are reconciled.'

'Aye, Rupert.'

'We should not wrangle when we may find our judgement day tomorrow.'

'I will tell Ferris.' He backed away from me. My spirits rose, for he had left the pot in the fire. I lay down again, feigned sleep and waited for it to be rescued. Gently, humbly did I rehearse words of loving-kindness against my friend's coming.

He came without speaking, to the far side of the fire. Like Nathan, he bent over the food, and the light showed up his disfigured face, now much thinner than when we first met on the road. I sat up and waited for him to notice me. He met my look at once, without a bow or even a nod.

'Yes, he's told me,' he said. 'And I'm come over, not to see you, but because he's mortally afraid to fetch a pot of pease while you are there.'

'The Bible,' I said, holding it out to him as he wrapped the iron pot in a cloth.

He made to take it, then backed away. 'I'll come for it later.'

Perhaps he wished to sit down with me. But no, it was only because he needed both hands to manage the pottage. He went off with the smoking mess to a group of men some distance away; I knew without looking that Nathan was among them. Sitting on the ground, my knees drawn up and head on my arms, I was wretched as a child none will play with, having said nothing to Ferris of all the fine words I had framed in advance. I snatched up the Bible and put it back inside my shirt, then lay down again. Fat Tommy would still be with him: I shuddered at all the tales *he* could invent about one Cullen who was run away from his master. No truth so ugly it can't be made worse. Now the men were calling me bad, and Nathan was afraid to come back to the fire. A shivering, fierce as an ague, took possession of me when I thought of Ferris giving ear to Tommy.

When I looked up my eyes went straight to that knot of men and I caught my friend staring at me. He at once looked away.

After this I was afraid either to see Ferris or to miss him. As often before, I escaped misery in sleep. I was asleep while the rest were still eating and talking, and for a marvel, I did not dream, though I was constantly waking through the night.

Once, looking about me in the early hours, I saw the guard wall ripple as men dropped from it in the moonlight. I should have raised the alarm, but something told me these were no skirmishers but poor wretches hoping to escape the Armageddon John Paulet had brought upon himself and all that were his. They were servants, as I had been, and I let them go.

Before dawn I awoke again, unable to lie longer. I felt in my shirt: the Bible was there, warm in the darkness. The moon was behind cloud. I crawled to the fire and took out a brand, then, blowing on it for light, picked my way across the grass. I saw Tommy, and heard his snores; for a moment I thought of putting the brand in his spiteful mouth, but this was not the time.

At last I came to the one I sought. Ferris slept on his back, breath quick and shallow. His soldier's coat, despite the cold, was open. Nathan, lying beside him, had rolled so that his head rested on my friend's chest and Ferris's arm curled over the boy's shoulder.

I took the Bible and laid it on Ferris's shirt front, brushing away a few strands of Nathan's hair. When I again raised my eyes to his face, Ferris was looking directly at me. We stared each at the other, his gaze black in the firelight and so level, it might well be unseeing. Perhaps, I thought, he was rapt: one of those who dream eyes open. Then Nathan shifted, pressing his face into my friend's breast, and Ferris drew his coat over the boy's head as if to shield him from me.

I backed away. Men swore as I stumbled over to my own place by the fire. Lying down again, I drew my knees up to my chest to ease the pain that was there.

I must have slept again, for soon after came the call to rise, and for the first time, most men around me prayed rather than cursed. I heard them on all sides, imploring God that they might come safe through the assault, be worthy, get home soon to Margaret or to Father. I made no such prayer, but held Caro and my brothers a minute in my heart, and then stood, pierced by the usual aches. Someone had fed the fire nearest Ferris during the night, and the flames gave off just light enough for me to see him rise and the Bible fall from his chest. He picked it up, and before he could stop himself, looked over in my direction. I bowed. He turned away.

TEN

Golgotha

THE BITTER GLOOM before dawn was thick with the rustling of unseen men, ghosts condemned for some hideous crime perpetually to arm themselves and fight. The officers got us into formation with the aid of *dark lanterns*, that is, lanterns which showed no light on the side of the enemy, and part of me thought, as calmly as if I were a scholar studying a sermon, what an apt name *dark lantern* was for false religion. As the soldiers filled their bandoliers, and rinsed their throats with drink, the stench of powder battled with that of Hollands. This liquor I had always refused, being disgusted by its smell. Now men passed huge flasks of it back and forth as they waited for Preacher William Beech to furnish them with more spiritual comforts.

'What's this?' I asked as I was handed a weapon.

'Pikemen are to have brown bills for today,' said the man in charge. 'And swords.'

I looked at the bill I had been given. It was shorter than the pike, and hooked. Evidently we were in for much mauling and grappling. My heart began to knock in my breast.

'Swords also,' the fellow insisted, passing a baldric round my neck.

'Here.' The man next to me pushed a flask into my hand. 'Get that down you.'

I took a pull at the foul stuff and it seared my throat. Spitting, I made to pass it back but he would not let me. 'Drink, soldier. It gives courage.'

Gasping, I let more of the poisonous brew into my belly.

'And blunts pain. Good lad.' My comrade took the flask, upended it at his mouth and downed all that was left.

William Beech was begun. He waved his arms at us as if herding cattle, stamped the earth and had evidently a month's mind to his work.

'They are open enemies of God,' he called in a hoarse voice which seemed to have got the damp of the place into it. Each time he passed before a lantern I saw his words fly away in clouds to join the mist which lay about us.

'Papist... vermin... deserving of the fate of all who stand against His might...'

His urgings came to me in drifts, cut across by coughs and wheezes on every side. Staring about for Ferris, unable to see him, I wondered how he looked, angry or despairing, as he listened to that sermon. My eye fell on a man nodding and clenching his fists: this was Colonel Harrison, whose hatred of recusants and other 'vermin' outwent even Beech's. I had reason for noticing this officer, for on an earlier occasion some soldier had pointed out Harrison for his pure, fierce love of God, and I had seen Ferris's jaw set with loathing. Now I saw God's Executioner breathe hard as he strained to catch the sermon through the raw air and the barking of soldiers trying to clear their throats.

'... the fate the Lord of Hosts justly meted out to Sodom and Gomorrah...'

Men swilled down as much Hollands as their sides could hold. Beyond the crowd, the land, hacked up and trampled, lay desolate.

There was a great 'Amen' roared out. On every side I saw helmets pulled on over caps, a wisp of straw stuffed into the hole at the back as a field sign. I weighed the brown bill in my unpractised hand.

Commanders moved along the lines, making sure we were in our right order. First through the gap were to be unhorsed cavalry, who were the freshest of the troops and had good buffcoats beside. It came to me that by the time I got there we would be treading the wounded underfoot. Then the commanders went back to their posts, and something like a shiver ran through the field. My mouth grew suddenly dry, so dry I could scarce swallow, and I felt I must piss at once, let go there and then unless I would do myself some hurt. Fumbling with cold hands in my breeches, I realised that the man next to me was untrussing likewise.

He observed my surprise and said, 'It is always thus before battle,' in the harsh voice of our shared thirst. 'Look about you.'

I did so, and observed a frenzy of pissing among the ranks. Steam, smelling of stewed apples, rose from the mud. It was a practice, like that of the Hollands, never read of in Sir John Roche's drill manual.

The church bell tolled six, and was followed directly by four cannon shots. I thought my heart would come out of my mouth.

'Christ be with you! And no quarter,' cried my neighbour. The drummers gave the order to advance; the troops began moving forwards, walking at first and then trotting until we were in a headlong run. I could no longer hear any drum and it was all a man could do to keep level with his fellows. When we were halfway across the park the gaps in the wall suddenly filled with soldiers, ready and waiting.

Men were screaming, '*For God and Parliament!*' I saw the first of ours run up the breach and fling himself on the defenders. There were flashes, followed by the sounds of musket fire, and screams. I struggled to run with my weapon upright and not fall over it. At the front I could see a great mass of men packed and heaving together. A little further forward and we were pressing into the breach, those inside jabbing at us with bills. Slashing back, I laid a face open. Muskets fired on us from the upper storeys, hand grenades rained down and I saw a man's head shot to bits in front of me, felt his blood and brains fleck my skin. Those in the gap, lacking time to reload their muskets, had fallen to clubbing one another. Men fell screaming and were pressed onto the stones, the scrape and clatter of their helmets adding to the hellish noise. The drum struck up again nearby but was straightway drowned in shots and cries. A sudden warmth bathed my leg: someone was bleeding on me. He fell backwards against my chest; I saw brown eyes turned up to mine and blood on his teeth before he sank beneath our feet.

The defenders could not long hold the breach in this wise, and at last gave ground. Our men burst in like the Flood, though the heathen strove to make them pay for every foot gained, and Paulet's men fled to the houses.

There was now no order but a desperate struggle. A new cry was everywhere heard: '*Down with the Papists*'. We scaled the sides of the house, every instant losing men to granadoes and shot, and entered by the windows of the first floor where their apartments were situated. Once inside, the brown bill was useless, so I cast it away and put my hand to my sword. Men jostled one another as at a fair, hard put to it to draw arms, but where they could wield their weapons freely, they cut and slashed so that I was like to have lost my footing in the slime. There was a hideous stench which I could not place; when I understood it was the stink of slit bowels, my guts worked and I near vomited.

Opposite to me I saw a great fair-headed fellow all plumes, and while he was engaged with another of ours I put my entire might into driving the sword into his neck. So did we fell him between us. Many times was I heartily glad of my helmet. One of theirs tried to lop off my hand – all he could reach – and left me with a bloody cut across the knuckles, which I saw but felt not. Sweat ran into my eyes. The place rang with clashes and screams; slowly we moved forwards, slowly the enemy gave ground. As they dropped, more would present themselves, and I saw there must be an army of them hidden in the inner fastnesses of the house, where we would have to smoke them out.

It was scarce a time for looking about me, but even a glance showed that Basing far excelled its fabled greatness, and made our old house, which I had thought so rich, a dungheap in comparison. The great hall by torchlight was now a gilded slaughterhouse, with pictures everywhere, filthy idolatries in paint and in stone. I glanced up in blinking the warm water from my eyes and saw wood carved fine as lace. Velvet and gold tissue ran with gore or were caught on pikes and torn from the walls: men were blown up and fell in gobbets through jewelled windows. I saw one soldier ram a sword down another's throat, and heard the scream grow shrill and then choke off as the blade was driven home. Above them, high on the far wall, a marble Christ pale in death looked down from the cross upon His people.

All this time I continued pushing blindly forward, for there was nothing else to be done, cutting at a man here, being shouldered by another there. A burning in my thigh told me that I had been stabbed; though badly frighted and harassed by pain, I was unable to examine any of my wounds for fear of catching worse. Drill, which I had thought such war-like preparation, had been a country dance to this.

Paulet's men being at last unable to stem the flow, our soldiers rushed the stairs, swords out. I let myself be borne up with them, and found another fight going on before some chamber doors. Servants and gentlemen of the household barred the way, but being utterly unequal to so many adversaries they were spitted against the door and kicked aside. We shouldered the panels until the bolts burst off. There was a wailing from the inside, and I knew we had found the women of the household. They huddled together like rabbits in corn: I did not want to touch them. I looked round quickly for Philip and saw him not. I little doubted to see the females violently abused before my eyes, but the men dragged them out and down the stairs. Some, resisting, were kicked from the top step to the bottom and their screams were fit to tear flesh. An old woman's leg was shattered by the fall, and I saw her near the bottom of the steps, trying to crawl between men's feet as they gouged one another.

More men, come up with me by this time, broke open the door of another apartment and found therein an old man in strange priestly garments and a young woman, both on their knees before an idol in manifest defiance of God's commandments. The woman was ill dressed for prayer, in a pale green dress the colour of milk infused with mint, gleaming like metal in the candlelight and cut so low that she might almost have suckled a child without disarranging it; and in this wise she had knelt before God. I saw a beauty in her, in the black gypsy eyes and hair of bronze, but also that arrogance of carriage which has been the downfall of many in these times, and so it was hers.

One of our lads made to take captive the man, and seeing him reach towards a chest, thought it best not to wait to see what was within, and fired first. There was a great scream from the wench as she saw the old man wounded and clutching at his shoulder; she jumped up and commenced railing, calling us 'Roundheads' and 'traitors'.

A soldier straightway gave her his sword across the head. She gasped, and clapped her hand to the wound; and then he ran her through. I heard the crunch of the blade, saw it disappear into her, and yet she remained standing, looking into his face, and reached down softly, as if to adjust some portion of her dress, until her fingers circled the steel. He at once wrenched it out, slitting her hand, upon which she held the bleeding palm up to her face and her lips worked as if she would cry. There was red coming down her neck from under her hair, and I saw a blotch spreading through the greenish, milky cloth over her belly. Suddenly blood streamed out from under her skirts. The old man shrieked like a dog that is scalded. The soldier whose work it was glared upon the girl as if he could have torn her in pieces for outright detestation. She looked at me, seeming to appeal for help, then softly folded downwards until she laid her cheek on the carpet. I watched her lips draw back and her shoulders rise and fall. The back of the gown was beginning to stain.

The man turned to the rest of us. 'And so will the proud and vainglorious be utterly pulled down and vanquished!' His voice trembled with passion; indeed, his whole body shook as if he had encountered with Satan himself. I nodded, feeling nothing but intense cold within me.

'Tie the old one,' he ordered.

I could see nothing to tie him with. Another man prodded with his sword at the girl's silk girdle, now clotted with blood. Her hair brushed my hand as I pulled at the fastening. At last it was off and I began tying the prisoner. Then the first soldier, still not finished, knelt and stripped her of every garment until she was naked under the old man's eyes.

I finished binding the priest. Speechless and wracked with dry heaves, he was left for the time being to contemplate the corpse. The woman's destroyer, having tied her dress round his neck by the sleeves so that it hung from his back like a cloak, went out 'to hunt up more wolves', the others following. I leant against the wall, fingering my wounded thigh and sweating, until I could stand straight. When I left the old man's gaze followed me to the door.

There were many passageways, many chambers leading off each. Men surged back and forth, pushing prisoners before them, slashing the images in their great carven frames, shattering the statues. I saw one soldier with strings of bloody pearls about his neck. Others bore off plate and cloth, or tore jewels from women's ears. They tripped over the dead and dying, slipped on their blood and vomit, trampled their intestines. The air was foul beyond anything. I beat off a man who hacked at me, until he thought better of it and went to find someone smaller.

Directly beside me was another door. Opening it, I found myself in an empty bedchamber with a key, which I turned, on the inside of the lock. The urge to piss again came violently upon me, so I stood next the window, looking out of it as I relieved myself against the wall. The scene outside blurred and I understood by this that tears were rising in my eyes, but knew it in a blank, insensible fashion, like an idiot that cannot say why he laughs or weeps.

The window gave onto the courtyard, which was evidently under our control. Below me stood four priests, roped together; in another corner huddled the flock of women, now stripped to their shifts. I could not see the one with the broken leg. Their dresses were heaped upon a cart, and men were bringing other garments out of the house to add to the pile. A feeble daylight made it possible to pick out the colours of the pillaged clothing, but it was still bitterly cold. On the ground lay some old sick creature in a blanket, his naked legs like string.

There was a door opposite: I went through it and found myself in a short corridor which was eerily empty, though ringing with the sounds of the most ferocious combat on all sides. At the far end there was a flight of stairs leading up. I went up to the foot of the steps; it was evident by the noise and the trembling of the ceiling that there was fierce fighting above, and the Marquess's men by no means vanquished even yet. I knew I should mount, and wanted more than anything to stay where I was.

As I hesitated, there was a *clang* of metal and two men came rolling and slithering down, gasping as the stairtreads battered face and back. One's head was caked in mud and blood, and he had lost his helmet, but I could see by his garb that he was one of ours. The other, big and thickset, seemed a manservant, and getting the better of it. They had both lost their weapons and had fallen to grappling one another, but though they were roughly of a height our soldier was much slighter in build and Paulet's man, having got on top of him, commenced banging his skull against the stairs.

I came up behind the big fellow, clutching my knife, and got astride his legs, then seized his hair from behind, dragging his head back. He tilted his face towards me and I drove the knife under his ear, pulling it through the flesh to the other side of his throat so that my hand ached. There was a smell of iron. He fell forwards onto the one beneath, who turned his head aside, mouth closed against the warmth spilling onto him. A snorting, bubbling sound came from the Papist, but he continued to struggle, trying to throw me off. I held on tight and put the knife in him again, in the back; he cried out something that might have been 'Mercy' but we were long past that. His war ended in a drumming of the feet.

The smaller one pushed his dead opponent's face away from his own. I knelt back, dragging the body aside, and let the Parliament man sit up to wipe the fresh blood from his chaps onto a sleeve. A part of the mud came with it, and I started. There was something – the lips—

'God requite you!' he wheezed. His eyes were clenched shut, tears seeping from under gummy lids. I strained to place the broken, breathless voice. Then, as I stared at the slime plastered over hair and face, the eyes unsealed and showed themselves flower blue.

Nathan.

It was hard to breathe for the lurching of my heart; the throat's drag on the blade still stiffened my arm; my thighs remembered the dying man's struggle against their embrace.

Tears and blood ran off Nathan's chin. He rocked back and forth in an attempt to rise, but was too beaten to pull himself up.

'Rupert, God bless you!' He held out a palsied hand to me.

'Brother, saviour.' The jewel eyes turned full on mine, not with the crafty glance of the night before but with a look of adoration. That look coming after the girl's death staggered me, drove me back. I knew it for what it was, a momentary outpouring of his love for his own life, yet despite myself the surge in my flesh began to ebb. I stood baffled, hand on my sword. A group of our soldiers burst into the corridor at the far end.

'Jesus fights on your side all right,' I said, frighted at the cracked sound of my own voice. 'Where's your weapon?'

'At the top of the steps. I'll fetch it.'

I helped the boy to his feet, then ran away from him towards the new arrivals who were trying all the doors to see if any Papists lurked within. There was banging and screaming from above. I burst into a room on the right: a bedchamber, empty and cold. Even against that grim and cloudy sky the windows shone bright, with three medallions in fine scarlet glass let into the leads. I let out a great bellowing sob, and taking up a stool from the bedside, I hurled it straight through the middle design, the finest. Glass fell to the floor like drops of blood.

A cry went up from outside and I ran to the broken pane. People below glared up at me. Glittering scraps lay on the stones, and among them the stool, still in one piece. I stepped back into the room. The shards put me in mind of Sir Bastard's goblet; I took up one of them and read scratched upon it, *Loyaute*. Snatching up a linen cap that lay on the bed, I carefully wrapped the glass, and laid it in my bosom. As I did so a scarlet blot formed on the linen, and I understood for the first time that the liquid stinging my eyes was not sweat: my shaking fingers found a split across my forehead to make me a pair with Ferris. Someone had dealt me a cut right under the edge of the helmet without my feeling it. A rising roar warned me that the corridor was filling up again, and I pushed out into a rush of men heading back towards the courtyard.

The idolaters, flushed from every corner of the place, were being herded outside. They staggered, some howling with burnt flesh from powder and shot, others with broken heads or limbs. The soldiers showed them no mercy. I saw one man, blinded, rest against the wall and one of the New Model break his nose with a musket butt to teach him more speed. Even those who were not much hurt wept openly as they were forced along, guessing what tenderness would be shown them. Our men, too, bore marks of hard fighting. I was somewhat ashamed to have had an easy time of it, and so I made a show of goading the captives on their way.

~

Soldiers bustled about in the cold, stripping or tying folk according to the will of the officers. I wandered from group to group and heard men say there would be nigh on three hundred prisoners, though I could not see anything like so many.

'Will they be killed?' I asked the man who had charge of the four priests.

'Not here. They'll be sent to London.'

I knew what that meant: they were to be hanged, drawn and quartered. The guard told me that several Papist priests were already dead in the assault. 'They had better fortune than these,' he added, and I thought there was pity in him. He went on, 'There's every degree of prisoner. Did you see the old rat? Naked under the blanket?'

I nodded, remembering the frail legs I had seen earlier.

'Inigo Jones,' said the guard, but I could not tell who Inigo Jones might be.

~

Ferris waved to me across a group of men, beckoning me over.

'Look here,' he said without greeting. He knelt and raised the head of an enemy officer who had been shot in the chest and whose strange, comical face looked to be laughing. The eyes, bold and mocking, outstared anything men could do to him. Ferris thumbed them shut.

'They call him Major Robinson,' he said. 'I knew him as Robbins the actor.'

'*You* knew him?'

'I saw him once on the stage.' My friend lowered Robbins's head onto the wet stones. 'They say Colonel Harrison shot him.'

'I have never seen a play,' I said.

'Do you know what he said as he did it? *Cursed be he that does the Lord's work negligently*. You and he are of a mind.'

'If I was ever of his mind, Ferris, I am not so now.'

My friend raised exhausted eyes to mine.

'I have killed but few,' I said, 'and one of them, I think you would be glad of.'

'If it was you or him, then yes. I'd not let a man put a sword through me neither.'

I wondered should I tell him just then about Nathan, but decided to wait, for had the boy been dispatched by another, there would be no proof. We regarded one another in silence. From behind him came the strange sound of prisoners muttering to themselves in Latin.

Ferris said, 'Forgive me. You are not Harrison.'

'Tell me,' I answered before I could stop myself, 'I beg of you. What has Fat Tommy—'

A whoop went up from the men: a gentleman, in a richly embroidered shirt but nothing else, was dragged from the house and was brought before Cromwell himself.

'Paulet,' said Ferris. We strained closer to see and hear. The man was shaking so that only his captors kept him from falling, but he tried to stare down every soldier there present. Hugh Peter, newly arrived from London and standing at Cromwell's side, asked if the Marquess did not now think his cause must be hopeless? And the other, holding himself more upright now he was come through the first shock of that crowd, but still trembling in his linen, answered that had the King no more ground in England than Basing-House, he would venture it as he had done and maintain it to the uttermost. I thought he looked a very hardnecked old sinner. Orders were given to take him to London, to the Tower, and to keep his sons away from him so that they might be raised in a pure religion.

'He was in the bread-oven telling his beads!' shouted one of the soldiers who had brought him out. There was a general laugh as the Romanist was marched away.

'They still put faith in their idols, even when it's all up,' said a man in front of us.

I heard Ferris mutter, 'Would you have him utterly comfortless?' so I asked him what comfort there could be in false religion.

He answered me impatiently, 'That's the very question he'd fain put to us.'

~

I soon came to understand my error in smashing the windows, for we had fought for more than just prisoners. There were garrison supplies, and treasures fit for a Solomon, which this reprobate had bought in France, Italy and other corrupt places, and hoarded here where thieves break in and moth and rust do spoil.

The plunder began even before the assault was over, and once the prisoners were secured the entire army gave themselves up to it. Men ran through the rooms snatching up any gold or jewels they could lay hand on, stripping off their filthy linen and putting on good clean stuff found in the chests; many a friend fell out with his friend over a bag of money not shared or later stolen while he slept off the wine filched from the cellars. Costly perfumes were poured over lousy shirts; in the stores and kitchens men crammed their sacks and boots with dried fruit, cheeses, anything within snatching distance that no other fellow had got to first.

We had been ordered not to wantonly spoil anything, for it would be sold to pay and feed us, but where food and gold were concerned the men preferred helping themselves, as being the surer way. Even Ferris grabbed what he could, and I saw him lay hand on a purse and two shirts, one of which he straightway gave to me. In my sack I had three bottles of wine, a necklace set with rubies which I had found thrust under a pillow, and two fine silver candlesticks. All this was picked up in the chambers and apartments, after which we made our way to the barn and brought away as much food and drink as we could carry. On the way we passed some of the hotter sort slashing at Romanist pictures or statues, which were to be broken and not sold, but most soldiers were starved for comfort rather than set on destruction, and their most sacred mission was to fill their bellies.

We found rows of sweet wax candles, like ghostly rushes, in the idolaters' chapel and took them to one of the chambers where there was a fire. To the troops it was morning, noon and night rolled into one. Our candles once lit, we sat in a blaze of light, other men soon joining us with provisions of their own. There was a deal of victual captured from the great barn and we had the wine, some hams, cheeses, salt beef, sausages and pies in the room with us. Someone was cooking eggs in a helmet over the fire. All were merry: each had a sack stuffed with plunder and a bellyful of drink.

Russ was nowhere to be seen. No more was Nathan, and I wondered if I had spared him only to afford another the pleasure of the kill.

'Have you seen any of – the rest?' I asked, not liking to say 'our friends' lest he challenge the words.

'None.' Ferris was flushed. He threw back his head and swilled the wine, eyes shining. 'Here, give me your knife.' The clumsy way in which he cut the ham put me in mind of Mervyn Roche. We gorged the meat without bread, washing it down with wine. Ferris pulled a bolster from the bed, where men were already asleep before midday, and laid it on the floor so that we could sprawl there in comfort.

There was singing, of the bawdiest kind. Someone had set to music a filthy thing I had never heard before:

An Elder's maid near Temple Bar
Ah what a Queen was she
Did take an ugly mastiff cur
Where Christians used to be...

Not even coarse-minded Peter at Beaurepair would have sung that. Ferris seemed hardly to notice it, by which I saw how far gone he was in weariness and drink.

'We are in for trouble if an officer hears,' I said to him under cover of the final verses which the men roared out fit to split the ceiling. '"*An Elder's maid*", that is not only lewd but against our own side, surely!'

'Picked up from the Cavaliers,' he murmured. 'This is not a time for psalms. Cromwell has turned the place over to pillage. That means drink, and drink brings all the rest.'

'Why does he allow it? Because Paulet was a Papist?'

'And put us to the trouble of a storm. Besides, the soldiers are owed this for Winchester, for good conduct.'

'Men must have something.'

He nodded. 'The women of the house have cause to thank Cromwell. He hangs any that rapes.'

I blushed at that word, and even more when he said, 'I will say one thing for you, Rupert: concerning pillage you are innocence itself.'

The wine spoke up before I could stop it: 'Is there nothing else you can say for me?'

Such pleading was in the words that his look softened at once. 'Much. You have strength in you for anything.' Then his face hardened again; he frowned. 'But you are altogether too fierce.'

I had known it. His mind was poisoned. 'What has Tommy told you?'

'Tommy? Nothing.'

'I beg of you, Ferris, don't lie to me! I know he—'

Ferris held up his hand to interrupt. 'When have you seen me sit and blacken another's name?'

'But they tell you things?'

'You should rather ask do I give ear to them. Our quarrels, Rupert, are between us two.'

'You gave ear to Nathan.'

'That *was* my quarrel. I had already begged—' He broke off and I saw that he was backing away from a dispute with me. 'Nathan is a boy, tender, gently raised. He should be home with his mother and sisters.'

'We talked of this before,' I said.

'Let us try it again. You are a man, why crush him in your fist?'

'He comes between me and you. I have no other friend.'

Though I waited for him to say, 'You must make yourself friends,' he took another pull on the wine, then handed over the bottle saying, 'Give me some cheese.'

I watched him eat. The room was hot with the fire, with men's bodies and with flaring candles; there was a shine on his brow and the sides of his nose. I ached to tell him how I could have made my teeth meet in Nathan, but had saved him instead.

'I could gladly drink myself to death,' Ferris said, closing his eyes.

I started. 'Is this a time to be sad?'

'O yes.' His laugh was harsh.

'But you are come through the siege,' I said, 'and in one piece.'

'I were better cut in two.'

'Are you afraid for Nathan?'

'More afraid than you know.' He opened his eyes and turned them on me. 'He may be safe and well. Let us not kill him yet.'

'With all my heart.' I offered him the wine again; he drank off the rest of the bottle and asked me to fetch another. There was one opened and left untouched by the fireside, and I gave it him. None protested. Though the odd man whispered or swore here and there, the roaring stage was past. Several had been sick, their heads hanging out of the chamber window. Not all of them were got so far, and the unlucky ones had been roundly cursed by their mates. A fug of wine and vomit hung on the air as the fire burnt down and the revellers sank into sleep.

When I ceased staring round the room I saw Ferris looking at me very hard.

'You have watched in the field every day,' he said.

Unsure what to answer, I held my tongue.

'Nat told me,' he added.

'Nathan?' Now I suspected Ferris of trying to reconcile us through lies. 'He told you of my doings? Why?'

'I asked him.'

We regarded one another. A silence grew between us, and did not frighten me; I looked him in the eyes longer than I had ever done with any man, save Izzy.

'What a thing is wine,' he murmured.

The next minute there was a shout; two of the men, grown quarrelsome, were begun pushing at one another, jabbing their sleeping neighbours into the bargain. Since they would not lie quiet, those of us who could still stand pushed them out into the corridor and turned the key on their threats and oaths.

When we lay down again Ferris arranged himself for sleep, injured cheek upwards. I at first settled beside him, but my hips, which had pained me so sorely till now, were no better for the warmth, so I went to the bed and found one side of it empty. It seemed that after months of longing for a mattress, most of the men had been too drunk to get onto it. Still wearing my boots, I stretched out next to a man called Bax sprawled on the other side, and was asleep before I could strip or get under the covers. Some time later I woke to find Ferris crept in between me and Bax.

~

Around noon our rest was broken up by a hammering at the door: hucksters and merchants come for anything worth having. Basing was to be flayed, then picked to the bones. What we could not eat from the garrison was sold off to the local folk; the pictures, together with missals, rosaries and wicked sculptures, were packed upon carts for public burning, to show our contempt for a religion that was half superstition and half Mammon. Whatever the soldiers could not pocket up fell prey to dealers: carpets, hangings, plate, linen, beds and other furniture, clothing, slipware and glass. There was enough to furnish two palaces, and crows aplenty come to fat themselves on the carcass. The very flesh of the building was devoured, for Cromwell bade the country people help themselves to brick and stone. Paulet having razed their own homes, this was a thing they were mighty willing to do.

When Ferris and I rose from the bed, stepping over the men half dead from drink, we were ordered to the great hall and there put with one Rigby, our task to count, and sort, the gowns taken from the women. My head ached, and Ferris looked bruised round the eyes. Rigby too seemed as if he could have wished for more self-governance, or a stronger stomach.

We had scarce begun piling the garments up on the table when Nathan came up to us and asked if he might help; the captain had told him to make himself useful where he could.

Ferris brightened at the sight of the lad, kissed him on both cheeks and said he was right glad to see all his limbs in one piece. Nathan beamed at me in a fashion I could ill endure and I almost thought he would come over and kiss *my* cheeks as recompense for my saving of him, but he stayed himself at smiling.

'Let us make three piles,' offered Rigby, 'gentlewomen's, servants', and one where the stuffs are spoilt.'

This seemed a good plan. Ferris was a sound judge of the linen, and Nathan evidently a keen observer of ladies for he pronounced upon which were the rarest cloths and costliest laces.

Laughing, Ferris asked him, 'How does a lad get to be such a proficient in silk?'

'O, my sisters: they were mad for robes, always on at Father to buy new stuffs. And they are brave, these things, are they not?' He held up a dazzling crimson skirt. 'I'll marry no dull mouse, she must be bright and beautiful.'

'A noble lady?' Ferris teased him.

Rigby joined in, 'A princess!'

We were as merry, for a moment, as I had once been at home. But then Ferris held up a shining green robe with a deep slit in it, and around the slit a blackening crust of blood. Flies buzzed away as he shook it out. Nathan's laugh stopped short.

'Not hard to guess what happened to her,' said Ferris.

'I saw it,' I said, feeling the same cold within me as I had then. 'She gave our man a sharp answer.'

'And he gave her another.' He spread out the glistening, ruined stuff. 'I wonder who will they find in London to buy *that*? Some thrifty citizen—!'

Rigby looked sheepish at this talk. I said to him, 'He cut her down for nothing.'

'Not doing God's work?' asked Ferris, but his voice was gentler than it would have been two days before.

'Rupert did God's work,' said Nathan.

I bridled up but got command of myself, and it was well, for he went on, 'He saved me in the assault. I had otherwise died, there was a fellow all set to knock out my brains.'

Ferris stared at me, lowering the gown without knowing it until his hands rested on the table. I raised my eyebrows, as one who says, *Well?*

'There was none other there, he was my only help,' Nathan prattled on, making my happiness complete.

Ferris seemed dazed. I took the wounded gown from him and laid it to one side.

'You had *great* good fortune, Nat,' he said quietly. 'Let's all hear the tale, but first could you take that green one and ask the captain what we shall do with it? He's somewhere upstairs.'

Nathan bounded off like a deer.

'The man's outside,' said Ferris. He pulled me over to the corner, away from Rigby; I was surprised at his vehemence. 'Can this be possible?' he whispered. 'Why did you? And don't say it was for love of him.'

'I don't say so.'

'So why?'

I glanced round. Rigby was staring after us curiously. For once in my life the right thing came to me by nature, as it would have come to Zeb. I pulled out the woman's cap from my shirtbreast and gave it to Ferris.

'Look inside,' I said.

He unfolded the cloth, found the glass with its inscription and hung his head. I listened to his breath as it came fast and then slowed again. At last he looked up to me, smiling on the good side of his mouth.

'What shall I do with you, Prince Rupert? It seems I cannot stay angry for long.'

'For a start, call me by my own name,' I said. 'I'm not myself without my name.'

'What man can be himself here?' He scratched his head. 'So what would you be called? Cullen?'

'I can't go from Rupert to Cullen.' I had never liked my sir-name in any case. 'Call me Jacob.'

'And what will you call me?'

'You are Ferris.'

'Jacob.' He tried the name against my face. 'Jacob, I have something I must tell you.'

'This is about Tommy,' I said. 'He told you my name before.'

Ferris hesitated, then drew me further from Rigby. His lips worked an instant before he stuttered, 'I, I am—'

'Say it!' I cried.

'I am – leaving. Leaving the army.'

I had known one day he would say this. My loneliness had whispered it in nightmares; I would dream he was run away, gone out of the New Model and lost to me.

'May – God – be with you.' Each word cut me as it came, and after the last I felt my throat close. I knew what that presaged, and indeed the water was already in my eyes. I raged inwardly that at such a moment I should dissolve like any mewling girl, like Nathan, and so be remembered. 'I guess you go to London,' I forced out, tongue strangling in my mouth.

'We will go,' he said. 'Do you think I am so cruel, to tell you and then leave you behind?'

The tears burst out then. I smeared them away with the palm of my hand, and begged him to say it again.

'Come with me,' he said. 'If you will,' and I felt his smile go warm through my blood.

I was panting, laughing and crying together as I hugged Ferris to me; over his shoulder, I saw Rigby's face duck down to the linen.

'If! If!' I cried, light and free through all my flesh. It was the feeling called happiness, which I had near forgotten.

Ferris put me away from him. 'The army is bad for you,' he said. 'I got you in, I must get you out.'

'When shall it be?' I asked.

The door was kicked open and Nathan burst in upon us. Ferris laid a finger across his lips. 'Nat' was not to know, then. I was a soul in bliss as we went towards the table where Rigby was trying to look as if the piles of clothes occupied him entirely.

'He says to cut out the stains,' Nathan called, 'but keep the rest to be sold in pieces.'

We went on with our work, the boy ripping at the bloody stuff with a swaggering relish born of fear. I wondered why Ferris had chosen to leave him behind, perhaps because Nathan had Russ and other comrades. I hoped it was because he had to choose between us, and though turbulent and troublesome, I was the friend with whom, in the end, he could not part.

ELEVEN

The Man of Bones

TOWARDS EVENING a chill breeze sprang up. Men complained, after their drunkenness, of aching heads; weariness possessed the camp. We sprawled in the park, on a heap of blankets we had found, mocking Nathan's tale of a miraculous fish.

'I tell you true,' Nathan insisted. 'Twenty pounds' weight.'

'Who weighed it? Does he carry scales with him?' Russ mocked.

'Aye, fish scales,' offered another.

Ferris rolled his eyes in disbelief. 'No matter for the weight. But as to the rest—'

'Will you listen to me?' Nathan was flushed. 'This was witnessed – sworn to – there was a paper in its mouth, and this paper said—'

'Throw me back in!' a man shouted. The rest laughed.

Ferris asked, 'Nat, how could they read a paper all wet?'

The day had been too long; none was in the mood for foolish stories. Hoping to stop his mouth, I handed Nathan a piece of cheese, my thigh wounds paining me as I did so.

'My thanks Rupert, and – but will you *listen*! This paper was a prophecy, that the war should end with the Second Coming—'

'Aye, to be sure,' said Russ. 'It won't go on after it, at any rate.'

The others grinned. Nathan, sulking, bit into his cheese.

All around stood barrows and carts stacked with goods. Most of Basing had already been devoured, though men still crawled over the skeleton.

'Look there,' said Russ.

An orange light was sprung up inside the pillaged house.

'He's had it fired,' Nathan exclaimed.

Ferris said, 'But there was stuff yet left to sell.'

I admired the fragile sparks floating like angels in the deepening blue sky. The orange light dimmed, and a pale smoke began pouring from the windows as the flames found doors, carved panels and beams. Some things, at least, would escape the dealers, and I was glad, for though I knew that they paid for what they took, yet I resented their easy scuttling off with what we had won with sweat and blood.

But I could not feel much anger. Though it was hours since Ferris had made my happiness, the excitement was scarce gone down. I sat gloating.

'And so an end to Basing,' Russ said. 'What are they doing, there?'

Soldiers were running towards the ruin. The crash and crackle of burning drifted to us on the wind, then swept away.

'I shall go and see,' exclaimed Nathan, making to rise.

'Nat—' Ferris clutched at the boy's jacket. 'Stay here.'

'Be easy, I won't go in!' Nathan wriggled free and ran towards the crowd.

'Nat!' Ferris called after him. 'Nat – wait—'

I stood to get a better look. 'There's Cromwell riding up,' I told Ferris. 'What is it? Do you know?'

'There are wounded under the rubble,' Russ answered for him.

I stared at him. 'How do you know?'

'Why else would—' He broke off as the wind again veered in our direction. The sounds from the burning house grew louder and I could distinguish shouts and screams. Ferris, his eyes on the retreating Nathan, sat biting his lip.

~

All was packed and ready for the next day's march on the West Country; soldiers sat around, glancing from time to time at the ruins. The sky was now black except for the orange-bellied smoke clouds over Basing.

'I must show you something,' Ferris whispered to me. 'Go to the courtyard. I will stay for you.'

I waited awhile, making a point of talking to others as he rose and walked off towards the carts drawn up for the night. When I judged it right I went directly to the place, where I found my friend in talk with a man I had not met before, the two of them leaning against a cart and their voices very low. There was a stink of scorched brick and of something else which I did not choose to name. The man looked up and froze as I approached. 'My friend,' I heard Ferris whisper.

'Lord, how big is he?' the man exclaimed.

'Not too big,' Ferris answered. He called to me in a more natural fashion, 'Jacob, this is Mister Bradmore, a carter. Mister Bradmore, Jacob Cullen, that some call Prince Rupert.'

At this the man wheezed rather than laughed. We bowed to one another.

'Are you buying?' I asked Ferris.

'Carpets,' he replied. I thought his voice strangely loud. 'They are in here, and this,' tapping the side of the cart and whispering again, 'is your bedchamber for tonight.'

'Sleep here?' I turned to Bradmore. 'To guard it? What will you pay?'

'He doesn't know,' Ferris murmured to the man. 'Aye, Jacob,' again his voice swelled, 'to guard it.' He beckoned me closer and breathed into my ear, 'He will take us out of camp hidden beneath his load.'

'Why in a cart? We could cross the camp on foot,' I hissed back.

'*This* cart goes to London,' Ferris answered. 'We will come back when all are asleep.'

'Why not now?'

'I have business to attend to. And Jacob, we must keep sober tonight.'

'Not a drop,' I promised.

'Until tonight then,' Ferris whispered to the man.

'Fear me not,' replied Bradmore. He spat in his hand and clapped it to Ferris's, then to mine.

We went back to sit with our group of friends, Ferris again walking in front. From a distance I saw a soldier hanging his head and looking into the fire. He scarce moved as Ferris went to sit beside him; I knew him for Nathan when I saw my friend's arm go about the soldier's waist.

As I came up Ferris raised pitying eyes to me. 'There were men burnt alive. Nat heard them.'

'Romanists,' I said. 'Enemies of God.'

'Where have you been all this while?' Ferris began stroking the back of Nathan's head and neck. 'We were in the courtyard—'

'Our own men!' the boy cried. 'Crying for quarter – they thought it was us set the fire—'

Under the smuts and the smears of blood his face showed white as if poisoned.

'But you tried to bring them out,' Ferris said.

The boy covered his eyes.

Ferris sighed. 'He's shivering like a dog. Here, Nat, try to sleep.' He took off his coat and put it across Nathan's knees, tucking it round him for warmth.

~

Watching and waiting was misery. It was almost worse than the assault, for I had nothing to do and everything to think on. Ferris and I had made a point of sleeping on the outer edge of the group and away from the fire, the more easily to get away. Now cold air washed over me and I shivered worse than Nathan.

This was the first time since the fight I had lain down with no drink in my guts. Whenever I turned over to ease my back and hips each wound pained me by rote. The thigh constantly opened up and bled, causing the stuff of my breeches to stick to it; wincing, I pulled away the stiffened cloth once more. The hand that plucked at the breeches was stiff and sore. My knuckles, rimmed with an ugly yellow, were not scabbing over as fast as I would like, my brow was hot where the blade had slit it, and I suffered sharp aches in the breast.

Even after the terrible sights I had seen, women run through, men trampling in entrails, I could find it in me to hope I would not be much scarred, so selfish is the flesh. I thought of the mark of Cain, and of Ferris, unable to lay down his torn face in sleep, and how little I had reckoned with his suffering.

There was a moon. I did not know if this was good or bad for us, but thought it most likely bad. Still wrapped in Ferris's coat, Nathan muttered in sleep, perhaps talking in his dream with the friend who was leaving him.

I woke with a violent pang in the chest: someone had touched my neck. I must have slept at last, for Ferris was risen without my knowledge, his hair white in the bluish light. He was in shirtsleeves. Clutching my snapsack, I rose and followed him across stiffened mud which crunched beneath my boots. As I did so I felt a familiar stab and trickle: the thigh wound opening. At the entrance to the courtyard he stopped and waited for me to come up.

'You've left your jacket,' I hissed, trying to still the thumping of my heart.

He put one finger to his lips, then pointed. Not ten yards off men lay asleep.

I could not see our cart and bent to whisper in his ear, 'Now where?'

'Follow me. If you hear anything, if they wake, stop dead.'

We passed between heavily laden wagons, the inside of my shirt all sweat and my mouth as dry as ever it had been before the assault. From inside my snapsack came a *clink* and I bit my lip, expecting the guards to rise up roaring. This was where the priests had been tied. Now there were so many carts there, a man could see nothing but their sides. London was licking her lips for the fruits of sin. Ferris pulled me alongside a covered wagon and out of the moonlight. I jumped, feeling his fingers on my face in the dark; he tugged at my hair to make me decline my head.

'There are men in these,' he mouthed into my ear. 'Yonder is ours.' He turned my jaw with his hand and I saw a cart standing in the full beams of the moon. Something moved next to it.

'The guards are there,' I gasped.

Ferris at once pinched my lips together. He pulled my head down again and I knew then what a fright I had given him, for his breathing came fast.

'Our friend. Come on.'

He stepped out and I was very content to let him go first. Surely moon was never so bright before, nor frost so crackling. As we drew near, the thing I had seen shaped itself into the ghostly driver of a ghostly cart. I thought of an old wives' tale told in the country round Beaurepair, of the Man of Bones: to see him was to die within the year. The apparition remained motionless until we came up to it, and then pointed to where we should mount. Ferris stepped up delicately and lowered himself onto some sacks. I tried to do the same. The wood groaned under my weight and the base of the thing tilted; sweat sprang in the palms of my hands so that they slipped along the rail. The grey man covered his face. Then I was in and lying beside Ferris, seeing his breath curl upwards to the moon.

My friend reached down and pulled what looked like a carpet over him, offering one edge to me. The rich thing showed oddly dulled by moonlight, as if silvered and soiled by some monstrous snail. Between us we silently tugged it this way and that until we were covered. It shut out some of the cold, but the dust from it put me in a terror lest I sneeze. *If we are caught,* I wondered, *will they shoot him before my face?*

The Man of Bones moved silently about, tying and untying. A hood was hoisted over us, and he lay down at the opening of it as if to sleep.

'Rest.' Ferris's breath warmed my cheek. 'If I snore, wake me, and if you hear anything else, pull the carpet over our heads.'

'Trust me for *that*,' I whispered back. 'What if I need to piss?'

'Don't.'

'Would you had told me before.' My knees knocked into his; I tried to get more comfortable. The smell of carpet took me back to the hangings at Beaurepair; I saw Izzy smiling, swishing about with his Turkish withy, and sent up a prayer that he might be safer and warmer that night than I.

~

It seemed but a minute before the carpet slapped at me, pressing on my face and limbs so that I feared to be smothered. I screwed my eyes shut against the dust. On opening them again, I observed a frail subterranean light trickling in. Ferris, roused by the sudden movement, had raised an edge of the carpet on his fingers so that we could breathe. More weight slammed onto us: the man was loading up.

'We'll suffocate,' I whispered.

'Be still.'

Metal jingled; the man was hitching up his horse. Next we felt the cart rock as he mounted, and the whip cracked.

We were on our way. Under the carpets Ferris's other hand pressed mine for courage, as I had once pressed Caro's. Something scuttled across my scalp. When I shifted, trying to get at it, the breeches pulled the scab from my thigh once more. We lay silent, jolting to the *clop clop* of hooves, listening as best we could to those about us who went on with the morning life of the army. Most of the time the sounds were padded, indistinct, but some things came sharp and clear: the click as a catch was tried, a sword clattering on stones, and most of all, men's voices raised in complaints or exultation: this man was recounting a jest played on one Joseph, another was being scolded for not minding his weapon. There was a strangeness in it. We were already out of that life, and would no longer speak its language. No more weevil cheese, or pike drill, or lying in fields. No more Rupert Cane. I allowed myself a smile in the dark womb where Ferris and I crouched beneath the carpets, waiting to be reborn.

~

'Here's one still alive, at any rate.'

The hood was back; the carter's face, upside-down and haloed by blinding sun, grinned at me. To my left Ferris groaned, dusting the motes and straws from his cheeks.

'Let me out a minute,' I cried, struggling from under the layers of stuff. Leaping down onto the grass, I at once relieved myself against the wheel. Ferris followed suit, and while standing there asked the man how far we were come from Basing.

'Two or three miles,' came the reply.

As one, we turned and looked back down the road. A blackness hung on the air above the horizon.

'You see that,' the man said.

Ferris nodded. 'Still smouldering. That's slighted it.'

'Slighted?' I asked. It seemed a gentle word for what we had seen.

'Burnt it, broken it utterly. There were not men enough to hold the place.'

Feeling my bowels move, I went behind a bush at the roadside for even after the army I hated to be seen at such private business. I fancied I heard the carter laugh at my finicking ways. We mounted again and this time rode on top of the load.

I patted the carpets. 'Who will have these, friend?'

'Any that can afford them, your nobility, citizenry,' he called back. 'They look brave on a table.'

'Did you pick them up cheap?' I asked.

He shrugged. 'I buy for another. There's two or three lots gone already.'

Ferris stretched on top of the load and gazed at the sky. I whispered to him, 'What did you pay this man?'

'Nothing. We spoke awhile; he took to me.'

'You could give him that other shirt you found.'

'I gave it Nat, last night.'

Something now struck me, and I stared at him. 'Ferris, where's your coat?'

He crossed his arms.

'You gave Nathan that too! And your snapsack – the purse you got at Basing—'

'Remembrances,' he muttered.

'But did he not guess—?'

'I put the snapsack under his head, to find when he wakes.'

His eyes told me to leave off. I did so.

The land peeled away on either side of us, the hillslopes steaming like the flanks of a beast. From time to time we saw empty carts coming in the opposite direction, the drivers laying on the whip in their eagerness to seize some of Paulet's jewels and plate.

'Eaten up already,' Ferris bawled maliciously after the first to pass us. 'Picked clean and a fire set in the ruins.'

The driver never looked back but went straight on.

'O well, let him make the journey,' my friend said, flinging himself down on the carpets. He was out of humour and I could guess at his contemplation: *Nat has missed me by now. How does he take it?*

'Do you know this country?' I asked, to distract him.

He shook his head. 'All I know is that this is the wool route.'

'What shall we do in London?'

'Live with my aunt, eat, sleep. Go from brutes to men.'

I thought how it would be to wash after all this time.

'We must get you some new garments,' Ferris went on, looking at my botched-together coat, and again I recalled the one I had worn for the betrothal, and lost.

'That means a tailor,' I said. At Beaurepair we were allowed three suits a year, but these were often hand-me-downs, except those for myself, whom no other man's clothes would fit.

'We will get you a tailor directly. But my uncle was near as big as you. Some of his things will do until yours are made.'

I was struck by the decision in his voice. 'Ferris, are you rich?'

He hesitated. 'I am not poor. You need not trouble yourself about tailors.'

In that speech I heard how little I really knew of our coming life, and I shivered with hope and fear.

~

We were three days journeying to London. It might have been quicker but for a thaw that set in, softening the roads and sometimes obliging myself and Ferris to get out and help clear the wheels. I hated doing this, for the heaving and slithering was horribly like that time when I had helped drag the pond.

'Watch the goods, lads,' said the carter warningly as we struggled back into the cart after a long hard push that left my legs trembling. We tied my boots and Ferris's shoes to the horsegear and spread my coat, inside out, upon the merchandise to keep off our muddy hose and breeches, before falling asleep. Our powers of sleep astonished me; I was seemingly making up for every hour lost over the past month, and passed in and out of the day like one in a fever. Ferris, who looked worn to skin and bone, did likewise, and in this way we both of us escaped our wounds awhile.

My snapsack was buried in the carpets, out of reach of prying hands. No pay remained to me at all; we had been promised our arrears in November. However, I still had the ruby necklace and the candlesticks, which I thought would serve for Ferris and myself at the inns. Our deliverer, however, put up at houses that he knew, and when the horse was securely locked away Ferris and I were left sleeping under the hood to guard his merchandise. This suited me well, for I kept the plunder for myself.

The first night was passed at the house of a Mistress Ovie, and Bradmore's relations with her it were better not to enquire into. To be sure, she kissed him in full view of us, and not coldly neither, as the cart set off. We were greeted by a woman the second night also, but this one was evidently his married sister. The husband, one Walters, came out to see the cargo and gaped to see men stored along with the goods, at which Bradmore laughed heartily.

That night I slept deep and dreamless. While the sky was still grey I woke, and found myself full of a blind joy, the like of which I had not felt since the *blessed time*, as I privately called that part of my life unsoiled by Walshe and my later doings. Ferris, as usual, slept on; I had already observed how he hated to rise of a morning. I studied his face. Though too thin, it was a good one. With the scarred cheek turned away from me and thus unseen, there was grace in his looks, and strength. His mouth curled upwards as if his dreams were happy, and his eyelids fluttered; I wondered what he saw, and wished he would wake. My wish was granted, for he straightway mumbled something and began an awkward scratching of his neck.

'O, I am eaten alive,' came his voice, thick with yawns. His eyes opened on mine. 'Crawling. Are not you?'

'Ever since I joined up.'

Ferris now smiled. 'Today—' he broke off to claw at his thigh, 'there will be clean linen. I have not let myself think of it till now, for fear of weakening. Feather beds, coal fires. Conserves.' He stretched himself out under the canvas hood. 'But most of all, clean linen.'

'To each his Paradise,' I said. '*Methinks the proverb should not be forgot*—'

'—*the wars are sweet to those that know them not*,' he finished. 'But where is Bradmore?'

'He is not late, but you are early this once,' I told him, amused by his impatience.

'This is London day! Ah, Jacob, when you know my aunt—'

He raised a finger for silence. The horse was heard crossing the cobbles towards us and a minute later Bradmore pulled back the hood, letting in a crisp new air that made us blink.

'Here, lad, catch hold of this. For you, from my sister.'

I took what he thrust at me. It was a pasty and a piece of cheese, wrapped in a paper.

'Your sister is a true Christian,' said Ferris.

'She is indeed, though it's I that say it.' He laid a jug of ale next us. 'No drinking that on the road, eh, or we shall have spills. She would have fetched you in the house last night, only I told her you were needed out here. "Lord, sister," I said, "they're young men, soldiers. The ground's as good as a feather bed to them."'

Ferris grinned at me.

Bradmore had by now backed the horse between the shafts. His sister came out for a last embrace and kiss before we pulled away to the sound of her little ones crying, 'Farewell, Uncle Harry.' As soon as we were out of their sights, I pissed from the back of the cart, kneeling on the folded-down hood; I had wanted to do this ever since the idea was come to me the day before.

'Pray do not bring your army ways into my aunt's house. Strive to be mannerly,' said Ferris, but he was laughing.

My friend spent the rest of the day in a growing excitement. I envied him, for I could not but compare this innocent happiness with my own guilt and fear that time the New Model came within sight of Mulberry Hill. The land grew flatter as we approached the city; we stopped awhile at a place called Staines, where there was a deal of water, and there we got out to shit and also drank off some of the ale and ate the pasty. After that, Ferris was rapt much of the time, for he began to know the names of the places we passed through. His constant cry to me was, *Jacob, this is such-and-such.* I was at first puzzled, for as we were not in London, I could not see what any of them might be to him, until at last he made me understand that his mother had been born in these parts and that his aunt had often talked thereof.

'She will be glad to know I have seen it,' said he. I turned my head away to hide a smile, for to my mind, there was something very like a boy in this talk.

Towards the end of the afternoon, I did observe something worth noting: the sun, now low and lying behind us, lit up with its red a mighty wall strengthened with towers, which lay some distance off against a blue-black sky.

'What estate is that?' I asked him.

'Is what?'

'The wall. Whose is it?'

He cried, 'A wall?' and I learnt again the excellence of my own sight, for Ferris was unable to distinguish even the towers. His eyes glistened as he said to me, 'That is the city defences.' A look of pride came into his face and he watched me, to see was I as impressed as I ought to be, when he added, 'You know someone who helped make them.'

I was very much minded to humour him, and so cried out, 'Brave Ferris,' upon which he tried to appear as if it were nothing.

'So when was this?' I asked.

'It started three years back, after Turnham Green. It was thought the King would move on the city. First came ditches, and chains against cavalry. We were digging directly, men, women and children – all in a terror – and the fool never came!'

'And was the wall put up then?'

He shook his head. 'It took a year more. First the forts, and then the lines of communication between. It goes all round the city.'

I gasped. 'All round? Every part?'

'Every part. We will go through, and you can see how it is.'

I had remarked in the army how some of the London men would speak of saints, by which they meant the Precisian, or Puritan, citizens, and it struck me how much might be brought about by a people assured of God's favour.

It took us some time to come up to the wall, and this afforded opportunity for as much amazement on my part as he could ever have wished. As we drew nearer, and Ferris saw better, he clutched at my elbow, pointing out a great fort.

'That one is at Hide-Park Corner, Jacob.'

Bradmore here putting in that we would enter near Hide-Park, I thought Ferris would burst from anticipation. We went over a wooden bridge and my friend told me we were crossing the defence ditch. I leant out to see this famous thing, which might be some five yards wide, and one-and-a-half deep, and thought how women pioneers helped dig it. Shortly after, we passed through a gate in the wall.

I could now see the inner part, London itself, and my heart leapt at it. We moved steadily forward, the houses thickening and crowding around the waggon as we went, and Ferris pointed out all the spires against the darkening sky.

'This is Fleet Bridge,' he told me, some time after the houses, together with a certain foulness in the air, had closed all about us.

I saw some pale thing struggle on the black waters of the Fleet.

He went on, 'This place is Ludgate – and there—'

'Paul's Cathedral,' I put in to show my knowledge, which came out of a picture at Beaurepair. To tell the truth, my spirits were oppressed by the vast bulk of this sacred edifice, which reared up to shut off the end of the street. It was hedged about with a scum of other buildings and with petty shacks that had seemingly grown against its sides. Though our picture had shown it standing proud to the eyes of every man in the city, here only a part of it could be seen. I was much struck by the fact that, owing to the narrow ways and penthouses leaning over us, nothing could be seen of the city except what lay nearest to hand; we were forever passing through a tunnel, one where the air was unwholesome.

'We will go to Paul's churchyard for books – see there—' and he pointed out the house of some famous man. Never, not even when he talked once of the great work to be brought about in England, had I seen him so animated.

'I thought you disliked London,' I ventured. 'At least, I am sure you once called it a Sodom of cheating. Did you not?'

'And so it is, yet that's not all – O, Jacob, look—' and he was off again, until Bradmore at last set us down in Cheapside.

Thus we entered in to the City of Saints, or to Sodom, what you will.

PART III

TWELVE

At Liberty

I WAS NOW TO SEE the house where Ferris had lived, the shop (since boarded up) where he had traded in his linen stuffs, and all the things which had made up his life before I knew him. It was also the place, and this I did not forget, where he joined his life with that of Joanna Cooper, and took her into his home and his bed, and watched her die.

I knew this dead wife was with us as soon as he got out of the cart, for he broke off in the middle of a laugh. We trudged along, sore and stiff in the chill darkness, until Ferris stopped, saying simply, 'This is our house,' but he turned straightway to the one opposite, and I saw another face, boiling with some inner hatred, bubble up through his own. My friend stood silent, fixed, as I hopped from foot to foot in the cold.

'Don't offer yourself as a spectacle.' I plucked at his shirtsleeve to get him away. He gasped and I realised he had been holding his breath.

'Aye.' That was all he said. He permitted me to lead him to his aunt's door.

She came to answer the knock herself, tall and thin and upright, leaning forward in the dark to see who we might be. She held a taper, and I saw her mouth twist as the rays fell on his torn cheek; then, wasting no words but gathering him to her breast like a mother, she half dragged, half carried him inside.

I followed them up the stairs and saw my friend pushed into a chair. His aunt bent forward and fingered the scar, moaning; when he flinched she snatched her hand back as if burnt. As for Ferris, he seemed struck dumb; but I saw that he was trying not to weep.

The aunt at last noticed me, pressed my hands and bade me make myself at home. I was unwilling to sit, being all bloody and stinking, but she would have me do it nonetheless. The warmth of the fire was so grateful that I shed a few tears of my own, even without an aunt to bring them on.

'Blue with cold, not so much as a coat, where's your coat?' she wailed, chafing his arms.

'I lost it,' said Ferris.

The maid was shouted for and ordered to boil water, bring victuals, lay fires, open some wine, make the beds and prepare simples for mending the skin, all at once; she shrugged and said she would do what she could with one body, and would first bring something for washing hands, and after, food and drink. She seemed not to know Ferris, nor he her.

Warm water arrived, and a cloth. The aunt said nothing when, wiping our hands and faces, we turned the linen from white to black. Soon after, the girl brought up food: some mutton, pickles, wine, and for bread a fine white manchet. I saw her look at me sideways in going out.

We swallowed down the meat as fast as our knives could cut it. Ferris said, 'Aunt, you have brought me back to life. Jacob too, see how he eats.'

The aunt scolded him for teasing a guest. I tried to chew more daintily and take smaller draughts of wine, but my belly cried out so loud that politeness was deafened. Besides, I had remarked that Ferris ate as greedily as I.

'We are a brutish, filthy pair,' he said.

She replied, 'I kept all your clothes, Christopher.'

I started to hear his given name.

'They'll be too small for your friend, but Joseph's coats may do for him. We must get you washed and something clean on your backs.'

'Before we make the whole place lousy,' said Ferris. He spoke through a mouthful of mutton, and smiled on her with wet shining eyes.

'Rebecca is heating the water,' said the aunt. 'I'll have it put in your chamber, and a fire lit, and one for – I beg pardon, sir.'

'Jacob Cullen,' I told her, glad to lay Rupert in his grave.

'I'll have a room warmed for you, Mr Cullen, and some water taken up.' She eyed my empty plate and pushed the dish of meat towards me.

'You are too kind, Madam.' Though somewhat ashamed, I could not stop eating. It was more than I could do to rein it in.

When we had finished she led us in a prayer thanking God for our safe homecoming. I bowed my head and wondered if God might indeed look lovingly on me.

Ferris was first to go up and wash. His aunt sat gazing at me with her hands perched in her lap, her eyes eager as a young girl's.

'How did you get here?'

'On a carpet.'

She laughed, shaking her head. 'But come, tell me! Have you walked?'

'A carter brought us privily away.'

Her face fell. 'Privily—? You're not in disgrace?'

I shook my head. 'He was sick of it.' That 'in disgrace' of hers, after the brutal victory we had won, touched me by its innocence.

'They say it's almost over,' she went on. 'One time all the men and boys were crazy to go out, now folk are thinking more of the peace.'

'Mmm.' That would be the folk who had had a taste.

'Were you at Naseby-Fight, Mister Cullen?'

'Ferris was there.'

'And was that where he got his wound?'

'No, Winchester. Mine was at Basing-House.'

'Yours?' She got up and came over to me; I lifted the hair from my brow and saw her stiffen.

'You must suffer greatly!' she cried.

'Not so very much. There are cuts in the thigh pain me worse.'

I saw her eyes travel down my body until she came to the blackish blood congealing on my breeches. Her hand went to her mouth. 'Lord have mercy on us! The surgeon shall come tomorrow.'

'I think,' I said, remembering the army surgeons, 'that if the wounds were but washed, and cleanly dressed, they would do very well.'

She promised to give me an excellent healing ointment she had.

'And were the battles so savage as they say?' she asked.

'Christopher will have much to tell you,' I said. 'I would not spoil anything he wished to relate by saying it before he has the chance.'

She nodded and said she would leave me in order to look me out some clothing.

After she went I must have dozed, for I jumped as Ferris came back into the room, translated from soldier to merchant. The garments hung loose from his bones, but he was otherwise the picture of a citizen, right to the deep white collar. A sobersides. I stared at this man who like me had lived a life before the two of us had met up in the army. His hair shone; only the slashed face and coarsened hands suggested he had ever done aught but fold cloth and count gold. The hands would soften again, the scar fade. I could see him calling at Beaurepair to pay his respects to My Lady. She would have despised him – and perhaps ordered me to wait on him.

He smiled uncertainly, gathering up the loose folds of his clothing. 'Look here. The army has eaten me.'

'You'll put on flesh,' I said.

I went up next. The aunt showed me to a room where the girl had already laid a fire and made up the bed. She was, I thought, worth her wages, but then London people were said to be very yare and sharp, able to draw and roast a fowl before a countryman could catch it.

There were towels by the tub of hot water, and a lavender washball. When I stripped off, the clothes were stuck to me in places, and crusted with other people's pain as well as my own. I laid them in a heap and once off my body they looked like beggar's rags. I scraped the washball over me and rubbed at the blood and sweat as best I could. The water ran red as it came out of my hair, and my feet were in a sorry condition, blistered thick. I went on scrubbing till my skin was sore, taking off the army along with the filth, except for those tender wounded places where I dreaded skinning myself yet again.

The knuckles itched as I put my hands in and out of the hot water. When I had soaked and dabbed away the crust on my thigh, I saw that the cuts were as I had thought, not green or stinking but in a fair way to heal if only my blood-stiffened breeches were no longer pressing on them. That was great good fortune, and I again gave thanks to God. It might be that in His mercy He still valued my filthy soul, and would not cast me off just yet.

I ran my hands over my body, wanting to know what I was become. Like Ferris, I was thinner, but dense and tough like hardened wood. There were small cuts and bruises everywhere, but these hardly counted beside the real trophies of the assault. My forehead was ridged under my fingers: I would let my hair grow now. Standing up to dry myself, I felt the wounds sting.

The aunt had laid me out some clothes belonging to her dead Joseph, and with a little dragging at the buttons I was able to make them go on, though I feared they might give at the seams. Especially welcome were the hose. Though I had to put my feet back into the same old boots, they seemed less cruel now they no longer pinched my bare flesh.

I had often remarked that new attire renders the wearer uncommonly happy, foolishly happy, for the gloss soon wears off and the man knows that it must be so. Despite my moralising, this was also the case with me. When I came down both Ferris and the aunt admired me in the husband's garments, she saying that it was good to see them being worn and not eaten by the moths, Ferris that all I needed now was shoes. His face glistened with something oily which the aunt had spread on the injured cheek. She came to me and daubed some of it on my forehead also. It hurt, and smelt bitter, but her hand was gentle on me and felt like love.

'He has thigh wounds,' said Ferris.

The aunt said that she knew it, and offered to dress them, but I did not like to give her that work and said I could very well do it myself.

'Then you must take some of this unguent to your chamber,' she told me. 'Becs shall tear you some linen strips.'

Ferris was not as happy in his own clothes as I was in another's.

I observed that he drooped his head, that he fiddled with the cold mutton bone and looked into the fire. His aunt watched him gravely and bade him go to bed if he wished, there would be time aplenty to give her his news.

'Do you have my packet still?' he asked.

'Of course. I'll fetch it.' She hurried out.

I asked Ferris what packet that might be.

He answered, 'Things I asked her to keep.'

The aunt returned with some objects tied up in cloth. Ferris put the bundle on the table and began tearing at the ribbon. The first thing he revealed was a heap of white linen, which I supposed to be padding: however, he laid it aside with great care, and I saw it was a woman's nightgown, richly embroidered. Next came a gold case on a chain: he opened this up and stared into it as a man might gaze into a necromancer's mirror. I strained to see it.

'Here,' he said abruptly and tossed it across the table. It struck against the wood, and I wondered he was not more careful, for it was very prettily enamelled.

'Take care, Christopher!' said his aunt, sounding as if she were more afraid for him than at any hurt which should come to the jewel.

It was a pair of miniatures. On the left, a joyous Ferris I had rarely seen, full of defiance too: I would have wagered my life it was painted on the occasion of the marriage. The lips were parted as if to speak, the eyes full open and very straight at the onlooker: a man saying what he liked, to whom he liked.

On the right, his Joanna. She took me unawares. For one thing, she was beautiful, with brown eyes and fine golden hair not unlike Caro's, where I had pictured her sallow and plain. But while Caro's glance was sometimes mocking, Joanna's were the eyes of a saint. I had seen just such a look at Basing, on the face of Christ's mother as her portrait blackened and shrivelled on the bonfire. As I closed the case, folding their miniatures together, she turned her pure gaze on her husband before her lips were pressed to his. I pictured their images forever kissing within.

'Aunt painted them,' said Ferris. I glanced up in surprise.

She nodded and smiled. 'My mother was a limner before me.

There was a man-limner in our district too, a very handsome one; he ruined a silly lass whose parents left the two alone. That brought *us* a deal of trade.'

'Not from the married women, however,' Ferris put in. '*They* found him a master of his art—' he caught and kissed his aunt's hand as she made to slap him, 'practised and cunning in his technique.'

'A very loving gift,' I said, turning the case about. 'And skilled.'

'So I think.' Ferris got up and put his arms round her neck. 'She's my mother and my father too,' he said. His aunt closed her eyes, resting her cheek on his arm.

I said, 'You're lucky to have her.'

He started. 'Jacob! Forgive me! You said once you would tell me your story after the siege, and we have never talked.'

'Any time for that,' I said.

Ferris turned to his aunt. 'Jacob lost his wife too.'

'Well, you're both of you fine young men,' she said. 'And if a body may say so – without seeming hard – you'll marry again.'

'*You* didn't, Aunt.' Ferris kneaded her hands. 'Did you grieve for him a long time?'

She laughed. 'Well, we weren't like you. Your grandfather chose for me – though yes, I was sorry when Joseph died. Yes.'

They regarded one another an instant.

'But I've no call for a new husband. Besides, he'd cut you out of my money.' She wrapped her arms round him, and squeezed. Ferris remained solemn. The aunt went on, 'I had never such grief as you, and provided you outlive me, I never will.' She turned to me. 'He didn't eat for a week or sleep for a month. The minister could do nothing. But I wouldn't let go of his soul. I hung on to him.'

'The minister upbraided her, for being soft with me when I should be learning Christian resignation,' Ferris said.

'He thought it right, child.'

They swayed back and forth, rocking in love. I remembered how Izzy and I would press our faces together, reconciled. Did we learn it from Mother? I could not recall.

'Never was a better husband than you,' said the aunt softly to my friend. 'And be assured she knew it. *Knows* it still, in Heaven.' She kissed his hair. 'And now mayhap you should go to bed, that's enough for your poor friend to listen to for one night.'

I knew what was wanted and said I would go to my chamber. The aunt pressed the bottle of oily medicine into my hand and called to the maid, bidding her take up some linen strips torn large enough to bind a leg.

I found my room pleasantly warmed by the coal fire and an embroidered nightshirt of Joseph's laid ready. The maid knocked and entered with the strips, bidding me a good night as she went out. The nightshirt just fitted. I smeared the stuff over my cut thigh, feeling the wounds burn, and tied the bandage round it. Then I got between the sheets and stretched myself out in the shape of an X, arching with pleasure to feel the fresh lavender-scented linen on clean skin. My flesh felt heavy and supple as if dropping off my bones, and I fell asleep straightway without hearing the other two come upstairs.

~

The next day I woke early. I had none of the pain in my hips that had plagued me in the army and the warm bed was unspeakably comforting after lying out, cold and wet, under the sky: I rolled and wallowed, the very picture of sloth. Despite this appearance I was full of vigour, so that when I heard people stirring in the house, I dressed and went downstairs. There I found Ferris's aunt inspecting some wine bottles. Her eyes gleamed as she looked up at me, and I saw that any friend of 'Christopher' must be a favourite.

'We will celebrate all the time you are here,' she said excitedly. She was dressed in a plain dark robe, but her face shone with anticipation. It seemed not all citizens were gloomy.

'I'll bring you some breakfast,' she went on.

'After bad rations or none,' I said, 'good things to eat. A Paradise.'

'Then be happy in it.' She bustled off, and as she opened the door onto the stairs there came a clattering noise: the girl already cooking, down below. I had suddenly a great longing to see Ferris and talk to him, get used to his new ways, old ways. I climbed the stairs to his chamber, the one at the front where he had slept with Joanna, and tapped at the door.

'Ferris?'

Silence. I opened the chamber door and put in my head.

'Ferris, we're all dressed, I would talk with you. Will you come down?' On his not replying I walked over to the bed, parted the hangings and reached with my fingers towards his face in the dark. I touched nothing but linen. Jolted, I ran my hand over the coverlet: it was entirely flat. A thought came to me. I felt between the sheets: they were warm, and on sniffing the pillow, I found the scent of his hair. Then he must have got downstairs without my knowing it, and be at this moment talking to Aunt (for I was already permitted that familiarity, to call her by that name). But when I got down again I found a bowl of caudle on the table, Aunt sitting by the fire, and no Ferris.

'Christopher's not in his bed,' I said to her.

'Ah.' She looked down at the tiled floor. 'He'll be gone to the grave.'

'What, before daybreak?'

But she was right. He came in, damp and cold, while I was finishing up the caudle. His aunt bade him sit by the fire, but he came and sat opposite me.

'I'll get you some food,' she said, 'and if you don't want to see me in a passion, you'll eat it. It's too cold to go trailing around in the dew.' She laid her hand on his head and went out; I waited, hoping he would speak. He stared through me as he had done the night I woke him with Nathan. A bird called outside, over and over.

'Ferris,' I said.

The bird continued to call as he slowly raised his hands and covered his face from me. Then he got up from the table and went back upstairs. I heard the slam of his chamber door.

~

He was gentle with me that autumn, and on some days cheerful, but mostly there was a melancholy in him replaced the satire I had seen in Ferris the soldier. I came by degrees to see how, fleeing the solitary bed he had once shared with Joanna, he was run into the New Model – and how, the army having beaten him back at last, he was come home only to find himself still raw. Not even I could look on him and be jealous. Jacob Cullen was patient! – and I think I loved him during those months as I never loved friend before or since.

He would walk each day, saying it helped him sleep, and I more often than not went with him. I took great pleasure in learning the names of the buildings, which were the most noted and so on. The tailor who came to measure us had told me that if I cared to call at his establishment I might see there a rare piece of work, a suit worked in slashed and perfumed leather, ornamented in gold. I did call to see it, and it was precisely as he had said, nay, more wonderful. Like all tailors, goldsmiths and suchlike he had a sharp eye for who held the purse, and had understood that Ferris paid for my garments. He could not have judged me likely to bespeak such a thing as a suit in leather; I could only think he was so proud of the craftsmanship, he must needs show it everybody. I told Ferris of this marvel, asking him what else was to be seen, and he showed me the fashionable streets: not only his own Cheapside, where the costly gloves and hose astonished me, but the Strand, Paternoster Row and Cordwainer Street.

Ferris made faces, gasping and gaping in imitation of my lumpkin ways. 'I never thought you would be so taken with these vanities,' he said. 'Are you pining after ribbons and feathers?'

I laughed and said it was only that everything was new to me. He took me another time to London Bridge, and when I was several times gone up and down, jostling in the crowd and half drunk on the fascination of the place, he told me there were dead men's heads there, stuck on poles.

The weather was notably foul that year and we often talked of the men still fighting, their trials and victories. Ferris fretted at times about Nathan, whom he now wished he had brought away, and I bore with that too. By mid-November he had long since told his aunt everything of his own campaign days that he thought fit for her to hear, and delighted in bringing back news from others. Any little thing about the Parliament or the latest fortunes of the army he picked up for her instruction or amusement, and with his natural courtesy got a great deal from the most unlikely men. In this way, he found near the end of November that Colonel Robert Blake had the Royalist Francis Wyndham under siege in Dunster Castle.

'I had it from a fishmonger,' he told Aunt as soon as we got home. 'A letter came from his brother but yesterday.'

'I never heard tell of Dunster. Would that be Devonshire?' she asked.

'Somersetshire. The West is all but fallen.'

Aunt offered up thanks, and in the same breath a plea that the war might soon be over.

However, I discovered he did not tell her of all his encounters. One day as we were turning out of Cheapside at the very start of our stroll, I saw an erect, dignified old man coming towards us, wearing a dark blue coat and red plumes in his hat. He saw Ferris in the very instant that Ferris saw him, and at once turned down an alleyway. My friend immediately walked faster and turned down the alleyway likewise.

'Who is that? What are you doing?' I asked. Ferris marched at such a pace as to make my legs ache though they were longer than his. The greybeard knew we were following him, for though he did not run, yet he walked so fast that his back rocked from side to side. My friend loped along, relishing the chase.

'Ferris, for the love of Christ!' I cried. Our quarry must have heard me, for he stepped out even faster and I saw Ferris's face set like a dog's just before it fights. I thought to catch him by the sleeve, but he must have sensed it in me, for he straightway broke into a run. I was not going to do the same, but instead stayed behind to see what would follow. What did follow staggered me. My friend ran past the old man – who flinched as he went by – and whipped round to stand in front of him, barring the way. At this the fellow turned, and saw me still bringing up the rear. He stopped dead. Then Ferris ran up to him and spat hard in his face. Not a word was spoken. My friend backed away, still glowering at the enemy, and circled round to me. The man made no protest. Wiping his mouth and lurching a little to one side, he scuttled through an archway and was gone.

Ferris glared up into my eyes as he rejoined me. I had seen that look before, when he dared me to break him of having friends, and the questions died on my tongue. We continued in silence until we were almost at London Wall, when I halted and put out my hand so that he stopped also. Both of us were hot and breathing fast.

'I know not what to think,' I said. 'Who—?'

'Mister Cooper.' He spat again, on the ground this time, and slowly walked on. I followed, beginning to understand the speed with which the elder had taken to his heels upon seeing us.

'You go for him whenever you meet?'

He said nothing but the set of his shoulders told me I had guessed right.

'He is old, Ferris. Death will level him soon. Why should—'

'It pleases me,' he said stonily.

'But how did you marry his daughter if—'

'Not then, you fool! *Then* I had to be meek, so I could get her away.'

I remembered the bold stare of his portrait. Perhaps Aunt had painted him not as he was, but as he longed to be.

'Her death freed me from that,' he added.

'Should you not try to practise forgiveness? For your own sake,' I added hastily, for his eyes sharpened as if I were Cooper himself.

Ferris snorted. 'You weary me, Jacob, and you are the last man on earth who should preach forgiveness. When did you ever stop at spitting!'

I was afraid to go on. Yet when we got back to Cheapside, he squeezed my hand and entered the house without even a scowl at the windows opposite, his humour seemingly purged. Aunt, who was cutting up some cabbages within, remarked on our glowing cheeks and said our walk had surely been healthful. Ferris said it had been most enjoyable, and Jacob's conversation as good as a sermon.

~

'Farming's like the army,' I said. Ferris and I were sitting at the table, face to face in unalterable opposition. 'Graft every day, the ground muddy except when it is hard, sweat, shit and injury.' The idea of field labour filled me with dread, for besides knowing what suffering it brought, I was now enamoured of London.

'Under a taskmaster, yes,' Ferris said. 'But there will be none such in the colony. We will be our own men.'

'The earth's your taskmaster,' I retorted. 'The cruellest.'

It was our constant quarrel. This friend of mine, so gently raised and so utterly ignorant, was wild to get away the following spring and dig the commons, an idea he had long debated even before his army days. In vain did I endeavour to impress upon him what had been ground into my bones while I was still a child: the stubbing up, burning, ploughing, harrowing, planting, hoeing and dunging; the war against crows, snails, blight and whatnot which brought such weariness that no bed could be too hard; and then the back-breaking Harvest when the workers went on until there was no more light. I told him how I had seen men drop to the stubble and sleep without food or covering. My breath was entirely thrown away, for Ferris saw only the means of a glorious triumph. Smiling, he assured me that he took good care to school himself. Did he not study his Gervase Markham and his other writers?

'Let Markham persuade you if I cannot!' I cried exasperated. 'If there be any truth in the man, read only what he puts as to digging, setting aside the rest. It is slavery! I wager you *anything* that on that point your author chimes with me.'

Ferris said that a man of my size had surely endurance enough.

He had friends of a like mind, most of them as unskilled as himself and as full of these madcap notions. They would come and drink wine and scribble on little papers. To Jeremiah Andrews, a gardener wizened as one of his own apples, who like me had some conception of men's daily fight with the land, I could listen without too great a trespass on my patience. But then there was that great fool Roger Rowly, a journeyman tailor whose own breeches were wearing out at the arse from a lifetime's sitting. *He* deemed it no hardship to plough, scatter, build, harvest, do everything ourselves, and the women, for all I could tell, to give birth in the open fields.

One day he talked of digging turf.

'That takes more strength than any of you reckon on,' I said.

'We can't all be pikemen,' Ferris put in, so that the others laughed.

Recalling how often my temper had shamed me, I calmed myself and went on, 'Men can only endure such toil if they know nought else.'

'We can learn to labour if we have to,' insisted Rowly, who looked about strong enough to lift needle and thread.

'Our people put us to better trades,' I urged.

They were completely deaf to me, and for the rest of that afternoon I held my tongue.

Another time, when we were joined by Harry and Elizabeth Beste, I gained more support. These two had three small children, one still at suck. Like Ferris, they had read and been fired by writings that claimed men might work the common land, and so live free; unlike Ferris, they could see shadow as well as sun.

'While we are building, the babes may fall ill,' said Elizabeth. 'They need warmth.' Her husband nodded. Rowly was there also, and he raised his eyes to Heaven but to no avail, for these two were respected. Elizabeth was comely, with a skin so white the veins showed blue on her forehead, and thick hair like dull gold. She had a deep soft voice which soothed quarrels and gave hope, and her husband, who was a blacksmith, also spoke softly but was so big about the arms that not even I would willingly have fought him. Harry's eyelids drooped, giving him a lazy look, but he was more wide awake than most.

Now Rowly was talking of strolling women and their children, the living proof (he said) that babes could lie out in the cold provided only they kept close to the mother. I said that grown men had found it hard enough in the army and challenged Ferris to deny this, which he could not.

'It blights the little ones,' said Elizabeth. 'Vagabond women have thin and ugly children.'

'I hope—' I said, and broke off. The rest stared at me.

'Go on, where are you now?' asked Ferris.

I saw Caro trudging forward, over mud, through snow. By now, if my seed had rooted in her, she would be heavy with child. 'I consider that a woman – a woman without shelter—' I stopped, for to my surprise and horror my voice was thickening. There was silence. Ferris seemed eating me up with his eyes.

'Pray excuse me.' I walked out and up to my chamber, tears already slipping onto the boards as I climbed the stairs.

Like Ferris, I had a ghost-wife. Our talk, so like the meetings at Beaurepair, had called this ghost to table with us, and the mention of vagabond women had finally given her flesh. During those weeks of lying in the rain I had more than once wondered if Caro lay cold and wet likewise, and each time I had hardened my heart. Now was the reckoning. I wept with the abandon of one who can make no restitution, and after sprawled on the mattress watching the sky grow dark.

At last I heard their farewell calls and laughs far below. He came upstairs at once and tapped at the door.

'Come in.'

Ferris entered with a candlestick which he placed on the mantelpiece before seating himself on the edge of my bed. 'So. Who is she?'

'You know.'

'Do you fear she is dead, Jacob?' Ferris took my hand between his; I let it lie in his grasp.

My voice sounded cold as I answered, 'She was half naked, travelling the roads.'

'And you must not be found,' he squeezed my fingers, 'else you would write and enquire?'

'We are wanted for theft.' As soon as the words were out I remembered Fat Tommy's big mouth. 'And I killed a – a man. In self-defence. He went for me in the dark.'

Ferris's eyes held mine. 'It seems scarce justice to be hunted for that when the whole country's at it.'

'She's most likely dead.'

'I fear you are right.' Sighing, he again pressed my hand. 'Will I ever hear the whole of this tale?'

I shook my head.

'Come down.' He loosed my fingers and felt in his sleeve for a handkerchief, which he held out to me. 'My aunt is back and it's much warmer than up here.'

I blew my nose with an ugly farting sound. 'What was decided after I left?'

'O, the usual, to put by money until we could agree what to do with it.' He smiled ruefully. 'We need more people.'

'More women,' I suggested.

Ferris raised his eyebrows. 'Aye, why not! Are you looking to remarry, Jacob?'

'I meant, bring in men with wives. It's not to be the army again, is it?'

'But *do* you want to remarry?'

'Not yet. And how can I?'

'These are strange times,' said Ferris. 'There'll be thousands disappeared, not known for dead. Folk must live.'

We went downstairs.

~

Ferris was not the only one musing over my right to marry. Sometime in early December I noticed that the maidservant, Rebecca, had a liking for my company. She was eager to bring in the breakfast to me, and would stand watching me eat, asking me was it good, and so forth. At these times she looked keenly into my face, her voice taking on a curve that flattened out entirely when she spoke to Ferris or his aunt. I was flattered and amused by this humble courtship but hoped for her sake she would soon cool, for though she was not an ill-looking girl, black hair and clear pale flesh, she stirred me not a whit. She could have come to my bed – well, perhaps not. At any rate, I was courteous with her, but never more, and she neither took offence nor grew bolder. My hair was growing back, and Aunt said I was handsome in a gypsy sort of way, and all this puffed up my vanity. Thus all of us went on peaceably enough until we came to the Eve of Our Lord's birth.

THIRTEEN

Eve of Nativity

'WHAT, JACOB, up early again?'

Sitting alone, I shrugged and smiled as Aunt came in. The windowpanes, entirely black, reflected my candle flame in their magician's mirror. Aunt put down her candle next to mine, and the window caught that flame too, and doubled it, so that there were four. She sat down beside me in the kindness of their yellow glow.

A silence followed. We needed few words, being easy with one another. Looking at her, I thought she must have been comely once, with her nephew's light hair and clear eyes, but time had creased and dried her blondeness into sand.

'Rebecca shall bring some caudle.' She knew I could not get enough of this broth, which I had never tasted before coming to town. Leaving the light for me, she went to tell the girl; I stayed, watching the flames jiggle and then draw themselves up into white-gold angels.

The room where I sat so idle and somewhat melancholy was comfortable, with that solid plainness which is commonly called 'Dutch' and breathing the cleanliness of that people also. Black and white tiles on the floor, dark cases full of godly books. I had searched in vain for those pamphlets of which Ferris had boasted.

Over the fire was a painting of the late Joseph Snapman, whose sober dress, like that of a minister, could not disguise his sharp, busy face. Aunt, as his widow, owned the house outright. Her sister Kate Tuke had married Mister Henry Ferris, but they both died of the plague when their boy was but two years old, so little Christopher came to live with the childless Sarah and Joseph. In their house he grew to manhood and took a wife; from their house he left for the wars.

Soon after Rebecca had brought me my broth I heard him banging down the stairs. By that time, I had grasped that whereas I was either asleep or awake, Ferris passed some time in twilight before and after sleep, a kind of living ghost, and it was thus that I had seen him – eyes open, mind shut – that night with Nathan. He was clumsy in the mornings and had once fallen down the stairwell, crying out with the fright of it. Now he trod heavily and scuffed the door open with his foot.

'Good day, Rupert,' he said, and shambled away.

I called, 'Ferris? Will you not take anything?'

He came back, sheepish, saying, 'Be so good as to ask Becs for a bit of bread,' before disappearing again.

'Ferris! Come back!'

In the end I followed him downstairs. He was in the back room, shivering in his shirtsleeves.

'Would you help me get this clear, Jacob?'

I saw a machine half buried in firewood, broken crates and soiled ends of cloth. These we pulled off, and I saw that it was a press. I had only seen them in pictures before. At once I felt my ignorance, for I could not even guess which part of it to hold.

Ferris noticed my look. 'You'd like to learn?'

'Very much.' I walked around it trying to see how the different pieces went together. Ferris found a skin bag and inside it a clout which he stroked over the metal parts, sighing to find so many rust spots. The stink of pig grease filled the room.

'It's too damp,' he remarked, 'but there's nowhere else. Look here,' and he pulled up a greenish stack of paper. I took the mouldering mass in my hands and read, *On the True Brotherhood of Men.* As I opened it the top sheet of the pamphlet flipped away and went whirling to the floor. Inside I read an address to the Members of Parliament exhorting them to grant every poor man or woman a cottage, pig and cow and four acres of land. It was dated 1643, and signed *A Friend to England's Freedom.*

Ferris laughed. 'You didn't believe me, eh? But come, I'm starving hungry,' and he led me upstairs again.

Rebecca brought in some rolls for both of us and a jug of beer. I said, 'Thank you,' and tried not to look at her. Ferris chattered on like a natural, holding his roll in a napkin so as not to get pig's grease on it.

'Won't you wash your hands?' I hinted.

'O it's not worth it, I'll be back there directly – we can get sowing by the spring, if there be enough of us, that means starting now and selling them from the house, but wait, there's a bookseller at Paul's takes pamphlets—'

He dropped crumbs on the table, picked them up with the point of his tongue. Rebecca stared at him and he began to snort with laughter, spraying the bread out again. 'You'll not tell Aunt, will you Becs? What a pig I was? Jacob's no pig, is he Becs?'

The girl flushed and walked out.

'What ails her?' cried Ferris.

'What is become of your discernment?' I asked hotly. I was embarrassed for the girl, and for myself.

'What, you and Becs—!' He was merry in disbelief, but then he saw my face and stopped. We stared at one another, and I thought there was displeasure in the look he gave me.

After this the rest of the day held something of an edge. I relished it notwithstanding, for it was new to me to celebrate *Nativity* and not *Christmas*, and to be a guest instead of waiting on others. I helped Aunt, was especially kind to Rebecca (though this might not be wisdom, still the girl's blushes merited gentleness) and made small talk with neighbours who came to give the compliments of the season, viz. to gossip. I learnt that Mister Cooper was selling up, perhaps weary of dodging Ferris in the street. Not a single visitor arrived drunk, and I wondered if the Roches could have recognised the religious feast at all.

Ferris mostly avoided the company. He scrabbled about in the back room, coming out covered with grease. From time to time he would look in, bow and smile, but decline to shake hands on account of being 'all over muck'. The visitors seemed a little offended, and indeed I think I would have been, in their place. They departed with much dignity, sighing out their wishes that the young master might live to be the man his uncle was.

'They have never understood him,' his aunt said. 'Up and down! Up and down!' she went on, as his feet shook the stairs.

Ferris was straightway back again, wiping his hands on a linen napkin. 'The press is not too stiff—'

'Christopher!' His aunt snatched the cloth from him.

'O, I'll make good whatever I spoil. Let's kiss and be friends,' and he hugged her to him in a bear dance. Then, without a word to me, he was out of the door again.

'Did you ever see such maggots!' But she was laughing. 'He hardly knows we're here,' she said. 'He was just this way as a child, charging about . . .'

She was delighted to see him less melancholy, let the neighbours say what they would.

My own feelings were not so happy. There is a very particular way that a man looks upon another who has just disgusted him. He feels the eruption of hatred from within, and you may even see him place his hand on heart or belly as if to support the body against the scalding of the spirit. Yet at the same time no movement, paling or even breath of the other escapes notice, and the loathed object is seen vilely *revealed* as if on the Day of Judgement. I had shivered at Ferris's expression when I tried to drive away his friends, for he had looked at me as if my whole life lay open to him and he found it an ugly spectacle. I had also received other kinds of looks: Caro's promise of herself, Nat's stupid gratitude, the crooked smile Ferris had worn when I gave him the *Loyaute* glass, even the dog's gaze that Rebecca fixed on me while I was eating. None of these served as preparation for the way that Ferris left without seeing me. I was become nothing but the audience to his play, and had not felt so discounted since I jumped to the orders of Mervyn Roche.

Aunt looked over at me sitting by the fire and seated herself nearby. 'It won't last,' she said. 'He'll weary himself.'

'Why is he so – so—?'

'O, because it's Nativity tomorrow, I guess. It's a cruel season for a man who's lost his wife. He's killing the hours.'

'Will he really use the press?'

'Why not? He knows how. Go down to him if you wish; I have Becs for company.'

I stayed where I was. If he asked me to help, I would gladly do so, but I would not lie ready to his hand. A tool can be used, a man must be asked.

We had supper: boiled salt pork, pickled cabbage and cider followed by stewed apple. Ferris scarce spoke, and when Rebecca put the dish of apples on the table he jumped. Since he did not serve himself, Aunt set out some fruit for him. 'These apples have kept well,' she said to me. 'They are our own, from the courtyard.'

'Ginger,' murmured Ferris.

I watched him eat. His face was heated, perhaps from the spice, and he lifted the apple absently to his lips. His eyes were not on us but on the future. Before Aunt or myself had half finished, he dropped his spoon *clack* into the dish and rose to leave.

'Will you not stay and talk with us?' his aunt demanded. 'It is almost Nativity.'

'When will the press be ready?' I asked cunningly.

He sat down again. 'It is not too rusted. I've got all the letters cleaned and polished. You can be my crophead prentice.'

'To do what?'

'O, set up the type. You'll learn to read backwards.'

'I meant, what are we going to print?'

'I told you! To draw like-minded men together – women too—'

Aunt's face darkened. 'What, Christopher, are you still talking of leaving here?'

'I have to, Aunt, it's all I've wanted since I joined the army. The New Jerusalem.'

I sighed and covered my eyes.

Ferris stamped back down the stairs to his press.

'You know,' I said to Aunt, 'if he wishes to break virgin ground, he should be at it *now*. Better wait another year and plough in good time.'

She chewed on a thumbnail. 'He can't wait to leave me.'

'I've never seen him like this,' I told her. 'He's not the same man.'

'That's what it does.'

'Excitement?'

'Drink.'

I stared at her.

'Couldn't you smell it on him?'

We went down together. He was bending over the machine as I had once seen him crouch over a pot of beans, and made a feint of not seeing us. That was like the army too, when I waited by the fire for him. So much of a man is wasted, I thought, wasted on the watch for that look which says, *Welcome, at last.*

The empty bottle was lying just inside the door, and a freshly opened one under the press. Aunt seized it straight off. 'You're never going to finish this?'

He stood up as if he would bandy words with her, but she at once cut in, as if speaking to a young boy. 'You'll hurt yourself fooling with a press drunk.'

'I know what I do,' Ferris said.

She took both bottles away without further talk. Her nephew sat down on the dirty floor and sighed.

'Why don't you leave it until after the holiday?' I coaxed him. 'Two days is nothing.'

'I want to get started.'

'Yes, but two days?'

'I want—' and then he choked. I thought, *Out it comes*, but he was not sick of the drink. He seemed to be crying. I stepped towards him and he turned away from me.

'Why don't you go to bed?' I asked. 'I'll get Rebecca to put the warming pan in for you.'

He shook his head.

'Your aunt fears for you, Ferris.'

At this he turned to me, blinking. The tears, if tears there had been, were already dried. I led him back to the upstairs room, he kicking the stairtreads as we went, I wondering if this would now be the pattern of our life. He swayed into a chair and sat quietly by the fire while the bed was being warmed.

'Are you sick at all?'

'No. Now sneck up! You're worse than Aunt.'

I dropped the hand I had offered to him and when the girl came to say the bed was heated, I let him fumble his way up the next flight of stairs alone.

'How did he get like that?' Rebecca asked me, hearing him thud on the boards above us. A slam informed us he had dropped onto the bed if not beneath the coverlet.

I shrugged. 'The usual way. Best keep the cellar locked.'

'What, will he go on like it?'

'How should I know?'

She took a long look at my countenance and went, '*Pfui!*' evidently taking me for an unfeeling friend. If only I were Nathan, who in pain shows so soft and tender: misery only renders my face more rigid. And yet just then I could have wept and had she but given me *one word* of kindness I would have put my head on her breast like a babe. God alone knows what might have been the sequel, so perhaps He hardened her heart against me. Aunt came back from the cellar and I told her Ferris was abed.

'He's not taken so much, only the bottles we found,' she said. 'Here, help me finish it.' She banged down the opened bottle, and two goblets, in front of me.

It was good wine, and I said so. She told me it was from Ferris's own cellar. 'The wines weren't sold off, he gave them to me.'

'So can you lock them from him?'

'Whether I can or not, I have done so.'

We sat drinking and watching the fire, and O, the gentle song of comfort the drink set up in my soul, *Suffer no more*, so that I very well understood its charm. My eyes began to feel sore and red as if I had been in a smoky tavern.

'Will you go with him into the country?' Aunt asked me.

'If need be. He'll never make a farmer.'

'I don't know,' she said. 'He seems to get no further forward here. If he is going to drink, then best he go.'

The sand of her cheeks glistened. I gently pressed my palm onto her fingers, all knotty with their stiff bones and raised veins: the coarse, honest fingers of one who has always worked. That razor, pity, began chivvying in my breast. And as always, I felt myself a poor comforter. After a while I kissed the sad hand and walked up to bed. The stairs were unsteady beneath my feet, and in my room I felt the walls drag after me as I turned about.

~

I was fighting for my life with a cruel yellow beast somehow got into my chamber. It ran over the walls and across the ceiling, talons skittering, and its cry was the savage mating call of cats on a summer night. I knew it for an emissary of the Devil, waiting for me to sleep in order to smother me. At last I griped it by the tail, and having forced it to the window, dropped it out there. I saw it shatter to powder on the cobbles, but turning back to my bed I found someone in it, evidently dead, for all was bound up tightly in cerements, even the features. I was now grown young and called out for my mother but Caro came in instead, dressed in her bridal gown, and said that the dead man was Zebedee. I knew at once he was all corruption under the graveclothes. She began to unwrap the face, continuing though I screamed at her to stop. I covered my own face so as not to see. Then Isaiah (who like Caro was of full mature size though I seemed much smaller) came up behind me and, with a strength he never possessed in life, tore my protecting hands from my eyes and forced me over to the bed saying Zeb had been killed in a weapons drill. Still I kept my eyes shut but soon felt his fingers plucking at them and screamed for Mother and Father and his nails now began to dig as if they would blind me and when I next tried to scream my tongue was dry and stilled so that I could hear that there came a rustling from the bed—

I was greased with sweat. There were stabbing pains in my chest; I put my hand over it to feel the heart punch against my ribs and I thought, a man may well die from a dream. The candle was lit and this sent a flash of fear through me until I understood that I had forgotten to snuff it. The back of my neck was awash; I turned over the bolster to find a dry place.

When I finally lay still and assured that I was awake, I caught some little noise in the room. I at once thought of the cat-beast, for there was something of a whimpering sound to it. I glanced round and even under the bed: no cat there. Then it came again and I realised it was from the next chamber, where Ferris slept. It grew louder, and I knew it, now. Though preached against as the sin of Onan, unnatural and a filthy vice, it was heard everywhere we had made camp; to wake any night was to catch the rustling and some man's quick furtive breathing. Russ had called it the lullaby of the army... Ferris was now groaning, must be greatly carried away. I wondered if he would end by waking Aunt. Despite myself I smiled at that thought. And then came a thought which splintered my smile. The maid slept by herself in an attic room. I recalled his laughter, picking up the crumbs with his tongue, calling her 'Becs' and making her his witness that he was a pig, while I was not – his quickly masked displeasure at my hint that she liked me. All of a piece.

That he could play the widower by day and do thus at night! I was glad of the candle now. The latch of my door lifted sweetly, sweetly, and as I stepped out into the corridor his noise seemed so loud I was amazed to be the only one roused by it. His own door – O, the heedlessness of lust! – was open, standing in a gilded frame of candlelight. I extinguished my flame and crept forward. The door yielded to me silently and I saw a woman's dress lying over the chest in the corner. *Judas!* I thought. I sprang to the bed and ripped back the hangings and covers. His candle flared to show me Ferris, alone, his head partly framed by a heap of linen. I recognised the white cloth as Joanna's nightgown. Her widower lay, face pressed to its soft folds, his cheek smeared and shining. When he looked up at me, it was with eyes desolate and defenceless. I heard him fight to calm his breath, unable to speak or look anger, but only because he was too brutally torn from his grief.

Ready to cry out in horror at my vile mistake, I dabbed at his face with the shift, pulled the coverlet back over him and blew out the candle. Then I sat silent and unmoving on the edge of the bed, confounded, waiting for him to sit up and tell me to leave his house. My face burnt in the dark.

Ferris did not move. It even seemed to me that his breathing grew quieter. I began to hope that the sudden darkening of the room would send him off to sleep. Come the morning, he might believe it all a dream. But no, he had been awake, pressing her shift – pressing *her* – close to him in his lonely bed as he must have done every night since we came to London.

I have no idea how long I stayed there. Sobs rose in my own breast, so that keeping them down was a strangulation. I bit my hand to get mastery over myself. At last his breathing lightened, and sounded as if he might be going off, when there came a clicking from his throat. He might wish to speak to me. Most delicately did I raise myself from the bed and go to stand over him. I peeled back the coverlet. It felt cold and slippery on the outside, hot and dragging where he had wept into the underside of it. Without the candle I had so foolishly extinguished I could not tell if I was exposing a sleeping face or one which looked up through the darkness and could distinguish me. At once a very Flood of tears rose on me. Like Izzy had he befriended me, like Izzy had he paid for it. The more I tried to battle back my crying the worse it came on: I hiccupped and forced my breath. At length there came a sigh, and a rustling from the bed. I lay down on top of the coverlet and brought my face level with his.

'Forgive me. I'm the Fool of Fools—'

I could not say it. Speech rose in me but was dammed at the throat. Atonement. I craned forwards in the dark until I could press my streaming face on his as I used to with Izzy. The scent of sleeping flesh, of hair and neck, came up to me; his face was blubbered and slippery, warm under the cooling salt. His nose hurt my cheek; there was a smell of wine on him. A cluck rose from his throat as if he would start sobbing again. 'Hush,' I said. I licked his tears away, in the dark. For atonement. And so it happened that while drinking the tears I licked some from his mouth, which was open and tasted of sour wine and salt. Wet hair trailed on my neck. He mumbled something. *Hush.* I pressed on his lips to quiet him, pushing deeper, tasting his spittle. I wanted to lie still with him and let him know he was as welcome to me as myself, burrowing into him in the safety of the darkness.

There was a gasp; he pulled away and the kindness of our mouths was ended. I froze in the darkness, a child torn from the nipple, one great ache of loss, *Let me, let me*. His breath faded against my lips.

'Jacob?'

His voice was sleepy and unsure, but my own name struck violently into me. I felt doused in cold water, or as if looking round I had suddenly seen the rest of the household watching us. I got up from the coverlet, groped for the shift and pressed his hands into it. He breathed fast, but made no further sound. I could still taste his mouth inside mine. The air of the chamber striking chill on my wet face, I laid my finger on his cheek, dragged the covers up over his head and left the room.

Fighting the sheets in my own bed, I could not conceal from myself that my blood was up and that this – comfort – had stirred the animal spirits in me exactly as an encounter with a woman might. I ran my tongue round my teeth and swallowed. His mouth had already been open when I – the word *kiss* was enough to so inflame my face it was a wonder it did not light up the chamber. At the thought that I must meet him at breakfast I groaned inwardly.

Nor was this the worst of my torments: the Devil refines upon these things and hones His barbs for each particular soul. Now He whispered to me, *And if he had not pulled away . . . ?* The question was put *inside my head* with a dry and sandy merriment, His very voice, I swear. And with this whisper He set up such a tumult in me as to starve me of sleep all the rest of the night.

FOURTEEN

An Incubus

POOR AUNT. The next morning, when we should have been prompt and merry in our celebration of Nativity, her nephew and myself were so evidently not right that she hardly knew which of us to coddle more.

Ferris was at the table and already eating when I entered. My eyes went straight to him and though my bowels turned to water, yet I feigned (I hope) a passable smile in giving him good morrow. He returned my greeting civilly enough, but his eyelids being much swollen I could not tell how he looked at me.

Aunt came up to kiss and wish me a happy Nativity. On seeing my face up close she gave a squeal.

'Do you mark this, Christopher! What a sight for Our Lord's birthday!'

'We both of us look ill,' said Ferris. These harmless words had me quivering like a fern in a moorland gale.

'O, the wine,' I said hastily. 'You know I seldom, ah . . .' I broke off, all in a terror lest Aunt's chatter set off some echo in her nephew's head.

'First I tell Christopher that he must take care,' she went on, 'and now I find Jacob in the same case! Is it possible, a big man like you? You had no more than myself!'

'It troubled my sleep. I dreamt my brother was dead,' I returned shortly, and then could have torn out my tongue for the word 'dreamt'.

'Ah, I am sorry!' Her face softened.

'I saw him laid out.' I shuddered: that at least was unfeigned.

Aunt pinched my cheek. 'Sit you down and eat something. We should be joyous today.'

I wondered how many times I would be told 'Be joyous' before I died. Can a man arrange the sorrows and joys of his life to the Christian calendar? But of course, all particular and temporal sorrow should melt before Salvation's timeless sun. I gave her a hypocrite's smile before closing my eyes to say Grace. Opening them again, I kept them fixed on her, as in gratitude; anything was easier than looking at Ferris. I took a roll and some butter, carefully placing myself so that I was not opposite to him.

He picked out two boiled eggs from a dish and proceeded to crack the shells.

'Jacob, did you come into my room last night?' Directly before Aunt! My mouth seemed full of clay as I answered, 'No, not I.'

'Ah . . .' he put pepper on the first egg. 'No matter.'

'Is something gone?' I made myself ask.

'No.' He took butter on his knife, pushing it down into the yolk. After a minute or so he announced, 'Aunt, I think we should leave off that wine.'

'*One* of us might drink less of it,' she replied. 'It is not the quality at fault, methinks, but the quantity.'

'I'm not talking of sore heads,' Ferris insisted. 'My head is clear, at least, it is now. That wine provokes dreams.'

'Not in me,' said Aunt. 'And I drank my half bottle with the best of 'em.' She winked at me.

'Jacob had a dream. And I – well, it was either a dream or an incubus!'

'A what?' asked Aunt.

I did not want to hear him tell her. My face felt scalded and I was convinced they must both remark it.

Ferris patted the table as if the wood needed calming. 'A dream. A dream.'

'Is an incubus a spirit?' asked Aunt.

He rubbed his eyes, smiling. 'Aye. But this was a dream.'

'Dream of what?' Her face was grown uneasy. 'Not another death?'

'No, no. I'd be hard put to tell—' He burst into outright laughter. 'Your nephew's a wondrous wanton dreamer.'

Aunt pursed her lips; Ferris continued to laugh, shaking his head incredulously. A wanton dreamer. I felt warmth return to my hands, arms, belly; I sat back in the chair and was able to taste the bread again.

'No wantonness *today* if you please,' said Aunt. 'Of all days.'

'Agreed,' said Ferris. 'Or rather, no *more* of it, for a man can't unthink what's been thought – eh, Jacob?'

'I beg your pardon,' I fenced, 'I was not paying attention.'

'I was saying one can't unthink a wanton thought.' He took the spoon out of the eggshell and shifted slightly in his chair so that his eyes were full on me. 'But Jacob, why fear a dream?' He held up the spoon for emphasis. 'It was the wine working. My life on it, you've lost no brother.'

'I would I knew that for sure,' I said.

'Nor any friend,' he added.

His voice was gentle. I tried to thank him for this reassurance but my tongue cleaved to the roof of my mouth; I could bring out nought but a confused babble. He bent his head over the egg and began spooning out the yolk. I would have undergone public penance to understand him aright. I dared not ask... did he know I was there in body? Who, to his mind, was really the wanton dreamer? Who had the wanton thought a man can't unthink...?

~

During divine service I stood next to Ferris and heard the minister speaking a long way off, as I studied the shape of my friend's hands, and how he clasped them. I could smell his skin and hair in the cold air of the church, and stood aching, my face a devout mask stretched over a rotten soul.

On the way back I talked with Aunt, and felt better; but as we approached the house I started a toothache. The warmth of the fire indoors only made it worse, and the twinge grew to a clamour, until at last a torturing demon began jabbing the tooth with a hammer and chisel. Chewing cloves took the edge off it awhile, but they burnt my tongue. Meanwhile we ate goose, patties, a pumpkin pie, nuts: every dish spiced with pain. By the end of the afternoon's celebrations I was groaning aloud.

'Which one is it?' Ferris and Aunt stood before the glass with me, each in the other's way. They made me sit, held little mirrors and tried to shine candles in my mouth.

'Nothing,' said Aunt. 'No black anywhere, no bloody gums.'

'Perhaps a wisdom tooth,' suggested Ferris. He spoke softly, his face creased up with my suffering.

'At the front,' I moaned.

'Which one?'

'It feels like all of them.'

'That's the way with teeth,' said Aunt. She flung herself into a chair. 'You can't have the lot drawn!'

Ferris felt inside my bottom jaw and pressed each tooth in turn. 'Here? Here?'

I was quite unable to distinguish. All I could do was to hold on tight to the sides of the chair, and keep myself from sucking his fingers.

'Would that my teeth were as good,' he said. 'Had we best fetch a surgeon in any case?'

'We'll try simples first,' Aunt said. 'There'll be no surgeon willing to come out today, not for a tooth.'

Tinctures were produced. They drowsied me so that I would fain have slept forever: but through it all the drum of pain throbbed on. Hot and cold objects were held to my jaw and produced no effect. Aunt shook her head, puzzled. It was still only six in the evening.

'You are lucky, one way,' she said. 'You won't be any prettier with a front tooth out but at least he won't have to pull your head off.'

'Is a back tooth harder?'

She nodded vigorously. 'Agony. I had one out once and I'd say it was a fair punishment for any crime!'

'I don't want to be gap-toothed.'

'O, you're bonny enough.' I must have frowned, for she added, 'Jacob! Vanity!' and then kissed me on the forehead and said, 'Forgive me, child. Let's see what else there is.'

Infused valerian was poured down my throat, but failed to shift the pain.

Aunt paced the room. 'It must be worms in the teeth.'

'Get him to bed while he can still stand,' said Ferris. I remembered Zeb with his broken rib. They helped me upstairs, for the various draughts had rendered me clumsy, and stripped me to my shirt. I perceived no timidity in Ferris's handling of me but was scarce in a state to observe it. In my tired and drugged condition I should have melted at once, yet the agony crept by degrees into my upper jaw, my ear and the side of my skull. Lying on my side – my back – my front – with my face buried in the bolster – it was all of no use, for in the dark chamber torture blotted out my world. Fists clenched, I imagined my skull lit within by a brilliant white, which blazed out at my ears and eyes into the night. Illumination by suffering! I smiled at this theology but straightway the throbbing swelled, turned hotter and uglier and commenced cracking my skull from within, hatching from it as a chick from an egg. I beat my head on the pillow and cried out to Jesu. Again I heard the hurt men at Winchester. Well, I was not yet calling out to Mother.

Aunt came in with a candle, Ferris walking behind her.

'Here,' she said, holding out a pewter cup.

Poppy. The scent of it was familiar from Beaurepair. I drank the lot.

'You'll rest now,' she told me. 'Christopher will fetch the surgeon as soon as it's light.'

Ferris touched the side of my face. 'He'll get it out for you.'

'Once it mounts into your head it's a devil—' Aunt's whisper was cut off as she closed the door on me. Unseen, I shed a few tears, but soon after the poppy at last swept me away.

My dreams were not so much wanton as disordered. The dead girl from Basing was in the chamber with me and asked me to give her her gown again. She was wearing it, stains and all. I said I had no such garment and she pulled back the bedcover to show my body fully clothed. She then took a knife from my belt.

'Is this the one?' she kept asking. I said it was. After that she touched my hand. She was cold and wet and I knew she was come from the pond.

'Will you see the place where he cut me?' she asked, and fell to unlacing her gown. I told her No, and she replied, No matter, she could show me *here*, and bending right over me she showed me a bloody hole at the base of her neck. I put my finger to it and she laughed and called me Doubting Thomas. My father was there but I cannot recall what he said or did.

When I woke I could feel nothing at first. Then I understood that Ferris's hand was on my cheek and he had brought up a candle. The pain leapt in my jaw.

'Aaah! O no, no!'

'The surgeon's here, Jacob.'

'It's gone to the back of my mouth!' I was in a terror lest we end by drawing my every tooth.

'Mister Chaperain will know where to have it,' he replied. He did not sound very sure. 'I'll tell him you are coming down.'

I dressed palpitating, fearful as any guilty soul entering Hell's Gate. I told myself I was lucky to have reached man's estate and no worse pain than this, yet how can philosophy soothe bodily anguish? I knew then, and have often confirmed it since, that be a man never so trusting in God, yet he cannot hold his hand in a flame. Nature will not support it. The girl at Basing, she who was come to me in the night – what had she felt when the sword minced her entrails? She did not scream, was that only to cheat us at the last?

The toothache had indeed moved. It seemed gone into the lower jaw on the right side, a white flame of agony, and what games it now played me, licking round the jawbone as if to burn me out. I tore at my clothes in the haste to don them and at last went down in my shirt and breeches. Ferris stood by the fire. Aunt was there, looking sick, and a little balding fellow with black curls round his ears. He was solid as a bull-dog and had monstrous knotted calves setting off his bandy legs. A chair stood in the centre of the room.

I nodded to the bull-dog. 'Mister Chaperain. Good morning, Aunt.'

'Will you sit down, Sir?' He turned to Aunt. 'I see it now, Madam.'

'He means,' said Ferris to me, 'that you are too big to hold and had better be tied.'

'I will keep still,' I said indignantly.

'With respect, Sir, my experience tells me that even the bravest gentlemen cannot do so,' murmured Chaperain. 'Unless you will consent to be tied I cannot perform the extraction.'

Had I not just been considering that Nature will not permit self-torture? 'Very well,' I said.

'We will not bind you *yet*,' he smiled at me. I sat down in the chair, feeling I think more frightened than ever I did in the army or of Walshe, either. A man may laugh when there is only the chance of pain, but not when he sees the rack and screw laid ready for him. Tied down. The sweat was already starting under my arms.

'I'll give you something,' soothed Aunt. She pressed my hand and left the room. The surgeon now took a small hammer and began tapping at my teeth as if trying to crack hard-boiled eggs. One of his taps had me directly up and out of the chair.

'Ah! That will be the fellow,' he murmured to himself. 'Pray be seated,' and he again tapped in the same place. This time my arm flew up and I drove the heel of my hand into his nostrils.

'Pardon me,' I mumbled as we both rocked and held our faces.

'No matter. That's the one. Sir! I shall lay out my *batterie*. You see the necessity for tying the patient,' he remarked to my friend, who looked mighty sick already.

'Poppy, quick!' called Ferris. To Chaperain he said, 'Pray give him time for it to take hold.'

'I have other patients—'

'You'll find it worth your while.'

Aunt came in with another jug of poppy mixture. I drank it off at once.

'Courage, man, it will soon be over,' said Ferris. He looked down on me with a kind of gentle grief. We sat awkwardly until the mixture began to take effect. I seemed to be dreaming while awake and slid sideways in the chair.

'Now,' said Aunt. I was pulled upright and felt rope go round my arms and legs. I asked if they were tying me up so that dog could bait me. Ferris enquired of me, which did I take myself for, a bull or a bear? and when I laughed they put wadding in my mouth on the left side which stopped me closing my jaws. I felt them laying stuff over my neck and chest. Something metal scraped along the teeth on the right side. I shut my eyes and kept them shut.

'No need to screw up your face like that, we're not under way yet,' came a voice.

'Alas, poor lad!'

'Get a grip of his head! Ready?' Someone seized me in a head-lock from behind – it must have been Ferris – and the surgeon sat astride my lap to weight me down. I could smell his own rotten teeth, and the fingers which thrust between my lips tasted of herring.

'Give me a clout, there, he's drooling on me—'

Red hot, white hot, wire driven deep through the quivering jelly beneath the tooth. Some eating poison thrown in a soft, open wound – I howled as well as I could through his fingers and the suffocating wad which was partly got into my throat and was like to choke me.

'Madam, could you kindly hold the chair legs?'

A crunching, splitting sound like the heart of an oak as it is felled. I was drinking my own blood. I tried to spit it out.

'Stop that! . . . Give me the clout again!'

'Let him spit,' Ferris said. 'Jacob, spit.' He let go of my head so I could bend to the bowl Aunt was holding. The bull-dog was wiping his face.

'Once more and we're done. Get ahold, sir.' My head was pulled back. Then came a cracking and tearing as though the whole jaw was being ripped out. I screamed from full lungs, over and over again.

'There,' someone said.

The crunching stopped and pain, tasting of rust, pulsed over my tongue. Then I understood that too was blood. I opened my eyes. The little man was holding up the tooth, which to my fuddled sight seemed a huge belegged thing like a mandrake root. He got up off my thighs, his face all gory freckles.

'You'll be easier now,' he said.

Aunt came to me and wiped my mouth; I felt something wet and heavy being peeled off my chest.

'Lord, Lord, the poor lad!' she lamented. 'And look – we should have taken off his shirt.' I looked down and saw my linen brightly spotted where the blood had soaked through.

'Do they all bleed like that?' asked Ferris. He came round to the front of the chair and put some water to my lips. I opened my jaw to show I could not drink with the wadding, and he fished it out. Aunt was untying me.

'O, they all bleed,' said Chaperain. 'Would you like to keep the tooth?' he asked me. I nodded. 'Keep it for a marvel,' he went on. 'It's the soundest I ever pulled.' He showed me the thing without hole or flaw. And then I fell asleep in the chair.

My head was loose inside. 'Sick,' my voice said and Ferris rose from the corner and snatched up a pot. I heaved violently and a thread of blackish stinking stuff came trickling out of me. He stared at it, frowning, and called out, 'Aunt!' I heard her dress swish against the door as she hurried in.

'He's casting up!' Ferris cried. 'Look here.' He pushed the pot towards her: she took it and swilled the contents about, sniffing at them.

'Well?' Ferris urged.

She put down the mess and wiped my brow, then lips, with something perfumed.

'Blood, gone black in his belly. What he swallowed.'

'Will there be more?'

She shrugged. 'Keep nigh him.'

But there was no more. I had been asleep two or three hours, for they had eaten. I could smell boiled fish in the room.

'I want to go to bed,' I said.

'Becs shall put the warming pan in,' said Ferris.

'Now. I want to go now.' When I stood up I was weak, but steady enough, so they contented themselves with mounting the stairs behind me. My feet dragged. A clean vomit-pot came with me and Aunt made me take a finger of cordial before I undressed.

'What with poppy and lack of sleep you're almost done for,' she soothed. 'All for a tooth, eh?'

'It's gone,' I said. A dull ache nagged at my jaw. Where the tooth had been was a torn jelly which I tried not to stir with my tongue, for whenever I touched it the blood would well up into my spittle, like wine in water. I was as ready to sleep as an overladen beast, and no sooner had the sheets warmed to me than I was gone again.

I slept all the rest of Boxing Day and woke, with a burning desire to make water, in the dark of the next morning. Having relieved nature I came back to bed all goosebumps and lay rubbing my feet together, but had no longer any wish to sleep and so waited, curious to know what o'clock it was, namely four, as I presently discovered by the bells of Paul's.

I rested quietly in the darkness and from time to time put my tongue into the tooth hole. The flesh there was tender and ragged: prodding at it brought a sullen twinge. That was no great matter. What tormented me now was that I could not see my way how to speak privily with Ferris and to know whether he truly believed himself a drunken dreamer. That *incubus* had been his jest. He knew how the incubus was called, he had uttered its name in the dark. But did he understand I had indeed been there? If he did, my talk could be only apology and excuse, and he, how could he answer me? Or, supposing him ignorant, why break it to him? He had said that I would lose no friend, and he had acted friendly by me since, yet I might still see him turn from me with disgust, or even put me out of the house. I thought of Nathan, and of the whisperings of the Voice. But the Voice was full of lies. I lay rubbing my butchered jaw.

It did strike me in the midst of these benighted musings that there was One whose judgement I should fear infinitely more than my friend's. The Jacob of the old pamphlet-reading days – who was come in his place? Until the night when I dispatched Walshe, and even after, I was wont to consider myself a good man. Caro had thought me quick to anger, but noble-hearted and upright. Yet I had not sorrowed for her as I ought. Other husbands were not so cold: again I saw Ferris bury his face in Joanna's old shift. This brought me back to the question – *had* I committed an act of filthy lust? I recalled the violent flutter within me, and as I did so pleasure, that pimp to the Devil, suddenly spread in me like a stain: my prick stiffened and without thinking I put my hand to it.

I had my answer. I made myself unclench the hand and think of scraping boots, a task I detested, but it was a long time before my blood would lie quiet. Shame festered inside me like the black vomit. There was one thing I could and would do, namely keep myself out of drink until Satan grew weary and the strength of it went down. I decided to write a letter to my mother, and did indeed write it in my fancy, and in this way gradually composed myself to sleep.

But the Evil One, being rich in snares, at once spread his nets for me sleeping. Ferris lay with me in the wood. He was amorous like a woman, took my hands and put them inside his clothes. From this I suddenly started awake almost dying, unable to hold off any longer. The thing was done while I was still drowsy and the pleasure, shot through with a flash of pain in my jaw, sharp in the extreme. For a long time afterwards, I lay afraid to go back to sleep, wherein there now lay a danger. I had an incubus of my own, and already it bade fair to master me.

FIFTEEN

Broken Men

WHEN I FINALLY went downstairs that day, I found Rebecca lying in wait for me as usual, full of questions about my health. I assured her that the toothache was gone and said I thought I could eat something now. She at once announced that she would bring me some of yesterday's pie of preserved fruits, 'So good it were a pity to have missed it', which she had saved expressly for me. I said that was very kind, and when she left the room I let my head droop forwards onto the table, thinking that wherever men and women lived together their desires cut away the ground each from under the other. It needed only for Ferris to fall amorous of Becs to make our misery complete. The notion afforded me a tight smile; I straightened up and it was thus that she found me on her return.

'I am right glad to see you merry,' she said. 'The Master and Mistress were saying what pain you had, for a good tooth too. Mistress said it was a shame.'

She had arranged the food on a pretty Dutch dish and brought some salep without being asked, setting the whole before me with a flourish. *O child*, I thought, *look elsewhere, I am sold twice over*. I said, in common politeness, that the pie seemed very good, and this was enough to bring on an ogle. Taking some of the salep, I carefully mumbled the piecrust into the left side of my mouth.

'Look, Sir.' She was holding something out to me: the tooth. I disliked seeing it in her hand, and took it from her only to lay it down by the side of the dish.

'It's sound as marble,' she said. 'Mister Chaperain said your teeth were all excellent.'

'Excellent!' I snorted.

'Are they not?'

'Does he think I gave myself a toothache, for the pleasure of seeing him?'

'O no, Sir. He meant only that you had good teeth.'

I knew myself churlish and wondered why she so grated upon me. Hoping someone would soon call her away, I took up the pie and nibbled at it, halting to ask, 'Where is everybody?' – this being as near as I could get to telling her I did not want her company.

'Mistress is gone to see Mistress Osgood.' This Jane Osgood I had heard of more than once, a young wife with child and grown so huge it must be twins at least. The confinement being her first, she was horribly afraid.

'Is she brought abed?'

Rebecca shrugged. 'Mistress didn't say, but she's very near her time.'

'And Mister Ferris—?'

'Is here.'

I blinked.

'Working the press,' Becs explained. I had made an error in questioning her, for be the talk never so dull it gave her cause to stay. I therefore addressed myself to the pie and she at last tripped out of the room, casting a roguish eye backwards as she did so. There was a new boldness in her, and I sighed. *1646*, thought I to myself, *will be like the year before, a chaos.* Chewing away in this humour, I let a morsel of the crust dig into my gum. My eyes watered and the fruit was sauced with blood.

'Jacob!' Ferris put his head round the door. I thought I saw pleasure in his looks. 'How long have you been up?'

'Not long.'

'Will you come out when you've eaten? To Paul's Cathedral?'

I nodded, flushing with happiness, and he sat down to wait with me. He need not have asked, for I counted it one of my best pastimes to walk in London with him. I sometimes ventured out alone, but although there was much to admire, such as the markets, the churches, the palaces and the quays, yet the crush of people in some parts, especially down by the river, unnerved me, and I was forever in fear of pickpurses. Then there were what they called *ditches* and *kennels* but which any countryman would have called by their true name, moving cesspits, for the water could scarce crawl along for filth. All the streets were wet with more than rain, as the jerries were emptied into them, and a terrible stench breathed from the sweating, greenish stones. Even after weeks in town I marvelled at the way the inhabitants contrived to step over black vegetables, rotting cats and bubbling crusts of shit, seeming neither to see nor to smell them. Despite my distaste, however, I never lost the chance of seeing any new thing, and if Ferris were able to show me a famous building or two I felt I was growing in knowledge and, if not a native, might one day make a citizen of the place.

Near though it was, I had not yet been inside Paul's. The outing promised well, for Ferris seemed amused by my excitement and when in this mood he was often especially kind to me. I pushed aside the pie without finishing it.

It was as miserable a day as I have seen, dark and blustery. Most of the time we were shielded from the wind, for the houses were built on three or four storeys, each projecting further into the air than the one beneath it, so that in the end a mere crack of sky remained overhead for light. I thought our progress was more like digging a mine under the earth than walking on top of it. Despite the cold there were still plenty of folk about. Many men, like ourselves, seemed going to the area around Paul's Churchyard, to the shops there, and some of these had a scholarly look, but others showed more boisterous, loud in their calls and whoops, running along fired by drink and folly. There were women, too: sutlers selling hot chestnuts and pasties from little stalls, others who hurried along, head down, who might perhaps be midwives, going to Mistress Osgood. Two of these stalked rapidly before us for the length of one street and their talk was borne back by the wind; I heard one say, 'She cannot be married for she cannot lie dry in her bed,' and the other reply, 'What! Sixteen years and such a baby!' 'Aye,' says the first, 'And her mother says it is nothing but a trick...'

I heard no more of this poor wretch. From time to time a foul-smelling gust found its way through an alleyway or round a corner. I gaped to see a man ahead of us wearing four hats together, one atop the other, and somewhat perplexed as to how to keep them on.

'Is he a lunatic?' I asked.

Ferris laughed at me. 'They are for sale.'

No sooner had we got free of this coney-warren than we were swallowed up in the scum of little shops around Paul's, many of them pasted up against the walls of the place itself, so that its fabric looked to be completely smothered. I stopped and said to Ferris, 'We had an engraving of this. It showed the whole. But where could the artist have stood?'

He considered. 'I don't know. There's nowhere I know of where you can see it complete.'

Puzzled, we made our way towards the booksellers, Ferris saying that we were come to do business though he would gladly take me into Paul's afterwards. He stepped into a kind of shack propped against the cathedral wall. Inside we found a young man of a sallow cast of countenance, whose hair was so black as to be near blue. He seemed hiding in the dark at the back, but stepped forward when he saw Ferris.

'Welcome. I've not seen you this year,' he said.

'I've been in the wars,' and my friend touched his cheek.

'More welcome, then.' They clapped each other on the shoulder. 'There are some new things here which might please,' he went on, 'will you do me the honour...?' He bent to pull out some material from a stack of papers at the back. Ferris went forward and started to browse through it, frowning from time to time. Other customers stood here and there, unfolding maps or reading plays with a finger on the page, quietly mouthing the words. One tall sanguine gentleman seemed much taken with his reading matter and I determined to know what that might be, but on my coming closer he shut up the volume with a look of no good will towards me and held it to his chest as if to say, *Go off, impertinence*, so I withdrew having seen nought but the name of the author, one Aretino: I thought this might be a Spanish name, and the writer perhaps a monk. Repulsed by the tall gentleman, I examined the contents of the shelf behind the counter, mostly sermons and political pamphlets, but without recognising any of the titles.

'*Liberty No Sin*,' I heard my friend say. 'Please you to wrap it.' There was a rustling as his purchase was stowed against the wind.

'Will you come and dine with us as you used?' Ferris asked.

I looked up. The young man hesitated. 'I – I have wived since you left.'

Ferris shrugged. 'No reason not to come.'

'And my father died.'

'I am heartily sorry to—'

'He left me the shop. Here I stay, now.'

'Not even a cup of wine between friends.' Ferris smiled ruefully. He raised his hat to the man, who blushed. We went out into the darkening day. Outside he turned his back to the wind and carefully inserted the thin package between his shirt and coat, then swore. 'I forgot to ask him about paper.'

'We can go back.'

'Too late,' he said. 'Too late altogether. Shall we go into Paul's?'

I dithered. It was so cold that I most of all wanted to go home, but I might not get another chance to see the place with him.

'We can come again,' he said, seeing me hesitate. 'Now, there's something I want from the New Exchange.'

I lumbered unwillingly along by his side. When we got there, however, there was so much to be seen that I asked Ferris if I might wander at large. He at once agreed and I had the impression that he was glad to be rid of me awhile. Having seen all the jewels, stockings, pots of perfume and stacks of books, I came back to find him clutching a roll of paper as well as his precious *Liberty No Sin*.

'What might that be?' I asked.

'A secret just now.'

We again burrowed into the maze of streets and alleys, their stones now slippery with drizzle. It was like the reign of Old Night: steps rang out long before the eye could discern any human form and

I tensed each time a man passed us in the way, my heart labouring under all my accustomed fear of footpads. I thought how strange it was that my size availed me nothing against this dread. In the darkness I almost took a pratfall, having trodden in something both brittle and slimy the feel of which on my shoe made me shudder. I was loath to examine the mess and walked on dragging one foot a little.

At the end of the street shone a faint amber light and I heard the clink and hum of a tavern. A man stood in the doorway spitting and seemingly looking out for someone.

'Eh, Christopher!'

'Daniel, my lad!' Ferris ran up to embrace him.

'You'll take some canary with us, f-friend?' Daniel asked me over Ferris's shoulder. He put me in mind of a carrot-haired owl, but his face, despite the gloss of drink upon it, was humane and spirited. As soon as Ferris released him he seized my hand and pumped it up and down.

'This is Jacob Cullen,' Ferris said. 'And no, lad, it grieves me but we must go back. My aunt awaits us. But how have you been living?'

The man sighed. 'I wasn't meant for a stool-arsed Jack. The fencing school – now that was an occupation.'

'Why don't you—' I stopped. Ferris and Daniel were both looking down. I followed their eyes and saw what I had not perceived earlier owing to the gloom: Daniel's left leg was of wood.

'I beg your pardon, sir. I hadn't remarked—'

He clapped me on the arm. 'And why should you!'

'So, no more swords,' Ferris said. 'But can you handle a spade?'

'Don't know, I never did before.' Daniel roared with laughter. I wondered how far gone he was in drink.

'I propose to dig the commons and raise crops.'

'Ah, we're onto *that*, are we?' Daniel clutched at my sleeve. 'Are you another one?'

'Another—?'

'Another dreamer.' He turned to Ferris. '*Your* man is Richard Parr. Mad as the man in the moon.'

'He wants to start a colony?'

'Not his own, perhaps; but he'd go along with yours. Able-bodied, but poor. Lodges at Twentyman's.'

'I know it.' Ferris's look was gone inward. He roused himself to ask, 'Will you come and eat with us, Dan?'

'No, thank you kindly.' The man's eyes glistened. 'Too f-far on this leg.'

'Then shall we come one day and see the new babe?'

'When you will.' But he seemed now not to want us. I expressed likewise a wish to have his company at some future date and we left him. Passing up the street I heard some men within roaring out the ballad of the 'Mercenary Soldier'.

I come not forth to do my country good,
I come to rob and take my fill of pleas-ure...

'The rain's stopped,' Ferris said. It was thin comfort, for the streets were darker than ever and the air nipped my flushed cheeks. We walked on some yards without speaking, until I asked, 'Will Dan stay there all night?'

'They ought not to let him, if the landlord wants to keep his licence.'

'I never thought of you having a toper for a friend,' I said.

'What, you don't think I've ever been in a tavern, neither?' He laughed, but stopped and went on more soberly, 'Dan was no toper when first I knew him.'

These broken men, I thought, *are everywhere. Who will gather them up and mend them*?

~

Rebecca opened the door. 'I took you for the Mistress,' she cried on seeing us. 'She won't stay much longer, surely?' She hurried back to the kitchen whence issued a strong smell of roast goose.

'Mistress Osgood must be brought abed,' said Ferris. He shuddered at the warmth as he unfastened his coat and laid the parcel from Paul's Churchyard on the table. I stood before the fire, crushing my purple hands together and thanking God for the comfort of coal on such a bitter night.

Ferris picked at the parcel, hissing with annoyance. 'My fingers are too cold.'

'Mine also.'

'We should get us dogskin gloves.' At last he was able to peel back the outer wrapping. 'There! A treasure revealed.'

Liberty No Sin looked a strange enough treasure, showing Adam and Eve but without their coats of leaves, standing to face the reader naked and unashamed on either side of a spade planted upright in the ground. The handle of this spade seemed to have taken life and spread into a goodly tree. Indeed no such tree was ever seen, unless it were that Papistical tree at Glastonbury that the cunning monks professed sprung from the staff of Joseph of Arimathea, for this spade-tree had fruit and flowers together on the branch. I knew at once what manner of reading I was in for, and groaned inwardly.

Ferris saw it. 'Wormwood, eh?'

He could not hide his disappointment, and I was at once ashamed of myself and my stubbornness.

'We'll read it together, as soon as it please you to start,' I said, and he brightened directly, and said we would get warm first. He took the other package, the scroll, and stored it carefully within the bookcase, locking it after.

'So will you tell me what that is?' I asked.

'I have told you, a secret for now.'

He stuck his head out of the door and called downstairs for Rebecca, who came, poor girl, as promptly as she always did, and embarrassed me again, for she fairly ate me up with her eyes before she looked at Ferris. I remembered that I had left her special offering of pie unfinished, and blushed, and could then have kicked myself to think what interpretation she might put on my reddening cheeks, and so blushed worse.

'Will you bring us some wine up?' he asked her.

I said, 'Ferris, I don't want any.'

'Well, I do.'

I coughed. 'We – Daniel—' trying to be discreet in front of the listening girl.

'And some of that cheese we had yesterday, Becs.' She curtsied and left the room.

'Ferris, don't.'

'I'm not Dan. I'm me, and I'm cold, and I want warming through.'

I held my peace. Rebecca brought in the wine and two goblets. She poured one; I straightway bade her take the other away again: I would wait until we had the goose.

'There's bread and cheese coming,' she said, misunderstanding me.

'I'll have some salep, if there be any,' I went on. 'Is there?' She nodded and went out again.

'Salep's just as warming to drink as wine,' I said.

'If you say so,' he answered. 'Shall we have a look at *Liberty No Sin*?'

He lit a fair new candle and propped the pamphlet on the table, taking up his wine and sitting down to the paper as to a feast. Part of me wanted to laugh, but I pulled my chair up next to his and endeavoured to keep a respectful face. It had been easier to escape the wine than I had anticipated – I had been afraid he would urge me – and I felt calm, certain I would not shame myself in any way. Ferris read aloud, pausing from time to time:

'*Whereas we know that in the beginning He created them man and woman, that is to say that Adam was the grandsire and Eve the grandam of all mankind, none excepted, and that man and woman is to say, all men and all women, how comes it that since then are sprung up so many Kings, Lords and Squires that tread their fellows under foot and are loath to call them Brother?*'

I looked through, not at, the pamphlet, and listened to his voice. He pronounced the words wonderingly, as if granted a vision of divine light and overpowered with its sweetness, even at times with a little catch in his throat, when, looking round, I would see a glitter in his eye that might be a tear. Zeb, I thought, had a softer way of speaking, more beguiling, but this halting, passionate way of Ferris's made it impossible for a friend to break in upon him. I had heard him only once before with this ache in the voice, and that was when he had told me how he rescued Joanna out of her bondage and brought her safe home. But the time he told me that, he had not been drinking.

'*And so the earth was given to mankind that all might enjoy it, and though Eden may not be regained, yet by labour and by just dealing one with another we may build a happy and prosperous Israel. And to those lovers of kingly power that will say, You come to throw down all rank and degree, we answer without shame, being none other but your dispossessed younger brothers, Aye, we do, and know you not that you are our own flesh and blood, and are you not ashamed to lord it over us so long? And yet we do freely forgive you, if you will but lay down the wealth you wrongfully hold, and join with—'*

The door opened. 'Here's the cheese,' said Rebecca. 'And your salep, Sir, and extra nutmeg in it for the cold.'

We thanked her and she went out, again casting a longing look at me which made me fairly flinch. Ferris laid down the pamphlet and cut some bread and cheese for us both, for though I would not tipple, I could eat.

'Well, what think you?' he asked, sawing through the manchet.

'It seems to me,' I answered, hesitating, 'that it is a curious thing to be reading such matter as this and have a woman serve us. The last time I read such things I was a servant myself, and now I have one, or rather,' for I saw the chance of a jest against him, '*you* have one. Are we not lording it over her? I could fetch bread or make salep, could not you?' I took a bite of cheese and waited.

Ferris frowned; he chewed slowly, turning the bread about over in his mouth and moistening it with wine. 'I know not what to say,' he confessed at last. 'Do you think, Jacob, that the man who wrote this has servants also?'

We sat in silence, for although I had meant only to tease him, on reflection I found it a matter worthy of serious thought.

'She is my aunt's servant,' he went on uncertainly. 'Not mine.'

'But we both of us give her orders.'

The salep was very good, steaming hot and full of spices. Becs was showing me how well she could look after a man. I drank it off and continued: 'We have no wives, and she does many things for wages which our wives would do naturally for us were we married.'

Any man but Ferris would have cracked a jest here, but instead he demanded of me, 'Does that not make a wife a species of servant?'

'No more than a husband, who also labours without pay for the household.'

'But this means unmarried men and women will all have servants – no, hold, Jacob, we are out of our way. Married persons also have servants, which shows it is not a question of being married, but of wealth.'

'Would you call your aunt wealthy? She works near as much as Rebecca.'

'Because idleness is a sin. She is far from poor.' He poured out another goblet of wine.

'Would you receive Rebecca into your community?' I asked.

'Yes,' he replied without pause.

'Then why should she serve us now?'

Ferris rubbed his ear. 'Because of the way the house is ordered. That's why we must leave. If I call Becs upstairs to talk with us now, the goose burns, and there's my aunt angered, because she and I want different things.'

'You could mind the goose yourself. Labour with your hands!' I teased.

'No, no. If I call her upstairs now, with us two, it makes her a kind of wife.'

It was my turn to feel ill at ease.

'Whereas,' he went on, 'in a colony, with many men and women, she would be more like a sister.'

'Are you so convinced of that?' I asked. 'When I lived as a manservant we had men and maids working together and – and – they were not like brother and sister. Not at all,' I added, recalling Zeb and Patience.

There was another silence. I felt a tightness in the air: we were got upon dangerous ground in talking of wives, and it was my fault. If only Ferris would stop drinking. He picked up the pamphlet and made to go on, but I said, 'Let me read it quietly for myself; here, move the candle,' and so we settled again and I went on with my salep as well as *Liberty No Sin*. It did occur to me that the thing might very well have been written by Ferris himself; I saw him smile several times as we continued to peruse it. It was all much the same stuff. Like my friend, the writer thought the only way was to break free of custom and go build the New Jerusalem. At last Ferris came to the end, with a great sigh of satisfaction. 'Have you finished?' he enquired, moving the candle nearer to me.

'Yes,' I lied, seeing that the end of it was nothing but exhortations.

'Would you *like* Becs to come with us, Jacob?' he suddenly shot at me. Surprised, I raised my eyes to find him studying me closely. Did he mean come with *one* of us? If so, which?

'I had not thought about it,' I said. 'I spoke but for the sake of argument.'

Someone was banging up the stairs. I got up – gladly – to open the door and saw Aunt outside, swaying with fatigue. She came in pale, bringing the chill of the wet streets with her, and sniffing the air of the house.

'O, the goose!' she cried. 'Believe me, I'm ready for it!' Ferris kissed her and moved to stir up the fire. Her eyes went to the wine bottle, then rested on me, reproachful: I shrugged to show I was helpless.

'Welcome back,' I said pointedly, and her look changed to one of understanding.

'Well, Christopher,' she said, sitting down near the fire and unfastening the strings of her cloak, 'are you not going to ask about Mistress Osgood?'

'She's well, I hope?' Ferris left poking the fire and came to sit by her. 'Brought to bed?'

'There's a boy born. As we thought, there are two; I left her with the other little one about to come. She's been in such agony, poor soul! – I'm sure I prayed as hard as her own mother would, were she alive. And so afraid!' She twisted her fingers together. 'It's as the minister said last week, when you see what a weak woman can bear if she has to, a man should be able for almost anything!'

'Except toothache,' said Ferris. I was surprised at his lightness; then I noticed his face, how stiff it was, and saw Aunt's look of pity. Joanna was in the room with us again.

Ferris took his aunt's cloak. 'So who's with her now?'

'Her mother-in-law, and the midwife. She's well looked after.' Aunt pressed her hands to her drained cheeks, kneading colour into the flesh. Ferris rose, poured some wine into his own cup and handed it to her.

'We've been to Paul's today,' I said as she sipped and sighed.

'Paul's? How did you like it?' She turned her tired, gentle eyes on me. I prudently suppressed Daniel, telling her instead about the bookseller and Ferris's new pamphlet.

She took up *Liberty No Sin* and flicked through it, staying a while on the picture of Adam and Eve; but without a candle right up to the page it was too dark to read the print.

'Shall I tell Becs to send up the goose?' asked Ferris.

His aunt nodded.

'Aye, give her her orders,' I put in. He looked hard at me, but went, coming back to say it would be up directly.

It was perhaps the quietest meal I ever had in their company. We were all tired, and ready to sit companionably without much talk. The goose was very tender, and fat; but even so I would as soon have slept. I observed that Ferris ate as much fowl as anybody despite having had the lion's share of the bread and cheese. He continued drinking, but did not slur his words or grow quarrelsome. I would take nothing but beer with the meal, and Aunt cast approving looks at me, anxious ones at her nephew.

'I'll call on her tomorrow,' said Aunt suddenly; the words were swollen by a great yawn, and then we were all yawning. Rebecca stacked the plates at the side of the table.

'I could sleep now,' said Ferris.

'The pan is already heating,' said the girl.

'Becs has second sight,' said my friend. We all laughed, but I thought Aunt's laugh was not very hearty or happy. Rebecca took the plates out and shortly after we heard her stamping up towards her chamber. Ferris poured himself more wine.

'Leave it, my dear,' implored his aunt.

'Aunt, you can't think I am intoxicated?'

She put her head down and scratched at a scab of candlewax on the cloth. Rebecca was heard coming down again, and put her head round the door to tell us all the beds had been thoroughly warmed. Ferris at once stood up, keeping hold of his goblet.

'Good night.' He kissed his aunt and took a fresh candle, lighting it from our dying one. 'Good night, Jacob.'

When we could hear he was got to the upper floor she whispered to me, 'When did he start?'

'Not long before you returned,' I answered.

'We had this just before he sold up,' she said. 'If only he would wive again.'

I said that in my opinion he was, indeed, missing Joanna. Had she a suitable woman in mind?

She shook her head. 'Half the neighbours think he's mad, anyway. Poor lad!' She looked and sounded close to tears; I went to her and kissed her forehead, telling her that night and weariness darken our spiritual vision along with the bodily one, and that in the morning she would see things in truer colours.

She squeezed my hand. 'Go up. I'll follow you.'

Taking another candle, I blundered up the stairs like a man in armour, so groggy that I twice let the candle flare in my face, right under my eyes. *You will end by blinding yourself,* I thought as I reached the top. Then I stumbled on the last step, crashing to my knees. I hissed with pain and dropped the candle on the boards. It rolled away from me and died, and I was at once made aware that Ferris had not yet extinguished his light. A pale yellow shimmer outlined his door and I could see a strip of the wall inside. I felt a now familiar rush of shame, but then took comfort: he had not seen fit to bar his chamber.

A thick, sleepy voice called out, 'Jacob? Have you hurt yourself?'

'No, no.' My voice boomed; I cringed. Groping for the candle, which was come to a stop some feet away, I glanced through the crack of the door, and jumped. The bed hangings were pulled back and he was sitting up, eyes wide open but apparently unable to see me in the darkness of the landing. I froze, in case, seeing something stir, he should think I was spying on him; I waited for him to lie down again. He stayed exactly as he was. I could not fathom his expression, which struck me as intense, somewhat perplexed; or it might be that waking sleep of his. Then I realised that, having heard me, he would know by sound that I was still outside the door. I must go away forthwith. I grabbed the candle, rose, and went directly into my own chamber, where I undressed in the dark and said a hasty prayer about dreams. It was answered, for I underwent no temptation that night.

SIXTEEN

Hope

I WOKE FROM a dream-free sleep and remembered that this day we were to call on that Richard Parr, lodging with Mister Twentyman, of whom Daniel had spoken. Unlike Ferris, I had no itch to exchange all our comforts for a thorny wilderness, but if we must, then I saw the need for men of sense, if only to put down the likes of Roger Rowly.

The grate was full of ashes. Icy air shot into the bed as I lifted the cover, and I hurried to don my clothes. Sudden hail pecked at the glass. What I most desired was to sit downstairs and have Ferris teach me to play chess. Let Richard Parr keep for one day, I thought, as the sound of the hail swelled to a drumming and the yard outside grew white. On the landing, I thought Ferris's door was shut: I could not tell if it was bolted. A faint snoring buzzed from within. The stairs were near as dark as the previous night, and having no candle I felt my way down.

Below, the fire was lit, and the moving zigzags of flame made a pretty show in the room. Aunt must be still abed; Becs, having probably heard nothing, would stay in the kitchen if I were quiet. Just then I craved solitude and peace, and to sit gazing on the fire, more than any food or drink. The pattering against the glass slowed and stopped. Outside, a sparrow sent up thanks.

Quiet. My body melted heavily into the chair; I heard a cart go up the street. The room grew suddenly big with meaning. Something was about to happen, was happening: each object in the room seemed perfect of its kind, its kind being just its one self. The moment split into Eternity and I went with it: I had neither skin nor bones, but flowed into the world, sacred along with everything else, and was lost.

A door opened downstairs. The joy faded; I felt myself staring about like a madman, and breathing fast; I blinked to get back to my right senses.

'Are you well, Sir?' Becs was arrived and staring hard.

'Very well.' My voice sounded strangled.

The girl came and stood over me. 'What will you have?'

Her nearness was an affliction and it was an ordeal to answer, like struggling up from the depths of a dream. 'Bread, eggs, beer,' I mumbled, willing her to go so that my ecstasy should return.

But when she was gone, I found that I no longer filled the room; my skin was grown back round me. I was left shaken, unsure what this vision might portend, or was *portend* the wrong word? For the thing seemed complete in itself. I had been touched. And then my heart really did leap in my breast in just the way I had heard men describe. This was surely the Grace of which they spoke and wrote: I was one of the Elect, the Saved, after all. And the incubus? A temptation merely, the last snare of a desperate Devil to lure me away before Grace could take hold. None may know he is saved *unless he receive Grace.*

Though I had sinned most grievously, it was not too late.

I knelt at once, thanking God for this sign of his infallible mercy, and vowing to mend my life. My knees were stiff but I forced them to bend. I should find a way to write that letter to my mother, and thus discover the whereabouts of my wife and brothers. Every unclean thought I would put resolutely from me until the besieging Devil saw himself powerless to corrupt; I should show myself more grateful to the friend who had plucked me out of the army by aiding him in his dear enterprise. For what reason, it suddenly came to me, was I there with him but so that I might give my strength and experience in setting up the colony? He did not know how men live in the country; but I did, and considered together we were not lacking in skill. I should serve him to the best of my ability and God would bless our endeavours.

I opened my eyes. Becs was standing in the open doorway. I rose with a smile, my knees cracking, and she advanced with the tray of food. As usual, she stayed to watch me eat. My appetite was excellent, yet still she shifted from one foot to the other, and at last whispered, 'I hope you are not troubled in spirit, Sir.'

I assured her I was never further from it, and laughed; but she continued to scrutinise me and shuffled out at last with a sober gait as if quitting a sickroom, which made me laugh more.

No food ever tasted so good, even in the army after a shortage of rations, for I was eating in a new freedom and the certainty that things were to go well. When had I last felt such conviction? Not since childhood. I pushed aside the dirty plate and kissed my own hands and arms for the sheer joy of living. There was a candle stub on the mantelpiece and I lit it at the fire, took up some paper and a quill and straight off began to write:

Dearest Mother,

I hope this letter may not distress you too greatly. Fear no beseechings for money or other aid; would that I knew all of my family to be as safe as I am at present. Could I only impress on you how sorry I am for the suffering I have brought about, then I think a mother's heart might pity me. Though I wished very much to write earlier (here I could not resist softening the truth for her sake), *it was plain that no good would come thereby, for, being in the New Model Army and mostly ignorant of our future whereabouts, I could not stay for your answer. I feared also to bring more trouble upon you. I pray that Sir John leaves you in peace, and that the dust of the affair now begins to settle.*

For the shame I have caused you, Mother, you have every right to cast me off, yet I hope you will not, or if you do, will first do me a service considered right for felons, that is, to show me the full extent of my wrongdoing. I beg of you, let me know if you can what is become of my wife and brothers. I would make some reparation, if I may, to those I have wounded, or if it be too late to do so, understanding will at least fit me for repentance. I repeat, this is all I ask. Should your forgiveness come with it, then am I blest indeed, but a man who has done so ill must not look to be pardoned.

The direction I give you is that of one Mrs Snapman, whose nephew, being a friend, permits me to lodge with him under her roof. She is a virtuous lady, and ignorant of my—

I heard Ferris stumping down the stairs and at once made to hide the letter, then reproached myself with this deceit as unfitting my new resolution and took it out again from under my shirt.

'What, scribbling?' said he when he saw me. 'May I?' and he took the letter, frowning as he read. His eyes when he looked into mine were thoughtful. I was afraid he would begin to question me about my *wrongdoings*, but he only asked, 'Are you not afraid someone will come after you?'

'Though my mother be angry, I hardly think she will set them on.'

'That's not my meaning. This may be intercepted by an interested party before it reaches your mother: they may be waiting for you to write. Does she receive many letters?'

'No,' I admitted, seeing where the talk was leading and not liking it.

Ferris went directly to the place I dreaded. 'If you value your skin, you were best not send this.' We both of us sighed, and he added, 'You endanger my aunt too.'

'I have put that she is innocent.'

'What's your word worth, to them?'

He was in the right of it, but it was hard to have my ideas knocked cold when I was full of the joy of self-abasement and had actually written my letter. More, there was something in him which was not quite Ferris.

'You said not long back that Caro was most likely dead,' I ventured. 'Here might be a way to know for sure, yet you say I should not write. You weren't so timid when we sent Tommy over to Beaurepair.'

Ferris ignored the mention of Tommy. '*You* said she was most likely dead. I merely agreed.'

That was true. Yet when I opened my mouth to beg pardon I was struck by his guilty look. *He is ashamed of his fear*, I thought. Risk had been our daily bread in the army but in London it seemed he was afraid of people troubling his aunt, and perhaps scotching his plans for the colony. But then I thought, he was not bound to shoulder my sorrows, having ample of his own.

'I won't send it,' I promised. As earnest of my good intentions I crushed the letter into a ball and, stepping up to the grate, tossed it into the flames. *God reads it*, I thought, as it drew itself together into a black rose, then delicately broke apart.

Ferris came up to me and squeezed my hands. 'You're grown very biddable since we left the New Model,' he said. 'What has quieted you?'

I shrugged.

'If I can think of any safe means, Jacob, be assured we'll use it. Let's both give it our best consideration.' He patted my arm. 'Meanwhile, I've something to show you. Sit down – no, not there. At the table.'

Biddable, I sat where I was told.

'Clear all this away to one corner.' He was fumbling with the lock of the bookcase. 'Why are these dishes still here? Where's Becs?'

'I've frightened her away,' I told him, stacking plates.

'What, did you catch hold of her?' He stopped jiggling the key and looked back at me. 'Eh? Kiss her—'

'No!' I almost shouted. 'Nothing, I'll tell you later.'

'Be sure you do.' He grinned. 'I count myself the protector of that girl's virtue. It is a fearful thing to see your lust battering down her defences—'

We both laughed. The bookcase door swung open with a thin squeak and Ferris lifted out the scroll of paper he had brought back from the New Exchange. Easing off a narrow ribbon he unrolled the thing and then whirled round to slap it down on the table in front of me.

'There!'

We faced one another over a masterly engraving of the cathedral itself and all the city round it, finer even than that we had at Beaurepair, and serving also as a map, for it showed the names of the roads and streets. Ferris smoothed it flat against the table, holding down the corners with his elbows.

'This is where we went—' and he traced the route with his finger, as well as he could, for he was reading upside-down and some of the smaller ways were not marked. 'And here, Cheapside.'

Fascinated, I picked out one of the tiny houses. 'Is this ours – I mean yours—?'

We bent down to look closer. Warm-smelling hair brushed my face. The shirt fell away from his neck and I drew back a little.

'Hard to say,' he replied. 'Wait a minute,' and he took up and inked the pen I had been using, then bent again and turned the map over, writing on the back, *To Jacob Cullen, a New-Year's gift from his friend Christopher Ferris, 1645–1646.*

'There,' he said. 'Though somewhat early.'

I flung my arms round him. 'Many, many thanks! The best gift I ever had—' And so it was, not only the gift itself but his having noted my interest in such things, and picked me one out with such care.

'Something to remember me by,' he said as I released him.

'It needs no gift for that.'

Ferris came to sit next to me and watched, amused, as I traced out upon the map all the places I had visited.

'I shall never tire of looking on it,' I cried. He turned to me, smiling, a tiny movement in his eyes as if he were searching in my face, then rose abruptly.

'I wonder what ails my aunt! Will you get Becs to fetch me something to eat, Jacob, while I go and see if she be well?'

I agreed to brave Becs, and going downstairs I asked her to bring up Ferris's *something*.

'You look more yourself now,' she said.

'Is prayer so unusual in this house that it's counted an illness?' I teased her.

'Kneeling on the tiles is.'

I discovered she did not know why Aunt was so late that morning, but on going back to the fire I found Ferris full of intelligence.

'A chill,' he said. 'Rheumy eyes and nose. She'd best keep her bed.'

'Should we call in a doctor?'

'She says no. I'll take her some ginger after breakfast.'

We sat down at the table again in silence, side by side. I carefully rolled up my map and replaced the ribbon. 'Ferris,' I began.

'Yes?'

'I – something very strange happened to me this morning.'

'Becs put her hand on your knee?'

'This is no jest. Pray hear me out.'

He moved back to the chair opposite me.

'This morning, when I came down and no one was here, I – I had a vision.'

Ferris's eyes grew perplexed. 'What, an angel? A ghost?' There was suddenly a hunger in his voice and in his look. I knew what it meant, and was sorry to disappoint.

'No. Nothing like that. But I saw the room – the world – *felt* it – translated.'

'Translated!' He frowned. 'How?'

'I can't say!' I was beginning to wish I had never started. 'I was happy, and – methought I was with God. It was so strong, Ferris, like nothing I have known since I became a man.'

'How long did it last?'

'Perhaps a minute, I could not tell. Becs broke into it.'

'That was what scared her?'

'She found me kneeling in prayer.'

'That would scare anybody.' But there was no heart in his mockery. He leant forward and took me by the shoulders. 'So, why did you pray? Does it signify, do you think? About the colony?'

'There was nothing about that. But I knew myself forgiven for all my past sins. Now I have to do right.'

'Make restitution.'

'Aye.'

'Stay here.' He rose and went to the bookcase, whence he pulled out a little blue and green volume.

'What's that? A book of visions?'

Ferris shook his head. 'Sermons. Look here,' and he ruffled the pages with his finger. 'Here.'

I took the sermons and read: . . . *the desire for salvation is in itself a most certain proof of salvation, and though diverse there be who feign it, so that they may deceive their fellows, yet any man who doth yearn and travail in his heart after salvation, even that man who grieveth for that he holdeth himself damned, that man is saved. And though none other knoweth it, or considereth the man worthy, this proof doth hold. For what wicked creature did ever desire to be saved? The evil wish only to continue in their evil, and to be thought good. The fool hath said in his heart,* There is no God. *But to say,* I am a sinner and desirous of salvation, *that is to say,* I am every good man. *Take heart therefore, and continue in the ways of virtue.*

'This is all that was wanting,' I said, laying aside the book.

'Did you not tell me in the army that you wished to make restitution?' Ferris asked. 'You grieved for your sins then; it needed no vision.'

His voice was gentle, but I thought I heard mockery there, deep down.

'More than grieved,' I insisted. 'There was terror of damnation – temptations—'

'We are all tempted,' he said. 'Are you a Christian, and still to learn that? Every single man that lives—'

'Not every man hears—' I cried out, then stopped. I was afraid to put to him the question that racked me: *And if some – thing – came privily to you? If it showed you foul pictures, and spoke to you in words – in words—! Would you not fear for your soul?*

'Hears what?' asked Ferris.

I shook my head.

'Take comfort,' he said. 'Lay the past aside.'

'So you do think I have received Grace?' I begged.

Ferris gave a crooked smile. 'I guess that if Elect there be, you are one of them. And being Elect, you stand in no need of my say-so.'

I saw he did not like the talk. For one moment, when he had thought I was speaking of a ghost, his longing for the dead had charged my *vision* with a quickly fading glory. He was now recalled to himself and to a familiar scorn. His own dreams were of brotherhood and justice on earth: visions and enthusiasms he associated with Ranters. When Becs brought up the food Ferris began to talk of the printing press, and we spoke no more of the thing I had witnessed; though I was sure I had been given a sign, and glowed inwardly with resolution, yet I felt I should never have told him of it. For I was Jacob, and there was room for just one prophet in our house.

~

It fell out as I had hoped: we did not visit Richard Parr. Having taken up some ginger in hot water, Ferris found the sick woman more wretched, and sat with her until she went off to sleep again.

'Becs can't do everything; besides, Aunt gets comfort from me,' he said. 'I'll go and see her every hour or so, unless she wants more.'

'Let me help,' I said, glad to risk a sickroom provided I could only stay shut up on such a foul day.

'I have more need of you than Aunt. Get your coat.'

'Coat?' I thought I had heard him wrongly.

'For warmth. Today your apprenticeship begins.'

The room at the back of the shop was bitterly cold. Ferris ran about fetching logs and quickly made a fire. The grate did not draw very well, and the air soon grew something smoky.

'Here.' He threw me a leather apron and tied another round his own waist. 'You'll get ink everywhere until you're used to it.'

There was a slanted wooden shelf which I had not noticed before, and on it a kind of frame filled with metal blocks.

'This is your typecase, and the type pieces with the letters on. What do you notice about them?' he asked.

'They're back to front.'

'Right! A very quick boy. Now, you have to read and set everything in reverse.'

Ferris pulled something from a drawer underneath the shelf. 'This here's your stick,' and he put a piece of wood in my hand. It had corners to it, and looked nothing like a stick. 'I want you to set up my name, yours, and Aunt's, all in one line. Like this,' and he showed me how to wedge the little squares of type in place. 'Off you go.'

I searched for the letters and found J-A-C-O-B-C-U-L-L-E-N. It was easy work laying them out on the stick, and I went on with Christopher Ferris and Sarah Snapman in the same way. Ferris meanwhile fiddled with the screw mechanism on the press, flicking oil onto it with a feather.

'Finished,' I said. He came and took the stick from me and smeared a little ink over the type with his finger, then pressed a sheet of paper over it. When he peeled the leaf off, I read:

SIRREFREHPOTSIRHCNELLUCBOCAJNAMPANSHARAS

'First mistake,' he said. 'Everybody makes it. Try again.'

'You could have let me know after one name.' But I settled down to work out the problem in earnest. It was much slower going the second time, but at last I managed:

CHRISTOPHRFERRISJACOBUCLLENSARASHNAPMAN

'Better. Now,' he went on as I picked at the muddled letters, 'to space them out, you take these,' and he showed me some little squares which were blank. 'Put spaces between them, and points,' showing me the stops.

All my life I have had a horror of being thought clumsy or stupid; even when I toiled beating carpets and polishing pewter for fools, I wanted my fellow servants to see how well I did it, and Caro's neatness of touch, shown in her skill with My Lady's hair and with laces and pot-pourris, was one of the things that drew me to her. I grinned with pride when his next print-off read:

CHRISTOPHER FERRIS. JACOB CULLEN.
SARAH SNAPMAN.

'Excellent!' He was boyish, excited. 'So far as composing goes, practice is all – getting handy at it. So I'll give you something to set up.' He handed me a printed sheet. 'The Lord's Prayer. Set it up, and justify the left, exactly as it is here – you see?'

I nodded. 'Where are the big letters for the title?'

'In these cases here. They're all laid out in order of size, see the names: ten point, twelve point.'

'And what happens when I've finished?'

'It goes in the form.' He showed me how the type was fixed into a metal frame. 'Then you can see it printed off. Put your name on the bottom and we'll hang it on the wall upstairs.' He went off to see if Aunt was awake.

How I laboured. Yet at the time I scarce noticed, for I was no longer working to please Ferris alone. There was a delight in it. No one had taught me such things before, my job at Beaurepair had been simply to serve. Then there had been handling the pike: that was a butcher's job, needing only size and strength. But this work was what they called a *mystery*, a skilled trade. My eyes watered in the smoky room; my hands were stiff with cold and most likely very clumsy with the letters compared with my friend's more delicate fingers, but I kept on without a thought of stopping until I heard the door open.

'Jacob, come eat something. Aren't you hungry?'

I at once knew that I was.

Ferris came over to see my handiwork. 'Bravo, Prentice! We should cut your hair again.'

'What, and break Becs's heart?'

'Give her a lock to keep.'

We were laughing as in the army, the early days. I almost expected Nathan to stick his head up from behind the shelf of type-cases. Ferris's spirits were high, I knew, because he saw my willingness as a sign I was coming over to the idea of the colony. His happiness was so pleasant to me, I resolved there and then never to thwart him if I could help it. If I could not atone to others I could at least be a means of good to my friend, and though I could not interpret my vision to him he might yet benefit by it. And I at once had some success, for as he ran up the stairs ahead of me I remarked how graceful he was, and another thought following upon this, I straightway cut it out at the root.

'Jacob is one of the Elect,' announced Ferris as Becs brought in some boiled bacon and pease pottage. 'So be sure and serve him properly.'

Becs sniffed.

'From now on he will lead us in saying Grace,' Ferris added.

'You would not talk thus if your aunt were here,' I said. I most definitely disliked this teasing, which seemed to hint that I had lied to him.

'Becs understands,' said Ferris. 'She knows what Elect means.'

The girl stared at him.

'The Chosen,' he went on.

The poor thing clattered the dishes in laying them before us. When she went out I said, 'Why so unkind, Ferris? What harm does she do?'

'O, she knows I mean nothing by it,' said he.

'She knows no such thing. She will think I complain of her to you.'

Ferris hummed a tune.

I put down the cup of cider I was tilting against the tabletop. 'Come man, she wants a husband and I'm thrown in her way. She does no wrong.'

'And suppose she had money and were offered you, would you have her?'

'She has no money – has she?'

Ferris shook his head. We chewed on the bacon, which was tough.

'I wish spring would come,' he said suddenly. 'It seems years since I tasted green salad.'

'You won't be eating it here.'

We both fell silent. For my part, I was overcome at the thought that the place would then be well known to me, which now I was unable to see.

'You'll print off the Lord's Prayer this afternoon,' Ferris said. 'Shall we go talk to my aunt first?'

She was lying propped up when we pushed open the door after tapping. I could see the flush on her cheeks from the other side of the room. Ferris put some cordial to her mouth but she pushed the vessel away, so he set it by the bedside.

'I'm not dying, so you needn't come in looking as if you're going to lay me out.' She blew her nose and I heard the catarrh rattle in her head. 'How is the girl doing? Have you dined?'

'Bacon and pease. Be at rest, she is doing well.'

'I'm hot and cold, Christopher. No comfort at all!'

'Will you have some of the bacon?'

Aunt pushed herself up in the bed and dropped back again. 'I can't taste anything, every bit of me aches. Hold me up, Jacob, so Christopher can turn the bolster.'

Her back was slightly humped, the bones pressing on my palms through the thin stuff of her shift. I held her in an awkward embrace while Ferris beat the thing and turned it over. Dust and feathers made her sneeze as I laid her down and pulled the coverlet over her shoulders.

'Good strong arms you've got,' she coughed out, voice cracked with phlegm. 'A prop to a woman.' I must have shown my surprise for she laughed and added, 'Don't take fright, Jacob, you're safe with me.'

I smiled and kissed her hand.

'He's setting the Lord's Prayer,' Ferris told her. 'When it's done I'll bring it you.'

But she was already drifting off. Her nephew put his hand to her forehead.

'She's hot,' he said on the stairs. 'But I doubt it's more than a cold. Let's check your typesetting.'

He found only two errors, and I had composed as far as *Thine is the Kingdom*. When the whole thing was properly justified and my name added in a smaller point at the bottom (which I thought was like the ending of a young girl's sampler), he took me over to the press.

'This is a Dutch one,' he said. 'The frame is wood and as presses go it's not heavy.'

'Was your uncle licensed to print, then?'

'No. He got the press as part-payment for a debt, took it as a commodity, you might say; then he got the itch to use it, and paid a licensed man to run off lists of his goods, and so learnt.'

'But he did not use it himself? That would be against the law.'

'They were but lists. I did the same when I traded in linens.'

'And you, you –'

'– Have no licence. Don't look so sick.' He placed his hand on part of the machine. 'Here. This is the bed – it rolls in and out so we can get at the type and ink it. Put your form onto the bed – like this.'

I watched him fix the form, with all my labours in it, to the flat bottom part of the machine.

'See that? Now, we ink the form with these inkballs.' He put them in my hands. 'Run them over the type.'

'They stink,' I said, passing them back and forth. Their smooth leather surface gave off an odour like rotting kidneys.

Ferris laughed. 'I piss on them. To keep them sound.'

'Make me not your story!'

'Ask anyone in the trade.' He grinned. 'Your privilege to piss on them tonight.'

The form was inked and he arranged a little frame about the lettering. 'This is what you call your frisket. It stops ink getting where you don't want it. Now, paper. There's some behind you.'

I reached for the top sheet of a pile.

'And don't paw the rest of it!' he cried.

'Yes, Your Lordship.' I held out the sheet to him.

'Don't give it me, put it there. That thick thing is the tympanum – it evens the pressure—'

'I won't remember all these names.' I laid the clean white sheet atop the tympanum, as he called it, and Ferris showed me how to work the hinges so that the paper was bedded between two layers. Then the bed was rolled underneath the enormous screw at the other end of the press.

'Now, pull the lever to bring your platen down.' He showed me the way I should bend my arm. I took a firm grip and dragged the metal bar all the way.

'When you let go, the thing will move back of itself, because there's a counterweight,' he warned me. 'Right, let go now.'

I watched the lever return to its original position. The platen rose. 'Is that it?'

He nodded. 'Do you remember how the paper comes out?'

I was excited as a child with a gift, undoing all I had seen him do until at last the paper came off the form. He came to look it over with me.

The Lord's Prayer stood out clearly, properly pointed, and my name underneath like a real printer's. I capered in the smoky air.

'Let it dry,' he warned. 'Lay it here until the ink is set.'

A thought struck me. 'Did you go back for the paper?'

'Roger Rowly brought it.'

'Ah.'

'And why, *Ah*? This is good quality merchandise . . . now, load another sheet while I watch.'

After a few false starts I was able to set up the machine and print off correctly. Ferris, ink blotching his unscarred cheek, made me say the name of each part of the press as I handled it. Though he watched like a cat all the time I was performing my tasks, in the end he could not fault me. Five copies of the Lord's Prayer lay drying on the stand.

'That's plenty for one day.' He rubbed his eyes and gave himself another smear on the other side.

'Ferris?'

'Aye?'

'Does your scar still hurt?'

'It itches sometimes. Now, your prentice's privilege. Take the inkballs into the back courtyard and wash the ink off.'

He was serious. I went out and pissed on the things, turning them about and shaking them. Coming back I held them out for his inspection. He looked up from the type which he was poking at with a little brush, and nodded approval. 'Next time you complain of the stink, remember whose it is.'

We wiped our hands on rags, laid by the heavy aprons and went upstairs to wash off the remaining ink a more civilised way.

~

For once, sitting by the fire with him, I consented to share some wine.

'You have to do a lot more to be a printer,' Ferris explained to me. 'There's the printing of several pages on one sheet, all in order.'

'What, one – two – three?'

'No, but so they come out in order after being folded. And all properly justified and nicely finished off – no blanks, no widows or orphans.'

'Widows and—?'

'Bits left over, stuck alone on the last line. Looks ugly.'

I asked if he could do all that himself and he said he could manage some part of it, but nothing like the skill of a real craftsman. 'Go and look in the bookcase,' he urged. 'The big collection of sermons on the top shelf.'

I did as I was bidden. There were frontispieces and borders and different typefaces: a lovely piece of work. He said not every master was as skilled, and some let their prentices do too much too soon and thus spoilt the volumes. It was hard to listen to this and think of those slovenly prentices. Why was I not born in London, I found myself thinking, and raised in a trade where a man can set up for himself? Put to it early enough, I would have made a good printer. But there is no profit in crying out against the will of God. How fast do we forget our resolutions! That very morning I had been touched by Grace, yet like treacherous Simon Peter, I was already denying what had been revealed. I reminded myself that all was well.

'More wine?' Ferris held out the bottle.

I shook my head and for good measure pressed my hand over my goblet.

'I shall go up to Aunt soon,' said he. But he stayed, staring into the fire.

'Go now, if you're going to drink,' I urged him. He looked annoyed, but I went on, 'You take my meaning.'

'Yes, yes! She dislikes it.' He got irritably to his feet. 'Not the only one, is she? Will you come up?'

'Later, when you're tired.'

'When I'm drunk, you mean.'

I looked exasperation at him.

When he was gone up I must have dozed off. I was picking fluff off someone's coat and fitting it into a form no bigger than a miniature when a dull *thunk* woke me – Becs banging the dish against the door panels – and I smelt the fishy stink of eels. I sluthered up in my chair and blinked my way over to the table.

The things were lying in a mess of onions and parsley. They were not ill cooked but I have never liked them, no matter how prepared.

And be it noted here, that few people will allow a man his natural dislikes, but instead folk are always crying up some new receipt supposed infallibly to give delight: *Sure, you've never had them done in the Venetian manner.* I could see from Becs's face that it was her fixed intent to impress upon me her skill in eel cookery. Ferris sat opposite me and observed my difficulty with amusement. I feared he would laugh, but he kept his countenance quite civil as long as Becs could see it.

'Please to give me some of that wine,' I begged, thinking to wash the things down.

'Finished,' he returned sweetly. 'Shall we have some more brought?'

'Not for me. Becs, some ale please.' As she closed the door behind her, Ferris and I pulled faces at one another.

'They'll get cold,' he said. I poked at the smallest eel with the serving fork and it flaked apart. He took the fork from me and dumped two of them on my dish, then spooned the greenish sauce on top. Having done the same for himself, he began eating with relish. I took small gobbets and crushed them on my back teeth, carefully sparing my tongue. It was slow going: I could only manage one to his two.

Becs brought me the ale. 'I'm taking supper to the Mistress now,' she announced, depriving me of my hoped-for escape. 'Do you want anything?'

Her eyes lingered reproachfully on my plate. Ferris beamed at her and crammed great lumps of the slimy flesh into his mouth, closing his eyes in a mock ecstasy.

'Unkind,' I hissed when she was finally gone.

'I'm not Elect like some. Here,' he relented, 'try the wine,' and he fetched the bottle from its hiding place behind the chair where I had been sleeping. It did take off the worst of the taste. But I was careful not to indulge myself, swallowing just enough to enable me to clear the platter. I was glad when the girl returned. She presented us with a hot apple pie, and smiled as she gathered up my empty dish.

'He knows now what he's been missing,' said Ferris, turning an angelic face up to her. I fumed silently as she lumbered off with her pile of plates.

'You want her to serve them again!' I exploded when we were left alone.

'I like eels. And she would most certainly give them you anyway.' He laughed. 'Don't you know what eels do to men?'

'Make them sick,' I said. I had a most pestilent queasiness coming on. Once back in my chair by the fire I dared not budge, and while waiting for the odious feeling to pass I again fell asleep.

~

The fire was low. I could not tell what o'clock it might be, but there was nobody in the room with me. My left hip stabbed as I got up and went slowly downstairs. The kitchen was all in darkness, and Becs long gone to bed.

Bed. From the kitchen to the top of the house seemed a weary long way for my heavy limbs. This was worse than Beaurepair, where at least the great hall was on the same level as the offices and kitchen. I fumbled my way up the first set of stairs, lit a candle from the dying fire and started on the second lot feeling sorry for myself and hoping Becs had put something in the bed to warm it. Just as I reached halfway up the second flight the bells at Paul's chimed eleven. I had thought it later.

At the bend of the stairs there was more light. I felt the rush of blood in my cheeks which heated me whenever I recalled the night of my *mistake*, as I called it. What if Becs were really in there, now? Should there be any noise I would go quietly to my chamber, hearing and seeing nothing. I turned the corner. The light was from Ferris's room, as I had known it would be. Again the door stood ajar. A full five minutes passed: the flame of my candle grew tall and clear in the motionless air, and the candle being tilted, wax piqued my hand before hardening into a second skin. Grace, I repeated inwardly, Grace; but since the morning it was become an empty word, a woman's name. Go away, I told myself. Walk, cripple, walk.

There was a creak from within. The sound struck a cold blade into my chest and my heart beat painfully as if pierced. The coverlet rustled. I could not move now: I had to stay put. He might go back to sleep. In agony I waited, knowing myself free all the while to walk to my own chamber, except that I could not do it.

I saw fingers fold round the door-edge. Ferris stood before me, clad in his nightshirt, eyes big and black in the yellow light. We stared at one another.

'It's you,' he said stupidly. I thought, *He took me for his wished-for ghost*. The battering of my heart began to go down: I managed to say, 'I am sorry to have—' then my tongue dried. He was pulling at his hair, running it through his fingers and stroking it down on his neck. I had seen others do this while looking on me: Caro, and Becs. I had seen Patience do it while gazing at Zebedee.

I stared at Ferris's parted lips. He was again the incubus. I could step up to him – force him over to the bed as I had once dragged the boy inch by inch towards the pond, feeling his struggles weaken until he was helpless, make him cry out—

Deliver me from temptation, O Lord, let me not – not—

'Do you want me for anything?' Ferris asked.

The Voice laughed deep within my head. My sense sharpened to a cruel ache. It was all I could do not to pitch forward into the doorway.

He went on, 'Sleep evades me.'

The dry, knowing Voice of the Evil One whispered to me, *Tire him out*.

I closed my eyes.

'Well, Jacob.' His voice was unsure. I opened my eyes again and, looking down, saw my fist coated in candlewax. Ferris stared at it, saying, 'If you've nothing to say to me, best go to bed.'

The door shut in my face.

I undressed and lay down in tumult, my head brimming with foul images. No question of calming the blood this time, I was charged like a musket, and the seed fired off so hotly that I groaned; too bad if he heard it. Afterwards I lay calmed in body but racked in mind. Was this always the way of it, that a man climbed towards the angels only to drop into the midden? And he – *he* – I went over every look and gesture which had burnt itself into my memory. This, of course, was another snare. For it was a short way from what he had done to what I would have had him do; and once more I felt my weight bear him down and saw him grind his teeth, and then – in short, I was defeated afresh. The gushing forth of the spirit did at least bring on sleep, and sleep wrapped me up a little while from fear and shame.

~

Waking brought back the knowledge of my filthiness. Things could not go on as they had; I dressed and considered what to do.

It was possible I had seen my friend through a glass darkly, the image twisted by my own murky desires. Then I bethought me of the hand smoothing the yellow locks of hair; but this time, being on the alert, I at once felt the snare closing round me in the sudden tightening of my loins, and I straightway put the thought to one side.

It wanted yet an hour to the time when the house would begin to bustle. I looked out on the black courtyard, now my familiar view, yet unforeseen in the New Model, undreamt of at Beaurepair. In the spring I would leave for something clean different, and this too would join the dead lives I had put behind me. At the front of the house was Ferris's window and his view was stranger still – firstly, the place where he had remarked a pretty girl; then a secret communication with a room become her prison; later, he had looked out on the night with her before taking her to his bed; and still later, the steep walls fenced in a ghost's walk.

I wondered what the view was to him now. The field where he hunted Mister Cooper? A walk shared with his comrade and friend? Did he lie lonely – snare, snare, snare. I fell again on my knees, impelled by fear, and spoke aloud: 'Help me, Lord! I am not equal to the task; be Thou my strength!' and in the silence I heard that I must wait and trust as better men had done before me.

Fully clothed, I got into bed so as to sleep out the time. When I next opened my eyes the sky was dark blue: once risen and at the window, I could distinguish the boundary wall of the courtyard. I took a few deep breaths and after braving the landing, made my way downstairs without looking at the door next to mine.

They were all risen before me, Ferris sitting at his usual corner of the table. He looked up as I entered; I turned my eyes away in confusion. Aunt wished me a good morning and went back to slicing bread. Becs was on her way out as I went in, and stepped back to ask me would I like the new eggs. I said yes, and would have said the same to a dish of spiders.

'Good morning.' I paced awkwardly to a chair. Aunt raised her head to smile. Plainly she was still unwell, her cheeks an unnatural red and the skin round her nostrils tettered and cracked from constant wiping. I saw from the corner of my eye that her nephew bent his head over his plate. When I stole a glance at him he was crushing a slice of bread in one hand, biting off pieces as if to punish it. I prayed briefly and then remained silent, not because I was resolute in keeping my vow, but because I could think of nothing to say.

The maid brought me some eggs fried in butter and Aunt put down a hunk of white bread next to the plate. The eggs were excellent, and spiritual turmoil had actually given me a hunger: I devoured them in silence, and scraped the dish. Afterwards, I bethought me that taking less victual might be of help in curbing other appetites, but by then it was too late.

'It is good to see you well again,' I said to Aunt as I mopped up the last shreds of egg.

'I don't know about well,' she said. 'Still, I made use of my time, lying there. Thinking.' She tapped her head. 'Christopher, will you come to my chamber?'

Ferris nodded. His aunt got up from her chair, and he rose with her.

'Not just yet,' she said. 'In a little while.' Ferris did not return to the table with me, but went over to the fire and the bigger chairs, and flung himself down there. Silence settled on us like a pall. I was ill at ease lest he should think me unfriendly, so I went over to the other chair where I had him in full view. He flushed deeply and began to fidget, crossing and recrossing his legs.

At last he said, still not looking at me, 'Have you something to say?'

'I'm always fain to talk with you,' I said, and then remembered that I had not spoken to him the night before, when he had said he could not sleep. Perhaps he thought me selfish. That might be it, for his expression was wary as he said, 'Aunt has something to break to me.'

'I know,' I replied. 'She said as much.'

'Indeed.' His voice trembled. We each looked into the fire. He went on as if attacking me, 'It concerns you.'

'Well, tell me what it is.'

'Such innocence!' His laugh was a harsh bark which filled me with pain. Stunned, I watched him rise and leave the room.

SEVENTEEN

Brothers and Sisters

MISTRESS WOULD SPEAK with you.' Having delivered this message, Becs withdrew before I could gather my wits and question her.

Stung by curiosity, I bounded up the stairs. On my tapping at the door I was at once bidden to enter. She was propped against a reddish cushion, the empty salep cup by her side, and at the first glance I saw she was certainly not angry with me.

'Come, sit down.' She patted the quilt as if inviting me onto the bed itself, but I guessed she meant me to take a chair, and did so. The room smelt of orris, and on the table I remarked an untidy heap of papers which had slithered onto her comb and hairpins.

'May I speak frankly to you, my lad?' Her voice was grave. Without waiting for a reply, she went on: 'When you left the army, what did you bring away with you?'

'Bring away—?'

'Money,' she supplied with the directness of the Cheapside trader she was.

'You want me to pay my board?'

'You are Christopher's guest. But please to answer, as you would a friend.'

This made no sense. However, I obeyed. 'No money. Our pay was in arrears, due in November, so Ferris and I lost it. I had some plate and jewels from Basing.'

'Nothing else in the world?'

'No property unless it be a share in my father's house, but – I cannot come by that.'

'And how do you like London?'

I wondered what this had to do with arrears, but answered, 'Wonderfully well. How could I not, after so cordial a welcome!'

Aunt smiled. 'Do you see that?' She pointed to the pile of papers.

I went over and found, on the very top, my prentice work, the Lord's Prayer.

'Don't tell Christopher I said so,' she warned me, 'but you learnt to set up much faster than he did. You could turn your hand to any work.'

I smiled feebly, unable to discern her drift.

'Do you think if you stayed in London he would give up his colony?' Her eyes, lifted to mine, were grown very bright and searching. My cheeks fired up at once.

'I can't say,' I mumbled, dropping my gaze. I did not want to be the means of entrapping Ferris in the city. Was this what they had talked of earlier? If so, I cursed him for leaving me so unprepared.

'You could do well here,' she said.

'Your kind encouragement is most flattering,' I hedged. 'But Christopher's heart is set on the colony.'

'O, there might be ways to make him see sense. And make your fortune.'

I stared at her.

'We'll talk of it again.' She sighed and turned over, ready to sleep: I had been dismissed.

I slowly descended the stairs. A crazy suspicion dawned that she was about to propose marriage to me: my youth and strength in exchange for her wealth. Widows were commonly rumoured to be insatiable. But I could not reconcile this notion with her character, nor with her manner to me, which was anything but wanton. And would a woman consumed with lust want to give private audience from her sickbed? No, no. I shook my head with disgust that I had entertained such an idea. No one, seemingly, was safe from my diseased imaginings.

Ferris was scratching away with his pen at a great rate when I entered, so intent upon his work that he did not hear me at first, and jumped violently on looking up to find me there. He at once stopped writing and flung sand onto the paper.

'Well – well?' he faltered.

'I don't understand her.' I sat down at the opposite end of the table. 'Questions about my estate—!' I waved my hands in desperation. 'Ferris, what did she say to you?'

'She wants you to stay in London.' I saw a crafty relief in his face: there was still something he had not told. He rose, rolling up his paper, and went to the bookcase. 'Where's your map I bought you?'

'I took it up to my chamber. Why?'

'I just wondered.' He went to the door. 'There's a book upstairs – excuse me—'

'Ferris, what's that writing?'

'Only the pamphlet. The one you saw.'

'Don't you want me to read over the last bit?'

'Er – later.' He was gone.

Everyone in the house was mad.

~

Company was expected that afternoon; I was doomed to endure the colonists and their ravings. Harry, Elizabeth, Jeremiah I could at times give ear to, but Roger Rowly never. If God kept throwing myself and Rowly thus together, I thought, He must be thirsting to greet Rowly in Heaven. Ferris, never idle where he could be foolishly busy, had written to that Richard Parr of whom Daniel had told us. I sighed upon hearing inwardly to hear that Parr was to make one with the rest.

At noon Ferris came down, without his sheet of paper, and we dined on roast goose and salted cabbage. I could scarce digest it, my stomach was so jumping about. For some reason there was no apple sauce. Ferris ate savagely, not like himself, clashing his knife in the dish so that the noise set my teeth on edge. Becs, scenting rage in the air, stepped demurely in and out of the room, not setting her wits to ours or even looking back at me as usual. I found that I missed those attentions which had so grated on me before. Perhaps Aunt was right, and I was vain.

'Becs should find a young man,' I said when all the plates were cleared and Ferris was casting about for his draft pamphlet.

He snorted. 'Don't you worry about her, she can look out for herself.'

I spotted the draft propped against a fruit dish and we settled down to read it through one last time before they arrived. A blessed calm spread through the room; we sat harmoniously side by side as Izzy used to sit over a book with Caro. For once my sense was sleeping and I could be close to him without the usual pangs.

'There is nothing about children,' exclaimed Ferris. 'I forgot.' He scribbled in the margin.

'Did you note what we said about tools?'

'Aye, see here. But not in full.'

This puzzled me. 'I thought you were putting it in while I was with Aunt? On that bit of paper?'

'What paper?' He looked around the room as if it might be hiding there.

'The paper you were writing when I came down from Aunt's room. You took it up again with you.'

'Ah. That.'

I stared at him. 'So, if this be the fair copy—'

'Yes?'

'—where are the notes on children? On the other sheet, the one upstairs?'

'Yes.' Ferris was avoiding my eyes. Such a debate over a paper was ridiculous, and yet I could not let it go while I felt he was keeping something from me.

'So go and fetch the other sheet,' I urged.

'I have the matter off by heart,' he snapped. In another minute we would be jangling outright.

'Then nothing's lost. I only wished to be sure of it.'

He tapped his forehead, saying 'Everything's here,' then gave a rueful smile. 'All ready for Rowly.'

'Why must we have him, Ferris?'

He spread his hands. 'The man can make clothes.'

'Could not the women do that?'

'Is that what you want, a lass to measure you for breeches?'

'Let's have a tailor by all means, just not that one.'

'He's over-keen; but we need men who have the root of the matter in them. Experience will sober him.'

Over-keen? He's not the only one, I thought, eyeing my friend's shoulders, which showed none of the bulk which fits men for heavy labour. In all his travels through the wretched, war-stripped countryside he had learnt nothing from the sight of those farmworkers, cursed with weak bodies and lack of provision, who buckle under the weight of a bale of straw. If ever he came to that, I promised myself, I would carry him back to London by force. Aunt and I should keep him prisoner.

The knocker downstairs clacked: the first inhabitants of the New Jerusalem. Harry came up, bringing the scent of smoke and horses with him, followed by Elizabeth carrying her littlest babe. Both parents smiled to me as well as to Ferris, and I began to feel the meeting might not be so bad.

'How's trade?' I asked them while Ferris was downstairs seeking out some canary.

'Coming on a bit,' said Harry. 'More are staying at home, now. But I swear they're eating their horses.'

His spouse's face bore a look of wifely patience; she had clearly heard this more often than she could wish, and I was sorry to have brought it on again, since it irked her.

'Is the pamphlet ready?' she asked, holding the little one upright so it could stamp its feet on her lap.

'In draft,' I said. 'I'll set up the type tonight.' To my ears, this speech rang with a thrilling authority, especially when Elizabeth looked at me with respect.

Ferris brought up some little hot cakes with the wine, observing in an undertone to me, 'Becs seems to think we need sweetening.' While the cakes were being passed round I heard the clack of the door again and the maid at once bawled up the stairs, 'I can't go!' as she sometimes did if she were frying or something of the sort. I went down and found Rowly bowing to me on the step; resisting the temptation to close the door in his face, I bade him enter.

'You look weary,' he observed as he stepped in. 'Nothing amiss?'

Despite myself my mouth twisted up at the memory of the previous night's goings-on. Rowly might be surprised to know the half of what was amiss in this house.

'I hope you sleep well?' he persisted. I looked blank at him, and he smirked. 'Not weeping still?' So that was it: Caro. He thought to have found a way to bait me.

'Stop there, rag merchant.' I barred his way to the stairs. 'The next time you speak of that, you find yourself outside the house. Do I make myself clear?'

He bristled up. 'Does Ferris let you throw out his friends?'

'I am Ferris's friend. But just hold you there.' I rolled up my sleeve and showed him the arm which had carried an eighteen-foot pike. 'See that?'

Rowly looked at the muscles and raised his eyes back to mine. I could see fear in them now behind the mockery, and I pursued, 'Want to lay your arm alongside it?'

He lowered his gaze. I made a sudden feint at him with my fist, and watched him flinch.

'Well,' I went on, 'this arm says I can put you out with one hand and hold off Ferris with the other. So remember.' I let him squeeze past, leaving just enough room for him if he pressed up against me, and he went through meekly, head lowered and body folded together. A warmth spread through me until I remembered that I was supposed to be furthering God's will. But perhaps God's will was that I should protect my friend from such twopenny jacks.

Before I could get to the top stair someone was hammering at the door again; I descended and found Jeremiah Andrews, and a young man with him who could only be Richard Parr. This last had blue eyes glittering with joyous lunacy: by the look of him, he had none of Rowly's insolence but even less contact with the earth beneath his feet. I welcomed Andrews and then had Parr fall on me, clapping my back and chuckling with pleasure at *our great design*. He babbled like a river: What was my name? Where was Ferris? Was I to be one of the brethren?

Sighing, I mounted the stairs. Parr scampered to the top, Jeremiah grinning at us both. Our new friend was an enthusiast if ever I saw one, and Jeremiah saw it too, for he clapped his hands over his face in mock despair behind the young man's back.

Parr burst into the room ahead of us; when I got there I found him kissing Ferris on both cheeks. I thought he presumed too much on my friend's good nature, but then he did the same to all the rest of the company.

'An Italian custom,' he chirruped as he finally subsided into one of the fireside chairs.

Seeing a space next to Rowly, I took great pleasure in seating myself in it.

Ferris was just handing about the last drinks. He held out a cake he had kept for me, and invited the guests to propose a toast.

'To the New Covenant,' cried out Richard Parr, slopping wine over Elizabeth's sleeve. 'In which we shall be saved eternally by the Christ rising in us.' He stared about like one distracted and I suddenly remarked the beauty of his jewelled eyes, which put me in mind of Nathan. More than one member of the company, forgetting to raise the glass and drink, gazed back at him as at a lover. 'An end to punishment, whore to Mammon! The beginning of the New Jerusalem, under the guidance of a man of vision!' His eyes flashed admiration and I was vexed to witness Ferris's returning look: it seemed he was not proof against the flattery of an idiot.

The guests drank, praised the quality of the wine, and received more.

Elizabeth asked, 'What shall be done with murderers and violators if we are not to punish them?'

'To let them go free were licence, not liberty,' put in Jeremiah.

'The thing is to avoid undue force,' said Rowly. 'Working all of us together, we could capture a man without stabbing or broken bones.'

'How, in a net?' asked Elizabeth. The men here laughed, and she protested, 'It was no jest!'

I could not resist. 'So, Roger, were I a violator, or murderer, you see no difficulty in my capture? Provided you had company.'

'Working together we might capture even the most brutish,' Rowly struck back.

Ferris glared at me.

'Why talk of brutes? Where people live together, you'll find always disagreement,' said Harry. 'Sooner or later, a man will be arrested.'

A chill settled on the room.

'We are to live like brothers,' pleaded Ferris.

'Brothers don't always agree,' said Jeremiah. I thought how right he was. Ferris, his aunt's sole darling, had no conception of those wars fiercer than any fought for King or Parliament.

'A prison, then?' asked Harry.

Ferris looked troubled. 'I thought transgressors could be put to work the fields.'

'In chains? For if not, they'll run off,' said Harry.

'He wants the work of making the chains,' said Rowly, raising a general laugh against the smith; the latter joined in the mirth along with the rest, but said afterwards, '*That* I would gladly put in free, if 'twere wanted; but is it wanted?'

'Are we leaving London to build a prison?' cried Ferris.

'It grates, I know,' said Harry. He patted Ferris's shoulder with his great calloused paw.

'God will direct us in time. Our task is only to have faith in the cause,' insisted Parr.

'I see you were never in the army,' I told him. 'You'd have had a bellyful of causes, there.' A sickening prospect of such disputes stretched away from me like mirrors in mirrors; all the future taken up with fools' parliaments, and never again to talk to Ferris alone.

Miserable, I looked round for my friend. He was opening up more wine to further confuse our Babel. They fell on it eagerly, evidently considering his cellar as part of the common storehouse already. How could this turn out a noble project? For the first time my belief in my vision wavered: every hair of me shrank from a life passed in such company. Just to look at them was to know this was not God's meaning. I would pray again, I decided, as soon as I could get decently away; I would pray and wait on the spirit.

'Are there any more of those cakes?' asked Rowly.

'No,' I said.

'I'll go and see,' said Ferris at the same instant. But Harry putting some question to him just then, he called to me, 'Jacob, could you see if there are any cakes downstairs?' so that I found myself manservant to Roger Rowly.

I went down and discovered to my vexation that Becs had indeed made a second batch. She arranged them on a dish and gave it to me, brushing my hands with her own.

'I'm not taking them up,' I barked at her. 'You do it.'

She blinked at me, fearful lest her little game of fingers should have given offence. I had never before shouted at her. I shoved the dish into her hands and saw them quiver; she curtsied before silently mounting the stairs. I followed, cursing myself for being as great a brute as Rowly would have me. It needed but the swearing to make me Sir Bastard.

As she pushed the door open before us, the racket from the room poured into the stairwell. The babe was crying and its yells added to the hubbub, the little wretch seeming to sense we were getting nowhere. The company were all risen and were standing about, arguing. Becs edged her way to the table and put down the cakes. As she came back I shot her a contrite look but she received it coolly and upon going out, slammed the door.

'O-ho! I see how it goes!' It was Rowly; if he could see that, why couldn't he see his danger and how much better he would have been away from me? But having gargled as much wine as he could at Ferris's expense, he was more than half drunk. I turned and looked my contempt at him.

'No good pulling that saint's face to me, I *saw* you,' he smirked, putting a whole cake in his mouth. His cheeks puffed out; he chewed noisily and sprayed out a few crumbs. 'So she's cruel to you, eh? Well, friend, she's not so very bad neither; but if I'm any judge of women, you'll be unlucky there.'

I took a cake for myself. I knew I ought to go away, yet there was a fascination to me in his loathsomeness, and besides, he was so far wrong that as yet, he failed to exasperate. He could not touch me on any nerve about Becs while I knew myself desired.

'You're free to try your hand with her,' I said airily.

'Never trust a tailor with a woman. We tailors are a privileged breed—'

'Tailors! I never heard—'

'Most certainly. Few secrets a man can keep from his tailor!' He drew closer to me and tapped the side of his nose, before continuing in a hiss, 'We see it all, you know – who's deformed, who's poxed, who's impotent—'

'Charming privilege,' I muttered.

'Ah, but my dear Sir, consider. That means we know whose wives are most in need of *comfort*. Oh, yes!' he exclaimed, evidently considering me put down and overawed, while I marvelled at the vanity of the man: Roger Rowly, the cure for greensickness!

'And stranger things—' he looked round furtively. This, had I but known, was my last chance to move away, but my evil angel whispered me to stay and hear it out.

'When *he* was married,' he jerked his head over at Ferris who stood at the far end of the room, 'she wasn't right, you know: she'd been tasted before she was bought, and who do you think it was—?' He leered like a face reflected in a troubled pool.

'Enjoying his wine, are you?' I asked.

'Hoity-toity! But listen, man—'

'Not another word. Be warned—'

'But listen! It's a tale to warm a corpse!' He was shouting now, his belly full of Ferris's drink. '*They* lived opposite, and—'

I threw him across the table. The room at once grew silent; the company froze. Rowly lay shaking among the spilt wine and crumbs, and I took hold of his thin, oily tresses the better to bang his head on the wood. I was calm, as in battle when a man is too tired to fear and everything happens slowly. Each time I cracked his skull down he shrieked with pain, and I then raised him up again to get a good strong slam. Spittle flew out of his mouth on the downward swing, and he tried to twist off my fingers as I pulled out tufts of his hair.

'Jacob!' Ferris was first to cry out. Shrieking almost as high as Rowly himself, he ran up and tried to pull my arm away by the elbow. I sent him flying into the glass front of the bookcase; I was defending his name, and later he would know it. Richard Parr came up on my other side, plucking at me and whining 'This can't be the way, pray have patience,' until I stamped on him as a man would a worrisome terrier.

A pain in my wrists bringing my attention to Rowly again, I found that he was clawing them, for which courtesy I brought my fist down and smashed in his nose. Elizabeth, who up till that time had been turned to a pillar of salt, ran to stand in the corner, clutching her babe to her neck; Jeremiah skipped about, his jaws working silently. I saw Rowly's feet drumming in the plate of cakes, and heard Ferris scream out 'Harry! Harry!'

Turning to see what Harry was doing, I found his face almost touching mine, his mouth open in a great O. Everything went red, then black.

EIGHTEEN

The Uses of a Map

MY FATHER WAS GOING to punish me, for I had done something terrible, written some foulness in the Holy Book, and he had found it out. I started awake in a wash of sweat and at once shuddered in terror: this was not home. Then it came back to me, and my shame and dread were not put to flight but increased.

I was lying on the black and white tiles, near the table. It was dusk. My head and shoulders ached; the shoulder muscles grated on my bones and one eye was sticky and would not open properly. There was firelight in the room and I rolled towards it. At once my heart stabbed violently, for there was a figure, silent and unmoving, in one of the fireside chairs. His head, seen in profile and lit by the flames, was held stiffly upright, the jaw set hard. I shook inwardly at the averted face.

'Ferris—'

'Harry laid you out. Before you killed someone.' He was hoarse with bitterness. I tried to drag myself up off the tiles, to comfort him, and fell back groaning.

'Are my ribs broken?' I panted.

'I hope so.'

'Is this—' I fingered my swollen face '—Harry's work?'

'Not all. Roger gave you plenty, once you were down.'

I was shocked at the picture thus presented. 'You didn't help me, Ferris?'

'Me? I was lying with glass in the back of my head.'

I had forgotten smashing him into the bookcase. More shame came up over my soul, in foul, suffocating waves.

'It was vile. I am vile, I know it now.'

'You always know it *after*, Bad Angel.'

My heart sank at the despair in his voice. I said with a sense of having nothing to offer, 'Would I could undo it! I have my punishment: my head and chest are agony.'

'Good,' he said and I saw the word drip from an icicle. He rose to his feet; I tried to rise too, but gasped with pain and finished by kneeling doubled on the tiles.

'My aunt is lying upstairs, crying,' he said in that same toneless icy voice. 'It's the army all over again. Roger has left us, and Richard, most likely; even Harry is not sure now. Where will we find another blacksmith? I could beat you myself.'

I watched his feet go out of the room. He closed the door softly, as if walking away from one already dead.

~

When next I woke I was in bed, with no remembrance of how I got there. They fetched a surgeon to me, not my old friend Mister Chaperain, but a fellow with sickly fish-white flesh and no chin; he pronounced my limbs and skull uncracked, and having also attended Rowly, told me that person was gone to stay near Bunhill Fields with his sister.

'So I've not killed him,' I said, somewhat sullenly for a man supposedly lashed by guilt.

'That I wouldn't swear to, as yet,' he corrected. I could tell that he did not like me. 'There was a deal of bruising. It rarely does a man *good* to knock his brains round the inside of his skull.'

'So why have I not been summonsed?'

'That I can't say, Sir.' *But I think it a pity*, his eyes added.

I knew it was fear which held back the little snot-nosed tailor from bearing witness against me. But what did he matter? Ferris was keeping away. Aunt and Becs came in with soups and ointments. Their long faces showed plainly that they had been spared nothing of my exploits. One of Aunt's friends sat with me and read me some improving matter from the collection of sermons, about hasty wrath. He was a thin white-haired man, and looked to be the kind whose temptation is all in cowardice, rather than the other way; I lay staring up at the ceiling until he was done. Becs dressed the cuts and bruises on my chest, while I wondered how she liked her work. Her former playfulness seemed melted away.

'Is – is he ill?' I asked her the second day I woke up in bed, having passed the first in constant expectation of a visit.

'All cut with glass,' she returned shortly.

I considered this. 'Does he keep his chamber?'

She made no answer.

'Becs, I must beg his pardon.'

'Lift yourself.' She beat up the bolster behind my neck, her small fists thudding into the feathers.

Like the army again, Ferris had said; but to me this was worse. Once the first pain eased, there was less to distract me, and this was the first time I learnt that one pain can numb another; the reason, it might be, why lunatics tear themselves. I feared to offend him more, so set myself to wait patiently and read the rest of the sermons; very bloodless stuff they were too, and made me melancholy as a sheep.

At last, about four days after the fight, unable to hold off longer, I asked Becs for the wherewithal to write. When she had brought the things and gone, I settled myself as well as I could with my aching ribs and began on a letter to Ferris. Several times I proffered my apologies, and as often crossed them through, for they seemed either sly or presumptuous; at last, abandoning them altogether, my labour produced the following:

> *Ferris – He was insulting and slandering your Joanna in the foullest manner, exulting in her misfortune, making your love unto her the complaisance of a wittol, and your marriage bed a brothel. I gave him fair warning, but was mocked at. Now tell me what I ought to have done? Were my own wife so traduced I would defend her. I did all for love, and in defence of love, and am beaten black and blue for it, and would do it again if I saw a hair of your head threatened.*

I folded it up and called Becs back. She looked curiously at the note as I bade her take it to Ferris.

'Read it if you like,' I said, wanting to hurt her.

'What do you take me for?'

She descended, probably to the printing room, since I guessed he would be with his press. I waited, fingering a yellow-brown contusion on my forearm to see how much pain was left in it. The door at the bottom of the stairs opened: I strained to hear. Becs. I slumped disappointed onto the bolster.

His reply was on a sheet of paper from the press, and had a dirty thumbprint on it.

The hairs of my head are more than threatened: they are bloodied. Violent love eats up what it does love, and is mere appetite.

I scribbled on the bottom of this before sending it back:

I would sooner cut my own flesh than do you a hurt. You should not have tried to get between us! But only come to see me, and another time I will stand and let him beat me to a mummy.

Becs's sharp eyes took in what I had written and she gave me a pitying look. I was at once ashamed of my unkindness. I had wished to punish her for being cold, for up until then, her face had remained unfeeling even while she was dressing the war wounds received at the Battle of Cheapside. As she turned to go down for the second time, I said to her, 'You're a jewel,' and had the pleasure of seeing her smile.

The next time the door opened downstairs, I knew it was Ferris, and tried to calm myself as he neared the chamber. When he did appear, his expression was not encouraging.

'Tell me, Jacob,' he began, having seated himself on the edge of the bed, 'were you sincere in what you wrote in your note? The last one.'

'Try it – bring him back and tell him to set about me.'

'And now tell me how that would help us.'

'I only meant that I was sorry,' I said, feeling tricked.

He frowned. 'Well, if you ever feel such anger at another of our company, you must do what you wrote to me, stand and let him beat you to a mummy. You make great protestations: you'll do this, and this. Next time stand off before you hurt the other man, not after.'

'I did it for you.'

'For *me*? Did I not beg you to stop?'

I was silent, and not only because it was impossible to deny the truth of this. Again I heard Caro's shocked gasp as I told her I had slain the boy for her sake, followed by her scrabble to get away from me in the dark.

'Well, did I?' Ferris asked crossly.

I nodded my head.

He went on, 'Should he die, what will become of you?'

'I was only—'

'You make no attempt to hold yourself in.' Ferris turned his face away from me. 'Look here.'

I winced to see the bloody hair at the back of his head. 'He stirred me up – he called your wife such names—'

'*You* told *me* not even to spit at Cooper!'

'I hit him for love of you—'

'For love of mastery! By God,' he spat, 'Nat was lucky!'

Luckier than you know, I thought, rocking myself in agitation.

Ferris cried, 'And don't tell me violence is an affliction to you! I saw your face!' He paused, calming himself, before saying more quietly, 'It would go better with you, Jacob, had God seen fit to make you small.'

We sat in silence a few minutes and I saw his wrath going down, now that he was in the room with me and had spoken his mind. 'Yes,' he said at last. 'And made *me* tall and strong.'

I sighed. 'I know. You would be patient and set me a good example.'

His mouth began to curl up. 'On a quarrel like this? I would beat you senseless.'

~

We were reconciled, of course we were; things were now too far gone between us to be broken for a Roger Rowly. But it was not the same. I had never before hurt Ferris; he now felt the possibility of my doing it again, and as his aunt knew what had happened as well as anybody, I was no longer her darling boy.

For Aunt however, looked at another way, the news was not all bad. Ferris had spoken truth when he said that I had scared off others besides the tailor. The next day, when I came down, I found him writing letters in an attempt to pull together the remaining colonists. His aunt was out and perhaps he thought it a good time to resurrect the project, for I was sure she would have made the most of our setback as a sign of God's will. He had just signed a most diplomatic missive to the Bestes.

'Surely Harry's not afraid of me after knocking me down,' I said, attempting a laugh.

Ferris answered, 'He has a wife and children.'

At the thought of Elizabeth I felt a twist within. Up until this time she had thought me sober and discreet, a man to repose trust in. I hoped never to see her again.

'Will we find another smith?' I asked.

'I'm trying for one.' Ferris showed me a new pamphlet which he had run off while I was abed: it appealed for men and women to join our colony and especially for any who could farm or work with cloth or metal. 'We'll see what God sends. After all,' he threw me a sardonic glance, 'He sent me you.'

Becs entered with a bowl of warm water and a poultice for his head, to draw out the remaining splinters of glass embedded in the skin. I made to leave, but Ferris said, 'Stay and see this.'

So I sat, wretched, and watched the water grow red; saw him wince as she dabbed at the back of his head with her poultice.

'I can't get at it,' she said crossly. 'Why don't you let me cut your hair!'

'Cut it then.'

Becs jumped; I guessed she had asked before, and been refused. She hurried off for the scissors before he could change his mind. The two of us sat in silence until she came pounding back upstairs.

'Now,' she said, arranging herself with comb and scissors behind his chair, 'are you sure you want this?'

'Want it? I want my head to heal, that's all.'

'Then I cut.' She put the comb to his temple, but Ferris turned and gently took the implements from her. 'No, Becs. Let Jacob do it.'

'I can't cut hair,' I stammered. 'I've never, never.'

'But this is a job you've earned,' he said. 'I'm not asking you to cut your own flesh, am I?' I started at the words from my note, and understood: I was to know the whole of what I had done to him, right to the shearing of his hair.

'If you botch it, Becs will tidy me up,' he added.

'Very well.' I put the comb into his hair and pulled it through to the end. He ducked, and I pushed his head upright again. 'Keep still.'

'You pull too hard,' he said fretfully. Becs snatched the comb from me and showed me how to tease out the knots, starting at the bottom and working up to the top. I copied her and was doing well until I touched the comb on a hidden cut and saw redness seeping through the roots. Sickness rose in me like the spreading blood. I snatched up the front hair and combed out the ends of it into strands, working my way up as the girl had shown me. Some of the hairs stood quivering away from his head or stuck to my sleeve.

'Strange how it does that,' said Becs. 'You always get a few fliers after it's combed,' and she smoothed them down again. Strands of dark gold lay on his neck and shoulders.

'I don't want to,' I repeated.

'It must be cut so my head can be poulticed,' Ferris said, relentless.

I started at the back, holding up handfuls of the shiny slippery stuff and hacking at it, unable to keep it still against the blades. Becs watched critically, coming over from time to time to adjust the angle of the scissors. The hair crunched and squeaked as I struggled to keep level. Two big handfuls were severed, and laid on top of the pamphlet on the table, and then I could see the back of his neck and the vulnerable dip at the base of the skull. The sight pained me, and to avoid looking at it I came round to the front of him, chopping at the side locks which had once trailed on my face.

'It's done,' I said. It was a mutilation. My thumb trembled from the unaccustomed wrenching of the scissors.

'Not for a poultice,' said Becs. She took them from me without consulting Ferris, and snipped away until he looked like a dandelion. The hair was jagged and stood on end; she blew on it and laughed.

'There. I'd best put the poultice on, I know where the sore bits are.'

'Throw the hair on the fire,' ordered Ferris.

I kept back not a single strand, but gathered it all up and let it drop together like a tangle of gold thread onto the greying coals in the grate. It flared in an ecstasy of sparks, shrivelled to black, sent up a stink and went to join my letter to my mother. Becs was slapping some greenish mess on the back of my friend's head.

'How soon will it bring the glass out?' I asked meekly.

'O, a few days for what's left.' She wrapped a warm cloth around him in the style of a turban before carrying away her poultice.

We sat subdued, reading and sometimes talking of this and that, and so wore away the morning until the meal was served. Aunt joined us for it, feigning to admire Ferris in his Moorish headgear. It was clear she thought it a great pity the hair had been cut.

When we were risen from table, and she was gone to see Mistress Osgood and her two little boys, Ferris asked me to go up to my room and consult the map he had bought. He spoke as if short of breath, and looked so strangely at me that I asked him if he was well.

'Quite well,' he answered, pale and sweating. 'I would know where to find Abbot's Gardens. Andrews tells me there is a man there called Samuels, who can raise potatoes.'

Afraid he might be starting a fever, I went up to my chamber but before looking in the map I lay down to rest my back and chest, which still ached from Rowly's kicks, and I at once fell asleep. When I awoke and came down later, he was sitting by the fire, unfamiliar in his turban, and I thought he looked at me even more strangely than before.

'Is something amiss?' I asked.

'Did you look in the map for me?'

'Abbot's Gardens isn't there.' I brought out the lie without thinking, because I had little desire to eat potatoes, and no desire at all to climb the stairs again.

My answer fell like a blow on Ferris. I saw his chest rise and fall as if he were running.

'So – what I want – isn't in the map—?' He seemed unable to understand me. 'Do you mean, that is – are you saying – no?'

'Is it so important?' I demanded.

He rose to his feet, agitated. 'Jacob, did you really look? Tell true – you haven't looked, have you?'

The interrogation vexed me. 'I looked,' I said slowly and distinctly. 'The answer to your question is *no*.'

He flinched; I saw one hand go over his heart before he noticed what he was doing, and let it drop. Then he seized the poker, driving it into the coals in the grate until he had fractured most of them and thoroughly spoilt the fire.

'You set your heart too much on things,' I soothed, wishing to God I had not lied.

He turned from the shattered coals, flushed and rigid, and said bitterly, '*Don't* finish what you start then. It won't save you on Judgement Day.'

'I start and not finish!' I cried. 'Not finish what?'

He stared at me as Christ might have stared at Iscariot just after the kiss. All this for Abbot's Gardens and a few seed potatoes.

'You are not well,' I said. 'Not yourself. What ails you?'

'I would I knew!' he shouted. He got up and ran out, leaving me, baffled, to repair the fire.

~

Such strange days; such a sadness in the house. None came in pursuit of me, we were spared the disgrace of the officers taking me out in chains; for all I knew, Rowly was mended as well as ever and most likely a lot wiser. Aunt spoke kindly to me again and showed willing to forget, Becs likewise.

But after this talk of ours, Ferris grew increasingly melancholy, seemingly in mourning for his colony: he scarce ate, took no pleasure as formerly in his pamphlets, barely spoke to me, and refused even the offer of chess.

I took the pamphlets out to the bookseller at Paul's for him and we received several letters from interested parties, but after a week Ferris had yet to answer a single one. His hair still poulticed and turbanned, he lurked in the house like a wild thing caged. Each day, Becs examined the back of his head, lifting away the glass as it worked its way out, and each day he complained pettishly of her clumsiness. There was also something amiss, something I could not fathom, between him and Aunt. Whenever she and I spoke together, Ferris turned his face away, and I noted that she did not court his attention as she might have done before.

At mealtimes especially, when the conversation flagged under the heavy weight of his sulks, I wondered how much longer I could go on living there, but always came back to the same thing, namely that I had nowhere else.

The day came at last when the turban was cast aside, and Becs washed the poultice out with soapwort. I went up and touched his cropped head; he turned away slightly, but said nothing. How strange new-washed hair is. His was soft as feathers, prettily yellow; it had lost its intense smell. He sat by the fireside to finish drying it and Becs laid a piece of linen over his shoulders. I sat down in the other chair. There were old bloodstains on the linen cloth, and I thought it was the one they had used for my toothpulling.

'Would you like a fricace for your hair?' the maid asked me. She had moved rapidly from cold through civil back to saucy. 'I've a rosemary rinse would put a shine on it.'

'Nay, I'm not a lass,' I answered.

'It's good for the brains,' she went on. 'Here—' and leaning over behind me she put her cold fingers on the nape of my neck, making me jump. She giggled and I laughed with her. She was too forward, and I knew it, but I was starved of merriment.

Twisting round to speak to her, I found my face almost in her bosom. She was a full-bodied girl with rounded shoulders and arms, and the sight of her leaning over me gave me the first real pang I had felt for a woman since Caro. Confused, I stopped laughing, and looking up saw that, although it had all passed in an instant, she had missed nothing. I glanced across at Ferris: he was staring into the fire. Becs gave my back hair a long, soft tug and went out, leaving me confounded.

Towards the end of January Ferris at last roused himself to read his letters and make a memorandum of the correspondence. To prevent as much strife as possible, he explained to me, we would both examine them equally and if I took a strong dislike to any person then he or she should not be part of our commonwealth. I was sensible of just how much he was giving way to me in this, and said so. In return, I solemnly promised not to beat anybody, howsoever provoked.

'So it's a bargain?' he asked, opening his hand.

'Done.' I spat in my palm and clapped it to his. 'Christ, Ferris! You feel like Fat Tommy. You'll never build the New Jerusalem if you don't eat more.'

'I lack appetite,' he said frowning.

'You know the proverb? One shoulder of mutton drives down another. You were fatter when you left the army.'

'You exaggerate.'

He looked about ready to snap in two, but I bridled my tongue and studied the list which he had drawn up. There was one good thing: we had more people this time and in particular, more women. The writers were altogether various, and I noted their offerings with some interest. Ferris had a good clear tradesman's hand, so that I easily made out what he had written; he stood in any case by my side, pointing out important details. I read as follows:

Jane Seabright, prophetess, given to speaking in tongues.

'No other calling?' I asked. Ferris shook his head.

Nathaniel Buckler, formerly weaver. Lost right thumb and now living with his sister's family in London. Accepts any work that offers.

Wisdom Hathersage, manservant to Mister Chiggs, some private savings; unable to meet save on the Sabbath.

Jonathan and Hepsibah Tunstall, servants, one boychild aged two. Able to tend plants and trees, and to cook.

Benjamin Botts, formerly army surgeon (Ferris's eyes lit up as he pointed out this piece of intelligence), *now working as a toothdrawer* (my own eyes watered).

Catherine and Susannah Domremy, sisters-in-law, Mister Domremy dead of the plague. Dairymaids. Readers of pamphlets. No children.

Alice Cutts, her husband an ostler and dead at Naseby-Fight.

Antony Fleming, employed to drive coaches to Durham and back, not a smith but knowing something of the mystery (Ferris again hopeful).

Eunice Walker, claims to have great skill in cookery and cures; sweet-smelling paper, quill very fine, sealed with a device of a thorny heart.

'A thorny heart?' I asked. 'Why do you note that?'

'I fear she may be a Papist. Look here,' and he showed me the seal. It was indeed a heart, but he had mistaken the rest of the device.

'Those are arrows,' I said, sniffing the paper, which breathed roses over the names of the other colonists. 'Your Mistress Walker is a votary of Cupid, not the Pope.'

'Well.' He pursed his lips.

Jack and Dorothy Wilkinson, just married, the man lately come from the war and the wife with child. Weaver. The letter written by the wife.

Christian Keats, tailor. Able to bring stuffs. Lately widowed, three children, now with his sister-in-law.

Ferris laid the letters one on top of the other, and then side by side. 'Some of these will come out bad,' he said thoughtfully.

'Jane Seabright?' I had taken against the 'Prophetess' at once.

'Aye. And I fear Eunice Walker.' He held up the letter and wafted it towards me so I again caught the scent of rose otto. 'Does *that* bespeak a hardy, God-fearing woman who'll work the fields with us?'

I said there was cause to doubt it. 'But we're losing the women already. At least let us see them.'

'The only way is to bring them all here together. If we are to work and live as a community, each of them must have the chance to meet all his fellows, not ourselves alone.'

I hoped Wisdom Hathersage would be able to come, for I had taken a childish liking to his name, and he was the only one to mention openly that he had means. I pointed this out to Ferris.

'We'll get mostly folk with very little,' he replied. 'If a man is doing well, and content, why should he change? Our commonwealth will be but a common poverty to start with, all our riches still to strive for.'

'Ought we to ask Hathersage to put in money, though others put in none?' I asked.

Ferris grinned. 'Perhaps he too has none. Best ask a small sum of each, what think you? But this should be agreed by all of us.'

He was happier than I had seen him since I attacked Rowly, and I prayed that this new company might prove more congenial to me than the old. Ferris and I were still not right with one another. I perceived that he was nursing some hurt, but could never get him to speak of it, and once, upon my pressing him, he had shouted, 'Did I not swear, never to enter upon this subject again?' as if referring to some vow. I could remember no such occasion, and thought one or the other of us must be subject to bouts of lunacy.

I helped him draft and copy letters to all of these persons requesting them to present themselves the second Sunday in February (this was done for Hathersage) at the house in Cheapside at noon, there to meet their fellow projectors. A boy from next door was hired as messenger, and Aunt was informed that the house would be invaded by strangers.

'Of what quality are they?' she enquired, already fretting over what hospitality to offer.

'Working people and masterless men,' said Ferris. 'Here.' He passed her the letters. 'Meat pasties and cabbage will do very well, and were they kings I see no reason to offer them more.'

She took this meekly, pleased to see him more active and cheerful even if it meant the resurrection of the hated community.

'And canary,' said Ferris.

'*No*,' said I. 'We don't yet know how these people conduct themselves when they drink.'

'Do you mean they'll bang each other's heads on the table?'

That silenced me.

'He's in the right, Christopher. They can have beer, and all manner of cordials,' said his aunt.

'Very well. We'll have the bookcase door repaired in case any of them are light-fingered.'

I thought that was meant for me too, and resolved to shame him. The next day, having enquired of Aunt as to what tools there were in the house, I myself repaired the bookcase, something Ferris had not known me able to do. He watched me pick out the broken glass and fit the new pane, adjusting it with care.

'A neat job,' he admitted grudgingly.

Resentment suddenly flared in me. 'When you found me on the road that day,' I snapped, 'did you think me fallen from the sky? Since then I remain under your tutelage, but let me tell you there wasn't a job – not one! – in my former life that I couldn't complete to perfection.'

'Perfection?'

'Perfection! I was like to be steward when the old one died.'

Ferris raised his eyebrows as if to say, *Well! You never told me this before.*

'And had the fairest woman to my wife. There, an end to my bragging,' for I was beginning to sound, even to myself, like Roger Rowly. I wiped my hands and began packing away the tools.

'You're proud as Lucifer,' he said wonderingly.

'Bad Angel,' I shot back. Then I put away the tool-box and after went straight up to my room.

Perhaps I should leave him. Our amity was grown so twisted and soured by errors and mistakings that I was hard put to see how it might ever come clear again. I wished I could start over from that first day, when I opened my dazzled eyes and found him giving me water. Then I fled to him from the prentices and he took me up again, and charmed me by sheer goodness: that was the time to go back to, and live in. Or perhaps even before that, sitting with Caro in the maze, no blood on my hands, no man's kiss in my mouth. But there would still be Walshe, and the pamphlets. It was all pre-ordained, there had never been a place where I could have leapt free of the net.

I came to myself with a sense of hopelessness and found I was looking out on the courtyard without seeing it. In place of my vision there stretched before me a blue-grey life of city winter and darkened rooms.

Someone was shouting below. I stepped softly onto the stairs, and by straining could pick out Ferris crying imperiously, 'Do it yourself! I don't—' (here I lost some words) '—but may I rot in Hell if ever I do it for you!'

Aunt's voice next, faint and querulous: she seemed to be pleading with him. My friend grumbled something which I could not catch, and then, venomously, 'I know what this is for!' along with further angry speech which was lost to me. I had never heard them talk so to one another. I went back inside the room, sat down on the bed and covered my ears, miserably certain that my sin of wrath had infected the whole house.

~

In the end Aunt called me and I had to go down. The supper was on the table; I descended and found Ferris deathly white and Aunt very red, but full of praise for my work on the bookcase door. Her nephew listened in a sulk until she asked him, 'Is it not beautiful, Christopher?'

'Perfection,' he replied bitterly.

She gave up and we sank into silence. The meat was stringy, and I chewed on the ox-tail as the wretched animal must once have chewed on the cud. Becs had never again subjected me to the eels, but I felt she had not forgotten. Now, picking gristle out of the hole in my jaw, I almost wished Eel Day were come.

'Jacob, Christopher has something to discuss with you after supper,' Aunt said into the tense air. I looked up in terror: surely this was the end, and he was telling me to leave.

'Let me hear it now,' I begged, as if the message would be less cruel with Aunt there, or as if he would not dare deliver it. Striving for calm, I heard my voice squeak like a lad's. Ferris shook his head, as if warning me. He looked as afraid as I felt, which was some encouragement: perhaps, after all, he would not put me out – perhaps he had changed his ideas on the colony. That did not matter. Whatever he wanted, so long as I was there to share it.

Aunt rose to clear the table.

'Where's Becs?' I had not missed the girl until that moment.

'With her family. I've given her a half-day. Open the door for me, Christopher.' Aunt disappeared down the stairwell. Halfway down she called out, 'There's a spiced tart,' her voice floating up eerily to the upper room.

'Now,' I said, turning to face him.

'I can't.'

Those were the only words we spoke. Aunt reappeared bearing the tart, and with it mulled wine, full of cinnamon, which I drank deep for comfort, picturing it lapping round my heart. Ferris ended by eating three portions of the sweet pastry, which I was persuaded he did not want. His aunt served them up to him with the calm of the nurse who sees the child will soon tire and will end by doing what she wishes. He was unable to eat the crust of the last piece, and sat head down staring at it.

'I'll just take these to the scullery and then I'm straight up to my bed,' said Aunt. 'Goodnight to you both.'

'Goodnight,' we chorused. She gathered up all the dirty crocks and I thought how even women, those soft creatures, can be masterful at times; it is just as well God made them weak in body. I trembled as the door closed after her.

We sat each staring jealously at the other. My face felt hot, my hands cold. Ferris got up and I rose also, thinking to move to the chairs by the fire, but he bade me stay where I was. Taking more candles, he lit them and lined them up, two near his left hand and two near his right, then seated himself directly opposite me.

'Are we going to read?' I asked.

'No.'

'Then why the lights?'

He said nothing and I realised it was my face he wanted to illumine. After glancing at the table two or three times, and much opening and closing of his lips, he began. 'I am to make you an offer. You know what it is.'

'Aunt wants me to go?'

He shook his head impatiently.

I tried again. '*You* want—?'

His eyes narrowed. 'So I'm not to be spared anything, not even saying it.'

'You'll have to, for me,' I said. 'I don't know what your offer is.' If it was not an order to leave, I was baffled, and his face, full of a hurt I could not interpret, gave me no help.

'Right,' he said. 'Since you will have us play the game, Aunt wants me to broker a marriage.'

'A *marriage*!' I gave a gasping laugh. 'I've neither house nor money, what makes her think I'd wive?'

'She has ways round that.'

'I can't marry your aunt!'

'Come, come, Jacob! You know she's not the woman.'

It came to me at once. 'Becs.'

'My aunt sent her out purposely.' He spoke in a cool, determined voice and sat back in the chair to observe my stupefied expression.

'But she has no money either,' I stammered.

'And that's your objection?' asked Ferris, stern as the Recording Angel.

'I wasn't thinking of myself.' Though a lame answer, it was a truthful one: not avarice, but simple astonishment had spoken in me. 'What I would say is, why will Aunt have me marry her when we have nothing to marry on? Where's the, the—'

'Profit?'

'Aye! If you remember it was *your* word. Where's the profit?'

'Well, I can see where Becs's profit lies,' he mocked. 'How often have we joked about it?'

Again I felt her fingers tangled in my hair, pulling my head back, and heard her low laugh.

'She thinks now is the time – she has talked with your aunt,' I mused.

'And why might that be?' demanded Ferris.

'Eh?'

'Have you given her cause to hope?' He leant forward as if to snatch at my answer.

'Not I. But I've seen her more – forward – of late. Yes indeed.'

We were silent a moment. I both saw and heard him take a breath before he went on flatly, as if reciting a hated lesson, 'She is to have a dowry of twenty pounds, and you can live in with her as servant here.'

I sighed, for it was a fair prospect to a masterless man already disenchanted with the colony. No more living on Ferris's bounty. A good, kind mistress to work for; a pretty young wife, clever at what she did, who felt for me all that a woman may feel for a man. I would become a citizen of London and not lie in turf huts nor dig drains. But Ferris being gone, I was not sure what it would all taste of.

'My aunt and I have fallen out over my telling you this,' Ferris said. 'She *would* have it come from me, as being more persuasive. I refused at first.'

'But then yielded to her? Why was that?'

'Something she said cut the ground from under me.' He looked at me almost with hatred.

I lowered my eyes and studied a mark on the table. 'Yes? Something she said?'

'She said it was no matter my refusing, if you didn't. She as good as dared me to put the question.'

'She is sure of my acceptance, then.'

'You haven't refused,' he pointed out. I thought I heard scorn in his voice and looked up to tell him that poverty opens as many temptations to a man as do riches, but seeing his compressed lips, was ashamed to offer such an excuse. Instead I said, 'Is your aunt doing this just to help Becs to a husband?'

'She says she gains a man in the house, and that's good against thieves if her nephew goes.'

'If? You are already set on going.'

'So I am; but Aunt imagines *your* staying would hold me here, too. That's the root of the matter, though she never says it.'

I remembered her eager quizzing of me from her sickbed, and especially the hint that Ferris and I were bound together, which had made my face so fire up.

'But she is wrong?' I asked. 'You would go without me?'

He nodded.

I went on, 'So I'd never see you again.'

'Not never; I would come to see Aunt,' he replied. 'But I would meet you as her servant.'

I pictured myself waiting at table, silent while others were privileged to sit and talk with him. I would brush his coats and lay out his shirts: that image so pained me that all I could do was repeat, 'But you would leave.'

'*You'd* have made *your* choice!' he flared. 'What would satisfy you – that I should give up the colony to secure you twenty pounds?'

I hesitated, shamefaced, for had there been no woman in the bargain, it was exactly what I did want: money, and the two of us in London.

He went on, 'And that I should drink to you at your wedding?'

I pictured Becs and myself together, squabbling, but always over little things, while I rotted away at the core from love of Ferris.

It was hopeless.

'Here.' I laid my hands on the table, palms up, and jerked my head at them, 'put yours on top.'

Ferris did not move.

'Please,' I said.

He laid his cold hands on mine and I curled my fingers, folding his within them.

'Now,' I said, 'I've neither accepted nor refused. Speak it out plainly, tell me and I'll do it.'

He cried, 'Don't put it onto me! Choose for yourself.'

'This *is* choosing. Tell Aunt I will do whatever you'll have me do, and that's my answer.' I kept hold of his fingers. We stayed there silent and motionless for some time, while the candles burnt down.

At last he said quietly, 'It is a lot to give up.'

'Well. My history is bad enough without bigamy,' I replied, at which he smiled but made no reply. The candles were half burnt. I took one and rose.

'Goodnight, Ferris.'

'Goodnight, Jacob.'

As I climbed the stairs I could hear him behind me blowing out the rest.

The Devil had again struck at me, not through the flesh this time, but through that love of money which is the root of all evil, and for once I had bested him. I would be neither bigamist, nor husband to a girl I did not love; instead, I would master my laziness and love of ease and I would help build the colony. I had vowed it before, but vows are but a paper study for a monument in stone, to be carved out with much sweat, perhaps not without injury, before the thing stands to be admired. To the colony I should go, and give of my best for it, and live kindly with my companions so that Ferris should see my worth.

On entering my chamber I put down the candle and fetched the map from the shelf, being now of a mind to do anything, provided I did not like it, in order to lay up riches in Heaven. Though the printing was too fine to search by candlelight, I was ready to blind myself to find Abbot's Gardens and so redeem my meanness concerning Samuels and his potatoes. As I unscrolled it, something dropped out, bounced off my shoe and skittered along the floorboards. There was a paper, too, rolled up in the map. I pulled it out, and pressed it against the wall behind the candle flame, to read the following:

> *You avert your eyes from me. What should I think? For some time I believed I had understood you, and even now am not sure, but begin to fear I am fallen into a horrible error, and blush to think of that whore's trick of leaving the door unlatched. What is become of me? Do not believe I forget my spouse, neither. My nights are cruel: I lie unfitted to sleep. Now I find myself solicited to plead the cause of a rival, and to help put her into your bed. Have you the heart to stand by and see it done?*
>
> *Or will you come to me?*
>
> *Were this to be printed, I could not keep back those words. I swear this is the last time I shall ever break the business with you. I cannot talk of it face to face; try as I will, I find each time that my tongue is nailed down. What is wrapped in this paper, let it*

plead for me, as once it pleaded for you, saying, Deal with me kindly. I have had no rest since a certain dream that you know of. Waking, I thought (pardon me the resemblance!) that the scales dropped from my eyes: had I died then, I had died happy. Speak to me, Jacob, do not play the tyrant. Speak to me.

The air was become as water. A sea pressed me down, my ears roaring, lungs choking on salt heaviness. I stood motionless, only my eyes going over and over the message like those of an unlettered man who feigns to read. He had struggled long in these same waters, until his strength had given out. My breathing was hoarse against the silence. *Wrapped in this paper*. Taking the candle, I knelt on the floor and found what I had known would be there, the sharp-edged glass diamond marked *Loyaute*. It needled the palm of my hand.

His letter was dated some fortnight earlier, about the time he was become so insistent that I look in the map. I remembered the paper I had seen him scribbling at, and which he had snatched from my sight, the day I paid out Rowly. Here, then, was the root of those bitter and mysterious words about *vowing* and *being spared nothing*.

I was out of the room before I knew it, and opened his door without knocking. Ferris was still up, fully dressed; he started as I burst in.

'Yes?'

I waved the paper at him and he frowned. 'Well, what is it?' In my foolishness I had thought he would know the letter at once. I showed him the red glass in my other hand.

He winced. 'For shame, how can—'

'I have but now found it! I didn't look in the map! I lied, Ferris, I didn't look—'

He touched a finger to his lips and I realised I was shouting. There was anguish in his face; he was telling me something but the roar in my ears blocked it.

'It says, will you come to me,' I went on, throat very dry. 'So—' I threw the letter and the glass onto his bed, the sea swell pulling me off balance. He came closer and from his eyes I thought he was about to embrace me, but instead he went to the door and bolted it. As he turned back into the room, I caught him round the waist.

That was how I first went to him.

NINETEEN

Possession

I WOKE IN MY OWN BED, dazzled in my senses, invisible prints and tracks on my flesh. After such thirst, to have him lie on me and drip kisses into my mouth; later, to feel his sweat and trembling, and to remember all this now, with his scent still on me: delight, delight. Certain embraces, certain cries and pleadings in the dark coming to mind, I turned over and cooled my burning face in the bolster.

Aunt was to receive her answer today. Ferris had perhaps told her already; I was quite unable to give it thought. A star revolving in my own sphere, I was remote from earthly troubles. Everything courted me; the very sheets caressed me. I dressed slowly, waiting for my soul to seat itself back in my body.

As I was leaving his bed in the darkness, he had pulled me down to him, and whispered that we had so far only tasted our banquet. At that I almost got back in, but he laughed and said I must wait until the next night. Now I looked on the day ahead as an Eternity to be struggled through, full of business and meals and manners, before I could again enjoy him and he me.

The first person I saw on coming down was Becs, smiling at me as she put bread on the table. I smiled back and she asked, 'Have you slept well?'

I said, excellent well. At that moment Ferris came up from the lower stairs.

'Thought I heard you,' he said, nodding to Becs on her way out.

'Were you working on the press?' I asked him.

'Mmm.'

'On a new pamphlet?'

'I'll show you.'

Throughout this babble I was trying to catch his eye. He was flushed, and kept glancing down. At last I said softly, 'Won't you look at me?' and received a full gaze that made me hot all over. Without thinking, I rose, but he shook his head.

'Not here.'

The bread which I found myself chewing had no taste in it.

Ferris took nothing, but watched me eat. 'My aunt is at the market. I haven't spoken to her yet.'

'When will you?'

'Perhaps tonight. Or do you wish to tell her yourself?'

I threw down the bread. 'I'm not hungry. Let's see your pamphlet.' Getting down from table, I knocked the chair over backwards. We left the room without picking it up.

Once behind the printroom door, I pushed him against the wall and put my hands in his clothes. Becs was just along the way in the kitchen, and Aunt might return any minute. Almost as soon as he laid hand on me it was over, and he held out no longer than myself. Hearing his moan, like astonishment, I knew that embrace for the madness it was, and moved away, terrified by the risk we had just run.

We straightened our dress, regained our everyday selves; he spoke unsteadily of the work before us and I steeled my mind to printing. The new pamphlet was for the benefit of the second group of colonists, and set out some questions to be considered. There were also new copies of the previous one to be printed off, setting forth his basic principles, notably that of *no force* which I had so notoriously violated on an earlier occasion. It was fortunate that Ferris could not read my mind, for I smiled to recall the thrashing I had given Rowly. Let him come back now and try dividing myself and Ferris; I enjoyed privileges he would never—

'What's happened to your justification?' asked my friend mildly. I frowned at the case I was setting; the characters seemed crowding away from the left-hand side.

'Something's distracting you,' he said, and we burst together into crazy laughter. 'Aren't you happy in your work, prentice?'

'A fool's question.'

Feeling strong enough to choke a bear, I worked away, setting three pages of type before I began to grow weary, and making sure that everything was justified. Ferris whistled, seeing how far I was got. He took up a case and searched it for errors, but could find none; I was triumphant. The smell of salt beef drifted into the room and I realised I was passionately hungry.

'They'll call us in a minute,' he said, taking off a print to dry.

I determined to finish the last line before wiping my hands.

'Jacob?'

'Mmm?'

'You're not worried—?' His voice was gentle, as if I were ill.

'About what?' I wanted to hear the words in his mouth, a confession; I hoped he would blush like a girl.

'About the Devil,' he answered.

I almost dropped the case. 'What!'

'You think much on him. Don't you?'

'No more than others do.'

'Is it him you talk to in your sleep?'

'I slept in my own—'

'In the army. We heard you.'

Bad Angel. Now I understood it. 'Well! Something has made *you* forward,' I returned, not sure that I liked this care of my soul. 'Are you saying we've let in the Devil?'

'I don't believe in the Devil.'

'That's terrible!' I cried out before I could stop myself. 'If you don't fear the Devil – well, it means you're—'

'Look at me, Jacob. Am I one of the damned?'

I did look at him. He was gentle as always, and I remembered all his kindnesses to his fellow men. I shook my head, but went on, 'We see good striving with evil all around us. How can there be God without Satan?'

'I'm not persuaded there, neither. That there's a God.' He faced me calmly, waiting to see what I would do.

'You're building the New Jerusalem, and you don't believe in God?'

'That is but a name, a name people can understand. The place will be made of sweat. So are all dwellings, and everything.'

I saw that he was out-and-out Godless, and had only said 'I'm not persuaded' to spare me. 'Have you always thought this?'

'No. It took time. Basing-House finished God and me.'

'But you pray – you give thanks at meals.'

'I do it for Aunt. If there be no God, what does it matter?'

I gaped at him.

'But to the purpose,' he continued. 'I feared you would be miserable this morning, and I see you happy. Long may it continue! That's all my meaning.'

'Perhaps I am hardened! Sin is our condition,' I said.

'Say rather love is our rightful condition.'

'You talk like – you *are* a good man! But how can you be good without God?'

He grinned. 'Not so good, neither. But what virtue I do have is in me and of me. Men deny the good that comes from themselves, calling it God. So they do with their own evil, calling it the Devil.'

I tried to see how this might be.

'There is no Hell, Jacob.'

'And the Bible?'

'Was written by men like ourselves.'

He was frightening. At the idea of there being no Hell I had felt a breath of something like freedom, but it was illusion. I marvelled at his foolhardiness, feared it, and loved it.

'Ferris, why tell me this now?'

He mocked, 'Perhaps you may have remarked some changes between us since yesterday?'

A scuffle followed, and I again pushed him up against the wall.

'Here,' he panted, 'bend your head down.' On my doing so, he licked my mouth and said, 'If you like that, don't give it up for a sermon.'

Despite my fear, I was amused at the idea of being able to give up, when only the nearness of Becs stopped me from rolling him on the ground. He saw this, and teased, 'Or be like Augustine, who prayed, "Lord make me chaste, but not yet"!'

'Aren't you afraid of dying, Ferris?'

'I'm afraid of not living.'

There was a *clang* from the kitchen: Becs was about to take up the food. Ferris clapped his hands together, as if to say, an end to all this. 'You like salt beef, don't you? Let us eat.'

I followed him up the stairs. I was a fornicator, of unnatural appetite, in thrall to an Atheist. I repeated the words in my head and tried to feel the shock of them, but they remained strange and cruel, far removed from Ferris and me. It was simpler to say I was in love.

~

'Perhaps he's with child!' cried Aunt. 'What do you think, Christopher?'

'Stranger things have happened,' he agreed. 'He took nothing at breakfast: that might have been the sickness.'

Beef. One mouthful and I could have cleared the whole dish by myself. I had never suffered such a craving since the night of our arrival, when after months of rations I had fallen on the cold mutton. Ferris and Aunt watched, my friend looking amused, as I worked my way through two large plates of salt meat.

'It'll give you a thirst,' Aunt warned. 'Don't blame me when you can't stop drinking.'

Ferris said slyly, 'He'll be up all night,' but I held back the laugh he wanted.

'You're both of you strange today,' Aunt said, her voice grown thoughtful. Ferris had not yet made report of how I had received her proposition, and to her anxious eyes our foolishness might signify that I was to marry, and Ferris stay, or that we had joined forces against it. I drank freely to wash down the beef, and felt the wine lift my spirits. Not that they needed it – I was hilarious as a lunatic. My friend looked on, happiness lighting his face like sunlight thrown up from water.

'Will you be in the house tonight?' Aunt asked. We gave assurance that we would, and she went on, 'I should like to talk with you when Becs is not there.'

So that was to be the time. We nodded our assent, and I think she knew then that disappointment would follow, for she seemed to grow older and more tired, so that for a moment I felt pity.

But I could not think on her long. Down in the printroom I felt the impossibility of working with him all afternoon, and begged that as a good prentice I might have a half-day holiday. He said that in that case the master must have one too.

'Let us go out,' I implored.

The weather was hard and windy. Warmed by wine, we wrapped ourselves in cloaks and set out in a cold bright sunlight. He led me north, and it was not long before we came to the edge of the city. Looking about me to know if we were alone, I saw tiny green knots on the bushes. Birds hopped about with straws and scraps of wool, carrying them home, and I thought of the fields around Beaurepair in summer. The clouds were fine and white like old men's hair. We wandered, as full of foolery as boys, pushing and jostling one another (a game at which Ferris was beaten every time) and he consented to sing. This performance had me in tears of laughter, for he sang out of tune without knowing it.

'My aunt has always praised me for a sweet voice,' said he indignantly.

'Does deafness run in the family?' I mocked.

'You sing better, then!'

I gave him *Barbary Ellen*, and he found all manner of fault with my voice, but I sang on, happier I think than ever before, my legs aching from the unaccustomed exercise. Breaking off after a while to bend and rub my calves, I said, 'I am grown soft since we left the army.'

'Digging will cure that.'

Joy lapped me in sparkling waves and I cared nothing for digging. We leapt small ditches and hunched over ponds looking for fish; I saw a toad stumble away from us and wondered if it truly had a precious stone in its head.

'We had better turn back,' he said at last, tilting his face up to the sky. In place of the white wisps I saw black chains of cloud coming in from the east, and there was a chill dampness in the wind. I wondered what o'clock it was.

We set out in earnest and were just arrived within the outskirts of the city when the rain began clapping on the house walls. Shutters were heard slamming above. We made good progress by clinging to the shelter of the dwellings on one side, and mostly kept our cloaks dry. A woman dressed in brave pink silk stood in a doorway unwilling to move, confounded I guess by her own vanity, or else duped by the shortlived sunlight into coming out to be soaked. Some children herded past, splashing my shoes and hose.

At the corner of Cheapside I bought a slice of plumcake from a sutler. It tasted sour, and on turning it over I found a green fur growing on the underneath. We went back, but the man was gone. Ferris grinned at my vexation.

'Here,' I said, 'don't waste it!' We tussled back and forth as I tried to push the horrible stuff into his mouth. Choking with laughter, he spat it out, but I kept a mouldy handful at the ready, and threatened him with it all the way home.

Happiness makes the heartless man, someone told me when I was a child. We arrived home happy and heartless. Becs opened to us and by evil chance she caught from me an amorous look. It meant only that I was returning home with Ferris, counting the hours until bed, but when she took the cloaks from us I could tell from the way she held mine that she expected, very shortly, to hear something to her advantage.

It was too dark for setting more type but we went into the printroom to clean off the equipment before the evening meal.

'We were slack,' said Ferris cheerfully. 'We should have finished up before going out.' He ranged the little boxes of letters and looked over the dry pages. 'You can do the inkballs.'

I took the things out to piss on them while he wiped over the press. The sky was patched, black and stringy grey, with a bright blue piece, the size of a loaf, above the chimneys. I was careless and at first pissed on my hand, which made me jump, but soon the leather was shiny and clean.

The printroom when I took them back in was grown darker, and there were no candles. I found my friend rubbing the hinge of the platen with the greasy cloth.

'We can get it all done tomorrow,' he said as I approached. 'Then comes our meeting.'

'We may not want to stay in tomorrow,' I replied. 'Did you see the way Becs looked at me?'

'I can picture it.'

'Then don't you think we may want to go out?'

Ferris shrugged. 'The weather's changeable. Let's see.'

'Will you wash that stuff off your hands?' I asked.

'Why?'

'I hate the smell of it.'

He continued greasing the metal, while I wrinkled my nose at the stench. 'Best not come in tonight, then.'

'Don't tease me.' The slightest hint and I felt the blood, the ache of my body drawing itself together.

Ferris laughed. 'Why, what will you do?' He began sliding his shirt up over his belly.

'Don't.' I went out of the printroom before desire vanquished my common sense, and sought refuge with Aunt beside the upstairs fire.

He did wash off the grease in the scullery, but he did not stop teasing me, even during the meal. We sat opposite one another, under Aunt's nose; when I looked up from the fish he was eyeing my mouth and licking his lips.

'Still hungry?' he asked.

I said there was a draught on my neck and moved to the same side of the table as himself, where I could fix my eyes on Aunt.

'You're right,' he said and moved his chair closer to mine. 'It is warmer here.'

'The fish is – is very good done like this,' I said desperately, seeing his left hand slide below the board while his right innocently mopped up sauce on a bit of bread.

'Excuse me,' said Aunt. 'We lack a knife.' She got up and left the room.

'Did she see?' I breathed.

'No, no. Calm yourself.' He was laughing.

'*Calm* myself! That's your wish, is it?'

'O come on, it's all part of the sport!'

'I don't like your sport.'

'What, never played before?' He smiled and twisted in the chair to kiss me. My lips opened to him although I would gladly have given him a slap. Then we heard the downstairs door and he drew back, leaving me thwarted.

Aunt returned with a large knife, and shortly afterwards Becs brought up a dish of venison. I avoided looking at her, and she went back downstairs.

'You don't eat as heartily as you did,' Aunt remarked, seeing me take a small portion.

'Jacob bought a mouldy plumcake,' explained Ferris. 'I wonder he's not poisoned.'

'But why did you eat it?' exclaimed Aunt.

'I – er – only a little,' I replied, unable to talk about cake while Ferris sat decorously beside me, awaiting his chance. Thirsting to pay him out, I fidgeted in my chair. There were hours before bedtime. I hoped at least that he, too, was suffering since the kiss.

'*You're* eating more, Christopher,' Aunt remarked approvingly.

'Am I, Aunt?' He set down his knife with a clink.

'And right glad I am to see it! You'll need to put on flesh before you go off digging.'

'I'm well enough. You'd be surprised what weight I can carry.'

I closed my eyes, then opened them again to beat back the images. Aunt was watching me, and did not look away when she saw herself observed. Confused, I dropped my own gaze.

'Well, Jacob, you have had much to think about, today,' she began.

I said that I certainly had.

'You said we'd talk when Becs was gone,' protested Ferris. 'She will be back directly.'

'She was told to serve the meat, then keep her room.' Aunt drew up her chair. I was not ready, and neither I think was he, but begin we must.

At first I hid behind pretended ignorance. 'Does she know—? Is she waiting for an offer?'

'She and I have talked, yes.' Aunt pressed her lips firmly together and waited for me to speak out. I glanced to my right, at Ferris. He was watching his aunt, his lips unconsciously compressed like her own.

'The matter requires thought,' I began. 'Christopher and I talked of this last night. We went over it. Over all of it.'

I hoped, coward-fashion, that she would interrupt and let me off saying the rest, but she remained silent, her face stern.

'She is a good girl,' I smiled lamely, 'skilled in her work, comely, honest...' (What to say? What?) 'and the offer you make is generous, yes indeed, far above my deserts...'

'So it seems,' she cracked out at last.

'But I wish first and foremost to go to the colony.'

Her mouth pursed up and the skin round it grew furrowed; her eyes contracted to slits which reminded me of Ferris when he was angry, and her thin old lids pressed down in an attempt to hold back the water seeping from under them. Ferris sighed. He reached across the table and tried to take her hand, but she pulled away, sniffing loudly as she did so.

'He doesn't love her, Aunt,' he soothed. 'Becs can find a good man who does, a manservant with more money – a tradesman—'

'He would come to love her once they were wed. The man doesn't know his luck – there's health and good temper, beauty too – what more does he want? A penniless soldier!'

'Now, Aunt, how can you—'

'*She's* fairly sick for *him*.' Aunt glared at me.

'His first wife may be living,' pleaded Ferris.

Watching her face crumple, it came to me how selfish she was. I had known, of course, that this had little to do with Becs and her happiness, though Aunt was glad to serve her by the way; it had been clear to me for some time that I was to be the decoy to keep Ferris at home. What I had not reckoned with was her persistence. We might as well be dogs she had determined to wall up in a yard.

Ferris caught hold of her fingers. 'Aunty, Aunty,' he crooned. 'I'll send word to you, I'll come back and see you.'

'If you loved me, Christopher, you'd help bring off this marriage,' she snuffled.

He dropped her hand. 'Nay, that's too much. Must I be of your mind in everything?'

She wept afresh. Ferris mouthed at me. I was at a loss to understand him, and shook my head, until he said aloud, 'Jacob. Why don't you take the plates downstairs?' I needed no second bidding but began piling them up while he went round the table to stand next to her. As I bundled together the dirty knives he leant his neck against her hair, pulling her in towards his breast, and the two of them rocked softly as they had done on my first night in London.

'You are my mother,' I heard him whisper just before I passed out of the door.

Awkwardly, fearful of stumbling on the dark steps, I felt my way with my feet until I reached the open door of the kitchen, where to my relief Becs had left a candle burning. I laid my burden on the table next to the scullery and wondered when I should go up again. Ferris could best bring her round by himself – at least, I hoped so. Now that I was no longer her hero, I was in a fair way to be cast as villain, luring the heir away to the colony, no matter that he was the one luring me.

I picked up the candle and held it high to see round the room. There was pewter put on one side to be polished up; I could have helped Becs with that. We would have made a good pair of servants. Her outdoor cloak hung from a nail. Curiosity led me to bury my face in the folds: they breathed wet wool and smoke, no trace of her flesh. This, then, was as close as I would come to the girl who hoped to be my wife. It was hard on her. Nothing could be done about her liking for me, but I hoped, by a respectful demeanour, to spare her pride a little. I put my face into the cloak again and felt a strange tenderness spurt up in me. Izzy once scolded me for that my backwardness had made a fool of Caro. Women's happiness is all bound up in us, can any man tell me why that is? Ferris upstairs kissing his aunt's hair, a young man comforting an old woman, there we see it: women never learn sense. Reason is weak or lacking in them: Grandmother Eve makes them impulsive, batted back and forth by their passions.

I recalled Ferris's teasing of me and wondered had he done the like with his wife. Or others? Up till now I had never asked him if he went in to her a virgin, never given it thought. Men, had he been with men while he lived here? Again I saw Nathan's ardent face turned to him, then the boy's sleeping head pillowed on Ferris's breast. I should have killed the little fool when I had the chance.

Well, he was gone, most likely dead. I would go up in a minute. A thought came to me, and I passed the lamp rapidly along the shelves of stores until it shone on a small jar. This I opened and tasted a little of the contents on my finger. Honey. I passed on to another, and this time was luckier: goose grease. I put the jar into my sleeve, and taking the light began slowly climbing back up the stairs.

~

That first night, I had torn at his clothes; after, I learnt to stroke and kiss as I eased them off, heir to tendernesses he had been taught elsewhere. I breathed his scent, slid my hands over his supple back and round to the front, caught and held him tightly. He stared into my eyes, and pushed at me as if trying his strength against mine. I laughed, loving his fierceness, and tightened my grip.

Afterwards he lay licking my neck and stroking me with his hand. I reached for the jar, which I had placed next the bed, opened it and gave it him. Ferris looked at me in surprise, then scooped up the stuff on one finger and spread it over his palm.

'Here.' His hand closed round my prick; I jumped at the slippery feel of it. Ferris smiled and continued his stroking.

'Do you want me underneath? Mmm?' He kissed me, pressing hard and stirring me up with his tongue, then knelt by the bedside.

He is practised, came a whisper in my head.

My throat dried. I gazed on him, seeing beauty in his slender boy's hips and the long curve of his thighs; seeing also dogs and bitches. Nathan. Other men, their faces a blur above greedily jerking bodies.

The smell of grease unnerved me.

'Jacob?' He ran his hand down my arm where I still lay on the bed, pulled me towards him.

Closing with him, I trembled; he whispered me what to do and I tried to hold back until he was ready. But then, as I kissed the nape of his neck, he twisted to offer his mouth, whorish. I was at once on fire to possess him, no holds barred. I went into him relentlessly, grappled him to me and let him feel all my strength. When he flinched, sparks shot up into my belly.

'What's my name?' I demanded.

Ferris groaned, and I filled with hot delight hearing what it cost him to take me. I slid out a little, and then as soon as he shifted under my weight, drove in at full length. 'Say my name.'

He panted, 'Jacob.'

I gave a hard sharp thrust which almost finished it for me. 'Again. Say it over and over.'

'Jacob. Jacob! Jacob!'

It was done. I was burnt into him.

TWENTY

As Meat Loves Salt

IT WAS EASIER facing Becs the following morning than I had feared. She neither snivelled after me nor turned sour and combative. Instead, she was grown distant. I was no longer favoured with smiles or languishing looks.

'Will you have some bread?' she asked me, setting down a bowl of caudle.

'Thank you, Becs, I will.' I met her eyes and kept my voice pleasant and level, for I was resolved to treat her with respect and never to seem as if I presumed upon a liking.

Aunt was more difficult. Ferris had done his best the night before to persuade her of his unaltered love, but though she had softened to him she evidently still regarded me as a Judas. When I came down to eat she barely returned my salutation, and left the room almost immediately. But it was easy to forgive slights just then, for I had never felt so strong and so well, and I understood how the sight of my satisfaction, considered as a triumph over her wishes, might be a standing provocation to her.

Ferris came down after me, having gone first to his own bed to rumple it and warm the sheets. He jerked his head towards the door and raised his eyebrows, as if to say, *Where is she*? I pointed downwards to indicate the kitchen below. He stood against the opposite wall and watched me drink my beer as if he were trying to find something.

'Sit down,' I suggested.

'Use your wits.'

I flushed.

'*And* my back near broken.' He lowered himself carefully onto a chair.

Before I could think what to say the door opened and Aunt came back; she smiled at Ferris, nodded frigidly to me, as she brought in some small loaves and honey. I waited until she had left the room and her steps were heard going right down to the kitchen before I whispered, 'Forgive me.'

'And next time?'

'I will hold myself in more.'

He raised his eyebrows as if to say I had better. I caught hold of his hand, pleaded the spur of desire, vowed to curb my strength, until the fingers I was clutching finally relaxed in mine, then curled round them. Footsteps were heard on the staircase. He let go of me, split a loaf and spread the end of it with honey, then cut me the honeyed slice. We continued to eat, unspeaking, staring at one another.

~

All that day we finished up odds and ends of pamphlets. Ferris left me to print off the last batch, while he went to talk round Becs and his aunt, for the next day was to be the first meeting of the new colonists. He wanted to make sure there would be enough for them to eat, and I think suspected Aunt of some skulduggery intended to drive away this lot as effectually as I had driven away the first.

'You look weary,' I said as he came back into the printroom.

'Aunt has been there before you,' he replied. 'She has just asked me do I sleep well.'

Rain tapped at the printroom window as we sorted pages and folded them together; stacking the new pamphlets in piles, we stopped to listen to hail stoning the panes.

'Just as well Aunt hasn't thrown us out,' observed Ferris.

It was easy working with him, doing as I was told. Everything seemed simple: just we two and the press. Despite his complaints of a stiff back, the movements he made were graceful, unlike my own, and I delighted in watching him.

'I am happy,' I said aloud.

'What?' He cupped a hand to one ear; ink had got onto the side of his nose.

'I love you.'

He came up to me and we kissed. The soft, searching voluptuousness that is kissing began at once to work on me. Some men, they say, are not much moved thereby; it may be they got used to it young, while I had to wait. Ferris had some difficulty in freeing himself to say, 'Tomorrow—'

'Tomorrow?' I was fearful; perhaps he was putting me out of his bed till then.

'*No fighting* at the meeting.'

'Never.' I meant it; I saw no cause why I should ever fight anyone again.

~

I was mad. Love *is* a madness, but there, it is hardly an original observation. I seemed to recall having heard even at Beaurepair, most likely from Godfrey, that all the great scholars of ages past thought love and folly the same thing. Whoever said it, I remembered Zeb's retort, at which I had laughed along with the rest: that to a cold onlooker, a man lying with a woman might present a foolish sight, arse waggling and face screwed up, but the folly was all the spectator's own, for the actors were as near Heaven as anyone gets on earth. Now, whether standing close to Ferris or keeping away from him, I was translated. By day it pleased me to be prentice, letting him play Master, but my soul, like a bat, waited wrapped in itself for the night. No bat so blind as a man bound up in the urgings of the flesh.

I was staggered, at first, to find my idealist so wanton; but this was simply my own ignorance. He had already told me that, once he went to Joanna as a husband, he had loved her passionately, with that worship of the body which we promise in the marriage service. I had never had the smallest reason to think him a Christ. We have all of us a secret being, mining deep and invisible within, opening out at our mouths when we kiss, and I had touched him there. If Nathan had done likewise Ferris gave never a sign of it. This did not stop me, sometimes, fermenting my madness by picturing them together.

At other times I tormented myself in the knowledge that I could not always tell lovers from simple acquaintance; I had not even known that Patience lay with Zeb. For all I knew, then, Ferris and I were shouting our delights from the housetops. What would we do, once under the eye of the colony? Attempts at secrecy must soon wear thin. How much better to stay in London with its substantial walls and solid beds, to enjoy one another and let the world go hang.

We passed a third night together, and he bade me whisper; I did so, but later burnt with pride when he himself cried out loud, unable to hold back. The momentary intoxication past, I found myself listening. There were no muffled steps in the corridor, not even the sound of a bolt, yet I was sure they must have heard.

~

Our future companions came the next day to talk dreams, drink ale and eat meat pasties. Aunt was keeping away, leaving Becs to serve everything, and so all the duties of hospitality fell on us two. I was eager to redeem my past wickedness, and would have welcomed any idiot as a brother had Ferris told me to.

Eunice Walker, she of the heart and arrows, arrived first, in a gown all of pink stuff. A servant brought her to the door, but was not suffered by her to enter: I wondered if her visit was being kept a secret from someone at home. The lady was in her forties, plump and coquettish, and ogled both Ferris and me straight off in one practised glance. I saw she was so accustomed thus to flirt at men, it was become her ordinary way of looking. The bowing and curtsying over, she began:

'How many men and women will you have under your command, Mister Ferris?'

'Not my command,' he hastened to correct her. 'The thing is to be fraternal, no trace of servitude or the army about it.'

'A very good notion!' She walked up to the bookcase and examined the titles quite openly, as if offering to buy them. From behind I noticed that she wore false hair: the few strands that had slipped out from her cap were much greyer than those framing her face. 'So,' she went on, 'how many persons?'

I began to smile to myself. 'There might be perhaps five women, Madam. Be assured you will not lack for the company of your own sex.'

She eyed me behind her smirk. I recalled seeing her or someone very like her, stranded in pink, the day we walked home in the rain.

'We have about equal numbers of men and women,' said Ferris more kindly. 'Persons of all conditions: spinsters and bachelors, married and widowed.'

She nodded in acknowledgement.

'What draws you to this meeting?' he asked her. 'Have you skill, er—?'

'O, I excel in salting, pickling and all kinds of preserves,' she answered.

'But Madam, the work at first must be rough: there will be the ground to break, and all still to plant and sow,' Ferris urged.

She smiled, showing black teeth. I was now sure that this was the woman I had seen sheltering in the doorway.

'I'll tell Becs to start bringing up the drinks,' I said. On the way down I allowed myself a quiet laugh.

The girl was lounging in the kitchen, reading a letter. She looked up eagerly as I entered, then her face blanked over and she drew herself up tall.

'There's a fine sight upstairs,' I said to her. 'A pink galleon. Pray bring up the ale and you'll see it.'

Becs folded up her letter, laid it on the table and turned to the stone jar of ale. I saw her jaw set as she tilted it to get a hold.

'Let me take that,' I said. She let it rock upright and went immediately, without thanking me, to get the drinking vessels from the shelf.

'Are we still friends?' I asked.

'You have no need of me,' Becs replied.

'Nor you of me, I guess. But may I not help anyway?'

She ignored this and went out of the room with the cups. I followed with the jar.

When I entered the room Mistress Walker's eyes darted towards me; she wasted no time on the girl. Ferris seemed ill at ease. My arms trembled as I set the ale down on the table.

'Could you bring up some of those little pies you made?' Ferris asked Becs. She curtsied demurely and turned to go.

'Mistress Walker has just been telling me—' he began, when there was a knock at the door below. Becs ran down stairs. We all waited in an awkward silence, lapped in smiles, until the upper door opened to admit a gentle-looking young man, hatless and dressed in sober black.

'God give you good day, Masters! I trust this is the right place? My name is Wisdom Hathersage. Good day, Madam.' I wondered what was become of his hat.

'I am Christopher Ferris, this is Mistress Walker and this my friend Jacob Cullen,' my friend rattled off. We all made a leg; I wondered how many times we would go through the same thing. Mistress Walker seemed rather taken with Hathersage, whose features were delicate. He had a brown skin and very dark eyes, almost not English. Put Zeb and himself side by side and you would see a great difference, my brother being altogether superior in beauty and vigour, but describe them both to another party and he would conclude they were much the same.

'Tell me, Mister Hathersage, was it difficult for you to come here?' I asked, remembering what he had written.

'My master is in poor health,' he answered. 'If I wish to leave the house for any length of time he needs another man in, and that requires notice.'

'Could not a maidservant help?'

'He falls. The maid is not strong enough to lift him.'

'Ah,' said Ferris.

'But you can leave him on the Sabbath?' I asked.

'Yes, I am at liberty for church or other godly pursuits, because his sisters come on that day. Between them they manage.'

'Poor, poor gentleman!' sighed Eunice Walker. 'Has he been afflicted since birth?'

'Why, no, Madam. He was cut in the head during the war, and has never been the same since.'

'Is he much deformed?' She shuddered fleshily.

'No.' He turned to Ferris. 'I am not sure, Sir, what you are seeking in those who are to live alongside you.'

Ferris hesitated. 'We must mostly take one another for better for worse. But there's no use starting unless all will do heavy work.'

'I know something of gardening,' offered Hathersage.

Ferris began, 'And can you—' but was interrupted by the arrival of three persons together, the Domremys and Christian Keats, and we had the round of introductions to go through again. I poured ale for everyone.

Catherine and Susannah were fine-looking, the first young and the second not yet old. They were as alike as sisters, the late Mister Domremy having, after the fashion of many men, married a woman resembling those of his own family. They had the clear unpocked skins of milkmaids everywhere, and the hair which dropped forwards out of their white caps (which were laundered very fresh) had a reddish sheen to it. Eunice Walker studied them for half a minute before going to stand close by Keats.

These younger women were excited at the thought of our venture, and it seemed to me that, like Ferris, they were much taken with fantastical notions. The late Mister Domremy had been a great lover of harewitted pamphlets, deeming them wholesome even for women's light brains. Now Catherine and Susannah held forth freely on their ideas, and perhaps showed more sense than some of the men, for they could undoubtedly do useful work. They spoke in particular of a new receipt they had discovered for a cheese which matured early and made excellent eating, and of the use of simples to cure diseases of the udder. An innocent good humour shone from them – their enthusiasm was not of the sour-faced kind – and I thought that women so sanguine and practical would be able to turn their hands to most things.

Keats, the widower, was a very different type of person, and appeared to be suffering from melancholy. Like Hathersage, he was of a brownish complexion, but in his case the skin was a sickly yellow and gave him a liverish look. There were deep sags beneath his eyes, yet to judge by his coal-black curls he was, or should have been, in the prime of manhood. He turned his drooping countenance shyly, but not unkindly, upon the Domremys as if wondering how anyone could be happy in this vale of tears. When he told me that his youngest child was but three months old I understood him better.

'Your wife departed this life three months ago?' I asked.

'Two. She never recovered from her last lying-in. The Lord giveth and the Lord taketh away.'

'Amen,' said I.

Keats bowed his head. 'God be praised in all things. He has seen fit to try me in the furnace of affliction.'

I ventured to think Ferris would find him dispiriting company: I had never yet heard my friend thankful for the spiritual benefits of Joanna's death. But, I reminded myself, this man's bereavement was very new, and Ferris no longer hot and bleeding.

All this time Mistress Walker was prowling near so as not to miss a word, and she now began speaking to Keats of the great sorrow she had felt when her own dear husband, a veritable Saint, had passed away of the fever. As she spoke she drew nearer to Keats, edging between him and myself, until she at last cut me out altogether. He did not seem sorry, so I left him to her consolations.

More folk arrived: Jonathan and Hepsibah Tunstall, the woman carrying their boy. The child was a roguish little thing, and once set down he rolled about the floor, crowing and unfastening the company's shoes, which caused much laughter. The parents were both strongly built, clearly used to hard work: they looked much as country servants do, if their food be good. Ferris caught my eye and I could see we were of one mind.

'Why would you leave your employ?' I asked of these two, for they had spoken of their master as being a decent man.

'London is not for us,' the husband answered. 'The Master came into a house and business here, but we had rather be in the old place. Without offence, Mister Cullen, the filth oppresses us. We would rather dig and sow.'

I thought how it had oppressed me also, at first; and yet there were most precious pleasures to set against the stinks. I guessed the Tunstalls must be like those plants that, once moved from their first plot, never thrive: no matter how starved the soil, it is what they know.

Ferris asked, 'Could you not return where you were, and seek a place?'

Surprised, Jonathan returned, 'That were to throw ourselves on the parish,' and I thought how poorly my friend, for all his goodness, understood a servant's life. 'Besides,' the man went on, 'if we are to do farm work, we may as well work for ourselves. Who knows, if things go right, Parliament may grant us the land.'

This answer pleased Ferris, for it was exactly to his own tune. I longed to ask him why he thought Parliament should concern itself with us at all, but could not put the question in company.

There were also Jack and Dorothy Wilkinson, these two somewhat older than the Domremys and the woman pretty far gone in pregnancy. For all that, she was evidently the keener of the two; when I remarked how the husband kept shaking his head and saying, 'I know not, I know not, best let see,' etc., I saw how it was that their letter was come from the wife, and felt that they would not join us in the end, or would not stay, for his heart was not in it. But they were pleasant enough, and the meeting might tip him one way or the other. They stood a little apart from the rest, examining the room and the company and conversing together in low voices except when addressed by some other person.

Alice Cutts came up and at once showed herself too old and feeble to do the work. Ferris spoke with the utmost gentleness to her, showing her what manner of hardship she must undergo, and made her take a pie and some ale before she departed.

The next to appear were Fleming and Botts, and by ill luck these two not only arrived together but knew and disliked one another. Fleming might be twenty, and affected as much dash as was possible for one neither a Cavalier, nor rich: a stained jacket, most likely some man's cast-off, with brocade down the front, and a pair of bucket boots. He swept off an elaborately trimmed hat to reveal pale curls which he kept pushing back from his brow with a languid hand. The effect was somewhat spoilt by the smell of horses which clung about him and reminded me of Harry Beste. His letter had said he knew something of smithing, but he looked too frail to beat out metal. I asked him could he shoe a beast. He replied that he should think he could, for he was experienced in most things pertaining to horses.

'I drive the coach to Durham and back,' he told me.

'Not all in one go,' put in Botts, whose flat voice grated.

'No.' Fleming was evidently peeved at admitting it. 'I take some of the stages.'

'How many days from London to Durham?' asked Ferris, curious.

'Four days, more. No time is guaranteed.'

'That's a fearful long journey,' put in Keats.

'Near four hundred miles.'

If Fleming could work in metal he was valuable. But I could not see this man trenching, or sleeping in a ditch with his fine feathered hat over his face. What a fool I had been to lose us Harry.

Fleming and Botts could have been exhibited as examples of natural antipathy. All the time that Botts was standing near me I could catch that peculiar sweetish whiff which exhales from red-haired people. He was red altogether: red hair, jowls adorned with spreading scarlet grog-blossoms and inflamed blue eyes, the whites of which appeared to be bleeding. He had the build of a barrel. His unfortunate clothes strained to hold in the flesh pouring from the neck and sleeves of his jacket, swelling into a great bulbous head and hands meaty as pig's trotters.

'You assisted in surgery on the battlefield?' asked Ferris, rigid in face and body. I judged him to be gripped by as violent a disgust as my own.

'Aye. Seen a few sights there—!' He downed the ale in one gulp and held out the vessel to me. I filled it, wondering did he take me for a servant: Ferris had introduced me as his friend not five minutes before.

'Man with the whole of his face shot off, nothing left but shreds. In the end we found a hole in it – the throat.'

I shivered at his *in the end*, wondering how long those clumsy paws had prodded and probed.

Botts went on, 'All I could do was pour wine down. We marched the next day.' He shook his head, as if to say it was a bad business, yet his face gleamed. 'I've seen men cut in pieces, and some half burnt to death – there's this smell—'

'I beg of you, no more,' said Ferris, whose upper lip was sweating.

'Ah well, that's it with you civilians,' said Botts contemptuously.

'Civilians? I was at Naseby and Basing-House.'

'Then you'll know I speak nothing but the plain truth. You'll have seen it.'

'It is *because* I've seen it—' my friend turned away, understanding that here was a man devoid of imagination, and consequently incapable of mercy. Botts seemed not at all offended, and made his way over to the Domremys, who backed off a little as he approached.

'I wouldn't let him lay hand on a dog,' Ferris whispered to me. 'Who's missing? Apart from Jane Seabright.'

'The one with the thumb?'

'With no thumb. Nathaniel Buckler.'

He called the guests to order and requested everyone to sit round the table. There was much scraping of chairs. I observed that Mistress Walker had attached herself to Keats, and that none wished to sit by Botts. Hathersage interposed himself between that gentleman and the dairymaids, for which I liked him the better, for I was sure he relished Botts no more than I did myself. Hepsibah Tunstall was on my right, and Ferris on my left. On Ferris's left was Jack Wilkinson, staring anxiously at my friend as if afraid he might be Beelzebub in disguise. His wife's eyes roamed about the table, noting the disposition of the company and the alliances which had formed in this short space of time.

Ferris stood. 'Well, friends,' he began, 'not all of us are here present, but it seems best to proceed. Please to take one of these pamphlets,' he laid his hand on a pile of our best efforts, 'and read to see if we are at least in some sort of agreement. Will that suit?'

Keats put up his hand. 'It behoves us to start so great an undertaking with a prayer.'

Hathersage and the Domremys nodded.

'You do right to remind me' said Ferris smoothly. 'Be so kind as to lead us, Mister Keats.'

The tailor stumbled through a lengthy plea for mercy, which I was sure must irritate Ferris, and just as we seemed got to the end he announced time for each of us here to search his heart and put out any worldly or unclean thought. The result of this pious wish, for me, was that the prayer time was filled with unclean thoughts, and again I wondered how we could possibly live with these people, doing as we did.

At last we were done praying. I handed each guest a pamphlet, and, since some of the company were unlettered, Ferris read *The Rules of the Community* aloud.

> 1 Every man to be considered as equal to every other man, women not excepted: none is to be considered the servant or inferior of another unless by some wrong or shameful action he do forfeit his freedom, and even in that case he must first be given warning and only deprived of freedom after repeated warnings and for a limited time, unless the act that he has committed be so grave (such as *rapine* or *murder*) as to render him a danger unto others.
>
> 2 All property to be held in common, including Harvest, which is to be kept in common storehouses.
>
> 3 Women to be free to choose their husbands, as men to choose their wives. None, man or woman, to be forced into an unwished marriage, and in place of dowries the common storehouse.
>
> Ferris was still looking after his Joanna.
>
> 4 Children being the jewels of a community, all must keep them safe.
>
> 5 No force to be used in our commonwealth. Nor should violence be offered to oppressors, for to strike back is to sink to their level, and at worst will but furnish them with a pretence that they must needs defend themselves; under which they will do us greater injury.

'And if they be sent by the landlord,' added Ferris, 'why, we know which way that battle will go. Best not engage.' He laid down the paper. 'This is rough, and not as well expressed as it might be. More follows, but shall we talk over this first part now?'

They bade him read it again. All the men looked happy at the first rule, glad to be the equals of their one-time betters, until they understood that they were also to lose their inferiors, and more especially the women.

'The Bible says woman is subject unto man,' said Jeremiah. Harry, closely watched by Elizabeth, maintained silence.

'Their bodies are frail because their minds are likewise,' said Botts. 'Women lack full reason and have only a shallow imitative cunning.'

'My aunt is as clever as anyone here,' Ferris said. 'Has an ox more wit than a man, only because it is bigger and heavier?'

Jeremiah frowned. 'Given freedom, they may run wild.'

'Begging your pardons, I've as much liberty now as I'd have digging the land,' put in Susannah Domremy. 'Catherine and I earn our own bread and are as chaste as married women – nay, chaster than many.'

Fleming sniggered.

'This will be a life of hardship, not dissipation,' Ferris said. 'There will scarce be time for running wild. What is more, if our sisters wish to embrace that life, and we oppose them, it may be that we oppose a working of the spirit. Shall we give direction to the Lord God where He must pour His Grace?'

This, for the time being, settled the matter. I admired Ferris's adroitness.

'Shall we have tobacco?' asked Fleming.

'I had not thought to forbid anything,' Ferris answered. 'But there will be little opportunity to obtain it. Our time shall be spent working, not sitting about.'

'What about strong drink?' asked Tunstall.

Keats glanced at him nervously. 'Do you fear intemperance and disorder?'

'Where wine, Hollands and suchlike are permitted there will be drinking to excess,' Tunstall said. 'I had rather we did not allow them.'

'Wine is a useful medicine,' put in Susannah Domremy.

'Is there anyone here,' asked Ferris, 'who holds wine an absolute necessity of life?'

No hands were raised.

'Then we are unlikely to quarrel,' he concluded. 'We can settle on wine, or no wine, later.'

I smiled, thinking that the person most likely to feel pinched for lack of wine was Ferris himself.

My friend now produced a clean sheet of paper and asked the company to say when they could come away and begin digging, and what they could bring into the community. Hathersage promised ten pounds and some seeds from his master's kitchen garden, the Domremys a milch-cow, in calf, and some four or five large cheeses. The Tunstalls thought they could persuade their master, who was kind, to give them some turving and drainage spades, hoes and flails packed up by accident and still kept at home but never used since the family came to live in London. Fleming suggested a small anvil and hammers, Botts his surgical instruments (I shuddered) and *materia medica.* In addition, everyone was to bring clothing and bedding for themselves and any extra that they could spare. Eunice Walker said she was unsure what she could contribute, and would think about it. I was convinced we would not see her again. Keats promised to bring all the stuffs he could fetch away, and particularly the heavier ones such as wool for cloaks and canvas for tents. The Wilkinsons were silent, considering.

Over the date of their setting off, the company were much less forthcoming, and here methought I smelt duplicity. Our best chances were the Tunstalls, the Domremys, Hathersage and Keats. Hathersage thought he could come in a month, that is, in mid-March; the man and wife said perhaps six weeks. The young women and Keats, being masterless, thought they could manage it soonest. Some of the others, like Fleming and Botts, were so vague that I felt they did not mean to come at all, and I rejoiced at it.

Ferris, quick to learn, anticipated Keats by saying Grace before we had our pasties and cabbage. Afterwards we drank toasts to fraternity, and to the future under God's guidance. I was bored with the food, the company, and the whole idea of the colony, and grew increasingly silent as they chattered on. Ferris glanced at me from time to time. The cabbage was oversalted, and I left it on my plate.

~

When they were all gone I took up the list from the table.

'What's it worth, think you?' my friend asked.

'Nothing, most of it.'

He nodded wearily. 'Some few are honest and able, the rest—'

'You need not go,' I risked.

Ferris stared away from me out of the window.

'Have you thought,' I pursued, 'what will happen to us – to *us* – among so many? Are we going to lie in the fields?'

'Men did in the army.'

I bit back the question that at once rose on my lips, and instead replied, 'We'll live side by side with them for months, years.' Bitterness rose in me. 'That *was* the army, never alone with you.'

'You were too jealous,' Ferris said. 'Too harsh with the men.'

I put my hands on his shoulders and turned him about so I could look him in the eye. 'You knew what ailed me.'

Ferris returned my look. 'Aye, but did you?'

'You let me suffer.'

'Unjust,' he said. 'Had I offered myself, you would have despised—'

'You didn't want me – you had Nathan—'

'But now we understand—'

'Ferris!' I was exasperated; I forced myself to lower my voice. 'We've had three nights and you want to throw it away.'

'No, Jacob! I—'

'It will never be as you hope! You saw what came of such things in the army – you see these people, how they are – *will you not give the thing up*?'

'Call it pride if you like.' His face was grown noble. He terrified me, for I perceived that, thought being painful, he had ceased thinking.

'Isn't pride a sin?' I urged.

'There's pride and pride. You and I are different kinds of men.'

I was offended and left him.

~

During the next two weeks he began putting in order his lists of things needed for working the soil, lists made long before and often looked over, but never finished. I was sent on errands to bring home various tools, and to bespeak an ox-cart and plough to be collected nearer the time. All this time I was utterly sick of soul. He called me into his chamber one morning and showed me a small box full of gold.

'This is a part of my savings,' he said. 'The rest will stay home with Aunt.'

'If Hathersage is putting in all he has, should you not do likewise?' I asked unkindly.

'We don't know it is all he has,' responded Ferris. 'This is still more than anyone else is putting in, and is not just for me but for all of us. To be buried and kept secret in case of dire need.'

'What need?'

'O, supposing you were hurt,' and he looked at me so lovingly that I was ashamed. What right had I, eating his bread and living like a lord, to say anything at all?

Ferris said, 'I had a key made for you. Here, take it.' He held out a ribbon and I ducked my head; Ferris pushed the key inside the neck of my shirt where I felt it slip down my breast like a drop of cold water.

'I'll be out this evening,' he announced. 'Dan and his wife have invited me to dine and rest there the night.'

'I'm not invited, then?'

'The house is tiny and the babe fractious. They entertain none but old friends.'

I felt that if invited, I would hardly enjoy it. Yet the prospect of dining with Aunt brought no pleasure neither. The more Ferris sent me out for boxes, vessels, skins or seeds, the more she seemed to blame me for the whole affair.

In the afternoon, Ferris poring over his lists again, I took a walk down by the river to kill time. The wind was bitter, and so strong as to almost push me over.

~

'I have told you already.' Ferris stood up and rubbed the small of his back. 'Let's not quarrel. I leave in half an hour for Daniel's.'

'Where's Aunt?' I suddenly realised I had not seen her since the day before, and then only briefly.

'She keeps her room.'

'That makes two of us miserable on account of your colony.'

He went back to scribbling his latest list. I paced up and down, unable to settle.

'Now you are jealous of Dan,' said Ferris. 'I knew this was coming.'

I snorted. 'What's it to me if you drink yourself sick?'

'Peace! I won't be sick. You shall see.' He folded up the list. 'Do you think you could learn to sew tents, if I got you a pattern?'

I considered. The idea interested me, but I was not to be so easily won over. 'Let me practise on some cheap stuff,' I said at last.

'That's the way!' He rose, spat in his hand and clapped it to mine to seal the bargain. 'I may get a pattern tonight. There's a man coming who put up tents in the army.'

'Pity we never got under any,' I said. 'You won't stay longer than tomorrow?'

'For shame, Jacob. What did I say to you last night?' He cocked his head to one side, smiling, teasing me. 'Does a man who says *that* want to stay away?'

The memory of his praises and pleadings made me flush up. Looking at him, I thought how much more beautiful is a man's smile than a woman's: more force and fire. He left the room unopposed, my kisses drying on his mouth.

Sitting alone, I took comfort against jealousy in going over everything he had told me as we lay together the night before: all about our first meeting, how I had at once wounded him, how when I stripped by the fire he could scarce breathe for delight, and for fear of my noticing – recalling it, I could scarce breathe myself. After a night and a day I would have him safely back, privileged now not only to gaze his fill but also to lay hold of me and possess me entirely.

And then it came to me that fiercely as he might fling about in my arms, yet he wanted to go to a place where we would have to keep off from one another. It seemed that, like wine and tobacco, I was delicious, but still not reckoned a necessity of life.

Becs brought in salt beef and mustard; I ate it reading over what he had left behind, a pamphlet on ploughing and setting. Using the setting board looked to be weary work. The house was dismal. I retired early, and lay abed wondering what he was doing just then, and if he thought of me at all, and what it must be like to be him, and not believe in God nor the Devil.

~

The next day was bright. Aunt was downstairs before me and had evidently determined to be civil for all our sakes. She greeted me cordially and I readily returned her good will. Even the farming pamphlet seemed less disagreeable when spread under the sunny window and I further sweetened its lessons with spiced cake and some cider. The little key lay against my heart like a jewel.

'You'd be more comfortable at the table here,' said Aunt. 'Becs will clear it directly.'

'No, no, Aunt. I'm very well where I am.' My window seat showed the street leading to Dan's house. I knew myself laughable, but what did it matter? After half an hour the front door slammed; I jumped, but at once saw Aunt herself step out with a basket, picking through the idlers on her way to market.

It was another hour before I had my wish, but I was lucky: Ferris had only just turned the corner when I glanced up and saw him ambling along, boyish next to a burly man who crossed his path. I was able to watch him the whole length of the street. He was smiling, eyes slitted against the white spring light and his arms full of papers and bags. I saw how he remarked everyone who passed and from time to time turned his face up to the sun. Evidently he was happy, and with a pang I wondered if he was often so happy without me. Though I willed him to look up at my window, he passed below, face hidden under his hat-brim, and I heard a key in the downstairs door.

When I descended he was setting out his treasures on the table, while Becs gaped at the bags.

'Seed samples,' he announced as I went in. 'Look: carrot, onion. We can grow beans and grey peas too.'

I prodded the seeds and pulses, put my nose in the pouches of coarse sacking and sniffed. 'So, can you tell good from bad?'

'Dan came with me to the seed merchant's and told me what to look for.' He gloated over the tiny heaps of seed as another might over sacks of gold. 'And there's grain, too. Here.'

I reached into the bag he had pushed towards me and examined what lay in my palm.

'Dredge,' I said. 'Oats and rye.'

Ferris stared in surprise. 'You know it?'

'Too well.' Again I stood, filthy, among the furrows, heartsick to see my work stretching to the edge of the sky. 'And this,' I went on, casting another grain upon the table, 'is the pure rye, and this, bullimong.'

'What's that last?' Ferris pounced upon the bag. 'The man told me buckwheat, has he cozened me?'

I shook my head. 'They are the same.'

'Another time you shall come with us,' he said, excited. 'There was much to see, we had not time even though we were there before the rest.'

'You rose early then?'

'No sottishness, I told you! And look here!' Like a child thrilled by some newfangled thing, say a furred caterpillar, he implored my attention. The marvel turned out to be a thin book, entitled *On the Cutting and Stitching of Tents, With Diverse Plans and Examples Taken From Antiquity*. The frontispiece was of the Apostle Paul, cutting cloth.

'Examples from antiquity! A lucky find indeed,' said I.

'What's that?' Becs asked.

'No find, but a gift. Dan asked his friend for something a man could learn from, and this is the one James – that's the friend – learnt from himself. Take it.' He folded my fingers over the book. 'And now I think on, there are bales of stuff still in store that might do. They were too marked to sell. You can cut out in the courtyard.' He looked ready to hug me to him in the ecstasy of sudden good fortune, but the girl's presence kept him orderly. All this time she had held her face neutral as a mask. Ferris whirled towards her.

'Becs! Do you think you could show Jacob how to hold a needle?'

'Like this.' She pinched finger and thumb together in mockery. 'But if he's going to make tents he'll need to know a sight more than that.'

'But will you teach him? Ah, Becs – please? Please, for me?'

I was glad he did not say, 'For Jacob.' Becs hesitated, and it came to me that she might not want to hasten our departure.

'I will ask the Mistress,' she said at last.

'There's my best girl,' said Ferris. I did not quite like the way he spoke to her, so coaxing and all the while her secret and successful rival. He must know what it cost her to be constantly with me. It seemed that like his Bad Angel, where he was jealous, he too could be unkind.

Ferris produced maps. 'See here, the very latest and best. This one shows common and enclosed lands, dry and marshy, look—'

We all three of us bent over the table as he unscrolled them. A chill crept into my belly at the sight of these alien fields. Some carried ominous names: Marsh End, Breakback, Starveacre. I pointed these out to Ferris.

'You want a good black loam if you can get it,' he replied. 'Or clay.'

'Clay is cruel to work,' I told him. 'All round Beaurepair was clay. It gets hard as—'

'Jacob!' Ferris screamed.

'What, man!' I cried. Becs clapped a hand to her jolted heart.

'Beaurepair – I had almost forgot – Jacob, there was a man in the tavern called Zebedee Cullen!'

I sat down on the nearest chair, feeling as if I had been shot in the chest. 'How do you know? Did you speak to him?'

'We drank in that place you know of, where we went with Dan, and I heard someone call out "Cullen" but thought little of it. Until I saw him.'

'He's like me?'

'Not so big, but – yes. Same skin, same black hair.'

'Oh God.' I rocked back and forth. 'And did they also call him Zebedee?'

'That name was used too—'

'Was he proper? Pleasing? Much more so than me?'

Ferris hesitated.

I banged on the table. 'Come on! I've heard it all my life.'

He nodded. 'The best-looking man I ever saw.'

'Zeb.' My eyes were filling and even brimming over, why I could not say; I was not sad, nor was I joyful. Across from me I could see Becs's hands tumbling one over the other, never ceasing, like a madwoman's.

Zeb. The more I knew it the less I could think. Ferris observed me, waiting for some other speech. At last he said, 'He had no woman with him.'

So he had guessed that part.

'Did you speak?'

'Aye.' He coughed towards Becs, who at once left the room. 'Now Jacob, be wise for once and hear me out. He was in the company of gypsies—'

'But did you talk with him?'

'I had to wait my chance. They drank to freedom, so I let him see me raise my glass with the rest, and then I asked him had he been in the wars, and so fell into talk.'

'Yes, but to the purpose—!'

'Well.' He turned on me the gentle eyes which had pitied my thirst. 'Don't grieve at it, Jacob. He said that he had one brother. Isaiah.'

I measured the hatred that would deny me even in tavern talk with a stranger.

'He has a gold ring in one ear,' Ferris went on. 'I asked him was that to show himself a gypsy, and he said it was his wedding ring.'

'His what!'

'Those were his words.'

I tried to make sense of what I was being told. 'Did he seem well, and happy?'

'As happy as a man usually is in his cups.' Ferris stroked my hand, saying, 'For what my advice is worth – and in speaking of a brother, perhaps that's not much – Zeb is best left alone.'

'I would know what is become of my wife.' I laid my head on my arms, pushing away a bag of seeds.

'Will he tell you if you ask?'

'I don't know,' I moaned. I was horribly afraid of meeting unprepared and of what he might say to Ferris. My face flushed with self-pitying tears.

'The old sorrow,' Ferris said. He laid his hand on the back of my neck. 'The one you never tell me.'

I lifted my head. 'Shame.'

'Can there be shame between us two?'

'Easy for *you* to say.'

His look showed hurt and disappointment. He doesn't believe in Hell, I thought, because he has never put himself there. He thinks he can love me better than I deserve.

We stayed silent awhile. I wondered should I go to the tavern alone. Zeb had every reason to seek revenge. Suppose Caro were sitting there with him?

'Very well, we go tonight,' said Ferris, breaking in on my thoughts. 'And start cutting out tomorrow, eh?' He began rolling up the maps and tying up the mouths of the seed bags. I rose and picked up the book on tents.

'I am sorry,' I said.

He looked at me enquiringly.

'You were happy when you came in.' Again I saw him almost dance along the street.

'I *am* happy. And I chose. I could have kept it from you. Anyway, where shall I put all this? The printroom is too damp for seeds.'

'Not the cellar,' I said. 'Put it upstairs.'

'Aunt is out,' Ferris said.

We looked at one another.

He was stretched on his back, eyes closed, shirt up and breeches open; I lay further down the bed, playing the whore. I was come to understand him pretty well by now. I knew how to break his defences, when to draw back and make him beg, and it fired me up to hear my high-minded friend reduced by me to the words any man might use. I was planting kisses on his belly, not letting him have what he wanted, while he, lacking the strength to force me, twisted his hands in my hair.

A draught cooled the skin of my face and neck.

'Say you love me,' I ordered.

'As meat loves salt.'

I took him inside my mouth until I felt him quiver, then pulled away. Looking up to see how he liked that, I thought, not for the first time, how pleasure and pain resemble one another. I licked the sweat from the inside of his thigh and my fringe fell into my eyes.

'I'm going,' he panted. 'Jacob – please—'

I let him in then, and held tight as a hound who pulls down the stag.

Downstairs the clock chimed. Presently I raised myself and took off my shirt; Ferris ran his hands over me and kissed my chest. At that moment I felt the draught of air again, stronger than before. Looking up, I saw the door ajar, and in the opening Becs, a statue in servant's dress.

TWENTY-ONE

Discoveries

WE LAY CONFOUNDED. Ferris was pale as the bedsheets which I kept crumpling in my hands, then smoothing out again, until he shouted at me in Christ's name to stop.

'I could kill myself for not bolting the door,' I said.

'Why you?'

'This is my chamber.'

'O what does it matter!' He rolled away from me.

'Will she tell your aunt?'

He shrugged. 'How should I know? Bad enough that *she* saw.'

'I think Aunt knows.'

'Not like this. O God, God.'

So he too could scald with shame, and even forget that he denied God. His garments were still undone, and I pulled the coverlet over his nakedness, then sat on the edge of the bed watching clouds through the window. It would soon be time for the midday meal. Was Aunt already come in? Were the two women even now in the kitchen, Becs savage in disgust, Aunt trembling at her revelations of our foulness? My fault, my fault. How could I have forgotten the door? Every night I had checked, only to betray us at this much more dangerous time.

'She will go to the officers,' I whispered. Ferris buried his face in the bed as the room suddenly filled with the roar of furnaces, the delirious sputter of fat in flames, In Hell you are as if alive.

'No. She would not.' The words came half stifled from the bolster. He rubbed the back of his neck and I pictured that gentle hand charred down to the bone.

He went on, his voice hoarse, 'She won't do that to Aunt.'

'But suppose she does,' I urged. 'We must prepare a defence.'

He turned wearily towards me. 'There's none but denial.'

I considered. 'Spite? She hates me because I didn't take her.'

'They will ask, why didn't you?' he countered. 'She came with money, you have none. It's not as if she were ugly or poxed.'

'I have a wife not proven dead. You said as much to Aunt.'

Ferris's eyes were shrunken up with misery. 'Becs loves her. That's who she'll tell, if any.'

Rage rose in me, at myself, at Becs and at all spies: I bit into my knuckle until the skin broke, leaking blood onto the sheet.

'Jacob.'

'Aye?'

He pulled himself up in the bed. 'Let's to the tavern tonight. No matter what.'

I saw he was contemplating an escape into drink, and remembered how Aunt had confiscated his wine from the printroom.

'I'm going down,' he added. 'She mustn't find me here.' He smoothed the shirt down over his hips and tucked it in.

'You drink too much these days,' I said.

'There's Zebedee to look for.'

I hesitated, torn between my desire to find Zeb, my fear of his speaking with Ferris, and an awareness that of late my friend was grown too fond of bottled comfort.

He reached for my hand. 'Will you brave it with me?'

We descended the stairs padding on our toes and listening out for angry women's voices. Our luck improved, for while we were still coming down we caught the sound of Aunt entering by the front door. Ferris almost fell down the stairs, so desperate was he to get to her before she could hold converse with the maid. I scrabbled after him.

She was already in the kitchen, but the two were got no further than salutations before we burst in. Aunt turned round in evident surprise. Her arm was still hooked through the basket she used for marketing. Becs was gutting a large fish.

'Well, what's put you in such haste?' Aunt laughed.

Ferris hesitated.

'Christopher has all manner of things to show you,' I said. My everyday voice came out quite as usual. If we were not to arouse suspicion, I must act the man.

'Seeds, maps, you know,' Ferris offered timidly.

'Oh, that.' Her lack of interest was unmistakable, yet he pressed on,

'And a book on tent-making. Jacob is to learn to sew.'

'Learn to sew!' She giggled like a young girl, seemingly quite caught by the idea. 'Do you teach him, Becs?'

There was a sharp squeeze about my heart as the girl looked me over, unsmiling.

'Nay,' she said. 'Some things are for women, and men should keep off.'

'But tent-makers are men,' said Aunt.

'I doubt there's much any woman could teach him,' said Becs. She ripped out a long necklace of fish guts.

I felt she would not tell, or at least not yet. While Aunt was unpacking the basket I tried to signal Becs my thanks, but it was hard to make her look at me, now that she knew what it was I preferred to herself and twenty pounds down.

'I'll get the things out and show you,' said Ferris and fled upstairs. Aunt took butter into the scullery.

'God bless you, Becs.' I leapt forward and seized the girl's slimy fingers.

'Hands off!' she hissed, whipping them away. 'And get out!'

Upstairs I found Ferris pacing up and down, maps and seeds forlorn on the table.

'She won't tell,' I said.

'No?'

We set out the bags as he had done that morning.

'Does Aunt want to see these?' I asked.

'What else can we talk about! I feel I'm going mad.'

I was unhappy, for after lying apart the night before we had left my bed before I wanted to.

'Ferris!'

'What?'

'You will let me in tonight, won't you?'

He stared at me in silence.

'You said I was not to give you up for a sermon, Ferris.'

The door opened downstairs. He shrugged helplessly.

'I'm coming in to you no matter what,' I whispered.

'Then bolt the whoreson door!' he hissed back.

Aunt gave ear briefly to the many virtues of the several seeds, and looked over the maps with keener interest. She wished him to dig not too far from one of the coaching inns, so that she might see him in London again or even travel to the colony.

'We must be far enough from enclosed land,' said Ferris. 'We are not asking for a fight, though I wager they'll be hot to give us one.'

They both liked the look of a place called Page Common, where there was a stream and a wood nearby. It was just two miles from an inn whence there was a coach to London. I came and examined it for those fateful names that warn of long toil and little profit, but instead I found places marked Fatfield and Bull Bridge.

'This could be the one,' said Ferris to me, his face drawn.

'As soon this as any,' I returned. 'You look spent. Come out with me this afternoon.'

'Did we not agree to go tonight?'

'The streets are safer by day.'

'Come with you? Where?' asked Aunt. 'Christopher, clear these bags now, the meal will be up soon.'

I piled the maps and seed pouches into his arms and he took them off upstairs.

'Where are you going?' she repeated, fixing me with her eyes.

'To a tavern where Christopher thinks my brother may have been last night.'

'O Jacob! What good news!' She squeezed my hands.

'It may not be the man,' I warned. 'And we are scarce friends.'

'A brother's always a brother! I pray it be him.'

Aunt had seemingly forgotten Cain and Abel. Her eyes filmed over with visions, which doubtless stretched to Zeb keeping me, and thus Ferris, in London.

Becs brought up the fish some twenty minutes later, and stood as far from me as possible. Disgust quivered from her like noise from a struck gong. Ferris came down and Aunt prayed aloud not only that we might be thankful for all that was placed before us, but that, God willing, Jacob's brother might be restored to him.

'Amen,' chimed in Ferris.

I ate in a species of trance. Too much had happened too quickly, and I could not properly take it in. More than once Aunt had to call my name several times before I could understand I was being spoken to. At last we rose and Ferris went directly for his cloak and mine.

'We may be late, you were best not keep food hot for us,' he warned Aunt as he handed the garment to me.

She nodded. 'Late, but sober.'

'Just late.'

The glory of the morning was vanished utterly away. We fell in with a crew of returned soldiers whistling to a jackdaw in a woman's window and teaching it to curse: one of them called out, 'Stay, my son!' to Ferris as we passed and they shook hands.

'I know Tom from before the wars,' my friend explained. I looked up and saw the woman come to the window, lift the cage inside and pull the shutter to, while the men called out, 'Sweetheart! Come down to me!' and even, 'I saw him in camp, my angel, and he lies with all the whores.' Ferris coughed and I could see he was glad when they moved off from the house.

'How's it with you, Tom lad?' my friend asked his acquaintance, a comical individual, whose face drooped like a hound's and who rolled, rather than walked, along. Plainly, all of our companions had already drunk deep.

'My wedding's off. Some fool tells her I'm dead – I get back and find her married!'

'Didn't you write?' asked Ferris.

'Can't, can I? And my brother's dug up the fruit trees. Was man ever cursed with such a family! What's worth living for, eh, Christopher?'

I said, 'Get yourself a wife with an orchard.'

'Never mind a wife, my hearts,' said his companion, a fat man of about thirty. 'A maidservant, that's the thing. Get yourself a little honeypot on the premises.'

At the word *maidservant* Ferris at once turned scarlet.

'Hey-hey! Look at this one, lads, blushing like a bride! What, your maid's kind, is she?'

'No indeed,' said my poor friend.

'I can see it in your eyes, you dog—'

'*He's* got his feet under the table—'

'Is she dark or fair?'

'We *have* a maid—' began Ferris.

The men cheered.

'—but she affects Jacob, not myself.' His cheeks were cooling, and I saw he had mastered the rush of shame.

'Jacob, eh! And is she worth the whistle, Jacob?'

They now turned their fire on me and I amused myself in stirring them up. I had a bedfellow to tickle any man's taste: graceful, with yellow hair, the firmest, whitest paps a man might glimpse through a chamber door – at these words I saw Ferris jump, but I ignored the pleading look he turned on me and went on to boast of her waist, so slender and supple that she wore no stays.

'Easy to strip?' leered Tom.

'As a man,' I replied. 'And everything down below—' Ferris's eyes threatened murder – 'firm, gentlemen. Tight and – best of all – eager.'

'You make pretty free with her,' Ferris said as the rest of them howled, as is men's way, urging me on: *Damn scruples!* And yet I would swear that all the time they took me for a liar, even as they praised my boldness and assured me that a woman likes a man to be master.

'No wonder she likes you, then,' said Ferris out of the corner of his mouth.

'But Christopher,' asked the one called Tom, 'surely I heard you're married now?'

'She died in childbed. The babe too.'

The fellows were silenced.

As we approached the tavern, Ferris said to me, 'We will end by all going in together. You can keep to the back.'

'You forget I'm tallest.'

'Can't be helped. Or shall I go in with them and you wait outside?'

This seemed a better plan. We dropped behind and let the rest put some distance between themselves and us.

'Ferris, you'll pardon what I said?'

'Of the maid?' He laughed, and turned on me such a look as must have infallibly discovered us had any man been watching.

The little crowd tramped into the tavern. I paced outside the windows, peering in at each place where a pane had splintered from the leads. On the left I made out the shoulders of our company, and further right some tables with a few drinkers, none of them Zeb, and one sluttish woman.

I heard my friend say something about seeking a man, and my eyes followed him across the room and round a corner out of sight. I tried to read a name some sot had scratched on the glass with a diamond: it looked like *Fubsy*. Then Ferris reappeared and beckoned me in.

'What kept you?' asked the fat man as I rejoined our group.

'A neighbour passing by,' I said vaguely.

Ferris pulled up two stools and laid hold of my arm. 'Jacob, a word.'

The other man turned to where some cards were being dealt.

Ferris went on, 'He's not here. But there's one in the back who was with him last night.'

Behind me the men were shouting their bids. By rights the landlord should lose his licence, permitting the use of cards; perhaps he had the officers in his purse. I pushed open the oak door leading to the back room. The air was foul with tobacco. There seemed none there to serve. I called for ale, and sat with my back to the window so as to see the company better, feigning meanwhile to be engrossed in a ballad which someone had left on the table to my right. I saw a grizzled man before me, not unlike Walshe but much thinner, his hat limp and shining with old grease. He had a weary, frowzy look, but shouted uproariously at something his companions were saying. With him were a lad, whose lardy cheeks were not flattered by his prentice's crop, and a horse-faced woman, her hair uncovered and hanging matted down her back. She had pulled her skirt up, so as not to trail it in the tobacco spittle which streaked the floor, and seemed not to care that her calves were on view. To my surprise she got up and went to the hatch; coming back directly, she served me with my ale.

'You are the tavern-keeper, Mistress?' I enquired.

'Aye, Sir,' and she hawked and spat.

'That is your husband, then, and your son?'

She stared at me as if suspecting some trap, then snorted. For my part, I paid for the ale with the exact sum for I felt she was the kind of hostess who might forget a reckoning.

'Aye, Nolly's my son.' She swept up the coins from the table top. 'My husband's dead.'

'Forgive my forwardness, it was an idle question.'

She grinned, showing dark brown teeth, and went so far as to say she hoped I liked the ale and might drink there again. I took a sip of the drink and was pleasantly surprised. Having served me, the woman did not move off but seated herself nearby, and it came to me that she liked my looks.

'Mistress,' I began, smirking. 'You do good trade here. Is it the cheer or the pleasure of your company—'

Before I could push on with the rest of my flattery a man came in and called for a pipe. The woman rose again with a loud uncivil sigh, and as she served him I felt my courage dissolve. I finished up the ale and left.

In the other room I found Ferris sitting with the rest, being dealt in for a game of cards. I bowed to the assembled company and told him we must be going.

'I'll cut out then lads,' he said.

A man protested, 'We've just begun, my arse has scarce warmed the bench!'

Smiling, Ferris shook his head.

'Just one hand – Jacob shall play too.'

'Some other time,' I said. 'I've urgent business.'

'Aye, Blackamoor there wants back to his maid,' one said in my hearing.

Ferris came out with me to the street outside, where I at once smelt the tobacco on my coat.

'What did you hear in there?' he asked. We walked in the direction of the river, for by unspoken agreement we had no wish to return to the house.

'Nothing.'

'No?'

'They talked of other matters,' I said, seeing in his face that he suspected some bungle. 'Did you wish to go on with the cards?'

Ferris shook his head. 'Let us try some more places. I've enough in my purse to sit all night.'

And fall senseless, I thought. I said I needed to consider, so we went down by the quay and admired the ships that were come in.

I told Ferris that I loved to look at the sea.

'This isn't it,' he replied. 'The Thames merely.' Suddenly he stopped and whirled round to face me, eyes bright with mockery. 'Jacob's never seen the sea!'

He could not stop laughing.

'As good as. Well, is it any different?' I demanded.

'You can't look across to the other side of the sea, you lumpkin—!'

I knew that, from maps. He need not have mocked me, for it was no fault of mine I was country born, and I had in fact thought a deal about the sea, in particular that time when I hankered after Massachusetts. Sometimes, when I pictured how big it was, curling round the earth, I got a splitting sensation in my head that forced me to stop. It was easier to look at the people who made their bread from it, though these were almost as strange to me as the sea itself. The sailors were so wild, so outlandish, to my eyes they were scarce Englishmen at all. I said as much to Ferris, who was come to the end of his laugh. He said they had a way of living entirely their own, so in a way they were inhabitants not of England, but of their ships only.

'As a boy I had a great idea of being a mariner,' he said. 'What did you dream of?'

'Nothing. For my father to come back.'

'He left you?'

'Died. Later I thought of going to Massachusetts. But if ever I cross to America it'll be in comfort, with money.'

We watched a man twist together what looked like a snare of ropes.

'You would make a good mariner,' he said. 'You have to be strong, and it helps to be tawny.'

'How, pray? To pass for an Ethiope?'

'The fair ones get flayed by the sun. I talked once with a red-headed man sailed on the *Bluebell*; he said his back came off in pieces.'

We walked on in silence. A sweet smell, like to a fruited cake, drove out the usual stench of the quays.

'Tobacco. I could drink a pipe of it now,' said Ferris. Pale and frowning, he eyed some men loading a crane.

A tenderness rose in me. 'Are you afraid to go home?'

He hesitated. 'Somewhat.'

'Then we'll stay out until you're ready.'

We walked on awhile and then doubled back on our steps. The warmth within me grew.

'Ferris?'

'Mmm?'

'You said this morning you loved me as meat loves salt.'

I think he knew what I was leading to, for he glanced at me and kept silent.

'Ferris, you will let me come to you?'

'Even if I am miserable?' he answered.

'I have to come in, I have to.'

'You have to. Jacob, how do *you* love *me*?'

'With my body I thee worship.' That was half a jest, but only half.

'Say rather you love the meat that loves the salt.'

I could not understand this directly, but when I did, I felt the insult. I walked on awhile, picking my phrases, and said at last, 'When *you* penned that letter bidding *me* come to *you*,' my voice quivered and I took a few steps in silence, in order to recover it, 'you wrote you could not hold back those words, even if they were to be printed. Where's that courage now? Are you changed?'

'Plainly, you are not,' he flared up. 'Nothing but your prick and its wants! I don't lack courage, Jacob—' he hesitated, and went on more calmly, 'nor love neither. But don't you see I can't just put Aunt out of the way? I live with her as well as you. Nay, I love her.'

'You love me,' I insisted.

'Is there no room here for discretion?' he cried.

'Yes. Yes—' I thought him cowed by a petticoat, but some men do set too much store by women and I knew that on such matters there was no reasoning with him.

'We will use all discretion. Only let me in, and we will be silent,' I begged.

We walked on again. I could feel him yielding, and no wonder, for despite what I had said I knew full well that he did love me like salt. If he shut me out one time, I could the sooner wear him down another.

Ferris tugged at my sleeve. 'Quiet.' He tilted his head. I saw a man like Zebedee just turning out of an alley before us and evidently going the same way we were about to take. Ferris whispered, 'Is it—?'

The stranger had long black hair hanging down his back, and my brother's walk exactly. Either the man ahead was Zebedee, or my father had played false.

'I'm not sure.'

'Go on then, go up to him.' Ferris jogged my arm as if to urge me forward.

'No. No it isn't.'

'Won't you look?'

'No. Let go of me.'

I jerked away from him and we stood facing one another. My legs were drained of blood.

'What of your wife?' Ferris asked.

'I want to go home. To bed.'

~

The house seemed more than ever an Egypt. Becs was cold as a corpse to us, turning on her heel and stalking off to the kitchen as soon as she had let us in.

Aunt sat in the chimney corner with some crewel embroidery. She was civil but distant, saying that we were earlier than she'd reckoned on, and that we stank of smoke. Ferris made to kiss her, but she flinched away from him. His face fell, and I wanted to hit her. He went down to the kitchen himself, bringing up two bottles of red wine. His aunt sighed as he set them down on the table.

'Will you join us, Aunt?' I asked.

She said she would take a cup for her stomach's sake. I was trying to discover if Becs had talked while we were out; on the whole, I still thought not.

'You didn't find him, then,' she murmured.

'No,' I put in before my friend let anything drop.

For some time we sat ill at ease, politely talking of everything and nothing. Though the wine was not of the best, Ferris swilled it down almost as fast as that night when I found him wrapped in Joanna's shift.

'Becs has given me notice,' Aunt announced after her first cup and while I was pouring her a second. My hand shot forward and splashed the cloth with purple. I dared not look at Ferris.

Aunt went on, 'She says she is needed at home.' Her face added, *And I blame you, Jacob, for refusing her.*

I met her look full in the eyes. I was in no mood to be blamed or controlled.

'We'll find a girl as good,' said Ferris.

'Who's *we*? You'll be far off by that time,' she whined.

'You then,' I said.

Dinner, which we ate by candlelight, was minced beef baked into a pie. Becs served briskly but with sufficient civility to satisfy Aunt. I had, after all, refused the girl. Pie, cabbage, baked custard: all savourless and heavy. I ate what I was given but asked for no more.

'I shall miss Becs,' Aunt said when the girl was gone downstairs. 'So neat and handy.' I nodded, understanding all the while that I was under attack.

Ferris, already halfway down his fourth cup, sighed and said, 'A kind mistress like you, Aunt, will never lack for servants. I'll print you off a handbill, *Maidservant required.*'

She sniffed. 'This isn't the season for hiring. A good maid will be in place by now.'

'Nay, there are folk thrown out of work everywhere. They'll come in droves, you'll see.'

He bent himself too much to the humouring of this old woman. I wanted to get up and tongue his mouth under her jealous stare.

'You lack sleep, Ferris,' I said.

Aunt stiffened. 'It's early yet.'

'O, he'll only stop drinking if he sleeps,' I went on. 'We walked a long way today. I shall go early to bed also. Here,' I put a candle in Ferris's hand, 'move yourself.'

'I've not finished my drink—'

I drained my third cup and pulled him upright. 'Come on. Good night, Aunt.'

'Good night,' she breathed, eyes wide.

'Good night, Aunty.' Her nephew smiled, innocence incarnate, as I marched him towards the door.

All the way upstairs I held him close. Once in his chamber I laid him on the bed and kissed him soft and deep, tasting wine and burnt tobacco leaf. As soon as he breathed fast and ran his hands down my sides I pulled away and went, laughing to myself, to my own room. I had but stripped off my coat when the latch lifted and he came in to me. Later, I thought I heard the floorboards creaking out in the corridor, but by that time the bolt was securely driven home.

TWENTY-TWO

What's Past Repair

GOD GRANT THAT we remain ever thankful, and ever mindful, Lord, of Thy presence, Thou who seest our most secret doings.'

Aunt was excelling herself over the morning bread and beer. I said nothing; Ferris answered with a simple Amen. We ate in silence, and when I had finished I put down the cup and went to fetch my cloak.

My friend looked at me in surprise. 'Stay, Jacob, I'll bear you company—'

'I wish to be alone.'

'Very well,' said Ferris, hurt. 'But it is early.'

'I know that.' I donned my hat and went out.

In the street I felt shame. The night before he had been so loving with me, I had been nearly mad with the joy of it, and now I was cold with him as a man might be with a woman just paid off. I walked fast, staring at every man who approached until sure he was not Zeb. Most fellows dropped their eyes.

First I tried the tavern I knew best. An ancient purple-faced fellow lay sleeping off his debauch in the ashes. It seemed he was the woman's tapster, for he woke with a snort, raised himself on an elbow and wheezed to me, 'What's your will, Sir?'

'Hold your peace.'

Not another soul was to be seen though I strode through to the back and looked all round there. The air of the place was exceedingly sour. I could hear the old reprobate's cracked cough as he voided his phlegm into the hearth.

I was glad Zeb was not to be found in that midden. But then it came to me that he might be lodged upstairs. I would come back later.

The cloak rose behind me like a wing as I cut up the next street; there was such force and spirit in me I felt I could walk forever. As I went, I tried to picture Zeb as I might soon see him, unshaven, surly, perhaps threatening. But the image softened until what I had before me was a laughing boy. Try as I might, the face refused to harden, so from this ghost's ear I hung a gold ring. As for speech, I had by now rehearsed my first words to him in every way; be he sorry or sly or full of wrath, I was ready, yet still my heart clenched whenever I saw a fellow with a swarthy face.

I next tried the tavern where he and Ferris had talked together, but found the door barred, so I went along the quays again weighing up every man. Fallen into a rhythm now, I continued walking until the Thames banks grew green and soft, when I knew I was out of my way; then, sitting down awhile, I rubbed my calves, which were stiffening with the exercise. A scent of decay came off the river mud. A conviction settled on me that it was useless going back to the taverns, but I resolved to do it anyway, and turned back, going more slowly now on my tiring legs. The green banks smeared again into trampled mire, shabby boats were hitched here and there, and the buildings thickened until the foulness of the wind assured me of my return into the city.

I now became aware of a difficulty. Ferris might think I was concealing some meeting from him; he might not believe that I had failed to find my man. 'Not a sign of him, nothing at all,' I was saying to a stone embedded in the mud, when I looked up and saw Zeb standing in an alleyway, watching me go. I stopped dead, and raised my hand as he turned to run.

The ground seemed to fly up towards me as I ran over the street. I felt my hat fall as I thudded after him, my legs limp, my cloak a lead weight; though my breast laboured I could not get up speed. But Zeb was also hard put to it, and I was gaining on him. Several times he glanced back, and each time he did so he fell back a little. Men leapt to one side as we tore along, and once he tried a doorway let into the stones, but it was locked. When we were almost level I saw that the alley ended in a blank wall. He must have noticed it at the very same moment, for he stumbled. At once I was up with him and had hold of his hair. He whipped round, and straightway getting hold of my little finger bent it backwards until I let go of him; while I was shaking my hand from the pain he kicked full on my shin as if to crack it. My eyes watered in agony. Panting, we stared at one another. I guessed he would try to run past me, and dodged left and right to show him he could not.

'Stay! Stay!' I cried. 'I won't hurt you.'

'I'll see to that.'

'Trust me, Zeb.'

'You! I'll trust to this,' and he pulled out a knife. 'Now stand off.'

Unarmed, I hesitated before my unknown brother. There was the gold earring Ferris had made report of, but that was nothing in comparison with the way his countenance had aged and hardened.

'Stand off,' he repeated. His eyes had never left mine, and for the first time in my life they cowed me. I moved back a yard.

'Now speak,' Zeb ordered.

'I have been looking for you,' I began, 'to make peace, if I may.'

'That'll take some doing,' he sneered. 'Looking for me? How did you know I was here?'

'A friend saw you and heard your name.'

'Ah yes, the one with the questions. Jacob's spy!'

I hated to hear him speak thus of Ferris. 'Don't put my crimes on him, brother,' I said. 'He's as good as I'm bad.'

'O, I'd say he was a *very* loving friend.' His laugh brimmed with spiteful meaning. 'And you to him, I'm sure.'

I tried not to look as if I understood.

'I have had ample time to think about you,' Zeb went on. 'And cause. I have met folk who could tell me what you were.'

I was frighted by this speech. Did he mean that Ferris and I were noted in the town? But I dared not question him, and asked instead, 'You are better?'

'I'll never be what I was. Still, I have my admirers. Your friend among them. Stripping me naked with his eyes, did he tell you *that*?'

I felt a stab in my chest.

Zeb smiled. 'Well, well. It seems we are jealous still.'

I would not answer this and turned my face away until I could regain my dignity. But the task proved too difficult, and it was in a trembling voice that I at length began again, 'You see I will use no force.'

'Nor would I in your position,' he observed. His gaze travelled downwards, taking in the heavy cloak and good shoes. 'Quite the citizen, aren't you? Living with him on Cheapside.'

I gasped.

'I've known your whereabouts for some time,' he added.

'O Zeb, I have been in agony wondering what became of you! Why, why did you not come to me?'

'Because I've taken my last beating from you!' he shouted, eyes black and possessed. 'Because you knifed Walshe, and fucked Caro – like a beast – under my nose! Because, because! Did you forget I was there, *Brother*, or did you reckon me as already dead?'

I dropped to my knees. 'Forgive me. Forgive me! I want to make reparation, only tell me what to do!'

'Make reparation!' He spat. I stayed kneeling, beseeching him with my eyes, and at last he put up the knife.

'I can get you money,' I pleaded.

Zeb looked thoughtful. I noticed how tattered was his sheepskin coat, and stretched out my hands in supplication. 'Let me take you—' I had almost said *home*, when I checked myself and went on, 'into one of the taverns here. So we can talk further.'

He nodded. 'Just don't lay hands on me.' He eyed my outstretched palms. 'I learnt from the gypsies ways of dealing with big men. They do it so well, they end up burying them.'

'I understand.' I got up on my aching legs.

He would go nowhere with me unless he chose the place himself. Despite the Puritans and the community of the Elect, there are so many of these holes round the docks it is a wonder the sailors keep any of their pay. We sat by ourselves near the window; I now remarked that he leant a little to one side. The only other customers were a weary-looking woman, perhaps a trull, and an elderly man with a basket of eels.

Zeb sat with his back to the wall and demanded wine. When it was served he raised a cup and bade me drink to brotherly love. He had put off the sheepskin, and in shirtsleeves, his hair curling round his face, he soon had the serving-girl simpering like an imbecile. I saw that his shattered rib had put hardly a crack in his beauty.

'Did you know that Mervyn is dead?' I asked.

Zeb's face lit up. 'Excellent! Killed in the fighting?'

I shook my head. 'Poisoned. Or drunk himself to it.'

'Would I could have nursed him!' my brother cried, and again I remarked a savagery in him that had not been there before.

'Zeb,' I said, 'ah, Zeb—'

My brother waited without speaking.

'Zeb – where did you get the earring?'

He laughed. 'That's what all the world wants to know. Citizen Whore, and now you.'

'His name is Ferris.'

'And what does he call you? Husband? Ganymede?'

'I go by my own name.'

We drank a little more wine.

'So, the earring,' I tried again.

'He's told you it's a wedding ring, and so it is. Yours.'

I stared at the shining loop in his ear. 'That ring was thrown away.'

'We found it in the morning and I persuaded her not to be a fool. Later she had it worked into an earring for me.' He sat back the better to observe my expression.

'Zeb, where are you living?'

'Here and there.'

'You're not with her any more?'

'Before you start, *she* left *me*.'

'Do you know where she is?'

He drank lazily. 'No. We parted company after coming to London.'

I shuddered inwardly at the thought of coming up against her in the street. 'Why did you part?'

He considered. 'That I won't tell you.'

Clenching my fists under the table, I stammered, 'Were you—? Were you, ah, did you—?'

He laughed. 'She fastened her wedding ring in my ear. Work it out for yourself.'

I covered my face; my shoulders heaved. I should never have sought out this shame and pain. He was more her husband than I. It seemed I could do nothing for Caro, and would not be permitted to do anything for Zeb.

'You don't deny killing Walshe,' he said at length. 'I knew that was it. By God, you picked your time to tell her.'

I lifted my head from my hands. 'That's past and gone.' I was not going to rehearse the boy's death with him. 'I hear that Izzy was whipped and turned out,' I added.

It was Zeb's turn to flinch and look away. I recalled something he had said earlier. 'Why did you say I beat you?' I demanded. 'I have never beaten you.'

'You've a short memory,' he replied. 'When we were boys.'

'Never.'

'You near skinned me once. In the orchard.'

Memory stirred: the two of us, and a rod in my hand.

'You were standing in for Father, you said.'

'But why did I?'

'Aye, why did you?' He stared at me. 'That's a thing I should ask your friend perhaps, your Herris.'

'Ferris,' I said and then stopped. The room seemed tilting; I could scarcely breathe.

'He's not as pretty as I was,' Zeb went on, as sickness spread in me. 'But slight – no match for you, eh? Are you rough with *him*?'

'I don't know what you mean,' I whispered.

'No?'

I was on my feet. Zeb's knife was out at once, but I wished only to be away from him and that room before I suffocated: chairs and tables barred my path to the door and I bruised my shins and thighs as I ran through them, furniture falling on either side of me like the Red Sea. I heard the girl call out something as I crossed the threshold. Out in the cold air I whirled round in case he had followed me, but I was alone. I walked on more slowly, saw folk staring at me and realised I was groaning aloud like some baited beast. In this condition I stumbled back to Cheapside, seized from time to time by the dry heaves. To get home, to run to earth. I must get home.

I could not find my key. Ferris let me in, and was as gentle with me as I had been curt with him earlier in the day. Everyone else being out we sat together, his arms round me, as I told him some of what had passed. My hands were icy and from time to time I had shaking fits, as if poisoned.

Having heard that Zeb disowned me and had taken up with my wife, he patted my hand, and murmured, 'You need never see him again.'

'He knows this house! No—' in answer to Ferris's face, 'I didn't tell him, he knew it before. I am not safe—'

'Does he mean harm to you? To all of us?' Ferris asked anxiously.

'Not you, I think.' I met his clear kind eyes with a kind of terror lest he see the guilt in my own. 'It is me he hates, and in a – a – brother's way.'

'We will soon be gone,' said my encouraging friend.

He had news of his own: Becs was come to him, and had said that she would keep silence. Upon his trying to thank her she had cut him short, and said she considered him the bigger Judas of the two, for that he had actually promoted the marriage, which was nothing but a cheat to get money and a place for his filthy darling (her very words), a trick that even his he-whore (her words again) had stood off from.

'But you hated the thought of it,' I protested.

'What could I say? In the end I told her that at the time I proposed the marriage to you, we were not – not in the same relation,' he went on. 'Dear God, was there ever such an explanation offered to a woman!'

'Never mind that, has she taken it?' I urged.

'She said she would not shame Aunt.'

'Otherwise she would see us burn?'

He smiled bitterly. 'Me, perhaps.'

'Not the he-whore?'

Ferris looked pityingly at me. 'She would have you tomorrow.'

I had passed all of the morning and eaten nothing since some bread at breakfast; nor could I eat now, though Ferris fussed over me as if sworn to act as Aunt's substitute. When he found I was adamant, he agreed to set out the material for cutting so we could look it over together. I swept a corner of the court and he brought down the bales of stuff from the loft.

'I lost badly on this,' he said, throwing it down. 'But there, I could afford it.'

I unfolded the first bale, which like the rest was a coarse linen, marked all over with green and the edges pulled uneven. It was some three yards wide. We looked at it, then at one another, and I opened the book given us by Dan's friend Robert.

'Where shall I start?'

'We must measure exactly,' said Ferris. He ran into the house and came out with Aunt's workbox, from which he took a tape and a fine pair of scissors. The book showed various kinds of tents, and we chose the simplest, with sloping sides and no decorations. I wrestled to expel thoughts of Zeb and attend to Ferris's instructions as we folded the stuff between us like maids folding bedsheets, snapping out the edges to straighten puckered threads.

'Spread it on the flags,' said Ferris. He picked up a large beetle and placed the creature on the apple tree, out of the way.

'Now, if the weather holds, we'll get it done before night. Measure six feet, so,' and he stood back to let me get to the linen. 'No, not like that, you must go with the warp.' He showed me how to line up my shapes with the edge of the cloth.

'Am I doing this, or are you?' I asked as he snatched the scissors from my hand.

'Don't be crabby. I've worked with the stuff, you haven't. Look, this is how you do it.'

I watched as he cut the first few threads and then ripped the open blades through the material as if impaling someone on a sword. 'You'll soon have the feel of it. Always cut straight.'

I marked and cut the next piece while he watched.

'Is that right?' I challenged, knowing it was.

'Like your other handiworks, Jacob: perfection. No, truly, very good,' for I had caught hold of him and was dragging him towards the pump. We tussled, and I got the water flowing, but let him go without putting him under. After this foolery I felt happier. Panting, we came back and folded up the pieces completed so far; Ferris marked them with a pencil. The ground was uneven, so that we would have been better at a big table. However, we began to get on, and apart from the crouching, which made me feel my stiff calves, I enjoyed it. He showed me how to lay out two or more pieces at a time, and how to mark them showing the name of the part, which was the outside and which way was up.

'Can you make clothes?' I asked him.

'I never have. But I used to watch the maid do it when I was a child, and she marked her pattern pieces thus.'

'You could stand in for Roger Rowly, methinks.'

'Nay. You'll soon know as much as I do.'

The stuff was not broad enough to cut out all the pattern complete, and some parts had to be pieced. I watched fascinated as he took needle and thread and stitched them together.

'It is not very beautiful,' he said frowning. 'I wish we could have got Becs to help you.'

'She will never help me more,' said I. He hissed suddenly and I saw red from his hand stain the linen.

'Here.' I put the wounded finger in my mouth. He tasted of my tooth-drawing.

'If we start, it is better than nothing,' he said. 'We can tack it together for someone to finish off.'

'What's tack?'

'Put it together loosely, to see how it fits. Then you stitch it down good and tight.'

I watched, thinking that I had seen Caro and Patience work thus, but had never known what it was called.

'Get hold.' Ferris put the needle in my hand. 'In and up like this, and don't let the tail of thread get tangled. In and up. No, in and up.'

I was clumsy and the linen was soon spotted with my blood as well as his.

'Ah.' He examined the bloodspots. 'Perhaps you should go back to cutting, and I'll join.'

We worked on peaceably. If this were the way of the colony, I thought, it would not be too bad, and I would never again meet Zeb. If only I were able to get to Ferris when I wanted. I reflected that work was no problem to me, for I had been raised to toil alongside others, from beating the hangings – but here I baulked at some obscure pain in the recollection, and fixed my mind instead on typesetting. I was quick to learn, had ample health and strength for labour, but I could not bear to work alongside him all day and lie apart at night.

'That's it,' said Ferris. His voice lilted with pleasure. 'The last one!' He held it up like a trophy before folding it on top of the rest. I saw he had made a neat workman-like pile of the linen pieces.

'Just in time,' I said, glancing up at the darkening sky. A drop fell on my forehead.

'The cloth!' Ferris wailed. We gathered all up in a frenzy and had barely got in our harvest when the rain fell straight down like a curtain. Ferris ran out in it to get the book and other things while I carried the unused material back to the loft. When I came down he had lit a lamp in the printroom and was laying the pattern pieces where he dried his prints. Yellow light swam over him and the cloth; drops ran off the ends of his hair. At my coming in he smiled up at me and his skin sparkled with the wet. Just then he was more beautiful than Zeb, and after I never lost that picture from my mind. It was burnt in for good, like his thin profile forming out of the darkness as he brought me back to life on the road, his return to me warm and living, though with a slashed cheek, at Winchester, and the sobbing sound he made as I took hold of him that first night, the night I found his letter.

~

We ate with Aunt that evening and there were no references to secret acts. Becs served us as quickly as possible – she never lingered these days – and I chewed silently on my salt pork and beans.

The other two talked of news. The last month had been one to excite, especially if a man were ignorant of the suffering that is war.

Chester had fallen some weeks back, having been reduced to a state of near famine, so that the citizens trailed at the heels of Lord Byron, begging him in tears to come to terms with Parliament before they were all starved to death. Even so, the city had endured until the third of February. With the Parliamentary troops safely installed, it became known that the King had raised three thousand Irish soldiers and would have landed them at Chester had Byron held out a week longer.

'The hand of God plain as anything,' said Aunt.

'Say rather the King's stupidity,' said Ferris.

She tutted. 'And Torrington? Was that the King's doing too?'

'No, Hopton's,' Ferris teased her. 'He was the one fired the church.'

'God works through men, Christopher,' she reproached him. 'To ignore His help is to provoke His anger.'

'Very true,' Ferris answered. He filled his mouth with pork, as one who is done talking.

I knew about Torrington. Fairfax had fought his way into the town a fortnight earlier, and as the Parliamentary troops advanced towards the church the sacred edifice had 'gone up like a powder keg', which indeed it was: nearly two hundred barrels of Cavalier gunpowder stored in God's house, which their commander, Hopton, did not scruple to demolish. Fairfax himself escaped injury from the stone, lead and burning timber that rained down upon the earth like World's End. Hugh Peter, likewise, lived to preach amid the rubble in the marketplace the following day. Aunt was delighted by the extreme good fortune of these two godly men. I tried not to think about what must have happened to those around them.

Instead I worried over the words Zeb had flung at me earlier. Feeling sick, I continued to chew on the tough cut of pork as I rehearsed my memory, over and over. It was now clear to me that I had taken Zeb into the orchard (his shirt on? off?) and there beaten him over the back and shoulders. Then – a blank. Further than that I could not get, I could remember nothing of what followed. Surely I would, if – if—

It was all nonsense, an accusation born of spite. A man could not do such a thing and forget it. Suddenly, a dry voice I had heard before whispered, *Why did you take him into the orchard?*

'Jacob?'

I started guiltily. Ferris was leaning towards me.

'We are talking of you and the tents; I told Aunt how well you get on with the cutting.'

I forced a modest smile. 'Less well with the stitching.'

'There we come to it! Aunt, will you be so kind as to show him?'

I thought he was rather too quick. She looked unwilling, and even setting aside the awkwardness between us, I had scarce the air of a likely pupil.

'Plain sewing?' she enquired. 'Cannot Becs do that?'

'She has not sufficient leisure. Besides, Jacob must learn for himself, and you are the better teacher.' Ferris made a pleading face.

She pursed her lips, considering. I wondered what she saw whenever she looked at me.

'He needs to learn tacking and how to make seams and turn over edges,' urged her nephew.

'If you know what's to be done as well as that, can't *you* teach him?' she shot back.

'Knowing and doing are different things. He needs someone practised.' Ferris sat like a schoolboy begging a half-holiday, until she laughed at his earnest countenance.

'Tomorrow,' she agreed at last.

'Praise her, for her price is beyond rubies,' said Ferris. He took and kissed her hand.

'I thank you most sincerely,' I said, dismayed at the course of study my lover had prescribed. It came to me that Ferris had hit upon a means of occupying my time while he busied himself with preparation for his dear colony.

The three of us were easier together than we had been for some days. I decided that if Aunt had guessed at us, which was by no means certain, she found it simplest to turn a blind eye. She played at chess with Ferris, while I looked over the more complicated kinds of tents by the light of a single candle. My head began to ache, so I left it off; but as soon as I shut up the book I felt Zeb's black gaze boring into me, so I watched their game instead. Aunt won, and was exultant. They set up again so that her nephew could get his revenge.

~

The hangings were encrusted and Godfrey said I might use only a stick to cleanse them. I did well enough with the first and second pieces, slashing away until sweat polished my skin and the devices showed clear: the Lady and Unicorn, a Garden of Delight. One that stood by, watching, said I was a fine workman. When I laid into the third and last, the stick thudded dull against something sewn up in it, like a moth sealed in a leaf. I unfolded the tapestry to find Caro and Zeb looking up at me. They were lying packed about with a greyish dust, which dust flecked the air and stuck to my sweat. It settled on the hangings I had just cleaned, and when I turned to flog it away they laughed, so I raised my stick over them to teach them cleanliness. Caro shielded her face and turned her body away from me, into the folds of stuff. I brought the rod down on her back; she rolled deeper into the cloth and was gone. Searching for her I found stains and smears across the design and these came, I saw, from something stinking, which I was afraid to look at, on the ground nearby. At once I was in the orchard and come to beat Zeb. I turned and found him running at me with a scythe—

I leapt out of sleep with a cry.

Ferris was shaking me. 'Jacob! You're here, it's all right.'

I looked round wildly. Zeb was gone.

'What were you dreaming? You were throwing yourself about.'

'A fight.' The comforting solidity of the chair, the grip of his hands on my shoulders brought me back to myself; I put my arms and legs around him and pulled him close in to me. Laying my head on his breast, I heard the heart beating clear and calm.

'What time is it?' I muttered into the warmth of his shirt.

'Eleven. Aunt's long gone to bed. Here, let me go,' and he fetched me some cordial from the sideboard. 'I thought you would have a fit.'

I tasted the stuff with the tip of my tongue and found it pleasant enough. The misery of Zebedee settled back on my soul.

'Do you think, Ferris, that people know what we do? Do we betray ourselves?'

'No,' he answered at once. 'Tom and his friends don't know. Nor Dan.'

'Zeb saw it in you when you talked to him.'

'Indeed?' he asked with quick interest.

'He said you admired him.'

Ferris laughed. 'Your brother is used to admiration and is grown to expect it. He fancies himself a lady-killer, that *I* could tell on first meeting.'

'He has cause.' My jealousy was a little soothed, but not my fear of discovery. 'Zeb knew about me, too,' I added.

'He's known you for years, who better?'

Following Zeb's accusations about beating, this was as comforting to me as a peach full of needles.

'Try not to think on him,' urged Ferris. 'What do they say? What's past repair is past despair.'

'He could have us burnt.'

'Is that what's giving you nightmares?' He came over and took my hand. 'It needs evidence. He wouldn't get any, Becs loves my aunt too well.'

I was silent.

'I forgot to tell you,' he said coaxingly, 'but I had a visitor while you were out.'

'Ah.'

'Won't you guess who?'

'Keats?'

'Botts. You know, we may have to take him.'

I groaned. 'In God's name, what for? All he offers is physick. I'd sooner fee a doctor in the ordinary way.'

'That's where you're wrong,' Ferris answered. 'What we need most is *hands*. Forget professions. We need people to dig, and strong ones – the women will help, but we need men.'

I grudgingly admitted to myself the sense of this. 'Who have we got? You, me—?'

'Botts, Hathersage, Tunstall. Five in all. Then the women: Catherine, Susannah, Hepsibah. I can't see anyone else coming in.'

'Jack and Dorothy?'

He shook his head.

I was wide awake now. 'Ferris, why would a man like Botts, a surgeon, want to join us? There must be something amiss.'

'He's friendless,' said Ferris. 'By the look of him, I'd say his only friend is drink.'

'And you still think we should take him?'

'He'll find it hard to carouse where we're going, and if he does – well, an end to his time with us.'

'I suppose you'll ask *me* to throw him out.'

'Jacob, Man of Peace,' he pronounced in a ringing pulpit voice. 'But consider, it could turn the fellow round. That's a noble thing.'

'I see it is decided,' I said, remarking the familiar far-off shine in his eyes. 'But he'd best dig like a slave for I'll none of his medicine. If I find *himself* a leech on my side, I'll burn him off.'

'Give the man a chance,' said Ferris.

'He's a toad, an offence to the eyes.'

'Not a Christian objection. Come,' he asked slyly, 'would you rather he were a golden lad?'

There was no disputing that point and I saw it was simplest to give way, since Ferris would surely tire of him in due course. We talked a while longer before bed. Ferris wished to go to Page Common the next day and look about for a good place, while I stayed in Cheapside 'learning to make my sampler' as he put it. While I was willing to stitch like a little maid if need be, I thought him unfitted to choose land by himself. We agreed he should go about business in the city and we would go to the common the day after that. Though the printroom was near piled to the beams with stores, there was still plenty to attend to. Harmonious, we went quietly upstairs.

I woke in an agony of fear, clammy, my eyes stinging, cheeks awash with tears. In my terror I had pushed the sheets away, and the air was cold on my damp flesh. I reached out to touch Ferris. He was gone, and I remembered he was returned to his own couch.

I rose and felt the wet hair stick on my forehead as I dragged the covers up from the boards, wrapping myself tight. They, at least, were dry: they warmed my chill, slippery skin with the dumb comfort of familiar things. I lay motionless in my dark burrow, breathing his smell. I would have given much to have him hold me and talk to me then, but a grown man is not driven to another's bed by a nightmare. Besides, Ferris did not believe in the Devil.

~

Morning came, and was sunny. I was up betimes, more cheerful for the light at the window, and raised the latch of his door. Ferris had drawn back the bed curtains and was lying awake, hands behind his head. He threw me a look of innocent contentment. I saw directly that he was already full of the day's business, and would come home with more seed samples, diagrams and schemes for planting. Never such an industrious man, if his heart were only in the work. And kind, for he wished to recall Botts from the vice of drink. He is as good as Izzy, I insisted silently to the Voice, which had whispered in my ears all night, promising I should watch him burn.

'Are you well, Jacob?'

'Just bad dreams.'

'That won't do at all. We need you strong for the needlework.' He looked at me with amusement. 'Who was that Greekish hero, another big fellow, had to sew like a woman?'

'More of that,' I threatened, 'and I lay down my needle.'

'I'll get cords for the tent today,' he said. ''Twill be a fine thing to see it go up.'

I would have liked to stay and watch him dress, but knew it was best not to, so closed the door and descended the stairs.

Aunt sat at the table, evidently just served; she nodded to me, her mouth full of bread. In front of her, some of the very best manchet. After saying Grace, I took a large piece for myself.

'Shall we start this morning?' she asked, pleasantly enough. I said I was ready and at her command. Ferris joined us before I had finished the first bit of bread, and had the aspect of an angel – not an angel of vengeance like Zeb, but a warm one, still dreamy from his bed. His evident happiness tugged at me and I could see Aunt was drawn likewise. Impossible to look coldly on one who breathes joy.

My life on it, he is not damned, I thought. I watched him eat the bread; he had an excellent appetite.

'I shall be out all day,' he said on getting up from the table, 'unless I get too tired or have too much to carry. But tonight, you'll see marvels!'

'Not the first man to promise marvels,' said Aunt.

'And I shall find Jacob fit to clothe the Pope of Rome.'

'If he wears tents,' I said.

Ferris kissed his aunt and made eyes at me from behind her chair. I could not help but laugh as I wished him a good day. He rammed his hat on askew and was gone.

~

At ten – that is, after an Eternity – I was permitted to take some salep, provided I brought my stitching with me. The pieces Aunt had set me to join were now bloody as a soldier's bandage, but none could say they were not fairly tacked together. As for me, I felt ready to run or fight, do anything but sit down and bend my strength to such fiddly work. It was far worse than cutting out. What patience Ferris must have, to have learnt to sew.

'My hands are too big. I will never be able to do it right,' I told her.

'There speaks sloth. Anyone can do it in time.' She drew up her mouth. 'I made that sampler behind you when I was nine years old.'

I nearly said, 'And a very great loss of time it was,' but stopped myself. There was no need to examine the sampler, for there was so little ornament in the room that I had often looked it over and knew it off by heart: a row of bandy gentlemen, all sons of the one rickety father, advanced upon a line of ladies with waists long and thin as bedposts, perhaps to ask the ladies to dance, perhaps to snap them in half. In the centre of this masterpiece were the alphabet and numbers up to ten, the words 'SARAH TUKE HER WORK' and the date – the only thing I could not call to mind without looking – above the words, *A Virtuous Woman Is A Crown Unto Her Husband* stitched in faded green.

'A splendid piece,' I offered. 'How many years had you been learning?'

'I can't remember when the needle was not put in my hand directly after breakfast.'

'Admirable.' I wondered at the resilience of girl-children; perhaps such labour was to their taste.

Aunt took up my cloth and unpicked the seam I had just made. I cried out in protest.

She laughed. 'Did you think I should frame it? Now, do it again, and less bloody this time.'

I sat in the window, taking care that the stuff was invisible from the street. A door slammed downstairs: perhaps Ferris was come back. I bent my head industriously to the task.

'Mister Beste,' announced Becs. Her voice trailed off to see my occupation; I know not who was more surprised, herself or me. I had thought never to see Harry again. He was through the door before I had time to lay aside the work.

'Mistress Snapman, good day.' They bobbed at one another. 'And Jacob, well met!'

It was a fair enough greeting. He took my hands between his and I saw no ill feeling in him.

'I shall leave you gentlemen to conduct your business,' said Aunt. She hurried downstairs to stir Becs up to hospitality.

'Pray be seated,' I said nervously. 'Ferris will be out most of the day.'

Harry settled back in his chair. 'I am glad to catch you alone,' he began. 'I have apologies to make.'

'I should rather give you thanks. My good fortune was you stopped me before I killed him,' I answered.

'I would be sorry to see you hang for such a braggart fool.'

I smiled, knowing he had floored me for Elizabeth. 'Your wife is well?'

'Aye. It was she bade me come. We are willing to start again – pardon my blunt words – on the express understanding that you govern your wrath. Without that condition,' he shook his head, 'I fear nothing can be done.'

'I school myself in patience,' I said, my cheeks and ears hot. 'Do you see my task?'

Harry took up the white cloth, amused. 'What, are you doing penance?'

'I suffer enough for it. He has me stitching tents.'

'And how do you like the work, Mistress?'

'Worse than the army.' We laughed together and I began to feel at ease. 'He thinks of setting up soon,' I went on. 'We are to look over some land tomorrow, Page Common.'

'Of course, you must plough.' Frowning, he pulled up a chair to join me at the fire. 'Elizabeth and I will give it thought.'

'He will be overjoyed to see you again. After you left he was so grieved he said he could beat me himself.'

Harry grinned. 'Shall we come with you tomorrow? I can shut up shop.'

'I'll ask him – no, come with us. If we were to meet here at nine? I don't know if he means to hire a coach or walk.'

'Nine, then. Her sister will take the children.'

Becs pushed open the door with a tray. On it, a flask of wine, cups and a large venison pasty cut in two pieces. She laid them on the table without looking at me and went straight out.

'Cream gone sour *there*.' Harry stared after her. 'She looked at you in another style altogether when last I visited. Have we tasted the goods, Jacob?'

'Something like that.' He would not have talked so before Ferris; I prayed Becs was not listening behind the door. The wine she had brought us was the cheapest, not normally served to guests, but Harry drank it down with seeming pleasure. The pasty was good, crisp and hot.

When he had eaten we shook hands and he left. I was in a rare excitement and could scarce wait to tell Ferris. Even when Aunt set me to slave at my third seam I lost no time in sulks, but instead turned out a pretty straight line and only two bloodspots. My reward was paltry, for she announced that I should next go on to backstitch, but I was given leave to take a walk, and availed myself of it: up and down Cheapside to take the air. I heard a young lass tell her friend that I was a proper-looking man and came back to the house with my head swelled, taking Vanity's pains to walk straight and tall, and very glad my admirer did not know of my course of study.

Backstitch was even more of a torment than tacking. My needle bred herringbones where I wanted straight lines. At last I was freed by the failing light. Aunt lit the candles and said we should stop.

'Christopher is late,' she complained.

At once I saw him with Zeb, his gentleness spitted on a knife-blade. I suspected that, despite his savage talk, my brother had no special hatred for Ferris; yet the vision frighted me. *Zeb is more like me than I knew*, I thought to myself.

But Ferris came in unscathed. Though tired, he had evidently carried his joy with him all day and brought it safe home again.

'What have you bought?' I asked, for I could see nothing but papers.

'I have put in orders for drainage spades, to collect next week. And a yoke for the ploughing. And . . .' here he listed a great many things. I waited in patience till I could get his attention.

When I told him of Harry's return he clapped his hands together and crowed.

'Excellent good fortune! Let's drink to it!' He seized on the wine left by Harry and myself. I thought the taste might give him pause, but not a bit. Aunt, however, was not pleased when she took a mouthful of what Becs had seen fit to serve with her good venison pasty and she went downstairs to tell her so. Ferris hugged me and the vinegary wine spilled over my linen and its backstitch. He snatched up the work and pored over it, laughing.

'I will get better,' I protested.

We talked of the journey to Page Common, my aim being to secure some companion who, like me, had knowledge born of experience and not pamphlets, for I knew that nothing I said would be listened to. Ferris was pleased to see me take an interest, and by consent I sent next door's boy with a note to Jeremiah Andrews, the gardener, requesting the pleasure of his company on our great expedition. Aunt had brought up a better wine and it went round pretty freely, so that by the time the rest of the venison appeared in a hotpot we were all three foolish and cheerful. We dined well, played cards for love and retired early.

Without the friendly warmth of the drink I might have turned melancholy, for to me the drainage spades were almost as ominous as the spiteful whisperings which had begun, once again, to infect my sleep. Afraid of the nightmare, I crept into Ferris's room and folded my arms about him. He sighed happily and pressed against me, and I kept him as close as an amulet. Clasping him thus, I felt myself safe; my dreams were innocent, and upon my asking him in the morning had I spoken or struggled, he said no, I had been still and quiet all the night.

We set off for the common in time, and Jeremiah came in answer to my invitation. He seemed modestly pleased to see us, a little stiff with me at first but that wore off and he was soon lamenting the dearth of corn and other things, caused by so many crops being trampled down and the fields rained into mud. I had suggested to Ferris that we hire a coach, for it was a weary long way and Harry's youngest child being still at the breast had to be carried with us. When the Bestes arrived, however, Harry was driving an ox-cart. Ferris's eyes shone at such an addition to the common storehouse, until the smith told him that the cart had been borrowed.

Jolted along greasy alleys, I craned at parts of the city I had never seen before and would never know now. I watched Ferris's face grow eager as we neared the place, and by the time we got down at the inn he was breathing as fast as a fever patient. Looking about me, I saw a soft, wet, rolling country with marsh grass and buttercups on the downward slopes and in the bottoms. Less than two miles off the ground rose and the grass and bushes darkened into trees. Towards these we walked, strolling along with no great idea how to proceed.

As always, I was between amusement and despair at my friend's lack of knowledge. Harry and Elizabeth were nearly as bad, and sending for Jeremiah was perhaps the wisest thing I ever did, for Ferris's ignorance was only outgone by his stubbornness. Having been told by me that a green plant found everywhere among the grass was a kind of buttercup, and would show bright yellow come May, he was much taken with the idea. He remembered to have seen buttercups, and thought their brightness must show a good fertile place.

'They mean the soil is wet,' Jeremiah and I answered together. Harry nodded, as if to say he had known this all along.

'Here is too lush, it will turn rank,' Jeremiah went on. 'The clay may be under water in the winter. We could put a cow on it, but—' he shook his head.

My shoe leather was sodden. We trudged on to a place where the land was stonier and more uneven. There was space for several strips before it dipped down again to the treacherous buttercups.

'Better, apart from the stone,' pronounced the gardener.

'Stone has its uses,' said Ferris. 'We can put it in the ditches and soughs.'

Jeremiah said, 'You have been reading, I perceive.'

Ferris looked up quickly but it was not Jeremiah's intention to make a mock of him.

'Don't you think it a good plan, Jeremiah?' I asked.

'It's well enough.'

'When we drained a piece of land at Beaurepair,' I recalled, 'we stuffed the ditches with hedge trimmings.'

'That's good too.'

'What is a sough?' asked Elizabeth, who unlike Harry had no fear of revealing her ignorance.

Ferris glanced over at Jeremiah. 'You will correct me if I go astray? A sough is a hole dug under the ground, Elizabeth. You first dig a pit for a man to stand in, and then he goes round and round with his spade and digs out all the earth underneath. And so you get a hole like a narrow-necked vessel, broad at the base but with a small opening at the top, and the turf mostly left in place.'

'But the turf would fall in, surely,' said she. 'Suppose a man walked on it? Like the crust over a bog.' The child choosing this moment to plunge in her arms, she caught it and held it fast.

'You pack the hole with hedging,' answered Ferris.

Elizabeth still looked puzzled, and Jeremiah took over: 'Then the water can drain out of the soil and into your sough. It flows round the twigs, or stones, or whatever, and stays there. And so you get a drier field.'

'At Beaurepair the land went down by a foot in the end,' I recalled. 'And from being spongy, it got so that you could drive a coach across it.'

'Surely your Master cared nothing for land drainage,' said Ferris.

'He did, when I was a child,' I answered. 'I guess the drink grew on him later.'

Strange, the memory of Sir John sober and purposeful. And Godfrey – I saw him younger, full of authority, ordering the digging. He it was who had some snap brought out to the workers, bread and cold beef and cider. Pain stirred in me as I recalled that in those days I looked up to him, loved him even. He was childless and craved a son, which made him kind to all of us Cullens. Me he called a fine lad; he let me beg food in the kitchen, made much of me. Some fifteen years ago. When did I first look on him with the young man's scorn for the greybeard? Of the three of us, only Izzy honoured him in later life.

'All decays.' I jumped, unsure whether I had spoken aloud. But none answered me, and I thought Ferris, walking in front, had probably not heard.

The ground rose and then flattened again as we approached the trees. Here, the grass had a different feel.

'This is your place of choice for corn,' said Jeremiah. 'It needs a drier earth. Put beasts to graze away the weeds from the top here, then plough, and keep the stock where the grass is lushest.'

Ferris said, 'I thought to sow dredge.'

'That might be well elsewhere, but your new-turned clay is no good for barley. I'd put down rye the first year—'

'Peas and vetch also?' Ferris asked. 'And what think you of beans?'

Jeremiah nodded a guarded approval; evidently he thought Ferris, inflamed with study, in need of calming rather than encouragement.

Ferris began, 'When I have dug the sough—'

'We must dig latrines as well as soughs,' I cut in. 'Nay, before soughs.' The thought oppressed me at the heart's root, not for the labour, but for the return to army days, the filthy crouching and the stink. Ferris and Jeremiah turned to me in surprise.

'Latrines! That's well thought on,' said Harry. 'Where should they be placed?'

'I am for having none,' said Ferris at once. 'It were a waste not to dung the fields.'

Elizabeth looked grim, and for myself I could have wept. Shitting in a furrow, in rain and snow, that was the very thing to appeal to him; and I wondered, as I often did, why one decently and pleasantly raised must needs set comfort at nought.

'We will talk of it another time,' I said, resolved to dig a place whether he would or no.

We explored the woods, slipping on roots and fallen branches, serenaded at every step by the snapping of twigs. Evidently few or none gathered the timber. When we found a spring with a deep natural basin beneath, there was a general cry of delight at our good fortune, especially when all had tasted the water and judged it good. Ferris clapped Harry and me on the shoulders. I knew then that the spring had sealed our fate.

Walking back, I was saddened by thoughts of Godfrey. But as Ferris had said, what was past repair was past despair, so I addressed myself to Jeremiah, asking him if he thought this spot a wise choice.

'As good as most,' he answered, disappointing my secret hopes. 'You'll get something out of it. How many are you?'

'Five. Men, that is.'

Jeremiah frowned. 'Have you cattle?' The women he evidently considered as not worth asking after.

'We are promised a milch-cow by some women that would join us. Ferris is to buy us oxen and he has bespoke an ox-cart for carrying tools and suchlike.'

'He pours out gold.'

'He's one that can't go by halves.' Sensing some caution in Jeremiah, I said slowly, 'The last time we were in company together, I disgraced myself, for which I beg pardon.'

He bent his head in acknowledgement.

I went on, 'I have sworn to Ferris he shall never witness such a scene again; or at least, I shall not be the actor.'

'That were well,' he said shortly.

'So,' I went on, 'what think you – would you consider joining with us again? Now you see the land?'

He paused, tongue pressed to his top teeth.

'If the enterprise will fail, 'twere best to say so,' I pleaded.

'No reason it should fail,' he replied, surprised. 'Many live off worse ground. 'Twill be what you make it, but methinks you need more colonists.'

'More men?'

'Skilled men.'

'And if we find them, will you join us?'

'I will consider it.'

That was as much as I could get from him. Should I press further, he would shun me as being still too masterful, so there was no more to be done.

We climbed back onto the cart. Elizabeth drew her cloak about her and put the babe to her breast. I wondered would she be honoured by the fruits of her body in old age. No child would ever honour me. Or blame me, neither; but I was like to go hungry in my dotage. I imagined myself weak, patiently swallowing insults for lack of a defence. Harry, meanwhile, talked of ploughs, their wooden and iron parts. After a while I became aware of Ferris watching me, and understood that his mournful face mirrored my own. I forced myself to smile.

At the end of Cheapside, Ferris, Jeremiah and I descended from the cart together. Each colonist had sobered on the journey back, now that the New Jerusalem had ceased shining with amethyst and pearl and had shown itself of the earth, earthy: a place of soughs, stones and dung. Harry and Elizabeth went off briskly, wishing us a good night. Jeremiah came some of the way home with Ferris and me, talking of the pamphlet on setting which Ferris had found and had bidden me study. The gardener thought this new way might shield the seeds from birds.

'Bird-starving is a kind of work to drive you mad,' he commented. 'What you need is a boy to do it and do nowt else until the grain has had a chance to get going.'

'But if we set, there'll be less grain lost?' asked Ferris.

'A man would think so. I use a dibble in the garden and I find it answers.'

'A stick for poking holes in the earth,' I put in before Ferris could ask.

Jeremiah halted. 'This is my turning. God be with you, gentlemen.'

'And with you,' I replied. Ferris smiled and nodded; we all bowed. I watched Jeremiah go, his even, springy steps giving him the gait of one much younger.

'A valuable fellow,' said Ferris. 'Would he would come back to us.'

'I have asked him to consider.'

'Well done.' He linked my arm as we made our way along the road. It was dark, and the cold meant there were few folk about. I thought lovingly of the fire at home.

'This weather doesn't help us,' Ferris lamented.

'It doesn't help the weeds, neither.'

'Right you are, Colin Clout.'

'Who's he?'

'A name for a shepherd. Countryman.'

'Ferris, don't take offence if I ask something.'

'There's a warning! I don't promise. Ask.'

'When I was in the army, I heard that some of the London men, first time out of town, ran in crowds to see the cows. Was that you?'

'I'm not ashamed of it,' he answered, laughing.

'I can't believe a man can get to full age and not know a cow!'

'I know a man grew to full age on an island, and never saw the sea.'

'He's not ashamed, neither. Wonderful, to think how these wars have been a – a revelation to people.'

'So they have. But some things that were revealed—' he sighed.

'What are you thinking of?'

'Lots of things. Basing-House.'

I heard flesh-flies buzzing in the folds of a bloodstained dress, and then the faint screams of men against the crackling of fire. As if by agreement, we walked in silence the rest of the way home.

TWENTY-THREE

Coney-Catching

THE TENT CAME on apace, although not nearly as fast as Ferris had imagined. I found that by the use of darts (for I had mastered that trick too, and felt myself a perfect knight of the distaff) the thing would hold its right shape: the pattern pieces now being perfected, we needed but the hempen cloth called canvas to cut out the tent proper. I was pretty sure I could finish the whole thing before we left, and so I made a special effort to obtain the canvas, by paying a visit to Mister Keats's shop and demanding it gratis. I considered he owed my friend that much. Ferris was told I had bought it elsewhere; and since I naturally refused payment in money, things went on merrily between us that night.

Sitting somewhat heavy-eyed at breakfast the following morning, I heard Aunt offer up special thanks for the great mercy shown to the household. Ferris and I exchanged puzzled glances.

'Great—? What mercy might that be, Aunt?' he asked once the *Amen* had been said.

'Becs has said she will stay on,' she answered. To me, that hardly seemed a *great mercy*, but then I recalled how attached Lady Roche was become to Caro. To an ageing widow a change of maidservant might be a serious matter.

'She finds that her family are able to do without her after all,' Aunt exulted.

'An excellent servant,' I said. I meant it; it must have been cruelly hard on her, waiting for Ferris and myself to quit the house. She rarely smiled these days, and the eyes she turned on me, when she thought it safe, were dull with shamed disappointment, wincing away directly my glance met hers. Plainly, she now thought of my strength and apparent mettle as decoys laid to take women. I also thought that Ferris was right, and that a part of her yet struggled in the snare, for she held herself very stiff whenever I was in the room. I was sorry. I could not myself have explained to her how the thing was, even had I thought it wise to try.

Everything needful was ready by the end of March, and Ferris itching to depart. Our first ox was purchased, and stalled until we should call for him. I went one day to see the creature and stroked his mild snout. He seemed a good beast. I was now sunk to the neck in this scheme which I dreaded, weighted down by loyalty and love.

The Mistresses Domremy came and passed an evening with us; they talked of pasturing and buttercups. Aunt indulged us with a stew of rabbits. Watching Ferris talk, his lively expression and the deft movements of his hands, I compared him favourably with any man I had ever seen: he was all grace. He listened keenly as the women went over their plans.

'There can be no cheese made without slabs we can scald,' Susannah explained.

Catherine added, 'And keep the sun off, after. That will not be for some time, but if we set up a cow and calf on the common we could let the calf suck and when it was weaned sell the milk.'

Whether this was a good plan I could not tell, and I am sure Ferris could not. He had that shine on his countenance which both charmed and exasperated me. The charm was also working on Catherine, the more talkative of the two women. Her face glowed with a passionate warmth; I saw that she had misinterpreted his tender looks and the yearning sweetness of his speech. There needed someone to take her aside and explain that he would have shed the same radiance on a dead dog, had he seen a use for it in the New Jerusalem. Becs, who stood by awaiting orders from Aunt, watched the poor girl with the air of one who could, if she chose, tell much.

We accompanied the women to their lodgings and exchanged many good wishes before turning back to Cheapside. On the way home, I warned him not to smile so often or so kindly on Mistress Catherine.

'Don't you see,' I said, 'she thinks you have a liking for her? Time was, you would perceive such a thing at once, but your head is stuffed with enthusiasms.'

'I did perceive it,' he replied, amused at my vehemence.

'And can you not disabuse her?'

'She will learn in time,' Ferris answered. 'Be easy, I have no temptations that way. Here, read this.' He waved a letter at me.

'It is dark, Ferris,' I explained with marked patience.

'O, very well. Jeremiah writes: he will call on us, and has many tools of his own, including dibbles.'

'And what are dibbles?' I asked sternly.

'Sticks to make holes in the ground,' he recited. 'In the ground we make holes, Brethren, and do make these holes with sticks, and these same sticks, that we use to make holes in the ground, do with many folk commonly go under the name of—' he leapt back, but too late, for I had his hat and proceeded to knock it out of shape while holding it out of his reach.

'A warped hat for a warped head,' I said, letting it drop. 'Now, take care with the Domremy.'

'Fear me not!' He smoothed out the squashed felt. 'I have not time for the devouring of virgins.'

~

Botts came to the house another day. He was unexpected and I was on edge lest Ferris invite him to dine, but my friend contented himself with offering cake and canary.

'I am come to let you know how matters stand,' Botts announced.

Ferris blinked obligingly and poured out more drink. It was wonderful to see how the good doctor got through it, with no ill effects save a slight wheezing as he explained to Ferris that he had so regulated his affairs as to be ready at a week's notice.

'We have now four oxen,' Ferris said. I started, for this was the first I had heard of it. Botts inclined his head by way of compliment, saying, 'I see you are no idle chatterer.'

'Actions before words with Ferris,' I said. 'Nay, sometimes no words at all.'

I tried to breathe through my mouth whenever Botts turned towards me, for he smelt no more wholesome than formerly and there were now gusts of garlic added to the original perfume.

'There's a nobility in action,' Botts said. 'To dream is one thing, but to do—! That's another.'

I could not help asking, 'What do *you* propose to do?' even though it meant he must blow his stinking answer into my face.

'I have already said I will bring my instruments,' he said. 'Those aside, I will dig and sow as necessary.'

'Should we need to butcher one of the beasts, your skills would be priceless,' I said. The man hesitated, unsure whether he was being mocked.

Ferris, more experienced in my ways, made slit eyes at me behind Botts's back.

'Jacob hardly understands these things,' he said. 'When first he came here, he took the Thames for the sea.'

I was silenced. Ferris was plainly angry, and I wondered would he bolt his chamber door that night. Luckily the doctor could not stay long for he had an abcess to lance. My relief at his going enabled me to smile as I repeated, 'God be with you,' remarking meanwhile that he lacked a neck, so that his head swelled directly out of his body. Ferris bowed deeply. Botts went off leaving the ghost of his pestilential stench to sicken the room and Ferris threw himself crossly into a chair, legs across the armrests, feet dangling in the air.

'Four oxen!' I cried. 'You said nothing of that to me.'

'I forgot. What do you care for such – O Jacob, what in God's name shall we do with Botts?'

'Why ask? You have accepted him.'

'I won't have a man driven off with mockery. But I don't want him, Jacob. I don't like him—'

'Why will you do these things?' I pleaded. 'Let me go to his house and tell him he's not required. There's still time.'

Ferris frowned. 'I don't know. Who else is there?'

I went on, 'The women won't take to him. Suppose we lose them?'

'We need men more than women,' he said, biting his lip.

~

There was indeed a lack of willing hands, and Ferris feared we might lose some of the friends we had. He fixed on two days, the first to visit Hathersage and the second to hunt up Buckler. We set out for Mr Chiggs's house, where Hathersage served, directly after breakfast, the weather bright but cold.

'Will his Master like it?' I asked. I knew what it meant to be a servant, subject to whims and vapours.

Ferris laid a finger alongside his nose. 'Master can't walk. Not likely to step along and see us, is he?'

'Machiavel.'

Hathersage himself opened to us. Ferris, sweeping off his hat, bowed deeply. I watched fascinated as he assured our friend we would not take much of his precious time, for we knew it was not his own and he had many duties – in short, under the guise of politeness, he cunningly recalled to Wisdom Hathersage the bondage under which he lived. We were bidden enter, and I could see the young man was glad of our company. I guessed loneliness must make up a great part of his life. He took us to a room that was entirely of polished wood. What looked to be a real silver service, not pewter, shone on the sideboard. All was richly carved and perfectly appointed, but the air smelt as if no food ever came there.

'A brave room,' I said.

'It was made over in the new style for dining, just before Mister Chiggs joined up,' said Hathersage. 'Now we hardly use it.'

We seated ourselves around a large oval table.

'Not much company?' asked Ferris.

'Only when his sisters come to town.'

'How many others in the household?'

'The cook, and a maid. Both married,' and he smiled shyly. 'A very respectable house. O, and a gardener. I rarely see him; he might beg my help once in a while.'

'That's not your work, surely?' I asked, surprised.

'I don't mind. It is a change, out in the air.' He sighed.

'So, the life is respectable,' Ferris returned. 'But somewhat flat? No wife, little masculine company save the master?' He studied the face opposite with gentle gravity, before going on, 'Would you grow old in this life? If a man is equal to freedom, in the end he must have it.'

Hathersage lowered his fine dark eyes.

Ferris leant towards him imploringly, his voice now very soft as if he feared hoarseness. 'We are far forward already. Cattle, grain, plough, cart, all manner of implements, and we have found a good place not too far from the City – a man might walk there in half a day. Since you came to the house we have a smith and a gardener in our company.'

He waited. Hathersage looked up and met his gaze, and as he did so Ferris tilted his head a little to one side, as if pleading, and so made it hard for the other to look away.

'I have had second thoughts. About the – money,' Hathersage jerked out. 'It took me years to save.'

'Is that all?' cried Ferris. 'Then leave it with some trusted friend. Bring yourself, your garments and bedding. Our first work must be digging, and all the money *that* takes has already been laid out.'

A flush rose in the pale brown cheeks; the fellow's eyes glistened. Which way would he go? His lips quirked upwards, straightened again.

'You'll have like-minded friends about you,' Ferris urged. Hathersage pressed his hands fanwise on the table to cool them.

'All the rest have been asked to bring something. You see how I value you,' my friend went on. Hathersage stared at his splayed fingers; I scarce breathed. Ferris laid his hands over Hathersage's. The young man stiffened, but Ferris held him there and gently turned up the other's palms. I saw them open, peeling back from their sweating prints on the polished wood. Ferris's own palms folded over them, their clasped hands much of a size. I thought how it would be to break first Hathersage's fingers, then Ferris's.

'Come to the house,' exhorted Ferris, 'see what we offer to share with you. Come any time, without notice, you'll find yourself welcome.'

Hathersage stared at him, lips parted. 'I shall speak to my Master this evening.'

'God helps those who help themselves,' said Ferris. 'You can always come back to London.'

'I can't leave while there is none here to care for him.'

'That shows a good heart; good hearts make loving friends. So we shall see you soon, agreed?'

'Agreed.'

Ferris was first to pull his hands away.

'An honest fellow,' he said to me as we came away from the house. 'With his second thoughts. No *If it please you, my money was stolen*, but the truth, straight off.'

'Mmm.'

'What, you don't think he's honest?'

I was certain Hathersage was all he should be, and felt the more miserable for it.

'He didn't change his mind because of his moneybags, and not for a plough and cart neither,' I said at last, turning to face my friend.

'We have to like one another if we're to live as brothers,' said Ferris. He skipped nimbly over some wine vomit.

'Paddling with his fingers like that! You courted him.'

'I persuaded him, and for a good cause.' His eyes invited me to laugh. I very nearly did, and stopped abruptly, shaken to find myself so obedient. We trudged back to Cheapside, ill at ease.

Once at home, I withdrew into my chamber to cut out canvas on the floor there, and while bending over the pieces I gradually came to a clearer mind. On consideration, I did not really suspect Ferris of any yearning for Hathersage, but this made me no happier. A virtuous young man, so easily caught. I recalled Zeb's *Stripping me naked with his eyes*. Had Nathan, I wondered, been thus taken? Sleeping each night with Ferris twisted round me like ivy, I no longer doubted what I had blundered upon when I found them lying wrapped in one another. Now, I had even sourer cuds to chew on than jealousy of a lovely boy. Right up to our climbing onto the cart, the *sprig* had thought to keep his friend, but one morning he had woken to find Ferris run away with another. That idea had tickled me once. Now, it clawed.

~

'Do you love me?'

I put the question before I touched him, before even getting into bed, for I wanted something more than those cries of love which are torn from the flesh. He lay eyes closed as if asleep, but on hearing me he sat up, pulling the cover round his shoulders.

'Jacob,' he whispered, 'I'm not amorous of Hathersage! If you're going to be like this, best not have him. I warn you though, if we keep him and you lay violent hand—'

'Keep him by all means. Do you love me?'

'I bring you to live in my house, make you a gift of all my goods, take you into my bed and my body. I let you come between me and the woman who is a mother to me, and I run the risk of the gallows. Can you not interpret all that?'

'Won't you say—'

'What's that ribbon round your neck, Jacob?'

It was the key to his money chest. I was ashamed, but not eased, and undressed with sullen clumsiness. 'You won't say the words,' I accused.

'I love you, I love you! But what does it prove? Words are easily said.'

'So they are.'

'*This* says I love you.' Ferris pulled back the covers to show himself. 'And it never lies.'

'*That* can love thousands. What counts is the heart.'

'But why should you doubt my heart?' he cried. 'After all I've just said?'

'Only tell me this!' I paced up and down the room. 'Did you love Nathan?'

Ferris appeared to consider. He patted the mattress. 'Come in. A man can talk just as well warm as cold.'

I got into bed and lay without touching him. He propped himself on one elbow, and observed me through cautious grey eyes.

'Did I love Nathan. How, love him?'

'I know you fucked him,' I shouted.

Ferris flinched and put his hand on my arm. 'Keep your voice down.'

'Did you *love* him?' I moved my arm away. 'From the heart, the place that counts.' I was bleeding within; until that moment, I had not known how much I still hoped he would deny the thing.

He rolled onto his back and glared at the ceiling. I recognised the withdrawal, the refusal to be held in my stare. When he turned to me again it was with the warning look he had given me in the army, when he felt I kept off his friends.

'Do I order you to tell me how you lived before?' he demanded. 'Do I put you on the rack to know who you love more, me or your wife?'

'Why will you not tell—'

'Have you told *me* all *your* past doings? The truth, now.'

My heart thumped. What had Zeb said to him in the tavern?

He went on, 'It was never a secret that I liked Nat. Now forget him, he's past.'

'Loved him.'

'Aye, then, loved him!'

'But you left him behind.'

He looked at me with sudden understanding. 'Have you really forgotten? I had to choose between him and you.'

'We were friends only.'

He sighed at my stupidity. 'If you say so. We already belonged to each other.' He lay back on the pillow and put his hand on my chest, stroking me. 'Very well, I loved Nat. But I *belong* to you.'

At these last words my blood came up very hot. I pulled him tight into me and took possession of what was mine.

~

The next day we finally got the canvas tent up in the courtyard. It stood only slightly crooked. Ferris explained it was for storing our grain and other gear; for our own protection from the elements we were to make little dwellings something like a charcoal-burner's hut. I wondered at him, so wise and so foolish, to have lived with me all these months and not know that the worst storms break *inside* a man.

In the evening we had a visit from the Tunstalls, come to inform us they had received permission to take away drag-rakes, spades, and other tools. Being orderly people, they had written down on a paper all their treasure and now handed the list to Ferris. He embraced both of them, which (I laughed to see) made them jump, but when they came into the sitting room and saw the wine jug they understood. We were celebrating the tent, that is, we were drinking off our fears. Aunt rose to greet them from the corner where she sat looking over a soiled coat of Ferris's, brushing at the mud spots.

'Pray let it alone, Aunt,' my friend begged. 'We will be all over mud, there's no help for it. Be seated, friends.'

They needed no more encouragement. I saw the eagerness with which they eyed the wine jug and thought that most likely they got little wine at home, for it seemed the appetite of novelty rather than intemperance. Ferris fetched glasses from the sideboard, purchased new the week before as a farewell gift to Aunt, though he had not called it that.

'Where is the little one tonight?' I asked.

'My sister has him. She has no babe of her own,' said Hepsibah. Like her husband, she drank slowly, setting the glass down as if to feel the effect of each mouthful before going on. 'We thought to leave him with her until we have a place fit.'

Ferris wanted to know when they could leave. Jonathan said there would be no difficulty. The young man being gone to the wars and the girl recently married, there were fewer servitors wanted. Their Master and Mistress would certainly be glad that here were two who would go willingly, leaving places for the rest. Again I noted how healthy and solid they were, and how alike, as if brother and sister. On my saying so they laughed.

'We are cousins,' explained Hepsibah.

They were brown people, brown of eye, skin and hair, made like sparrows to blend with the soil. There was none of the swarthy glitter of Zeb or myself, but a much quieter style of physiognomy. They might have been carved from wood, like a doll the Mistress at Beaurepair showed Caro once: it was her own in childhood, and afterwards saved for the daughter she never had.

'You don't speak like Londoners,' said Ferris.

'Indeed we're not: we came from the West with the family when they sold up and moved here.'

'Why would they do that?' he asked.

'The times,' said Jonathan. 'They are Parliament people, and most of the neighbours Royalists. Then there was free quarter for this army, free quarter for that, and the last lot of soldiers used us so barbarously, the Master was afraid for his wife and daughter.'

'They have connections here,' added Hepsibah. 'As good sell, as leave it to be stripped bare.'

'Why bring drag-rakes to London?' I asked. 'To farm the streets?'

They laughed politely.

'Pay no mind to Jacob's airs,' my friend advised. 'He arrived here a few months back knowing as much of the city as a cow.'

'Mister Ferris,' I informed the visitors in awed tones, 'has seen cows in pictures.'

'Most of the tools were packed up by mistake,' said the wife, turning the conversation. 'They were left out of the lots to be sold. Yet now, how clear, the hand of God! Praise the Lord.'

'Praise the Lord,' Ferris responded promptly. He went round again with the wine jug.

'I have got your coat clear, Christopher,' came his aunt's voice.

'God bless you, my dear! Though I wish you would rest.'

''Twere a shame to let it be spoilt. You are handsome in it.'

'Nay, Aunt, my vanity!' He bent and kissed her, taking the coat on his arm. 'Here, I'll lay it in the chest.'

When he went out Hepsibah turned to me. 'So, Mister Cullen, you are come from the country to be with your relatives here?'

'Not so, I am a friend of Ferris. We met in the New Model. Before that I served in a big house, like you.'

They looked at me with fresh interest. 'Were they a great family?' asked Jonathan.

'Of noble birth, but the men were clowns, sots.'

'And the Mistress? Was the Mistress still alive?'

'Yes. A sad life,' I said piously.

'So you fought and never returned home,' said Hepsibah. Aunt watched me curiously. I wished Ferris would hurry back from laying away his coat.

'I did not wish to continue as a serving-man, and Ferris would have me come back with him to London.'

'Are you married?' asked Jonathan.

'I – I lost my wife.'

'Poor man!' exclaimed Hepsibah.

Aunt could not restrain herself. 'He's not a widower. Are you, Jacob?'

I shook my head. 'She left our home under my protection, but we were separated, and I can come by no news of her since. I pray she escaped insult from the soldiers.'

Jonathan said to Hepsibah, 'Show them what was done to you.'

'O, no, Husband! They won't want to see that!'

Aunt said, 'I had rather – that is, I—'

'I mean nothing indecent,' Jonathan urged. 'Go on, Hepsibah.'

Hepsibah lifted off her cap and for the first time I noticed that her hair was cropped beneath it, shorter than mine and almost as short as Ferris's. I had never seen a woman's head in such a condition. Aunt's eyes were wide with pity and horror.

'Was that apprentices?' I asked, fascinated to find that we shared a misfortune.

'Cavaliers,' her husband answered. 'Because she couldn't get them the wine cellar key. Did you ever see such senseless – such—!' He shook his head.

'Thank Providence it was no worse,' his wife reproached him. 'They debauch women for a joke. Maid, mother, no odds.'

'She's right,' I said. '*That* would have come after the wine cellar.'

Ferris entered the room and found us all staring at the woman's despoiled head.

'The Cavaliers did to Hepsibah what the prentice lads did to me,' I told him.

Almost proudly, Hepsibah put back her cap.

'Your hair was cut?' Jonathan asked me.

'He can't remember it,' said Ferris. 'We – the New Model – found him on the road, half dead, and some of the young lads cut his hair off.'

'But why?' asked Jonathan. 'How had he offended?'

'Do such fools as that need a reason? They said he was Samson to the Devil and must be shorn or he would rise and slay the camp. A good thing for them the corporal didn't hear their blasphemy.'

'You never told me this before,' I said.

'I wanted no revenges. What does it matter what they said? They cut your hair because it was black and shiny.'

I glowed within to know he had measured their envy.

'It will grow again, my dear,' said Aunt. I looked round eagerly but she was talking to Hepsibah.

'Let me see the list,' I said. Ferris passed it over. The Tunstalls had put down sickles, flails, seedlips, all the usual stuff; also a breast plough. This last made me sigh. There was no need for it, since we had oxen, but I suspected that once carried to the common, sooner or later it would be put into someone's hands. The thing took a strong worker and I had a good idea who that worker would be. With a man's sweat to oil it, it might take a week to turn as much earth as an ox team could plough in a day. I laid down the paper. 'Have we need of a breast plough?'

'It is a gift,' said Ferris. He turned to the Tunstalls. 'Will you bring these and put them on the cart?'

'When will you depart?' asked Jonathan.

'We thought the tenth of April. High time to be sowing,' said Ferris.

We thought. I had not heard the date before.

'That's late. The ploughing should have been done in the winter,' said Jonathan, voicing one of the very doubts which tormented me also.

'And next year we will,' I answered, obediently singing Ferris's tune. 'But there we are, it is all unbroken. Not much manuring to do; we have that on our side.'

They agreed to bring round their implements a couple of days before the time, and to walk with us to the common on the tenth Ferris went downstairs with them, clapping them on the back and calling out to them as they walked down the street. I stayed behind, looking over the hated list, aware of Aunt's inquisitive gaze on my face.

I was finding myself more and more in this position, promoting what I feared. Sometimes, in my sleep, I heard myself offering explanations to the Devil, who listened in mocking silence and then for answer turned to our precious crops, his fiery laughter scorching them up to withered gourds.

~

I should have been like the dead after all the packing and stacking that had gone on, but I was sleepless on the eve of departure, lonely even in beloved company. Ferris rolled about in bed; he muttered and laughed and once said, *Joanna*, but still he slept. Dreading wakefulness, I had left the candle burning and brought another up with me. I passed my time in watching him, the candlelight being too dim for the Bible which still lived by the side of his bed. Besides, all such reading now frightened me, ever since I had opened the book at random and my eyes had at once fallen on: *If a man also lie with mankind, as he lieth with a woman, both of them have committed an abomination: they shall surely be put to death.* Later it came to me that most likely Ferris – or Nathan – had halted at Leviticus before, and pressed the page open; but *then* it seemed an omen to strike terror into my soul.

The Judas cry of hundreds of birds told me the sun was coming up outside. I turned down the sheets to gaze on Ferris, to commit him and the room to heart. He lay on his back, arms flung wide, as if in welcome: he was slender as a boy, only his scarred cheek to show he had borne arms. I stored up his grace, and his sleeping innocence, for old age.

Feeling the cold, he frowned and rolled towards me. I pulled the cover over us both. Every delight I ever tasted with him pierced me like a knife. I locked my arms about him, caught him between my thighs, burrowed my face into his neck. He struggled and woke. I saw that he knew what day it was, for he said nothing but at once put his arms round me. We lay pressed together, unmoving.

~

Our loving neighbours were out to see the fanatics depart for their field. Some looked on with a discreet – very discreet – admiration, but on most faces I saw that hard completeness which has no time for newfangled notions. *Mister Cooper need not have sold up after all,* said their eyes, *for the young madman has quit. Good riddance to him and his hulking ill-mannered friend.*

Our companions were come and the fellow had brought round the oxen as promised. We all waited in the courtyard in the flat light as Harry fitted the yokes. The beasts stood quiet.

'This one is Reuben, and that Pharoah,' said the man.

Elizabeth patted his snout. 'Pharoah, Pharoah.' Thomas, the eldest of the three Beste children, stared in awe at his hooves. The other two were called Diamond and Blackboy.

'Have we overloaded the cart?' Ferris asked nervously.

Harry made an inspection: it was hard, indeed, to see how more could go on there, or even how we had fitted on all that there was: rice, cheese, salted butter and beef, bacon, poor-john, dried beans, oil and beer, not to mention clothing, grain, seeds and implements. A plough lay on top of the pile, handles projecting from the back. Jonathan, Harry and the Domremys had smaller carts of their own, while the other colonists carried bulging packs.

When everything had been checked several times the terrible moment came. Aunt was still in the house, weeping. I hesitated, then realised that everyone apart from Ferris and myself had gone through this already. I looked round to see how well they had survived it. Botts seemed happy as a man just sat down to a roast goose. The women all had swollen eyes, but each smiled at me, while the men stood quietly acknowledging that it was a blow, a blow indeed. I knew too well how the married couples must have kissed and clung earlier on.

'Go say your farewells indoors,' I suggested to Ferris.

'You go first, then.'

At that moment Aunt came out, looking so pinched and old that I would not have known her. A dreary pleasure passed through the gaping neighbours, and one woman came and took her hand in sympathy. Aunt wrenched it away and threw both her arms violently about Ferris. I was reminded of our arrival in London; she heaved and moaned. He sent me a look of helpless misery over her shoulder, then buried his face in her neck. I looked away, surprised to find myself so pained. The woman who had offered her hand stood stiffly to one side.

Someone touched my sleeve. Becs. She jerked her head towards the house and I followed, oppressed by a faint dread. Once in the kitchen she stopped and turned to face me. I could find nothing to say or do but wait.

She had on her best gown, dark and close-fitting; her wet cheeks showed very fresh over the brilliant white collar. It was a shame, after all, for her not to have had the man she wanted. I was about to beg forgiveness, when the girl rapped out in a strange, fierce voice:

'She'll never know what I saw.'

'O—!' That was my breath going out, the breath I had not known I was holding. My thanks were still unspoken when she went on, 'Take care of him, he's her life.'

'He's mine also.'

We stared at one another. Then she stepped up to me and raised her face, imperious, as if I were the servant. *Very well, a truce.* I touched my mouth to hers. It was a dry, brotherly kiss and we did not cease staring. I made to raise my head, when suddenly her arms coiled round my neck, pulling me down; she closed her eyes and the tip of her tongue pushed between my lips, soft, coaxing. I held back, refusing to join her in it, but then came a treacherous excitement. Panicking, I again tried to raise my head and she at once hung with all her weight on me, pushing right into my mouth, her blind, wilful eyelids shutting out my fear. To my horror, I felt a springing in the loins. She must be stopped at once. Praying Ferris would not come back into the house, I slowly but firmly prised her arms from my neck.

She bit me, and as I pulled away she hit me a ringing blow in the face. I was too shocked even to strike back. There was a taste of blood and I knew she had split my lip. We stood quivering, Becs with clenched fists, I fingering my mouth. I almost said, 'What's the meaning of this?' but instead I bowed to her – bowed! – and stumbled out of the room, closing the door on her violent crying.

At the door I met Aunt, who did not look me in the eyes but seized my hands and muttered, 'May God take you to His care. This house is always open,' and then pushed past me, staggering, on her way upstairs. I stepped out into the sun to see our company waiting for me, Ferris very white.

'You've cut your lip,' said Hepsibah.

I wiped it on the back of my hand and took up my bundle. Harry, bearing Thomas on his shoulders, passed the handles of his cart to Jeremiah, then jerked the reins and clicked to Pharoah. Elizabeth carried the baby in her arms; her middle child, who looked to be about a year old, was held by Susannah Domremy. The carts squeaked on the cobbles and the onlookers parted to let us through. At the end of the street Ferris and I turned round, as one, to look back at the house. There was the window of his chamber, with the two women in it, waving. We waved back. I wondered if Becs could taste my blood. The neighbours stood motionless, watching us go.

PART IV

TWENTY-FOUR

Of Snares

THAT FIRST DAY, when we set down at the edge of the trees and Harry halted the beasts, we stood silent and still as those we had left behind. As soon as the cart stopped creaking I was struck by a mighty squawking of birds, and looking up, saw the spikes of a monstrous rookery in the top branches of the wood.

Then Hepsibah took the hands of the two sisters, one either side of her, showing we should all do likewise, and having made a circle each bowed the head at the great thing we were about. My lower lip was swollen. Some skin was come off and the raw place had been healing, then bursting open, all the day: a loving remembrance.

'Look with favour on our labours, Lord, and grant that they may be a sign unto the times.' The rooks screamed through Hathersage's pleas; each of us echoed, 'Amen'. I remarked that Ferris closed his eyes in prayer to the God he disowned.

We all turned to the cart. Harry unyoked the oxen and tied them, allowing the creatures plenty of rope. I took the weight of the plough as Ferris, atop the cart, slid it down to me, while the others pulled away stuff from the sides. I saw Jonathan unload the hated breast plough and add it to the pile of implements he was building on a level piece of grass. The seeds and small items were in wooden chests. At the very bottom, lining the cart, was the tent, oiled against rain.

My coat and shirt were damp, and had been so throughout the walk from Cheapside. In my pack were some washballs and a cloth; I was already resolved to keep as clean as I might. There was spring water, which meant the battle was half won already, and should it prove too difficult to strip off in the wood, I would fill a bucket. City ways. We were to be peasants now, even my soldier-merchant who stood flushed with sun and with pride at the sight of his purchases all new and unused. He helped me put up the tent, while the rest, instructed by Jeremiah, went to mark out where our strips should be cut, or to fetch back water or timber from the wood.

'Your nose is burnt,' I said.

'Ah, no!' He rubbed at it crossly. 'Once the skin browns it is all right.'

I wondered how would he trench and sow under the sun. We got the tent up more easily than I expected and secured it with stakes, then ran back and forth carrying the chains of our bondage into it. I gave him some of the most awkward stuff to lug, seeing no reason to take it all on my own back. Standing in the printroom, he had said the New Jerusalem would be built of sweat: let him find out what that meant. When I loaded him up with a big pack, so heavy it gave me pause, he locked eyes with me and his jaw set. I watched him go slowly, painfully, to the tent, expecting him to sink to the ground. He did not, but when I followed him in I found him still standing, unable to cast his load without losing balance, and I took pity on him, supporting the load while he slipped his shoulders from under it.

'The strength will come with the work,' he proclaimed.

'Most folk find strength *goes* with the work,' I mocked.

Then I was sorry for my discouraging words, he having borne his burden, after all. 'Come,' I said, 'I'll be your packhorse.' We cleared the rest of the things between us according to their weight. When the last box of tools was safely stored I put my head out of the tent: all the others were some distance off, and I could hear the women, the nearest, shouting to one another about a water-pot.

I caught Ferris by the sleeve and pointed to my mouth. 'See this?'

'What . . . ? Ah, that! Did you bite yourself?'

'Becs bit me. This morning.'

His eyebrows rose. 'You were kissing her?'

I told him what had happened and he snorted with laughter.

'Yes, laugh,' I said. 'I'd have you know it has pained me ever since.'

'You'll live.' Ferris kissed the split lip. 'Chew thyme, that will help it.'

'There's some in the wood,' I offered craftily.

'Jacob, even I know that thyme grows in meadows. But we'll go in the wood,' he ducked away from me as I tried to kiss him properly, 'to hide this.' He pointed at the money chest he had brought from Cheapside. 'You have your key?'

I nodded.

'I'll bury it, and none know where it is, except ourselves.'

'Not in common, then. Your best notion yet,' I said.

'You'll come with me?' He winked, and methought at least there would be no Aunt or Becs.

It was not bad. I took up a small spade; we went very deep into the trees and found a place where we were certain the bushes covered all, Ferris having walked right round it while I lay within and having glimpsed not so much as a shoe. From inside I could hear him moving about, even several yards off, so we stood little chance of being surprised in there. Clutching his money box, he crawled under the foliage to me and, setting it down, pulled my hands under his clothes. It was my dream of months back, that he lay with me in a wood, then seemingly an impossible delight: that remembrance put me in excellent good humour. I indulged him, until he grew hot as an inexperienced boy; I let him bully me, and play the young prince. Later came the pleasure of paying him out in kind. All this time there was a constant chatter of birds above our heads, and the scent of crushed grass.

We buried his treasure under the place where we had enjoyed one another, and came out from the wood bearing bundles of timber.

~

The remainder of that day was passed in going over the strips, removing stones and uprooting with mattocks any tough weed or bush that might hurt the plough. The oxen were set to eat all the scrub that they could, and were the only ones among us to enjoy a rest. When it grew dark, we took cheese, bread and beer under the stars. There was much laughter and some teasing; spirits were high. We all of us slept fully dressed in the tent, side by side, army fashion, and rose with aching limbs to more bread and beer.

The second day we were to make ourselves huts. The turf should rightly have come off with turving-spades, but we were bound to act as quickly as we could, so the beasts were put back to work, breaking the sod while I walked beside Harry learning how the thing should be managed. I was determined to follow this plough and none other, let Ferris or Jonathan do what they would. At Beaurepair the turf had been burnt and scattered back on the soil with lime, to manure it, but we needed ours for shelters. As we went up and down between the lines Jonathan and Hepsibah had marked out, the women followed, gathering up the grass and stones in baskets. These they took to Botts, who made a pile of stones and stacked the turf clumsily on wooden frames cut by Harry. Every so often the smith took his axe and went to cut fresh poles, leaving me to guide the plough. On coming back he would roar with laughter.

'Did you say you had worked the fields?' he demanded.

'Not like this,' I answered, ashamed to see my wavering line after his clean furrow. Worse still was when he found the plough standing motionless, for the oxen felt my unpractised hand.

Hathersage was digging a pit for a fire, constantly wiping his forehead on the back of his hand; his fine brows were fixed in a frown, giving him the air of a good child set to an irksome task. His coat was already off and I saw that his shirt was soiled at the wrists, though elsewhere starched very clean. The earth lay in a neat pile beside the firepit; from time to time he patted it down with his spade. Ferris and Jeremiah were in the wood where Ferris was learning how to set snares, whither Elizabeth and her children were also gone to seek fruit and nut trees.

The sun glared into my itching eyes. Jonathan went ahead of me, hacking at any shrubs which remained before the plough came up to them. The stiffest and thorniest scrub, which the beasts turned from, he laid aside to be used in lining Ferris's drainage sough.

I could barely keep pace with him, and felt my humiliation. My hands and arms trembled; the plough stopped dead and Pharoah flicked his tail at the flies.

'Poor beast, he's tired,' said Susannah.

For a moment methought it was me she meant. Scrubbing my wet face against my sleeve, I saw the linen come away brown with soil and sweat; no breeze sweetened our labour. I watched Catherine fit a slice of turf into her basket, her bronze hair all dust. Both sisters were pink with sun and effort, Catherine's face sprinkled over with fine dark freckles, while her companion's showed paler, more patchy marks, like shreds of October leaves.

'What's this yellowish stone called?' asked Susannah. Nobody knew. I wished I had one of the other men gathering turf, since I could hardly ask the women to take a turn with me on the plough, and I envied Ferris the cool darkness of the wood.

Perhaps he would get us a rabbit or two. Despite the stale heat my mouth ran at the thought of flesh and I realised I was hollow with hunger. I felt faint directly, and stepping back from the plough, I said I must have some food and drink if I were to go on working.

Catherine came with me into the tent and opened one of the cheeses she had brought, finding also a bit of bread. I saw the blackish print of her fingers on the fresh-cut cheese, and my own hand that received it was ingrained with the soil. We each looked down at the dirt, then at one another, seeing our new life take on flesh. Ugly flesh. I drank deep of some warm beer which I found in a big pottery jar, probably the property of Botts. All things in common.

'Where is Christopher?' Catherine asked shyly.

'Setting snares.'

'Once Wisdom has the fire going we can cook.' She picked up the jar but had some trouble with the size and weight of it; I supported it for her so she could take a pull. From her gasping I should say she was drier than myself; I wondered how long would she have gone on without a word. She tapped the jar to tell me to stop, and the beer slopped down her face and neck, onto her bodice.

'Sorry,' I said.

She rubbed at her wet face and the dirt peeled away in tiny black shreds. 'The cow calved yesterday. In a day or two we can fetch her.'

'What, walk her from London? It is too soon, surely?'

'Nay. She's in the next village! All that was arranged weeks ago.'

She eyed me curiously, probably wondering why Ferris had not told me. I could have enlightened her: he knew that I would be bored. The spilt beer having left a white patch on her chin, she looked like a man who shaves off his beard in high summer. I felt no anger towards this innocent rival, perhaps because she was beaten beforehand, or because I had lived too long with Becs. It was soothing to see myself reflected in Catherine's eyes: Jacob, neither bad angel nor filthy darling, but a poor unlucky man who had bitten his own lip.

When we returned to the field Harry was back, looking lazily down the sides of his nose as usual. The oxen laboured, stretching their necks to take the strain.

'Would you like to do something else?' Harry asked me as we stumbled along by the side of the beasts. 'Carry stone? Susannah can help Ben with the poles.'

'Let me help Ben,' put in Catherine. She walked over to him before anyone else could offer, and knowing how he revolted her, I could not understand what she would be at, until I saw how she kept glancing from the hut into the forest. If she could stomach that man for the sake of keeping an eye on her sweet Christopher, she was deeper in than I thought.

'My sister-in-law is young,' said Susannah as we bent together over the baskets. 'She relishes frequent change of occupation.'

I smiled and nodded. Black beads with legs twinkled over the torn soil; cut worms curled upwards as if imploring our mercy. I tried not to touch them. Crouching down was even hotter work, and the warm wet shirt on my back began to sicken me, so at last I took it off. I would now tan like a peasant, but there was no help for it. Susannah laboured on in her woollen gown. It was stained in great swathes beneath arms and breasts. Looking at her made me itch.

'See here,' she exclaimed. In her hand I saw a slab of yellow stone about the size of a brick, but roughly triangular, and embedded in it a scallop, real as on a fishmonger's slab.

'Look, everybody!'

They were all glad to leave off for a moment. Susannah passed round the stone. 'What do you say to that?'

'Elves,' offered Catherine.

'Superstition,' Hathersage sharply corrected her. We passed the scallop about, pressing the stone. I ran my fingernail between the smooth ribs; Harry spat on the object and rubbed at it.

'I have seen things like this before,' I said.

'Have you indeed!' cried Harry. 'Just so?'

'Like great flat snails. There were lots of them buried in the land at home; the farm men built them into the walls for luck. One was the size of a cartwheel.'

'Lord have mercy!' cried Hathersage.

Botts put on a doubting face for superiority. 'And was *that* built into a wall?'

'It was left in the church porch,' I told him. 'There to this day.'

He sniffed, annoying me, for every word was true.

'I have seen such things too,' said Hepsibah. 'Sticking out of clay banks after a hard rain. When I was a girl the village children used to keep them.'

'They are devilish things,' said Hathersage. 'Animals turned to stones – that's either some witchcraft, or a punishment from God. Do you think this might be from Sodom and Gomorrah?' He stared round anxiously.

'How would it come here?' gibed Botts.

'Not Sodom, but the Flood,' I suggested. 'The waters covered the face of the earth, and this was left behind when they went down.'

Hathersage's face cleared.

'But why is it stone?' asked Catherine. 'Could we find stone dogs, or kine?'

Botts wanted to know was it stone all through.

'Break it and see,' suggested Harry.

'No!' cried Susannah. 'Don't spoil it!'

'Put it back where it was,' said Hathersage. Susannah frowned, evidently considering the scallop as her own.

'What do you think?' I asked Jonathan. He shrugged and said it might be some fluke or sport of nature; as a man's seed spilt on the ground grows into a mandrake, so this might be a sea creature spawned in stone. A scholar could perhaps tell us.

In the end Susannah laid the scallop aside from the pile, to be put in a prominent place when we built our first true walls; she said it was too pretty to bury again. I saw Hathersage was unhappy at this, but he did not take it from her.

~

I am black, but comely, O ye daughters of Jerusalem.

Thus Ferris's poor attempt to raise a smile. I was grown into that very Ethiope I once jested of when we spoke of mariners, and I was ragged to boot, ragged as Rupert Cane as he lay on the road with nothing worth taking but his hair. After a day or so, I laid by my heavy cloak for the winter. As I closed the trunk lid on the Cheapside citizen in his coffin, I recalled my mother's poor beaten pride when My Lady raised me from the furrow and got me the place at Beaurepair. A man's last state is often worse than his first. Printing, strolling about the city: all that brief glory had burnt itself out. The only riches I was like to see now were the stones glittering in the sun.

Our latrines had been dug behind bushes for decency. I had made a shallow trench with the fresh earth piled up alongside. There was a shovel to hand so that folk could cover up their leavings, filling the trench as they went. The stench was not as bad as I had feared, for the colonists were both fewer and more cleanly in their ways than the New Model Army. Ferris was displeased, considering it a waste of both labour and manure, but I could sooner bear this than making the open furrow my privy, and I was not the only one.

'Do I ask you to squat under another's nose?' Ferris cried in exasperation. 'All you need do is go to the far end of the field, that is decent enough.'

'I dig and plough at your command,' I replied, 'but you will *not* tell me how to shit.'

The colonists had been turning up the ground two weeks and a half, which came to roughly two acres; practised labourers would have made it more. We were laying down rye, turkey corn, dredge, and bullimong as well as some peas and beans, carrots, onion, leeks and turnip. The grain was mostly rye (for neither wheat nor barley would thrive in a newly cultivated field) and so the strips had to be harrowed before sowing. I was glad to see that Jeremiah had things in hand, and had soaked the grain, all except the rye, in cow dung and water well mixed. We all of us took turns with the wooden harrow, and as soon as each row was turned Ferris and Jeremiah got to work with the setting board.

I watched Ferris kneel on this board, pouring seed down through the holes; he was so busy getting Mother Earth with child, Catherine might have thrown herself naked in the furrow and he would have rested his knees on her. As the plough followed the oxen, so the poor girl followed Ferris, making many small approaches to him, all of which were gently repulsed. He had been right in what he told me in London: Catherine, at least, could not see how it was between himself and me. Of Hathersage I was less sure. Botts, methought, noticed none but himself, and we had none of us much time for observation. Even the children were given rattles and put to bird-scaring, though being so young, they lacked skill. The sight of them among the furrows filled me with a pain which I kept to myself. Ferris would not understand. *That* wound had been inflicted long before I went to war, and the only man who had measured the depth of it was Izzy.

For most things, it was Jeremiah who had the best notions. To keep off birds he twisted up black rags in the form of crows, laying pack-thread along the furrows. Having once spied ants within the tent, he made it his special care to search out the anthills and discovered many under bushes and trees. After sundown, which was in a manner of speaking the ants' curfew, he carried water to these nests, scalding the inhabitants, who would else have carried off our grain on their backs.

Though I hardly liked to admit it, my friend's endurance surprised me. When he was not sowing his slight figure would be found, as often as not, down by the sough. This sough, a kind of covered drainage pit, had long been a most precious project of his. He had always wanted to construct one, poring fascinated over diagrams during the winter months and comparing different designs. Now it was begun he preferred to carry out the work alone, at times asking Jeremiah or Jonathan for counsel but refusing all offers to join him in the digging of it. The thing itself was placed in one of the bottoms, where the grass was rankest and made a sucking sound if anyone walked across. Ferris had already cut drainage channels into it, to dry out the land nearby, but the special delight of the thing was in the construction of the sough itself, and that was but begun.

'I'll hollow it out just after the fashion of the plan,' he explained to me one morning as we repaired a hut which had collapsed during the night. I passed him up a piece of turf and he went on, 'It has to be deeper, and then widened on all sides and the brush and branches put in.'

'Will you want pulling out afterwards?' I asked.

'Aye. Today I'll finish the pit – there'll be no getting out after that without help. Tomorrow I'll put the stuffing in it.'

'That's a two-man job. You'd better catch it from below and I'll take the weight of easing it down.'

He frowned. 'I'm strong enough to lower boughs.'

'The top man has to pull the other up,' I reminded him.

Ferris nodded stiffly. I had already noted that since we were come to the common, he envied me my strength as he had never done in Cheapside.

'After eating, then?' I coaxed him. His face brightened, for early that morning, before starting on the repairs to the hut, we had gone round the snares and found three rabbits.

Hathersage's firepit worked most excellently. He had banked up the earth in a ring round it, thus permitting air to get to the flames, yet not to blow them out. A trivet made by Harry expressly for this purpose swung over the pit and held Elizabeth's kitchen cauldron. Hathersage toiled back and forth with logs, all over smuts like a sweep's boy and with little Thomas Beste trying to swing from his shirt-tail. I wondered if, labouring thus, the young man thought back longingly to the boredom of Mister Chiggs's house. The infant lay snorting on the grass, punching at the sun.

Ferris smiled on Elizabeth as we approached. 'And how do the rabbits swim?' he asked.

'In their own gravy,' she replied. 'Jacob, you look to be dying of hunger. They are as good as ready, if you will call the rest.'

I set off to round up the other labourers; Ferris stayed to peer into the cauldron and tease Hathersage about his sooty skin; the words *black as Jacob* drifted to me along with the gusts of steam. I quickened my steps.

Hepsibah and the Domremys were in the tent, examining salt meat and going through the jars of beer to see how many had been broached.

'The cheese goes nowhere, we should have brought more,' Catherine was saying sadly as I entered.

'There is something better than cheese waiting for you,' I told her, smiling. Her fine skin turned from pink to dull red, and I perceived I had made an error. Backing out of the tent, I added, 'Elizabeth expects you directly. Be so kind as to fetch the beer,' and fled to seek the men.

Jeremiah and Jonathan were sorting the piles of stones into big and small. It was dreary work, and when invited to eat they left off without further ado. Jeremiah grinned at me and I noticed that the smile-wrinkles fanning out from his hot blue eyes went right back to his hair. What did he get from our experiment, I wondered: had he perhaps fled some ill-doing or debt? I had been slow to consider such things, except in the case of Botts. Now I realised that we did not know for sure why any man or woman had joined us. I could read nothing in Jeremiah's bright gaze.

'Harry is cutting wood,' he offered. 'Shall I go for him?'

'My sincere thanks – where is Ben?'

The men looked at one another, then at me. 'He's not well,' said Jonathan finally. 'The sun's got to him. What he needs is rest.'

I set off towards Botts's hut. The others remained where they were.

'Jacob, don't!' called Jonathan suddenly. He came running after me. 'Let him be, eh? The more rabbit for us.'

I looked on his earth-brown face, the face of one who will buy peace at any cost. 'I shall at least see,' I answered.

But I had no need to see, for the stink of ale and vomit farted out from the hut even with the door closed. I spat. 'How long has he been like this?'

Jonathan shrugged. 'Maybe an hour. He was well enough at prayers, you saw him same as I did.'

Wondering how much drink he had swallowed, I made to open

the door, but Jonathan laid his hand on mine. 'What good going in now? He won't know you. Shall we not eat?'

I hesitated.

'Not eat your fine rabbits?' he added. 'Ben will wait.'

'True.'

We walked back together companionably enough. 'Is this the first time?' I asked.

'The first time he's been this bad.' He looked up with clear sad eyes. 'The man's lonely; that gives an opening to the demon of intemperance.'

'He's with all of us, all day! What more does he want?'

'What every man wants, a particular friend, a woman, children.'

'I have no woman, no more has Hathersage, or Jeremiah,' I said hypocritically.

'No; but you've a friend. It's having *nobody*—'

'Well, stinking of spew won't help that!'

'You are hard, Jacob.' It was a plea, but there was no hint of cringing or truckling to me; he was not made of earth after all, this brown man.

'Hard, because I am galled!' I said. 'I saw this coming, but Ferris would have his way.'

'He's not an easy man to refuse,' said Jonathan. I turned to see his eyes fixed on mine, mild, inoffensive. For a second I thought there was pity there too, but then he smiled and shrugged. We walked to the cauldron in silence. Harry and Jeremiah were just emerging from the wood. Hathersage's cheeks and mouth had been wiped clean.

There was a rough table made by Harry next to the cauldron, bearing a large dish, wooden bowls and some greyish cloths. I saw strings hanging over the cauldron side. Elizabeth pulled on one, and brought up a jug, the lid sealed with pastry; this she lowered onto the table while Susannah and Catherine pulled up another two, sealed in the same way.

'Hot, hot!' Susannah shouted to Thomas, who made to finger one of them as it swung near his head. Hepsibah took the little boy by the hand, pulling him back. The other women deftly handled the scalding vessels, in that way women have, and cut the pastry seals. A cloth came out last, with something green in it, and was laid on the grass to drain; there was rabbit in the air, in everyone's nose and mouth. I felt a gnawing in me and secretly determined to eat my fill one way or another, for at times I received the same portion as Ferris and it rattled around my empty guts like a dried pea in a drum. The meat, done very tender inside the jugs, was scooped into the large dish and thence to the wooden bowls.

'Did you call Ben?' asked Elizabeth, flushed and hesitating over his dish. A drop of sweat from her chin just missed falling into the stew.

'He is ill and wants none,' I replied, thinking too late that a sharper man would have offered to take him his food. She pushed another forkful of meat onto the little heap in my bowl; Susannah handed out slices of cheat bread. The cloth was untied and I received some boiled greens: nettles and fat-hen. The company sat to eat, digging in their clothes for knives and spoons. I looked down at my spoon. It was the one Ferris had given me at Winchester.

'Well done, wife,' said Harry.

The rest joined in praising Elizabeth's cookery.

'Wisdom built me a good fire,' said she.

Hathersage blinked modestly, heard Ferris say, 'Brave Hathersage,' and received the jar of beer from Catherine, which should have made him completely happy. There was quiet except for his gasp as he took a pull at the drink, and the clack of cutlery. Ferris sucked meat off the bones. I rose, picked up a pastry seal from the table and put it on top of my bowl: Harry did likewise. Elizabeth gave the remaining piece to Thomas to chew on.

'If you please, the beer,' I heard Ferris say. Hathersage promptly relinquished it. Ferris drank so deep that a man might think he knew of Botts's condition, and was trying to forestall further indulgence by emptying the jar. Then he lay back on the grass, his empty bowl on his chest.

'Is there any cheese left?' asked Jeremiah. Susannah went off to fetch it; I sat up, ready for more food.

'We should thank Christopher, too,' said Catherine, 'since he snared them. You must set more snares, Brother Christopher.'

'Or check them more often,' said I.

Ferris smiled, lying with his eyes shut, lashes very fair on his brown cheeks.

After the cheese, I went with him to examine the sough. I was in a good humour, having for once eaten my fill. Piles of earth lay around the hole, nakedly black until the grass and weeds should clothe them.

'See how deep the pit is,' urged Ferris.

He was tipsy with beer and sun, wanting me to admire his prowess and to say I could not have shifted more soil myself. I looked down into the hole, which was disagreeably like an upright grave, but could not see how far off the bottom was, for it reflected sky and our peering faces, his head level with my breast.

'It is draining already!' he cried.

'And how deep might that water be?' I was not happy to think of him going into it.

'Perhaps a few inches, Jacob. But all since yesterday!' He took off his shoes, then his shirt, tossing it impatiently onto the grass. 'Come back in a while, will you?'

'You don't want help to get in?'

'Nay.' He frowned; I had said the wrong thing. 'The spade's still down there.'

'Ferris, have a care! How will you—'

'Look,' and to my shock he leapt down the shaft.

I ran to the edge and saw him gazing up, laughing. 'It's just over my calves. Did I frighten you, Jacob?'

'Indeed,' I said, accepting my punishment for being bigger and stronger than himself.

He looked quite comfortable in his pit, his head some three feet below the grass.

'How did you get out last time?' I asked.

'Harry pulled me.' He measured the height of the walls. 'It grows harder to throw out the earth. Jacob, could you draw it up?'

And so while Harry and the women continued with the plough, and Jeremiah knelt to set the carrots and onions, I lowered a bucket on a rope and raised the soil which Ferris scooped out from the sides of his burrow, hollowing out a full-bodied, narrow-necked pot.

'That's the last one!' he shouted as I dragged up a sodden heap of roots and worms. 'Next is me!'

I brought him up sitting on the bucket, the handle lengthways between his thighs, hands black on the rope. There was a scuffle at the lip of the sough as he kicked himself away from the edge. While he was crawling over the grass I spat on my palms: the inner sides of my fingers were creased and hot.

'The lining goes down tomorrow, then it is complete.' He dusted off his hips and arse. Water running off the legs of his breeches made two dark patches on the earth.

'And very glad I am to see the end of the thing,' I said. 'An open ditch would have served.'

Ferris sniffed. 'Shall we cut some wood for it?'

I took a saw and followed him hopefully under the trees but we spent the time until supper lopping branches. Then it was bread and cheese again, and afterwards bed, alone. I could only get to sleep by laying hand on myself and making believe that Ferris did it with his mouth.

In the morning Botts appeared, greasy and half stunned. None spoke to him of his debauch.

~

While I was not precisely in Catherine's plight, I could scarce style myself happy. For a start, the huts were wretched: it was foul and brutish to sleep under turf and find worms dropping off the underside of it during the night, or spiders descending, and the bedding we had brought from London was soon damp. I spread mine on the roof of the tent every day we had sun, which took out some of the wetness but not the smell of earth. I tried not to think about autumn rains.

Then, our homes were without any real defences. True, they were raised up close to each other (a torment to me, for it meant every little noise on either side could be heard) and each hut had a kind of door knocked together by Harry and Jeremiah, but these were more hurdle than portal. I kept a knife always by my side at night, and told the women to do the same. Catherine and Susannah slept in one big-sized hut for safety, with Hathersage one side of them and Jeremiah the other. Harry and Elizabeth shared a turf dwelling with their little ones. Jonathan and Hepsibah also had one roof over their two heads. As far as I could tell, Jeremiah, Botts and Hathersage lay in solitary confinement like myself.

I yearned after Ferris for days at a time. The morning we finished the sough, I stood for hours lowering branches and twigs to him as he stood half naked in the rising water, then pulled him out, supple and gleaming, and watched him put his shirt on.

'You are shouting it,' he said coldly, 'remember we are observed,' and walked away. Stung, I would not go after him, but stayed lying on my belly with my head hanging over the edge of the drain. Below me were wet twigs, and beneath these I could just glimpse the bigger pieces which I had supported while he positioned them. I wondered how he had balanced on the lining even as he built it, but of course he was more agile than I. For what seemed a long time I concentrated on the sough and its construction, shamming, even to myself, an interest, and all the while pressing my hips to the ground in frustration.

On occasion we went out at night and lay in the field, not the wood with its hidden foxholes and branches. In the utter blackness of a country night it was too easy to fall and make a deal of noise, which would infallibly rouse our companions. To take a light would have been madness. I would grow urgent first; he would bid me have patience, and this I suffered up to the point where it was as dangerous to leave him as to go to him, when I would glance up from digging a trench or cutting poles to find him staring at me, when after days of *Jacob, hold off* I would find him pleading, silently, at my elbow. That look, I thought, must betray us to any knowing watcher, and I would propose we go round the snares. Checking the places too often, filling the wood with our scent, we most likely lost us many rabbits. Ferris laughed at our strange piebald flesh – I was now very dark down to the waist, he all white but for head and forearms – but I saw nothing to laugh at in our coarsening into peasants. We would come back squeezed empty, sticky and pleasure-drunk, and for the moment it was enough; yet it never sufficed me long. I wanted to lie in a bed, for him to keep a hold on me all night as he used, to watch him sleep, and wake. Sometimes, furtive like one performing a guilty action, I would carry my washball to the spring and cleanse myself as best I could. The scent of rose and lavender came to me as keen as when I had first washed myself in Cheapside and put off my old rags. Now, however, I put my rags back on again and returned to my labour.

The bad dreams were grown more frequent, and I woke always alone, the Voice intimate and insistent inside my skull. Often, of late, I flew in the air over Hell and looked down on the damned, whose punishment it was to mine rocks with picks and spades. They flowed over the black surface like ants. From time to time a flame would lick up and burn some of them off. The rest kept digging.

~

The cow came. Her calf was thriving enough, and prettily spotted. Hathersage named it *Fight-the-Good-Fight* (soon shortened by the women to *Fight*) while the mother went by the less stirring name of Betty. The dairymaids were at last happy to go on with their old trade, even though there could be no cheese as yet; they inspected the beasts daily for any sign of sickness or injury, but found none.

Ferris and I were standing near the sough one day when Catherine brought some milk in a pot. I watched her cross the patches of corn and potatoes, holding her offering before her as if it were the best wine. The grass around the sough glittered in the searching light; though dew still clung here and there, the sun was already hot to the skin.

She went directly to Ferris and gave the pot into his hand.

'Why, thank you Catherine,' he replied and put it to his lips. I watched her watch him drink it.

'Is there some for me?' I asked. Catherine did not deign to look at me but Ferris stopped drinking and wiped his mouth.

'Excellent,' he said. She beamed.

'Have some, Jacob.' Ferris handed it to me. Catherine's smile stiffened.

I put my head back and let it down my throat. That milk was the first thing ever made me glad to be out of London, for there was neither chalk nor water in it, just its natural sweetness, thick with cream. I drained it to the bottom, and said, 'I could drink that again,' by way of praise.

'You've drunk more than your share as it is,' she said, snatching the pot from me. As she stamped off, Ferris and I exchanged smiles. Too late I looked up to see Hathersage, some distance away, watching us. He turned his head aside.

I had by diligent observation made a discovery of my own, namely that Hathersage was amorous of one of the Domremys, but he was so timid and backward I could not tell which; all he would do was to stay with them when he could, and show great courtesy to each, as if courting the two. When I imparted this intelligence to Ferris, he said, 'Maybe he *is* courting the two, to see which will come out good,' but I judged the man shy rather than sly. At first he had clung to Ferris and myself, but that had stopped very early on, before he fell in with the women, and methought he had understood something.

Now he coughed, straightened his garb and went after Catherine. At a distance, I saw him beg some milk of her. She spoke to him as if in anger. He looked to be soothing her, and she pointed in my direction. A pot of milk was handed to him and he drank it slowly, not throwing his head back as I had done but sipping.

'See there,' I said to Ferris.

He grinned. 'Will he cut me out, think you?'

'Not with everyone.'

'Now,' said Ferris, bending over the sough, 'to business. How much would you say has run off into here?'

'We should check the snares this morning,' I said.

'You think of nothing but snares, Jacob.'

'Because we've left them too long.'

'I want to try this first. Snares *later*.'

That was the fourth time in two days I had pleaded and been refused. By 'try' he meant descend into the sough, to see how it was draining the land. For a fortnight he had talked of little save this underground pond of his creation.

'It's not safe,' I said. 'Water sucks you down.'

'Tie the rope round me then.'

He had one ready. Unsure how it should be done, I waited until he had stripped to the waist and then looped the rope under his arms. Hathersage was strolling back to us across the field, smiling sleepily to himself. Catherine was evidently his first choice, and, I thought, he might strike home: a woman who could fancy Christopher Ferris might well look kindly on Wisdom Hathersage, each being delicately made, gentle towards the female sort and with a head stuffed full of maggots. We waited while he came up to us, and when he was about ten feet off, he called to me, 'Shall I help hold the rope?'

I shook my head and, standing a few paces from the edge, steadied myself for the strain.

Hathersage watched as Ferris lowered himself into the sough feet first, until his buttocks perched on the edge.

Ferris grinned at me. 'Let it out.'

I saw the sough embrace him, easing over his hips and up his chest. His arms shook. With a gasp he let go of the earth on either side and first his head, then his hands, dropped out of sight. There was a crash, and the rope shot through my fingers, burning them. I clawed at it, cursing, but it slithered across the dry grass and then suddenly stopped, limp in my grasp.

We ran forward and bent over the hole.

'Brother?' called Hathersage.

Ferris shouted something. I could hear a thrashing in the water, and a crackling, snapping sound: the branches.

I got down and lay on my belly peering into the dark. 'Ferris, are you hurt?'

Hathersage towered over me; I saw a crease in his breeches picked out against the brilliant sky.

Somewhere, not in the sough and not in the field, I heard a laugh and the word *Drowned*.

'Ferris!' I cried, more loudly this time.

There was a scream. Then I heard 'Jacob', and other words, indistinguishable but childish with fear.

'I'll pull you up!' I bellowed into the hollow beneath me. 'Hold on!' I stood and braced myself, but then I heard three words clear:

'No! Don't pull!' The voice rose to a scream at the end: he sounded like an injured wrestler begging an opponent for mercy.

I would have to go down to him, and someone pull us up both.

'Fetch Harry,' I shouted to Hathersage. He stared at me.

'Shape yourself! Move!' I yelled. He turned and stumbled away towards the wood. There was a dull crumpling sound. The grass gave way under Hathersage and he was thrown forwards, clutching at a thorn bush. As he scrabbled to safety, clods and stones rattled down into the sough and loaded the branches; I heard them drop through into the pit, *gloop gloop*, and knew the water was deep.

'Ferris—!' I bawled.

'Get away from the edge,' cried Hathersage, who was pulling himself upright.

'Are you still here? Fetch Harry before I break your neck—' I collapsed onto my knees. If I went down the hole I might crush him. 'And bring spades!' I shouted to Hathersage's back, then turned my attention to the sough. Earth and stone; water beneath. Perhaps over his head by now.

'Ferris, speak!'

Silence.

'Tell me where you are!'

There was a sound like sobbing. I craned forward trying to place it: all I could tell was that it was somewhere near the bottom. I began to descend, clinging to the side which had collapsed, trembling at every pebble that rolled away into the hole. Once halfway, I began grabbing up bits of rock and turf, anything I could get hold of, flinging it all upwards through the mouth of the shaft.

'Careful there below!' came a voice over my head.

'Get Harry down here!' I screamed back.

I could hear the sobs more clearly now: he was alive, and not crushed beneath me. A shadow fell on the rubble. Harry.

'Is it safe for me to come?' he called.

'Stay away from *there*,' and I pointed out where I thought Ferris lay. The smith came scuffing down and handed me a spade.

The two of us began to dig as a team. From time to time I would heave up a rock or branch and Harry would raise it out of the pit; he later told me that Hathersage bruised and cut himself as he strained to clear the stuff at the top, but at the time I never lifted my eyes from what lay below. We dragged away whatever lay nearest. My hands were torn by the crisscross of branches; parting them, I saw that the water beneath was fouled, dulled from glass to a brownish stone.

There was a scratching noise, and I looked round to see a clod of earth unfold itself, put forth fingers and arch like a spider.

'Harry!' I whispered.

My helper pressed the earth-spider between his palms, comforting it. I was unable to touch the fingers from my side, and dared not cross to them; I thought I would faint. Harry began scooping out the earth round the imprisoned hand with a sharp stone. A forearm was revealed, caked in dust which was turning red where Harry's stone had pierced the skin. Tightly packed twigs lay across the upper part of the arm. These Harry snatched up and flung aside.

'You can come closer,' grunted the smith, 'I see where he is now. Keep this side.'

I picked my way over and saw branches under where the twigs had been, and lower still, a sheen of pale hair. We bent to heave up the boughs, but could get no purchase and I sweated with fear lest we slip and drop them on him. Stooping, I saw a thin face tilted up at us, eyes closed. He was powdered with earth – light coloured. Dry earth. Not drowned. Not drowned.

Father of Lies.

'One of us will have to go under and push up,' said Harry.

'I will.' I brushed aside small branches until I could see what to do: I would have to slip into the water beside one of the large boughs.

My shirt caught on the branches; I tore it off, swearing, and threw it into the darkness. Bark scored my skin as I lowered myself, arms aching, until I could go no further. I took a deep breath and let go: the water came up to my chest and was so cold that I cried out, but my feet touched bottom.

'Can you get a grip?' Harry called.

'This one!' I shouted. I braced myself under the left-hand bough and pushed. It rose slowly, with a sucking sound; my legs trembled and I had a flash of terror, but then the burden lightened as Harry took hold and lifted.

'Over that way!'

We swung it around and away from Ferris. I lowered the branch gently, going completely under the foul water in the process, and surfaced to see him slipping down, about to drop under likewise. I splashed back and caught him, holding him upright. I could feel the rope, heavy and wet, dragging round my feet.

'I'll pass him up to you,' I called. I heaved Ferris into my arms like a child and waded towards Harry, who had now inched his way further down. 'Here.' Unable to see, with Ferris's back pressed against my nose, I held him up and felt Harry take the weight. There was a tug at my ankle; I freed the rope, and saw my friend carried safely out of the shaft. I had still sufficient strength to drag myself out of the icy water and crawl up again, the debris slipping away beneath me.

Ferris was lying on the grass, Harry wiping the unconscious face with a wet sleeve. I knelt beside my friend's outstretched body, clutching his wrist, and suffered a violent qualm, weeping like a woman. I had just enough self-command not to grapple him to me and kiss him.

When I was able to look up I saw Hathersage, rubbing his sore hands and watching me, then Elizabeth standing next to her spouse. Little Thomas Beste danced about as if in celebration. Botts was arrived, lugging a case of instruments. He bent to listen for the heart.

'Brother Christopher may think himself fortunate,' he said.

'Not least in his friends,' said Harry. He laid his hand on my heaving back. Botts smirked, thinking the words were meant for him, until Harry went on, 'If he values you aright, I'd say this wipes out the Rowly business and two more like it.'

The Tunstalls were hastening towards us across the field. Ferris opened his eyes; they were dazed, innocent as when I saw him that night with Nathan, but they slitted when he found Botts crouched over him. He turned his face away from the surgeon's.

'Jacob?'

His lips scarce moved; his voice was so faint that I was not sure what I had heard. Botts ignored his attempts to speak and pressed hartshorn under his nostrils: Ferris flinched back from it.

'He doesn't need that.' I shoved the vial aside and bent over my friend, whose lips were working: I put my ear to them and caught the whisper, 'Let him not hurt me.'

I shook my head. Botts had just finished rooting out two scalpels and was holding their edges up against the sun to see which had fewer nicks in it.

'Letting blood will help lift the swoon,' he proposed excitedly. I laid my hand on Ferris's arm and turned my face up to the surgeon.

'He doesn't wish to be bled.'

'Nonsense,' Botts returned. 'I must at least examine him, else we lose precious time.'

Ferris turned a dog's eyes on me.

'No,' I said. 'He suffers too much pain.'

'It is the nature of a patient to suffer.' Botts was laying out implements; I saw screws on some of them. 'Is not the word itself derived from the Latin *patiens*? That is to say, *suffering*,' he translated for the benefit of the rest of us. 'But the professional man's way is not the way of sentimental ignorance,' here he cast scornful eyes on me, 'for he cures the sufferer *despite* the pain. Will you help me by restraining him?' He took hold of Ferris's left arm and lifted it; my friend gasped. I saw sweat darken the dust on his brow.

'Lay that arm down – softly – softly!' I ground out between my teeth. 'Touch him again, and you'll be in need of a surgeon yourself.'

Botts raised his eyebrows. He pushed his bloodshot features into mine. 'Some might call this usage ill advised. I would go further, sir: I would call it barbarous.' He stood up and looked round for succour, but the others dropped their eyes, all except Hathersage, who had never stopped watching me.

I stood up also, very close to Botts, as a gentle persuasion. 'Well then,' I shrugged, 'barbarous I am. But I keep my promises. Harry, do I keep my promises?'

'I fear he does,' Harry said dryly. 'Best leave things for now.' He took the surgeon by the arm. 'Mister Botts, have I leave to talk with you a while?'

Botts glared up at me, flushed and sullen. I returned the glare. Either he would look away first, or I would black his pig's eyes for him.

'I beg of you, Mister Botts,' the smith whispered. Botts dropped his gaze and I exulted silently, fiercely, as Harry led him away.

I knelt again by Ferris. 'Can you walk?' I asked.

He struggled to sit up, but failed.

'I can support his back,' suggested Hathersage.

I went on, 'Will you let me lift you? With Hathersage's help?'

He moaned, 'Don't pull me by the arms!'

'Then roll over and kneel,' I told him. At last, though with cries from him that wrung my innards, I arranged him over my shoulder.

'Give him cold compresses,' urged the women. I asked them to make us some and they set off in search of cloth to soak in the spring.

'I will see what I can do with the sough,' said Jonathan, who had remained silent until now. He walked off to the edge of it, and stood contemplating the ruin.

I took the way to Ferris's hut, where I intended to stay a while, for I was not going to leave him where Botts might return to the torture. Halfway there I stopped and adjusted his weight on my shoulder.

'Where are you taking me?' he asked faintly.

'To bed.'

He giggled.

'Sshh. Rest.' I nuzzled my face into his side. As I did so I glimpsed something dark: Hathersage walking a yard behind us. My heart jerked, but it was possible he had understood nothing. I turned and asked him would he be so kind as to fetch my blankets from their airing place on top of the tent. He set off willingly and without any knowing look. I then carried Ferris into his own hut and laid him next the bed. There was a bucket of water there, and a dirty linen clout. I sponged the muck as best I could off his face, arms and breast. His head rolled to one side.

'Cold water and rags, here.' Susannah stood at the door. 'Shall I put them on him?'

'Let us wait until he can show us the pain.'

Susannah nodded. 'You know where I am to be found.' I had thought she would stay and insist on nursing him, but she left without further talk, ducking out through the door just as Hathersage arrived with my blankets.

'My sincere thanks,' I said, bending to unfasten my friend's soaking breeches. Sinking now into sleep, he made no attempt to help me. Hathersage averted his eyes.

'It was nothing,' he murmured. 'Shall I fetch *you* some water also?'

'To drink?' I looked about and saw a stone jug. 'There's beer here.'

'For your face.' I stared at him, puzzled. He awkwardly went on, 'Your tears have washed two great channels in the field-dirt.'

'Thank you, Susannah has brought some.'

He bowed and went out.

Pondering the meaning of that extraordinary last speech, I stripped my patient. The heavy wet breeches took some time, for though he was light, I feared injuring him further by too brisk a movement. His flesh beneath the cloth was cool and damp, his feet muddy. I washed that off as best I could and the flat scent of pond water filled the hut.

Laid out thus, Ferris showed himself even thinner than formerly, his belly drawn in high under his ribs like that of a starving dog. Only his shoulders had swelled slightly: the compact, stringy muscle of a lean man. His face was now brown, though it would never darken as deeply as my own; his hands and forearms stood out sharply against the fair skin elsewhere. I did not find him improved. The Devil had granted my wish to watch him sleep, but granted it in his usual cruel fashion, making a pain of a pleasure. Yet pleasure there was. I still desired to watch over him, be his dragon against Botts.

Catherine tapped at the door of the hut. 'Jacob? I've brought more compresses.'

I pulled the blankets over Ferris's nakedness. 'Thank you most sincerely, but he sleeps. Leave them with me.'

'Let me see him.' That was forward, for Catherine. She pushed in and gazed on his sleeping face. By the look of her, she ached to pull back the covers, or slip her hand under them and run it down him. I was struck by the similarity between us.

'Catherine,' I said. She turned to me, eyes big and fearful lest I forbid her entrance to her holy of holies. 'Would you be so good as to fetch us our food when it is served? I shall stay near him for a day.'

'Of course. Jacob—'

'Yes?'

'Forgive my churlishness over the milk.'

'You did right to check me when I drank Hathersage's share.'

Her face softened. I asked myself why I had spoken thus when we both knew the milk was not for Hathersage. Why had I spared this girl? Even Ferris, always gentler than myself, had been spiteful to Becs. But that was when he feared her. I was not afraid of Catherine. The woman who could draw him away from me must be very different from this creamy innocent; perhaps only a man *could* draw him now.

Ferris woke with a confused cry. I stroked his brow and bade him rest; he lay dozing while Catherine put a compress on his head and neck, where he said he had a hurt. She was so gentle, one watching might be hard put to it to guess which of them felt the touch more acutely. I recalled Becs pushing me about and scolding me after the fight with Rowly; different females act after their different ways, but surely it is fire to gunpowder, letting women nurse men. This one, having served her god, departed full of happiness. He lay blinking at me from under flaps of wet linen.

'Now,' said I, 'how do you find yourself? More comfortable?'

'My head aches still. Will you put something on my shoulder blades?'

'Another compress?' I took up some linen she had left ready in the bucket. 'Can you raise yourself?'

Ferris heaved himself up, gritting his teeth; I ran my hand over his back, feeling it all ribs.

'Softly there!' he cried.

'I barely touched you.' I remembered the anguished squeal which had so terrified me floating up from the shaft.

'The muscle's pulled both sides.'

I arranged a compress under him and held a cup of beer to his lips. He drank greedily. Then I moved him back into a lying posture, not without much gasping and whistling through the teeth on his part.

'What happened down the sough?' I asked.

'I dropped too fast – I should have bidden you let the rope out slowly—'

'I should have done it without telling.'

'No matter – I went too fast and found myself wedged between those two large branches we put in there. The water was already up to my waist and I couldn't feel the bottom with my feet. I was frightened of falling further.'

'Why didn't you pull up?'

'Couldn't get any purchase. In the end my own weight dragged me through. It was tight – I felt my shoulders give.' He made an agonized face. 'I think I screamed then, did I scream? What with that and the water coming up over me.'

'Could you see and hear me?' I asked.

'There was some light but once you're under the branches and bushes – methinks now I should have heard you, but I was in a terror, stirring the water up like a fool.'

'I heard you splashing about as if you were drowning.'

'Then you said you would pull me out the same way—!' He laughed ruefully.

I shuddered.

'And *then* the sough fell on my head.' He was still laughing at the horror of it, almost with tenderness. 'I saw your feet – kicking about in the sky.'

'Hathersage's.'

'His! I'd have given something to see the rest of him!'

'How can you laugh about it, Ferris? Don't you know you almost drowned?'

'Who better? The water was up to my armpits, nothing under my feet. A very good sough.'

'The last sough you dig,' I said. 'Open ditches, or none.'

He put his hand on mine and we rested a few minutes in silence. I saw his eyelids begin to droop.

'You'll keep him off?' he murmured. 'Botts.'

'You *would* have him with us,' I reminded him.

'Don't scold me now, Jacob. Be kind.'

'I'll sleep here. If he sets foot inside the door, I'll kill him.'

'There's my fierce lad.' He closed his eyes.

I stayed by his bed the rest of that day, offering drink, holding a pot for him to piss in, placing cold compresses on his shoulders where he said the worst pain was. All he lacked was rest: though he had given himself a bad wrench, his shoulder blade was not out.

'You won't need a bonesetter,' I said that evening. I was sitting on the floor of his hut, watching the sunset spread itself over the turf walls and light up the pamphlet which I was reading to him: tedious stuff again, this time about manures. In a corner of the hut stood a decoction made by Elizabeth, supposed to loosen muscles and ease pain.

'Look here.' He pulled back the cover and I saw bruises like giant blackberries, one staining his flesh from the pit of his neck right down the breastbone.

'A wonder your chest isn't stove in,' I said, appalled.

'I'm lucky.' He burrowed under the blankets and slept, snoring. I lay down on the makeshift couch that was even more primitive than my usual bed. There was no ointment to dress bruises with. By and by I would get up and make a fresh compress. By and by.

~

In the silence of night I was woken by someone in the hut. Then I understood it was Ferris, and stretched out: my hips ached as they had done in the army. He shifted on his bed and I heard the intake of breath; he was awake. I rose and felt for his face. It was greasy with sweat.

He sighed. 'Talk to me, Jacob. Take the pain off.'

'Is it so bad?'

'I can't lie comfortable.'

In the dark I found the bucket of water, and pulling back the bedcover, carefully unwound his compresses and soaked them afresh. Lastly I replaced the cold cloth under his shoulder.

'Will you sleep now?'

'Perhaps.'

'Yes. I'll bring you sleep.' I began to stroke him on the neck and chest, then lower down.

'Jacob, no. I can't!'

'Sshh. Just lie still. I'll make you sleep.'

I did, and was very gentle; I took nothing for myself, and the only force I used was at the end, when I put my hand over his mouth.

~

In the morning he was able to rise, with help, walk a few steps and eat. The other colonists came and stood about, offering to help lift him or bring some victuals which might tempt the appetite. Ferris, making a royal progress round his hut, smiled grimly on them all, yelping from time to time as a muscle spasm forced him to halt. At the end I helped him back into bed, gave him some cheat bread and came out to give the others a report on his health, saying the compresses had been most beneficial.

'All quite bootless,' rumbled Botts, choked with resentment at being baulked of his victim. 'He has had a fall and is already half recovered; had I bled him he would be up and working by now.'

We were just outside the hut, Ferris inside; I pictured him chewing on the bit of cheat and listening to the attacks made on us. Our companions looked from Botts to me, and I thought they did not like me least.

'He's pulled all the muscles round his shoulders,' I said, 'and been battered by the landslip. Here,' and I waved Botts into the hut; the rest followed. Ferris looked up fearfully, but I stepped between himself and Botts before holding open the front of the patient's shirt.

'Lord have mercy, his chest's black,' said Hepsibah. The other women clucked their tongues; I saw Hathersage purse his lips in pity.

'Poor fellow,' murmured Susannah. Her sister stood rigid, eyes wide, as if learning the blue-black pattern by heart.

'A man doesn't die of bruises and pulled muscles,' pronounced Botts.

'I know that,' I said.

'But if there be too much blood,' he went on ominously, 'his recovery may be slowed. Why should I not undertake the care of him?'

The jackanapes wearied me to death; he would not leave well alone.

'Because you've not been called upon. He doesn't want you,' I said. 'Good Lord, man, don't you wait for your patients to call you in? Or do you go about blistering and bleeding willy-nilly?'

We were beginning to square up to one another. Harry, who was just arrived, caught my eye warningly.

'Jacob, your promise,' came an anxious voice from the bed. I turned away from Botts and when he was gone pulled the door shut behind him.

'You look dejected,' Ferris said. 'You should wash your face.' I realised then I was still in the tear-stained dirt which had so struck Hathersage the day before.

'My lower back gripes me horribly,' he added.

'You've given it a pull, that's all.'

There would be no work done by me that day. I sat cross-legged and talked with him, not letting him sleep so that he would be the drowsier later, when it was dark.

'You need not watch over me any longer,' he said suddenly.

'I like to.'

'I thought Hathersage would offer, but he keeps back.'

'Does he guess?' I whispered.

'Guess what?'

'*Filthy darling*.'

'What, pure-minded Wisdom?' He grinned. 'Jacob, remember when I tended you?'

'In the army?'

'I meant the tooth-drawing.'

'Holding me down for the surgeon! I am kinder to you.'

We giggled together and he tried to shush me. When we were both quiet there was a feeling of peace in the little hut.

'Ferris, what became of that letter you wrote me?'

'I have it somewhere,' he said dreamily, contemplating the turf roof. 'It seems long ago, does it not? And there's a thing I always meant to ask *you*: what became of your vision?'

'Vision?'

'You saw something strange in our upstairs room at home. Do you remember? The Elect!'

'It never returned—' I broke off. How could it? I was unfit.

'Are you sorry?'

I hesitated. 'No.'

'But you want to go back.'

'I miss things.' He must surely know what.

'To my way of thinking,' he said, turning to face me, 'the great design we are putting into practice here compensates for much. Work, but no master. That's swords into ploughshares, Jacob: a new England. Think how it will be when the cottages go up.'

If ever they do, I thought silently, but said only, 'Build as many as you like, we'll still not live together. What *I* think on is that, that and the winter.'

'Poor Jacob. And we never got to the snares.' He began to laugh silently, shoulders shaking despite his pain.

'I see I should not have comforted you last night,' I said in a huff.

'Jacob.' His voice was coaxing, enticing. 'Come winter, we'll go visit my aunt.'

'Visit—?'

'For a week.'

'Say a fortnight!' I lay next to him and put my face to his. 'Two weeks; that's not long. Say two,' I begged.

'Ah . . .' he spun out the answer, teasing me, 'that will be a hard thing to bring about . . .'

We gazed on one another.

'Black but comely,' he whispered. There followed a silence during which we both listened. The wind carried voices from the rye field; there were no footfalls on the grass outside.

Ferris raised his eyebrows questioningly.

'No,' I said, already giving way with desire.

'Put the wedge in the door.'

I leapt to do his bidding.

'Take care – my shoulders—'

I stretched out beside him. We kissed with the practised tenderness of old lovers, the terror of new ones: it was perilous just to lie there, letting him caress me inside my mouth, hearing his murmurs of pleasure as I grew bolder. Our danger sharpened the kiss to a delicious edge.

He pulled back from my face to whisper, 'Will you keep silent? Promise?'

I nodded, feeling a hand slide down my belly.

'Know what this is?' he whispered. I shook my head, panting. He gripped me hard. 'A snare. You're caught.'

I scarce heard him for the delight beating like a wave up my body; he pressed closer and stopped my mouth with his tongue. My flesh held fast in the snare, I thrashed about, more and more wildly, and poured out my life.

TWENTY-FIVE

Things Broken

THE CREEPING BUTTERCUPS, so tall and thick as to hide the cow when she lay down in them, delighted Ferris; the horse-chestnuts in the wood pushed up their tender finials, hiding the rookery for another year. Each tree was a city of birds, and I pictured myself a rook, rising free of bog and stone to fly direct at the sun and look down on poor diggers. Alone in an entire sky, the way as long or short as wishing. Men are very snails in comparison. It was like thinking on the sea, I soon felt myself overwhelmed. Why me? Could another have lived all this out in my place? I was stitched down by desire, and I could not leave without tearing myself. It might be that the white-pink blossoms of the chestnuts were hateful to the birds, that they too were stitched, through eyes, heart, wings.

The colony was settling into a community. A fashion was sprung up of calling one another *Brother* or *Sister;* it seemed to me foolish but innocent and I joined in when I could remember.

We met for prayer, now, every morning. My Atheist modestly declined to lead, so Hathersage was granted this honour by the other colonists and evidently deemed it a kind of glory. Botts went through with the forms of prayer decently enough, though he seemed to me as unbelieving a man at bottom as Ferris, and not one tenth as good. Elizabeth came to prayer dragging her boy with her; she was much occupied with this eldest child, who was growing wild running about in the fields, and with keeping the little ones cool. Jonathan or Hepsibah helped her at times by holding one of them: they sadly missed their own babe, and began to talk now of reclaiming him from his aunt's care. Harry and the Domremys prayed quietly, sincerely, without parade.

As for me, my prayer was always the same: Forgive me. Many nights I dreamt of Hell-fire, and more than once my screams had woken the others and brought them to my hut. Ferris always made sure he was among the last to arrive, claiming his back made rising painful; he would then stay talking long after the rest had left – never long enough, save one precious time when, hearing snores all about us, he lay down and offered kinder comfort.

We were now got further with the work than I had thought possible. Two acres were planted with the several sorts of corn and without much loss of seed, thanks to Ferris's newfangled reading. We had vegetables in hand, too, and much of our time was spent weeding the rows. Vetch was got into the rye, which crop being hard to rake out, all we could do was bend over the furrows, backs aching, in order to snap off the curling fronds at the root. Ferris had a wooden nipper for pulling up weeds but to my mind it did no more than a quick-handed man could do with a glove, and after some time he abandoned it to the women. Directly we had saved the rye, grasshoppers crept into the corn, and spoilt it. We drove them off with wormwood, but not before we had lost part of our crop. There were also some of those unlucky potatoes which had come so close to undoing Ferris and me. I had now double cause to dislike them, and left their cultivation to others whenever I could.

In other ways we had cause to be thankful. The cattle had ample feeding, and were plump; Catherine and Susannah took milk from the cow each morning. Elizabeth had found a number of fruitful trees in the forest, including cherry and walnut, and her husband continued to chop and stack timber against the winter, when we would need a goodly pile ready made.

One day Ferris walked over to Dunston Byars, the neighbouring village, to see if the people there would be willing to buy our milk or barter anything of theirs. He had not been sanguine, for the place was nothing but a straggle of rotting cottages, their inhabitants stupefied by poverty.

The weather was cool. I was hoeing, glad for once to don my shirt, stink as it might. From time to time I glanced up from the weeds, hoping to see the familiar figure crossing the pasture. Instead, I observed Botts weaving over the rows at the far end of the field, and kicking down the young plants.

'The sot! He's had as much as he can carry,' I said to Jonathan, who was working near me.

He looked up with a bunch of grass in his right hand, and crying, 'Merciful Lord! He'll have them all ruined!' he ran towards Botts, still holding the grass but taking care to step between the rows.

I set off after him. As we got nearer it was clear that the surgeon did his work wantonly, and not simply through any accidental swaying or clumsiness brought on by drink. He glared up at me and I wished, not for the first time, that I had never promised Ferris I would keep peace. Jonathan he seemed not to notice, even when the latter cried out to him across the field, 'Brother, mind what you do! Brother! 'Tis your own food!'

We had now reached the imbecile and I caught him by the arm, marching him off the ploughed land onto the fallow. He was heavier than I had imagined, but too unsteady to resist me. Again I smelt that curious sweat of his, and the lighter scent of brandy-wine on top of it.

Botts tottered and pushed at me. 'Whoreson thief! Thieving blackamoor bastard!'

'What ails you, man?' cried Jonathan angrily. 'How is he a thief?'

'*He* knows,' growled Botts, jabbing one stubby finger in my face. 'Where have you put it?' he screamed to me. 'Who's hiding it for you? Saint Christopher Cutpurse?'

I was dumbfounded, too astonished even to feel anger.

'Got what, man?' urged Jonathan.

'Ask him,' and again he pointed at me.

'I tell you what,' I said to the stinking beast. 'We'll leave you here till you sober up. Either hold your peace or go elsewhere. And keep off the crop!' I shouted, 'or it'll be the worse for you.'

'I might fall and break a few,' he said slyly. 'Or I might go to your hut, Blackamoor, and find where it is.'

'You'll keep out of any hut but your own.'

'Afraid, eh? I'm going there now.'

Clearly he was one of those who love to torment, who from their earliest childhood need only be told, 'Bounce is a good dog, pray do not kick him,' to fall a-kicking. I began to think this was an exceptional case, it would be such a pleasure to feel my fists thud into his sodden bulk, when I saw, over his shoulder, Ferris coming across the field, returned from Dunston Byars.

Smiling, my friend strode across to our little group. He was carrying something, a chicken upside-down: it brushed the grass in rhythm with his walk. All three of us stopped and watched him approach, walking with a slight swagger in the freshness of the day. I heard Botts mutter, 'Weasel, weasel.'

'Hey, you!' he bawled out. '*Brrr*other Christopher! What say you to a thief in our midst?'

'Thief?' asked Ferris, seemingly not at all surprised to see him so far gone in drink. The chicken, which I now saw to be two, both alive, jerked in his hand as he came up to us, and Ferris shook the birds incompetently in an attempt to quiet them.

'Are their wings clipped?' I asked.

He peered at them. 'Aye. At least, she said so.'

I cast an eye over their feathers: 'she' had not lied. 'Set them down,' I suggested.

Ferris placed his chickens on the grass and unshackled their scaly legs. The fowls wheezed, expanded and stalked onto the ploughed earth.

'Now,' I said to fix my friend's attention, 'Brother Ben thinks I have taken something of his.'

'What is it you say, Brother?' Ferris turned amused eyes on Botts.

'He's taken my brandy-wine. I was weary, had a pull to ease it and settled down just to clear my head – saw that sneaking fellow coming up the field – then I wake and all's gone. It was him. he's had it. You want to send him home.'

'That was a very wrong thing, Jacob,' said Ferris.

'Seems to me he's had ample,' I said. ''Twere a good thing if he were weaned. But,' I held up my hand in rebuttal, 'someone else took it, not me.'

'Nor me neither,' asserted Jonathan.

'You hear that, Brother Ben?' asked Ferris.

'That's right, side with them when you weren't even there,' spat Botts. 'But you two,' he glowered round at Ferris and myself, 'always stick together, you'd swear black's white. An honest man's got no chance. But answer me this: if it was not him, who was it?'

'I myself,' said Ferris. 'You were dead drunk and I took the bottle from you.'

Botts stood a moment puzzling it out. He put me in mind of a bull trying to think, so that I had to hold in my laughter. At last he said, 'Mayhap it *was* a drop too many. But you'll do the Christian thing and give it back.'

'No. It's all gone, Brother. No use asking for it.'

'*You've* never drunk it.' Botts was incredulous. 'There was half a bottle left. It'd overset a pinch of a thing like you.'

'I've turned it to profit,' said Ferris. He stood quietly and gave Botts a steady look. 'There it goes,' and he gestured at the two birds scratching along one of the furrows. Jonathan jammed his knuckles into his mouth, near choked with baffled laughter.

Botts stepped towards Ferris. I saw he was about to do what he had long wanted, get a grip on the piece of insolence who had snubbed his professional aid, and I was afraid for my friend's tender back and shoulders. However, before I was obliged to give Botts a drubbing, he became aware of me closing in, and stopped dead, staring at Ferris. I watched entranced as his skin seemed to boil on his bones; he could have been flayed, so crimson did he become. Ferris seemingly shared my fascination, for he regarded Botts with sympathetic horror rather than the tense wariness of a man who anticipates a tussle. He even craned forward a little. Jonathan was frozen, still holding his hand to his mouth, but no longer laughing.

'You are not well,' I said to the gasping surgeon, for it had struck me that he might suffer a paroxysm or even die, leaving us to dig his grave. 'Pray go and lie down. We can talk of this later.'

'That's a light-fingered whoreson nobody,' he burst out, still glaring at Ferris.

'Come, we'll discuss it later.' I caught hold of his shoulder, as gently as my vexation would let me; he looked up dazed into my eyes and his lips contorted to a bitter smile. He was, however, come a little to himself, and allowed me to lead him to his own hut. There he dropped onto his evil-smelling blanket and straight fell to snoring.

I dawdled back to the field. Ferris stood close to Jonathan, holding himself more upright than was common with him and laughing from time to time, as if he felt himself watched. As I drew near methought he eyed me stealthily. Jonathan, distressed at the way the thing had ended, stopped his talk as I came up to them and turned his eyes on me.

'Is he well?' he asked.

'Asleep.' I waited for Ferris to say something; he smiled, shuffled his feet and feigned to be looking for the hens.

Jonathan glanced from one of us to the other. 'I shall bind up the plants, if I can,' he offered and walked off across the furrow. Ferris lifted his face and flashed me an admiring smile. 'Well, Jacob! You save me a drowning, and now a beating.'

'And if one day I left you to your folly?'

His smile died at once. 'Folly? I said that Botts must not carouse here. Should I not have stopped it? He would else be quite mad by now.'

'You've put another madness in him,' I answered. 'He wants revenge, and that will last longer than a sore head. What possessed you to bandy his drink for chickens?'

'We need chickens,' Ferris insisted.

'I heard none begging for them.'

We stood silent a while, until my friend said more softly, 'Maybe not. But do you think he will come right?'

'He'll never come right, Ferris. He must go.'

'But we need him.' He caught hold of my arm with one hand, waving the other in the air. 'I can persuade—'

'Oh, you think he's another Hathersage?' My voice came out like spiked metal. I was straightway sorry for it, but too late.

Ferris dropped my arm and glared at me. 'Could *you* sweeten him?'

'I've no call to. I need no protection from any man.'

I walked away towards my hut, thinking I would lie for a while until I could compose my thoughts. Before I reached the door I heard Ferris huffing after me. He ran in front and turned to face me as I once saw him run in front of Cooper.

'Let's not quarrel,' he panted. 'I'll send him away.'

I stood looking at him. '*You* will send him away? How will you do that?'

He spread his hands imploringly.

'I see. Jacob twists his arm.' Bitterness filled me. 'I thought I was to keep my fists by my sides? But you will tell him, Ferris. Either the order comes from you, or you shift him yourself.'

'I'll tell him tomorrow.'

'In front of the others,' I insisted.

'In front of the others.' His head drooped; he was humbled and my indignation cooled as I looked on him. He added, 'You are right. It could never have come good.'

I sighed. 'You meant well by him.'

There was now no need to go to the hut, so I walked away to the field and rejoined Jonathan. Ferris did not walk with me. When I looked back, he stood defeated, no longer the man who had so jauntily announced the exchange of the brandy-wine. I shivered as I bent over the crushed green shoots. His false step in dealing with Botts was not like him, he who could play a man as an angler plays a fish. Then I found myself smiling, grimly, as it came to me that he might have foul-hooked the surgeon but he had lost none of his touch with me, for I had agreed to rid him of his unwholesome catch, without recompense.

~

Botts departed the next morning. Ferris was as good as his word and bade him leave us, speaking out in front of the whole community, as soon as prayers were ended. The Domremys' faces were so blank that they could only be glad, and while some of the others looked surprised, none spoke in his defence.

Botts heard Ferris out in silence, and then said, 'You took what was mine and disposed of it; in my book that makes you a thief. I sold up to come here, and have laboured without pay. You might have let me drink, I troubled none.' He was paler than usual, and evidently afflicted with the headache; his looks were actually improved thereby.

'Come, let us not part enemies,' said Ferris. 'Your ways will not fit here, but I bear you no ill will.' He spoke as tenderly as he had to Hathersage. 'Will you forgive me, Brother Ben?'

'No,' said Botts. He trudged away to his hut, and as I watched the forlorn, graceless figure duck under the doorway I felt a sudden stab in me. We all stood round waiting for him to come out with his pack.

'Could we not give him another chance?' Harry asked Ferris.

'He was destroying the crops,' my friend replied.

'Won't you speak for him, Jacob?' Harry persisted.

'Me?'

'We let you off Roger Rowly.'

At last Botts came out of his hut, a bundle tied across one shoulder. I hoped he would go straight off, but he came back towards us, searching our faces as he approached.

'Farewell, Brothers and Sisters. Not one with a word to say for me?'

The other colonists contemplated the grass, all save Harry who regarded the surgeon with frank sympathy. Botts went on, 'You've a strange notion of brotherhood, Mister Ferris.'

My friend frowned; the two of them locked eyes and I saw a dogged nobility I had never before remarked in Botts, in the straight opposition of his ugly head to Ferris's fine one. Seconds passed, and he did not look away. Ferris glanced in my direction; I edged closer.

Botts laughed and turned to me. 'Are you going to drive me off?'

'Not unless you make me.'

'And who would you say was the stronger, me or you?'

'Leave now,' I said, 'and you can go off believing 'tis you.'

Ferris lowered his gaze, as if to say this was between me and Botts, and none of his choosing.

'I'll go directly,' the man replied. He bent forward to me, breathing foulness into my nostrils. 'Weak I may be, Brother Jacob, but no man masters *me* with a look.'

Ferris's eyes flicked wide open.

'Who'd look at you?' I asked Botts. He turned away. My throat stiffened, and the stab I had felt earlier, when he went into his hut, pierced me again. It was a familiar feeling, but not one I had ever felt for Botts; I could not quite place it. I stared at his thickset back, trying to read the answer there.

'What did he mean, master him with a look?' asked Hepsibah.

'Not to be stared down,' said Ferris.

The others were silent, awkward; I kept my face turned away from Harry. We watched Botts diminish as he crossed the fields, and it was not until he disappeared altogether that I knew the stabbing in my guts for what it was: envy.

I passed the next few hours degraded, wretched. Despite my repeated warnings that the new growth was too fresh and the pennygrass still moist, Ferris had decreed that we should try for an early hay crop, so we were all of us slashing at that part of the meadow with the fewest buttercups, showing our skill, or lack of it. I tried to quieten myself by getting in more grass than anyone else, but my spirits were further oppressed by the fear that our hay would be damp. The rest glanced round at me from time to time and kept their distance.

At noon Ferris brought me a piece of bread and some black-smeared cheese.

'Here, thundercloud.'

I looked up but did not cease working.

'You look set to kill me. You don't regret Botts, surely?'

'No.'

He sat down by my side. 'Rest a while.'

I went on with my sickle.

'Jacob? Don't you want to eat?'

'Not at your command.'

He looked round hastily; none was near enough to hear us. 'That was no command! I thought you might be hungry.'

'I'm thirsty.' I straightened and rubbed my shoulders. 'Get me some beer.'

Ferris hesitated.

'What keeps you?' I snapped. 'Must you always be the one to give orders?'

He stood up, staring at me and wiping his hands on his shirt, then walked off. I continued to cut the grass. After several minutes he appeared again, jug in hand. This he held out to me without further speech.

I laid down the sickle and sat down to drink. The beer was cool; I looked at him.

'I put it in the spring,' he said, lowering himself to sit cross-legged opposite me. I drank again, and snorted, and choked.

'You're—'

'No.' I finished the beer. 'I've cried too much already.'

'Are you so unhappy?'

I looked at him, at his face formed for gentleness, and knew that should I speak, he would say, *I am sorry for your suffering but, but, but.*

'This is to do with Botts,' Ferris said.

There was a strickle in my bag. I pressed sand into it and then scoured my sickle, cleaning off the sap and setting a new edge.

He watched the blade clear into brightness. 'Could you handle a scythe?'

'Not on this uneven ground.' I took up the sickle again, held the coarse grass and cropped it in one move.

Ferris smiled. 'You're a good reaper.'

'I'm your dancing bear, that's what I am.' I cut again, more clumsily. 'Botts knew it.'

My friend waited while I got his harvest in for him.

'We will not visit Cheapside,' I went on. 'Come the season, there'll be urgent business in hand. I begin to know you.'

'You've known me some time,' said Ferris. 'We never agreed I would give up my life to you.'

The others were all far away in the field.

'I gave you mine,' I said. 'You will say, you never asked it.' He nodded, and I laid down the sickle. 'Ferris. You said you belonged to me.'

'You know what that meant.' He touched my foot. 'It still holds, I want none other.' Then, with a flash of anger, 'You talk as if it were me pulling away from you, and not the other way round. Be straight with me, Jacob. If you want to leave I'll give you half the money chest. Or you can stay with Aunt until—'

'Until I marry Becs?' The grass stalks blurred beneath my eyes.

'I might be her husband now, only you wrote to me begging – begging—'

I could not go on.

'I did, I begged you to come to my bed,' he said gently. 'But not to direct my life.'

'Once I came to you my life *was* – directed. Your aunt's offer was all I had.'

'I don't wish you to leave!' he cried. 'All I say is, I will give you money if *you* wish. Should you want to go back and marry Becs, well, I would make it worth her while.'

'You wouldn't care?' I stopped cutting and sat down the better to see his face.

'I would suffer crucifixion, Jacob,' he said slowly and emphatically, 'but I wouldn't keep you from her if that was what you wanted.'

We were silent a while. He took my hand, and after glancing round him bent his head to kiss the palm. I began to feel better.

'Shall we go to the field tonight?' he asked.

I nodded.

He went on, more hesitantly, 'When we lie together – then – you know, then, how I love you?'

'I know.' It was as he said, he belonged to me. I wished I could share his vision of the future, for it must be a dazzling one, to curb such hunger.

Ferris chewed on a grass stalk. 'I would you were happy, Jacob. Without going back to London, I mean.'

'But we *will* visit?' I asked anxiously.

'Yes. As I said.'

I smiled, thinking that the weather here being by that time most likely cold and foul, two weeks of coal fires, of roast meat, and wine, and me bedding him every night, might do much to persuade my friend to give up digging.

'I'll build a house for the chickens,' I offered.

'They are run away,' said Ferris.

~

I woke stiff and aching the next day, having walked with him by moonlight right over the fields to a place where we could be heard by none, and there been sweetly, sweetly gratified. I stretched out, arching my back, remembering.

The next minute there were shouts outside the hut.

'Rise, friends! Here! Over here!'

I recognised Jeremiah's voice. Dry earth trickled onto my head as I wrenched at the hut door.

'Jacob! Put your shoes on.' Jeremiah was hoarse: he gestured towards the field and I saw five horsemen galloping over the young crop. My belly began to churn: again I saw Botts's face thrust into mine. I had fled from a group of men once before, and it had done me little good; besides, here was no means of flight. There was a creaking and I saw Ferris's door jerk open; he stood rubbing his eyes and then, glancing upwards, grew suddenly still. My fingers were thick and clumsy on the shoeties.

'Harry! Jonathan! Wisdom!' bawled Jeremiah in his cracked voice. Ferris, coming back to life, banged on the Domremys' hut.

The men were upon us. The three riding behind were sombrely clad and looked to be house servants, such as I had once been myself, but the first two, tricked out in satin and with a great deal of lace, seemed gentlemen. The horses, walking now, came up to the circle of huts and the men reined in, keeping on their hats; when I looked at the insolent plumes of the front riders, I wished I were not bareheaded. We stood before our turf homes, awaiting their pleasure, while the eldest of the five looked round at us as if committing us to memory. I returned the compliment: he had a handsome brownish face, marred by a broken nose, and grey hair beneath his black hat, where a tiny chestnut blossom was riding on the plume. Under the suit of maroon satin his body was heavy, tired looking; not so the fine Spanish sword on his hip. His horse's legs glowed with pollen from the meadow.

The man's glance circled us all and lighted on me. 'Is your name Christopher Ferris?'

'No.'

The fellow behind him, rigid in green, coughed and waved his hand in Ferris's direction.

'*You* are Christopher Ferris?'

'Who wishes to know?' returned my friend.

'What insolent reply is this?'

'You have offered us no civil salutation.' Ferris's voice was calm. I hoped the rider could not see the sheen on his brow.

'Are you Christopher Ferris?' The man's cheeks purpled.

'I'm not ashamed to own it.'

'Very well. This man,' and he pointed at Ferris as if none of us had seen him before, 'is a false prophet, my friends. He has led you into the desert, into Egypt. Given time,' he stared round at the colonists, 'he will lead you to a worse place.'

'We are here of our own free will,' said Harry, whose nostrils flared with dislike of the newcomers. 'And who might you be, to come and talk so to us?'

'I serve Sir George *Byars*,' the horseman replied, as if the very name were enough to strike us dead.

'Sir George Byars does not own this common,' Ferris said.

'He owns the manor, and the village is under his authority. He will not have ruffians digging up the common. That is the law.' The man's hand, big and veiny, strayed to the hilt of his sword. I watched Ferris's breast rise and fall beneath his grey shirt.

'The laws of England are the chains of the poor,' my friend asserted, once more the *Friend to England's Freedom* of his pamphleteering days. 'Where is it written in the Bible that your Master may build a manor, aye and enclose, too, if he see fit, and yet we may not plant corn to feed ourselves?'

The two men exchanged vexed looks. The one in green edged forward, so that his horse was almost on top of Ferris. He was handsome also, but in a cool, indolent way, with that complexion which is sometimes called *cream*. I could smell the rose-water on his linen. His soft reddish curls flirted with the breeze; he smoothed them back with fingernails a full inch long as he pronounced, 'These bedlams have plunged the kingdom into war by corrupting the unlettered. It were good they were torn up by the roots.'

The older one turned his eyes on the rest of our group, saying more softly, 'My friends, Sir George is a merciful man. Mindful that there are women and children among you, he bids you pack up and be gone within the fortnight. If, after that, you are found persisting in your folly,' he shrugged, 'rely no more on his patience. And, you women, he has a more tender care for you than you have for yourselves. You should learn to know your own good, for though you may whore yourselves to these, yet they—'

Here a gasp rose from the company. 'Fie! Fie!' cried Hathersage.

'Yet, I say, they will not—'

'Whore on your own mother,' shouted Harry. 'These are no such thing, but maids, wives and widows. But there,' he quietened into contempt, 'you know your own tricks best.'

'Where there is unruliness there will be immoral living,' the elder one rapped out as if knocking a nail into wood. He glared at each of us in turn, seeming to scent the corruption within, and though I knew it for a trick, a chill struck through me as he caught my eye. He went on, 'It follows as the night the day. I have delivered my message and you have heard it. Summon up what wisdom you have, and profit thereby.'

The last words were barked out. Elizabeth put her hand in Harry's. I studied the blank faces of the servants behind these messengers; the nearest to me held my eye and the flatness of his look melted to furtive pity. The man next to him turned in my direction and the kindly one at once looked away.

'If Sir George chooses to commit rapine and murder we have not the means to stop him,' said Ferris. The man in green spat at him, just missing his face; I saw the spittle run down his neck and inside his shirt. Ferris did not move, but glanced anxiously at me. I showed him my arms hanging limp by my sides.

The five of them turned and galloped over the cornfield, the pitying one hanging back a little until he could twist in the saddle and show his empty palm in a shrug of impotence. Dust rose from the furrows. My friend scrubbed his shirt against his skin.

'You should not have sent Botts away,' said Harry.

Ferris moved from one foot to the other, gazing at the departing men.

'What will they do to us?' Catherine asked him. She was trembling, lips pale in her brown face. Ferris turned away from her.

'They said we were whores,' whispered Hepsibah. 'That's what the soldiers do, they – they call the women whores, they—' she faltered into silence. As if by common consent we sank onto the grass.

'They will destroy the crops,' Ferris said, fingering the scar on his cheek. 'And arm the villagers against us.'

Elizabeth said to Harry, 'We must take the children to my sister.' Hepsibah began to weep, noisy tearing sobs, and her husband drew her head down onto his breast, saying, 'He is better where he is, my love.' He rocked her to and fro. Ferris bowed his neck, uncomforted, and I ached to embrace him.

'Come, let us talk.' I pulled my friend up by the arm and led him away. 'Into the wood,' I said when we were out of earshot.

'Do you think I want *that*!'

He came with me nonetheless, and we turned into the sweet green track leading past the spring, down to our usual place. I went in first and waited. He crawled under the bush and as he came through to my side I put my arms about him and kissed his neck where the horseman had spat on it.

'Don't, Jacob! You'll unman me.' He struggled away. 'I have to think.'

'Easy enough to understand,' I said. 'We go home, we let them ride over us, or we fight.'

'And fighting's your choice.' He smiled drearily.

'No indeed. I'd sooner go.'

Ferris sighed. 'In the army,' he began, then broke off. I again embraced him and this time he laid his head on my shoulder. 'In the army I had courage for anything.'

'You have.' I stroked his arm, seeing his profile uplifted against the dark coat of the horse.

He shook his head. 'Something is gone from me. Broken.'

'You are weary, that is all.'

'Do you think, Jacob, that what we do—?'

I stared at him. 'What we do?'

'Nothing. Nothing. Never mind.' He sighed again, and went on, 'I have drawn others along with me, promised miracles. They have laboured without cease. Now I see I cannot defend them.'

'They must defend themselves. They know it,' I replied.

'Then we all suffer.' He stared at me. 'But to give way – to submit to the likes of George Byars—'

'He has a village fighting on his side,' I replied. 'Our friends came freely, you heard Harry say as much, and can go freely back.'

'Harry can. What of the servants?'

'You have money enough to help,' I said. 'Let's go home, back to pamphleteering. I'll be your printer's devil.'

Ferris tried to smile. 'Incubus.'

'Whatever you wish,' and I folded him to me, comforting him as I had been comforted long ago, by Izzy. 'Don't make this your Basing-House. I couldn't bear it.'

We sat quietly and I soothed his back, my hand saddened by the bony feel of his spine.

'This is foolish talk,' he said at last. 'I knew it must come to this. We have set ourselves up for freedom. If we run away as soon as Mammon looks big on us and stamps his feet, of what use was it to start the thing?'

A bitter struggle was going on in me as we gazed at one another. I saw the shadows under his eyes; his lips were tight. A word from me now might break his courage and pull him back. Then we could go home; but he would despise himself ever after.

At last I forced out, 'Very well. We will face it like men, only, only—'

'Yes?'

'Should *they* want to go, for God's sake let us go. Promise me, Ferris!'

He squeezed my hand.

We came out from the wood silent, dragging our feet, and were at once spied by Jonathan.

'Brothers! Come here, see this!'

I strolled towards him.

'Nay, man, hurry!'

This was a sheet of paper folded over and addressed to Mister Christopher Ferris. 'You can read it,' said Jonathan to me. 'We all have. Brother Christopher, come on!'

I unfolded the paper and read:

Sir,

Though you will have some ado to guess at the writer of this epistle, yet your friend, he of the sallow complexion, may have an idea not so very far from the truth.

Ferris came up beside me, jostling for a view.

You have been cruelly used today and may expect further ill treatment. However, you should know that talk of a fortnight is but puffery, the plan being to let you go on, if you have a mind to do so, until the main crop is in, and then take it from you. Yours is not the first little commonwealth to have sprung up with the mushrooms hereabouts, and your enemies have found from experience that attacks too early in the year do not answer, while the loss of the corn, after a summer's labour, invariably proves efficacious.

If you are wise you will cease now; but if you must continue, your best hope is an appeal to Parliament, for Sir George is by no means a Parliament man, and not much loved by any party. He has a neighbour, one Sir Timothy Heys, who might be persuaded to uphold your cause for the mere hatred of Sir George, and who is now in London: write to him at the Palace of Westminster. Sir Tim. is a man of tender conscience and open-handed towards the poor.

By far the better course, however, were to quit now; that is the best advice that can be got from one who, though he dare not sign this, yet considers himself

Your Friend

Post scriptum: there is a taking up of mail from the inn, and paper and quills to be had there.

The rest of the community were now crowding round us. Ferris and I stared at one another.

'This was quick in arriving,' he said suspiciously. 'Who brought it?'

'Here,' said Hepsibah. She held up the hand of a little boy whom

I had not previously remarked, and who might be eight years old. 'He lives at the inn.'

'The innkeeper has heard them talking,' said Ferris.

'No.' I said. 'It's one of the servants that were here. See, "he of the sallow complexion", that's me. One of them was looking very kindly at me: that's our unknown friend.'

'It could be a trick,' mused Jeremiah.

'Tell us again who gave you the note, sweetheart,' crooned Hepsibah.

'A gentleman,' said the child. 'There was five come in for some sack and he said he had some business to write to his brother that was in London, and could he have a quill, and then he give it my Dad and said it was to go on the coach. And he give him a groat and winked, and wrote something else down on it. And when they was all gone my Dad says, Walter, go over the common.'

I turned over the letter. On the verso, we found the words '*By hand to the diggers at Page Common, I pray you fail me not*'.

'That's it then,' said Susannah.

'But this puts a different complexion on it,' Catherine cried excitedly. 'We must write to this Sir Timothy.'

'We must,' Hathersage echoed her. 'Who shall be the one to write?'

I looked at Ferris. His face was grey. He walked slowly into the hayfield, took up a sickle and began to cut.

'Let us all consider, and decide what's to be done later,' I said. I wandered back into the wood and went round the snares by myself. In one of them I found a rabbit, and in another a rook. The rabbit, caught by the hindleg, plunged in terror seeing its deathsman approach. It began to scream as I came within a yard of it and only ceased when I twisted its head nearly off the neck. The rook, luckier, was already dead and maggoty. I threw it into a bush.

When I went back, rabbit over my shoulder, I found the rest gathered round a dish of pottage, all except Ferris, whose back was still bent over the sheaves of grass.

'He doesn't wish for company,' said Hepsibah in reply to my look. 'Leave him, Jacob, and eat.' She lifted the rabbit and dropped it onto

Harry's makeshift table, then ladled some of the hot mess of lentils into a bowl for me. I hesitated, but in the end seated myself on the grass next to Jeremiah. Catherine, who was sitting opposite, seemed disappointed that I was not to bring Ferris back to the fireside.

'What have you been talking of?' I asked, wanting to know what kept my friend in the hayfield while others took food and rest.

'We think of staying here at least two weeks,' said Hathersage. 'If we get through that, well, something may happen in our favour.'

'Such as?' I cooled the pottage by blowing on it.

'Sir Timothy. We want Brother Christopher to write.'

'Does he want to?'

'Surely he will,' said Catherine. 'He brought us all together, he'll not abandon us now, will he?'

'He may not wish to endanger you, Catherine,' said Hepsibah.

I added, 'He wanted peace in this place. He's no swordsman.'

'He was in the army,' the young woman insisted.

'He hated it.' I was not come so far with Ferris only to see him heroically spitted. A coldness against Catherine was spreading within me, and I turned to Hepsibah. 'You think we were best depart?'

'I am unsure, Jonathan likewise. The letter does count for something, but—' she frowned.

'Harry?'

He did not hear me, for he was looking over at the figure crouched in the field, but Elizabeth pleadingly answered, 'The children, Jacob.'

'You do right,' Susannah soothed her.

Jonathan and Jeremiah examined their bowls and spoons.

'If we were right once, we are right now,' exclaimed Hathersage. 'God rewards the faithful servant. Our part is to labour in the vineyard, leaving the pay to Him. This I told Brother Christopher.'

'He needs no telling,' I heard myself say.

Hathersage ignored me. 'A glorious future awaits! He must not be suffered to fall back from the heat of the combat.'

'Do you mean a glorious martyrdom?' I asked. 'Seek it yourself if you please, I see no reason why he should drain the cup with you.'

The others were gone very quiet. Catherine regarded Hathersage with ardent eyes; he caught the look and took a deep breath to go on. *My poor Ferris*, I thought, *now you pay for charming these two.*

'My conscience demands I speak to him,' added Hathersage. He laid aside the bowl of pottage as if about to rise. 'Speak, and wrestle for his soul.'

'I hope you're a good wrestler,' I said. 'Because if you go near him now, much less preach, I'll break your arm.'

'Jacob!' cried Catherine. I looked about me and saw shock on the women's faces, all except Susannah, who was silently shaking her head at me.

'Not another Botts,' warned Jonathan.

'If you value this enthusiast, persuade him to sit in peace,' I hissed. To Hathersage I spoke no more, but fixed on him as a cat watches a mousehole.

'Why may Wisdom not speak with him or with any, the same as yourself?' pouted Catherine.

I felt myself on dangerous ground. 'Brother Christopher,' I hesitated at the feel of the name in my mouth, 'is in travail; he knows only too well all that you would say. Pray do not torment him.'

'But Wisdom wishes only—'

'Catherine, not a word,' rapped out Susannah.

Hathersage again made to rise and I sprang to my feet. He faltered and sank down.

'What!' I taunted. 'Is the heat of combat all for *him*?'

Hathersage burnt scarlet.

'Jacob,' said Jeremiah.

'Aye?' I screwed my eyes into Hathersage's.

'Suppose Brother Christopher chooses to stay.'

'Then he chooses.'

'He is coming,' said Harry. Ferris was crossing the field, slowly, shaking out his slender arms and rubbing his elbows. He squatted innocently next to Hathersage, who passed him some lentils. After one mouthful Ferris laid down the spoon.

'I have been thinking, friends,' he announced, in so humble a voice it made me want to weep. 'Whoever wishes to go must go. I shall write to my aunt to give you a consideration when you get back to London.'

'We shall not be wanting that,' said Harry promptly.

'And for those who want to stay, I shall write to Sir Timothy,' he went on. He did not look at me. 'But we may wait at least a month for his help.'

'Or lack of it,' I muttered. I held out my bowl for more pottage and ate it too hot, burning all the way down.

~

That afternoon, Harry and Elizabeth packed up their gear and left; they purchased a mule in the village, at great cost, and took with them the anvil and other gear on a cart.

'We'll not come to want, for he's excellent at his trade,' said Elizabeth, standing with her infant clutched to her neck and the eldest, suddenly tearful, by her side. 'It is you we think of, friends. I would you were all safe.' She kissed each of us on the cheek.

Her husband, the little girl on his back, bowed to us all; the child crowed at the sudden motion. He placed his hands on Ferris's shoulders and held his gaze. 'Be not braver than the times require.'

Elizabeth's eyes were wet. Her husband laid a hand on her arm as she said, 'Let us make an end. Take care of my sisters, you men. Brothers and husbands are meant for our protectors.'

I thought she looked at me, perhaps because, Harry gone, I was the only man of any strength. We stood and watched them depart just as Ferris's neighbours had watched us. Before disappearing behind a hedge at the end of the field they both turned and waved their arms as if to send us good fortune. I saw they had some trouble with the mule, and then the cart was round the hedge and they were gone.

The rest of us went silently to the field to ted the hay. I would say each felt himself diminished, for the Bestes had been loved. I owed Harry much, and in the days that followed I found, to my surprise, that I missed the prattle of their children.

That same afternoon, about an hour after their departure, Ferris leapt up from the field and went to the tent, not reappearing until the evening meal was served. After it, he drew me aside and showed me his work. He had scrubbed his hands, found some paper and composed two letters: one to his aunt, telling her nothing of his danger but only that she must reimburse, for their pains, any of our company who came to her; the other, not unlike one of his pamphlets in happier times, to Sir Timothy Heys. This letter to Sir Timothy he showed also to the other colonists, then sealed it up and joined in the haymaking.

We laboured on in the clear bright evening as the moon rose purplish-red. I watched it take the colour of an apricot, then turn to purest snow, cooling both sky and earth.

~

Ferris was up by moonlight to put his letters in the mail bag in person. Lying sleepless, I heard him stumbling around in the next hut, then his footsteps thudding over the grass. I opened my door and a low white mist came pouring in like the sea, a sea which parted in swirls as Ferris moved through it, a solitary wader in the darkness.

~

I rose shortly after sunrise and began feeding the embers for the new day's fire. The mist had lifted; a sharp wind fanned the flames into the pine cones and wood shavings I had laid as kindling. It looked to be a clear, dry morning. I fetched some beer and cold cooked beans from the tent; beans, beans, beans, like the army. Soon I had a good-sized blaze in the firepit; I swung the cauldron over it for an early start.

Susannah came out from the hut she shared with her sister-in-law. I thought how the colony had made a difference between the two of them, for while Catherine was grown more bouncing, Susannah had aged. Her eyes were rheumy and puffy, her skin daubed with yellowish splotches. She sat beside me with no more salutation than a nod, and I was grateful for the quiet. I passed over my dish of beans and we shared it, taking mouthfuls by turns.

'Where is he?' she asked, licking the spoon.

'Gone to post his letters.' I saw no reason to tell her he had set out in the dark.

'Can't you make him go home, Jacob?'

That was the first time I ever really saw her. I had examined Catherine Domremy many a time, taking stock of her beauty and how it might move Ferris, but in looking at Susannah I had remarked nothing save the injuries Page Common had done her complexion.

She went on, 'Catherine adores her hero. Wisdom is – unwise.' Her look was level. 'But the rest will hear reason.'

'I can make him do nothing.'

Her mouth sagged in disappointment.

I added, 'I never wished to come here.'

'*You* can be made to do things, Jacob?' She smiled wryly. 'You are too fond of your fists, my friend. Break Wisdom's arm, forsooth!'

'He merits it. Thanks to Hathersage and – and others, Ferris feels himself bound to stay.'

Susannah let out a long sigh. 'There *I* can do little. But tell me, is he not afraid?'

'Mortally.'

I put fresh branches on the fire. Susannah covered her eyes with her hands, yawning noisily through the soft O of her lips, before going back to the beans. I watched her smooth the hair back from her brow, and felt that this woman might be capable of good counsel.

'You were married, were you not?' I asked her.

'You know it.'

'I have heard that women can accomplish things by wiles.'

'Is this a man's wile? If so, it is threadbare. Out with it, what is it you want?'

'Susannah. How would you get him home?'

'Did I not ask *you* that?'

We finished up our breakfast in silence, then took our forks and rakes into the field, to turn the hay. About an hour later, Ferris came back to us, with a face so cold and pale he seemed still to be walking in the night mist. Susannah prevailed on him to rest a little before he took up work. The rest of the colonists hastened to turn as much as we might before the sun grew too hot.

TWENTY-SIX

Things Called By Their Right Names

IT WAS AS WELL, in the end, that we had the hay to deal with, for in raking, cocking, throwing together and the rest, we brazened out some part of our fortnight. I gave myself up to the work, and when I laid down my head to sleep the haycocks at once arose behind my eyelids.

But our labours could not blot out Sir George: the women wept for the slightest thing, and there were bickerings each day. Then, at the end of the two weeks, nothing having happened, a surge of joy burst out in our society. Hathersage praised the Lord at length. Our secret friend was evidently well informed, and I hoped he might find some way to warn us when the attack came – for that it *would* come, I never doubted.

The crop dried sweet and wholesome in the sun.

'God smiles on us,' sang out Hathersage. I checked that Ferris was out of earshot before asking him had he ever heard how the Devil sets snares for men, baiting them with good fortune. The light died in his face. He had not dared speak to Ferris about staying on, yet my heart had ever since been violently hardened against him, and we scarce exchanged a civil word. But I encountered with him in dreams. One night I lay between Hathersage and Catherine, and covered them both; they were my prisoners of war, and I was rough with them, as conquerors are. Waking, I was apprehensive lest I should have called out and been heard.

The next day I considered this dream, knowing full well what had brought it on. Ferris would not go to the wood with me, so that I was starved for him. Though I pleaded and even threatened, still he kept off. Once or twice I woke to hear him groaning in a nightmare, but could give no comfort. I knew that I would find the door of his hut closed against me, and I stayed where I was.

'I sleep ill since the horsemen came,' was all the explanation I could win from him. But after a week or so, I heard no more cries at night, his eyes were no longer haggard and he seemed more sanguine, even hopeful of a letter from Sir Timothy. Still he denied me. Daily one of our number walked to the inn in search of the letter; daily I besieged my lover, and was repulsed. But I could be cunning. The day after my dream, I lay in wait for Ferris and entered his hut just as Jonathan was coming out, closing the door behind me.

He raised his eyebrows as if to say, *This trick will not serve.*

'What ails you?' said I. 'Why do you treat me—'

'Nothing, nothing. I am worried.'

'It is ten days,' I pleaded in a whisper.

He regarded the floor, evidently ill at ease.

'Have you something wrong – there?' I went on. 'Some malady—'

'No, there I'm well enough.'

I put my arms round him and crushed him into me. 'Kiss me.'

He turned his head away. I cupped his face in my hands and put my mouth to his, feeling him passive, obedient, as if getting it over with. It was what I had done to Becs, and now I tasted the full bitterness of it.

I tugged on his hair, and none too gently. 'Beware, lest I bite.'

He made no answer. I paused, humiliated, then realised he was tensed, holding his body off from mine. Seeing my face Ferris immediately made to pull away, but I grasped him by the hips and held him tightly to me. It was as I thought: his blood was up. I wriggled against him.

'Jacob, *don't*!' he hissed into my neck.

Burning, I let him go. 'All right, into the wood.'

'No.'

'You want me.'

He was silent. I thought, this is not a thing to resolve by talk, or not this kind of talk. I kissed him again, gently prising open his lips to lick within, my hands stroking him under his shirt, keeping him close and not able to escape the taste or feel of me, until at last I felt myself kissed in earnest. When I pulled away from him he strained after my mouth. I tongued his ear, bit it, whispered into it a lover's name I only used when riding him and so far gone that my flesh was fused into his. He pressed tightly into the hand that I slid down his breeches; I could feel his ribs rise and fall.

'Shall it be here or in the wood?' I whispered.

He moaned, 'The wood.'

But it was too late for the wood. His surrender was complete.

After that he did not try to keep me off any more. His brief chastity remained a puzzle, one he would not speak of, but having conquered I was content. However, I made it my special study to please him, to make him feel in every bone the impossibility of doing without me. My cunning was rewarded: Ferris grew more amorous, and I felt myself safe. In the first heat of our reunion we worked side by side, so bound up in one another that every look between us was a promise. God knows what the rest saw or did not see. We ourselves were blinded to what was going on before our eyes, and it was with a shock that I glanced up one afternoon from the furrow and saw, at the end of the field, Hathersage and Catherine, locked in an embrace.

~

'How *will* they do?' Ferris's question was whispered, his smile lit by amusement; sitting by the fire after the evening meal, we watched the new lovers play with one another's fingers. 'Not in the wood, surely.' He stared at them, fascinated. 'What say you? A betrothal?'

'You're jealous,' I said, feeling myself heart-happy and for once, proof against all jealousy, for we planned a walk in the fields that night.

'*I'm* not the one who dreamt of lying between them,' Ferris replied.

'I should never have told you. Now you'll be teasing—'

'Shush, here's news.'

Susannah was approaching. She sat down beside me, her face perplexed.

'Is there to be a betrothal, then?' I asked, tipping my head in the direction of the turtle-doves.

'Who knows?' She pulled up bits of dead grass between finger and thumb. 'If 'twere hanging on my say-so, there'd be none.'

Ferris stretched out, handsome in the firelight. Since he was come back to me, he had eaten more, slept better, and it showed. 'I thought you liked him, Sister?'

'Setting aside the man, this isn't the time for betrothals, what with the trouble coming to us. And then to make young bones . . . ! Elizabeth Beste took her babes off to safety. She'd a sight more sense than poor Catherine.'

'Elizabeth wasn't young and new in love,' I commented. 'If Catherine asks, will you witness it?'

'O Lord! I pray she won't ask me just yet. Would you?'

'Not if you don't wish it,' I said, delighted at a chance to spite Hathersage.

'They won't ask Jacob or me,' Ferris cut in with certainty. 'It will be you, Susannah, then the Tunstalls.'

'I tried to reason with her,' Susannah sighed. 'She said I'd had my chance and she would have hers. I told her my chance lasted just a year, and I was lucky to have no little one clinging round my neck; I asked had she ever thought on that. But it's ill work preaching to the deaf.'

'They will never leave, now.' I watched as they got up and walked hand in hand to the wood, pacing in the dusk along the path which bordered it. As Ferris had predicted, they did not go in.

~

We had almost stopped hoping for a letter from Sir Timothy Heys. Either he was not in London, and our friend had been misinformed, or he cared nothing for the plight of a few ragged diggers, having more urgent business in town. Perhaps he had made it up with Sir George Byars. That idea infected me with dread. We might have entrusted ourselves to an enemy who amused himself, letting us wait, and yearn, and wait. The air which hung over our fields seemed charged with thunder; it was worse since the haystack was built, a standing provocation to any of his servants or cronies who should ride by. I felt we were living in the palm of Sir George's hand, where any minute he might choose to crush us.

About halfway through June I volunteered to take a turn at walking to the inn, in case our salvation was come.

'I will go with you,' said Susannah. We set off across the field before the early haze was lifted. I noticed she walked heavily, as if half asleep.

'Susannah, go back. You're tired already.'

'I can't sleep. Leave me be, I'd as lief walk as hoe.'

We went on a little. 'Is it Catherine?' I asked.

'If Brother Christopher would give her just a hint, it'd break the whole thing in pieces,' she cried out. 'Why won't he?'

'What makes you think he knows that?' I hedged.

'Stop it, Jacob. Everyone knows, except Wisdom. What do I say?' She laughed bitterly. 'Most likely he knows too.'

'That would be a kind of promise from Brother Christopher,' I said. 'What would he do once she loosed Hathersage? Take up with her?'

'Jacob, I don't—'

'Hathersage isn't the only man who can make young bones.'

Susannah turned her face slowly up to mine. 'Are you saying Brother Christopher would father a child on her?'

'Though I'm his friend that says it, he's a man like other men.'

'Is he?'

Uncomfortable, I returned her stare. 'Did you not know? He was already a father when he was espoused. She died in childbed, a few months after.'

She seemed nonplussed by this half-lie, and said at last, 'I only thought he might give her some cause to hope.'

I flushed when I remembered that he considered his taking of Joanna the best act he ever did in his life. Now I had slandered his care of her.

When we came to the inn the mail, perhaps owing to some accident, was not yet arrived. Susanna, cast down, wept and sniffled. I made her sit in the cool of the landlord's parlour and bought us both ale with some of the money Ferris had given me. After the glare of the sun, the dark wainscot made a little night of the room.

'To see the whites of your eyes!' she said suddenly out of our shared silence. 'You're every inch a gypsy.'

'I've a brother who passed for one.'

'I guess we both look like tramping people.'

'And stink like them.' I had been afraid the man would deny us the use of his parlour. Nobody else was in it, which might explain his toleration of such dirty folks as we.

'Do you still wash yourself in the spring, Jacob?'

I started and coughed.

'If we had another cauldron I would make us all washballs,' she went on longingly, and I realised with bitter amusement that it was not my flesh that she hankered after. Poverty makes the humblest things precious: I was not an ill-looking man and with my clothes off (to speak without false modesty) fit to stand beside anybody, and here was Susannah lusting after the paltry ball of fat and perfume with which I cleansed my skin. But I had scant time to muse on this for Susannah was back on the subject of her sister-in-law.

'We passed a woman on the road as we came up, alone and a babe in arms. I thought directly, *That could be Catherine in a year's time.*' She bit her lip and hugged herself.

'I hardly think he'll abandon her,' I said.

'My meaning was, Sir George might put him in prison. Or worse.'

'Come.' I downed the remnant of my ale, wanting to be away.

The sunlight gritted my eyes as we came out and started over the fields. I thought of Ferris, and how he would lift his head from the work he was doing and strain to see us, until we were close enough for him to read the slump of our shoulders. I remembered promising myself, in London, that if he were ever exhausted or ill I should carry him by main force back to Cheapside. That had seemed an easy thing at the time.

But, I reminded myself, he was now eating more, and (none was better placed to know it) was recently grown stronger. I recalled how he had given up his food to me in the army, so I could get well, and my heart twisted with love.

'Look there.' Susannah nudged me: there was a horse some way off, coming along the road. It put me in mind of Biggin and his henchmen.

'There'll be no letter,' I replied.

'We may as well wait after coming this far.'

There was reason in that. We turned back to the inn and I checked the contents of the purse Ferris had given me. I still had enough. We came up level with the inn just as the letters were being passed over, and stood to make sure there was nothing for us.

The host put a letter into my hand.

'Glory be!' cried Susannah.

I paid him what he asked and turned over the letter, weighing it, noting the direction, *To Mister Christopher Ferris*. The two of us stared at the seal: a common device, no motto.

'Sir Timothy Heys?' I asked Susannah.

She shrugged. 'Not like a gentleman's hand, is it?'

The thing might be from Aunt. But no, the writing was of a masculine type. Perhaps Botts had written to boast of his powerful friends, and to exult over us.

'I shall open it,' I decided.

'No, Jacob. Let him, it has his name on it.' She touched my hand and the touch was kind. I laid the paper next my breast, and we turned back towards the colony without further talk, wincing at the brilliant light full in our faces. Susannah kept up with me despite her shorter legs, and seemed to have thrown off her lack of sleep. We trudged across fields and clambered over the stiles, frightening birds as we went, and at every step I felt the letter weigh on me as if it were stone.

The haystack came into sight, and shortly after we could distinguish figures in the fields. I saw Ferris look up from the rows of carrots, just as I had pictured him; he was doubtless wondering if this could be the day of succour at last, the lamb snatched from the jaws of the wolf. It hurt me to see him, after months of planning and toil, waiting on a rich man's humour. By his side, Hepsibah in her cap, hoeing the ground. Against the surging of the windy wood, the colonists showed tiny and defenceless.

Ferris waved to us, gestured that we should come over. I saw Catherine leave her work group and cross the vegetable patch towards him; Hathersage stayed where he was. I ran across the last field, Susannah trotting by my side, encumbered by her skirts.

'There's a letter,' I shouted as I approached.

Ferris's eyes were as huge, their expression as intense, as when I first eased him backwards onto his bed in Cheapside. 'Is it from him?'

'We've not unsealed it.' I pulled the letter out, a little damp, and he snatched it from me and tore it open without considering the direction. His eyes leapt along the lines. I saw his lips tighten.

'Give it here –' I came alongside of him and pulled his wrist over to me. Ferris opened his hand and allowed the paper to drop. Susannah and I grabbed for it together. I took the thing up and read as follows:

London, at Mistress Coleman's, opposite the Sign of the Bull.
Brother Christopher,

My sincerest wishes that this finds you in good health and all of our brothers and sisters well, and loving one with the other. We are got safely back and think often on you all.

I will be brief in my salutations and compliments, having unluckily some sad news for you. We called upon your aunt in Cheapside, not to badger her for monies but to let her know that you are well. She knows nothing of Sir Geo. and his menaces, or at least not from us. Nor has Botts been near her, for all we can tell.

But to the matter. While we were there she suffered a species of fit, which has left her unable to move her mouth and very much weakened in the legs and chest. She is attended by an excellent physician, Doctor Whiteman, who said you would recall him. Once persuaded there was no immediate danger we came away and wrote while the surgeon was still with her. The maid shows herself an able and devoted nurse.

However, despite the tenderest care your aunt is much distressed and weeps whenever your name is spoken, which emboldens me to say that you would do well to return at once. It grieves me to be the sender of such ill news, knowing as I do how you are already set about by trials. We go to the house every day to do what we can, and if you require any aid, you will I trust call first on your own

Henry Beste

Ferris was gazing into the dust.

'This Whiteman, is he so good?' I asked.

'Aye.' He did not move or look at me.

'Who's Whiteman?' cried Catherine. 'Brother Christopher, what's the matter?'

'His aunt is ill,' I replied. 'It is Harry who writes to us,' and I passed her over the letter.

Hepsibah and Susannah pressed to her side.

'I can't read, what does it say?' urged Hepsibah. Catherine began reading the letter aloud. Ferris sat down just where he was standing, in the row of carrots.

'Take heart, man,' I urged. 'You see she is in no danger.'

'Thus my mother died.' He rocked himself back and forth, arms clenched to the sides of his ribs and his hands in tight fists. Sinews stood out in his neck.

I squatted next to him. 'You must go to her.'

For answer he looked about him, at the women with their pitying faces, the others further off in the fields, the huts.

'Yes, go to her,' Catherine put in impetuously.

'And if Sir George and his hired men should come while I'm away?' Ferris drew back his lips and clenched his teeth until he looked to be snarling.

'Your presence would not save us,' said Susannah. 'But wait, has she none other? No child of her own, no other nephew?'

'None.' He tried to lift himself from his sitting position, fell back. I straightened up and held out my hand to him.

'Will you help me pack?' he asked me as he hauled himself upright.

'We can help,' offered Catherine. Hepsibah nodded, while Susannah looked enquiringly at me.

'No, sisters, my thanks but you were better go on with the work.'

He turned away from them. I followed him to his hut, aware of Catherine running towards Hathersage and the others with the letter in her hand.

We paced drearily alongside the field.

'Here's a rare chance for you, Jacob,' he said. 'Direct my life. Tell me what to do.'

'I have done so. Go to her.'

He stamped on a clod, shattering it. 'I begin to wonder if there be a Devil after all.'

'What's devilish in this? You said yourself, a malady already known in the family.'

'Not the malady. Don't you see? Go or stay, I betray someone.' He smiled grimly. 'That's a real Devil's riddle, wouldn't you say?'

'You talk as if your going to her will bring on Sir George.'

'Bring him on. Yes, he's a kind of sickness.'

We were almost at the huts. I said, 'Well, you bid me direct you, but you're obstinate as ever. Don't go, then! Stay! Now I suppose you will go.'

'I am so weary,' he answered in a voice charged with tears.

I was ashamed. 'I will look after them for you.'

'No, Jacob, no.'

'You don't trust my temper?'

'If she dies I want you with me.'

There was little to pack up and he had not wanted me for that. He kissed and fingered me in the hut. I felt the depth of his trouble in those touches. But anyone might walk in upon us there, so I gently pushed away his hands.

That day's coach being gone some hours before, we were to make the journey on foot. I thought it might do him good. Our parting from our fellow colonists was as tender as any could desire: we were clasped close and our backs patted for comfort. Arms stretched up to me and for the first time I wished I had been of Ferris's stature so that people could embrace me heart to heart as they did him.

Catherine had been crying, and Hathersage supported her, his arm about her waist.

'Remember, we have your direction in Cheapside,' said Susannah to Ferris. 'If you see nothing of us, and hear nothing, believe we are well. You have cares enough.'

'The Lord looks after his own,' said Hathersage. I wondered was it meant for a promise or a threat. The other men clapped their palms to ours and wished us good speed and a safe journey.

'Your aunt is a godly lady,' Hepsibah called out to our departing backs. 'She has nothing to fear.' I pondered on those words as we fell into step, for it seemed to me that the Snapmans and Ferrises could not have been godly as most understood it, else they could never have made the man walking by my side. Aunt was not as innocent as a good woman should be; I remembered how she had thought to use me to tie Ferris to London.

My life on it, I thought, *she understood something,* and then, praying in my usual selfish fashion, *Let her not be dead before we arrive.* My father had taught me from earliest childhood that prayers do not demand things of God, but show our submission to His will. Nevertheless, whenever I heard people praying, they usually said, 'Thy will,' or 'Thy sake,' then asked God to bring about what they wanted. I prayed no better than others.

I will not say that God was obedient to my wishes, but a carter picked us up before we had been walking half an hour, with the farewells of brothers and sisters still in our ears. Ferris scrambled up and lay on the load of hay, face to the sky. I stretched on one elbow at his side.

'This is our entry to London all over again,' I said, growing more cheerful at the remembrance.

He murmured, 'When we come back, Hathersage and Catherine will be espoused.'

'Shame on you, you lost two chances there.' A feeble jest, but I was glad to hear him talk as if the colony would at least survive long enough to witness their union.

'I never wanted either of them,' he replied seriously.

'Jilt,' I teased, 'you promise more than you give.'

'So they will find.' His face clouded, and I could have bitten off my tongue.

The carter here cut in with a most gloomy recitation of deaths by plague. His brother's wife had taken the sickness, 'the buboes under her arms as big as *that*'. He let go the reins to cut buboes from the air with his hands. 'And then all their children, not a one left.'

'And your brother? Did he live?' asked Ferris, struggling to show interest.

'Aye, can you believe it? And lodges with our sister at Whitefriars. We think to have him with us next month. But he's down – sadly down.' The man seemed surprised at his brother's so easily giving way.

'Something new for you,' Ferris remarked to me. 'Summer's the plaguey time in London. The sun brings it on.'

'Why is that?'

'How should I know? Perhaps corruption in meat, perhaps sweating.'

'Anyway, there's no plague in your house,' I said, trying to cheer him. He did not reply.

~

Becs opened the door to us, and there was an awkward moment as we all paused, taking stock. I was struck by the deathly white of her skin, set off by purple beneath the eyes, while she in her turn stepped back from our filth and raggedness. I almost smiled at the difference in her demeanour from the last time I saw her.

'Is she—?' Ferris cried.

'God be with you, Master, she is well,' Becs answered more after her usual fashion. She bobbed to us and we stepped into the house. Ferris ran up the stairs.

'The physician is with her!' the girl called warningly. Then, turning to me, 'I'll heat some water and look out some clothes for the two of you.'

'My thanks.'

'He'd have been better to wash before going up to her, you're both dirty enough to bring on another fit.'

'I endeavour—' I stopped abruptly. I was not bound to explain to her that I tried to keep myself clean. Instead I said, 'And was I so disgusting when I left? When someone gave me a sore mouth.'

'Your mouth's quite safe as long as you are so dirty. When you are washed—' she paused.

'Well, what then?'

She met my eyes, all innocence. 'I'll turn down the sheets of his bed.'

I retreated after Ferris.

By *well* I suppose Becs must have meant that the patient still breathed, for Aunt was not well. I found Ferris with his head laid near her pillow, his tangled hair on the bedcover, much to the distaste of the grave and reverend fellow in attendance. Ferris's eyes were wet. He was clasping one of her hands and her fingers showed like wax against his brown and coarsened ones. Aunt's eyes were also moist but her face was otherwise frozen and I had no idea whether she had observed me. The doctor, who in his spectacles and furred gown resembled nothing so much as an owl, turned as I entered, brow furrowed with perplexity, and then paused, confounded at seeing a second scarecrow. Methinks he must have taken my footsteps for Becs mounting the stairs. I bowed and he returned the politeness, but seemed to find nothing to say to me.

'Here's Jacob, Aunt,' said Ferris.

Aunt still did not look in my direction.

'She's squeezing my hand,' he went on. 'She sees and hears me.'

A silence followed. The doctor and I stood awkwardly each in a corner of the room. At last he jerked his head to indicate we should speak outside. I padded out after him.

'What can your skill do for her?' I asked as soon as we got outside.

He replied as physicians always do, that the case was a difficult one, very difficult, and that such fits were highly unpredictable in their outcomes; in short, that should she recover it was all to his glory, but none of his fault if she did not.

'Will her nephew's coming help her at all?'

'It will undoubtedly give her heart,' he replied, 'but she must not be allowed to overexcite herself. She is of a sanguine complexion and I have already bled her and given the maid instructions for a cooling diet. In my opinion the superflux of blood has mounted to her head and caused some obstruction there.'

'Do you find her better for the bleeding?' I asked.

'She is no worse. I have not seen your companion Mister Ferris since he was a child. Is he also, as appears, of a passionate disposition?'

'In some respects. He is much taken with projects and schemes.'

The doctor frowned. 'You might make it your business to see that he does not act adversely upon her. This lying upon her bed—'

'You won't stop him doing that,' I said at once.

He frowned again and began to pucker up his lips.

'Though the nephew be impetuous, you will find him most tenderly disposed towards her,' I soothed. 'He freely acknowledges that he owes her all the duty of a son.'

But the physician was already exercising his intellect upon other matters. 'You have perhaps been travelling in – distant parts?' His eyes went over the full length of me. I must have stunk most unpleasantly in his nostrils, though to his credit he concealed it and went on, 'You have had a long journey, it seems?'

I smiled to myself picturing the fine play he had written us: myself and Ferris come from farthest India, robbed and left for dead once or twice. 'Not so very far. But we have been living and working as farmers. Virgin land, one of these schemes which so occupy Mister Ferris.'

He inclined his head and spread his hands as if he understood it all.

'How soon will she mend?'

'It will be slow. I must see her again, and more than once, before I can give an idea.'

So there was to be no end to Ferris's dilemma as yet. 'You have told the nephew this?'

'He has given me little opportunity.'

Evidently he hoped to disburden himself of his evil news onto me. If it came easier to Ferris that way, I was willing enough.

'Jacob,' said Becs. I jumped, not having heard her come upstairs. She went on, 'There is hot water and everything needful in your chamber. If you wish for anything else, call me.'

'Thank you,' I returned and bowing to the doctor, said, 'pray excuse me. A cleanly visitor must surely be more fitted to a sickroom.'

He returned my bow and went back into the chamber to coax Ferris away from his aunt.

The sheets of my own bed were turned down, no matter who Becs thought might lie between them, and the window had been opened. I closed the shutters, bolted the door – a precaution I would never forget, now – and for a second time stripped off filthy rags in that room. Last came the key he had given me, the ribbon stiff and grimed but the metal still bright.

It was as good as the first wash there, perhaps better. I took some time about it, scrubbing and rinsing every inch of me from the scalp downwards. My hair, free of dust and combed out while wet, showed blue-black again, and the tiny scars on my chest stood out pale against the darkening caused by the sun. I remembered the doctor's question about travelling in distant parts and laughed as it came to me that he had not taken me, at first, for English. What, then, I wondered, would he say to Zeb, whose eyes were jet.

Sitting on the bed, wrapped in the cloth she had left me to dry myself, I let my feet dangle in the bowl of cooling water a while before drying them off. A large shirt was laid across the bedcover, and over a chairback a pair of breeches, some stockings and a coat, with a pair of latchet shoes on the floor beneath: at first I thought they were more of Joseph Snapman's estate, but then saw they were my own, packed up as being too good to ruin in the colony. The linen shirt, sliding over my skin, made me gasp as if from some amorous touch. I tucked the key inside it. The bedcover, being turned back, revealed a snowy embroidered bolster. Gladly would I have consigned every colonist to the bottom pit of Hell to keep this bed, and Ferris in it. I ran my hand between the sheets, picturing us, until my flesh began to stiffen. Then I put on my breeches and stockings and shoes to go up to Aunt's chamber.

The physician was departed, leaving Ferris sitting upright, his eyes dry. He turned to me as soon as I came into the room, glanced down my body and gave a pale smile. 'Jacob cleansed of his sins.'

'Only the outer man. How is she?'

'As you see.' Aunt looked no different except that she had closed her eyes. Her tears, like his, had dried. 'I think she sleeps,' said Ferris.

'Becs will bring you some hot water for a wash,' I suggested.

He smiled again, acknowledging my wish for his comfort. 'I should like some wine.'

'You shall have it.' I made my way downstairs and pushed into the kitchen to find Becs heating water for a second grand cleansing. She turned from the cauldron and stared at me; I felt my drying hair spring up around my face, and remembered what Ferris had said about the army boys cutting it for jealousy.

'Let me have some canary for him.'

'Here.' She unfastened the key from a bunch round her waist. 'But lock up and bring it back after.'

'Don't you trust me?'

Becs rolled her eyes. 'Don't *you* remember anything?'

'I will keep him from sottishness,' I promised.

'He's in for a sad time.' She poured steaming water into a bowl and scented it with lavender.

'You're a good girl.' I meant it. 'Let me carry that for you.'

We mounted the stairs together, I bearing the hot water and Becs following with washballs and cloths. In Ferris's chamber she dug into the chest and laid out linen and clothing as she had done for me.

'Time to wash,' I told Ferris when I went up to the sickroom. 'You can have the wine later.'

'I'll take some now.'

I saw that Becs's warning had been wise, but said only, 'Come on, then.'

He kissed Aunt's cheek and went off calmly enough while I descended to the wine cellar and found him a bottle of canary, which I carried up with two goblets on a tray.

When I joined him in his chamber Ferris was just taking off his shirt. He stopped when he caught my eye on him, knowing that the sight of him raising the shirt over his head always whetted me, and then pulled it off quickly. I should have liked to stay and wait on him, wash him, hold the wine to his mouth. Instead I poured out a large goblet for myself and withdrew, bidding him scrub himself well.

Aunt still did not move when I entered. Her face was not hers without the sudden dart of knowing eyes, and her mouth, pulled to one side, put me in mind of a flatfish. I bent down to the pillow and felt her breath on my cheek, then took Ferris's seat by the side of the bed. *If she dies,* I was thinking, *he gets everything.* I wondered would that make him more or less willing to come back to the city, and tried not to wish that her recovery would take weeks, for I knew that while I would be every night in Paradise, lying between his legs, fear for his colonists would have Ferris in Hell.

Save for a flask of reddish liquid by the bed, the room looked much as it had the day she offered me my fortune, and that other day when I learnt to stitch. There was, however, an unfamiliar odour. After a time I knew it for the smell of sick flesh, lain too long abed. Someone had been burning rosemary to cleanse the air, and behind all this lingered the usual lady's chamber smell of orris.

I took her hand and thought she pressed my fingers a little. Putting my lips to her ear, I whispered, 'Aunt. I am here. Jacob.'

Yes, there had been a faint touch. I went on, 'I will look after him.'

I was unsure whether she had touched me that time. I folded her hand in both of mine. After a while my back began to ache so I straightened up – it was not for me to lie on the bed as Ferris did – and took some of the canary. It glowed on my tongue like warm rubies and I felt the beginning of hunger.

Aunt shifted very slightly on the pillow. I was at once on my feet, but she settled again in the same posture. In her unmoving features I recognised her nephew's long nose and full lips.

It came to me that Ferris would look thus on his deathbed, and that what I saw was his dying. I made myself think of comforts, of my friend splashing himself downstairs, of the kisses I would lay on his neck that night. Then, going from cold to somewhat too warm, I had to leave these thoughts also, but by now the journey, the clean linen, the watching and the wine had begun to act upon me, fading the room from my eyes. I woke with a start; the goblet had just started to tip its contents onto my breeches. Aunt was exactly as before. I downed the remaining wine and dozed off again.

~

Ferris was shaking me. I looked up into yellow hair, and his narrow face above mine.

'Water,' I murmured.

'What!'

I struggled to make sense of it. 'Like—' I felt myself blush. 'You found me.'

He said, 'You're still in your dream.' And then I breathed the scent of him and it was not the mouldy stink of army clothes, or the animal reek of linen sweated stiff, but warm clean flesh. I put up my hand to feel his breast through the shirt; he backed away and I realised we were in the sickroom.

Ferris took the empty goblet from my other hand. 'We are to go and eat,' he told me. 'Orders from Becs.'

'And Aunt—?'

'She's lying peaceful.'

Still drowsy, I shambled downstairs after him. I could smell the food from the top of the stairs, and though it was something I had tasted before there was a difference in it. Coming into the room I found that it was meat prepared after the foreign way called *fricassee*. Becs brought in the bread and having placed it on the table, held out her hand to me. I gazed stupidly at her.

'The key,' she prompted.

I groped in my clothing and then remembered. 'In the cellar door.'

Becs sighed.

'What was that?' asked Ferris when she was gone.

'I left the key when I took out the canary.'

'Well, there's none but us after all.'

He tasted the food. I did likewise and found it to be liver; I closed my eyes the better to savour it after the beans and cheese of the colony. Our diggers' food had brought about in me a great weariness, one might say disgust. Even rabbit had begun to sicken me; only the constant field labour kept me eating at all. Becs had cooked our repast very tender, with a spiced gravy, and there was more than enough for us both.

She brought in another bottle of wine and a goblet for Ferris. 'Have you need of anything else? If not, I'll be upstairs and take a look at her.'

'She sleeps soundly,' said Ferris. 'You could rest.'

'I can rest by her bedside. Stewed dried plums and cheese on the sideboard.' She left the room.

My friend gazed into the air as he ate. His hair was growing again. Soon it would tickle me when we embraced. I went to sit next to him, nuzzling his neck and relishing that scent which breathed from him and no one else. I felt him swallow.

'Jacob—' he took a pull at the canary, put his fingers on my jaw and kissed me; the kiss had wine in it. Looking into his eyes, I drank it off as if it were himself, then showed him the inside of my mouth warmed and reddened.

'No more down here,' he said, 'that's just a taste,' and laughed, but I saw he was stirred. I pulled him onto my lap, my thighs between his, took him in my arms and crushed him to me until he cried out.

'There's a taste for you too,' I said, 'since you play with fire.'

We kissed again and he darted his tongue in and out of my mouth. I began sliding his shirt up over his chest.

Ferris pulled away. 'Wait. I must sit with her before we retire.' He rose and fetched the fruit and cheese. 'What did the physician say to you?'

'Not much.' I struggled to suppress the ache he had started.

Fishing for plums with a spoon, Ferris said, 'He is not open with me.'

'He says he can promise nothing. Yet.'

'We may be here days, then.'

'Methought, weeks. Ask him yourself tomorrow.'

Ferris groaned and offered me the fruit. 'These are good, will you—?'

Shaking my head, I poured myself more wine.

He added, 'Becs looks all overwatched. What with the nursing and the house, she has too much to do.'

'We could relieve her as nurses,' I said, 'except that she wishes to do it all herself.'

He nodded. 'Then we must get another girl in to cook.'

'No,' I said.

He looked at me in surprise. 'Don't you see how weary she is?'

'Don't *you* see we don't want a stranger here?'

Ferris spat a plum stone into his dish and held out his hand for the wine.

'Am I a help in trouble?' The question was out before I had considered it.

'In the worst, you will be. Should it come.'

'Sir George?'

'That too. But I meant, should Aunt die.' He paused, picking his words. I waited, and he went on, 'I couldn't bear her dying had I no other love.'

A better man might have recalled to him the Divine Love, but I was none such, and besides, I knew him too well by that time to attempt it. Instead, I took his hand.

Becs looked as done for as her mistress when we went back upstairs. The purple marks beneath her eyes had smeared deeper and darker into the sockets since she opened the door to us.

'Get you to bed, girl,' urged Ferris.

'She may need me.'

'Does she have pain in the night?'

Becs shook her head. 'Only I hate to think of none being there.'

'Go to bed,' he repeated. 'Tomorrow we will each take a watch, if you like. She won't wake tonight, Doctor Whiteman gave her a draught.'

The maid rose. I heard the click of her stiff knees.

'There's a bottle of canary not all drunk,' he added as she left the room. 'Take some.'

But she did not go down to find the canary. We heard her stumble to her own chamber and slam the door.

'She'll drop onto the bed in her clothes,' I said.

'I'd not be surprised.' He was kneading Aunt's fingers. We both watched her face for any hint of sensibility.

'Nothing.' Ferris loosed her hand.

'The doctor will know more tomorrow,' I said.

He looked at me. 'You wish to go to bed.' He eased her arm under the sheet and we closed the door on her and walked along the corridor in silence.

When we reached my room I paused, hand on the latch. 'Will you come in?'

He shook his head, stepped to his own door. 'In here. I want it like the first time.'

'Why?'

He repeated, 'I want it like the first time.'

His room was not yet dark. He pulled the shutters across on one side to shield us from spying eyes.

'Now.' His hand was on the bolt. 'Remember?'

I remembered. I caught hold of him and kissed him as I had that night, with the hunger of months; we stumbled across the room and fell onto the bed. He called me *My delight, my honey, my Samson* and such talk being extremely rare with him, I knew by it that he was sweating for me.

'Take me in your mouth.'

I did so. He cried out and was gone almost at once, as if that time were really the first.

When he was quiet I said, 'There was another night after that.' Kissing, slipping against one another, we eased together, until I lost the knowledge of myself and became nothing but flesh.

~

'And if she were the same?' Ferris asked.

We sat at breakfast. He was eating eggs and white manchet, just as he had through the months before we left for the Common, spooning the yolk onto his bread and pressing salt into the yolk in precisely the same way. It amused me to see him as exact as ever. This was now the fourth day since our arrival and we were still trying to find our right course. The doctor had presented himself half an hour earlier and had again pronounced Aunt not better and not worse.

'If she were the same in two days we could write to Susannah,' I suggested. 'We could do it now.'

'Why Susannah?'

'She has excellent good sense. But for her I'd not have stayed for Beste's letter.'

He swilled down the bread with some beer. 'And because she is soft on you?'

'Wrong, there.' I recalled Susannah shaking her head at me as I shouted and threatened. 'She has measured my folly. But if you think me partial, write to Hathersage.'

He ignored this dart, saying simply, 'I'd sooner go back.'

'Had they been dispersed,' I reasoned, 'wouldn't they come here?'

'They might be unable.'

We could get no further forward. If Aunt got well, got worse, stayed the same, round and round we went. I tried to impress upon him that his being at the Common could do nothing to stave off an attack, but he answered that this would not excuse him in his own conscience, if the moment came and he were elsewhere.

'Masters!' Becs came running in. 'Masters, she can move her face. Come see!'

We followed her upstairs. I will never forget Aunt's mouth as first I saw it, the one side frozen while the other made grotesque moues and snarls. But her eyes presented a more hopeful aspect, for they appeared to fix on us as we approached the bed. Ferris craned his body awkwardly over it, seized her hand, and watched her face as if about to pounce.

'She's trying to say "Christopher".' His voice was thick. Becs stood to one side, hands joined and head bowed. After a short while Aunt seemed to lose strength and lay more loosely against the pillow, but her eyes still rested on us.

'The doctor must come again,' Becs cried.

I stood silent, ill at ease, as she hurried past me. Ferris kissed the patient's cheek. A drop fell from his face onto hers, though by his frequent swallowing I guessed he was trying to act the man. At last he stood upright with a great sigh and pressed his fists to the small of his back.

'Now be happy,' I said, hearing with dismay my thin feigned voice. Ferris appeared not to notice it.

'I'll stay with her, Jacob, until the physician comes. Suppose she should speak again, and no one there!'

'Then I'll watch with you.'

Ferris glanced at his aunt. Her eyes were now closed. I stepped forward and enfolded him in my arms. There was nothing carnal in that embrace. Putting my hand to the back of his head, I found with my fingertips hard little creases under his hair: the scars left by broken glass.

~

The doctor was sweating in his furred gown and I guessed that Becs, that nimble girl, had dragged him along on foot under the summer sun. Muttering to himself, he thumbed up Aunt's eyelids and scraped her tongue. Next he laid a heavily veined hand under her breast to feel the heart.

'Irregular,' he said and at this she moved a little. Finding her coming to consciousness he said he must now cast her water and Becs was given a glass flask and told to catch the patient's urine.

'If you would be so kind as to leave the chamber, gentlemen,' he suggested to Ferris and myself.

We waited outside, hearing grunts as they tried to raise her in the bed, and then the doctor to Becs. 'That will do, now hold it so.' There followed, 'Come, madam, just a little,' and 'Shall I press on her belly, sir?' at which last I wanted to laugh but, looking at Ferris, dared not.

Becs came out of the chamber and ran downstairs, going directly back into the sickroom with two jugs. We listened as she sloshed water from one to the other in the hope of stimulating the invalid to piss, and this time even Ferris did smile. At last there was an 'Ah!' from the maid and we caught the thin tinkle of liquid against the wall of the flask. Becs came out triumphant, bearing the jugs before her.

Ferris peeped round the chamber door. 'We can go in,' he announced.

Doctor Whiteman was sniffing the contents of the flask with a judicious expression. He held the thing to the light, and I gasped to see the deep orange tint of the urine.

'Is that blood in it?' asked Ferris.

The physician shook his head. I wondered how he could know.

'Is she truly better?' Ferris persisted.

'Have patience.' The man's look showed his irritation at our ignorance. He added, 'This is not a thing to be done as one might plant a turnip,' and I felt the gibe at my friend though Ferris himself was seemingly deaf to it. The doctor took a paper, and from it tapped some powder down the neck of the vessel; there followed a faint hiss. He continued slopping the urine about against the glass, holding it up to the window.

'Well?' asked Ferris.

'She will make a slow, very slow, recovery.'

I saw my friend's entire body quicken with joy, like a lamb put to the teat. He overpaid the physician, and gave him the direction for writing to us at the inn at Page Common.

'But you'll be here tomorrow, Ferris?' I cried.

'Yes, yes.' He told the doctor to call in that evening and accompanied him downstairs. Left to myself, I swore silently and then cursed my wicked selfishness.

Ferris rattled back up the stairs and flung his arms round me. 'Jacob, it cannot be long.' Not trusting my voice, I smiled and let myself be hugged.

We sat together in the sickroom, one each side of the bed. His eyes were dry now and they frighted me with that *shine* which I so dreaded. A curious weariness dragged on me and I found I wished very much to sleep despite its being so early in the day. Beginning to nod in the chair, I heard him ask was I ailing, did I wish to go back to bed, but I was already borne away on the dark and unable to reply. Towards noon (as I later discovered) the heaviness ebbed from me and I took a deep breath, feeling the air puff out my chest. I opened my eyes. Aunt was stirring; her nephew clasped her hand loosely and she was tapping her fingers on his.

'You see?'

I said that she had indeed made progress, but that we should not be hasty, but wait until the extent of her recovery left no room for doubt.

'The doctor has no doubt already. And are not doctors the most cautious of men?'

'But men still, and fallible.'

'Ah, Jacob, I know.' He looked kindly at me. 'I know. But the longer we stay, the harder to leave.'

'When, then?'

'I thought, the day after tomorrow.'

I cried out in protest. He bade me be quiet over the invalid's bed and we wrangled, that is to say, he reasoned and I pleaded, in whispers. He was, as so often, gently adamant, and I passed the rest of the afternoon in misery.

Come the evening I had better fortune. The Bestes chose this time to call and Ferris was mighty glad to see them again. After the first salutations they mounted with us to the sickchamber, but Aunt was asleep. Set against her twisted white countenance they seemed emblems of health, Harry's handsome lazy face bright with sun and blood and Elizabeth pearl-like, already losing the coarseness which had dimmed her lustre at the Common.

'Where are the children?' asked Ferris as we descended again.

'With Elizabeth's sister.'

There was venison roasting down in the kitchen, perfuming the stairwell, and Becs brought us tarts and wine. It took me back to the days when the colony was but a maggot in my friend's head, when guests came to drink and talk nonsense but went home again like sane folk.

Ferris told them of Doctor Whiteman's opinion and they drank to Aunt's health, but were scandalised to hear of his plan for our departure.

'You cannot go yet,' Elizabeth told my friend. 'Though your

aunt improves, yet she is still in a condition where she must wish her family near her, and you are all that family.'

Ferris looked uncomfortable, and I saw that three might accomplish what one could not. We hammered away at him, and by the time we sat down to the venison, had beaten him out to the length of a week. Elizabeth, with her woman's cunning, put in some of the most telling blows by citing mistakes that she had known physicians make. When Ferris at last yielded I could have kissed Harry and Elizabeth both.

The talk turned to their own doings, and they claimed to be now in a fair way to set up their old style of life. The anvil was come safely home, though the mule had needed very frequent persuading with the whip, and Harry had found a yard to let where the fire would be safe. Elizabeth's sister was come to live with them and help with the little ones, and Elizabeth had only quarrelled with Margaret (the sister) once, and that on a washday.

'Harry will soon be in a position to take a journeyman again,' said Elizabeth as Becs stacked the empty dishes.

'Would you ever take a prentice?' I asked.

'Mayhap, one day.'

'I could do prentice work,' I said.

'But Jacob, you are too old,' put in Ferris.

I found him officious, and went on, 'So I have no wife and do what I am bidden, where is the difference? Show me the boy who can do as much work as I can.'

'There are laws about these matters,' said Harry. 'Touching on age, and suchlike. But had I no journeyman – are we talking in earnest, now?' He grinned at me as he spiked a morsel of roast skin on the tip of his knife.

'Surely you'd want a man who had served his time?' Ferris asked.

'To help a friend, now – I could call him my servant. No need to ask could you handle a hammer, eh Jacob?'

There was a pause. Ferris looked sulkily down his nose.

'Wat might wish for his place back,' said Elizabeth. 'Should you not ask him first?'

Harry considered. 'He'll have got in elsewhere by now.'

'If the thing goes awry, perhaps I will come talk to you,' I said slowly. 'And Ferris, you would come back here, I guess?'

Ferris ignored my question and said to Elizabeth, 'First it was printing. He would learn every trade if he could.'

'That shows industry,' said she with a friendly look to me.

Ferris smiled stiffly.

Elizabeth, sensing some unease, began talking of Harry's brother Robert, who had worked as a manservant in a country house where he speedily discovered that the master was mad.

'The man's freaks were most curious,' she explained. 'He persecuted the servants – accused them of poisoning his bedclothes, and sometimes of trying to cut the faces out of the portraits in the great hall. Robert was walking in the garden, with the steward, Mister Cattermole, being instructed—' here we had to wait as Elizabeth choked with laughter and Harry, with his hand clapped over his mouth, was in no better plight, 'being instructed as to what he should do when the master was found naked in the corridors. "By kind words, oft repeated" said the steward, "we can generally persuade him to bed, provided it is not a night when the bed is envenomed." Robert would have asked what happened on those nights when the master broke cover from behind a bush, crying, "Out, Nebuchadnezzar" and shot at Mister Cattermole—'

Ferris and I gasped.

'Robert and Cattermole ran screaming into an arbour. By which you will guess,' said Elizabeth, 'that the ball had missed. The old man was disarmed by the gardener's boy (who showed more valiant than the rest of them put together) and led back to the house very penitent and confused. But that was enough, and Robert is come home to live with his parents.'

'And Mister Cattermole,' said I, shouting a little over the laughter, 'is he also departed?'

'Not he,' answered Harry. 'The man picks up a deal of money in the course of his work – you understand – and that makes it worth his while.'

Elizabeth wiped her eyes. 'And welcome to it,' she said. 'But alas, poor gentleman, to be mad – no laughing matter—'

We agreed with her, and then all burst forth in loud roars.

'Excuse me,' said Ferris as the merriment died down. 'I believe that was the front door. Becs will have let him in.' He went out and we heard him descend the stairs.

'The doctor,' I explained. Footsteps were heard again, continuing past our floor to the one above. As soon as the sound of the chamber door came to us Elizabeth bent forward over the table. 'Jacob, should he not stay here?'

'O don't tell me, Elizabeth. I am hoarse with persuading him. It is only what you and Harry said that stops him running off tomorrow.'

'I would have said he loved her more than that,' said Harry thoughtfully.

'He does love her, most dearly. He's torn in two.'

Elizabeth opened her mouth but we heard him directly, coming downstairs. I helped our guests to wine, filling their cups to the brim, and Ferris returned just in time for the fruit pie which Becs brought up.

'She's a better colour, and the heart is stronger,' he announced. 'And there are two kind of draughts, Becs, for you to give her.'

The Bestes offered thanks to God. I tried to look happy.

~

I could do no more than the three of us had managed together. Ferris would stay only a week, do what I might. I urged that a week was nothing in the care of a dear aunt, nay, a mother. He replied that he was leaving her to a trusted nurse, and would be sure to receive news each day. I argued that 'twere good the colonists learn to direct their affairs without him, each playing a fuller part in their little commonwealth, and he looked at me strangely and asked did I think he had crushed their spirit up till then. I put it to him that we might profit by our time in London: he nodded, and wrote me a list as in the past, of the seeds and knives, etc., he would have me purchase for the community's use, so that I found myself employed as errand boy while he watched at his aunt's side. Lastly I resorted to those arts which owe little to talk, but persuade a man more forcefully than eloquence. He came eagerly into my chamber, where he gave every token of a greedy and violent delight, then rose the next day ready to leave our bed forever. My powers were now bankrupt. Sometimes I would look up, catch his gentle eyes on me, and wonder what he was. I could, without much trouble, have broken his back, yet, for all the pain the colony brought to him, he would return to it, and I could not bend his spirit an inch.

~

At the bottom of my pack I laid as many washballs as I had been able to beg from Becs. Ferris laughed aloud when he saw them.

'Will you set up shop, Jacob? Or do you eat them, are you with child?' He tickled me round the waist.

I slapped his hand off. 'It is no pleasure to me, to stink like a beast.'

Ferris looked up into my face, more serious now. 'You don't stink.'

'Then there's something uncommonly wrong with my nose. Here, give me those shirts.' I would not smile at him and after a while he went out of my room.

He had purchased us places on the coach. He said this was to keep off the rain for he had a notion the weather would be wet, and besides we had much to carry. All of which might be true, yet I felt his unwillingness to walk with my sadness even half a day. For my heart was oppressed, and I made no show to hide it.

We were to leave at eight the next morning. After the evening meal, when the packs were bound up and Ferris had checked the knives and other implements were all stowed, we had nothing to do but drink and sit with Aunt. I took cup after cup of wine, feeling my heart all frozen. Ferris watched me with some anxiety and I returned his stare, daring him to correct me. The wine did nothing to warm the ice inside, and in fact I found it ill tasting, sour, but that seemed only right and fitting with all my joys turned bitter on me.

At last he said, 'I never knew you care so much for wine.'

'What makes you think I care for it? I spend my life doing what I hate.'

He sighed. 'Would you – would you sooner stay a while? I will go alone, if you wish. You can follow at your leisure.'

'You are all goodness,' I returned. 'But no, I continue to serve.'

His grey eyes winced, glanced uneasily at the sleeping woman. 'Be not so savage, Jacob.'

'When did *you* ever see me savage!'

The word '*you*' struck out hard from a deep place where the Voice was testing the walls of its prison, giving tongue to something long chained up. I felt a surge of terror and pleasure, mixed, for the Voice had never before spoken through me to another person.

Ferris made no sign that he had heard anything strange. He checked that Aunt still slept, then said mildly, 'Have you forgotten Roger Rowly? You—'

'That! – that was play.' I felt the thing inside me swell and swell until I was only just keeping it down. 'If ever I turn savage, you'll know. Now sneck up.'

'I meant only that—'

'*Sneck. Up.*'

I saw Ferris go rigid, and realised that I had locked eyes with him as I once had with Nathan. He had never caught that look full in the face before, and his cheeks grew pale.

'So, you're warned.' The pressure within slackened; my voice was my own again. I opened another bottle which I had carried up to the chamber with me. He held out his hand but I put the wine to my own lips and got down a good half of it without drawing breath. If he begrudged me drink, so much the worse for him. I was not under his authority.

'Jacob, please—' He leant forward to take the bottle. I kept my hand on it and he sank back into his seat.

'You called me savage. Don't you ever call me savage.'

There was a silence. Ferris contemplated the embroidered linen sheet. I observed his lowered eyes and suddenly felt the want of him in my bed, but getting up, stumbled over the chair. He did not laugh as I expected, and remained sitting as if I had not moved.

'Aren't you coming?' I demanded.

'If you wish.'

He rose at once and followed me out. We went directly to my chamber and there for the first time I held him silent and spiritless in my arms. I demanded caresses and he gave them without resistance and without desire, so that it was like bedding a corpse. Then I wanted him to lie under me and he would not, and I thought he took pleasure in the refusal. We struggled, and I punched him in the ribs and belly, then got on top of him and twisted his arm up his back. He tried to pull the arm free so I gave it a wrench and felt him jerk like a man who is branded.

'No followers now,' I breathed into his ear. 'Just we two.'

'Do it then,' he spat into the pillow. 'Make an end of us.'

I forced his arm up further and heard him gasp. Any more and he would cry out. I had got him, the *weasel*, he belonged to me and I felt myself his master for once.

'Let me in,' I said.

Ferris shook his head.

'Let me in.' I pressed with my knee, trying to get some purchase on him, and put more of my weight on the twisted arm. His muscles convulsed, then yielded, and I was between his thighs.

'What, no orders for me?' I began pushing outwards, spread-eagling him. 'Go here, go there?'

He would not answer. I heard quick breaths; he was trying to outwit the pain, so I let him have more weight on the arm and forced him to groan aloud. His legs were limp now, all the fight gone out of him. I spat in the palm of my hand and greased my prick with it.

His shoulder gave a faint *crack*.

Then all at once – it was perhaps that noise – the blood began to go down in me. I was unable to fuck him. All I could do was release him and lie by his side on the mattress; as I did so I broke into angry weeping. He did not speak to me or touch me. My mouth was grown too thick to speak properly but I mumbled at him, 'Why, why did you come in to me?'

'To get you away from her.' His voice quivered, not from softness but like an arrow newly shot into my heart. Having inflicted that wound he rolled away, and I lay staring into my own confusion and shame. From time to time there was the old rushing in my head, and words began seething up to torment me.

He does not love you.

No wonder. I have dealt brutally.

You already labour without pay. He will now make you beg for the privilege.

It seemed that I lay there for hours, but must finally have slept for at some point I found he was crept out of bed in the darkness. I knew this when I heard him bolt his door.

~

A jingling. The bed curtains were tugged apart. A weight slammed onto my chest and I gasped with shock.

'Ferris?'

He was astride me, on top of the bedcover so that my hands were trapped beneath it. I lifted my head to see what he was doing and something pierced my neck just under the chin.

'I'm kneeling on your arms,' he said. 'Move, and I cut you.'

I peered upwards into his face as I had never seen it before. The eyes looked bruised and were fixed on me as if on some poisonous serpent. His lips curled back from his teeth and I felt the thing in my neck push deeper into the flesh.

'Understand this,' he said. 'If you ever – do *that* – again, best kill me. For if you don't I will surely kill you.'

'You, kill?' I meant it as an appeal to his gentle nature, but in my shock the words came out coloured with contempt.

'I could do it now,' and he jerked the blade, making me wince. 'Give thanks to God that you are in my aunt's house and not in the wood.'

I thought, *He has considered it.*

'You could never overpower me in the wood,' I said.

'There are ways.'

I lay back and felt an ache, wages of my drunkenness, grip my skull. The probing of the knife in my skin was intolerable. 'Ferris, stop that! There's no call for it—'

'I am learning what it is to force someone.' A fine spray of his spit dampened my cheeks and jaw.

'I did not force you! My heart, I couldn't—'

'You were incapable, else you'd have fucked me till I split in half.'

I remembered the final wrench at his arm, when his very bones had cried out, and I felt sick. 'I was a drunken beast,' I muttered. 'If you knew how sorry—'

'O, but I know. Aren't you always sorry! First Nathan, then Rowly, and myself with a head full of glass. Each time I told myself would be the last.'

'It *will* be the last,' I pleaded.

'The last time you lie with me. Drunk or sober.'

I stared at him. 'Not lie with you?'

'You're possessed of a devil, your greatest joy is to hear me cry out.' Still he held the blade to my neck. 'You and George Byars are a pair. He's a great one for arm-twisting.'

'You told me there were no devils.' I tried to lift my hand and promptly received an excruciating jab from his knife.

'And I hold to what I said. A man's own evil is his devil and yours, Jacob, is mastery.'

I remembered the talk about devils, after our first night, when he was so enamoured he could scarce keep his hands off me. He had not been afraid of my strength then.

'So I am not to lie with you?' I sneered. 'We have danced this dance before, and it ended in you clawing my breeches.'

'Did you hear what I told you or is it all to say again?' His voice was icy. I began to feel afraid, not for my neck but for the many days that lay ahead of us. More humbly I asked, 'Are you very much hurt?'

'Your prowess is as great as ever.'

'Ferris, believe me—'

'You must leave the colony.'

At that I struggled to breathe and for a moment I thought his weight on my chest would suffocate me. 'Wait, Ferris. Wait.' The words jerked out from my throat. 'By tonight you will think differently.'

'Don't deceive yourself.' He shifted his knees and my breath eased a little.

'I can serve you against Sir George.'

'Serve me! That's not it at all. I want friends to work together, protect their own.'

'Can't you use my strength for a good cause?'

'Good causes are the most dangerous for men like you. That was one reason I took you out of the army.'

'If we are going to preach, let us call things by their right names,' I cried out, angered at this sermonising. 'You were on fire to get your big stupid friend back to London and break him in.'

'I don't deny it.'

He spoke as if I were some vice to which, having renounced it and repented, he could freely admit. Frighted, I tried retraction.

'Forgive me, I spoke unjustly.'

But Ferris was not listening. He said as if to himself, 'Lust addled my judgement. I should have taken Nat.'

That was a sword through me. I stared up at him and he steadily, unsmilingly, returned my gaze. The silence thickened between us. Then Ferris took the knife away from my neck, got up from the bed and went out.

And so it was that the coach journey back to Page Common outwent my worst imaginings. We ate bread in silence at half past six. My mouth was sour, my belly brimming with bitter yellowish stuff which from time to time voided itself by means of a retching so intense as to leave me all over sweat. I did not want the bread but ate it, and as I chewed my skull throbbed. From time to time I stole a look at Ferris and saw him pale with swollen eyes. I wondered had he wept in rage and humiliation after the beating. When he caught me watching him he turned his face away and I saw a small bruise on the side of his neck. At the thought of all the others beneath his clothes I shook inwardly.

Just after seven he went up to kiss his aunt once more. When he came down, it was with his pack already on his shoulders and he took his station near the street door without looking at me. I went to my room and shouldered my burden likewise, and on my coming down he whispered, 'I see you will force your way, as ever.'

Becs had been risen some time and she now came from the kitchen to stand with us on the doorstep. Perhaps she saw something of how the land lay, for she spoke gently with me almost as if in pity, from which I concluded that she had heard nothing of my monstrous performance the night before. Neither kisses nor bites this time, but decorous partings all round, while I was eaten up body and soul with wretchedness, like a carcass with worms. Ferris reminded her to write, or to make the physician write, and I started at the huskiness of his voice. As soon as he had finished his instructions to her we passed into silence. We walked down the street abreast, at the same pace, not looking at one another. I remembered our quarrel in the army, when he said he would not be my *thing*, and wondered would he ever love me again.

TWENTY-SEVEN

Things Not To Be Compelled

THE COMPANY in the coach was talkative: a husband and wife, the wife carrying a babe, and opposite these a great prattler, a schoolmaster in his middle years, harmless, tedious and happy. He struck up a conversation first with Ferris, next with me, and then had the idea of introducing us to one another.

Ferris nodded coldly to me and said in his broken voice, 'I had indeed the impression of knowing you, Mister Cullen, but find that I was mistaken.'

I could think of no reply. The rage that had swelled within me and almost burst out of my flesh was now shrivelled and blasted. Had I thought it would be of use, I would have kissed his shoes in the coach. Instead I sat inhaling the stink of damp clothing and garlic breath, trying to keep down my vomit.

The vehicle rattled on. From time to time I had to push past my neighbours to void my sickness from the window and while undergoing these torments I heard the coachman's curses floating past on the wind, damning the horses without cease even when the going was smooth and the road empty. I was astonished to find him so foul-mouthed, and for the sake of hearing my own voice I said so to our tiresome companion. He replied that the man had more than once been reported and suffered correction, but the habit was so grown into him that he could not shake it off.

Seeing that Ferris was listening, I said that an evil habit, say drink, might well destroy a man's happiness against his own will, and that such a case were pitiable. There was more cunning than I at first knew in mentioning drink by name, for even as I spoke I remembered that my friend could well understand this example. Perhaps, in recollection, he might judge my crime less harshly.

Ferris did not look at me but addressed his remarks to the schoolmaster. 'Whatever makes a man a beast also renders him pitiable. But it behoves us to be wary of these bestial men despite our compassion, for they frequently turn on their friends.'

The schoolmaster said that was very true, and an example might be seen in his sister's neighbour who beat his wife for no fault at all.

'And thus,' he said, 'he grievously injures himself, both in reputation and in the sense that they are, after all, one flesh.'

This piece of pedantry proving more painful to me than any I had endured as a boy, I was glad when his conclusion was lost in a shriek of laughter from the other passengers, who were talking, much more loudly than we, of jests played upon bumpkins newly come to London.

I wanted to take up Ferris upon what he had said. 'But you *are* compassionate to such men, Sir?' I pressed him, my breath struggling in my throat. 'For what our friend here says is true. Though guilty, the suffering caused comes back also on themselves, and so—'

'I think my friends would grant that I am compassionate,' Ferris replied. 'Long-suffering, even. But there are two things to be said here.' My stomach turned over at his measured tone. 'The first consideration,' he went on, 'is that a man must already have degraded himself in no small degree, to beg compassion where once he freely enjoyed the privileges of love.'

The schoolmaster was listening with interest and nodding. Never, I thought, had 'the privileges of love' seemed so like a lost Paradise, and never had Ferris been so cruel to me.

'And the second,' he continued, his voice hoarser yet still level, 'is that love and compassion have both their limits. I may forgive a friend seventy times seven for the love I bear him, but there are some things which, if a man resent them not, he ceases to be a man.'

'For the love I bear him.' I wondered had he meant to say that. 'Ceases to be a man' – looking up I saw his eyes contracted with pain despite the controlled voice, and the sight cut me with a terrible pain of my own.

'Let us take a case,' I began desperately. 'Suppose I offer violence to a dear, dear friend. I repent—'

The pedant cut in. 'You, Sir,' he cried, 'I hope you never do offer violence. I should fancy that when *you* resent something there are few men would stand against you!'

I tried to make myself clear. 'My word was *repent*, not—'

But the fool was listening no more than before. He invited Ferris to join him in roasting the stranger.

'I imagine our tall friend here generally carries the day. Crushes all opposition, hey?' He made to feel the muscles in my arm and I knocked his hand off my sleeve. How I did not knife him there and then is still a wonder to me.

Ferris smiled grimly. 'You would indeed do well to avoid his resentment. But suppose our friend – you understand I speak of him only for the sake of an example?'

The other man nodded. Ferris shot a look at me which filled me with dread, and continued, 'As you remarked, Mister – Cullen? – is well equipped to compel obedience. But friendship, love – these are not to be compelled.'

'But what has this to do with evil habits and repentance?' asked the schoolmaster.

'I mean that repeated offences, even when they secure forgiveness, drive out love. And from that I came to say that one may compel obedience but never love.'

'That's every husband's tragedy, eh?' smiled the other. 'Still, obedience is much in a woman.'

'A dog's virtue,' said Ferris, turning his head away as if sick of the talk. 'Those who would enforce it should marry with the beasts.'

The schoolmaster hawed, decided that my friend was joking after all, and settled back in his seat with a philosophical sigh as if to say, *Well, what of it.*

The darts Ferris had shot into me now poisoned my breast with the most intense fear and shame. I again felt the sheets pulling on my thigh as I ground my weight into him. A woman thus put to it can call for help. He could not, and as he tried to grapple with me I got a hold on his arm and set about enforcing *obedience*—

'Mister Ferris!' I cried. Some of the other passengers broke off their chatter at the sudden loudness of my speech. 'You are in the right – love is, is—!'

He raised his eyebrows in mockery and I remembered a knee in the small of his back. My throat closed up.

For a moment the sea-grey eyes rested on mine. I stared back, pleading with him, but he dropped his eyelids and shut me out. The coach staggered over the uneven ground and I had to go to the window, heaving and gasping with my own vileness. Back in my seat, my forehead wet with perspiration, I watched his head roll against the wood behind him, studied the shape of his mouth.

The schoolmaster was grown very quiet and had perhaps at last some glimmer of what he had stumbled into. Much I cared, just then. I was already burning alive.

~

Passengers got out, got in. The people with the baby left us and were replaced by a withered crone who stank of piss. At one stage, having nodded off, I woke suddenly with the feeling that something was wrong. Ferris had moved to the window. There he spent the rest of the journey, staring out of it, dull grey light clinging about his cheeks. Motionless, he put me in mind of a statue I had seen somewhere, but no sculptor would give his statue a face of such sullen intensity. The schoolmaster had long since reached his destination, leaving Ferris and myself strangers again.

A fine spray speckled the seats and floor near the window. He had guessed the weather aright. I saw the yellow hair darken, little drops running off the ends of it. Ferris stayed where he was. Once he had looked up to me with dripping hair, his face bright with candlelight, and brighter with love. When was that?

We slowed as the coach splashed through country roads brimming with ruts and rainwater, and the wheels sank into clay. At the thought of wet huts and clothes to endure along with my shame and pain, I was tempted to jump from the coach and walk back to London. I could seek refuge with Harry. But I caught myself in this delusion, that I had been secretly hoping that Ferris would leap from the coach after me. In truth I was more likely to stand in the mud and watch him go out of my life forever, staring back at me from the window with his statue's eyes. I was not made to be loved. The flesh was a different thing; once I had thought none would ever look at me (that was when I lived always with Zeb) but even then – I pulled my thoughts away from Caro. In the army was Ferris, and then the glances of the London people had told me that I was far from ugly. But I was afflicted with an ugliness of soul that no physick could correct. Though Ferris stayed unmoving at the window, he was leaving me, just as surely as if I were got down into the road while the coach rolled away.

~

The door was pushed open and he stepped down; I heard the *splosh* as he landed outside. The driver handed him his pack and he slung it across his shoulders as he marched away, slipping a little on the wet ground. My pack took longer to untie from the roof of the coach. By the time the swearing coachman had dangled it down to me and I had fastened the thing in place, Ferris was some fifty paces off. I followed without much spirit, trying to read his walk for signs of relenting. He held himself as upright as the pack permitted and went at a fierce pace, recalling to me that first day in the colony when I had given him too heavy a load and he had set his jaw and carried it. It came to me that with such resolve he had the makings of an excellent soldier. But then again I thought not, for soldiers must obey.

The first person I saw was Hathersage. He looked up from his hoe as Ferris approached and they waved each to the other, then Hathersage ran towards my cruel friend as if he were the Prodigal Son, shouting the news to the others so that in a short time Ferris was surrounded by an eager group. I saw hands clutched, embraces, kisses pressed on dear Brother Christopher. They waved to me, too, and smiled in my direction, but none would quit him to welcome me, such a difference they made between us. O Brother Wisdom, I said to myself, did you but know what this man, that you fawn on, did with me in London every night but one! The things he freely yielded who now, if we were in Hell together, would not give me a gentle look!

I came up with them. They still had hold of Ferris, who was answering their questions in his ragged voice. Aunt was in the way to recovery and we had brought back some newfangled tools. His sincere thanks for their prayers, which had doubtless been effective. Had there been any sign of movement from Sir George? Was all well with the crops?

The colonists greeted me with a civil but cursory word or two, before turning back to their darling. Only Susannah sought me, moving away from the huddle and holding out her hand with pleasant frankness. 'Well Brother Jacob, I trust you had good cheer in London? Brother Christopher says you have new knives and axeheads in your pack.'

'He says true.' I lowered my voice. 'And something for you, Susannah.'

'For me? A gift?'

I would be glad to get away from Ferris and his disciples.

Inside the dry space of the tent I laid the pack down and began unfastening the strings.

'I can't think what it can be,' she mused. 'Did I ask you for something?'

'Close your eyes and hold out your hands,' I said.

She did so. 'Hurry, Jacob, I'm mad with curiosity!'

'Now don't expect silver and gold, for there's none,' I warned her. 'Sniff, can't you smell anything?'

She snorted. 'Lavender, is it? You brought lavender?'

I laughed at her puzzled face. 'Here.' I put a washball in each outstretched hand.

'Ah!' As her fingers closed on them her eyes opened and she turned a smile of pure joy on me. 'You are too kind. Too kind.'

'An easy errand.' I had covered the rest of the washballs and did not intend to leave them in the tent. 'The only thanks I require is that you be so good as not to mention them to anyone,' I warned, for I had no wish to share with the others.

'Not even Catherine,' she promised, and at once stuffed the things between her breasts.

'Thank you, thank you, Jacob.'

She whirled about to go like a much younger woman, paused, ran back and kissed my hand before dancing out of the tent. I was left smiling despite the pain between myself and Ferris. I could tell by the business-like way she had stored my gift in her bosom, anything but flirtatious, that he was wrong about her being soft on me, but I thought I might count her a friend. The odd thing was that I had never intended to make such a gift, yet her fair greeting when the rest could scarce spare me a word, being all of them wrapped up in Ferris, had called to something in me – a sudden need to share and be thanked. How did men make themselves loved, I wondered. I had passed all my life with men who were loved but I seemed never to have learnt the lesson.

Left alone, I began to unwrap the axe-heads. They were beautifully keen and heavy. I balanced the largest on my palm and tested the edge with my thumb. No wonder, I thought, that lords and ladies chose to die by the axe rather than the noose. I laid out the deadly things on one of the crude tables knocked together by Harry, until there should be time to fit them with stocks.

I was just searching for a good place to store the knives when I heard the words 'such an assault' spoken by someone, perhaps Jonathan, outside the tent. It was followed by the words 'like the beasts' and I knew the second speaker, whose voice cracked with contempt, for Ferris.

There was not time to feel anything save the terrified certainty that he had accused me. Sweat burst out all over my skin and my legs turned to water. Trying to keep upright, I clawed at a pile of baskets near to me, and the two men entered just in time to see myself and the baskets drop together.

Jonathan and Ferris were kneeling either side of me, Jonathan fanning my face with my hat.

'All's well,' he said soothingly. He held up my hand and I saw I was clutching a long-bladed knife, as if I had been in a fight. I wiped my brow, letting the knife drop to the grass.

'You were lucky. Could've fell on it,' Jonathan explained as if to a child, and indeed I was very like one, a child confused and horribly afraid of being found out in my wickedness. His voice and manner, however, were gentle.

Ferris, on the other side, had placed himself a little further off, letting the other man touch and fan me. He stood up now, and, saying to Jonathan, 'He overdid the drink last night. That'll be the root of it,' went out of the tent.

Jonathan whistled. 'Have you and him fallen out, then?'

'Not for the first time.' I did not want his curiosity or sympathy, and I was trying to find a way round to the question burning my tongue. At last I hit on, 'Where were you? Just outside?'

'Aye. Telling him about Sister Jane.'

I showed my incomprehension.

'Didn't Susannah tell you? I saw the two of you come in here—' his expression grew sly. 'Perhaps you'd other things to talk about.'

'To the point,' I begged. 'You were talking of Sister Jane?'

'Sister Jane, or Mistress Allen as we called her at first, came to us the day you left for London. Myself and Jeremiah went to the inn to see was there any word from you, and on the way back we came on two men and a young lad, all set upon the one woman. In broad daylight.'

I almost smiled with relief, but kept a sober face to ask who had done the thing and why.

'None knows who they were. The lad was no more than twelve, a right little spawn of Satan *he* must be! Thought she had some money, it seems, but she had none, so they beat her right in the road. When we ran up they shogged off.'

'They were three against two,' I remarked.

'Not good enough odds for them.'

So Ferris had kept his humiliation to himself. I struggled to fix my mind on Jonathan's tale and show myself properly impressed.

'And Sister Jane is become one of us?'

'Oh yes.' Jonathan's head jerked up and down for emphasis. 'She's had to. She was in no condition to be wandering on the road – apart from being beaten, I mean. Even with one of us either side, she could hardly get along.'

'She was sick?'

Jonathan paused, enjoying himself. 'We put her with Hepsibah directly, for it seemed there was no time to be lost, and by night there was a child born.'

I gasped. 'And lived?'

'Aye, that he did! The beating brought him on too soon, but he looks set to live. God has sent us a good sign – the uplifting of the oppressed and the coming of a little child.'

It was extraordinary what I had contrived to miss in my brief time away.

'A great mercy,' I remarked. 'And will we see more of these heroes, think you? Could they be from the village?'

'Discharged soldiers, most like. Here, can you get up now?'

I took the hand he extended to me and found that I hardly needed it. 'She didn't greet Ferris,' I observed as I got to my feet.

'No, most likely feeding the child. She's not an ill-looking lass, under the black and blue, but you and I are spoken for, eh?'

Again the spear of terror through my side before common sense told me he meant Susannah. 'O, are you there? Ferris is under the same mistake,' I told him. 'You'll find out your folly in time. By the way, what of the other sister? Is she betrothed to Hathersage?'

'That you must ask her.' He smiled at me. 'There, a better colour in your cheeks. I'd best get back to my chopping.'

'Many thanks, Jonathan.' Again I turned to the pack and this time emptied it apart from the precious washballs.

Making for the door, I met Ferris coming in with his own pack. He stepped round me without a word, and I thought, *If you want me to beg you will wait a long time.* Yet had he said to me, *Beg,* I would have thrown myself on the ground, and I walked away from the tent straining my ears lest he should call me back.

Some of the washballs I had meant to give to him. Instead I packed them in my bedstraw, hoping they would not be eaten by the little creatures God sends to torment us. Having hidden them I opened the hut door, and in came a fine rain. Water dripped from the turf roof and I determined I would not work in the fields that day. Something disturbed the rooks and they swirled in a cloud about the edge of the wood and settled again. The whole scene filled me with disgust at this foolish project, the filth of our daily lives, the risk we were wantonly running from Sir George. I had blinded myself, delivered myself into the hands of the Philistines. It came to me that there is more than one kind of blindness, and I recalled the last sweet night we had passed in London, thinking that had I known it was our last I would have savoured it like a water drop in Hell. I had not known, and the joy was fled, and I had broken the thing between us. I lay on the bed, looking out at the colourless sky, and gave myself up to sorrow.

~

'Will you eat?'

Someone was standing at the door of the hut, a woman; that much I could make out though it was almost dark. I blinked and thought I recognised Susannah's build.

'Jacob, will you eat? I kept some back for you. Jonathan says you fainted.'

'Not exactly.' It was indeed Susannah. Behind her, a couple holding hands, who must of course be Catherine and Wisdom. *Only wait, my turtledoves,* I thought. *It never lasts.*

'Are you ill?' Susannah went on. 'Jacob?'

I sat up and considered my condition. The headache of the morning had unclenched and there was a sensation of faint hunger where before had been nausea.

'Rabbit,' came Hathersage's voice. 'Jeremiah worked the snares while you were away.'

At least it was not beans. I stood up and stretched. 'Thank you, friends.'

We squelched over the sodden grass, trying not to slip. I wondered if I must now square myself to having Susannah, and not Ferris, as my dearest friend. That would be walking on wooden legs, and I would choose London and Harry rather than bear it, or rather not choose, for I *could not* bear it.

The fire was lit and most folk, having eaten, were sprawled about in talk. Jonathan was singing and though his voice was sweet he had much ado to remember the words, so that I ended by wishing he would stop. It was like the army, looking round at everyone but seeking only one. He was nowhere to be seen, and I sat among my *brothers and sisters* eating my heart out with a pain I could not share.

Susannah put a bowl of boiled rabbit and greens on the damp grass next to my hand. 'Come, get this down and you'll feel better.'

'Will I?'

I took up the bowl however, and a spoon she had brought me, having now lost the one he gave me at Winchester. The meat was not bad, and – wonder of wonders – there was enough of it.

'Jeremiah has luck with the snares,' I remarked.

'Not bad,' she replied. Then, touching my sleeve very softly so that none but us two perceived it, she went on, 'Brother Christopher eats nothing.'

I considered this, and her touch, in silence. Jonathan began on a new song.

'Supposing a friend carried a message?' she asked softly.

My throat tightened at this kindness. 'Then you would be my messenger, Susannah. But there's nothing to be done.'

'Pray,' she advised me. 'Pray, and wait.'

I wanted to ask, *Pray to the Devil*? For surely God could not want things mended between him and me.

As if reading my mind, she went on, 'Implore God for the best thing for all of us. What that best thing is, let Him decide.'

'I am so sinful, have such difficulty in humbling myself to His will,' I replied, half smiling.

'We're all in the same boat there,' she said. 'As for humbling you, He can bring that about without your aid.'

'Food *and* a sermon,' I teased her. 'My thanks for all of it.'

'Here, have some cheat.' She offered me a chunk of the hard bread. 'I have been thinking of you this last week.'

'Of me?'

'I was reading in my Bible and I made a note of the place, look,' and she pulled out something from her bosom. I looked surprised and she laughed. 'I do take things out as well as put them in. The washballs are gone.'

I took the piece of paper she offered me but could not read it in the dark, so folded it and put it up my sleeve.

'He comes,' Susannah whispered. 'Behind you.' I could not resist turning my head, and saw him crossing the field towards us, the fire picking out his yellow hair. He must have seen me also, for he stopped and sat down where he was rather than come near. There was a woman with him.

'That's Sister Jane,' said Susannah, who had followed my gaze. 'We thought it right to take her in for she was in such a state, but we said she could not stay unless Brother Christopher agreed.'

'When we began, I thought we were to do without kings,' I said. 'Wasn't that his idea?'

'Unjust, Jacob. I would not call him a king.' She turned her eyes on the two of them seated at the edge of the firelight. 'They look to be friendly. I'd say he will keep her.'

'He has always detested violence.' Thus I laid the stripes on myself, a man like a beast, who should marry with the beasts. All I needed was a Bible, where I might search out Susannah's chapter and verse, to find myself back at Basing.

God would have His will one way or another. In Heaven is no giving in marriage, but a Jonathan might find his Hepsibah there and smile in her face for all eternity. Even cut loose from the flesh, I was sure that Ferris's soul and mine would never so much as join glances. It is said the Devil devises particular and peculiar tortures for unnatural lovers; perhaps whenever one man looks, the other is looking away. Forever. *That* was already begun, in Ferris's avoiding me. I deserved it, I was wrathful, and my very love a violation. Suppose I had never spied on Nathan sleeping in his arms, would we now be virgin to one another? Would he have left me in the army? I could not find it in me to wish the thing had never happened, which is to say I could not repent of the sin. My foul heart clung to it.

There was a noise like a cat and I twisted round until I saw it was the woman's child, bundled in her lap. To her, I guessed, I must show as nothing but a black outline and I took the chance to study her more carefully. She wore a greyish dress which I thought I had seen on Catherine, but I could see little of her person. She looked to be as blonde as Ferris, the hair bunching in knots.

Ferris said something to her and then glanced over to me. I should have turned away and not shown myself watching them, but my gaze was riveted to the woman. She swung the child over her head and I saw it was dark-skinned as a little Turk. As she raised and straightened her body to do so the firelight fell full on her face, on the rounded lips and eyes. As Jonathan said, not an ill-looking lass. As a woman Jane Allen was exactly to my taste, for I had already married her once. She was no stranger, but my own wife Caro. There was a drumming in my head, and the air was grown thick. I saw spots and swirls before my eyes.

'The sickness returns on me. Pray excuse me,' I said to Susannah, hardly knowing what I did.

'I am sorry. Remember, trust in Him.'

'In the Devil, for *His* jests are infinite,' I returned.

'My friend—' Susannah broke off as I stood up. Like a fool I was risen without thinking and as soon as I did so the distant woman saw my figure against the fire. I froze. Her head dipped towards Ferris; he gestured in my direction and seemed to speak. I saw her hand go to her neck. Raging inwardly at my own stupidity, I stumbled back to the hut. In the darkness it seemed suspended above the earth of the field. I dropped onto the straw incapable of thought, something screaming over and over in my head: *There is a child, a little dark-skinned child, O God O God O God.*

~

I saw Sir Bastard once at Beaurepair kick a greyhound that came running up to fawn on him. It ran under the table and stayed there a full hour, sighing and turning over. Izzy said it was grieving but Zeb said more likely easing the bruises, while Godfrey's opinion was that Sir B. had split something inside and good as killed it. The beast lay staring at a chair leg. Not caring that he made himself the mock of us all, Izzy crawled beneath the table and cradled the dog's head while he waited for it to die. At the end of the hour it rose and stalked off, mysteriously mended.

Now I lay in the stifling darkness of the hut, the gentle brother who might have cradled my head lost to me. Should I go back and speak at once to Caro, before she faded like the ghost she was? But here my courage failed. Just seeing her close to Ferris had made me want to run.

Then there was Zebedee. I wondered would she sing the same

song as he had, and if not, which of them I would believe. If they had travelled together then the child was his, surely. But then, some things he had refused to tell.

I might have a son.

It came to me that here was a woman I had wronged, a woman but lately attacked on the road. Where was my compassion? I was worse than her assailants, for I was her husband. The previous summer we had crept giggling into the bridal bower, full of joyous anticipation, until I saw the horsemen coming. All her troubles since then had stemmed from me, and here I was, seemingly emptied not only of desire but also of common pity. The reason was, I had given everything to Ferris. My very walking and talking belonged to him, and yet I was one flesh with this woman.

'They look to be friendly,' Susannah had said.

I knew now what the dog had been doing as it lay apparently senseless. It had been thinking, thinking, thinking.

~

I woke in pain, a flickering in the base of my skull. The Voice was back, wheezing ashes, rising and falling within me so as to blot out the silent camp.

I have been watching for you.

To do me wrong, I answered. I got up off the bed; some colonist might be still awake, to bear me company.

We are best alone. Stay and learn.

The words were known to me even as they formed.

I see a serpent, wrapped about by your pity and sharpening its fangs.

The word *pity* pattered on the inside of my skull, like sand.

Vermin are for the killing. Remember Basing-House.

Ferris was compassionate there!

Will you swear to that? You were not with him.

I do swear it.

You bleed for him, eh?

No!

Yet you have made him cruel. He will never be other with you now.

It laughed, a noise like bubbles in silt.

Your little serpent is now a widow. I put that lie in her mouth and sealed her tongue. Shall I unseal it?

I told him lies.

He lied also. The Father of Lies spoke through you both, and put you to bed together. I tasted him with you.

I covered my ears.

Sweet hero. In Hell are special embraces for him, hot, unbreakable—

'Jesus! Jesus! Help me!' I screamed to block out the words, and fell back on the bed.

The hut dissolved. Lightning impaled the ground and I saw a jeering crowd all jostling one another. As they fell back into night I caught the scent of burning. The dark-skinned infant fell wailing and I knew it for a boy and mine but my feet were fused to the earth. Flame swelled behind the child like a wave of the sea and in terror I turned to run, but found myself in a narrow way between trees, where I knew there were snares. The thorns held me. I heard a squealing which might be from men or beasts – saw Ferris leap in the midst of a circle of men, as the bushes which pulled at me grew soft—

I understood I was in the hut, my hands pressed to my forehead and the palms all sweat. The drag on my limbs told me that I was fully dressed; sunlight pierced the walls. *Too late,* I said to someone, to God I think. The pity of it, when once I had been a boy who woke to pray, then ran downstairs to Father, my life perfect, a shining bowl. Since then I had filled the bowl with desolation. Myself and Ferris damned.

It might be that he was one of the Elect. He would turn from me, and repent; he and Zeb would gaze down from Heaven, cold angels, while I was torn and broken on the wheels of sin. He and Zeb—

Something tickled my wrist. I scratched at it and found the note Susannah had given me the night before. She had written on it in a blunt hand, *I Samuel 20, 11.*

I wondered where she had found the pen and paper. Ferris's Bible lived in my hut – he never read in it now, and I only kept it because it was his. Digging it out from the pile of belongings, I found the place.

And Jonathan said unto David, Come, and let us go out into the field. And they went out both of them into the field.

So I had been right about her, she had in a manner understood and this was her way of telling me. I could have wept on her bosom like a child. As it was I felt her kindness flow into me like an access of Grace.

I was in sore need of such comfort. I lacked courage with Ferris, yet to quit without having tried every means would be madness. Once, as we lay in bed, he had told me that when we lived together but as friends only, he had been so hotly drawn to me it was pain. Very well, I should work alongside him in the field, and act lovingly towards him. His barred *delight,* his untasted *honey*, should be constantly before his eyes, and his flesh should plead my case.

It was time I discovered if Caro meant to stay. If so, I would be both dove and serpent, until I understood what best to do. Taking a comb from the side of my bed I pulled it through my hair and beard. I then wrapped two washballs in a piece of cloth and set off to find my wife.

~

The rain from the day before had cleared the sky for a bright hard sun more fitted to early spring. In the field I saw the Tunstalls, bent to the earth, and Jeremiah not far off from them. No other soul was visible. I turned away, silently rehearsing my first words to Caro.

Outside the tent I found the child squalling on the grass and yearning towards me with its arms and legs. It should have been swaddled, and in this laxity I recognised one of Ferris's notions.

'I don't know your name,' said I, taking it up. There was not much of Caro in it, only the mother's roundness of cheek and lip, but that all babies had, even those whose mothers were very deathsheads.

'Black but comely.' I held the babe away from me to get a good look. It ceased screaming and seemed to regard me with curiosity. It was a Cullen: the skin alone was enough to settle that. Then the hand: I could see it would grow to be square in the palm, with a long strong thumb. That was my hand, but it was also Zeb's, supple and capable on the lute strings. The eyes were blue, but again, my own grey eyes did not mean I was not my father's son. Did it know me, I wondered, and I folded it to my breast.

The tent door flapped open and Catherine came out. 'Ah, there's a sight,' she said. Before I could stop her she was yelling, 'Sister Jane! Come out here!'

There was no time to do more than try for a calm face and a level voice. Caro was out and curtseying to me, as self-possessed as if we had never met. Bowing awkwardly because of the child, I observed bluish-brown marks around her temples and jaw. A deep unbroken scratch began at her ear, crossed her neck and disappeared into her clothing. I tried not to stare at it.

'This is Brother Jacob,' said Hathersage, who as always these days followed practically on Catherine's heels. 'Brother Jacob, Sister Jane.'

'I am very glad to meet you, Brother,' said my wife. Her shyly upturned face put me in mind of her as a little girl, sitting on Izzy's knee and whispering in his ear that Jacob was *thwart*. I hoped I was smiling.

'The lad bids fair to be as handsome as you, eh?' asked Catherine.

'A very pretty one,' I replied, thinking that this was like acting a play in a madhouse. 'A boy? What is his name?'

'Dan, Daniel,' said Caro. I had been dreading *Jacob*, or worse, *Zebedee*.

We stood at a loss and I dandled the babe as best I could. Ferris was nowhere to be seen.

'Have they made you a hut, Sister?' I asked.

'Not yet,' said Hathersage. 'We were not sure – Brother Christopher was away, and Sister Jane was afraid the men who attacked her, you know of this—?'

I nodded.

'—afraid they might return, and so she has been in with Susannah.' He waited, triumphant, while I worked it out.

'Then you and Catherine are espoused?' I asked him.

'We are,' his wife answered for him.

'I give you good joy – why – you must excuse me, no one—'

'I told folk to say nothing,' Hathersage explained. 'I wanted to give the news to Brother Christopher myself.'

'Well.' I jogged the child up and down. I would not ask them why they had waited for Brother Christopher's absence. 'Well! May you be happy. And Sister Jane, shall you live with us? What has Ferris to say?'

'Ferris is Brother Christopher,' Catherine explained to Caro.

'He says I may stay.'

'Then everything falls out pat. I have no special work on hand, come with me and I will build you a hut. You shall help pass the time by telling me your tale as we work.'

'We were making buttermilk,' Caro said, glancing hesitantly at the new spouses.

'O, no!' cried treacherous Catherine. 'Go get your hut built. You'll find Jacob a quick workman.' I saw she could hardly wait to get back into the tent with her Wisdom, who was even then slobbering on her neck.

'Come then, Sister Jane,' and I walked away in the direction of the wood, keeping a firm grip on the child which might or might not be mine. I heard her tripping over the grass behind me but she took no pains to catch up.

'Now then,' I said, turning as we reached the first trees. 'None can hear us.'

She gasped and stared around.

I went on quickly, 'I mean only that we can talk. I will do you no harm,' and put the child, which had fallen asleep on my breast, into her arms. Caro watched me without speaking. I found I lacked the courage to begin at once, so told her to wait while I went back for an axe, which in my confusion I had forgotten to bring from the tent.

'Stay here,' I urged.

'Where would I go?' she replied.

I slowed my steps as I came near the tent, treading silently until I pushed through the flap. There was a scuffle as I entered. Hathersage turned his body away from me, I saw Catherine's skirt drop, and both blushed exceedingly.

I took my time finding a suitable axe-head, fitting it to a shaft and sawing off some rope from the smallest pile there. At the door I hesitated as if in thought, returned and selected a turving-spade. Hathersage glared at me.

'I may need more rope,' I told them with the sweetest of fraternal smiles. 'Be careful, don't spill the buttermilk.'

The infant was beginning to whimper as I again approached the trees. As I laid down the tools I saw Caro arrange a shawl over her bosom, and knew she was about to put the boy to her breast. My child or my brother's child, I told myself. We were once like Catherine and Hathersage, I put my body inside hers.

Caro fiddled with her bodice. Daniel ceased whining and began to snuffle. A part of me wished my wife would let me see her giving suck, and I felt as if haunted by my own ghost.

The work proceeded slowly, for I went for the straight, slender branches that Harry would have chosen, but did not hurry in cutting them. Instead, I made much play with the axe and then reined in the force of each blow before it pierced the wood.

'Our bargain was that you should tell me your tale,' I said. 'I know in advance it will shame me.'

She regarded me curiously.

'I am not the man I was,' I said. 'I would do what I can to make things right.'

'Make things right?' she interposed. 'How will you—?'

'As best I can. But be so kind, my dear, as to tell me the rest. How comes it you are alone?'

Caro drew her shawl more closely over the child's head. 'Some take me for a widow. I may be one.'

'What—'

'I was abandoned by my husband.'

I paused in mid-swing. 'Did not you abandon him?'

She made no reply and it came to me that by 'husband' she must mean Zeb. O, how could we get over that ground! I hacked at the branch harder than I had meant, severing it. Having propped it against the bottom of the tree I went on, 'So why are you come here?'

'To find him. Someone told me he lived on the common.'

With this woman, of all others, I dared not talk of beatings. Besides, my ear had fastened on her 'To find him'. Could it be that Zeb had lied to me, and given her the slip – it might be because of the child? Enquiring through the lanes and taverns for one dark-skinned man by the name of Cullen, she had been sent after another. I cringed to think of her wandering in the whore-infested warrens near the dock, being pushed up against the wall, pinched and squeezed by the drunken scum of the town.

Then I recalled that wives lie as well as brothers. I would try her a little further. 'How did you get to London? With the gypsies?'

She glanced up in alarm at this guess. I had perhaps given myself away and she would now know I had seen Zeb. 'That's how it falls out in the old tales,' I added casually. 'And you have no money?'

'All gone.' She seemed to have no questions to put to me. Zeb had known I was living in Cheapside, and at whose expense. I wondered how much of it he had relayed to Caro.

'I was in the New Model, and then in London, before I came here,' I said. No need to tell her that the common thread was Ferris. Unable to whittle it any longer, I hacked though another branch. She shifted the child from the left breast to the right.

'I am very sorry,' I said. 'You did right to leave me without a groat.'

'Leave you?'

'However you want to put it. Forced away.'

Her face was puzzled.

'Never mind,' I went on, 'I will help you as far as I can.'

'That is most kind,' she said. I took my hand from the branch I was about to mark and stared at her. There was no mockery in her expression.

'One thing I do long to know.' It was mayhap too soon and she might not tell me for spite, but I could not hold back. 'Mother, Isaiah – what became of them?'

'How should I know?' Her face was now grown anxious.

I set down the axe. 'Caro, I'd sooner have truth. No matter how cruel. Are they dead?'

'My name is Jane.'

I looked about. There was none to overhear. 'Surely between us you could be Caro.'

'Why, Brother?' Her voice was perplexed. 'Don't you like my name?'

For an instant I doubted myself. I stepped up closer and examined her. She was tanned and bore the marks of poverty and violence but she was Caro.

I took her by the shoulders, gently so as not to alarm, and crouched before her, our eyes on a level. 'Lord, wife, we are in a pitiful plight! Though the fault be all mine, we must pull *together*. Do you know anything of them?'

She shook her head.

'Did you know I was here before we returned from London?'

'They talked mainly of Brother Christopher. But why do you call me wife? My name is Jane Allen. Do you feel well, Brother?'

'You come from Beaurepair, do you not? Your voice! You talk like me.' *Why*, I thought, *am I arguing thus? We are insane—*

Forcing myself on, I spoke into her face: 'Caro. That little child is – is my child. We must decide what to—'

'O no, Brother. The child is my husband's.'

I was dumbfounded. Did she mean that she would never again acknowledge me, even in my private ear? That the child was Zeb's and she would go about saying she was *his* wife?

Caro continued, 'You are not my husband. Why, Brother,' and she actually laughed, a pretty, innocent laugh, 'when you were presented to me just now by Brother Wisdom and Sister Catherine, you called me *Sister Jane* to their faces! You never said I was your wife!'

She had me there. Either she was more cunning than I had ever dreamt, and determined that I should never claim her, or my poor wife had lost her wits along with everything else.

'What was your husband's name?' My head felt tight as if a band were being twisted round it.

'Thomas Allen,' she returned, her face clear as the infant's.

'Very well,' I said at last. 'The child is your husband's, I see it now.'

Caro nodded.

'Tell me, Sister Jane,' I went on, for now I thought to discern whether or not her madness was feigned, 'does your son have the same eyes as your husband?' My notion was, that if she were feigning she would not pass by this chance to stab me by hinting that the child was Zeb's.

Caro smiled at me, head on one side. Something stirred in me at the sight of her wide gaze and rounded, trusting lips. I thought of days sitting on the stone bench, teasing one another, and of the fullness of a woman's breasts heavy with milk.

'Your son has blue eyes,' I prompted.

She answered me, '*I* have brown eyes, Brother. Do you see?'

Confounded, I rose and turned to go. There was nothing I could do; but in time she might recover her reason. We might even make it up.

Look where she laughs. She has excellent sport of you!

I whirled about without warning and caught a squint of amusement before she could veil it. Though she at once dropped her eyes, that glimpse sufficed. Caro was very far from mad. Like the dog and like myself, she had lain and thought, but to greater effect. She had hit on this vengeance: I could never know her more, or make the restitution I craved. In our society, I saw, was protection for her, and I felt with horror my own impotence. She could live by my side, share my food and fire, and yet not be my wife.

TWENTY-EIGHT

The Stuff of Jest

'POOR GIRL,' said Ferris. He frowned from under his old felt hat at Caro strolling in the field, rocking the little one in her arms and talking with Hepsibah and Susannah as they fetched the pails of milk up to the tent.

'The rest carry the milk while she does nought,' I said.

'That's right, Jacob, you stand up for Susannah,' put in Jeremiah.

It was not worth the trouble of gainsaying him.

'Where's Catherine?' asked Jonathan.

'Gone to look at marble,' I said, while the other two jeered his ignorance for the talk that morning had been of nothing else. Catherine and Hathersage had taken the ox-cart to the village to bespeak some marble from a stonecutter there. I guessed Ferris had dug into his private purse so that the sisters-in-law could at last make cheese. Hathersage, that reed of a man, was to help load samples.

All of the men were engaged in building a dairy, using the sods as before. I marvelled that Ferris could think we would be allowed to stay long enough to use it. Though the weather was cooler than it had been, it was hot work, and the long narrow shape of the thing did nothing to strengthen my faith. Already it seemed to lean inwards.

I placed myself at all times by Ferris's side or opposite him where he might see me, and observed him at his work. Twice or thrice I caught him eyeing my body, but could not make him meet my gaze, for he constantly moved away or changed places with another man. I followed him as constantly. It was easily done as if by accident, circling about the hut, filling gaps here and there. Sometimes I would pause to watch him cut wood or stack turf. I always knew when he had remarked me at this game, for he at once lost his natural grace. Thus did I hunt him.

The men fell to talking of the new arrival, downright gossip as to whether she would work with the dairymaids or in the fields with Hepsibah, and of whether Catherine would continue to work with her sister-in-law or would fall in more with Brother Wisdom.

'You are as bad as midwives,' said I.

Unabashed, Jonathan went on, 'My Hepsibah says Sister Catherine dislikes Sister Jane.'

'Oh, aye?' Ferris turned sharply towards him. 'And why might that be?'

Jonathan shrugged. 'She sees it whenever they are in company. As to reasons,' he pressed together two pieces of turf, 'best ask Catherine.'

'As soon ask the cow there,' declared Jeremiah. 'There's no *why* with women.'

The talk no longer struck me as empty. I at once determined to hear Catherine and Caro speak together. Aloud I said, 'How will we prevent soil dropping from the roof into the milk?'

Ferris ignored me.

'Brother Christopher has had some thoughts on that,' Jonathan answered. 'There will be a roof of planks, packed very close together, with sod on top.'

Jeremiah was of the opinion that the thing would not stand firm enough.

'One day it will be stone,' said Jonathan. We were silent a moment and I wondered why everyone behaved as if Sir George did not exist.

'Jane Allen,' said Ferris. He bent to take an armful of turf and straightening, laid it across the frame as if dealing cards. 'We must be gentle with her. It seems her husband was as cruel as the beasts she met with on the road.'

I held my breath and looked into his face. There was no special meaning there, no freshly disgusted glance at me, and I concluded that Caro's husband was still named Thomas.

'He beat her excessively?' asked Jeremiah.

Ferris frowned. I knew it was for that word 'excessively' but he went on without taking up Jeremiah. 'Something like. He persuaded himself she was unfaithful.'

'Could he not keep her indoors?' I asked. Jeremiah laughed.

'It was his own brother he suspected her with,' said Ferris. 'They all three lived together.'

Jonathan shook his head.

Dissembling vixen, I thought. *Well go on, torture me*. Soon would come the Unsealing threatened by the Voice, and I would leave. Let them all be spitted by Sir George, and Caro first on the point of the sword.

'Am I the only man working here?' asked Ferris. We bent again to the walls of the dairy, straining our muscles to the useless task.

'Her tale is one a guilty woman might tell,' I suggested.

'She seems to me not wanton,' said Jonathan. 'More innocent-like.'

Ferris said, 'She puts me in mind of my own wife.'

'Her hair has something of that colour,' I agreed, 'but Joanna was more beautiful.'

He looked as if that were a matter for debate, but would not answer me. Instead he said to Jonathan, 'When I see her with the child, I think, had Joanna lived—'

'Your boy would have been fair, like you,' I told him.

He raised his eyebrows at me and I flamed hot with the sense of my stupidity. Now he would think I had forgotten, whereas I had often thought with admiration of the shame he had borne for his Joanna.

'And we – we should all of us remember,' he went on. 'When Elizabeth left, she said that husbands and brothers are for protectors to women.'

'Husbands? None of us can be her husband if her first still lives,' I said.

'Her brothers, then,' said Ferris.

'Or something else,' said Jeremiah. 'It has been known, even under the husband's nose. Shall I race you to her, Jacob?' He winked at me.

'You are welcome,' I told him.

I saw Ferris scowl, and it came to me why Catherine did not like Caro.

~

The samples of marble lay on the grass and Caro patted the palms of her hands on one of them for coolness, as Hathersage had once pressed his palms to a table. On that occasion, I recalled, Ferris had covered the hands with his own. Now he stood back, listening to Susannah and Catherine's opinions of the stone. The rest of us, having each said which we found the handsomest, bent down from time to time to stroke the blocks and perhaps remember the touch of city life. There were two whites, a rusty-hued marble like polished sandstone and an adamantine black.

'Each is good,' said Susannah. '*This* is what we used in London and we always found it answered, eh Catherine?'

'The other white takes a higher polish and is more easily cleaned,' Catherine replied. 'Sister Jane, would you—?'

Caro lifted her hands from the 'other white'.

'See, there are none of those little pocks in it,' pointed out Catherine.

Susannah turned to Ferris. 'The cheaper will do just as well, Brother Christopher.'

'Perhaps,' he returned. 'What do the rest of you think?'

'Marble slabs in a sod hut! Too dear at any price,' I said. Susannah looked at me as if I had struck her a blow in the face.

'I am sorry, Sister,' I went on. 'I would see you content, and I suppose I have as great a wish to eat cheesecakes as the next man. But fitting out a dairy, well, that argues long years of use from it.'

'All that we do here rests on faith,' Susannah's gentle voice reproached me. 'Drainage, ploughing, everything.'

'We have been in God's hand from the start,' intoned Hathersage.

'The slabs can be moved into a better place, when we make one,' Catherine pleaded.

'But will we?' asked Jeremiah. 'Suppose we should be driven off, will we be let to go carrying the marble? I can't see it.'

'We will gain by keeping more milk as cheese,' Hepsibah said. 'But not enough to defray the cost of the stone. Not in years.'

'Those of you who are against having any,' Ferris said. 'Why did you join in building the dairy?'

'I was not thinking on the price of marble,' I answered. 'Other matters have occupied me of late.'

Ferris scratched his neck. 'You have put a deal of labour into the walls. Is not that a kind of argument in favour?'

'None,' I said.

The women looked indignation at me.

'We should have only what we can afford to lose,' said Hepsibah.

They debated a while, while I held aloof as having said all I wished to say. Hathersage was for, Jeremiah very much against.

'Sister Jane,' said Ferris. 'Have you no thoughts on this matter?'

I watched Catherine. Hepsibah had been right. The young woman's face became tense with dislike as she waited for Caro to speak against her.

Caro dandled the babe as if thinking. It seemed to me that she saw, and understood, Catherine's fear.

'It were pity to have two of us unable to practise their craft for the sake of a piece of stone,' said my wife. 'Women so skilled, too.' She turned her brown gaze up to Ferris. Catherine, waiting, breathed out.

Caro pleaded, 'You told me, there was much the sisters might do here.'

Admirable, I thought, seeing him smile as if warmth were welling up inside and about to overflow at his mouth.

'I will pay for the marble,' he said. 'No one else shall be asked to spare a penny. But I hope you will be content with the cheapest kind.'

Catherine and Susannah ran to him and embraced him. I thought Caro might do so, but she remained sitting on the grass, beaming her pleasure at the other women's good fortune, to let all see that she, at least, was innocent of ill will. Her eyes, however, shot admiration at Ferris when the sisters had let him go. He blushed and looked away.

Hathersage and Jonathan each took two samples and carried them towards the tent. Jeremiah, not best pleased, shuffled towards the turf hut to begin again on his pointless labour and the women moved off together, seemingly all friendship.

'A word, Brother,' I said as Ferris made to go.

He cut in, 'Before you start, the money is my own.'

'Marble will always come in for tombstones,' I struck back. 'But I warn you, our new Sister is feigning.'

'You are jealous now of a widow and her helpless babe?'

'The mother's not so helpless. Take care lest you end as her servant.'

'Why would I? I was never yours.' He began to walk away. I followed, trying to find the words which would soften him.

'You're always at my elbow, these days,' he went on. 'Don't think to wear me down.'

'I love to look at you,' I said.

~

I watched the dust on my skin sift itself into the water, clouding it as the motes that rise from sieved flour cloud the air. The basin beneath the spring was just big enough for me to rinse and splash in it, and if I went in quickly with one great gasp the iciness of the water seemed less. The leaves overhead, warmed by the sunset, glowed as if held in the eye of God.

Near me on the grass lay two piles of clothes, dirty and less dirty, and one of the washballs I had meant to offer Caro, but in the end had kept for myself. No one knew where I was, for this cleansing was my secret celebration.

The dairy was complete, and there would be no more of that particular misery. Ferris had wanted windows, frames spread with cloth, so that the place might have more air and light than was needful for the other huts. Jeremiah said it would weaken the sides. We had struggled to shape and fit the things until Ferris, exasperated, flung down a hammer, almost crippling Jonathan, and I said only a fool would dream of windows in such a place. He yelled at me that he had proven himself a fool over and over again, and then suddenly quietened, seeing the others' faces.

We finished with two windows, facing one another for ventilation. The roof also had been done as Ferris wanted, though Jeremiah and myself still thought it would not endure. Jonathan had nailed cloth to the inside of the planks, proof against creeping things. That was a refinement I approved of, as one morning I had found a large spider in some milk I had begged from Susannah and had flung the cup away over the furrows before casting up all the milk with much retching. The creature had seemingly not enough time to impart its venom to the milk, for I did not fall sick, yet the disgust it caused in me took many hours to go off. The marble was also fixed in place, and by its side a stone sink. The sisters-in-law had brought the churn and butter pats out from the tent. I guessed they were that minute at work, laying out their tools and perhaps training up Hathersage to the mystery.

By lying back in the water I was able to lower my head into it until my ears were under the surface and my face an island. Gazing at the transfigured trees above, I heard the strange throb and squeal underwater as I scratched the scars on my thigh. When I closed my eyes the noises filled my skull. *Suppose,* I thought, *a man were to drown—*

No, no. I jerked upright and began rubbing the washball on my head. It did a poor job, but took off some of the stink from my skin. I thought of Ferris, dirty and clean, and his smell. By the time I had rinsed out the hair I was in London and he was sitting astride my lap. I made myself finish my wash and stand up. Lonelier than a solitary ape, I shook out my seed onto the grass.

I wondered did Ferris do likewise. Did he think of me because he could not help it? I saw no weakening in him. Far from giving way, he had sprung or sidestepped every snare I had laid. Once, working opposite him, I surprised him in a look of longing but directly he met my eyes his face closed and he changed places with Jonathan. During the construction of the dairy he had suffered some renewed pain from his shoulders, and had to rest a day. I had therefore waited and gone in to him in the morning, when the others were abroad in the field, for I knew that he could be lascivious on waking. On seeing me come in he had sat up at once and bidden me leave his hut.

'Let me just ease your back,' I had begged, only to be told that should I stay he would call out. Walking away from the hut I heard him put the wedge in the door. He often did this now – I knew that, for I had heard the others talking of it one day as we hoed. I was working a patch on my own and the other three were a few rows off.

'So what do you reckon he's up to in there?' The voice was lowered but I knew it for Jeremiah's, salacious and relishing.

Jonathan answered, 'Where I don't know I don't judge. But it seems to me—'

He broke off. I heard Susannah's voice, low and urgent, and concluded that she had silenced him. But, I thought, neither of the men seemed to know he was keeping me out, or they would have spoken much more quietly than they did.

That day of weakness was the only one when he did not go to the inn for news. Letters came more often than not; brief, for Becs had little time for writing, but to the point.

Susannah and Hepsibah enquired frequently after Aunt, so Ferris took to reading out parts of the letters at the evening meal. It seemed that the patient grew stronger and could speak a few words, only it was hard to make them out. As he recounted such details his voice softened, and since he looked always at the page, I could freely drink him in through my eyes. These readings were thus some of my happiest, and most painful, times.

Sitting wrapped in the cloth, I waited for my skin to dry off, not yet ready to go back to the rest. Fears distracted me, and there was none I could share them with. All the last fortnight, over and against the futility of poles and sods and planks, I had been sorely tormented by the nightmare. Unable to move, I saw Ferris run over the fields of Hell and there fall, dragged down by demons. The Voice had whispered again and again that my cruelty had made a desert between us, and my deceit would be the end of us entirely.

I was slowly, sadly getting by heart my lesson, namely that I would never again be privileged with him. The secret that was Caro was eating within me, yet how could I open it to him – such an ugly wound as that? I pictured myself telling him of the wedding night, saw his eyes sharpen with bitter understanding, and I shuddered.

There remained but one small and miserable hope. If I waited, practising humility, a day might come that would make us friends again.

The sun was now entirely gone from the wood. Beginning to feel cold, I dressed as quickly as my damp limbs would let me. There would be no talk of Caro. Sloughing off the skin of falsehood would not do, for as the tatters were peeled away they revealed fresh sores beneath. If he would only put his arms round me, press his forehead to mine as Izzy used to, and say, 'I forgive you,' I would serve for him as that other Jacob served for Rachel, not seven years perhaps but all the time Sir George allowed. All he knew now was that I had seized hold of him. He refused to remember that I had loved him soul as well as body, loved him in the army before there was anything fleshly between us. He could not see this, because the first time he found me stretched out and the boys cutting my hair he knew what I might be to him. Cruel, to put the water to my lips and then take it away. My lover was a good man, and passionate, and unjust.

~

We ate after darkness had fallen for the sake of the cool air. I sat apart, watching the cooking fire and the figure of a woman, who could only be Susannah, moving back and forth as she tended some rabbits being stewed in a pot over the flames. At least, I guessed they were rabbits, since we had rarely anything else.

Jonathan and Hepsibah were on the opposite side of the cauldron, facing towards me: I could see their cheeks all orange. From time to time Jonathan jabbed the air with his finger to give emphasis to his speech. Catherine and Hathersage, shameless, were still in the dairy. I wondered did he have his hand, or something else, up her skirt. Earlier I had heard Jeremiah telling Caro about a Christmas pig-killing he had seen done so badly that the meat had been spoilt, and the slaughterman's head plunged in the midden by the enraged family who had looked forward a whole year to the roast. Caro's squeals of laughter vied for loudness with those of any dying pig. But now they had moved themselves closer to the fire and I was free to rehearse a speech which I could never deliver, a confession and declaration of love in one. I repeated it until the words were grown into my tongue.

A body dropped wearily onto the grass at my side. Ferris. I was at once torn between the pleasure of his sitting there, and the fear that he would soon go.

My friend's face was mostly in shadow, but I could see the liquid gleam of an eye, and the edge of his mouth, curving upwards. A gentle look. I waited like a boy for him to speak.

'It is good to have the dairy finished,' he began.

'Aye.'

'A weary job. But for you, we'd be at it for weeks to come.' The smile had got into his voice.

My heart quickened. The words were something like praise of my strength, and that way lay everything I wanted. I could not help myself, but turned towards him eagerly. 'I do what I can.'

A few seconds passed. Ferris sniffed and laughed. 'Lavender! You've been scrubbing yourself again?'

'Yes, why not?'

'I never met one like you for washing. You'll wear out your skin.'

'You had your own bed from a boy. I always had to share with others and I didn't like their smell.'

'What, not your own brothers?'

'More when we went for servants. Too many men stinking in one hot chamber.'

'Everyone sweats.' He said more softly, 'I've seen you sweat in your time.'

Something in his voice made me think not of work, but of his thighs and belly slippery against mine. The scent of stewed rabbit blew across the grass, bringing spit to my mouth.

Ferris shifted position and breathed in sharply.

'You are hurt?' I asked.

'Only a blistered foot.'

'Rest it.'

'It is nothing. In any case, I must go for Becs's letter.'

'I will.' I tried not to sound as if I were begging. 'Let me go, Ferris.'

'That's a thought. Hold, Jacob, I can give you the money now.' He fumbled in the dark and pulled up a purse from his belt. 'Take whatever's here – and some drink at the inn, you'll have earned it.'

His fingers brushed my palm in giving the purse to me.

'Will we ever hear from Sir Timothy Heys, think you?' I asked, afraid he would now go away. My breathing was uneven; I wondered if he heard that.

He sighed. 'No. But Sir George will keep faith all right.'

There was a hollow *bong, bong*: Susannah beating the side of the cauldron to call people to their food. Ferris and I groaned as one, tired after the day's work and almost fain to sleep on the grass rather than rise and eat. We struggled upright. I waited as he stood stretching his arms and legs, until he was ready to walk back with me.

We sat down by the fire and I held out his plate for Susannah to put rabbit onto it. She took my own dish with a wrench and gave me no more than anyone else. Usually I hoped she would be the one wielding the spoon for in general she favoured me when there was anything good to be had.

'You have this,' said Ferris after a while, putting half of his rabbit stew by my knee. He sprawled on his back in the grass. Almost at once I heard his breath catch, the beginning of a snore, and his arm, suddenly outflung, narrowly missed the food. I moved the plate away and watched him sleep, so near, so open and undefended, that desire sharpened in me like the knife he had held to my throat.

~

'Come, Susannah,' I urged. 'I spoke the truth as I saw it, without respect of persons.'

Susannah looked up from the cauldron, which she was scouring as we spoke. I saw charred bones from the previous night's rabbit among the ashes. Fresh little clouds raced across the sky.

'Where's your loyalty?' she demanded. 'All we asked was a piece of stone, and you spoke against it!'

'You still got it,' I said.

'No thanks to my friend Jacob. The money wasn't yours! I guess you wanted him to spend it on you.'

I walked away a few yards to hide my anger. Ever since the debate about the marble Susannah had been cold with me. She was unjust; it had never been my intention to thwart her.

'Susannah, let us be reasonable—' I turned to see her scrubbing the pot so furiously that her cheeks shook in time with her hand. Her jaw was clenched and her skin shiny from hair to breast. I saw from this bodily frenzy that had I been a woman, she would have flown at me. Susannah and I would have torn each other's hair and might well be friends again after. Ferris had once warned me in the New Model that being so big I should bear myself meekly, for a man insulted by me could not strike out and get it over with. When I laughed at this he grew insistent, telling me of men shot by their own side on the battlefield to pay off some longstanding score. Now I saw that women were to men as those others were to me, and this was why they resorted to poison. I stared at the cookpot.

'Even Jane spoke up for us,' Susannah ground out between her teeth.

Before I could stop myself I said, 'Don't get in too thick with Jane.'

'I could say the same to others,' she grunted.

The breath caught in my throat.

Susannah started on the outside of the pot. 'You don't go to him any more, do you?'

'Susannah,' I implored in a whisper, terrified lest someone in the huts overhear us. 'Don't destroy me utterly for the sake of a marble slab.'

'Well?' She did lower her voice somewhat. 'Is it off with the old and on with the new?'

'There is nothing less likely,' I said. 'Myself and Sister Jane!'

Susannah stopped her scrubbing and stood hands on hips. She frowned as if about to say something.

'Well?' I said.

She shook her head and rolled the pot along the ground until she found a dirty part. She then commenced rubbing at it. I could not make her out. Perhaps Ferris had been right after all, and there was more in this than injured friendship.

'I may talk with her but that's as far as it will ever go,' I said.

'It's nothing to me what you do,' she returned. The frantic scouring slowed, softened, as if she were trying out her hand against the metal. At last it halted altogether and she stood staring at me. There was some obscure matter in that look. If it were a declaration of love, I thought, I would not stay to hear it.

'Enough of Jane,' I said. 'For the marble, I humbly beg your pardon – nay, more—' I knelt on the grass and smiled to her. 'Come, hit me, and be friends after.'

Susannah left the cauldron, strode up to me and stood within striking range. She rolled up her sleeves over full, fleshy forearms, sturdy from years of lifting, and it came to me that she might well break my nose.

'Understand me,' she said. I looked up into her face and saw the loose flesh hanging in swags, making her aged and ugly.

She went on, 'What I know I will keep close.'

'Your kindness, Sister—'

'You're not the only one to consider. But Wisdom has come close to stumbling over you, so has Catherine, and I decoyed them away. Now, you may watch out for yourself.'

'There is nothing to catch me at,' I said.

'I didn't say there was, I said I will do no watching out for you. Understand?'

I nodded.

'Remember, then,' she said.

'Enough! Come on, I'll close my eyes. Hit me and get it over with.'

I did close them, stiffening my jaw in anticipation of the blow. I heard her step back, and I clenched my fists. Nothing happened. The thought crossed my mind that she would kiss me instead, and at this idea I could not help smiling.

'You're a fine big fellow, eh?' There was new anger in her voice. 'Presenting yourself like that. Stinking with pride.'

'Do it,' I said.

She cleared her throat twice, raking the phlegm. Was she going to spit at me? I wanted to say, 'Hurry up,' but was prevented by a sudden fear that she was waiting for me to open my mouth so she could spit in it.

I heard a sound some feet away. Perhaps someone else was come. I raised a hand to cover my lips. 'Susannah?'

Silence, apart from a soft wind in the grass. I opened my eyes to see her walking to the cauldron. She began scouring it again, her back to me. Scrubbing dry lips on my shirt, I got up hoping none had seen us.

~

About mid-morning Ferris took me over to the sough.

'Supposing Sir George lets us live,' he began, 'we should consider winter drainage.'

'Jonathan says this is beyond repair,' I said.

He smiled at me. We were standing on the edge of the tumbled pit, the ruins of his first great project. Grass lay in limp ribbons over what had been bare earth, and at the bottom of the bowl there was a kind of quagmire, the water thick and greenish.

'A frog Heaven,' he said. 'Still, it drained off the field a bit. You can see the difference.'

'The frogs will put you down in their histories,' I answered.

'Though men will not. That's your meaning, eh? I will never be famous.'

'Famous men have bad deaths,' I said.

'This is a sough, Jacob, not the Tower of London. Do you think we could smooth out the sides and make it a pond?'

We walked around it. 'The field could do with more,' I admitted. 'But will we be here in the spring to profit by it?'

'No,' he said at once.

'Then why, in God's name?'

'To see the thing through to the end.'

'I don't see the good of it.' I hacked at the edge of the sough with my foot and some crumbling clods dropped away into the slime at the bottom. 'Unless Sir George has died,' I said. 'He's choleric, by all accounts. Or he might be gone to war.'

'The heir will be no kinder to us, God rot him.' Ferris clapped his hands together. 'Forget them. I have a notion of a long trough between here and the field, lined with tiles. There are Dutch ones to be had in London, an excellent design.'

He looked up at me, eyes bright, then faltered. The word 'London' festered in the air between us.

'You will go see Aunt and bring back some tiles,' I said, as a man might say, 'You will go to Paradise in my stead.' It was a feat of courage to bring out that word 'you' in place of 'we'.

'This time.' He looked kindly at me. 'But when Aunt is better, Jacob, you could fetch things. And stay a while in town, since you like the place.'

I nodded, unsure what London would taste of without him.

'Well,' he went on. 'I propose that we begin the ditch now. We will have to break off for harvest, but we should do what we can before the ground grows hard.'

'For nothing?' I asked. But I began to warm to the idea. Did he mean, I wondered, that the two of us would work apart from the rest? The hope aroused by that thought was agonising.

Ferris said, 'Worst of all would be to fail of our own cowardice.'

We walked towards the centre of the camp.

'The corn is coming on well,' he said.

'Too dry. We need rain.'

'Have you been for the letter yet?'

'I will do it now.' I went towards my hut to collect the money, feeling an unease somewhere at the back of my head. It was not the Voice, but something else, and it picked at me like a needle probing a wound. At the doorway I stopped and looked back.

Ferris was watching me. 'Are you going now?'

'As I said.'

My unease grew. Was it because he was come round so quickly after so great a rage against me? Or it might be an ill omen. I would be struck down by someone on the road, maybe even the three who had preyed on Caro: a cudgel on the back of the head and my peace with Ferris sealed forever. I started across the field towards the inn. At the hedge, where we had watched Harry and Elizabeth disappear with their anvil and mule, I looked back. He was standing motionless near the huts. Having rounded the hedge I waited a few seconds and then looked again. Ferris had moved off towards the wood. I hesitated. To go back for no good reason was to act the fool, and I should have the whole journey to make again. Best fetch the letter, if there was one.

It was hot work walking. I endeavoured to overcome the turmoil in me by admiring the swell of the hills and the deep colour of the fields on either side of the road. How wonderful, I thought, if a man could walk here and say, *All this is ours, for we work it*, instead of *This land all belongs to My Lord So-and-So.* Then we might stroll or dig or sit us down to rest with a fishing rod, and no one to drive us off. *This is ours, as far as the eye can see.* No working for hire, for the good things of the earth would be our own. Ferris had said no freedom by Act of Parliament counted unless a man could readily find himself in food and other necessities, instead of selling his body to another to get coins before he could feed. And he further said that it was surely no part of God's plan, if God there be, that the creation should not eat unless they could lay hand on a piece of metal (a thing in itself inedible) stamped with a tyrant's name and likeness. For what was the money, in comparison with the man starving for the lack of it, but a lifeless, soulless part of the creation? And the man but the finest and most precious?

Fine and precious he was. I crushed down certain images which, born of my heat and the few drops of encouragement he had lately sprinkled on me, were springing up more and more luxuriant.

The pamphlets were right, I reflected. *Though the reading of them brought us to grief, they were the work of righteous men.* Then I thought how the colony was also the work of a righteous man and would bring me more grief. With suchlike thoughts I tormented myself the rest of the way.

Heat swarmed up from the walls and flags as I entered the yard of the inn. A huge rambling rose clung wantonly to one wall, sweetening the blend of horses and sour yeast which hung about the place. As always, the inner part, dark after the sun, brought on an attack of blindness until the eye steadied itself. A pale young girl came down the stairs to tell me that the landlord was in the back talking to the ostlers, and did not allow her to give out letters to people.

'But he will be back directly he is finished,' said she.

'Then give me some ale if you please.' My throat was like sand. I went to sit in a corner booth and she brought me the drink. I could no longer shake off the feeling that had dogged me ever since I set out for the inn. Well, I had not been attacked on the road and I did not think it would come to that on the way back. Could there be a letter to say that Aunt was dead?

There was a juddering at the bar door as someone tried to come in but was hindered by the bottom end of the door catching in the frame. A crash followed as it flew open, freed by a kick, and banged against the wall on the inside.

'God damn it, go tell Hector he's to come and take care o' this *now*,' came an exasperated voice. 'I told him Tuesday—' the angry noise broke off and I saw the landlord's face behind the bar, peering over towards my booth.

'Come for letters,' the girl said. I swallowed the last of the ale and advanced towards them.

'Ah yes, sir, I recall you.' Though the man smiled, his eyes were all over my torn and stained clothes. 'Is Mister Ferris unwell?'

'Nothing serious. He has a blistered foot, and would rather I did the walking.'

'Very wise,' the man said. 'There *is* something for you.' I gave him the money and he groped under some cloths, brought out a paper addressed to Ferris and put it into my hand.

'Won't you read it, Sir?' he asked as I made to step away from the bar.

'I am not Mister Ferris,' I returned, puzzled at the question.

'I think you *should* read it, as you are a friend of his.' He was staring at me. All of my fears and premonitions rose in a wave until the small man at the bar seemed as sinister as the Destroying Angel.

I turned the note about in my hand. It was not Becs's writing, yet there was something familiar about it. Doctor Whiteman?

'Go upstairs, Nelly,' the man said. Nelly disappeared at once.

Then I saw the seal, and trembled. A common device, in red wax. Fingers shaking, I fumbled to get inside the thing, tearing the folded corners.

Sir,

You are to be rid from the common around the Seventh of July. I cannot be exact as to the date, so take the road now, while your legs are still unbroken. Believe me when I say I have witnessed the business before and wish never to see it again.

Your friend

I recognised the character, and the paper and ink. 'What date is it today?' I asked.

'Let us see.' He consulted an almanac hanging from a nail in the beam. 'Today we are the first of July. Shall I get you more ale?'

'No.' Six days. I stared at the initials JW newly carved into the wood of the bar. Perhaps I would meet with JW sooner than I had reckoned on.

'It was brought by hand,' the man said. 'Let me fetch you something.'

'No. Thank you – thank you—' I ran over to the door and out into the sun, blinded all over again. Out of the courtyard and on the road I kept running, from a frightened animal's need to move. *While your legs are still unbroken.* My bodily strength was all I had. To be crooked, to walk with a limp—

I slackened suddenly. When Ferris came out with me that morning to the sough, he had not limped.

It is nothing, he bound the foot up in rags, I told myself. But my prickle of unease was grown to a nausea. Again I heard him ask, *Are you going now,* and saw Susannah's hands move uncertainly on the cauldron.

Is it off with the old and on with the new?

Now you may watch out for yourself.

She had said enough, had I been able to hear it. I began running in earnest, loping along the road despite the heat and glare. Sweat drenched me, my breath came like an overworked horse's and the stitch in my side would have frightened me into stopping had I not been filled with a terrible rage which fed off the pain. I could have run barefoot over broken glass.

The flat dry earth made for speed. Soon the haystack came into sight, and the huts, rising and falling as I jerked my head about. Foam gathered at the corners of my lips. I charged at the colony, striking off from the earth, elbowing the air. The last field before the crops was downhill, and tussocky; I plunged over it, bounding unevenly until I came to the cultivated patch. Hepsibah and Catherine stood near the carrots. They turned and saw me, came towards me, and I ran between them, pushing through their shouts and along the furrows, over the last section of grass to the wood. I was staggering now. Down the green track I went, slipping, crashing, the brambles lashing at my hands and face. Then I was full length on the grass with a tremendous slam all the length of my body and an explosion of pain in my mouth.

Trembling from the shock, I raised myself onto hands and knees. At once there was a stab in my right arm. I had bitten the inside of my cheek in the fall, and my chest and belly were stinging from the ground. Heat surged in my face, blowing the skin full of blood. I felt I would never rise again.

It was cool under the trees. Birdsong trickled above me, and the air fanned delectably on my bursting head and neck. Gradually I ceased gasping, and was able to sit back on my heels. The inner part of my forearm had a blackthorn twig buried in it, the spines pressed full length into the flesh. Hissing between my teeth, I drew it out and stared, revolted, at six reddish-black punctures in the skin before rolling my sleeve down over them to take up the blood. At last, my breath under command, I rose, finding a painful scrape on each knee. Then I went forward slowly, quietly, some hundred yards or more, until I could just catch the sound of a woman's voice. For the last twenty yards I crept with extreme care so as not to frighten my turtle-doves. He was foolish – O, I would never have thought him so foolish! After all his care to decoy me away they were in our secret place, and in no condition to hear me approach. The run had emptied me of strength, else there might have been murder done. As it was, I stood and listened, and after a while I shook with silent laughter. For after all, it was the stuff of jest.

There was once a man who heard his wife and her lover together. He heard the secret things the wife whispered to the lover, and said only, 'Yes, that is she'. But then the lover pleaded to be touched, and the husband clenched his fists; and when the man cried aloud then the husband's nails cut deep in the palms of his hands.

TWENTY-NINE

Well-Loved Games

ON MY BED lay a stalk of the ripening corn. I took it up and tore off the head, then bent the straw into halves, and each half into three pieces.

First of July. Breaking the straw into six along the folds I had made, I inserted one of them into the earth at the side of my door.

Take up the head. It is the seventh. It lay in my hand, too dry no matter what Ferris said. I squeezed until the grains fell away, crushed. *It is to be a Golgotha.* The pieces of straw lay on the ground, condemned, until I should take them up. *You are, and always have been, My own. By this may you see it plain,* said the Voice. *How could any other head of corn come into the wall, here? The others may dance and shine in the field but the choice is made, unalterable, as between the wheat and the tares.*

He must know by now. Hepsibah and Susannah had seen me run into the wood. None was come seeking me these five hours though they were supposedly digging new trenches. Send Jacob to London. Ha.

Under a pile of sacking in the corner lay the note, blurred from rubbing against my skin but still legible. It might stay there and the hut be thrown down over it, until the day it dissolved into earth, like Christopher Walshe. I could present it to Ferris and watch him run about, bruising himself with terror. But then – I hesitated. Whatever came of the colony, if they both lived he would take Caro to town, and that meant he would never shelter me again. This sank into me with such iron teeth, and cost me such a gush of heart's-blood, that

I rested my head a moment or two on my knees. So soon, to go behind my back so soon. On that morning when Nathan found himself deserted, he probably woke from a dream of loving-kindness, thinking the pack beneath his head to be Ferris's arm.

I endeavoured to reason, to blunt the edge of my pain. I was not entirely powerless, for it lay with me whether they would marry. I had only to say a few words and put my hand alongside the child's. As for my wife, I had music for her ears also. His having so treasured his *honey*, his *Samson* that I ate at his table and lacked for nothing. His proficiency with mouth and arse.

There is a nobler and more terrible thing. Say nothing. Let them be taken unawares.

I stared at the scattered grains, and shivered.

~

When the cauldron was struck to tell us the food was ready, the day was far from over. I guessed the women, weary of sweated labour in the field, had begun their preparations early.

My mood was altered. The heat and blood of my grief were gone off; I was passed over to a colder mode of suffering, and seemed to walk as lightly as my deceiver as I went silently over the grass. Sitting nearer the fire than usual, I smiled at each person whose glance I caught, ready to sing or dance with anyone who would partner me, and slit their throat after.

Susannah was on kitchen duty again, and with her Catherine. The older woman doled out my share somewhat more graciously than last time but made no attempt to speak with me. *So this is it*, I thought. *You see me in extremis and say nought.*

We were back to the bad old days of pottage, flavoured with thyme from the fields. I sat between Jeremiah and Jonathan, both of whom were very Esaus in their relish for it.

'You were missed this afternoon,' Jeremiah said to me. 'We have begun the hutches for the grain. Come winter we'll raise a bigger store.'

'Come winter we won't be here,' I said. 'Tell Ferris to save his strength and yours.'

He stared at me. 'Susannah said you was sick.'

'I am sick. And we won't be here come winter.' I hated his mouth full of pottage, hated the half-chewed paste pressed up against his teeth and the snorting breaths he took as he ate.

'Do you think Sir George will drive us off, then?' asked Jonathan.

'I know it.' I turned my eyes in his direction, for he ate more daintily than Jeremiah. A stone crunched between my teeth and I eased it onto my tongue so as to spit it out on the grass. He went on, 'Where is Brother Christopher?'

'Why ask me?'

'We thought you were in the wood with him. You were not, then?'

'I have been in my hut.' It struck me that Ferris might be run from me while I was planning to run from him. But no, his stubbornness permitted no escape. I had him in a corner, and could inflict what injuries I pleased.

He was there. I saw him step over some tools lying by the fireside and look about to see who had left them. Caro was not with him. He glanced in my direction and went over to the cauldron to pull out the pot from inside it, helping himself before Susannah could rise from the grass, then sat down cross-legged to eat. I knew he had seen my eyes upon him. Let him wait, and wonder what form my vengeance would take. Since our fight in Cheapside I had understood that he had a particular fear of being *held* and hurt. The Voice had promised embraces hot and unbreakable. It knew.

Catherine came up to ask would I help Susannah, Hathersage and herself with the drainage ditch near the dairy; the ground, she said, was hard and they had found large rocks just under the surface. I answered that I would think about it. She was offended and went so far as to tell me I was eaten up with pride.

'I see you have been talking over my sins with Susannah,' I said. 'Did she tell you all of them?'

'I speak for myself, but I'll wager she thinks as I do,' squeaked Catherine.

I laughed at such assurance. 'And what *do* you think?'

'We should all help one another.'

'Help you empty Ferris's pocket! And I'm called proud because I won't do your work. What's Hathersage for?'

She muttered low, as if the words were themselves a betrayal, 'It needs someone stronger.'

I was weary of the Domremys and their preaching fool of a man. 'I tell you what,' I said. 'If Hathersage himself will come and ask me, using just those words, I will do it.'

'O Jacob, how can—'

'What!' I said, 'Surely he's not proud?'

Catherine rose without further speech and walked away.

Ferris ate with relish. He was perhaps recalling *her* praises and finding hope again for the future, when he should be thinking over the coming encounter with myself. Men are so stupid, so slow to learn that in the end this little fleshly hope means nothing.

He put away his bowl and took some beer from the common jug. I watched him walk over to me, a cup of beer in each hand.

'Here,' he said, and handing me one of the cups he lay down on the grass beside me. Taken aback, I found my face returning his smile. Clearly he did not know himself detected.

Susannah had not warned him, or had not known he was in the wood. Catherine, I was certain, would not have guessed what he did there, for though more jealous than her sister-in-law she was much slower witted.

'You had a hot walk of it today,' Ferris went on. He took a pull on the beer. 'Won't you have some, Jacob? You should, it's good for once.'

I drank to gain time and found he was right.

'What's that?' he asked. I frowned, not understanding, and he touched my chin. 'A bruise, or dirt? You look as though someone hit you.'

'A fall.' I held out my forearm and showed him the punctures in it, now reddish-blue and angry.

'Ah—!' He drew in his breath so that a man would have sworn the sympathy was honest, then stroked the pads of his fingers over the wounds. Hatred near choked me.

'We must get you some ointment,' he said when he had finished pawing.

'It is nothing,' I murmured, 'they are closing over already. And what of your blisters?'

'My blisters are – better. Yes, better.'

'So you will want to go to the inn tomorrow.' *Now I have you. And what of your dear aunt? You have not yet asked.*

His eyes skidded away from mine. 'I have still some pain.'

'Except when you're lying down?' I suggested. At this he could not help looking back at me, but I was ready with a face full of concern. 'They don't give you pain now?'

Ferris shook his head.

'I have something to tell you,' I said.

'Some message from the inn?'

'It needs privacy.'

Ferris hesitated.

'Shall we go to our secret place?' I asked.

He stammered something. I had again drawn blood, and was beginning to enjoy this game of pricking him. We got up and walked over to the trees, Ferris now going with a limp. The sight of it made me itch. I thought, *I could put an end to him, and none the wiser.* Make him beg for mercy. I considered what I would do after that, and saw in my mind's eye the basin beneath the spring.

'Jacob?' He peered up into my face. 'It grows late. This is far enough.'

'I can find the way back in the dark,' I said.

He sat down within sight of the others ana though he smiled, the joy was gone out of it. I saw he would go no further with me.

'Come, your message.'

'Not that precisely,' I said, seating myself next to him. 'But a confession. You being my truest friend.' That was another dig with the knife. 'You know I left home about a year ago.'

Ferris was silent.

I went on, 'I was contracted to a young woman, a servant. But I had to flee the house.'

He nodded.

'For murder.'

Ferris stared at me.

I said, 'A woman saw what I did, but she got away.'

'Got away?'

I waited and let my meaning sink in. 'Aye. She was a whore, with child by Zeb. He was best rid of her.'

Ferris winced despite himself. I smiled inwardly to think that had he understood me in full he would have got up and run. I continued, 'But my tale is all disordered, I must first tell you about the killing of the boy.'

'You told me,' he broke in at once. 'Self-defence.'

'Is that what I said?'

'Indeed you did.' His voice, breathless and thin, told me how his body had stiffened.

'I drowned him.' Here I paused, to enjoy the sound of Ferris panting. 'Kept a grip on him, held him down until he breathed water. He was small,' and here I paused again, before adding, 'like you.'

'You were – you said, a man – O God.'

'Would you like to know why?' I offered pleasantly.

Something like a sob came from him; I took it for 'yes' and brought my face very close to his. 'He thought to make me his fool.'

Ferris's eyes were grown dark against his bloodless cheeks. He made suddenly as if to rise but I was ready for that, and I caught hold of his arm.

'So we had to leave, for that and for some pamphlets we had. It was the day of my espousal. That was how you found me, in my wedding clothes.'

'Prince Rupert.' He bowed his head, then jerked it upright. 'Why tell me this now?'

'I want no secrets between us.' I smiled at him and though he could barely see me in the thickening darkness, the smile spilled over into my voice. 'There are none, are there?'

'None.'

He could not keep a quiver out of that word. The struggle in him excited me. I thought of dragging him into the wood and there forcing him to the ground, but I put it to one side for the time being.

'It's something that you talk to me again.' I patted his arm. 'And you let me go to the inn. But you were kind from the day we met.'

'I gave you water and got you a pike, that was my kindness. Now let me go.' So unnerved was he that he sounded like Nathan. I loosed my grip and Ferris was on his feet at once. Not even Sir George, I thought, could have frighted him better.

'Another time I'll tell you about my wife,' I called after him as he walked away.

He could have told me about Caro. He had chosen to keep the thing dark, and continue his double game. Very well, let him look to his cards, for the hand I had been dealt at the inn would sweep away card-table and all.

'Ferris!' I shouted, and dimly saw his moving figure pause in the dusk. 'Let me go for your letter tomorrow.'

'Yes, yes!' He quickened his pace.

Until I knew my own mind, he must be kept from talking with the landlord.

~

Morning, and the second stalk lay alongside the first, poking crudely out from the sod as if part of some lunatic scheme for sowing corn within doors. After a dream in which I slit the boy's throat and found that I had killed Ferris, I had woken in the dark and walked out between the huts for the air inside mine seemed full of my fear. Stopping by his, I heard a snore. At least he was not in the fields with *her*, but that brought him no nearer to me. The sky was clear, the stars brittle. *Where is God?* I thought. *Everywhere we see evil and misfortune.*

As a child I once asked God to give me a sign, promising that if I received it I would tell everyone. The sign I never received, and when I told the minister he said that I should be beaten for demanding such a thing, as if I were some juggling Papist. Did I not have the whole of revealed religion set before me in the Bible? If that would not suffice me, surely I would not respect a sign. Now I turned my face up to the Heavens. *Do You see me at his door? What will become of us?*

I went back to my lonely bed, and was seemingly not long asleep when I was called by my familiar incubus. He sat astride me, said I was forgiven for he had always loved me best, kissed and fondled me until I woke, wet and aching, to find I had poured out tears as well as seed.

Day leaked through cracks in the hut. It was worthless, for nothing remained to do. I had no wish to help with the work, no loves to prosecute, not even a farewell to utter. There remained five days, and as I lay in the straw scratching fresh bites I knew I could not face the time out.

The key still hung from my neck. The ribbon had originally been red, and was now a rusty blackish-brown. I would go first to the inn; let him get his amours out of the way. Then I would dig up the box of money. Should he want more, he had only to get to Cheapside. The rest must forage for themselves, it was the common fate in our times. I wondered what was become of Botts, and of Rowly. Eunice Walker was most likely Eunice Keats by now. Their lives had moved away from me like the roads around the common, over the hills and out of sight: they were all of them despicable, yet all of them skilled beyond me in that they knew how to live without Ferris.

If he married Caro he would raise the child. It was, I told myself, most likely Zebedee's. I only hoped Zeb might one day cross their path in town: I pictured his face on seeing Jacob's *keeper* with Caro and in charge of his own son. If Zeb wanted Daniel he would take him, and Ferris, being nowhere able for him in a fight, would be lucky to come off still walking. This thought, which once would have pained me, now made me smile, and that smile was the measure of my misery.

I rose and dressed. It was still early, for the day was bluish. I thought it would be cool and hoped we might have some rain, then remembered it would make no difference.

The fire was unravelling sulkily in smoke. Hepsibah bent over it, a soot-stained kitchen demon.

'God give you good day, Brother Jacob.'

'Is there any pottage over?' I asked.

'Look in the tent.'

I went in there and found a small bowl of it. There was a spoon lying nearby. I plunged it into the mess and ate three or four spoonfuls without tasting them. At once I wanted to retch, but by breathing quietly and taking a little beer in sips I kept the food down. I could not, however, swallow any more. I carried the things over to the fire.

'Thank you, Brother.' She came to take them from me, and paused, looking into my face, the pot only half given into her hand. 'Are you well?'

'I have been better.'

'Your eyes are bloodshot.'

I shrugged. 'Lack of sleep.'

'I can give you something to bring it on,' said Hepsibah. There came to me the memory of stroking Ferris to sleep and I pushed it away. She went on, 'We all of us need rest.'

'No, thank you. I have a most important work on hand, fetching letters for King Christopher.'

Hepsibah stared at me. 'You are not yourself. When he sees you I'm sure he'll not even send you for a letter.'

'Whatever he says.' I laughed, but she did not join in. 'Tell him I'm in bed,' I said, 'and under his command.'

Again she stared. 'I have valerian for sleep. Do you feel feverish, Brother?'

'No.' I must be haggard indeed, I thought, for as a rule the colonists never concerned themselves with my health, but treated me like a piece of iron.

As I crossed the grass back to the hut the early morning cold pierced me. My walk in the night, the dreams, all seemed to have cut into my strength. Perhaps I would fall sick unto death.

He will look into your grave, his hand clasping hers. They will feel themselves free.

Will he recall my kisses and embraces as they shovel the earth over?

What does it matter? You will be with Me.

In the hut I lay with my knees drawn up, arms across my chest, unable to get warm. The Voice continued in whispers as I lay half asleep.

I will use you at leisure.

Some time later I woke to find a jug by the side of the bed. I reached out and put my finger to it. It was no hotter than the surrounding air, and the light still fell into the hut but much more brightly and through different cracks. The flesh felt strangely heavy on my bones and the bed, with all its fleas, was become delectable. As I turned myself over there was an ache in my arms and legs like the beginning of cramp, or like a man's thumb driven into a muscle expressly to give pain. My skull suddenly tightened, but before I could lie down I felt a great longing to drink. The jug had what looked to be crushed roots in the bottom of it: valerian. I took a mouthful, then remembered that I had to get to the inn before Ferris, and that the potion would bring on sleep. I emptied the jug onto the earthen floor before I could be tempted to drink the rest.

Sitting on the edge of the bed, I tried my legs. When I attempted to stand upright, I fell against the wall of the hut and scraped my face on it. I dressed, wondering if Ferris and Caro were doing the same, and remembered they would have been up and afield hours before. I heard myself laugh aloud. *Go for the letter, Jacob.*

I stepped delicately out from the hut and shaded my eyes, the sun being overhead. They were engaged in digging the new ditches, and I saw at once that he was with them. Caro stood nearby. It was hard to cross the field keeping strong and steady in my walk. As I approached the line of diggers, folk stopped and leant on their spades, glad of some excuse for taking a rest.

Hepsibah came up to me, looking anxiously into my face. 'Did you find the medicine?'

'Aye.' I smiled at her. 'And slept better for it.'

'Brother Jacob!' That was Jonathan. 'We thought you were sick.'

'As you see, I walk and talk. I lacked sleep, that is all.'

All this time Ferris had kept digging as if I were not there, displaying to the whole colony the coolness between us. I wondered if Susannah had taken her revenge after all, and if some now knew it for a lovers' quarrel.

'I am very much better,' I said, 'but would not wish to dig just now. Perhaps, Brother Christopher, I might go for the letter?'

He reluctantly turned towards me. I saw by his face that he disliked that 'Brother Christopher', but I liked it just then better than 'Ferris', which to me meant love. He hesitated, full of mistrust, while Caro, thinking herself unobserved, glanced from one of us to the other.

'Jacob ought not to walk in this heat,' Hepsibah protested.

'What do you think, Jacob?' He regarded me solemnly. 'Do you find yourself well enough?'

'I will go slowly, and be the stronger for the exercise.'

Ferris unknotted the small purse he wore at his waist. He took out some change and paused; I watched him struggle with himself. As I had expected, lust vanquished prudence, and he held out the money. 'Pray do not hurry. Rest at the inn before coming back.'

'Have no fear,' I said.

As I turned and began my journey over the fields I heard him say, 'This ditch-digging tires us out of all reason. It is close on noon, shall we break for a while? I would sooner cut wood in the shade.'

This was a well-loved game, one that I knew by heart. Caro would not go to him directly, he would have tutored her too well for that. She might not even be able to join him. But he would be ready another time when she did come, and their delight all the fiercer.

I paced myself on the road to the inn, for I felt much weaker than I had revealed to the others. Most of the time I was as good as blinded by the light bouncing up from the stones of the road; once I almost sank down on the grass, but recovered. Let him go to her, let our place be theirs. I should take every gold piece in the box. Back in London, I should find myself work, and in time come to forget him.

I passed very quickly through the inn yard, with its rosebush and underlying stench. The pale girl was elsewhere. The landlord came in through the same door as last time, Hector having seemingly repaired the thing for it opened meekly.

'Ah!' the landlord said when he saw me, 'there is another of these,' and he handed me a letter. I saw at once from the paper and the neat hand that it was from Cheapside, and I paid him the money.

'There's a deal of writing to your friend,' said he.

'His aunt has been ill some time.'

'She'll be an elderly lady, as I guess?' He was inclined to talk, but I told him I was indisposed and should not be come out, and begged his indulgence if I seemed hasty.

In the road I examined the letter, wondering had Aunt died, or had the girl written to say that her cure was now complete. *What is it to you?* I heard the Voice say. *You will eat no more flesh in that house.*

I must know. I broke the seal and opened it, screwing up my eyes for the sun shining on the paper faded the words almost to nothing. The girl wrote that Aunt had taken a turn for the worse, and was unable to speak. Doctor Whiteman was at a loss; two others had been called in but none could rally her. She was sinking.

Here was a stay of execution given into my hand, for if I once showed it Ferris he would go directly to London and there be safe from Sir George. Not only would his bones be unbroken but the colony most effectively levelled in his absence. I stood paralysed, clutching the letter to my breast. Then I heard again his moans as he lay with Caro. My body shook with great tearing sobs as I crushed the paper into a ball and flung it away from me.

The man was drawing himself a cup of ale as I went back into the inn.

'You've already paid me,' he said. 'Are you well? You need to sit down by the look of you.'

''Tisn't that. I have a letter to send – pen and paper if you please—' I counted up what I had in my hand '—and a flagon of Rhenish.'

He raised his eyebrows at this unwonted debauchery, but my money was good, at least as good as the wine he brought me.

'Where do you come from, then?' he asked, seeing me drink but not write. 'You don't talk like folk do here.'

'I was raised near Devizes.'

'That's by Wales, is it not?'

I shook my head.

'Yes, surely it is, and they have their own tongue.'

'If you will.' I could not be bothered with them, nor with him neither.

'Are you Welsh?'

'English. The son of a gentleman, would you have guessed that?'

Evidently he would not have, for he gave no answer and instead asked me, 'Is it good country there?'

'Would to God I had never left it.' I drained my first cup of Rhenish and spread the paper on the table. At the top I wrote *My dearest Becs* then, losing courage, refilled the cup.

'*You're* going at it,' said the landlord.

The wine heated me and made my eyes itch, perhaps with fever, perhaps with unshed tears. I took up the pen again and continued:

> *It seems these are sad times for us all. I have to tell you that he is hurt in the leg with a scythe and the cut is grown very hot and has set up a fever in him, so it falls to me to open letters and to reply to yours. I have taken it upon me to conceal her condition from him. He is too weak and irrational to grasp it; besides, should the truth reach him we might have his death to answer for, while if he be left in peace and given his rest I feel persuaded he will soon be fit to return to London. Do not write again until I send word. Directly he is strong enough I will bring him. O thou good and faithful servant! Both Aunt and yourself have my prayers night and day. Believe that I hold myself your debtor,*
>
> *Jacob Cullen*

My fingers could scarce grip for sweat, and though I sanded the paper, still it showed all spattered where I had handled the pen like a ploughman.

'Here,' I said to the man as I directed it to *Mistress Rebecca, at Snapman's, Cheapside*. 'Let that go tomorrow. When will it arrive?'

He scratched his head. 'Not later than noon.'

I drank up the rest of the wine and pushed my way out again into the dazzling sun. My steps were unsteady, and my thoughts were as a cud that the cow chews on over and over.

There was a surging in my ears.

With money a man lives free, whispered the Voice. *There are places on the south bank where a man may purchase a boy—*

I will purchase none.

No? We must find you a slender yellow-haired lad.

It faded in laughter.

I walked on, my eyes on the stones before my feet. Whenever I looked up the fields quivered in the heat. A shimmering pool of water lay in the dip of the road, where there had been none before; it faded into dust as I came closer to it. Perhaps I would sink to the purchase of love, as the Voice said. Once such things have been tasted, how can a man say, *So far and no further?* Unless he had that iron resolve that will leave off food and drink sooner than break a vow once taken.

But I could end my misery at the colony. Ferris should never read his letter, and in a few days our slatternly village should be scattered to the winds.

And I? Where should I be?

THIRTY

Unsealing

'WHY SO LATE?' Ferris demanded. 'It is near dark! We went seeking you on the road!' He pounded his fist into the palm of his hand. The others stood around scratching their heads.

'I was taken ill,' I answered. 'I had to lie under a hedge and rest.' In fact, I had been sleeping off the Rhenish, and had woken hours later feeling all the better for my indulgence. Facing him now, I was almost well, my flesh soothed by the cool evening air.

'And that is all?' He turned on me, sensing something. I felt, rather than saw, Susannah and Jonathan stiffen. Whether they feared for him if it came to blows, or disliked it when their saint stamped about and looked ugly, I was unsure. Ugly he certainly looked, his face flushed and eyes pinched up with suspicion.

'Brother Christopher, be calm,' urged Catherine. 'Jacob has been unwell all day.'

He hissed, 'You are trying what you can to fright me. This is nothing but craft.'

'Craft, going for a letter?' I asked. 'Whose craft?' and saw his eyes flash. 'Have a care, Brother Christopher,' I said. 'Govern your wrath. That has ever been your counsel to *me*.'

Ferris was in such a passion as only I, of all the colonists, had seen before. He stepped up to me, making fists of his hands.

'Don't think I'm too sick to hit back,' I said.

He paused, glowering but not daring to strike.

'Well,' I asked, loud enough for the others to hear, 'do you want everyone to see you knocked into the ditch?'

'Brother Christopher, beware!' cried out Caro.

Ferris could well have done without that cry. Pushing his way between Jonathan and Catherine, he strode over to his hut and began throwing things about.

'Go and clear up in the dairy,' said Susannah to Catherine and Hathersage. 'And take Sister Jane with you.'

'I can help Brother Christopher,' whined my wife. Susannah grabbed her by the hand and took her by force over to Hathersage. Jeremiah had already begun walking away, and could be heard whistling softly in the dusk.

'There's more than a walk wrong here,' said a gentle voice. I turned to see Jonathan, and beside him, Hepsibah. He went on, 'What's ado, Jacob? Since you came back from London, everything jars between you and him.'

'That's just it,' I answered. 'Everything jars.'

'But you will make it up?' asked Hepsibah.

I shook my head.

After a pause she said, 'Will you have more valerian?'

'Thank you, I am much better now the heat is gone off.'

They smiled awkwardly.

'You have only to ask,' said Hepsibah, turning to go.

'Aye.'

I was alone. I looked about me and saw a lucky thing: in the excitement of seeing two of the Brothers almost come to blows, the diggers had left their spades in the ditch.

The path to the hidden place (I would have called it the secret place, but *that* it was no longer) showed in the fading light like a crease in the bushes. Carrying a spade, I picked my way between branches, recalling that recent visit when I had discovered just what a fool he had made of me. The punctures in my arm began to throb, as if remembering also.

I wondered had Ferris and Caro been back to their ferny bed that day. *Brother Christopher, beware.* Soon she would betray the two of them by playing with his fingers in company, or pushing the hair back from his forehead, and after that the rest of the colonists would naturally expect a betrothal. The secrecy in which her loves were conducted at present was sure to suit Caro. But what of this leader who carried on an amour by stealth? Did she find nothing lacking in her Brother Christopher?

The bush was thicker than when last I had lain there with him. I crawled beneath and found the grass freshly crushed, giving off the perfume of that day when I let him do whatever he would. I heard again his tender, astonished laugh and some words I had stored in my heart ever since.

He laughs with her, now.

I felt a pain in my chest.

Silence them.

I took the spade and tried to stand upright. It was more difficult than I had reckoned, for the bush was too close to the ground, so that a shovel would have been more useful. Pressing back the branches with my shoulders, I at last straightened up, got some purchase on the lug, and drove it into the ground with my heel. The money was buried just where the base of the bush broke the soil. Almost at once I felt a resistance to the blade, and threw the tool aside to grope with my hands. In a very short time I had the box. It was smaller than I remembered. He had wrapped it in linen so that beneath the cloth it was damp, but clean of soil. I drew up the key on the ribbon round my neck and fumbled for the keyhole. The thing opened easily, and I groped inside. Something pricked the pad of my first finger. I jumped, and it fell away from my hand and rattled among the coins. Putting the finger to my lips I tasted blood. Best not bleed on the papers: I closed the lid again, locked it and slipped the key down my shirt. The box went there, too, for none would see it in the near darkness as I crossed to my hut. I flung the spade away from me and heard it slash though leaves before hitting the earth. I would never use it again. The colonists should wake and not find me; by the time Ferris discovered his treasures rifled I would be on the London road.

Someone, a woman most likely, was calling my name. I stopped in the darkened path. The fools must be out searching for me, under some mistaken notion that I was wandered away in a fever. I went on slowly, not wanting to catch a bramble stalk in the eye. Let them disperse to their huts, not come crowding round me, perhaps to notice the bulge of the box under my shirt.

There were more shouts, angry ones, and it came to me that Ferris might have quarrelled with another colonist. I pressed forward more rapidly now, and as I came through a thickly ivied stretch of path I saw the cooking fire. But it was in the wrong place, and as I tried to understand how this could be, two black shapes ran through it. There followed a shot and a scream. I froze, unable to move or even think except for the one terrible thought which filled earth and sky: our friend had mistaken his dates, or Sir George's plan was altered. The day of reckoning was upon Ferris, and I was still here, to witness it.

Panting, I struggled forward as fast as I could towards the edge of the wood. Just as I came to where the trees thinned into shrubs, a brilliance out of Sodom and Gomorrah sprang up in the cornfield behind the huts, everything nearer to me showing black against it. I had been right, the corn was too dry, and a breeze took the flames so that soon all the field was alight and crackling, a sea of fire. Getting onto a tree stump, I saw we were completely overrun. They moved waist high in the smoke as if born of it, men armed with swords, muskets, clubs, dragging the colonists out of their shelters. Three of our people stood holding hands together, turning like poor sheep first this way, then that. I saw them prodded with staves, forced to kneel, and heard the coarse shouts of their tormentors. In the midst of the cries, again, someone calling, '*Jacob*'. Ferris was nowhere to be seen.

Men were kicking down the huts. I saw the door of mine pulled open and the contents ransacked before the thing was levelled to the ground. The destroyers then moved towards Ferris's dwelling. I held my breath, but he was not there. His possessions were tossed out and the men began snatching at this and that – I saw one man bundle up a shirt and stuff it down his breeches – before firing the bedstraw.

The dairy was next attacked, and I heard loud crashes as clubs broke up the marble. The cloth from the planks soared upwards in sparks like a prophet's cloak, then the planks themselves took fire and the whole thing slowly collapsed inwards. A sudden flare distracted my eye, followed by a spitting sound: the tent was in flames. A woman came running out of it. I could see men leading away our cattle, and shattering the ox-cart wheels with clubs. Bales of burning straw lay about, lighting up a man's face or hands and adding to the suffocating waves of smoke now belching from the cornfield.

Something thudded through the trees on my right. I whipped around and saw the back of Jeremiah, running. A black figure detached itself from the group who were demolishing huts and came hurtling after him. I ducked as the man approached the wood, and heard his hoarse breathing as he pushed after his quarry. Then he stopped some yards away. There was a click, and a scuffle of leaves as he steadied his feet. When the gun went off someone screamed, but whether it was Jeremiah or somebody near the huts I could not tell.

A woman was shrieking, '*Christ help us, Christ help us.*' She came stumbling from behind a hut as if drunk, and I saw the child, a black bundle against the fire. A man was in pursuit, and as I watched he caught at the back of her gown, swung her round and ripped the babe from her arms, casting it violently away. There was a terrified scream from the child and I heard Caro shriek, '*Christopher, Christopher,*' and then, '*Jacob,*' the knowledge of me wrung from her at last. Her cry was choked off as one of the men swung a club against the small of her back. I watched as my wife sank to the ground and her attacker bent to remove the purse at her belt. The child I could scarce see except as a heap of clothes, which might or might not be moving. O if it were mine—

Know it is not yours but your brother's bastard.

A man from the small group of colonists, who had all of them knelt helplessly until now, rose and started towards Caro. From his stocky build and the woman clinging to his arm, trying to hold him back, I knew him for Jonathan. He was laid low by a club before he could shake her off, and two of Sir George's men brought down their sticks as if on vermin as he rolled on the ground. Hepsibah tried to shield him from the blows but was wrenched away. Another man, still on his knees, lifted his hands as if to pray. I guessed this must be Hathersage. He was seized by the hair and a group of men lugged him over the ground and out of my view.

What I saw next gave my heart such a stab that I feared to drop. I recognised at once the graceful runner leaping the bales as he went, arms and legs flickering black against the inferno that was our corn. There were three men after him, each bigger than himself but not as fast. I held my breath. He might escape into the wood, where – but he did not make for the wood. Instead, he went to Caro, pushing aside the thief who now looked to be ripping open the neck of her gown. Ferris tried to raise her then turned, seeing the child, and made as if he would pick it up. I closed my eyes, but forced myself to open them again. The three men had piled on top of him. Ferris was jerked upright by his hair, and the man who had clubbed my wife, and was near as big as myself, leapt at him. Ferris lashed out and landed a blow, surprising me by his speed. But the other men were behind him, blocking any escape. His opponent had time to gather force and aim a punch that knocked his head back.

I stood hands clenched, at any moment ready to run from the wood and lay about me. Fists went into his ribs and belly, doubling him up. I was clutching a branch, or I might have fallen senseless, so violent was the struggle within. Caro was creeping on hands and knees towards the child.

All is meant. Did I not reveal it in a dream, the fire and the Devils that pulled him down?

I saw the man strike home again and again, and Ferris unable to recover.

He wishes for you now, My friend. There followed a laugh to splinter teeth.

Ferris was staggering, too dazed to keep up his guard. The man turned him around and pushed him towards another of the group. A fist went into his nose or eye; I heard him cry out, and the men cheered. He raised his hands to his face and one of his tormentors kicked out at his spine, crumpling him. There was a pause in which they stood back and watched him struggle to stand upright. It seemed he was bleeding into his eyes, but he was still trying to fight back, and I saw one of them mimic his blinded movements. They began knocking him from one man to the other, letting him find his feet for a few seconds and then starting again.

They know who they deal with, gloated the Voice.

I was weeping, muttering to myself, *Enough! Enough, for the love of God!* Yet I could not move towards him. The two devils furthest from me drew back to let through a horseman, come to enjoy the sport at close hand. He watched avidly, wriggling in the saddle, and I recognised the man of the perfume and the fingernails, he who had spat on Ferris.

Caro, forgotten in the excitement, reached the child and began crawling away with it.

Surrounded by four men, any one of whom outmatched him, Ferris was falling against them now, almost clinging to their fists. One tripped him and he sank to his hands and knees; another's boot cut into his mouth. Dropping to the ground, he curled into a ball, and they opened him up, and went for him again. I could not turn my eyes away but saw, and felt, every blow.

The horseman suddenly looked up. Light from the burning straw showed me his creamy, handsome face and his eyes were level with my own. They were full of a cruel ecstasy and it seemed to me that he saw me, and smiled in recognition, as who might say, *Brother*. Ferris lay completely still except that he jerked each time a man kicked him. The men paused, perhaps tired, and looked to their master for instruction. My breath came in great gasps. The horseman pointed at Ferris's outstretched body and two of them bent to pick him up. His head hung backwards as if the neck were broken, and the breast of his shirt was all over blood. Stretched between the two men, he showed pitifully slight. I could not tell if he was alive or dead as they carried him away, one holding his hands and one his feet.

The Brothers and Sisters were being driven off the land like cattle, with blows and screams. Caro was kicked until she got up from the grass, clutching the child to her, and was haled over to the small group where Jonathan still lay senseless. One of Sir George's men shouted an order and a thin figure was pushed forward to drag Jonathan by the feet. I thought I recognised Hathersage. Two of the women hastened to help from behind so that Jonathan's head should not trail in the dust, and thus the little group skirted the fires as they crossed the field.

When all that noise had died away I stood motionless, I cannot say how long, gazing on the ruined corn. There was no sound but the spit and crackle of fire. When I took my first step to leave the wood, my knees folded under me and I fell down. It was some minutes before I could raise myself and make for the road. Looking neither to my right nor my left, I crossed the camp, staggering as if I too had been beaten.

THIRTY-ONE

Treasures

LONDON WAS A charnel-house. The fairest streets brought no pleasure, for at every step I was mocked by a ghost. He crossed the road before me, turned down an alleyway or stepped into one tavern door as I came out by another.

I wandered about the familiar places, always fetching up outside a certain house in Cheapside where I dared not knock. I thought of Aunt lying stricken, impatient for a last look at her darling, her lamb, and I told myself he had most likely survived, and was even now turning the corner. Once, I walked behind him the full length of a lane before he turned and showed himself an impostor. As I went back the other way a group of gentlemen passed by, and in their laughter was mingled that of the Voice.

The city was grown cruel; I was glad to slip its jaws and go, go as far as might be. That meant a ship, and should the ship come to grief, I would end all my grief as I began it, in a drowning.

I purchased a place in the Southampton coach. There remained to me one last day in London, and I spent it lying in wait at the road's end in Cheapside, just in case. While there was daylight it was more than I could do to come away. When it grew dark I at last returned to my lodging, and the next day rose before dawn to begin the first part of the journey.

The coach smelt of mould and corruption; the other passengers were no more to me than the dead, and if one happened to address me I turned away. Soon I was troubled no more. We came out of London through one of the gates in the defensive walls.

You know someone who helped make them.

I never knew you, I answered. Looking back from the window of the coach, I saw forlorn streets, and houses crouched despairing under a meagre rain.

~

On arrival at Southampton I sought a lodging near the quay, and above all one where I might have a room to myself. Every kind of company grated on me, but most intolerable was the merry sort.

The search for such a hiding place brought me through some of the vilest parts of the town. Like London it has its warrens, places where I would never have ventured with *him*, though perhaps Zeb might not be entirely at a loss there. In one alley where the sky was no more than a crack above the houses, I was set upon by two whores who stood propping the sides of an ale-house door. There was an older woman who might be the *mother* as I believe these bawds are called, and a purple-faced girl of about sixteen, very drunk, whose thin blonde hair was plastered to her head with scurf. They tried to bar my way and when I pushed them aside, the girl ran ahead, raised her skirts and pissed full in my view. It is said some men's appetites are whetted thereby, but there could scarce have been a more monstrous sight than her veined flesh and swollen, matted privates. I knocked her into the muck where she belonged.

'Arse-merchant, he-whore,' shouted the other and with that the two of them started scooping up filth from the street and throwing it at me. I made a rush at them, and they fled. Being drunk, their aim was none of the steadiest, so that my cloak was only a little soiled.

After going up and down the streets, I found me a place in Cattes-Head Passage, a vermin-ridden rookery. In the tavern there they made offer of a miserable room, the walled-off end of a passageway, with an empty grate and the bed so narrow that not even my host could fit another wretch in it, so I had only the fleas and lice to share with. To get to the quay was no more than stepping to the alley end and crossing the road.

Having bolted the door that first day I lay perhaps an hour without movement, trying if I was any better for being out of London.

That was a vain hope, for I still breathed and felt. Again I saw Ferris bend over my wife and child, saw him pushed from one torturer to another in their sport; again the horseman smiled to me as to a fellow and a brother. There was a savage pain in my breast like to tearing or scalding, so great I would not have been surprised to look down and see myself butchered like a Jesuit on the scaffold.

Think not on him, urged the Voice.

I forced my mind towards money. I had of course Ferris's box with me, and had not yet fully examined what it held. There was gold lying near the top, and this had been little depleted by the price of my room and the clothes I had purchased in London. The woman who dealt in used apparel had told me I was in uncommon luck, for a man of my own stature had died two days before. I asked what was his complaint, not wanting to die of it likewise, and she said the heart.

Having bought a purse of the same woman, I poured out the gold onto the stinking bed, ready to be pocketed up. There was also silver that I had missed but now found jammed between the box sides and a lining of paper. All the coin taken together would pay my passage to New England. I had thought there would be more, but then remembered how freely he had paid out for the dairy. There was also a gold ring. In my first confusion I took it for Caro's, the one Zeb had boasted of wearing in his ear, but this was a ring I had never seen before, made for a delicate hand. Turning it about I found inscribed on the inside, '*CF & JC, 1645*'. So he, like me, had been betrothed with a ring. I pushed it onto my little finger.

The paper which lay at the bottom might be of some worth. Scrabbling to dislodge it, I felt the skin of my knuckle suddenly slit open and remembered that something had cut me as I held the box in the wood. I lifted out the sheet by another corner and found beneath it the fragment of scarlet glass I had given him after Basing-House. Holding it up to the light, I again saw the word scratched by John Paulet, that obstinate and defeated man: *loyaute*. There was a place where Ferris and I had failed utterly. I recalled his smile as he said, 'What shall I do with you?' and I threw the glass into the grate.

The folded document was a letter, spotted with my blood where the shard of glass had pricked me. As I unfolded it a twist of hair fell out, thick and black. I had never made him such a gift, and I wondered when this trophy had been captured. It might have been the very first day, when the boys cut my hair as I lay on the road. How I must have called to him. Months and months he lived alongside me, enduring it. And Nathan? I wondered. Had my hair replaced his?

I took up the letter. On seeing the first line I knew it directly, but could not hold back from reading the whole thing, not once but many times, for it was the only love letter I had received in my life. *Have you the heart to stand by,* he had written, *and see it done?*

The letter had been left behind, that first time, and Ferris had treasured it for the sake of what followed. Again I tightened my arms about him. Delight. He ran his hands over me, opened his mouth to my kiss.

Such a letter has no place where you are going, came the Voice. *Leave clutching at these rags.*

Keeping the thing folded so as not to read it again, I tore it in strips and then in scraps, but then hesitated, not liking to leave even scraps of it behind in the room.

Drown it.

The Voice was grown impatient. I crushed together the pieces in my hand and stepped out onto the quayside before setting them free. They fluttered on the air, some settling on the bosom of the water and other morsels sinking almost at once. Here and there a word blown back on land survived entire, waiting to be trodden into the mud.

~

The wind along the quay lifts my hair, drops it in my eyes and plays with the hem of my new wool cloak. Though cold, it is welcome, as it takes off the smell of rotten meat that hangs about the place. Dead cows, it might be: I watch as a crane dangles great boxes, the prisons of horses and cattle, over the deck of a transport. There are more than a hundred cows penned up, lowing their misery to any that will hear. Whenever the wind veers, the stink of carrion and the cleaner scent of animal dung are wiped away by a something like spiced cake, which Ferris once told me was tobacco. I remember his saying that as a boy he wished to be a mariner, and I said – I said—

Think not on him.

All manner of people are here, standing, sitting, crouching on their heels, and from time to time a squall of conversation breaks out, only to die down almost at once, for we are all weary. Somewhere behind me is a man whom I faced down last night over nothing, that is to say, over who should first pass through a door. It seems I am grown so thin-skinned I can scarce endure to be crossed; or it may be, I am looking for the one will put a knife in me at last.

Though the sun fumes in a mist over the sea, the man on my right tells me the haze will speedily burn off and the day be hot. This neighbour, sunburnt and thickset, is one Knowell, going to join his brother in New England. Mistress Knowell has the complexion of a woman brought up on whey, with a creased, patient face and very red eyelids. The Voice whispered me, when I first began talking with them, that the husband deals severely with her and that she merits it by her whining. She keeps up a constant chatter about seasickness and her determination not to yield to it, but whenever she falls silent she is visited by tears, which she blames on the wind drawing water from her eyes.

The line moves slowly as the boats weave back and forth, loading passengers and their goods to row them out to the *Fortitude*. The wind again dampens Mistress Knowell's cheeks with tears.

'Lord, Mercy, why must you?' cries the exasperated husband. To me he adds, 'We have a plot of land all cleared and made ready, Sir. My brother and his wife are gone before.'

'You are indeed fortunate,' I reply.

'Indeed! Yet my wife does nought but grizzle.' He turns away from us, looking outwards to the ship. Mercy Knowell, who has not the look of a spoilt or wilful woman, dabs her face on her sleeve. 'Husband,' she says.

He inclines towards his weeping spouse and I edge forward, for she is low-voiced and I wish to hear her over the fluttering of my hat set up by the salt wind.

'I am most grateful for James's work.' Her eyes glaze afresh with unfallen tears. 'But it is here that William and Anne are buried.'

He sighs resignedly, takes her hand. Tears spill over her eyelids.

I say, 'You must not weep for the past, Madam, but cultivate hope for the future.'

She turns a watery smile upon me. 'Excellent advice, Sir, and I wonder that you yourself do not profit thereby.'

'Profit? In what wise—'

Mercy Knowell wipes the back of her finger along my cheek and then shows it me. The finger gleams with wet.

'Nothing,' I say, 'an affliction of the eyes.'

It has now been three days that I weep and do not know it.

~

The boat rocks as I lower myself onto her boards. Packed in with the Knowells, with my enemy from the night before and two families, the anxious parents bidding their children sit still, I am cradled in a wooden shell. The mariners heave, bringing us little by little to our ship. How formless, I think, is the sea, swelling, folding upon itself, the folds dissolving as soon as seen. I look back at England, a heap of dead filth gilded by the early sun.

To my left there is a family where the youngest brother, fearful of the water, whimpers and snuffles like any girl. Someone says, 'Courage,' and I see Ferris take his wife by the hand and walk the length of Cheapside with her while the neighbours talk of shame.

Think not on him.

I see him in the army, defending Nathan against the Bad Angel he already loves more, and in London, composing the type for his uncle's press, his face bright with visions of a better time.

He betrayed you. Think not on him.

He sits alone, writing the letter which I scattered on the sea, and hoping I will not turn from him in disgust. He stands defenceless, in dispute with the green horseman, and I say nothing, but later kiss his neck where the man has spat on it. He raises his fists beneath the blows, while I look on.

Why did You bid me drown the letter? I have lost something that he touched, and the destruction of it has gained You nothing, for now I no longer read the words, I hear them, as if he implored me face to face.

Speak to me, Jacob, do not play the tyrant.

Speak to me.